THE GLORY

A NOVEL

LITTLE, BROWN AND COMPANY

BOSTON NEW YORK TORONTO LONDON

The Glory is a work of fiction set in a background of history. Israeli and other public personages both living and dead appear in the story under their right names. Their portraits are offered as essentially truthful, though scenes and dialogue involving them with fictitious characters are of course invented. Any other usage of real people's names is coincidental. Any resemblance of the imaginary characters to actual persons living or dead is unintended and fortuitous. The simplified map, of a region much subject to clouded boundary disputes, is intended only to illustrate the narrative. Further clarification of certain distinctions between fact and fancy appears in the Historical Notes at the end of this volume.

First Edition

Passage from "Sharm el Sheikh Song" by Amos Etinger is included by permission of the author.

Library of Congress Cataloging-in-Publication Data

Wouk, Herman
The Glory : a novel / Herman Wouk. — 1st ed.
p. cm.
ISBN 0-316-95525-6
ISBN 0-316-95527-2 (deluxe edition)
1. Israel — History — Fiction. I. Title.
PS3545.O98G58 1994
813′.54 — dc20 94-23281

10 9 8 7 6 5 4 3 2 1

MV-NY

Published simultaneously in Canada
by Little, Brown & Company (Canada) Limited

Printed in the United States of America

To

THE ISRAELIS

Valorous in War
Generous in Peace

Above All to Those Who Fell
To Save the Land

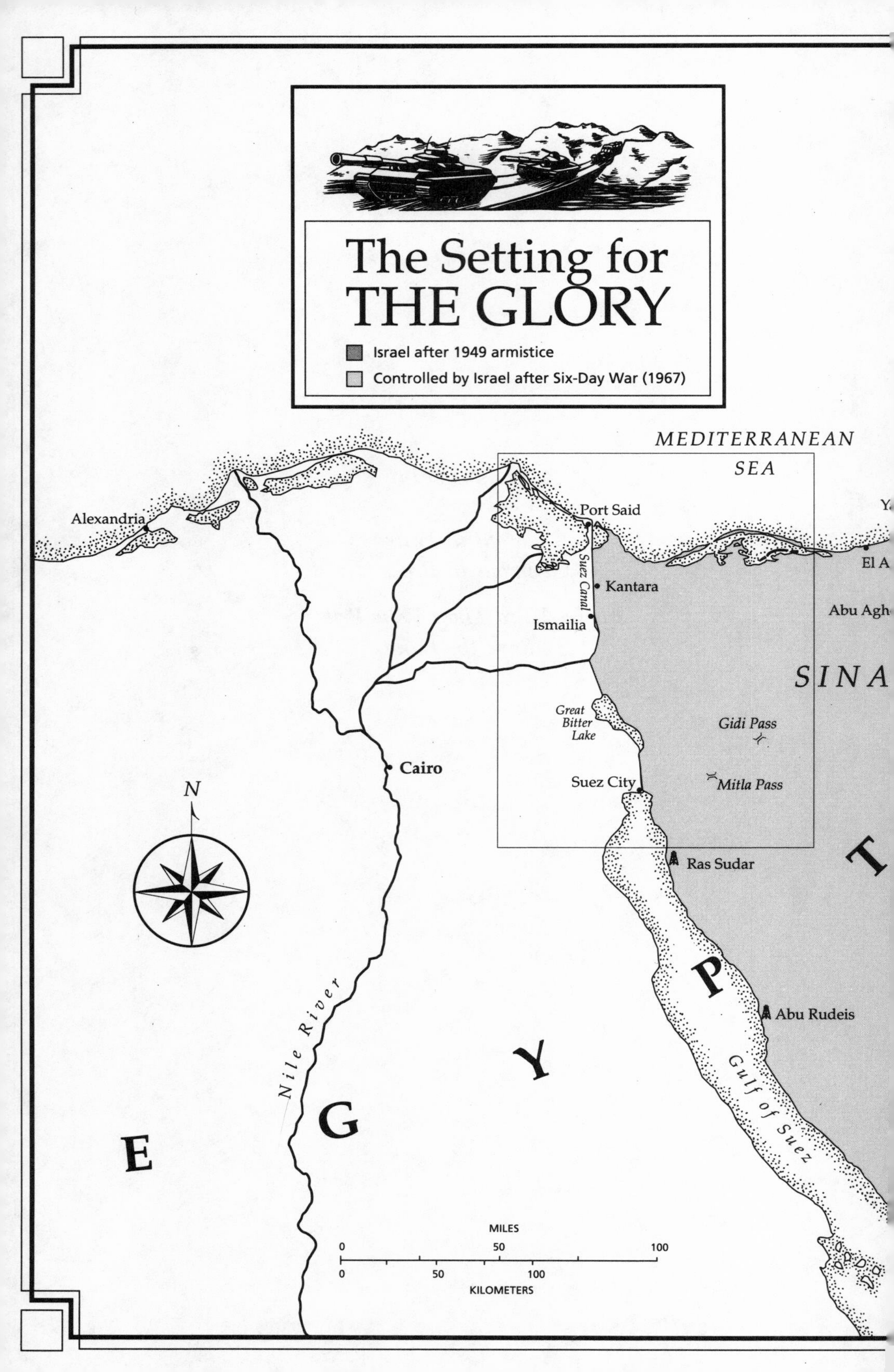

The Setting for
THE GLORY
Israel after 1949 armistice
Controlled by Israel after Six-Day War (1967)
MEDITERRANEAN
SEA
Alexandria
Port Said
Suez Canal
Kantara
Ismailia
El A
Abu Agh
SINA
Great
Bitter
Lake
Gidi Pass
Mitla Pass
Suez City
Cairo
N
Ras Sudar
Abu Rudeis
Gulf of Suez
Nile River
E
G
Y
P
T
MILES
0
50
100
0
50
100
KILOMETERS

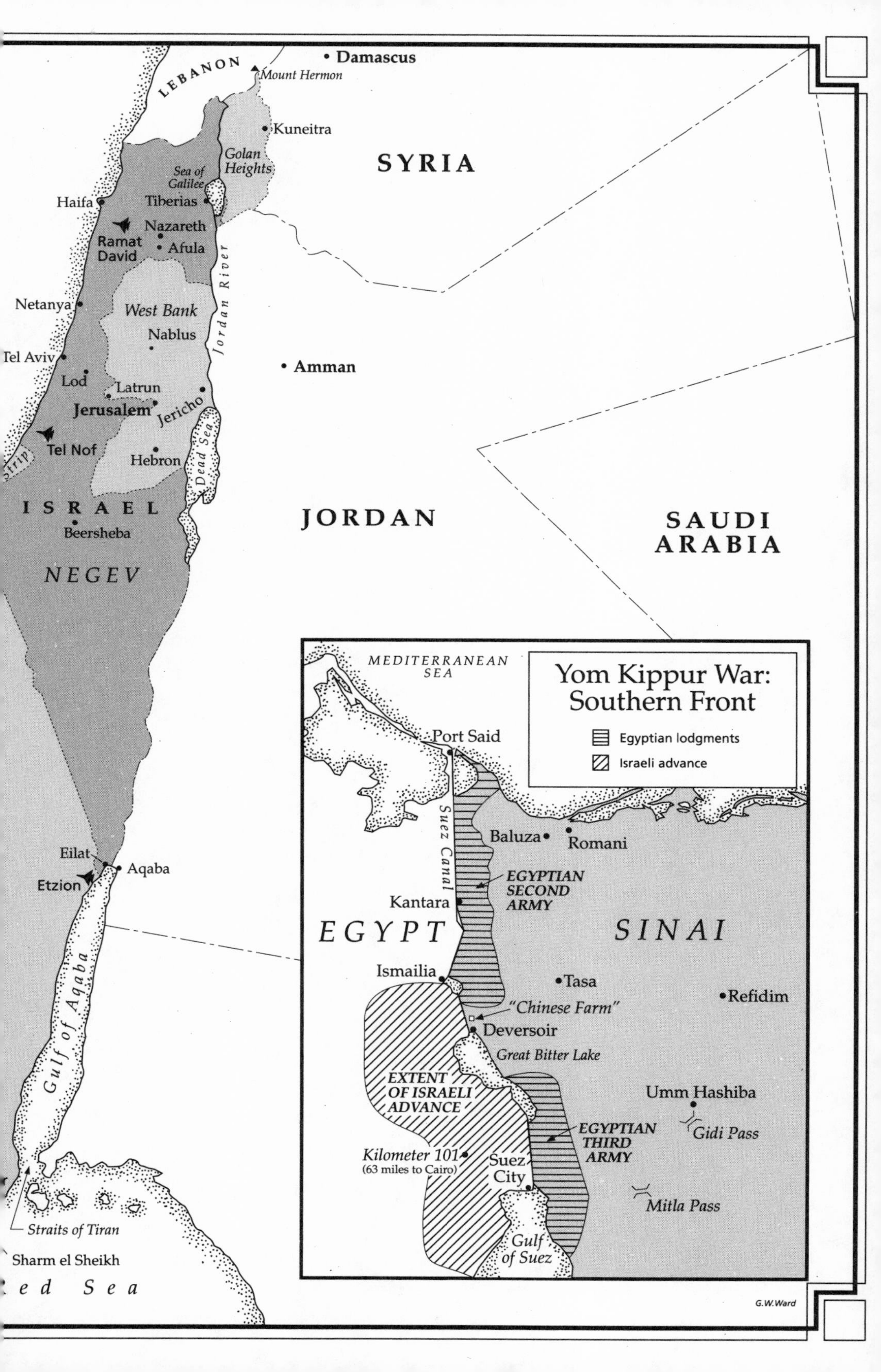
Damascus
LEBANON
Mount Hermon
Kuneitra
SYRIA
Golan Heights
Sea of Galilee
Haifa
Tiberias
Ramat David
Nazareth
Afula
Jordan River
Netanya
West Bank
Nablus
Tel Aviv
Lod
Latrun
Jerusalem
Jericho
Amman
Tel Nof
Hebron
Dead Sea
Strip
ISRAEL
Beersheba
JORDAN
SAUDI ARABIA
NEGEV
Eilat
Aqaba
Etzion
Gulf of Aqaba
Straits of Tiran
Sharm el Sheikh
Red Sea
MEDITERRANEAN SEA
Yom Kippur War: Southern Front
Egyptian lodgments
Israeli advance
Port Said
Suez Canal
Baluza
Romani
EGYPTIAN SECOND ARMY
Kantara
EGYPT
SINAI
Ismailia
Tasa
Refidim
"Chinese Farm"
Deversoir
Great Bitter Lake
EXTENT OF ISRAELI ADVANCE
Umm Hashiba
EGYPTIAN THIRD ARMY
Gidi Pass
Kilometer 101
(63 miles to Cairo)
Suez City
Mitla Pass
Gulf of Suez
G.W.Ward

THE GLORY

Prologue

The world is stunned. The eternal victims of history, the Jews, have risen in a single generation from the ashes of the Holocaust to win, in six swift days of June 1967, the greatest military victory since the Second World War.

In the West the media stammer astonished admiration. In Communist and Arab countries they rage against aggressive Israel and claim that American carrier planes took part in the air strikes. In the United Nations the Soviet Union leads a bitter fight to reverse the victory politically and force the Israelis back behind the old armistice lines of 1949. But various withdrawal proposals worked up by the Russians and the Americans are rejected one after another by the Arab governments, who in August have met in the capital of the Sudan and issued the Khartoum Declaration, embodying irrevocable NO'S — NO *negotiation with Israel,* NO *recognition of Israel,* NO *peace with Israel.*

In Israel, and among Jews around the world, all is light, gladness, joy, honor, and euphoria . . .

PART ONE

The Dreamers

WHEN THE LORD RETURNED US TO ZION,
WE WERE LIKE DREAMERS.
THEN OUR MOUTHS WERE FILLED WITH LAUGHTER,
AND OUR TONGUES WITH SONG . . .

Psalm 126:1, 2

1

The Cousins Berkowitz

On a blustery morning in October 1967, the destroyer *Eilat*, returning from patrol off Sinai, was approaching Haifa at a leisurely ten knots to conserve fuel. In the unsteady charthouse Noah Barak, a lieutenant of twenty-three with the haggard overworked look appropriate to an executive officer, was checking through a sheaf of navy yard requisition forms: hull repairs, engine maintenance, work on radar and signal gear, and — marked in angry red ink VERY URGENT — missile countermeasures.

The officer of the deck spoke through the voice tube. "Sir, collision course out here."

"Coming."

The day was fair, the sea moderate: rolling glittery blue swells, a few whitecaps, brisk chilly north wind. The sun was high over Mount Carmel, and ahead was the long stone Haifa breakwater. On the port bow some two miles away, a large rust-streaked white vessel was also heading for the channel entrance. Noah asked, peering through binoculars, "How long has he held course?"

"Since 0700, sir, no change."

Noah buzzed the captain. "Sir, request permission to go to twenty knots."

"What's up?" Noah told him. The captain yawned. "Well, so what? You say we have him to port. He's got to give way—"

"Sir, it's one of those Italian automobile ferries."

"Oh, *l'Azazel*. Those fellows never heard of the rules of the road. How far out are we?"

"Four miles to number-one buoy, sir."

"Very well. Go to twenty, Noah, and take her in."

The *Eilat* leaped ahead, smashing through the swells. The automobile ferry slowly fell back to port, then dead astern. When the *Eilat* entered the harbor and approached the naval base, the captain came up on the bridge, clean-shaven and in a fresh uniform, and took the conn to tie up alongside its sister ship, the *Jaffa*. These two old British one-stackers, purchased out of mothballs and reconditioned by the Israelis, were the capital warships of the Jewish navy, dwarfing the huddle of gray patrol and torpedo craft that made up most of the little sea force.

Noah shouted to the executive officer waving to him from the *Jaffa*'s bridge, "Shlomo, what's the word on the countermeasures?"

"The word is we have to sail without them again," Shlomo yelled back. The two destroyers spelled each other in the Sinai patrol station.

Noah uttered a pungent Arabic curse. "I'll go to supply section this morning and set fire to the place."

"Let me provide the kerosene and a blowtorch," called back the *Jaffa*'s exec.

By now the automobile ferry was inside the breakwater, slowing as it passed from foaming swells and sea winds to flat murky harbor calm. At the bow a young man about Lieutenant Barak's age leaned on the rail, dressed in a tan sport jacket, gray slacks, and a red racing driver's cap. He somewhat resembled the exec of the *Eilat*, and this was no coincidence, for they were distant cousins who had never yet met. Like Noah Barak the young man was broad-shouldered and round-faced though not as tall, and like Noah he had a thick thatch of straight hair, sandy instead of black. "I'm here," he was murmuring. "I'm here. Everybody thinks I'm crazy, but I'm the sane one, and I'm dizzy with joy."

The sight of the destroyer racing ahead of the ferry had thrilled him, an honest-to-God warship flying the blue-and-white Star of David, and this approach to Haifa was giving him a yet greater thrill, his first close look at the Promised Land: sun-drenched white buildings mounting the green Carmel slopes, a waterfront crowded with the parti-colored funnels of docked ships from many lands, a naval base lined with combat craft, and on flat ground to the north, imposing chemical plants and oil refineries. The whole panorama was stirring his blood like brass band music.

A deep voice behind him in Hebrew: "Beautiful view, yes?"

The burly speaker wore soiled jeans and an old leather windbreaker. His coarse jowly face was scraggly with black bristles, and his overgrown grizzly hair stirred in the breeze. On the three-day trip from Italy the newcomer had seen this man before, a loner of some sort, sitting apart in the dining salon or the shabby little disco, smoking big cigars.

"Ken, yofeh m'od." ("Yes, very beautiful.")

"Ah, so you're an American." The man switched to guttural English.

The young man laughed. "Three words in Hebrew, and you can tell?"

"You must be bringing in that new blue Porsche."

"That's my car."

"Tourist?"

"Nope, making aliya."

The pudgy face showed amused surprise. "You're coming to Israel to *live*? For good? From America?"

"Why not? For a Jew nowadays, this is where it's at, isn't it?"

"Oh, absolutely. *Kol ha'kavod*! [All honor!] But look here, you may run into problems with that Porsche at the *Mekhess*. You know what that is, the Mekhess?"

"Sure, Israeli customs. I've brought certified bank checks for the taxes, and all the required documents. Got them in the New York consulate."

"Really? Very wise. Do you have family here?"

"Sort of. Heard of General Zev Barak?"

"Our military attaché in Washington? Who hasn't?"

"We're related."

"You don't say." The Israeli pointed at the naval base. "The destroyer that just came in is the *Eilat*. His son's the second in command."

"So that was the *Eilat*? Well, Noah Barak's my cousin. I'll be looking him up. You're an Israeli, I take it."

"What else?"

"Were you in the war?"

"Of course, I'm not fifty yet. Antiaircraft unit in the north. Not much to do, since our air force wiped out all the Arab airpower on the first day."

"Yes, wasn't that marvelous? Christ, what a victory. Six days! Made me proud to be a Jew." At the Israeli's quizzical look he added, "Not that I wasn't proud anyway."

"And that inspired you to make aliya?" The Israeli's tone was warm, almost paternal. "The Six-Day War?"

"It tipped the scale."

The diesels growled, the deck shuddered, and the vessel churned toward the wharfs.

"And is your name Barak, too?"

"Nope. Barkowe." He added with a grin, "Both changed from Berkowitz," and he offered a card from his wallet: *John A. Barkowe, Attorney-at-Law, Real Estate*, with an address in Great Neck, Long Island.

"Real estate, hah? I dabble in it myself."

"I was just getting started."

"John Barkowe. Doesn't even sound Jewish."

"I know. My Hebrew name is Yaakov. That's what I'll be using here."

"Fine Israeli name."

Approaching a broad wooden slip, the ferry blasted its siren several times. "Here we go," shouted the Israeli, hands to ears. "Get into your car, and be ready to drive off." He handed Barkowe a card. "Have fun in Israel with that Porsche, Yaakov."

"Thanks. See you around." Barkowe glanced at the card and dropped it into a pocket.

The stream of debarking cars, mostly decrepit small European models, was directed by hard-faced men into an enormous shed, where the drivers after parking queued up at grilled windows along the far wall. A huge sign proclaimed in Hebrew over the windows

WELCOME, ARRIVALS

and below that, in much smaller letters

CUSTOMS

The Porsche came rolling in, attracting stares all the way. As Barkowe parked and got out, a tall bony man in a green peaked cap approached him, saying, "*B'dikah* [Inspection]." More men came up, surrounded the Porsche, and began peering into it and feeling the blue leather upholstery. Since this was happening to no other car that he could see, Barkowe mentioned the fact in his limited Hebrew to the inspector in the cap.

"*Ani mitzta'er* [I'm sorry]," said the inspector, who had a very pronounced squint; a suspicious look or a physical defect, the American couldn't be sure which. Another inspector was crawling under the car with a big flashlight, while a third banged here and there on the bumpers and fenders with a wooden club. Two more pulled out Barkowe's luggage, three fine leather bags, and began rummaging through them.

"What is this? Do you think I'm a —" Not knowing the Hebrew for "smuggler," he pantomimed cocaine-sniffing with back of hand to nose and a loud snort.

The squinter shrugged, frisked Barkowe head to foot, and stopped at a pocket. "Show please."

Barkowe handed him his wallet. The inspector looked at the credit cards, the driver's license, the wad of dollars, and the small stash of Israeli currency. "Tourist?" he inquired.

"Making aliya," said the American.

The squint was not a defect after all. It cleared away in a look of utter amazement, then returned more pronounced and suspicious than before. Lifting the hood of the Porsche, he squinted under it, borrowed the flashlight from the man under the car, crouched to squint more intently at the engine, and scribbled in a pocket notebook. Then he said, "Documents."

"Don't they go to the Mekhess?"

"I'm the Mekhess."

A shiny white Mercedes pulled up nearby and the Israeli in the windbreaker jumped out, seemingly in a hurry, for he went off toward the windows at a trot, swinging his overlong arms. Barkowe produced a rubber-banded envelope, and the inspector took a long leisurely squint at the papers inside. Meantime two of the other men were pulling up the floor mats, one was flashing the light into the gas tank, and another was kicking the tires. Long queues lounged and fidgeted at all the windows, but even while the inspector was glancing over his papers Barkowe saw the burly man lope back to his Mercedes and drive off through a gate into the waterfront traffic.

"New car?" said the inspector at last.

"Almost new. I drove around Europe a bit when I first picked it up."

"Where was that?"

"In Milan, Porsche agency."

"Ah good, no problem then." The squinter snapped the rubber band around the envelope and handed it back to Barkowe. "You can book return passage on this same boat tomorrow."

"Slikha?" ("Pardon?")

"You have to take this Porsche back to Milan."

"I don't understand."

The Mekhess man blasted a spate of Hebrew at him.

"Slower, please," said Barkowe.

The squinter said in heavily accented English, "Your model Porsche not available in Israel. No model in Israel, no car come in."

"Oh, so you do speak English? Fine. The New York consulate didn't mention any regulations about models."

"*Ani mitzta'er.* New regulation."

"Is that my fault? Look, let me make myself clear. I'll fight this up to the American ambassador if I have to, but I'm not taking this car back to Italy. That's an absolutely insane idea."

Squinting toward a chain-fenced area full of cars, the inspector said with a shrug, "Impounded vehicles park there. Storage charge, twenty American dollars daily."

When Noah Barak returned to the wardroom of the *Eilat* from the supply section, four officers at lunch burst into a popular new song of the war.

O Sharm el Sheikh
Once more we've returned,
Our hearts to you ever,
Ever have yearned . . .

Noah poured coffee from a simmering pot on a sideboard. "Look, isn't the joke getting old?"

"What joke? What old?" said the captain, a roly-poly lieutenant colonel (the Israel navy used army ranks), gesturing at a blown-up newspaper photograph taped to a bulkhead. It showed Noah, wearing only shorts and an officer's cap, nailing the Star of David flag to a pole atop a stone fortress. "Who else in this navy captured an enemy base singlehanded?"

It was in fact a very old joke. On temporary detached duty, commanding a patrol boat in the Red Sea, Noah Barak had led a landing force ashore at Sharm el Sheikh, only to find that the base had been abandoned in the pell-mell retreat of the Egyptians. So at negligible risk he had "captured" the deserted base, an army photographer had snapped the shot, and it had appeared next day on the front page of *Ha'aretz*. Aboard warships jokes tend to be durable. He had been serenaded off and on for months about Sharm el Sheikh.

Noah shook his head irritably and took the coffee to his cabin, where a telephone chit on his tiny desk read, *Daphna Luria called. Phone her 1800 tonight Ramat David.* He could seldom see the luscious Daphna, tied as he was to the ship and she to her duties at the air base, and just those dry words sent a warm flush from his scalp to his toes. There was also a hand-delivered letter on Dan Hotel stationery, from someone signing himself Jack Barkowe, who wrote in English that they were cousins, that he had come to Israel on aliya, and that he was having difficulty getting his car through customs. Could Noah recommend an agent in Haifa to assist him?

Noah was astonished. He knew that a branch of the family in Long Island had altered the Berkowitz name to Barkowe, but this was the first he had heard of the cousin, and an American making aliya these days was a real rarity. The newspapers were full of articles complaining about the failure of American Jews to start emigrating en masse to Israel, now that the Six-Day War had secured the Promised Land as the Jewish State once for all. What was wrong with those millions of American Jews? Here was the moment they and their fathers and their forefathers had been praying for three times a day, century after century, the glorious chance to Return to Zion! And American Jews were indeed coming to Israel in droves, to see sights hitherto barred to them — the Wailing Wall, Jericho, Hebron, Sinai — for three, five or ten days, depending on the tour plans. Tourism, yes, aliya, no. In and out. *Z'beng v'gamarnu!* (Bang and finish!) More power to this Long Island cousin, Noah decided, he deserved help at the Mekhess.

The captain leaned in the doorway as Noah was stripping to shower. "So, Noah, what happened at supply?"

"Again, no countermeasures."

"What's the delay this time?"

"*Balagan* [Foul-up], that's what. Balagan beyond belief. Captain, the requisitions I submitted sat in somebody's in-basket for *two weeks*. I tracked them down myself. They just went out Tuesday. I made a big scandal with the head supply officer, Colonel Fischer. You know what he said? He said, 'Lieutenant, calm down. Do you really think the Egyptians can aim and fire missiles? Anyway, whatever missiles they've got are Russian, they're bound to malfunction. You'll get your countermeasures by November, that's three weeks away. So what's the fuss?' "

"He doesn't have to patrol off Port Said," observed the captain gloomily. There was hard intelligence of Soviet-made Osa and Komar missile boats of the Egyptian navy in Port Said. But they had not gone into action in the war, so senior navy officers, unlike the two destroyer captains, were not taking them seriously.

Under the steaming shower Noah wondered how he could assist his American cousin. Haifa customs agents were all alike, except that some were more rascally than others. He couldn't leave the ship, but it occurred to him that Daphna might help the guy. She often got Friday off, and Barkowe might simply have a language problem.

Jack Barkowe ordered an early breakfast in his hotel room and sat at the window, delighting in the spectacular view of Haifa harbor. Like San Francisco, only prettier, he thought in his exalted mood. The Mekhess snag had not fazed him. His family and friends, trying to dissuade him from going on aliya, had harped on the notorious Israeli bureaucracy. Well, here he was, and he would lick the Mekhess and bring in his Porsche. It was as good a way as any to cut his teeth on his new life.

The door opened and in rolled a room service table ahead of a waiter smiling and singing the victory song that had swept Israel.

Jerusalem of gold,
Of bronze and of light . . .

"And where is *Adoni* [Milord] going today?" inquired the waiter, a little dark mustached man in a white coat. "Nazareth? The Golan Heights? The Sea of Galilee? The tomb of Maimonides, maybe? That's very good luck, the tomb of Maimonides. It's near Tiberias. I visited it, and my wife got pregnant with twins."

"I'm not married."

"Visit the tomb of Maimonides, and you'll get married. To a beautiful Israeli girl."

As Barkowe was finishing his breakfast the telephone rang. "Mr. Barkowe? You having trouble with the Mekhess?"

"Who are you?"

"Avi Shammai, of Shammai Brothers. We solve Mekhess problems. Our specialty is automobiles."

"Come right up."

Avi Shammai was a big stout blond man, in a striped short-sleeved shirt, brown pants, and sandals on bare feet. "It's no problem," he said. "We run into this all the time."

"How can you help me?"

Avi Shammai's English was rapid but cloudy. His proposal involved temporarily transferring ownership of the Porsche to the Shammai Brothers, who would take it to Cyprus, adjust the odometer to show more mileage, perform other alterations, and bring it back in as a secondhand car. Something like that. Barkowe found him hard to follow, but through the verbiage three points gradually became clear. First, it was no problem; second, the cost would be twenty-five thousand American dollars; third, Barkowe would pay twenty-five hundred dollars now, the balance when Shammai Brothers delivered him the car.

"When will that be?"

"In a month, guaranteed."

"What's your phone number?"

"Mr. Barkowe, Shammai Brothers is a busy firm. I've brought all the necessary documents —"

"Just your number, please." Barkowe pulled from his pocket the card the Israeli had given him on the ferry. "Write it on here."

Shammai took the card and glanced at it. With a strange expression mingling amazement and horror he said, "You know Guli?"

"Who?"

The agent extended the card, printed all in Hebrew except for two words, *Avram Gulinkoff*. "Him. Where did you get this card?"

None of this fellow's business, Barkowe thought. "Oh, friend of my father's. Why?"

Avi Shammai dropped the card on the breakfast table and hurried out, his sandals loudly flapping. Barkowe was puzzling over this bizarre turn when the phone rang again. Another helpful agent? Was his predicament the talk of Haifa?

"Dzeck Barkowe?" A girl's voice, peppy and sweet.

"I'm Jack Barkowe. Who is this?"

"My name's Daphna Luria. I'm Noah Barak's friend, and I'm here in the lobby. You're having problems with the Mekhess?"

"I'll be right down. Tan jacket."

"I'll find you, Dzecki."

Barkowe had never liked the familiar "Jackie." It was his custom to growl, "The name's Jack," when people used it. But *Dzecki*, as this girl said it, sounded sort of piquant.

The elevator door opened on pandemonium. From big snorting busses tourists were pouring into the hotel, and more tourists were pouring out into other enormous busses spouting black fumes. The lobby was festooned with banners — KING DAVID TOURS, HOLY LAND TOURS, SCHEINBAUM TOURS, PARADISE TOURS — under which mountains of luggage rose. Shouldering through the tumultuous lobby, looking for someone who might be Daphna, Barkowe heard a babble of tongues, English predominating. A tap on his shoulder. "Here I am, Dzecki." She was a smallish girl in a beige uniform, with heavy blond hair on which perched a little black cap. Her bosom was marked, her figure slender, her eyes lively and amused. A dish, at first glance. "Do we talk Hebrew or English?" she inquired.

"N'nasseh Ivrit," he said. ("Let's try Hebrew.")

"Ah. Very good. Noah thinks," she said, as they pushed toward the lobby entrance, "that maybe I can help you. He can't leave the ship until tomorrow, when the Mekhess will be closed." She glanced pertly at him. "Shabbat. Understand?"

"Every word."

"Lovely."

Soon they were riding in a small slanted subwaylike car going down a steep tunnel. "This is the Carmelit," she said. "Don't waste your money on taxis while you're at the Dan. We can walk from the bottom to the Mekhess."

They did, and found the huge shed vacant and quiet; no cars, no inspectors, all windows but one closed. "There's my car," he said.

"Which one?"

"The blue one."

The Porsche gleamed among the shoddy impounded cars like a sapphire dropped in dirt. Daphna widened amazed eyes at him, bluer than the Porsche. "That's YOUR car, Dzecki? What are you, a millionaire's son?"

He laughed. "I'm broke. It's a story."

At the open window, Barkowe handed his documents through the grill to a bald man with very big yellow false teeth. "Ah yes, the Porsche. Interesting case," said the man in passable English, his teeth clicking. "But the boat to Italy has left."

Daphna entered into a vigorous dispute which Barkowe could not follow at all, the teeth behind the grill clicking like castanets. "Well, you have a real problem," she said at last to Barkowe. "Let's go to the supervisor. This man isn't a bad person, he feels sorry for you."

"Sure. *Ani mitzta'er.*"

A glint of humor flashed in her sharp blue eyes. "Just so. *Ani mitzta'er*. You'll hear that a lot in Israel."

The paunchy supervisor had a large sad face and sat in a very small office, behind a desk piled high with scruffy folders. He nodded often at the pretty soldier as she rattled on, regarding her with benign melancholy appetite.

"You understand Hebrew?" he asked Barkowe in a hoarse rumble.

"Not the way she's talking now."

The supervisor almost smiled, and spoke slowly. "Sir, in strict confidence, by January your car will undoubtedly be admissible. A former high Treasury official plans to import this model, you see."

"*January*? I'm paying twenty dollars a day storage. Can't I post a bond meantime and use it?"

"No, no. Unheard of. Twenty dollars a day is a problem, I grant you. The next boat for Italy leaves Monday." At the look on the American's face he shrugged. "Ani mitzta'er."

As they left the shed Daphna said, "I've been useless to you."

"Far from it. Thanks a lot, now I know where I stand. I'm going to Tel Aviv and break down all doors in the American Embassy."

"Good for you." With a beautiful smile Daphna Luria held out her hand. "I think you'll survive here, Dzecki." She strode off to a bus stop, and looking after her, he thought he had seldom seen a more seductive swaying walk. Lucky Cousin Noah! There had to be other Israeli girls like Daphna Luria, and at that, he might yet try the tomb of Maimonides. Back in his room the breakfast table had not yet been removed, and there lay the card of Avram Gulinkoff. What could he lose? He asked the hotel operator to get him the phone number.

"Guli speaking," said the hoarse voice brusquely. "Who's this?"

"Mr. Gulinkoff, this is Jack Barkowe."

"What? Who?"

"The American on the ferry."

A peculiar sound, half a growl and half a chuckle. "Oh, yes, Yaakov. Shalom. What can I do for you, Yaakov?"

In dirty fatigues and a dirtier floppy cap, her hands and face black-smeared, Daphna was hurrying to the gate of the Ramat David air force base a few days later. A note had been handed to her: *Sergeant Luria — Unauthorized civilian at gate inquiring for you. Has no pass.* Outside the guard hut, a cluster of guards and off-duty soldiers all but hid the blue Porsche. Astounded, she pushed through. "Dzecki! By my life, how did you get it out?"

He stood by the car, tipping his red driver's cap. "Hi, Daphna, care for a spin?"

"You fool, I can't leave the base."

"Just joking. I'm on my way to the Golan Heights. I thought I'd let you know I've got my car, and thank you for your help at the Mekhess."

"Me? I did nothing. Who liberated it, the American ambassador?"

"You're not even close."

The enlisted men who surrounded them were all grinning. The visit would be the talk of the base, she knew. She was a marked girl at Ramat David, for her father, Colonel Benny Luria, had led a squadron of Mirages in the surprise air strike on Egypt, which — at least in air force opinion — had won the Six-Day War in the first seven minutes. "Well, nice seeing you, but I can't stay, I'm on duty."

"Right." He jumped into the Porsche and started it up with a rich purr.

"My God," she couldn't help saying, "how I'd love to drive that car."

"Anytime, Daphna." He tipped the cap and roared off.

He was soaking in a hot tub the following night, stiff and aching from ten hours of driving around the Negev, and from a bone-jolting ride on a camel at a Bedouin market outside Beersheba. *R-r-r-ing* went the phone by the tub. "Dzecki? It's Daphna Luria. I'm calling from my base."

"Daphna, hi. What's up?"

"Have you been to Jericho or Hebron?"

"No. I've driven all over, but not in the occupied territories. I'm too new here."

"Sensible. Well, listen. I'm free on Friday, and it turns out that poor Noah can't meet me. His ship will have to relieve the *Jaffa* a day early, it's got engine trouble, and we're both furious. I asked him about showing you around the West Bank Friday and he said by all means to do it."

"Great. What's involved, Daphna? Any risk?"

"Nothing to it. The Arabs are behaving very well indeed, I assure you. They're in shock. We'll have no trouble at all. Be here at seven, and that'll give us a nice long day."

"You're on."

It was a cold windy cloudy morning, the sun a low dull red ball, when Daphna came out of the gate and waved. Dzecki this time saw not a sloppy mess in fatigues, but the fetching girl of the Dan lobby, with one difference. Swinging on a shoulder as before was her blue leather purse, but slung over the other was a submachine gun.

"Shalom, Dzecki. We talk Hebrew, yes? Good practice for you." He jumped out and ran around to open the door for her. "Oo-ah, such a *gentleman*. How nice." She gestured at the gate guards, who were goggling at the Porsche and at them. "Those boors can't imagine what you're doing, or why. Probably never saw it happen before."

"Daphna, what's with the Uzi?" He got behind the wheel and started the car.

"Elohim, Dzecki, what a sound that engine makes! Like a tiger waking up. I'm signed out for the Uzi, and I'd better bring it back, or it's my head. Let's just get going."

"Okay. Where to?"

"Simple. Afula, Jenin, Nablus, Jericho. Straight run."

"Fine. You direct me."

"Now come on," she said as they started off, "however did you get this car out of the claws of the Mekhess?"

"Well, it's a story." He described his meeting with Gulinkoff on the ferry, then had her giggling with an account of Avi Shammai's visit, and his strange reaction to the man's business card. "After you and I got nowhere, Daphna, I thought I'd just call the guy, a shot in the dark. He was real nice, this Guli. He said he was about to fly to Switzerland, but he'd be back soon and look into it. He sure did."

"Oo-ah, such *protectsia*. Guli, you say? Noah must know him. A real manipulator. You were lucky."

"Was I ever! He called me a couple of days later and said, 'Go get your car, Yaakov.' That was that."

"Yaakov? Why Yaakov? Where did he get that name?"

As Dzecki explained she was smiling indulgently. "Don't be in such a hurry to change your name. Dzecki is nice. So! And the Mekhess simply let you drive it away?"

"Right. Four days' storage fee, and a twenty-shekel fine for violating regulations. And when I think what the Shammai Brothers wanted of me —"

"Good for you, Dzecki. Most Americans would have gone along with the Shammai Brothers."

They were entering Afula, a dusty quiet town where children watched with open mouths as the Porsche went by. The one light at the center of town was green, and they turned right into a stream of vehicles, mainly trucks of crated fruit and vegetables, and army lorries carrying bored or sleeping soldiers. Beyond Afula, on a two-lane asphalt road through green-brown farmland, the traffic gradually thinned. He explained as they drove how his grandmother Lydia, a lifelong Hadassah lady, had gone into ecstasies over his making aliya, and had presented him with his choice of cars.

"L'Azazel, I wish I had such a grandmother. How fast can this car go, Dzecki?"

"On the autostradas I've done a hundred miles an hour. But here —"

"Oo-ah, a hundred sixty kilometers! *Shiga'on!* [Crazy, marvellous!]"

"Daphna, I'm playing it safe here. Ninety is the limit, so I crawl at ninety."

"Oh, go a hundred ten, Dzecki. It's all right."

The car darted ahead and she leaned back, crossing her arms and sighing with contentment. "Ah-h-h! Both my grandmothers live on a moshav. Nahalal, actually Moshe Dayan's moshav. Never left. That's where both my parents were born, grew up, and got married. Moshavniks can't give away Porsches. By the way, Dzecki, we're just crossing over the Green Line."

"We are?" He glanced around in bewilderment. "Here? You mean we're entering the *West Bank*? It all looks the same."

Daphna uttered a hearty charming laugh, showing fine white teeth. "By my life, this is an experience, riding with you. Of course it's the same, what did you think? That it would be a different color, like on a map? It's all just Palestine."

"But no fence, no sign, nothing?"

"What for? The Green Line wasn't real. Nothing but a mark on a map. When Jordan attacked us in the Six-Day War, poof, end of Green Line. Gone." She laid a hand on his arm. "Say, when do I get to drive? You promised."

"Nothing doing. I've read the law. They'll confiscate my car if you're caught driving it."

"Read the law again. If you're in the car with me, no problem."

"You're sure? Say, it gets prettier and prettier out here, doesn't it?" He was glancing at a little Arab village snugged up on a rocky slope. "Real Bible scenery."

"Oh, the West Bank's lovely. We call it Judah and Samaria, the Bible names. Listen, Dzecki, the first big town we get to is Nablus. From there let me drive to Jericho, all right?"

"We'll see."

Nablus was a hilly town, wholly Arab in architecture and in populace. In the noisy central plaza amid food stalls and small open shops, half a dozen empty busses were lined up, and groups of sightseers were strolling about, shepherded by guides. Some Arab children stared silently at the Porsche, but the white-robed men in kaffiyehs and the bigger boys on foot or on braying little donkeys utterly ignored it, as they ignored the thronging tourists.

"Lock the car, of course," she said to Dzecki, as he parked in the plaza and they got out. Dzecki could hear the Israeli guides mostly talking English, with here and there some patter in French or German.

"Say, about that gun, Daphna."

"Yes, what about it?"

"Couldn't one of these Arabs grab it and make trouble?"

"You think so? Try to take it from me, Dzecki." He smiled skeptically. "Go ahead, I mean it, just try."

He made a quick sudden move at her, and even more quickly she unslung the Uzi and the muzzle was against his stomach. "See? Don't worry, we're trained. Anyway, look there." In a patrol jeep nearby, five soldiers in black berets sat surveying the scene through dark glasses, guns at the ready. "The Arabs have learned their lesson, believe me, for good and all. These tourists are as safe as they would be in London. Let's look around a bit, and drive on. Jericho's nicer."

He sniffed the air. "Exciting smells! Strange spices, strange foods, and —"

"And donkey dung, not so strange."

He laughed. "Popular sightseeing spot, for sure."

"Well, Nablus is really Shechem, you know. Very important in Bible history. Right there," she indicated a mountain looming over the town, "is Har Gerizim, where the Samaritans still worship."

As they walked down a main street a tall Arab boy in a shirt and slacks, with a broad tray of fragrant fresh flat breads on his head, passed by them and went into a gloomy alley of tumbledown stone houses. "My God, those smell marvelous," Dzecki said. "I'm starved. I'm going to buy one. For you, too?"

"No thanks, but listen, Dzecki —"

He started after the boy into the alley, which was full of Arab men and boys sitting around on stone steps. Behind him he heard harsh shouting, and over his shoulder he saw a lean gun-toting soldier running toward Daphna, berating her in rapid-fire Hebrew. She was answering back angrily. "Dzecki, get out of there," she called, and went on arguing with the soldier. Dzecki hastily backed out of the alley, and the soldier walked off muttering.

"That place is off limits for tourists," Daphna explained. "Not that anything would happen, but still — oh, come on, let's run down to Jericho. There's lots of good places to eat. Please, please let me drive. Look, I've brought my license. See?"

The appeal in the big eyes was not to be resisted, not by Dzecki. "Well, sure."

When she got behind the wheel of the Porsche, her face lit up like a child's. "Yes, yes, I understand, I see, I see," she kept saying as he explained the controls. "No problem, no problem. I'm ready to go, let's move."

"All yours," he said. "On to Jericho."

She started off smoothly. As the car passed the soldier who had made the fuss, he shook a reproving finger at them. "The road's better from here on," she said, "and the scenery's truly lovely." She drove carefully through the town, and spoke again when they were on asphalt highway, bowling along at a hundred twenty. "My God, what a glorious sensation. You'll have to let Noah drive this car one day."

"Glad to. Are you and he getting married?"

"Elohim, no. I've got more than a year of *sadir* to do, and God knows whether I want to marry a naval officer, anyway. I've *had* the military, up to here." She put a flat hand to her throat, and threw back her head in a wild laugh. "I just like him." Traffic was light, but there were trucks and horse-drawn wagons to pass. Daphna did so with nervy skill, concentrating on her driving. The play of her shapely thighs under the tight army skirt, as she worked brake and accelerator, caught Dzecki's attention and held it.

"I look forward to meeting Noah."

"Oh, you will." She gave him a quick glance. "You resemble each other, you know? Same round face. Same hairline and thick hair, same brown eyes. The Berkowitz face, I guess. General Barak also has it. He's the best-looking man I've ever met, though he's going gray."

"Like to meet him, too," mumbled Dzecki a bit thickly, watching Daphna's legs thrusting and rolling this way and that. Daphna was oblivious to this hot scrutiny of her limbs, or seemed to be, and he enjoyed the frustrating pleasure all the way to Jericho.

Unlike Nablus, where he had felt obscurely uncomfortable, Jericho charmed him. As the Porsche descended the winding mountain road toward the little city of palms, he felt a touch of awe. *Jericho . . . Shechem . . . Hebron . . . Jordan . . . the Dead Sea . . .* Far from religion though he was, Dzecki had breathed in with the American air veneration for these Holy Land sights. The pileup of busses, the tourists led about in clusters by guides, did not bother him here. The Jericho Arabs seemed friendlier, or at least not sullen and withdrawn as in Nablus. In fact the hucksters in the market stalls, chaffering with camera-laden Americans, were all smiles and gracious gestures.

"Tell you what," said Daphna, "we'll feed you first, then have a look around. You like humus and tehina?"

"Love it."

"You'll really love Abdul's. Best in Jericho."

She deftly turned and twisted through streets that even the small Porsche could barely scrape through. "Here we are." Beside a moss-encrusted low stone building, she pulled into a grassy plot. Shouldering gun and purse, she led him into a dark small eating place. "Too late for breakfast, too early for lunch," she said. "Nice, no other customers. I'll order for you."

"You're not going to eat?"

"Not me. Had a big breakfast." She rattled in Arabic at a fat aproned man behind the counter, and almost at once he smilingly served the humus with a basket of warm pitas and a bowl of olives. "Hearty appetite," she said. "I'll go and get the tank filled. It's a long way to Hebron."

"I've got to be with you in the car, no?"

"Pah! We're not on the highway. There are no cops in these back alleys." Dzecki shrugged, and she left. He scooped up all the humus and tehina with the pitas, washed it down with a beer, and was beginning to feel very good and relaxed when Daphna showed up, a man in a blue police uniform following her into the shop.

"You own the Porsche this lady was driving, Adoni?" the policeman asked him.

"Yes, any problem?" Dzecki tried for a light tone.

"It will be impounded. Please follow me," said the policeman, producing a notebook and going out.

Dzecki and Daphna looked at each other for a long moment, and she said softly in English, "Sorry, Dzecki. Sorry, sorry, sorry."

A sad laugh broke from him. "What you mean is, 'Ani mitzta'er.' "

She looked puzzled, then her face brightened, and she ruefully laughed too. "Just so. Only feminine, Ani mitzta'eret. Me and the Mekhess, hah? Noah will kill me for this."

"No problem," he said, "let's just hope Guli isn't in Switzerland."

2

The Telephone Call

"Green rocket to starboard," called the lookout on the flying bridge of the *Eilat*.

Pale in the setting sun, the rocket was arcing straight up into the sky over Port Said, beyond the horizon some thirteen miles away. The captain was dozing in his wheelhouse chair. Noah was navigating, checking bearings so as to stay well in international waters. The destroyer was slowly steaming the dogleg course in sight of the high Sinai dunes, which it had been patrolling turn by turn with the *Jaffa* for months. Shabbat routine, and the off-duty crew were sleeping, reading, or taking showers.

Noah's eye was at the alidade but his mind was on Daphna Luria, as it had been since they left port. What a rotten break, their cancelled Friday date! She had demurely told him, in one of their long telephone calls, that a girlfriend in Afula was going skiing in Austria, and had given her the key to her flat, where there were marvellous rock-and-roll records. That was all, but from the heated husky note in her voice, and from picturing the rest, Noah had been in a joyous fever for days. At last, at last . . . of all times for the damned *Jaffa* to lose an engine . . .

"What's this? Rocket to starboard?" The captain jumped from his chair, went out on the wing, and trained binoculars at a yellow light blossoming high in the sky. After a long moment he said, "Noah, what do you think?"

Noah was reluctant to believe his eyes, yet there it was, floating like a starshell but growing bigger. "By my life, they really may have fired one, Captain."

"It's possible. Battle stations, Noah."

Darting into the wheelhouse, the exec seized the microphone. *"Emdot krav, emdot krav."* ("Battle stations, battle stations.") The siren wailed, and sailors came swarming and yelling out of hatches and passageways and up ladders, some half-dressed, some naked but for shorts, pulling on life jackets as they ran. *"Azakah, azakah."* ("Alarm, alarm.") This was the emergency order to fire at will. The AA guns opened up at the swelling light with a deafening RAT-TAT-TAT and streams of red tracers.

"Left full rudder. All engines ahead flank." The captain's voice went strident. He took the microphone from Noah. "Now all hands, this is the captain. *TEEL.* [*MISSILE.*] I say again, *TEEL, TEEL, TEEL to starboard.*"

Through Noah's binoculars a small black shape became discernible in the yellow glow. One count against that son of a whore, Colonel Fischer, the Egyptians could fire a missile, all right. Now, was it really bound to malfunction because it was Russian? Intelligence said that this Soviet weapon, dubbed the Styx, was subsonic and radar-directed. That was all. Nobody in Israel, or indeed in the West, had yet seen a Styx fired. This was a first, a historic revelation.

"Look, Noah, isn't it altering course?"

"I believe so, sir."

The ship was heeling hard over, scoring a white curve on the crimson sunset sea, and the yellow light appeared to be turning with it. Its guidance radar was working, then. It was clear to see now in binoculars, a long delta-winged tube shooting reddish-yellow fire from its tail and trailing black smoke. The ship's guns rattled and boomed, crimson tracers combed the missile, but on it came. The evasive turn was futile, Noah realized, merely swinging the ship broadside to present a wider target. He plunged to grab his life jacket as the missile started its dive, and had it half on when a shocking CRASH! catapulted him across the deck of the wheelhouse. His head struck a projection, he saw broken lights, and all went black . . .

"You okay now, Lieutenant?" The helmsman was helping him to his feet. Putting a hand to his head, Noah felt warm sticky blood. His vision was misty and his head painfully throbbed. He peered around at the steeply listing wheelhouse, a chaos of overturned instruments, shattered glass, and tumbled books and charts. The wheel was swinging free, unattended.

"What the devil! Get back to that helm, Polski."

"Sir, it's no use, the rudder hasn't responded since we got hit, and —"

"Rocket to port." A soprano yell full of fright.

Shouts rose everywhere, and staggering out on a wing, Noah saw smoke and flame all over the ship and many arms pointing to a new light in the darkening sky. The *Eilat* was port beam to this second missile, and the captain stood staring at the expanding yellow eye, eerily reflected on the glassy sea.

"Captain, can't we maneuver with engines? We're broadside to again —"

"Ah, good, you're on your feet, but Elohim, you're a bloody mess! Maneuver? How? I have no rudder, Noah, only one engine, and I can't contact them below. God knows how many were killed. Sure you're all right? You were kaput for quite a while —"

"I'm okay. By God, sir, that thing's going into its dive."

"I see it. Hit the deck," shouted the captain, "nothing else to do now."

Descending through sparse gunfire, the second missile threw up a towering splash. Noah fell prone on cold metal, an explosion made the whole ship ring like a giant gong, and he felt it as a brutal blow on his chest and arms. Stumbling back to his feet, he saw a smoky column of new red fire rising amidships. Crewmen were running about and yelling, others were picking up the wounded. The power hum that was the ship's breath of life had suddenly ceased. The *Eilat* was a dead listing drifting hulk.

Getting up from the deck, the captain said to Noah in a curiously calm way over the clamor of the sailors, "We'll have to abandon ship."

"Why? We can call for help, Captain. Helicopters can be here in fifteen minutes and —"

The captain shook his head. "Don't you know our radio gear is out? Goldstein worked on it and we tried and tried, but we couldn't raise the army in Sinai, let alone Haifa HQ. The current is setting us toward Port Said, Noah. I've dropped the anchors, but they aren't holding —"

"All the same, we can stay afloat for hours yet, sir, and keep the crew together until —"

"Until *what*? The magazines can go anytime, and I have a lot of helpless wounded to think about. Look at those fires —"

"Sir, I think Goldstein and I can jury-rig a radio." Improvising an emergency set had been a classroom problem at which Noah had excelled, in an electronics course for officers.

"You can?" The captain gnawed his lips. "How long would it take you?"

"If we find the components, maybe twenty, thirty minutes. It's our best chance, sir. Otherwise the navy won't know for hours, maybe all night, what's happened to us —"

"Give it a try. But fast."

Scrounging in the wrecked radio room by flashlight, he and the handy little radioman Goldstein assembled tubes, wires, and batteries into a messy tangled contraption, its range for sending and receiving a total guess. A bright moon shone on the burning ship, down hard by the stern and listing more and more, when Noah commenced calling, *"IHS* Eilat *here. Mayday, Mayday. We are sinking. Request immediate help."*

Low crackling in the receiver, nothing more. Beaming toward Sinai, the radioman kept sweeping the crude antenna from north to south and back to north, while Noah repeated wearily, *"All Zahal units in Sinai. IHS* Eilat *calling. Mayday, Mayday. Does anyone hear us?"*

He and Goldstein were crouched by the anchor windlass at the bow, signalling from the highest spot on the foundering *Eilat*.

Smoke still rose from flickering fires all over the ship, though the worst blazes had burnt out. The crew was crowded on the steeply inclined forecastle, where the wounded lay groaning in rows on the deck. Everything that could float — not only rafts but spare life jackets, wooden cupboards, empty oil drums — was piled higgledy-piggledy at the lifelines, for most of the boats were smashed. Any hope short of abandoning ship now lay in the makeshift radio. Twenty minutes, and still no human voice had punctuated the weak static.

Noah had too much time to think, in the long agonizing wait. What a horror this was, his ship sinking under him, so many dead boys in the engine room, the terrible lineup of injured, moaning, crying sailors along the forecastle deck; himself half-numb from the shock of his own still-bleeding head wound, his mind drifting in and out of the nightmare amid dreamy thoughts of Daphna . . .

"IHS Eilat *here. Mayday, Mayday. We are sinking —"*

Barks of laughter from the radio. Noah's heart leaped as he came alert. A harsh tumble of Arabic, then crackling silence.

"What the devil was all that?" the captain asked.

" *'Go ahead and drown, Jews, and sink to hell,'* " said Noah.

The captain cursed.

Noah said, "Sir, sir, now at least we know we're transmitting. It's a break —"

Looking around at the jammed forecastle, his eyes puffed half-shut, the captain pointed aft, where dark waves were lapping over the canted fantail. He hoarsely exclaimed, "Noah, I've got to get my wounded off, and if we don't —"

A deep voice, calm and friendly, in clear Hebrew: *"This is army unit Aleph Dalet Three in Sinai. We receive you,* Eilat. *Go ahead."*

"Oh God! Captain, hear that?" cried Noah. Never in his life would anything sound as sweet or dear to him, he thought, as that response in Hebrew.

"I heard it, I heard it, keep talking to him —"

"Sinai, Sinai, do you receive me clearly?"

"Hiuvi, hiuvi [Affirmative, affirmative], Eilat. *Go ahead."*

"Sinai, we're northeast of Port Said, thirteen and a half miles out, clearly visible by moonlight. Hit by two missiles, on fire and sinking. Many wounded and dead. Two anchors down, drifting toward Egypt. Danger of being captured. Abandoning ship."

"Ruth [Roger], Eilat. *All authorities will be alerted. Rescue helicopters will come. Keep in contact."*

With his battery-powered bullhorn the captain roared this news to the crew. Cheers rose on the forecastle.

Taking the wounded off forced terrible choices on the ship's doctor, Noah, and the captain, as to who should go in the remaining boats, who on rafts, who in life jackets; quick cold-blooded decisions about the seriousness of injuries and the chances of men living through the night. At the order *Abandon ship* the boats full of the worst wounded were lowered, the crew threw everything floatable overboard, and then began sliding down ropes or leaping into the sea. The officers went last.

Noah's naked legs were plunging into cool water when he heard yells in the dark around him, *"Teel, teel."* Over the ship's bow, now black and steep against the stars, another yellow glare showed. He remembered to turn on his back. The explosion threw up a black fountain of water that foamed white in the moonlight. The *crack!* all along Noah's spine was like being hit by a speeding car. Then he thought he must be delirious, because it seemed he heard singing. Pulling himself up with searing pain on a floating jerrican, he saw shadowy sailors nearby clustered on a raft, raising discordant defiant voices:

Jerusalem of gold,
Of bronze and of light . . .

Seven time zones to the east, General Zev Barak at this moment was reviewing the navy requisitions for missile countermeasures, which had arrived at the Israeli Embassy in Washington by diplomatic pouch that morning. The military attaché was a prematurely gray officer in his early forties, an older heavier Noah, with lighter skin and bushier eyebrows. Noah had been beseeching his father by telephone for help. Now that the papers were in hand Zev Barak felt he could act. Procurement of such secret electronic gear would be tough at best, but he thought he might argue that countermeasures, being purely defensive gadgets, should not be embargoed as weaponry. The Pentagon was being damned obdurate on major replenishment long overdue. This might be a bone it would throw to Israel.

He pulled a greenish pad from a drawer and began a rapid scrawl in Hebrew of a draft memorandum. Unlike so much of the humdrum paperwork in this assignment, here at least was a labor of love, a way to be of use to his son out on the firing line. Barak was not happy in this job. He had never been. During his brief visit to Jerusalem after the great victory, the Minister of Defense had told him, *"What you accomplished in Washington, Zev, was worth two brigades in the field."* Coming from Moshe Dayan that was something, but words were easy. Barak's army contemporaries who had fought the war had leaped ahead on the *maslul,* the career track toward General Staff posts, sector commands, and the grand prize of Ramatkhal, Chief of Staff. Nothing Dayan said could change that. In earlier missions to Washington, Barak had earned a reputation of deftness at handling Americans, which now was proving a trap.

Writing up the memorandum absorbed him until his intercom buzzed. "General, your lunch with the Assistant Secretary is at twelve-thirty."

"L'Azazel, thanks, Esther." Finishing the draft would have to wait. He slipped on his army topcoat and drove to the Pentagon through the gorgeous autumn foliage along the Potomac.

Henry Pearson, one of several Assistant Secretaries of Defense, was a gaunt bureaucrat with a chronic cigarette cough, who fancied military history and liked to chat with Barak about Thucydides, Napoleon, and Garibaldi. Not today, though. Air force colonel Bradford Halliday was unexpectedly there in the office, and he rose to shake hands with the Israeli.

"I believe you gentlemen know each other," said Pearson.

"We're acquainted," said Halliday, cool and unsmiling.

"Nice to see you again," said Barak. In their awkward previous encounter, Halliday had been in civilian clothes. He looked taller, leaner, and more formidable in a blue uniform with combat decorations. It would have taken a sharper observer than Henry Pearson to discern that these two men were in love with the same woman, and had run into each other only once by chance on her premises, much to her embarrassment and theirs.

They lunched on curried shrimp at a window facing acres of parked cars, for Pearson did not rate an office with a river view. The topic of the lunch was forty-eight Skyhawk light attack bombers, contracted for by Israel some time ago and still not delivered. Pearson explained, coughing a lot, that since the United States was now embargoing all weapons shipments to the Middle East, and urging the Soviets to do the same, delivery of the Skyhawks at present was not feasible. Barak protested with heat that this was highly unsatisfactory, because the Russians, while pondering the embargo proposal, were continuing to rearm Egypt and Syria at an alarming rate. Halliday was at the meeting, it soon emerged, to help the easygoing Pearson stall off Barak. This the airman did with dry authority.

"General, Israel has wiped out all hostile air forces in your region," he said. "Your air superiority is absolute. You can't deny that. The urgency of our delivering the Skyhawks just now therefore escapes me."

"The urgency, Colonel, as I've just pointed out to the Assistant Secretary, is Russian resupply to our enemies. Clearly that compels us to start to resupply ourselves. Air superiority isn't a static thing. When Arab aircraft outnumber our squadrons three or four to one — we project a period of eighteen months from now at the present rate, with newer MiGs, by the way — our position could become awkward."

"Airplanes don't fly themselves," retorted Halliday, forking up curry. "Your air victory decimated their pilot pool, and it'll be a long time regenerating."

"With Russian instructors? Why?" Barak disliked shrimp, so he was picking at the bread and butter. "Arab manpower is infinite, compared to ours. Training a quality pilot takes a year."

"Zev, Russian instructors can't instill the motivation your pilots have," Pearson put in.

"True, because we fight for national survival, and the Arabs don't. Is that a reason to withhold from us the wherewithal to fight?"

Pearson coughed hard, and glanced at the impassive air force colonel. "Zev's a good arguer, isn't he?"

Halliday merely nodded. He had spoken his piece, nailing down the undeclared and unpalatable fact that President Johnson and the State Department were mending fences with the Arabs, and that Pearson, though friendly, was helpless. Barak wasted no more words on the Skyhawks, and the meeting ended with sparring about ammunition replenishment and parts for Patton tanks, during which Halliday was silent and Pearson vague.

Barak and Halliday left the office together. In the corridor Barak was ready for a cool curt goodbye, but Halliday surprised him. "General, where's your car?"

"Parking lot E."

"So's mine. May we talk a bit?"

"By all means."

Halliday told him as they traversed the tortuous Pentagon rings and stairwells that the superintendent of the Air Force Academy, his old wingmate, was eager to invite an Israeli squadron leader to lecture on the great air victory. "He has in mind Colonel Benny Luria. You must know him."

"Very well."

"Would you approach Luria? The superintendent wants him for sometime in November."

"I'm sure Benny would be honored, if he can do it. I'll have to go through air force channels, of course. Otherwise there's Avihu Bin Nun, another great squadron leader, also Ron Pecker —"

"The word is that Luria's an able speaker."

"That's the truth. I'll get on this at once."

"I'll be greatly obliged."

They came outside in a chilly mist, and Halliday surprised him even more. "Have you heard from Emily?"

Barak mustered all his calm to reply, "Not since she left New Delhi."

Emily Cunningham had in fact written him only once on her

round-the-world trip, mentioning that her correspondence with Bud Halliday was getting hot and heavy since his sidetracking from Vietnam to the Pentagon. Whether that had been a prod to elicit jealous regret, or just more of Emily's rattling candor, it had hurt.

"She writes genuinely amusing letters," said Halliday. "Of course you know that."

"Yes, we've corresponded off and on for many years. She's an original, Emily. Is she holding to her itinerary?"

"Apparently. Due back from Paris in two weeks. Here's my car." Halliday held out his hand. "See here, General, about those Skyhawks, entirely off the record" — Halliday paused, his face a trifle less forbidding than in Pearson's office — "holding them up is a temporary diplomatic blip. Denying them to you altogether would be bad faith. That won't happen. We're not the French, and the President isn't De Gaulle. Israel will get the aircraft. Meantime fussing by your government doesn't help. Save your energy — and the considerable political capital that you've gained with your victory — for other matters."

Barak seized the moment to ask Halliday about Noah's missile countermeasures. The airman listened with a knitted brow. "Well, you can get that so-called chaff on the open market. Window, we term it. It's a question of seaborne chaff launchers, which I wouldn't know about. As for the electronic stuff, that's my bailiwick, more or less, and in the air force it's highly classified." He shrugged, shaking his head. "About the navy, I can't say. Send me a personal letter, not through channels, and I'll bump it to a good navy contact."

"That will be very helpful."

The cold drizzle fogging Barak's windshield seemed to be drizzling into his spirit as he drove back to the embassy, angered by the turndown on the Skyhawks — though he had more or less anticipated it — and still hungry, for he had eaten nothing all day but that spongy Pentagon bread. Halliday's few words about Emily Cunningham had raked open a healing scar, bringing all too frustratingly to mind that strange winsome daughter of a decidedly strange CIA official, cut off from him by her own decision; the slender yielding body, the enormous clever bespectacled eyes, the disorderly halo of brown hair, the antic wit of her talk and her letters, the whole snaring presence which she had had even as a girl of twelve. Now she was reaching for a life beyond that of a girls school headmistress, and he could only welcome that, but he was discovering that loving two women — and he loved his wife as much as ever — did not halve the pain of losing one of them.

He had first caught sight of Emily Cunningham as a gamine with a tennis racket, scampering onto her father's patio, and later presiding gravely at the dinner table in her mother's absence; then showing him the fireflies on their lawn overlooking the Potomac, and prattling precocious romantic nonsense. Long afterward, in their rare encounters in Paris and in Jerusalem while she was studying at the Sorbonne, she had declared and insisted that she had an unshakeable crush on him. For long he had tried to laugh it off. But her beguiling and hilarious "pen pal" letters over the years had brightened his dogged army career and the constricted life in Israel. Then had come his missions to Washington, and the start of the affair. The unlucky assignment as military attaché had led to his getting in deep with her and — who could say? — perhaps even missing the war on that account . . .

Never mind, never MIND, stay off that quicksand . . .

He could more or less forget his breakup with that haunting woman in the drudging workload at the embassy, where the optimistic turmoil of victory still yeasted and bubbled. And why not? The Zionist organizations were happily swelling with members and funds, and clamoring for war-hero speakers like Dayan and Rabin; and these were not readily available, so the military attaché and the ambassador were winging all over the country as tolerable substitutes. That night Barak had to fly to Chicago to address a Zionist luncheon next day, and as he drove he was trying to work up some fresh angle for the talk, and to keep his thoughts from circling back to Emily Cunningham.

What could he say in Chicago that was really new? By now he had a memorized act. Quick review of the victory, to smiles and applause; cautionary words about enemy infractions of the cease-fire, about soldiers manning the Suez Canal line getting killed, about terrorists infiltrating from Jordan to mine and booby-trap the kibbutz fields — not what American Jews wanted to hear, so make that part short; then the exciting windup picturing Jerusalem and the West Bank after Moshe Dayan opened the borders, Arabs pouring peacefully into Zion Square to gaze with wonder at the shopwindows, Israelis thronging through the Old City bazaars to haggle for bargains and taste exotic foods, or joyriding in hordes to Jericho and Hebron, singing "Jerusalem of Gold"; all leading up to his personal anecdote of the graybeard Jew in a fur hat and ear curls, walking beside him through the Old City in a stream of Israelis on the way to the Western Wall, joyously exclaiming, *"MOSHIAKH'S TZEITEN!"* ("MESSIANIC TIMES!") He would certainly use that surefire finish again, however far he was from believing it.

He found on his desk a garbled telephone message from one Leon Barkowe, something about a son in Israel whose car had been confiscated. It took Barak a moment to recollect those distant Berkowitz relatives in Long Island whom he had not seen or spoken to in years. Another major task for the military attaché! But family was family, and even if the name was now Barkowe, a Berkowitz was a Berkowitz. He was about to return the call when a buzz on his intercom summoned him to the ambassador.

Abe Harman, a paunchy deathly pale man who sat in a perpetual slouch, and whose sleepy manner belied a razor-sharp alertness to every nuance of America-Israel relations, greeted him with a groan. "Always something. My wife's down with a stomach flu, and she's supposed to address a WIZO tea at the Mayflower this afternoon. She called me and said Nakhama should do it —"

"Nakhama? Abe, Nakhama's never made a speech here, her English isn't that good. Anyway, she's no speaker, forget it!"

"Zev, I've already talked to Nakhama, and she jumped at it. Sorry, but at three hours' notice I had little choice." With a foxy side-glance Harman added, "Will the world go under if she isn't a big hit? What did you accomplish at the Pentagon?"

"In one word, *bopkess* [goat shit]."

"Ah, so the goats are still grazing there." Harman heavily nodded. "Expected. Still, you lodged our protest against the breach of contract. Americans believe in contracts, live by them. They'll feel the pressure. So, you're off to Chicago tonight? I've got a major misery here at the Shoreham. Speech to a thousand Conservative rabbis. You're sure you don't mind about Nakhama?"

"Of course not. I'm surprised she's doing it, that's all."

"Zev, just when you think you have them figured out, they cross you up."

"Wisdom of Solomon, Ambassador," said Barak, and he went back to his office, where he began a letter to Colonel Halliday about missile countermeasures. He had not gotten far when a coding clerk phoned him. "Sir, General Pasternak is calling on the scrambler." It was like a red light flashing on an engine dial. Sam Pasternak, high in the Mossad and perhaps its secret head by now, had not used the secure telephone since the end of the war. Hurrying to the coding room, Barak shut himself into the soundproof booth, and Pasternak came through clearly.

"Zev? We have a serious development here." Deep solemn Pasternak tones, no trace of his usual irony. "I'm sorry to be breaking this news to you. The Egyptians have sunk the *Eilat* with a missile attack." Barak caught his breath, and Pasternak went on briskly, "Don't be too alarmed. Helicopters are out there right now picking up survivors, lots of them. Patrol boats are speeding to the scene. Chances are very good that your son is okay."

"Where and when did this happen, Sam?"

"Off Port Said around sunset. The missiles came from the boats in the harbor, no question. Abe Harman and Gideon Rafael have to be told right away." Rafael was Israel's ambassador to the United Nations. "The whole picture has changed, Zev. The balance of forces has shifted, and we're in a new situation. A new era."

Words from the Book of Job flashed into Barak's mind. *"The thing that I greatly feared has come upon me."* He had on file the intelligence about the missile boats in Port Said, and the navy chart which showed where the destroyers were patrolling off Egypt and Sinai. It had seemed to him a risky and provocative showing of the flag, and he had been concerned about Noah in that spot, but sea strategy was not his business.

"Have you been monitoring the Egyptians?"

"Yes. They've picked up the distress and rescue signals, and they'll call for a UN Security Council meeting tomorrow to claim the ship was in their territorial waters. Which it wasn't. They're bubbling with joy."

"Not for long," Barak said.

"Well, that's the big question now, how we respond. The Prime Minister is meeting now with Dayan and Foreign Minister Eban." The brisk dry tones of the intelligence man slowed and warmed. "I'll stay in close touch, Zev. I'll track the survivor list and let you know any news of Noah, the minute I hear."

"Thanks, Sam."

That was like Pasternak. Their friendship went far back to service together in a paramilitary youth group. Sam was a Czech by birth, the toughest of the tough, yet in his way a good Jewish boy, devoted to his mother and sisters, if not to an estranged wife. They had come a long way together in the army, before Sam had detoured into the Mossad.

Ambassador Harman's pouched eyes reddened and his pallid face turned a shade grayer when Barak told him the news. He said with a thick sigh, "So they haven't learned their lesson yet? Well, they will, believe me. I hope your son is all right. Ah, Zev, what a sad, sad business." He gestured at a typescript on his desk. "My speech is out the window. My title was 'The Coming Peace.' I meant every word, too." Narrowing his eyes, the ambassador went on slowly, half to himself, "I may be hearing from the State Department any minute. From senators, from Jewish leaders. Maybe I should call Dean Rusk myself. I'll think about that. Let me have a quick military analysis, Zev, the complications, the reprisal options. Something I can have in hand —"

"At once, Ambassador."

First Barak called Gideon Rafael in New York. Taking the news in stride, the UN ambassador asked businesslike questions about the attack, and said he would summon his staff that evening to plan Security Council tactics. On Barak's desk lay the start of his letter to Halliday. Too late, too late! He had an impulse to tear it up, but at that moment Nakhama came in. She wore a dark gray suit, and a feathered red hat was perched on her thick glossy black hair. "Like my hat? Zena Harman said the women at these things all wear hats. I just bought it at Garfinkel's. It was on sale. It isn't too much? Too *red*? Is the feather too silly?"

Should he tell her of the sinking? She was made up as for a party, and her eyes snapped with excitement. The idea of substituting for the brilliant Zena Harman had put her in high spirits. "It's a nice hat. What will you talk about?"

"About Noah. You know, how it feels to be a mother of a son fighting for Israel. About how we reacted when he first showed up in uniform. How we worried during the war, and were so glad when it was over. And for a laugh, about his capturing a fortress with nobody in it. How does that sound? Too personal?"

Rapid estimate before answering her: the tea should be over by five, the hatted ladies heading home for dinner. Even if the Egyptians claimed the sinking in the next hour or two, it would not make the network news right away. "Well, the question is, are you nervous?"

Nakhama threw back her head and laughed, and the hat fell off. "L'Azazel, how I hate hats!" she said, retrieving it. "Nervous? Why? It'll be fun. What have I got to lose? Don't worry, I won't disgrace you. Where is there a mirror?" She plopped the hat on her head, tilted it, and it looked very chic. "How's that?"

For answer, impelled by a pulse of love for her, he came and kissed his wife. Why panic her? Noah might well be in a helicopter right now, soaking wet but safe. That she was prettier than Emily Cunningham was an old story, but she was rarely this animated nowadays. Twenty-three years ago the sort of sweet faintly mischievous charm with which she now glowed had bewitched him into marrying a Moroccan waitress after knowing her for a week, over his parents' anguished objections. "Well, it sounds like a first-class speech. Good luck."

"Thanks. Poor Zev, off to Chicago tonight, aren't you? Will you have time to eat at home first? Galia and Ruti volunteered to cook dinner."

"That's a novelty I won't miss."

When she left it lacked a few minutes of three. He turned on his desk radio, and listened tensely to the bulletins. Not a word about the Middle East. Fine. The letter regarding the countermeasures still lay before him, and tearing it up, he realized, would be foolish. The *Jaffa* still sailed, and missiles could hit torpedo boats and patrol craft as well.

Awareness bore in on Barak that not only had the war with the Arabs entered a new phase; so had warfare at sea. No vessel had ever been sunk by a ship-to-ship missile until now, nor had any western country even tested such a weapon. Russia, the arsenal of the Arabs, had leaped at a stroke into the world lead in waterborne missile combat. Hard times ahead for Noah's navy, and a major shock on the global scene. The Soviet Union's massive edge in land armies was balanced off by superior American air and sea forces; but the Styx was suddenly a proven threat to the Sixth Fleet, and for that matter to all of NATO's surface warships.

Meantime, the wait for news. Zev's father had told him more than once that his hair had begun to turn white during the long silences of Zev's service in the British army, fighting Rommel in North Africa. At the time Zev, in the flush of soldierly youth, had shrugged off the old man's anxiety with some amusement; and now he was the old man worrying about his son. It had all happened fast. Who could have predicted that Noah would be hit at sea, by the first Arab blow after the Six-Day War? Nobody would be mothballing uniforms soon, that was now clear.

And what to say tomorrow in Chicago? By then the Egyptian coup would certainly be in the news. His standard act required drastic revision, and "*Messianic times*" was out for sure. On the other hand, it occurred to him that in this changed picture the forty-eight Skyhawks might be forthcoming.

He began scrawling rapidly in his clear Hebrew script on the green pad.

Sinking of the Eilat — *Implications and Options*

Egypt is militarily prostrate. In reprisal for this attack on the *Eilat,* our air force can sink every single Egyptian naval vessel afloat. It can level any targets in Egypt, from military bases to whole cities. Our armor forces can roll unchecked to Cairo. How then could

Colonel Nasser have dared to violate the cease-fire with such a major act of war? Is it suicidal lunacy?

Not in the least. To begin with, the sinking is a feeble first signal of Arab defiance in defeat. It proclaims that the "no's" of the Khartoum Declaration were not mere Arabic rhetoric, but hard policy. After the war our optimists were saying that it was only a matter of time before King Hussein or Colonel Nasser called Moshe Dayan on the telephone, offering peace for return of their lost territories. The telephone call came, all right, and it sank my son's destroyer.

The military loss is serious but endurable. The political damage to Israel's newfound world stature is something else. Our reprisal must be sure, swift, stern, and adequate to discourage any further such gross violations of the cease-fire agreement. For the Egyptian casualties, however heavy, that must result, Colonel Nasser will bear full responsibility, as he does for the lives lost on the *Eilat*.

As for the form of the reprisal, air strikes would cause an uproar in the UN and bring on Soviet threats which could get ugly. Back of the Egyptians always stand the Russians. That is why Nasser has risked this stroke. An armored raid in force across the Canal seems more likely. We lack bridging equipment, but a crossing on pontoon rafts against the demoralized Egyptian army may be feasible, razing army bases, industrial plants, perhaps Port Said harbor facilities before the Russians can intervene. But even such an operation will require a logistical buildup, and much planning and rehearsal. A reliable yet daring commander will be absolutely essential—

Barak stopped writing and stared at the opposite wall, where a picture of the Defense Minister, now a world hero, returned a one-eyed stare. An armor man himself, Barak was thinking how he would mount such a cross-Canal strike, given the assignment. A big challenge, a big opportunity; yet if things went wrong and the Egyptians put up any resistance at all, a big risk of an operational fiasco and political disaster. The sinking of the *Eilat* showed that their will to fight was far from crushed.

His eye fell on the weekend *Ma'ariv* lying on his desk, and there on the front page was the picture of just the man to pull it off.

Don Kishote! The news story was that Lieutenant Colonel Yossi Nitzan had been awarded the Medal of Valor, Second Class, for his risky and costly tank dash to El Arish, which had spearheaded the victory in the Sinai ground fighting. Kishote was now the operational officer of Northern Command, a long step upward on the *maslul* but a post very far from Sinai. There were able field commanders in Southern Command, but nobody quite like Don Kishote.

He put in a call to Pasternak. Sam knew and admired Yossi Nitzan, and he had Moshe Dayan's ear.

3

Reprisal

At about the time the *Eilat* went down, Lieutenant Colonel Yossi Nitzan was driving across the Golan Heights under lowering gray clouds, while around him tanks and armored personnel carriers roared and rumbled to their night positions in a haze of exhaust. Addressing the brigade after a dry run of a live-fire exercise, he had been hard-nosed and unsmiling, balancing brief praise for good performance with severe ticking off of sloppy lapses. No trace of humor had lightened his admonition that in Dayan's presence tomorrow, the hazardous drill had better come off without incident. To his army equals and to some women, Yossi Nitzan could be the prankish high-spirited Don Kishote, Hebrew for Don Quixote, a nickname he had acquired as a daredevil teenage recruit; but in the field he was the soberest of commanders, except when a rare combat situation called for savage boldness.

Back in his headquarters tent he was at a plank desk planning a last early-morning rehearsal of the drill, when Dayan telephoned. "Where is Dado, Yossi?"

"At Kibbutz Gal-Ed, Minister."

"Why there?"

"He felt he should go and talk to them. A tractor driver was killed by an infiltrator mine."

"I know about that. Tell him tomorrow's plans are changed. Cancel the exercise. I want to confer with him and with you. The Egyptians have sunk the *Eilat* with missiles. My helicopter will leave at dawn."

Dealing with military shock was nothing new to Don Kishote. "Many losses, sir?"

"We're still pulling them out of the water. It's bad enough."

Speeding to the kibbutz in a jeep, Kishote found the Northern Commander on his feet haranguing the weather-beaten old-timers and their gray-headed wives in the dining hall, but to his surprise the rows of chairs were half-empty. Evidently the younger kibbutzniks, who had been clearing mines or toiling in the fields all day, preferred sleep to a pep talk by the conquering hero of the Golan Heights. A stout old lady in greasy overalls raised a hand, stood up, and broke into Dado's speech.

"Pardon me, that's all fine, Dado, but when will it ever end? What is it all leading to? That's what we want to know. What was the use of winning a war? Every night my three grandchildren still have to sleep in the shelter. My daughter says she can't raise kids this way. She and her husband talk of moving to Netanya, where he has family. He's a mechanic, he'd make good money. What do I tell them?"

A murmur of agreement among the oldsters.

General David Elazar looked at her without words. She faltered and sat down. Even in silence Dado was somewhat scary: broad-shouldered, craggy-faced, with tumbled black hair, heavy black eyebrows, and a wide mouth that could curve in a fierce sudden scowl. "All right, Esther," he said in the warm voice he used with civilians, "I understand you, believe me. But if Jews like your family leave Gal-Ed because you feel life here is unbearable, we may as well disband the army and forget about having a country. *Because that's the one enemy war aim,* don't you see, to drive us out of our Land? Their defeats in battle haven't changed that aim one bit. Look, we routed them, didn't we? The Egyptians and Syrians were helpless after six days, crying to the Russians and the United Nations for help. I could have taken Damascus in forty-eight more hours. The Jordanians collapsed even before that, on the third day of the war, and already they're sending infiltrators here again —"

The stout lady interrupted from her seat with quavering bravery. "We know all that better than you. So what?"

Dado's voice hardened. "So last time the infiltrators paid, as you also know, Esther. We blew up their base and killed half of them. We'll take care of this gang, too. We'll make life unbearable for all your attackers. And where will it all lead to? To *peace*." He struck a heavy fist on a palm. "In your time, or in your daughter's time, or in your grandchildren's time, but *peace*! Because for us life will go on being bearable, and better than bearable, beautiful. And for the Arabs, in the end we'll make enmity unbearable. That I swear. The army will see to that. Life here on the border is hard, but this kibbutz is Israel. The army exists for you. So do I."

Kishote perceived, from the way the elderly kibbutzniks listened with moistening eyes, that this was what they needed to hear. Far from the victory euphoria in the cities, exposed on the farmland frontier, at least they weren't being forgotten. Other questions shot at the general about better army protection, newer alarm systems, government subsidies promised but not forthcoming. He fielded these briskly, and made an end with a wave to Kishote. The two officers partook of cake and soft drinks with the kibbutzniks, and soon left.

As they walked to the jeep and jumped in, Kishote told the general about the *Eilat,* and Dayan's change of plan. Dado took the news without comment, leaned back in the rear seat and closed his eyes. The jeep reached the main road and sped northward, tires hissing on rough tar. After a long time he spoke. "Missiles. A serious escalation. A new game."

"Dado, did you mean what you told those kibbutzniks?"

"Every word."

"How do you propose to make enmity unendurable for the Arabs?"

"Kill the terrorists they send in," Dado coldly growled from behind him, "and keep killing them. Grind the bones of their armies whenever they try war. War is crazy, it's horrible and disgusting, but we have to fight to exist. They don't. They can't get it into their heads that we can live in peace side by side. One day they will, when they become good and tired of dying for the Russians."

"That's not what they think they're doing."

"No. It'll take time for them to understand, maybe a generation, maybe two. But then peace will come."

Far down the road a lone girl soldier appeared in the headlights, gesturing for a hitch. "Pick her up," Dado said. She climbed in beside the driver without a glance at the back seat, a plump baby-face in baggy fatigues, juggling a rifle. "Are you crazy," inquired Dado from behind her, "breaking regulations, out here by yourself in the middle of the night?"

She pointed a pudgy finger at twinkling lights on a hill. "My boyfriend lives in that moshav."

"Then why didn't you stay the night?"

"We had a fight. I hate him."

"If you were brought up on charges before Dado," said Kishote, "he'd throw you out of the army."

"Dado?" She noisily yawned. "Ha! He'd just try to screw me."

Elazar gave Yossi a hard poke in the back. Yossi said, "Maybe you're thinking of General Dayan."

"Oh, the big brass are all the same," said the girl. "Sex maniacs. The higher the worse. How far are you going?"

"Headquarters Commanding Officer North," said Yossi. "Don't you realize that terrorists roam in the night around here?"

"So what? So I shouldn't go on living?"

"Life is bearable for you, then?" asked Dado.

"Life is fine since we won the war. That'll hold them for a while. They need a good bloody nose every few years. God, I'm tired. Wake me when you get to Afula." She snuggled down, the rifle between her knees.

"At your service," said Dado. After a while, when the girl slumped asleep, he said, " 'Every few years.' The kids know, don't they?"

"It's their skins," said Kishote. "Maybe the *Eilat* will wake up the others."

The helicopter thrashed to earth in a heavy rain, whirling streams off the blades. Kishote greeted Dayan and brought him to the Northern Commander's map-lined office, where Dado waited alone. "Forty-seven dead or missing from the *Eilat*," Dayan began abruptly, fixing them with his good eye. "More than a hundred wounded. The question is how we hit back. The American State Department is asking us to '*show restraint.*'" The crooked smile appeared. "Any votes for restraint?"

"I've been thinking it over. Sink the missile boats," said Dado. "Every one of them. Blow for blow, redoubled. Are their locations known?"

"Pinpointed in Port Said. The air force is ready to do it, but there are Soviet vessels in the harbor, including a cruiser and some destroyers. Nasser shot from behind that shield. Still, the Egyptian radio is warning the people to expect reprisal. Nasser knows we've got to do something."

Kishote asked, "Minister, how did he dare, when Motti Hod can level Cairo?"

"Don't be naive, Yossi." Dayan shook his head impatiently. "Levelling Cairo is nonsense and Nasser knows that. Politically, Egypt holds all the cards —"

"All the cards?" protested Elazar. "Why? How? We crushed them, we sit on strong defensible lines, and —"

Dayan interrupted. "I said *politically,* Dado. Superpower political odds, three to one for the Arabs — Russians a hundred percent for them, Americans '*evenhanded,*' fifty-fifty. Understand? Plus of course France, England, that whole European schmear, plus the Third World, whatever that amounts to, all entirely for the Arabs. And that's why we've got our hands full at the UN, just staving off a resolution for our total withdrawal. Like the vote after we won the Suez War."

General Elazar and Kishote looked somberly at each other. Dayan got up and walked to a wall map of Sinai and Egypt, and Kishote noted again how paunchy and unmilitary he appeared in his ministerial dark suit and tie. "So far, one idea has cabinet approval, and mine," Dayan went on, gesturing at the map. "A tank reconnaissance in force across the Canal, wiping out army bases, artillery emplacements, AA batteries, and so on. Military targets only. In and out with air cover, half a day. Southern Command is working on it. I want your views, Dado." He turned to Kishote. "And yours. It would take dash, like your run to El Arish."

David Elazar said, "It would also take time, Minister, and serious planning and rehearsal. A water obstacle presents major problems. Moreover —"

Abruptly Dayan turned on Kishote. "Well, Yossi? If assigned, would you organize and do it?"

"I have a different idea, sir."

"Let's have it."

"It's not practical now."

"Then why bring it up?"

"Because you made me think of it."

Dado remarked, "If it's Kishote's idea, it's something crazy."

"No, just requiring a lot more time. Use Russian tanks." Dado and Dayan exchanged sharp glances. "We've captured hundreds. Put Egyptian markings on them, and once across we could roll to Alexandria. Total surprise, total enemy confusion. Even in a one-day recco in force we could do tremendous damage with few casualties."

"Why can't we do that in the next week?" Dayan demanded. "Transfer seasoned Centurion crews? Train night and day? Assemble pontoon rafts?"

"Minister, have you climbed inside a Soviet tank lately?"

"Once. I could barely squeeze in. I've put on weight."

"It's not your weight, sir. They've sacrificed everything for low profile. The order went out, *low profile,* so they've got low profile, by God! Soviet munition-making. Those tanks must be manned by Russian midgets. They can draw on two hundred million people for small guys. Nasser, on fifty million. We'll have a problem, but it can be done, and it can be a stunning blow."

"By your life, Kishote," said Dayan, "let me have a study soon of such an operation. Meantime, Dado, what do we do?"

"Minister, even if the air force is out," said Dado, "one requirement remains, *swift response*. Slow reprisal sends a hesitant and mushy message."

"How about artillery, sir?" said Kishote. "Remind them we're not a hundred miles off in the Negev anymore, but right there at the Egyptian border."

Dado nodded. Dayan's good eye glinted. "We've been considering that, too, Kishote."

"This is a mistake," said Amos Pasternak.

He stood with his father in a sheltered observation post in the south of Sinai overlooking the deep blue Gulf of Suez, watching the oil refineries on the other shore blazing and exploding. Squinting in the desert sun, Dayan was talking to interviewers while cameramen filmed him against the background of the smoke and fire billowing over Egypt. The artillery exchange was still going on: distant flashes, staccato thumps, and nearby earsplitting thunder, rolling smoke, and pale flame.

"So, you're back from America a few hours, and you're passing judgment on national strategy." Sam Pasternak's tone was rough but not ill-natured. Despite his son's fine tweed jacket and flannel slacks acquired in San Francisco, Amos's Israeli look was unchanged; swarthy and thickset like his father, his heavy oval face almost boyishly open, his dark heavy-lidded eyes sparkling and sharp. He had telephoned at the first news of the *Eilat,* saying, "Looks like the war may be starting again, Abba. I'm not missing it, I'm coming home."

"You're a fool. There won't be war, the Egyptians are still helpless."

"They are? How did the *Eilat* sink? Some sailor pull the plug by mistake?"

"If you're interested in your army career, stay at Stanford."

"My career will be fine." And here he was.

After a deafening artillery salvo close by, the father said, "All right, military genius, why a mistake?"

"Such a public event!" Amos gestured at the reporters. "On

American TV, how will it look? Absolutely terrible. They won't show the *Eilat* going down, just the Jews bombarding peaceful industries. Only pictures count over there. Pictures!"

"Well, too bad there was no TV crew on the *Eilat*. The Americans know our ship was sunk, with big loss of life."

"They've forgotten already. Anyway, what kind of surprise attack is this? Major oil refineries within artillery range, civilians already evacuated? Zero shock. Nothing. Only shock can keep the Arabs off balance, Abba, and if Nasser calculated reprisal targets before he sank the *Eilat,* this had to be number one."

A white command car, with the blue letters UN painted on each side, was coming down the dirt road from the canal, raising a long dust plume. "Well, well," said Sam Pasternak, "the umpires are arriving to stop the fun and try to fix blame for who started it. Ha! There are no umpires at sea." He glanced at his wristwatch, and waved to his driver in a jeep nearby. "Let's get back to Refidim. A helicopter will be meeting me at twelve o'clock, I have to report to the Prime Minister."

"Great. I'm dying to surprise my girlfriend."

"Dvora? Is she still modelling for Yael Nitzan?"

"I assume so. I haven't heard from her. We had a tiff before I left."

"What about?"

"She wanted to come with me to Stanford."

His father grunted and was silent. After some minutes of bumping along the unpaved track in a whirl of dust, Sam Pasternak said, "For three reasons, Amos, that bombardment is no mistake. First of all, the Egyptians surprised us, we didn't estimate they'd dare such escalation, and politically something had to be done fast to shut off the Arab rejoicing. Not the Egyptians, they were pretty quiet, but the other countries were calling the *Eilat* sinking 'Israel's Pearl Harbor.' Second, our press and people were yelling for action. Third, our intelligence was that Nasser expected a reprisal in the Port Said area up north, so this was in fact a tactical surprise."

"Maybe, maybe. You know something?" Amos said. "California is the Garden of Eden, and this Sinai dust has the smell of Hell, and I'm glad I'm back."

Yael Luria, read the sign over the Tel Aviv shop in stark block letters, gold on white, for in business Don Kishote's wife used her maiden name. In the window were two ultrafashionable dummies, skinny and faceless, one displaying a blue leather coat, the other a miniskirted green suit. Inside, noisy American shoppers wore first names pinned to their dresses — *Marilyn, Connie, Isobel* — on small wooden Hadassah medallions shaped like Tablets of the Law.

"Good God," Yael greeted Amos, stepping away from customers. "You! You went to Stanford, I heard."

Amos had not seen Colonel Nitzan's wife in a long time. She looked as American as her customers, lean, well-coiffed, dressed in beige leather. Amos did not know exactly what had gone on between Yael and his father long ago. It wasn't talked about in the family, and he had heard only gossip, but whatever it was, he could understand it. "Well, I'm back. Dvora's here?"

"Dvora? Yes, she's with some rich Brit ladies in a private room" — Yael dropped her voice and looked oddly uncomfortable — "modelling lingerie. Will you wait in my office?"

"Why not? Congratulations on Kishote's Medal of Valor. How is he?"

"From the little I see of him, fine. He's up north now, he's Dado's chief of operations." She showed Amos into a cubicle decorated with French fashion posters, where a lean curly-headed boy was writing in a copybook at the desk. "And this is our son. Aryeh, this is Major Pasternak, a valiant warrior. I'll tell Dvora you're here."

The boy peered at Amos's tank corps emblem, and at the beret strapped on his shoulder. "If you're in tanks, why do you have a red beret?"

Sharp kid, this. "I'm qualified both as a tankist and paratrooper, Aryeh."

"But which are you?"

"Well, that's a story."

"Tell it to me."

Amos sat down in a wicker chair. "What are you doing?"

"English homework. My father is in the tank corps."

"I know. Colonel Nitzan is a famous tank commander."

Aryeh's face lit up. He had Yael's blue-gray eyes and snub nose, and with his thick blond curls he was pretty as a girl. He read from his open book in stumbling English.

Tomorrow and tomorrow and tomorrow
Creeps in this petty pace from day to day
To the last syllable of recorded time . . .

"*Zeh nifla, lo?*" ("That's wonderful, isn't it?")

"You think so? You have good taste."

"What do you really do in the army?"

"Special things."

"What things?

"You have to be clever and strong to do them. Maybe you will one day, Aryeh. Do you know what 'elite' means?"

"Sure. The chosen. The best. That's what I'll be."

"Then get back to your homework. First elite rule is, whatever you're doing, do it with all your might." The boy saluted, bent over his notebook, and resumed careful writing.

Amos sat drumming his fingers on the wicker. Three months was a long time to be without a girlfriend, and he had not found one at Stanford. He had met Dvora when she was finishing her draft service in the armor corps, and for a year they had shared a flat in Ramat Gan for weekends of shattering lovemaking. She had been given to kvetching — so Amos had dismissed her persistent protests — about this sporadic arrangement. She had wanted something more committed and positive, if not yet binding. Amos didn't. She was beautiful and sweet, but uneducated and lightweight, and as a companion for an academic year at Stanford University, all wrong. So he had judged, and he had been tough about it, resisting her cajoling, her tears and her threats. Now he had to make it up to her. He was thinking over an affectionate approach when here she came in a red bathrobe, her face all painted up for modelling, her lovely brown ringlets exquisitely arranged. "So you're back."

"Dvora!"

He jumped up with open arms. She threw a glance toward the boy and beckoned to Amos. He followed her into a small multi-mirrored dressing room, where she shut the door and stood with her back to it, hands behind her. "Didn't you get my letter?"

"What letter? I never heard from you."

"I wrote you a very long letter, Amos, back in September."

"It hadn't arrived by the time I left."

"What made you come back?"

"The *Eilat* news. I flew home as soon as I could."

"I see. So how was Stanford?"

"What was the letter about, *motek* [sweet]?" She was acting strangely, a bit stunned, perhaps.

"Oh, what you would call kvetching, I guess." Amos decided to cut through this nonsense, and made to take her in his arms, whereupon she whipped a hand from behind her back, and held it clenched under his nose. "About this, actually, if you want to know."

"L'Azazel!" The plain gold band was the very long letter in one stark fact. "You didn't really marry Ben, Dvora?"

"I said I would. I swore I would. You knew that." Her voice began to break, and her eyes to brim. "And I love Ben, and I'm happier than I ever thought I could be, and I'm two months pregnant. *B'seder* [Okay]? And I'll have to quit this job soon, and I don't care a bit, Ben makes a fine living with his filling station. So what can I do for you, Amos Pasternak?"

He took a moment to find his voice. "Just be happy, Dvora, that's all. Have a long happy life, and a wonderful family. Congratulations, and congratulate Ben for me, he's very lucky."

She choked out one word, "*Hazzer* [Swine]," and disappeared with a doorslam, leaving Amos looking at half a dozen nonplussed images of himself and thinking ruefully, *Talk about reprisal!* Threading through the Hadassah ladies, he left the shop and saw a new blue Porsche pull up at the curb, out of which jumped another romantic misfire of his, Daphna Luria.

"Amos Pasternak!" Sprightly tone, flirtatious smile. "Why aren't you in California?"

An Israeli query, that. He had not talked to Daphna Luria for nearly a year, and they moved in different circles, but here everyone tended to know everything about everybody else. Somewhat asphyxiating, at times. "Nice car," he said to the young driver as he got out, an American by his clothes, his haircut, and his callow look, not to mention the exotic automobile.

"This is Noah's cousin from New York," said Daphna. "Dzecki Barkowe. He's made aliya."

"He has? Kol ha'kavod," said Amos, perceiving the resemblance, but guessing that this fellow was no Noah and would probably not last long here.

"Actually, Amos might be the one to talk to," she said to Dzecki, as the men shook hands.

"What about?" Amos inquired.

Dzecki said in clumsy slow Hebrew with New York inflections, "My draft service. I'm thinking maybe I should go in now, get the three years over with. A crash course in being an Israeli, you might say."

"A real question." Amos shrugged. "Just don't be hasty. Once in, you can't get out. Daphna, how's Noah?"

"He'll be all right, but he's still in much pain. We're going to visit him after I pick up a new dress. My aunt gives me big bargains."

"Bad business, the *Eilat* sinking," said the American. "But I'll bet the Egyptians will be plenty sorry." He trailed after Daphna, as she went into the shop with a farewell wave at Amos.

Why had they never clicked, he and Daphna? Unlike Dvora she was mighty bright, extremely well read, sure of herself, maybe a bit too aware that she was a Luria, a squadron leader's daughter, and very pretty, if no Dvora; also given to leftish antimilitary patter, which she considered smart and he thought an unserious nuisance. Whatever the reason, their few dates had fizzled. Noah Barak was welcome to Daphna Luria, since she fancied him. *There* was a real mentsch, Noah Barak. Noah had had rotten luck, but at least he was alive and recovering. Amos meant to visit him soon.

What now? He decided to telephone Sue Weinberg, a divorcée in Kfar Shmaryahu, who was sure to welcome him with joyous warmth, a superb meal, and a familiar bedroom. Three kids, no future there, but somehow he got along best with older women. Girls made problems.

MAIMONIDES HOSPITAL

HAIFA

November 10th, 1967

Dear Abba:

You keep asking about Daphna Luria in your letters. Actually, she's been here several times. She couldn't be sweeter, and I could become serious about Daphna, but I doubt she's in that frame of mind. Not yet, anyhow. That dizzy relative of ours Jack Barkowe usually brings her here in his damned Porsche. She says he's just a pleasant kid, but she sure loves that Porsche. He let her drive it and the Mekhess nabbed it, but with protectsia he got it back. Was that your doing? As for the physical therapy, it's starting to work at last. My back pain is almost gone, except when I make sudden movements. I'll be out of here in a week, the doctor says. But then what?

Abba, I've spent a lot of time on my back, thinking about my future. If I do go on with a military career, I doubt it'll be in the navy. I'm disillusioned and disgusted. Yesterday we had a reunion of *Eilat* survivors in the hospital dining room, and the guys who weren't injured came and joined us. Strangely, it was uproarious. Everybody making jokes, insulting each other, even horseplay. Sheer joy of being alive and together again, we all felt it. Also shutting out our sadness about all the guys we lost. Anyway, it was something. The captain wasn't there. He's out of the hospital, but in terrible mental shape. So am I, Abba.

Do we even need a navy? It's a marginal branch at best, isn't it? That sense of being inferior, not crucial to Israel's survival like the tanks and the air, pervades the service. Slack, slack, slack! Slackness caused the sinking of my ship. Where we were steaming, the attack was no surprise. We should have been ready with countermeasures, but that's not the worst of it. In the Beersheba hospital ward where they first took us, General Gavish, Commander South, came and asked the captain why he was sailing within missile range, when

Southern Command had hard intelligence *that the Egyptians were preparing to fire missiles*.

The captain got so agitated they had to move him to a private room. Abba, that intelligence never reached the *Eilat*! My God, if we'd been warned, we could have been patrolling thirty miles out, far beyond missile range, and still performed our mission. The captain was always uneasy about our patrol sector so close in, but those were our orders. The other day at a promotion party for some officer the captain had a few glasses of wine, and he started yelling at the top brass, calling them idiots and murderers. He had to be restrained and taken home. I don't blame him one bit. My blood still boils when I think about all this. Whichever shlepper received the intelligence at headquarters probably tossed the despatch in his routine out-basket. Missiles, shmissiles! The inquiry is still going on, but they'll never pin down the guy who should hang. Not in this navy.

What's an Israeli navy for, anyway, Abba? We fight short land wars. All we really need is a coast guard to nab smugglers and sink terrorist craft. This shlepper navy is never going to match the Soviet Union in missile warfare, and no matter what Arab presses the buttons, the Russians are our enemy at sea. I'm ready to go into tanks, paratroops, even special services if my back will hold up. Amos Pasternak came in today, and we talked a lot about this. Amos says the tanks are Israel's backbone. They're your branch, and I'm just fed up with the navy. It's a blind alley. Maybe the white dress uniform got to me. Maybe you shouldn't have named me Noah! Anyway, I'll welcome your advice about what to do and where to turn. I'm at a dead end, and very depressed, as you may gather.

Love to all,
Noah

Rock-and-roll music bedevilled Zev Barak as he was trying to reply to this letter, for Nakhama allowed the girls to play records "low" while doing homework. A vague term, that "low," subject to very different constructions by the opposing parties, thought Barak — much like the words in the new UN peace resolution, under urgent grinding debate ever since the *Eilat* incident and the fiery artillery reprisal.

> . . . no argument, Noah, about your bitterness over the intelligence failure. It happens in the army too, God knows. You've learned in a tragic way that sea warfare has evolved to a new form. For Israel, no more large targets: destroyers, frigates, they're finished. But those Styxes were launched by boats tied up in port. Stable platforms. If fired from a tossing deck, who knows? Still, we must assume the worst. Russian-made boats of Arab navies, probably partly manned by Soviet technicians, will either dominate our coasts, or we must have a navy that can outfight them —

Barak's pen halted, and he ate pistachio nuts from a bowl by his armchair. Was he taking the right tone now, after crumpling into the wastebasket two starts which had tried paternal comfort and reassurance? But his son had not fallen off a bike, he had been blooded in a combat disaster. He resumed writing, as though advising any promising junior officer:

> — and remember, our longest border is not with Jordan or Egypt, it's our coastline. Interdiction of hostile sea forces has to be a seaborne mission. The air force has its own mission, *Clear skies over Israel*. It can't be diverted from that. Even if our navy is not a decisive arm, the *lack* of a navy is not an option for us. Granted, the navy is at a low point now, but don't for a minute assume that we'll never be able to contend with Russian missile boats. Jewish heads are hard at work, including Uncle Michael. Need I say more? I *strongly* recommend that you stick it out. Of course the tanks are vital, but you've made your mark in the navy, and your leaving now would hurt an already wounded service . . .

Barak broke off writing, wondering whether the reference to his brother was a security breach. The missile program was ultrasecret, and Michael Berkowitz as a Technion physicist was much involved. But it was only a letter to a very prudent young naval officer, so he let it stand.

"They're here." Nakhama poked her head into his small den, a converted maid's room. In came a skinny youngster with flaming red hair, followed by Colonel Benny Luria in blue dress uniform.

At Halliday's request, Barak had arranged for Benny to lecture at the Air Force Academy. Maybe there would be a return favor somewhere down the line.

"Elohim, is this Danny?" Barak laid aside the writing pad and jumped up. "Benny, by my life he's grown a foot."

The boy barely smiled. Luria embraced Barak, saying, "I couldn't resist bringing him along. It's important for him to see that Air Force Academy. He'll be the envy of every boy on the base, and I'd have brought Dov too, if he weren't tied up in the pilot course."

"So, Danny," said Barak, "you want to be a fighter pilot, like Abba and Dov?"

"That's what I will be," returned Danny in a new deep voice.

Barak's two daughters came gambolling in, crying, "Danny, Danny," and the boy's serious mien melted in laughter, kisses, and hugs. Galia, the twelve-year old, now hardly came up to his shoulder, though they had been wrestling and chasing each other as equals since childhood. She too was altered, by the beginnings of a bosom, and after the first rejoicing she withdrew from Danny, leaving Ruti to do the romping around him.

"He'll be taller than you, Benny," said Nakhama, smiling in the doorway. "He's shooting up. How come? Irit's not tall, neither is Dov."

The thickset aviator grinned and nodded, as the girls dragged Danny off to their room. "Genes, Nakhama, genes. Irit's father was a redheaded six-footer. Danny looks me straight in the eye right now. He'll have trouble folding himself into a cockpit."

"Let that be your biggest worry." Nakhama scooped up pistachio shells scattered on the desk. "Dinner in half an hour."

"Zev, what's really happening at the UN?" Luria dropped on the convertible couch. "A real katzenjammer, no, since we blasted the refineries?"

"More than a katzenjammer. The superpowers are pushing hard for a deal now, Benny. The Russians don't want the Arabs to take another trouncing, and the Americans have their hands full in Vietnam, and desire no more trouble in the Middle East. So they're negotiating a quick wrap-up resolution between themselves, behind the scenes, and we don't know what the devil they're cooking up. Gideon Rafael's very concerned."

"He should be."

"Well, meantime on the good side, the Americans are releasing those forty-eight Skyhawks, but —"

"Fantastic." Luria sat up. "They are? Two more squadrons!"

"— *But,* I say, also pledging fighter aircraft to five Arab countries."

"Ah. Evenhandedness."

"Exactly. Not to Nasser or Syria, since Russia's already supplying them in a flood, but to others."

"Pity the Russians aren't evenhanded too, I'd love to test-fly that new MiG of theirs." Luria took pistachio nuts from the bowl Barak offered. "You know, my Daphna's been visiting Noah."

Barak gestured at Noah's letter on his desk. "He writes me about Daphna. He likes her."

"Do you know she's acquired an American chauffeur with a Porsche, some relative of yours?"

"Yes, Jack Barkowe. What's he like? You've met him?"

"Yes. A youngster, maybe twenty-two or -three. Looks like Noah. Smart, but awfully immature. Says he's making aliya, and wants to be called Yaakov, like a real Israeli."

The telephone had been ringing and ringing in the foyer. Nakhama called, "It's Gideon Rafael, Zev."

The UN representative sounded hoarse and weary. "Zev, things are very bad here. How about that CIA contact you've dealt with, you and Sam Pasternak? Are you still in touch with him?" Barak had not disclosed Christian Cunningham's name to him, and Rafael had not asked.

"Not since the war ended. Why?"

"Because we've got a crisis on our hands, no mistake, and tomorrow comes the crunch. Maybe you can help —"

"Gideon, tomorrow Benny Luria lectures at the Air Force Academy, and I'm flying out there with him."

A pause. Voices off, in rapid Hebrew. Then Rafael: "All right. A courier will come to Washington on the next shuttle to bring you some papers. Meantime for God's sake, talk to your CIA guy."

"But about what, Gideon?"

"Just open the lines for fast action. Zev, a scratch of a pen at this stage, here in New York, can cost us our victory in the war." Rafael's voice shook. "Understand? The Russians are sticking on words fatal to us, they're being tougher than the Arabs, and the Americans are wobbling. After you read those papers, call me."

4

Two Little Words

Now that he had a reason to telephone the Cunninghams, Barak felt awkward. He tried the CIA man's office first. Not in, so he dialled the home in McLean.

"Hello?" Her voice, brisk and cool.

"Emily, it's Zev. Is your father there?"

"Zev! Oh, Zev, *you!*" She burst into warm jubilant laughter. "Golly, no, but he'll be here for dinner. My God, how are you? Where are you? Still in Washington?"

"Still here. I'm fine. Ask Chris to call me at home when he gets in, will you?"

"Sure thing. Say, know what? Bud and I are winging off tomorrow to Colorado Springs to hear your Colonel Luria lecture. They say it'll be standing room only at the academy. We'll be the guests of the superintendent."

"Luria's here in my flat. I'm coming with him."

"Honestly? Well then we'll see each other, won't we? High time! Bud told me you met at the Pentagon. My God, it's bodacious to talk to you."

The word was unknown to Barak, but hearing Emily's quick breathless voice was decidedly "bodacious," whatever that might mean. As a yeshiva boy he had joked with the others about a cautionary rabbinic saying, *"Woman's voice is naked sex."* Nothing truer, at least for him when the woman was Emily Cunningham. She went on in a more sober tone. "Zev, you told me your son's a destroyer officer. It wasn't his ship that was sunk?"

"It was, but he's all right. In the hospital, soon to be discharged. He was fortunate."

"Praise God. I had my hand on the phone ten times to call you. Then I didn't." Another pause. "Well, I'll tell Chris to ring you."

"Emily, maybe we'll have a moment to talk out there."

"Why, we'll *make* a moment. More than a moment. I've heaps and heaps to tell you, old Wolf Lightning." This was *Zev Barak* in English, her nickname for him. "Bye, dear."

The girls were setting the table and chattering with Danny. Nakhama brought out a soup tureen. "Dinner's about ready, Abba. Get Benny. Anything serious with Gideon?"

"I'll know more later."

With an odd look she went back to the kitchen, and he felt Nakhama knew he had been talking to Emily Cunningham. She had perfect pitch for variations in his telephone voice. But she didn't say anything, and neither did he.

At dinner Galia and Ruti plied Colonel Luria with questions about the air victory, and he responded in vivid detail while his son sat silent, a picture of filial worship. Zev thought Benny was testing his lecture on them. The battle incidents were especially exciting, and he would make a hit in Colorado, if only he could tone down his warrior pride. These were not Homeric times.

"Zev? Chris Cunningham. You called?"

Barak was still studying the papers Gideon Rafael's courier had delivered. "Yes. Chris, can I drop over and talk to you now?"

"Why not? I'm just watching a great Hopalong Cassidy. I guess I've seen it seventeen times. Come along. Em's still here."

"I'm on my way."

The autumn leaves glowed yellow and red in the highway lights, and an autumn chill was in Barak's blood as he drove along the Potomac. Would it never end, this Sisyphean task of rolling the stone uphill to military victory, only to have it roll back down the slope of superpower politics to diplomatic defeat? Gideon Rafael was dead right, the papers showed the crisis was at hand. At the UN the battle over the words in peace resolutions had been going on draggily since the end of the war, but now the pace had turned feverish, with the Americans anxious for a deal and the Russians unyielding. A hairy time for Israel.

He was in turmoil, too, at the sudden prospect of confronting Emily again. He yearned for it, he dreaded it, and he was baffled by their brief phone talk. The vibrant voice had been as loving as before, quite as though their breakup had never occurred. And yet, *"Bud and I are flying to Colorado Springs,"* so that relationship apparently was very far along, if not settled. What was going on?

She opened the door to his ring, a cloth coat over her arm. "Hi there. Chris is in the library with Hopalong Cassidy." Same naked voice, same twining of her fingers in his, same press of his hand against her soft side. Same affectionate look in those big near-sighted eyes, too, same careless cloud of brown hair. The purple jersey dress clinging to her slender figure showed no ounce gained in her globe-trotting. "Let me look at you, old Wolf. Well! God's gift to womankind, yummy as ever. How are you, dear, truly? And Nakhama and the girls?"

"All well. You're leaving now?"

"Got to, dammit." He helped her pull on the coat. "Thanks, sweetie. Twenty-odd French exams piled up in the Growlery, to correct and hand out in a nine o'clock class."

"The Growlery," he said, with a note of rue. This was the gatehouse of the Foxdale School, where she lived and where at snatched times they had made fierce hopeless love.

"Ah me, yes," she said. "The Growlery. *'Mais où sont les neiges d'antan,'* hey, old Wolf? The world wags on. Bud doesn't like the Growlery. Before Marilyn died they had a place like it on the Blue Ridge for years, so it brings back sad memories." She buttoned up her coat. "Well, then we meet again tomorrow in Colorado Springs! Is your air hero all set with his lecture? They'll eat it up, I'm sure, the Israeli air force is aces now in our military. In fact, Israel is."

"Benny usually does all right."

In a sudden movement she put her cheek to his and hugged him. "Ah, Wolf Lightning, seeing you is heaven, that doesn't change. Bye."

Glass in hand, Christian Cunningham was turning off the TV as Barak came into the library. "Hi, class-A fight at the end of that Hopalong. How about some bourbon?"

"Sure, Chris, thanks." Usually Barak declined, but this was an occasion when conviviality might help. "Emily looks grand."

"A little silly, Emily, like most of her sex, but good-hearted." The maroon wool dressing gown hung loose on the gaunt figure stooped over the bar. "Splash of water, you take, right? They're giving you a hard time at the UN, I gather. Cheers."

"Cheers. That's what I came to talk about, Chris."

"I'm listening." They sat down on a brown leather couch. Cunningham's wrinkled wise eyes, set deep in skull-like sockets and peering through thick horn-rimmed glasses, never left the military attaché's face as he summarized Gideon Rafael's handwritten memo which had come with the courier's pages.

"Your Mr. Rafael sounds a mite shook up," observed Cunningham. "All that checks out with what we know. The Arabs are on a roll, Zev, about to get an American-Soviet resolution calling for your withdrawal behind the previous lines."

"In return for what?"

"Some general language about all parties committing themselves to peace in the region, sometime in the future —"

"Okay, that's the Goldberg-Gromyko compromise," Barak struck in, "but the Arabs turned that down back in July."

"Well, this is November," said Cunningham. "The Arabs have thought it over, and now they'll take Goldberg-Gromyko."

"Israel can't go along, Chris."

"No? If the United States cosponsors it in the Security Council, what option have you?"

"The United States mustn't cosponsor it. Possibly you can help —"

"Hold it *right there*!" Christian Cunningham held up both hands and shoved them palms out toward Barak. "Diplomatic semantics are not my turf, Zev."

"Intelligence is your turf. What's the CIA's personality profile of our Prime Minister?"

"Eshkol?" Cunningham drank off his bourbon, and somewhat unsteadily went to the bar and poured more. "Shadowy weak successor to Ben Gurion."

"Utterly wrong, like some other CIA estimates. A mild-mannered compromiser, yes. But at any threat to Israel's survival he'll be tougher than B.G. ever was. Chris, he'll defy Lyndon Johnson over this. Does your President want that kind of trouble with Congress? Or with the American Jews?"

Cunningham refilled Barak's glass, handed it to him and sat down. "What's in that envelope, Zev?"

"Documents Gideon Rafael sent me. Abba Eban's clear and copious handwritten comments show why Israel will have to say no."

"Zev, what's the nub of all this? Where does your government draw the line?"

"You'll smile. At two little words."

"I'm not smiling. Go ahead."

"Goldberg-Gromyko calls for *'the withdrawal of parties from all the territories occupied during the war.'* Since the Arabs occupied no territory but ran away in all directions, that means only the Israelis."

"It sure does."

"Okay. Way back in June we offered withdrawal linked to peace treaties. The Russians and Arabs pounced on *withdrawal* and ignored *peace treaties*. That's been their game ever since. But that principle — withdrawal *linked to peace treaties*, not otherwise — is where Israel draws the line."

His eyes screwed almost shut, Cunningham slouched far down on the couch, and drank. "And the two little fighting words?"

" *'All . . . the . . .'* If we pull out altogether from the territories without treaties, what room for negotiating a real peace will we ever have?"

"*All . . . the . . .*" Slowly Cunningham nodded, rolling the words on his tongue. "True enough. If that wording stands, you've lost the war."

"You've got it," said Barak.

"Tough," said Cunningham with a bony helpless shrug. "A balk by Israel will go right up to LBJ. He's well aware of the Soviet threat in the Middle East, and maybe he sees Israel as an asset, but he's got Vietnam on his hands, riots in the universities, an election year coming up, and Bobby Kennedy snapping at his heels. He's not in a mood to be defied, and for better or worse, you're a client state."

"Can't you at least correct the CIA's estimate of Levi Eshkol? It's dangerously misleading."

Cunningham again held up flat palms. "I haven't been asked. Sorry."

"Well, thanks for the bourbon." Barak stood up, hiding his disappointment and not too surprised. "And thanks for hearing me out."

"My pleasure. Incidentally, can you leave those papers with me? At least the one with Eban's copious comments?"

On the instant Barak handed him the envelope. "Take them all."

"Why, thank you. Just curious. I'm a Middle East history buff, as you know. You can have them back tomorrow."

"Tomorrow I'll be in Colorado Springs."

"Right, for that air colonel's lecture. Well, when you return, then." The CIA man flourished the envelope. "Next best thing to Hopalong Cassidy, the Middle East nowadays."

Rows on rows of blue-clad air cadets rose to attention with a great clatter of seats when the slender tall superintendent, a gray-blond man with a big splash of combat ribbons on his uniform, entered the auditorium. Halliday, Emily Cunningham, Zev Barak, and Danny followed him. Benny Luria already sat alone on the stage. At dinner in his quarters the superintendent had been jocular with Halliday, his old wingmate, they had called each other "Bud" and "Sparky," but now he was all stern dignity, escorting the guests to reserved seats, then mounting to the podium beside a tall white screen.

"As you were, cadets." They slammed down into their seats, backs straight, eyes front. Looking around at these hundreds of intent bristle-headed youths, it struck Barak that the entire Israeli pilot force, cadets and all, would fit into the three rows in front of him. Sitting beside Emily, smelling the faint wildflower scent she favored, was a poignant distraction. So they had sat through the Mahler cycle and many a play and opera at the Kennedy Center, before Nakhama had come to Washington with the girls. But now there was Halliday on Emily's other side.

"Politics stops at the gateway of the academy, gentlemen," the superintendent began. "Not long ago the academy hosted the air chief of Saudi Arabia. Today we welcome Colonel Benny Luria of Israel, commander of Fighter-Bomber Squadron Twelve. Air combat is the cutting edge of the military calling in our time, cadets, something like a world brotherhood. The recent victory of Israel's air force is worthy of serious professional study by all modern nations. We don't expect Colonel Luria to disclose military secrets or plead his country's cause. He is here as a man of arms like yourselves, a squadron leader whose record betokens an integrity of purpose and a striving for excellence, which the fledgling eagles of the academy can well aspire to emulate."

The superintendent turned to Luria, and his severe mien relaxed. "Okay, Colonel Luria, now tell us how you guys did it."

The cadets rose, courteously applauding. The superintendent joined in. Walking to the podium, Benny smiled down at Danny, standing beside Zev Barak. Looking very mature in a dark suit and tie, Danny clapped hard and winked at his father, but Barak knew how nervous the boy was. Taking Danny's hand as they crossed the grounds, he had felt a very damp palm.

Benny thanked the superintendent, and all rustling ceased in a dead hush.

"At 0745 hours on Monday, June fifth," he began, "our air force struck simultaneously at nine enemy airfields. I led my squadron in a dive on the Inchas air base, through heavy AA fire." He looked around at the array of serious young faces filling the big bleak hall. "And let me tell you, it was scary, but I was less scared than I am right this minute." The cadets were surprised into hearty laughter, glancing at each other. Great start, thought Barak. Benny was b'seder, as usual. Danny's eyes shone. "Don't laugh, gentlemen,

I mean every word of it. When I was a student pilot, I never dreamed that I would one day address the United States Air Force cadet corps. My dreams were as modest as our air force was then. Fourteen planes in all, gentlemen, twelve of them operational."

He paused to let that sink in.

"Well, times have changed. There have been strange stories and rumors to account for our recent victory — electronic wizardry, secret weapons, even the ultimate secret weapon, American pilots." (Side-glances and chuckles in the audience.) "But in fact there was no mystery or miracle in it. Three unchanging requirements of successful warmaking were crucial to the way we won: *planning, rehearsal, intelligence*."

For the next half hour, sometimes using slides and a pointer at the screen, Benny Luria talked with calm candor about Operation MOKADE as a preemptive strike worked up for years. It was not much like Abba Eban's version of the attack at the UN, but Barak was unconcerned. This was a place for reality; the UN was a place for smoke screens. He could sense the absorption of the cadets around and behind him. Some of what Luria said was new to him; not so much the colorful business of waking pilots in the night to recite time of departure, distance to target, bomb loads, and so on — all that he had heard before — but rather the dry hour-by-hour, and sometimes minute-by-minute, narrative of Benny's own first day of combat. He had flown four sorties, the last late in the afternoon, to the most distant airfield in Egypt, where his four Mirages with fagged-out pilots had been jumped by MiGs on fresh full alert. In his picture of the dogfight that ensued there was no Homeric vaunting. Now he was Colonel Luria, an instructor among student pilots, dropping into a professional clipped monotone. Good for Benny, he knew what to say to UJA banquets, to children at a dinner table, and to the United States Air Force Academy.

"Those MiG pilots were proficient," Benny was saying. "Anybody who puts down Arab aviators, or Arab fighting men altogether, makes a mistake. They are brave able warriors. Their political leadership is something else, and not part of this discussion. The superiority of our pilots is due to factors of motivation —

and therefore of training — that are unique to Israel's air force. Maybe we do have one secret weapon at that, gentlemen, called in Hebrew *en brera*. Which means 'no choice.' "

A map of Israel flashed on the screen, with colored arrows and numbers. Slapping the pointer here and there, Benny said, "As you see, gentlemen, a MiG can cross my country west to east in about ninety seconds. So an Israeli pilot lives and breathes one mission, *Clear skies over Israel*. That's his reason for flying and for living. In combat he'll take risks, plunge into dangers, pierce the envelope of safe performance, because he knows that Israel's survival rides on his wings.

"Yes, we're proud — maybe a little too proud — of being Israel's eagles. I assure you we all hope for the day when our neighbors will make peace with us, and these wonderful machines we fly will be grounded as toys we've outgrown. Air war is wasteful and perilous. I've seen too many horrible crashes and lost too many dear, dear friends to believe otherwise."

All at once Benny Luria's voice weakened and went hoarse. He stopped speaking, and it took him a long moment of oppressive silence to recover. Danny gripped Barak's hand. When his father spoke again, the voice was quiet and firm. "So I confess to you almost in a whisper that nevertheless I've loved it, loved every minute of my service. I hope my jet-lagged son here in the fourth row, who has heroically stayed awake during this dull talk, will one day be a pilot, a *tayass* in the Israel Air Force, as his brother is now training to become one. And in a lower whisper I confess that I'm damned glad we're getting those forty-eight Skyhawks."

The cadets jumped to their feet. The applause this time was the real thing. Barak put his arm around Danny, who was applauding a bit too much. Emily leaned past him to touch the boy's arm. "How proud you must be of your father."

"My English not too good yet," said Danny with difficulty. "I understood most."

Speaking over the prolonged applause, Halliday asked Barak, "Where did Luria get his English? It's excellent."

"War college in England. Also, our generation grew up under the British Mandate."

"I see." An arid smile. "He managed to get in a little politics, at that."

"Target of opportunity," said Barak.

"Yes, indeed."

"Am I disturbing you?" Emily's voice again, low and charged. "It's late as hell, I know." Barak was bedded down in a VIP suite of the base guesthouse, and she was calling from the superintendent's luxurious quarters across the lawn.

"No problem. I'm in my pajamas reading. Reading Plutarch, as a matter of fact."

"Oh, sure." They had corresponded at length, off and on, about Plutarch.

"On my life. I found a beat-up Modern Library copy in this room." So he had, amid a shelf of faded best-sellers.

"Let's go for a walk."

He glanced at his travel clock. "At one in the morning?"

"Look, Wolf, I thought we'd talk over breakfast, but I'm not sure I can get away from Sparky and his wife. Anyway, I can't sleep. There's a mantel clock in this room driving me bats, every fifteen minutes going *bing bang bong* —"

"What about Halliday?"

"Bud? He must have gone to sleep hours ago. He has to run his five miles at dawn."

"Where do we meet?"

"At that eagle statue."

"You're on. Ten minutes."

There she was by the pedestal, a dark huddled shape in bright moonlight. The deep snow crunched under his tankist's boots as he hurried to her. "Hi, it's damn cold," she greeted him. "Are you warm enough in that sweater?"

"Our army sweaters are pretty good."

"Everything about your army is pretty good." She stripped a glove off her hand, and took his in a hard clasp. The chilly fingers interwove in his and tugged.

"Where are we going, Em?"

"To the chapel, first. That's where Bud and I will get married."

"What! When?" The news was hardly unexpected, yet the shock was real and physical, a tingle down his arms and back.

"Oh, pretty soon. You'll get an invitation, natch. I hope you can make it. You and Nakhama."

Creak, creak, creak of fresh snow underfoot, brisk wind sweeping dry flakes in the air. "Emily, that's beautiful news. Congratulations."

Her fingers tightened. "Bud's idea, doing it here. I'm just as glad to skip the Washington nuptial hoo-ha. My God, what a marvellous place to have a military school. Look at those mountains, will you?" The snowy range loomed high against the stars, bluish and jagged. "One of them is Pike's Peak, isn't it? And say, isn't the architecture of that chapel sublime?"

The beauty of the strange soaring structure, suggestive of airplane wings, was much enhanced by the chiaroscuro of glittery moonlight and black shadow. He said, "I've seen pictures of it, but they don't give the idea at all. It's wonderful."

"Zev, you don't suppose it's closed? Churches stay open for meditators, don't they?"

"Let's try the door."

It was open. The high interior was lit by a single golden lamp, and tall stained-glass windows showed faint moonlit colors in the gloom. They sat down in a rear pew. "Wow, what an edifice," she said, her voice echoing hollowly. "And I doubt we'll have fifty wedding guests. But Bud wants this. I told him about us, you know, old Wolf. No X-rated stuff, you understand, but everything. I had to."

Barak was fighting off an impulse to take her in his arms, for one last time. It was painfully sweet to be with her again this way. Queenie! The fey electric unforgettable Queenie, here beside him, her bespectacled face dim and lovely over a snow-flecked fur collar. That he had gotten in too deep with this alien oddball was a fact of his life. The rest was handling it. The marriage disclosure was an unquestionable relief. Why then was he taking it as a stab? He cleared his throat. "What was his reaction?"

"Sphinx-like. He just sat there listening, with stone eyes on my blushing face. We were in the Red Fox, actually. He'd driven out to the school the day after he popped the question, and we were having dinner, and I just came *out* with it. He did nod once. No, twice. I guess sphinxes don't nod, so let's say he was like the Commandant's statue in *Don Giovanni*. Then he talked about other things, as though I hadn't said a word. I doubt he was all that surprised. Surely he wasn't expecting me at my age to be a virgin — though I damn near was, you evil deflowerer, you. Maybe he was relieved that there was no more to tell. He's a deep one, Bud."

"Well, you're in love, and all set. That's the main thing, Emily. It's just great."

"You can still call me Queenie, chum."

"That seems outdated."

Four long years ago, during his first mission to Washington, the bartender in the cheap hotel where he was staying had taken Emily for a hooker, and had called her Queenie by way of being sociable. She had been tickled to death by this, and as a joke between them the sobriquet had stuck.

"It isn't. It won't ever be, not for me. Is it for you?" In the enormous gloomy empty chapel, his long silence was like a shout. "Come on, Wolf Lightning." Her voice trembled, her eyes glistened through her glasses. "Speak up, or forever hold your peace. Wasn't it on for years and years with not even a kiss? Just scrawls on paper crossing the ocean? And wasn't it okay?"

"It was okay, Queenie."

"Ah! That's more like it. The one point I made to Bud was that we'd probably go on corresponding. That elicited a nod."

"And the other nod?"

"When I said I wanted all the kids this rickety frame could still produce. That even brought a faint granite grin and —"

"Hello!" The voice reverberated off the walls and the vaulted ceiling. Benny Luria came striding down the aisle. "Hi there, Emily," he said, as though nothing could be more natural than finding these two together in the academy chapel, long after midnight. Israeli military men seldom showed surprise at pairings, however offbeat. "What a fantastic church! That architect had imagination, whoever he was."

Barak said, "So you couldn't sleep either?"

"I'll be unwinding for days." He dropped into the pew. "I'd rather fly five combat sorties than face such an audience again."

"One would never know," said Emily. "Your lecture was a wow. My fiancé wants to talk to you about it."

"I have a seminar with the faculty at ten. Be glad to see him before or after. Zev, how about this academy? All these wide low plain buildings, like wartime temporaries, and at the heart of it all this stunning church. Makes me think."

"What about?"

"Well, I'd been at Tel Nof base two years before I even found out we had a synagogue. When my mother died I went looking for it to say Kaddish. It was in a trailer behind the base kitchen. We're supposed to be the people of the Bible, aren't we? These Americans seem to be more biblically inclined."

"I'd call it pretty biblical," said Emily, "to return to Zion after thousands of years, and learn to fly jet fighter-bombers so you can stay there."

Luria turned to peer at her. "That's not bad. I'll remember it."

"Our air tickets are confirmed," said Barak. "You fly to Los Angeles at two P.M., and I'll return to D.C."

They left Luria sitting in the chapel. Outside the wind had sharpened, and fine snow stung their faces. "Well, this is no fun," she said. "Tell you what, let's pop by your digs. I'll pick up that Plutarch, I need it more than you. I'll smother that clock with a pillow and maybe I'll read myself to sleep."

"By all means," said Barak, his nerves quickening. *What now?*

When he closed the door of the suite she threw her arms around his neck, and kissed his mouth with gentle affection. "No happy hour, kiddo, if you're wondering. I do want to talk, then I'm tooling off with Plutarch. Don't make a pass at me now, there's a good lad, just sit down quietly."

"Why, it never crossed my mind," said Barak, dropping in an armchair.

"Ho!"

"Ho is right, Queenie. It's been a while."

Her eyes flashed at him. She threw open her coat and sat on the bed. "Well, curb the old beast, hon, it mustn't be on, you know that. Not that you don't look powerfully sweet to these longing eyes —"

"All right, all right. Curbed. Talk away."

"Fine. Good Conduct Medal for the Gray Wolf. Now *listen*. You just said I'm in love with Bud. Not so. He's a fine guy and we'll be all right, but falling in love has happened to me just once, and it won't again." Their eyes met, and after a silence she said in a roughened voice, "No, it won't, and it's hopeless."

"Emily —"

"Zev, it always was, but once I realized that Nakhama knew, it became intolerable. The more so, when she as much as said she didn't mind."

He shook his head. "I wasn't present when you two had it out, but it must have been something."

"It sure was, old scout. She was smart, decent, and mighty adroit. Lethal, one might say. In some ways that wife of yours can run rings around you."

"That's no news. Nakhama's never mentioned any of this to me, not once ever brought it up, so I have to take your word for it. Anyway, you're committed now, that part's over, and the rest is letters, right? As long as we live, if you like. Agreed."

"Not so fast. I want you to understand me, dearest. I was halfway around the world," she said, her voice faltering, "wrestling with this thing all the way, when I decided once for all in New Delhi that I'd done the right thing. That there was no solution but Bud. Out of the frying pan, into the freeze compartment."

"Oh, come off it, Queenie —"

"It's God's truth. That's when I wrote you from New Delhi. And that's when I wrote to Bud that I'd marry him if he really wanted me, once we met again."

"And he did."

"And how. And I truly like him. He's a gent, and patient, and bright as they come. Moreover, if you're into military types — which present company excepted, I sure ain't — he's a catch. A careerist who's going places."

The words obscurely jarred Barak. This tantalizing, disturbing presence of Queenie in his suite, on his bed, was not something to prolong. He picked a book off a side table. "Well, here's Plutarch."

"Throwing me out, are you? Not that I blame you." She accepted the book with a tart smile, still sitting there.

"Hey, stay till morning, by all means."

"No thanks, but there's just one more thing I must tell you."

"Shoot."

"It'll sound vain, maybe, but I swear I've become more seductive, or something. Result of having discovered what love is? On my travels, so help me, I was beating them off — guys on ships, guys on trains, guys on planes. How come?"

"What was the competition, Queenie?"

She burst out laughing, and jumped up. "Oh, go to hell."

He seized her, and their kiss was long and passionate. Then she murmured, "This sweater smells familiar. In fact you do."

"Shut up, Queenie."

"Okay. Just hold me."

And so this familiar slight body was pressed to his once more, no doubt as it never would be again. The Good Conduct Medal fell off, unregarded.

"Enough, enough. Too much, much too much," she gasped, pulling free. "We're out of the Growlery, Wolf, there's no going back."

Stumbling on his words he said, "See here, Queenie, we were being — what? — unfair to Nakhama from the start. And if you truly found out she didn't mind, as you claim, then why —"

Emily put warm fingers across his lips. "Easy. I think you're being very dense, but all right. I was a bitch who stole a bone. Ran off with it, got away with it, loved gnawing on it. But once she said she knew and didn't mind, I was a bitch under the table being thrown a bone. Get the difference? Good enough?" Emily picked Plutarch off the bed. "Fare-thee-well, for I must leave thee. I'll read the Mark Antony chapter, I can use a good cry. Over Cleopatra, of course, the original bitch who stole bones." They went together to the door, where she said, "Come no further, Wolf. I won't be mugged on the academy lawn." And she slipped out.

From the shelf of old scruffy best-sellers Barak took to bed *Arrowsmith*, in the familiar orange-and-blue binding. He had read it in his high school class in Vienna, but the first few pages seemed all different. They shut out Emily thoughts, which was all he was asking of Sinclair Lewis . . .

R-r-r-ing! R-r-r-ing! "Sorry to disturb you, sir. Base duty officer here. The switchboard has a call for you from New York, urgent official business, a Mr. Rafael —"

"Put him on."

Various clicks and buzzes. "Zev? How was Benny's lecture?"

"Gideon, isn't it three in the morning there? Benny did fine. What's up?"

"Have you talked again to your CIA man?"

"Yes. He phoned, told me he studied the papers and he totally agrees with your memo."

"What exactly did he say?"

"That '*all the* territories' is catastrophic, loses the war we won."

"Sharp gentleman."

"But, Gideon, he can do nothing about it."

"Can't he at least find out where the White House now stands? We think that unless the President intervenes, the State Department will sell us out on both words today."

"I can try calling him."

"You must do better than that. We know that Kosygin has sent Johnson a very tough letter, and Johnson's called an emergency meeting for this morning. When will you get back to Washington?"

"About six tonight."

"No good."

"Benny has a seminar in the morning, and —"

"Benny can take care of himself. You must get back by noon the latest. Hitch a ride on a military plane. Be there!" Rafael was not quite himself, a bit frantic or frazzled.

"For what purpose?"

"Do I know? So that you're not out in Colorado Springs if for any reason you're needed. Zev, it's possible that you'll do more for Israel in one hour today than in all your years in the field."

"You exaggerate. That's nonsense. But I'm coming."

At the Central Intelligence Agency building in Virginia, in a crowded room lined with clattering teleprinters, Christian Cunningham was reading a long printout when a boyish black runner came to him with a message slip from security. "Yes, I'm expecting General Barak. Escort him to my office."

Zev Barak fell into a doze in an armchair as soon as he sat down, suitcase at his feet, civilian clothes all wrinkled. He had driven a rented car through the mountains, to make a hairbreadth connection from Denver to Washington via Dallas. "I think you can use some coffee," he heard Cunningham say. He opened his eyes and saw the CIA man in shirtsleeves and suspenders, pressing a desk button.

"Definitely, thanks." Barak sat up, digging a knuckle in his eye.

"How did the cadets like your colonel?"

"Big hit. Chris, what's happened in the Security Council today, do you know?"

Cunningham frigidly grinned. "I know your people are fighting a classic rearguard action, right down to the wire. Also, that something's going on now at the White House."

"Something good? Something bad?"

"Well, not good, I'm afraid. But who can read LBJ's mind, till he speaks it? I'm waiting to hear, from an insider I trust." A young woman in a smock brought a coffee service, and put it on the desk. Cunningham said as he poured, "Incidentally, did Emily tell you she's getting married in the academy chapel?"

"She did."

"I'll have to drag my old bones out there, I guess. In the air force they say Bud Halliday's a comer." He extended a cup and saucer to Barak. "He may make general on the next selection."

"I respect him. A friend of Israel he's not."

The CIA man pursed his lips over his coffee cup. "Bud knows only the national interest. And his own career, to be sure. He has a lot to learn about the Middle East."

"Well, you're the man to educate him."

Cunningham hesitated, then blurted awkwardly, avoiding his

eyes, "Zev, let me say this. I long ago despaired of having a grandson, you know. Emily's a strange one, we all realize that. Now prospects open up. I'm happy and thankful. And I'm glad your navy lad's okay. The road ahead for Israel is long. You'll need your sons."

The telephone rang. Cunningham picked it up, and after a moment nodded emphatically at Barak. "Yes, yes, right, go on. . . . Really? Amazing. How definite is this? . . . Okay, many thanks. . . . Well, I appreciate that. I'll reciprocate one day." He hung up, and fixed Barak with an indecipherable expression.

"News, Chris?"

"I believe so. Call your Mr. Rafael and tell him that both words are out."

"*Out?*" Barak stared. "*ALL* and *THE*? Both?"

"Out. Both. Usually it's the Arabs who make a boo-boo and get you off the hook, but this time it was the Russians. More coffee?"

"Chris, for God's sake, what's happened?"

"Well, that was a hasty report, but it seems Kosygin may have overreached himself. His letter questioned Johnson's good faith, the clumsy Slav! To the effect, '*If you're sincerely interested in peace, Mr. President, you won't quibble over two little words like* all *and* the.' It infuriated Johnson. He shot back a letter referring Kosygin to his speech about 'Five Principles of Middle East Peace,' telling the Russian to take them or go to hell. I paraphrase, but that's what I'm informed, by a pretty good source."

Barak darted a hand at the desk telephone. "Can I talk freely over this line, Chris?"

"Why not? It's a free country."

Rafael was rapturous at the report. "*Gott in Himmel!* If that's so, Zev, we've made the breakthrough we missed in 1956, no withdrawal without peace —"

"I'm getting this at third or fourth hand, Gideon, remember."

"I realize that. All the same I'm calling Eban right now."

Cunningham took his coffee to a leather armchair, and sat down. "Is your Mr. Rafael pleased?"

"God, yes."

"Pure Hopalong Cassidy all this, what?" The CIA man sipped

coffee. "Assuming that report's accurate, the question is, Zev, did LBJ really blow his top at Kosygin's language? Or had he already figured he needed the Jewish vote in '68, and just jumped on the letter as his excuse?"

"Either way, Chris, Israel's out of a corner."

"Right, and Nasser's painted himself into one. My analysis is on file here, Zev. I estimated that he sank the *Eilat* to prod the superpowers into a joint resolution on withdrawal. He got it, all right." The CIA man's sunken eyes gleamed at Barak. "But he ended up without the two little words."

5

Golda

"The Prime Minister is dead, Sam." Shaky tearful voice of Eshkol's chief secretary on the telephone. "He died at eight-fifteen this morning."

"No!"

"Another heart attack. And he was so well and busy yesterday! The family is asking for you, so please come to the residence."

"I'm on my way." Having just arrived at his office, Pasternak still wore his old army overcoat, for the weather blowing into Tel Aviv from the sea was gusty and rainy. His desk calendar, he saw, read

FEBRUARY 26, 1969
9 A.M. *Coffee with Yael at Hilton.*

He buzzed his duty officer. "Call Mrs. Nitzan, tell her I can't meet her. It's an emergency, and I'll phone her soon."

"Yes, General."

He glanced through a few urgent papers and was walking out the door when the intercom buzzed. "General, Mrs. Nitzan's phone doesn't answer. Shall I call the Hilton, sir, and have her paged?"

"L'Azazel, I'll drive by there. It's simpler."

The morning traffic was thickest near the Hilton, and his driver had trouble getting through. Pasternak sat beside him, his mind running through the implications of Eshkol's death. Black, black day for Israel, another giant of the old days fallen. Ben Gurion, scrawling his memoirs in retirement, had outlived his successor, after all. The obscure Levi Eshkol, never a media figure, had been Pasternak's hero since their underground days. More than anyone, he had patiently built the infrastructure of the State and the army, always in B.G.'s shadow. Gone! The struggle for the succession would start at once, and it would be a dangerously divisive business.

Yael had trouble getting herself up out of the lobby settee, when she spied Pasternak and waved. That she was pregnant, let alone so far along, was news to him. But the dark gray leather suit was reasonably becoming, considering that she looked about ready to calve. He lent a hand to pull her to her feet.

"Thanks, dear, I'm monstrous, I realize. It's kind of you to come."

"Yael, Eshkol just died this morning."

"Oh God, how awful."

"So I'm in a rush to get to Jerusalem."

"Of course, of course, go ahead."

"After the funeral I'll call you. Probably late tomorrow."

"I won't be here. I'm flying to Los Angeles tonight."

"What? In your shape?" He looked her up and down. "A wild animal, that's what you are. Always have been."

"Sweet of you to be concerned." She caressed his cheek. "Just a short trip, and I'll phone when I get back."

"What's this all about, Yael?"

"Oh, Sheva Leavis business."

She had to say no more. Sheva Leavis was an Israeli from Iraq, now living abroad, who dealt mainly in Oriental imports, and covertly in munitions. He had once set Yael up in a Beverly Hills shop where she had made a pile, and now she looked after some of his interests in Israel. As to how far the connection went, Pasternak could only guess.

"Pardon, motek," he said with a gesture at her swollen girth, "but I thought you and Kishote were more or less separated."

"More or less, is right." A satiric smile, a pat on her stomach. "We still share the apartment, so . . ." With a look half-reproachful, half-amused, she said, "It happened to you and Ruth, didn't it? Twice, or so you claimed."

Even her pregnancy was an occasion to needle him, he thought, and disfigured as she was, she knew she could bewitch him if she chose. It was there in her eyes. This relationship was never over, only dormant. "Well, take care of yourself, for God's sake. Can my driver deliver you somewhere?"

"Thanks, I'm driving my own car."

"You are? And where do you put the steering wheel?"

"Between my teeth, where else?"

He reluctantly laughed. They walked out together, and she parted from him with a kiss on his rainy cheek. "I'm truly sorry about Eshkol, Sam. You were close, I know."

"We were. It really hurts, Yael. Have a safe trip."

The Prime Minister lay in the bed in which he had died, with tall candles burning at the head and foot. His distraught wife brought Pasternak in and left him alone with the body. There was a smell of medicine in the room, and a faint odor of death. From below in the crowded living room came the murmur of contending voices. Eshkol's broad face was greenish and still worried and weary, though the eyelids were shut in the last sleep.

"Goodbye, Layish [Lion]." Pasternak spoke the underground code name softly, after contemplating the blanketed body in silence. "You were a quiet man and a real fighter. You led us to win the war, but others got all the credit. Now you're in *Olam Ha'emet,* the world of truth, and there you'll be welcomed by the other great Jewish fighters, by Judah, by Joshua, by Gideon. Go to peace. I loved you."

In the subdued milling downstairs of cabinet ministers, generals, chief rabbis, bureau heads, family, and close friends, Pasternak found that all was confusion over funeral arrangements, beginning with where Eshkol was to be buried. As to who would succeed him, not a word was being spoken, though it had to be on nearly everyone's mind. The two foremost contenders were there, Moshe

Dayan and Yigal Allon, great army generals turned politicians. Allon was Deputy Prime Minister, but Dayan wielded the lion's share of the national budget as Minister of Defense. The groups clustering around the two were about the same size, Pasternak noted. Subtle currents of Israeli politics were swirling here. Allon had been a staunch Labor man always, whereas Dayan had once defected to Rafi, Ben Gurion's failed splinter party.

The former head of the Labor Party came in unnoticed at first, but as she plodded heavily into the room, holding her big purse and looking around, heads and eyes began to turn and the talking to subside. "Is there a problem?" Golda Meir inquired.

A pause of sudden quiet, then several people began to speak at once. She raised a hand to cut them off. "Who is handling the funeral?"

Wiping her reddened eyes, the widow said, "Golda, I've asked Sam Pasternak to take charge."

Golda kissed her, then glanced at Pasternak. He explained in a few words the burial dispute. Some said that Eshkol had wished to be interred beside his previous wife, the mother of his two daughters, at Deganya Bet, the kibbutz he had helped to found, and that the request might even be in his will. But others thought that his proper resting place as the head of state was on Mount Herzl in Jerusalem, in the space reserved for Prime Ministers, especially since crowds of mourners in the Jordan valley kibbutz might be exposed to terrorist assault with mortars and Katyushas.

"I see. Well, we will bury him in Jerusalem, of course," said Golda. "It is the right place, and we certainly don't want to risk any attack on the mourners, since there will be a multitude." The words were calm, not in the least argumentative. All around her people looked at each other and heads nodded. "But first of all, I must pay my respects to him. Where is he, upstairs?"

"Yes, Golda," said the widow, wiping her eyes. "Let me take you to him."

"Please. And after that, Sam," she said to Pasternak, "I want to talk to you."

As she trudged up the staircase the animated talk in the room turned to matters of detail — when to inform the public, how to handle the crowds, which heads of state to invite, and the like — and Dayan and Allon both took part, neither one trying to dominate. Here was history in the making, thought Pasternak. Out of the government for years, Golda had been a hard-handed political boss of Labor, but now she was presumably just a private citizen. Yet she had passed through this room like a queen, and nobody had been up to challenging her word. By all odds there would be no struggle over the succession, and the next Prime Minister would not be a military hero, but a seventy-year-old grandmother.

"I made one mistake. One *bad* mistake."

Thus Zev Barak to himself, replaying his mental tape of the Pentagon meeting just over, as he strode off on the five-mile walk back to his office, as usual criticizing his own performance. For better or worse, self-scrutiny was his habit of mind, perhaps a hobble to his ambitions. He did not envy his rivals who bulled ahead down the years with unshakable confidence in themselves. A man had to take himself as he was.

It was a breezy March day, the daffodils made splashes of dancing gold along the glittery Potomac, the exercise aerated his brain and blood, and all was almost right with the world, except for that one damned mistake. He had been summoned to meet the new Secretary of Defense, a good sign right there, for the incoming President Nixon owed the American Jews absolutely nothing. They had voted en masse for his opponent, Hubert Humphrey, and there was fear in Jerusalem that Israel might be in for a long Washington freeze. But Secretary Laird, a tall bald man with a hearty politician's manner, had said straight off that while he couldn't speak for the President, his strong sense was that Richard Nixon would honor Johnson's pledge to sell F-4 Phantoms to Israel. Barak had even managed to elicit possible delivery dates from him, a real step forward. The dour General Rabin, who had replaced Abe Harman more than a year ago as ambassador, might even be pleased enough to smile at that.

"Now, General, I'm interested in the military aspect of Mrs. Meir as Prime Minister, since that's my job," said the Secretary, having cheered Barak with his first words. "I'm informed that you're an astute officer who can talk straight. General Rabin's a diplomat now, and has to guard his tongue. Suppose you tell me, then, about a woman as your Prime Minister. Does that mean Moshe Dayan will be calling the shots?"

In reply Barak sketched Golda for Melvin Laird as frankly as he could: a formidable personality, he put it, capable of soft womanly charm but also of ruthless decision; less likely to compromise than Eshkol had been, because she knew so much less about arms and strategy; inclined to listen to Dayan and others, but in the end allowing nobody to call the shots but Golda Meir. Laird kept nodding, and seemed faintly amused by the picture.

Next he questioned the attaché hard about Colonel Nasser's newly proclaimed "War of Attrition." Barak pointed out that this was mere redundant posturing for his people, since the Egyptians had never yet ended the state of war against Israel declared back in 1948; agreeing to cease-fires only when routed in battle, and then persistently violating those until harsh retaliation made them desist for a while. Laird waved a dismissive hand. "You're talking legalities, General. This is something new. The man's words are clear and serious: *'What has been taken by force will be recovered by force.'* Our Cairo embassy says he means business. He's given the Russians a powerful naval base in Alexandria, a major problem for our Sixth Fleet, and in return they're rearming him heavily. How do you counter that?"

"With our army and air force, Mr. Secretary, which when last challenged crushed all our enemies."

Laird's further probes indicated that he had accurate intelligence about the Israeli defenses at the Suez Canal, a series of fortified outposts erected atop huge sand ramparts all along the eastern bank; Egyptian commandos were crossing the Canal and hitting Israeli forces, he observed, despite this so-called Bar-Lev Line.

"Nuisance raids, sir. Most of them die and we bury them in the Sinai sand."

"How long can you hold out in the Sinai behind that line, General?"

"Until the Egyptians tire of their futile policy, Mr. Secretary, and at last sit down to talk peace. If we have to, for a hundred years."

At that Laird raised an eyebrow, and ended the meeting with a pleasantry.

Barak winced to recall those last moments. *For a hundred years!* Bad, bad, *bad.* Boastful. Unprofessional. Journalistic. Why not something like "Indefinitely"? Up till then he had done well, but that lifted eyebrow! He had been stung into saying it, because Laird was prodding at his own doubts about the Canal defenses. Well, the words were said and gone beyond recall. The main thing, after all, was the Phantoms. Whatever the Russian rearmament of Egypt, a couple of Phantom squadrons should overawe Nasser — for a while.

Walking by the Kennedy Center reminded him of Emily Cunningham, naturally; of strolling with her under the stars on that overhanging promenade during intermissions, sipping tepid champagne from plastic glasses, talking about the music or the play, enjoying the sparkle of the lights of Georgetown in the black river. He would never hear Mahler again, he knew, without thinking of Queenie. But that relationship was fading off. After all her to-do about corresponding, she had written only twice in a year and a half; a joking honeymoon postcard from Hawaii, and a short letter months later, saying that she was pregnant, happy, and busy settling into their new home in Oakton, Virginia. Closed chapter, and just as well, he thought with a faint wistful pang.

Amid a pile of government mail on his desk lay a letter from his brother. He read it first.

Dear Zev:

I'll send this via the diplomatic pouch because there's news about the Gabriel seaborne missile, which you may not learn otherwise. Since the loss of the *Eilat* and the disappearance of the submarine *Dakar* put the navy command in such a rotten light, their obsession about secrecy approaches paranoia. But this Gabriel program has been going forward for many years despite all setbacks. It's now at a make-or-break point, and you may find a big job thrust on you one of these days. As you know, I've been involved right along.

Marine technology and weapons design are a far cry from high-energy physics, but if I can't fight, I can at least serve in this way . . .

Barak blinked when he read this. Michael, a congenital cripple, almost never referred to his handicap, though Zev thought it explained almost everything about him: his strange religiosity, his low self-esteem, and his marriage problems, especially since the couple's one child had been born with the same crippling muscle defect.

Some people found it hard to believe they were brothers, they were so different. In their Vienna boyhood they had both had a little yeshiva training, a concession of their irreligious socialist father to his Orthodox parents. The family's move to Palestine, barely ahead of Hitler's march into Vienna, had ended all that for Zev. His father had risen high in Labor Party circles, and Zev had gone the usual route of Zionist elite children, secular schools and then the army. Michael had diverged — or according to his appalled agnostic father, regressed — into a sort of shtetl orthodoxy, while flashing ahead as a mathematician and physicist of extraordinary brilliance. Zev admired his younger brother, though he was always somewhat baffled by him. The letter went on:

. . . Apropos, I've received a letter about my article in *Nature* (which you said you couldn't make head or tail of) from Richard Feynman, a very great Cal Tech physicist. It's an argumentative mess of equations, but then he ends by saying that my paper gives me a leg up on a Nobel Prize. Very nice, but I don't think he's right because (a) I'm an Israeli, and (b) I've put in far too much time and brainpower on stupid weaponry. No regrets, Israel's survival comes first.

Anyway, what has evolved is a small vessel fast and powerful enough to take on and sink the Soviet missile boats, and even their capital ships if they threaten our existence. Twelve of these boats (ex weapons, of course) were built in Cherbourg for us by the French, on a German design improved by our people, and we've used and upgraded matériel from all over Europe. Seven boats have been delivered and are now berthed in Haifa getting their weaponry installed.

However, De Gaulle recently slapped an embargo on the last five, although we've already paid for them. If the final test of the Gabriel succeeds, those five boats will become crucial to Israel's future. Maybe American pressure can get De Gaulle to release the boats, and it's worth a try, but Monsieur seems to be almost as sore at America as at Israel. The navy has other quasi-legal ideas to free those boats, which may bring you in directly —

Desk buzzer. "General, are you in to a Mrs. Halliday?"

Queenie? "Yes, put her on."

"Old Wolf? Hope I'm not disturbing your work." Emily sounded feeble, hoarse, yet exhilarated. "Guess what, chum, it's twin girls. About three hours old, and beautiful as daffodils. Only bright red."

"Why, good God, that's marvellous, Emily. And you're okay?"

"I suppose so. Just a bit broken on the wheel. You're the first to know, because Bud's off in Japan. If it had been a boy, I'd have called Chris first, but Bud and I will just have to try again. How are you, dear? Read any Plutarch lately?"

"Queenie, congratulations! My God, I'm terrifically happy for you. And for General Halliday, and for your father, too. He'll be ecstatic, I'm sure."

"Well, I guess he won't mind too much once he sees them. They're so pretty! I'll phone him next" — Emily's voice was weakening — "before the dope takes hold again. All well with you and the girls and Nakhama?"

"Couldn't be better."

"Bye, Zev, you rascal, it's partly your doing, you know. Don't tell Nakhama, she'll get a proper announcement."

"God bless you, Queenie."

"Oh, he has, he has, darling."

The roiling emotions that this call evoked made it hard to get back to Michael's letter. There was much more about the five Cherbourg boats, and some brief personal words at the end.

Thank you, by the way, for intervening in the matter of my former assistant's lost passport. Shayna's a remarkable mathematician, and there's a slot in my Technion department awaiting her return. Ever since that lowlife you call Don Kishote jilted her years ago — which I thought at the time was lucky for her — she's been half-alive. A bedeviled lady, and helping her to return home was a real mitzvah.

Lena and I have been having our own troubles, as I've reported, but now there's hope. I'll write you separately about that.

Love,
Michael

The last words were heartening. Michael's marriage to a kibbutznik atheist had always seemed to Barak a desperate business, what with Michael being crippled, and his wife so opinionated and far from pretty. They had made bizarre compromises, such as separate cooking by each one, kosher and unkosher sets of dishes and cutlery, Michael lighting the Shabbat candles, and so on; a shaky arrangement at best, but for a few years they had appeared to be in love and happy. Lately, however, Michael had been writing about a separation. If they could stay together after all, Zev thought, that would be best by far. Whatever Lena's drawbacks, Michael had a life with her. Not many desirable women would be eager to marry a pious divorced cripple, even one eminent in his field.

A shot of adrenaline flushed hotly through Yael Nitzan's nerves, as a comely black-haired woman of thirty or so walked into the El Al gate area at Kennedy airport. Surely this was Shayna, from whom she had stolen Don Kishote! Yael sat there with Sheva Leavis waiting to fly back to Tel Aviv, boarding time was only five minutes off, and here came Shayna Matisdorf, of all people.

For years after Yael had caused their split-up, this devout academic, a most unsuited match for the wild Yossi — at least in Yael's view — had languished in a single state; then, shortly after the Six-Day War, she had taken her broken heart to Toronto, there to mend it by marrying a rich Orthodox real estate developer. That was the last Yael had heard of her. If this was Shayna she seemed much older, she was not dressed like a rich man's wife, and she had an ashen woebegone look.

Why not go over and say hello, and find out something about her? Their relationship was coldly cordial, for during Yael's years in California Don Kishote had sometimes entrusted Aryeh to Shayna's care, and the boy adored "Aunt Shayna." Yael was slightly jealous of her on both accounts, husband and son. With Yossi's second child kicking around inside her, Yael had little to fear from the pallid woman sitting a few rows away, but she had never ceased regarding Shayna as a standing if remote threat. Yael was drifting along with Kishote much as Ruth Pasternak was doing with Sam, hanging on to a good thing as long as there was no urgent cause for a break. Next question: Was Shayna married? If so, why was she travelling to Israel alone? And if she was not married, why not?

"Are you all right? You look as though you've seen a ghost," said Sheva Leavis, startling her. He had been absorbed in the *Wall Street Journal*.

She patted her stomach. "This little no-good is giving me a hard time."

Leavis's eyes flicked around at the passengers, his glance rested on Shayna, and he gave Yael his peculiar smile, thin lips sliding up in a U-shape, conveying irony rather than mirth. It was uncanny, almost scary, for he had never met the woman. This natty little man with close-cropped gray hair, who looked like a nobody unless one could recognize a Savile Row suit, missed absolutely nothing.

When the flight was called Yael moved close to the woman in the queue of passengers. On the slim fingers of her left hand holding the boarding pass there were no rings. "Hello, Shayna."

Lustrous melancholy brown eyes rounded at her in amazement. "Yes? Is this *Yael*?"

"Have I changed that much in a year and a half?"

Shayna Matisdorf shook her head, as though to clear a mental fog. "Of course it's you. Sorry, but—"

"Oh, listen, I'm so bloated I shock myself when I look in a mirror. Coming back for a visit?"

"Well, not exactly a visit, no. How is Aryeh? I'm dying to see him."

"Why not? Anytime."

On the plane Yael preceded Sheva Leavis into the almost empty first class. As they settled into the commodious seats, Leavis said, "You really seem perturbed."

"I'm fine, thank you."

"And you're sure you haven't seen a ghost?"

"Sheva, let me alone, I'm very tired."

A sliding smile, as he accepted a *Ma'ariv* from the flight attendant and laid aside the *Wall Street Journal.*

In tourist class Shayna was sealed into a narrow window seat by a fat kerchiefed Hassidic woman with a squalling baby on her lap, and a big red-bearded husband beside her. As the plane took off Shayna resigned herself to a long night of misery. The glimpse of Yael Luria was reviving buried half-forgotten horrors, and when the woman familiarly thrust the baby in her lap, asking her in Yiddish to hold it while she went to the toilet, Shayna was glad of the distraction. The husband was immersed in a religious book, and had to be nudged to make way. The baby, quiet now, regarded Shayna with crinkling little eyes in a big red face. It was far from cute, but Shayna didn't care, she loved babies. That Yael should show up pregnant seemed somehow inevitable, given her role in Shayna's haunting misfortunes.

The start of them all had been her own fault, maybe. One small decision, right or wrong, can shape an entire life, and such had been her refusal to go to Paris with Don Kishote, when she was nineteen and finishing university, and they had been about to become engaged. Long before that, during the siege of Jerusalem, she had encountered him as a little girl. He had then been a crazy boyish stringbean of a soldier, a new refugee from Cyprus, and she had soon forgotten all about him. But years later they had met again, and an unlikely passion had blazed up between them.

Shayna's circle of friends in Jerusalem and at Hebrew University, strictly Orthodox like herself, had all disapproved of this Don

Kishote fellow, a veteran paratrooper of raffish reputation, and her parents too had looked askance at him. But she had braved it out until the Paris episode had blasted everything. Yossi's rich brother Lee, associated with the millionaire Sheva Leavis, had come from Paris to Israel on business, and had offered Yossi a birthday present of a trip to Paris with his girlfriend, not imagining that any Israeli girl would hesitate about jumping at such a treat. But Shayna's friends had been shocked at the idea, her parents had forbade her to go, and she had had to defy them all or anger Kishote.

What a dilemma, even in retrospect, it still seemed to her! Moral scruples aside, she had at that time never been out of Israel, she had no clothes suited to Paris, she had never eaten nonkosher food in her life, and the whole thing loomed as a scary plunge into the unknown. So she had backed out, and it might have passed as a minor lovers' dispute, except that Yael Luria had volunteered to go with Kishote instead; and in his irritation at Shayna he had taken her up on it. Months later had come his confession, which had stunned and almost destroyed Shayna, that in Paris he had gotten Yael pregnant, and on finding this out, had felt compelled to marry her.

And then, after ten long years, during the Six-Day War, a second smashing blow from Yael, who by that time was established in Los Angeles, making money hand over fist working with Sheva Leavis. Kishote had given Aryeh into Shayna's care while the war was on, and he had returned wounded to her Jerusalem apartment, on the very day the army was recapturing the Temple Mount. That day he had declared his unchanged love for her; and for a rainbow hour or two, Shayna had hoped that happiness might be dawning in her life. But Yael had arrived like a thunderbolt, returning because of the war, sweeping into Shayna's apartment glamorous as a movie star; and with bland irresistible self-assurance, she had then and there reclaimed her son and her husband. Gone, the rainbow, gone, the brief vision that joy might yet be possible for Shayna Matisdorf.

And now there Yael was again, up in first class, pregnant with Don Kishote's second child . . .

"Thank you. Was he good?" asked the woman, squeezing past

her husband into her seat, and taking back the baby. She felt its bottom. "Ah, nice and dry."

"He's sweet. I envy you."

"We have five more in Passaic," said the woman. "This one was too young to leave behind. The oldest girl takes care of the rest. She's eleven."

"You could have left him home, too," said the husband, not looking up from the book. "Malka's a better mother than you are."

"Maybe, but she doesn't give milk."

"When she does she'll give gallons," said the husband, turning the page.

"Malka's his favorite," the woman amiably said to Shayna. "She knows the Book of Psalms by heart."

"So do I," said Shayna.

The husband squinted at her. "You do? Recite Psalm 94."

Shayna recited it.

"You can't be an American."

"Did I say I was?"

Running through Psalms was one way to get to sleep. *"Happy is the man who walketh not in the way of the sinners,"* she began, and recited psalm after psalm to herself, her lips barely moving. She seldom got far, even on a bad night, without drifting into slumber. But the plane bounced, the baby whimpered, and she reached the last line of Psalm 150, *"All that have breath praise the Lord, Hallelujah,"* wide awake and not much comforted. Yael Luria would go on travelling first class through life, she was thinking, and for Shayna Matisdorf in tourist class nothing would ever go right. The Book of Job was the last word, there was no justice in God's world, not as the human mind understood justice. The wicked flourished like the green bay tree. *"Happy is the man who walketh not in the way of the sinners"* . . . Ha!

On this firm foundation of unyielding despair, Shayna at last dozed off.

Behind the thick glass barrier walling off the baggage area Don Kishote stood amid a throng of waving, shouting relatives and friends, looking for his wife. She had surely flown first class, so why wasn't she heading that stream of arriving passengers? Mulish woman, flying abroad in her eighth month on some stupid film business, in which she had even managed to involve him . . .

"Abba, there's Aunt Shayna! Look, it's her!" Aryeh clutched at his father's uniform with one hand, pointing. "And there's Imma now, next to that little man in gray." Indeed, here came Yael with Sheva Leavis. All men were briefly equal in Lod airport, so the multimillionaire was pushing a baggage cart. Yael was waddling rather than walking, otherwise she seemed all right. But Shayna! What was Shayna doing, coming to Israel alone? His old love looked preoccupied and worn, yet there she certainly was, and after retrieving one suitcase, she was already on her way out, while Leavis and Yael still were looking for their luggage.

"Let's go, Aryeh, we'll try to say hello to Aunt Shayna." At twelve the boy was too dignified to dance and caper, but he pulled his father by the hand in his eagerness to get to the terminal exit. Coming outside, they saw Shayna get into a car, a dusty blue Porsche. Aryeh groaned as it drove off.

"*Haval* [Too bad]," said Kishote. "Well, I promise that you'll see her while she's here."

Leavis and Yael soon appeared, followed by a laden porter. Aryeh ran to his mother and embraced her. "Hi, there," she said to Kishote, as he sauntered up and gave her a kiss. "This boy seems to grow by the week."

"So do you. Are you okay?"

"Perfect, thanks."

Peering here and there, Leavis said, "Mr. Greengrass is supposed to meet us with a car and driver."

"Greengrass telephoned me last night," Yossi said to Yael. "That's how I knew what flight you were coming on."

"What did he want of you?" Leavis asked.

"Well, with Golda becoming Prime Minister that whole film deal of yours seems to have gone on hold. He wanted to be sure that my tank units are still available."

Yossi's brother Lee had persuaded Leavis to invest in a movie about the Six-Day War, and Yossi was to assist in the tank battle scenes, if the project came off.

"Are they?" inquired Leavis.

"Depends. I may be getting reassigned myself."

"I hope this thing isn't unravelling," Yael said to Leavis.

"So? It wouldn't be my first deal to do that."

A black Mercedes pulled up at the curb. "Mr. Leavis? Mrs. Nitzan? Mr. Greengrass apologizes, and sends this message." The driver handed an envelope to Leavis, who scanned its contents and shrugged.

"Now what?" asked Yael.

"He's seeing your friend Pasternak, that's why he hasn't come to meet us. The car's at our disposal."

Kishote said dryly to Leavis, "Well, if anyone can help you with government commitments, Sam Pasternak can."

"I'll take Aryeh with me to the flat," Yael said, seizing the boy's hand.

"By all means," said Kishote. "I have to go back up north."

"Goodbye, then. Come along, Aryeh."

The boy said, following her into the Mercedes, "Remember, Abba, you promised you'd take me to see Aunt Shayna."

His parents exchanged a hard look as the driver closed the car door.

Many packing boxes were open in the disordered living room of the Prime Minister's residence. The pervasive smell of cigarette smoke identified the new occupant, and by heading where it was strongest Sam Pasternak tracked her to the kitchen. A pink apron over her cardigan and skirt, she was throwing chunks of meat and chopped vegetables into a black iron pot, with the gray-haired old cook of the residence and a Yemenite serving girl looking on. "I'll be right with you, Sam. I'm having eight for dinner, all family, for the first time. They like my soup, it'll make them feel a little more at home here." She shook in various condiments, gave orders to the grouchily obsequious cook, and took off the apron. "So, what did you find out about those crazy navy items in the defense budget? Let's go to the office."

In the book-lined room where a large regional map on one wall was flanked by portraits of Herzl and Ben Gurion, Golda sat down at the bare oversize desk, gesturing around. "Luxury, hah? I have to put up a picture of poor Eshkol. Go on, Sam."

A hush-hush missile program, he was saying, had compelled the navy for years to mask its cost with vague padding. Various budget directors had winked at the puzzling bulge, but not Moshe Dayan. On becoming Minister of Defense he had probed and found out that the army's General Staff had little faith in the sea force's missile project. A test of the weapon next month might decide whether the program would go forward or be scrapped for good.

Wrinkling her large nose at all this, Golda said, "I want you to be present at that test. If it fails, there will be a thousand excuses in a report I won't be able to wade through. You're to tell me in two words, *It worked,* or *It failed.* Understood? If it fails, that program's finished. Enough already. I'm shocked at how short of defense funding we are. For us the navy is very low priority."

"Permit me to disagree, Madame Prime Minister."

She fixed him with a cold eye. "Go right ahead."

"Assuming the missile works, those boats can change the entire equation in the Mediterranean."

As he described the design of the vessel, dwelling on its punch and its speed, she showed a trace of interest. "What are we talking about here, Sam, a pocket battleship or something? The Germans had those in the last war, pocket battleships. How can we afford them, or man them?"

Undeterred by her total ignorance — real or assumed, for Golda sometimes asked very dense questions on purpose — he explained that these were just patrol craft, beefed up to the ultimate. "For those Russian naval units based in Alexandria right now, Madame Prime Minister, the existence of a fleet of such Israeli seagoing scorpions will matter a lot, I assure you."

"I see. And what do you call a fleet?"

"Twelve vessels already built. However, there's a problem." He told her about the five boats interned in Cherbourg.

"Our good friend De Gaulle again," she said, shaking her head as she chain-lit a cigarette. "Holding back the Mirages we paid for isn't enough?"

"Well, he's not popular anymore, and he may fall in the forthcoming election. If he doesn't" — Pasternak paused, drooped his eyes almost shut, and shrugged — "maybe something else will happen with those boats."

"Sam!" She lifted an admonishing finger at him, her tone ironic. "Don't get us into any more trouble with the French than we are."

"God forbid, Madame Prime Minister."

With a knowing look, Golda flipped a hand at a sheaf of scrawls on the desk. "My first Knesset speech as Prime Minister. Do I take note of Mr. Nasser's War of Attrition or not? What's doing on the Canal? Anything new?"

"Not really. For a few days they stepped up the bombardment of the Bar-Lev Line, but that's been the pattern since the war ended. Sporadic violations of the cease-fire until we trade them blow for blow, with an extra measure that quiets them down. Temporarily."

"So I figured." Golda nodded. "I'll ignore his declaration. Just political noise. Now, should I visit that Bar-Lev Line, Sam? What is it, sort of a Jewish Maginot Line? We know what happened to *it*."

More pretense of ignorance, he thought. "Hardly a Maginot Line. If you go there, you'll see high sand walls stretching along both banks of the Canal, since they've raised a rampart to match ours. Crawling into one of our strongpoints won't tell you much. You'll find fifteen or so lads in a fortified bunker. The line's essentially a deterrent — an early warning system, well patrolled and electronically linked, so —"

"What deterrent? Boys are getting killed there, and I must acknowledge that to the Knesset." She tapped her speech manuscript. "So why aren't the Egyptians deterred?"

"They are, Madame Prime Minister." Pasternak took a grave confidential tone. "We have good access to their war plans and doctrine. *'Period of defiance, period of active defense, period of attrition, period of assault,'* et cetera. Soviet-style military planning, quite professional. They take the Bar-Lev Line seriously as a deterrent, believe me, and as a major obstacle in case of war. But their staff's not planning on war. Not now and not soon. They know they can't deliver the goods."

"Well, that's nice." Golda walked to the map and ran a stiff finger around the new borders, taking in the entire Sinai Peninsula. "Dayan likes these defense lines. So do I. Egypt signed Resolution 242, and as long as she flouts it we stay in the Sinai. So let them keep violating the cease-fire, let the big powers keep talking about imposed solutions, and let General Adan keep building our Sinai infrastructure — roads, tank depots, underground headquarters, bridges over the swamps and lagoons" — she suddenly sounded much less ignorant and much tougher — "and whenever they hit us, we hit back, and hit harder. It's not a solution, but until they're ready to talk peace it's a policy." Her plump hand circled the Sinai. "Meantime, could we have a better buffer, twice the size of all Israel?"

"It's the only policy, Madame Prime Minister."

6

The Test

A few days later a crisis meeting was in progress in Leavis's penthouse suite, looking out on the wrinkling whitecapped sea and the other tall hotels along the Tel Aviv beachfront. Rumor had it that Leavis owned this hotel, though he seldom came to Israel. The film producer Jeff Greengrass, a very fat young man overflowing an armchair in a voluminous black suit, was wheezing, "It's a hell of a blow to the project, Colonel Nitzan. But congratulations, of course, on your promotion."

"Is this final?" Sheva Leavis asked Kishote, who sported on his uniform fresh shoulder bars with three gilt leaves. "No chance you can do it?"

"It's final," said Kishote. "Sorry." He had not seen Leavis in many years. The man seemed hardly changed, perhaps a bit more withered; quiet, wispy, with watchful half-closed eyes, and the same strange smile.

"I *told* them it was final," said Yael, sitting beside her husband on a broad nubbly sofa, her distended belly in a green wool skirt resting on her knees. "I *said* that while you were a deputy you might find the time, but not when you command a front-line brigade."

"Then we must apply to the army all over again," said Shulamit, a big-bosomed redheaded lawyer who was representing Greengrass in Israel. "A pity."

"I can recommend other officers," said Kishote. "The job can be done."

"Well, there's a larger question here, Sheva," said Greengrass, "whether to proceed altogether."

Shulamit protested in thickly accented English, "Is that a question? Why? I have government approvals all lined up — Defense Ministry, Treasury Ministry, Jerusalem municipality, Arab Affairs, everybody's very enthusiastic, Mr. Greengrass, and —"

"Not according to General Pasternak. He says all those commitments are under review now."

"Oh, well. With Golda becoming Prime Minister, naturally people have turned a bit cautious. It may take a little time to loosen things up, but —"

"Shulamit, time is what's been killing this film," said Yael. "I found out that much in my trip to Hollywood."

A sad wheeze from Greengrass. "All too true, Yael, but not our fault."

"Explain that," said Leavis.

"Sheva, the movie should have been released a year and a half ago." The producer took short breaths and talked fast. "We had the script, I had the stars. Israel was hot then, on a roll, the admiration of the world. That's all been pissed away by the delays here. Now the Israel story is cease-fire violations, terrorist attacks, UN arguments. Downbeat, boring —"

"Is it true, Jeff," inquired Leavis mildly, "that the mayor of Jerusalem read the script and said — excuse me, ladies — that it was a lot of silly shit?"

"Yes, but we've got the mayor's approval, anyway," interposed Shulamit. "His deputy fixed that. The deputy was my law partner."

Kishote was looking for a moment to leave. This whole business had struck him from the start as preposterous; he had gone along with it as a favor to his brother Lee, and he had merely leafed through the script, looking at the tank episodes. In his view the mayor's comment had been a kindly understatement.

"Sheva, it comes to this," said Greengrass. "I can still make the film. Preproduction has run up to three hundred thousand dollars —"

"It shouldn't have," interposed Yael.

"No, but delays are murder on a movie. Production will now cost two million. To break even we must gross four and a half. That's where we're at."

Leavis gave Kishote his peculiar mirthless smile. "Colonel, how would you advise your brother Lee? Go ahead, or not? He's in this with me, you know."

"Why ask Yossi? He knows nothing about films," Yael expostulated, "and all he ever does — in everything — is go ahead."

"In my time I've done some retreating," said Yossi, "bringing out my dead and wounded." A short silence, and he went on. "I'd have advised Lee not to get into films in the first place. But then, I'd have advised him not to get into California real estate, and he's become a millionaire."

"Thanks to Sheva," said Yael.

Leavis shook his head. "Lee Bloom is sharp and very able, on his own."

"Furthermore, I'd have advised him not to leave his army platoon during a war," said Yossi. "In fact, not to leave Israel altogether. Lee and I think differently, so don't ask me how I'd advise my brother."

Another silence, somewhat unpleasant. Both brothers had been taken into the army back in 1948, on arriving in Israel from the Cyprus refugee camp; and Lee Bloom, then Leopold Blumenthal, had managed to get himself on a plane to America after only six weeks. A touchy business verging on desertion, and squared with some difficulty by Sam Pasternak so that the affluent Lee Bloom could now come and go in Israel. Which he seldom did.

Yael burst out nervously, "Oh, abort it, Sheva. That's what this is all about, and Jeff can't decide that. It's your three hundred thousand, yours and Lee's."

Greengrass said, "It's a hundred percent tax write-off, Sheva."

"All right. Abort," said Leavis.

"Oh, no! You're making a terrible mistake!" Shulamit's bosom heaved as though she might cry. "At least think it over —"

"Forget it, Shulamit," said Greengrass. "You've done your best, but it's over."

"Yes, that's that," said Leavis. "It's over."

Shulamit bitterly sighed.

"I'll tell you something, though, Sheva," panted Greengrass, "I've become hooked on this wild place, crappy government and all. There's a story here, a great story. You have to find the story, and none of this Jewish boy meets Arab girl — or Arab girl meets Jewish boy — horse manure. Romeo and Juliet it ain't. But there's a bloody fortune in an Israel movie. Only you have to find the story."

"Find the story and I'll find the money," said Leavis. "I'm not discouraged."

"I can introduce you to some brilliant Israeli writers," said Shulamit. "Like my nephew Chaim."

"Another time," said Greengrass. "I fly home tonight."

Don Kishote and Yael rode down together in a crowded elevator. When they emerged into the lobby he inquired, "Well, so what did the doctor say?"

She patted her belly. "I'm healthy as a horse. I could drop it in a field anytime and start licking it clean, but his best guess is two more weeks."

"Good. Have dinner with me?"

"Thanks, I've got to go over some accounts with Sheva. He's leaving for Singapore in a few hours. I'll have coffee with you." In the lounge she ordered a pastry with her coffee, laughing and slapping her stomach. "I don't want it, but this pest does."

They chatted about the film fiasco, Yael maintaining that she had always been against the idea but Lee had overborne her.

"How's Aryeh?" Kishote asked.

"Oh, he's in heaven." She touched Kishote's shoulder ornament. "When I told him about that third leaf he jumped to the ceiling. It looks mighty good, dear. Do you go to the Sinai right away?"

"No. Three days up north to turn over my post. Then before I report to Southern Command, a few days of rock-climbing in Maktesh Rimon."

"Maktesh Rimon? Kishote, that climbing is for kids, very tough kids. Be sensible, please."

With his old uncivilized grin he said, "*You're* telling *me* to be sensible?"

"Look, when I'm in the hospital having this baby, I don't want its father falling off a cliff in Maktesh Rimon."

He turned serious. "Maybe I should stay around until you have it. That can be arranged."

"Nonsense, why? You need recreation, Yossi, just stay off cliffs."

"I guess I can go skiing in Switzerland."

"*Much* better."

"Say, Yael, Shayna Matisdorf's here, and —"

Yael interrupted, frowning. "I know, we came in on the same plane. What about her?"

"I'm just thinking that while you're in the hospital, she might stay at the flat with Aryeh."

"Whatever for? He's a big boy."

"Would you mind?"

"You've already talked to her?"

"I'm not sure where she is now. I'm asking you first."

"That's thoughtful. Well, as you wish. I have no objection." She struggled out of her chair. "Thanks for the coffee. Tell me, don't you think Nasser will be tempted to start something, with that old yenta as our Prime Minister?"

"Not to worry. Ben Gurion once called Golda his only cabinet minister with balls."

"Ha ha! I hope he was right."

"He was. You'll see."

Shayna was staying in a richly furnished villa on Mount Carmel, owned by Guli Gulinkoff. Professor Berkowitz had parked her there on his rich American relatives, the Barkowes, who had reluctantly come to live in Haifa for a while because Dzecki had begun his three years of army service.

"He's our son, even though he's slipped his trolley," Leon

Barkowe had observed to his mutinous wife Bessie, when she tried to balk at the idea. "He can't be all alone while he's adjusting to army life. He needs support. We're going, and that's that."

Dzecki had appealed to Gulinkoff to house them magnificently and Guli had done so, at a very steep rent. Leon Barkowe, a mild-mannered balding little man, was finding Gulinkoff a congenial landlord. They shared a taste for certain Havana cigars unobtainable in Israel — except by Guli, who kept him provided — and they were even talking about investing in real estate together. Once a divorce lawyer, Leon Barkowe had made a lucrative switch to Long Island real estate, and he thought Haifa was full of opportunities, a view Guli was warmly encouraging.

"To me, she might as well be talking Chinese," Bessie Barkowe fretted. "I'm sorry, but I swear I can't stand the sound of Hebrew."

On a black-and-white TV set Golda Meir was addressing the Knesset, and an oddly assorted group was watching: unshaven Guli in his worn leather windbreaker, the skullcapped professor and his wife Lena in jeans and sweaters, and Shayna with a faded apron over an old housedress; whereas the Barkowes were holding to their Long Island style, tie and sport jacket for Dzecki's father, a smart black pantsuit for the plumpish mother.

"Never mind, she isn't saying much," observed Professor Berkowitz.

"She is too. She's brilliant," snapped Lena, in her most prickly kibbutznik manner. "That woman will save Israel. Shut up."

Leon Barkowe was giving the Berkowitzes cousinly help in their divorce process, working with a Haifa lawyer. The sluggish pace of Israeli law promised to keep them yoked for a while yet, and reconciliation had been Barkowe's forte, so he was working at it. Lena still seemed bent, however, on marrying an irreligious Australian Jew who exported kangaroo leather. She had met him in London, where she had gone to a sister's funeral, and he had come to hawk his wares. Sparks had flown, and ever since, letters from Melbourne had been expressing amorous impatience.

"You know something, Bessie?" said Dzecki's father in a soothing way. "Golda looks sort of like Lyndon Johnson — same big nose, little eyes, bulldog jowls, tough jaw. Doesn't she?"

"I wish Lyndon Johnson was still President," said Mrs. Barkowe, irked with the whole world, "instead of that Nixon. *President* Nixon! I still can't believe it. Everything's disintegrating."

"She's talking about him right now," said Lena.

"What's she saying?" Barkowe inquired. "Anything encouraging?"

Shayna freely translated, *"The American President is a man of peace . . . I welcome his new peace initiative . . ."*

"Oh sure she welcomes it. Like an attack of hemorrhoids she welcomes it," said Gulinkoff gruffly. "Be flexible and give everything back, that's what it'll amount to. It always does —"

Bessie Barkowe jumped to her feet and went to a window. "I think I hear the Porsche. Jack's coming."

The telephone rang on a side table by the professor's armchair. It was Noah Barak, calling from the navy yard to convey in cryptic words that the missile test had been advanced, at General Pasternak's request, by one hour; also that his boat would be taking part, substituting at the last minute for another vessel whose skipper had fallen sick. "Can you get here all right, Uncle Michael? Otherwise I'll organize a navy car for you."

"I'll manage. So the test is all set?"

"Affirmative. We just have to fire the thing and see what happens." Noah's laugh was a trifle uncertain.

In greasy fatigues, himself grease-streaked on face and hands, Dzecki strode in carrying a bulging laundry sack. The mother hugged and kissed him. "You're so sunburned, Jack! What have you been doing?"

"Daphna has to use the bathroom, okay?"

"Of course."

He went to the window, waved, and carried off his laundry to the back. With a smile for everybody, her blond hair in some disorder to her shoulders, Daphna Luria hurried through the room. When Dzecki's parents had first met Daphna she had been an impeccably groomed air force sergeant in uniform, but her service was finished, and she now wore the Tel Aviv bohemian outfit of the moment, a coarse brown skirt, a multicolored sweater, and many beads and bangles. Soon she passed through the other way, saying,

"Good old Golda! Still drivelling? Tell Dzecki I'll be waiting in the car."

"Young lady," Guli said, "you should talk more respectfully about Golda Meir."

Daphna stopped to give him an impudent stare. "Should I? Why?"

"Because you may be Prime Minister someday. Then you'll want respect from fresh youngsters." With a loud sniff and a toss of her head, Daphna walked out. "And who is that?" Guli asked Barkowe with a wolfish grin. "Your son's girlfriend? She looks like trouble."

The professor said, "She's my nephew Noah Barak's girlfriend. Dzecki just hangs around her."

"And very, very foolish of him," said the mother.

"But understandable," said Guli.

Shortly Dzecki reappeared more or less cleaned up, in slacks, a short-sleeved sport shirt, and sandals. "I have to drive Daphna to the navy yard."

"Right away?" complained his mother. "Eat something first, you're always starved when you come home."

"She's in a rush." He peered at the TV set. "Some Prime Minister! All the guys thought it would be Dayan or Allon."

"That's how she got in," said Professor Berkowitz. "Because of the standoff. Can you take me to the base, too?"

"Why not? Say, Shayna, can I talk to you?"

She followed Dzecki into the hall. "What is it?"

"Listen, you know this Colonel Yossi Nitzan, the one they call Don Kishote?" She rounded startled eyes at him. "He's coming by here today. He saw me pick you up at the airport last week, so he asked me where he could find you."

"But when and how did you talk to Yossi Nitzan?"

"This morning he turned over deputy command of the brigade at a relief ceremony, and afterward he called me out of the ranks." Dzecki shrugged and grinned. "The private with the Porsche. They all know me. I told him you were staying with my folks." Dzecki looked at his wristwatch. "He should be here in an hour or so."

"Ayzeh maniac!" Shayna went scampering upstairs, whipping off her apron, black hair flying.

When Don Kishote showed up she was in the living room, holding in her arms the Berkowitzes' crippled two-year old Reuven, a smiling chubby child, just awakened from a long nap. His mother and Bessie Barkowe were laying out cake, soda, fruit, nuts, and wine on the coffee table, though Shayna had begged them not to fuss, this was just an old friend dropping by. The red silk dress from Toronto and the hurried coiffure told them otherwise. They had cleared out the men, and the moment Yossi appeared Lena took her child and they made themselves scarce. "Then you're *not* married!" Yossi said when they were gone, giving Shayna a rough hug.

The hard arms felt inexpressibly sweet around her, and his chest muscles were like a wall. All but speechless, she babbled whatever came to mind. "Kishote, why are you so lean? Doesn't the army feed you? Have some cake."

"Sure, anything. Listen, I've been promoted. Full colonel, almost the youngest in the army." He pointed to the third leaf on his shoulder bars.

"Congratulations, let's drink some wine to your promotion."

"By all means. Shayna, my new assignment is command of an armored brigade on the Canal."

She stopped pouring the wine. "The Canal! There's been a lot of trouble there."

"Motek, it couldn't be a better assignment. Me, I'm drinking to your return. It's wonderful. Now, what to all the devils happened in Canada?" Yossi took a gulp of wine and dropped beside her on the couch.

"I don't want to discuss it."

"Come on! In two words, Shayna, why are you back?"

"In two words? Well, all right. In two words, HIS MOTHER."

"What about his mother?"

"That takes a lot more than two words." But Shayna ran on, of course. "Paul's family, it turned out, owns office buildings and shopping centers all over Ontario. His father's just a nice nebbish. Mama's the big boss. His older brother's a doctor, his sister's husband teaches at McGill, so that leaves Paul to take over, eventually. Therefore he can't settle in Israel. He can buy an apartment in Jerusalem, and come here for Passover and the High Holy Days, period. That didn't emerge until we began planning the wedding, then Paul had to choose between the real estate and Shayna."

"Well, you had to choose, too."

"I did. Actually Mama was very nice to me. Bought me a fur coat and dresses — *You're going to be a Rubinstein, get used to dressing like one'* — mind you, Canada's beautiful, Toronto's a big exciting city, and Paul is a good fellow, but —"

"But you love Israel," said Don Kishote, "and me."

She struck his arm with a fist. "Has Yael had her baby yet?"

"Any day now."

"How could you let her travel in that condition?"

"What have I got to say about it?" He pulled a key from a breast pocket. "Look, Aryeh will be alone when she goes into the hospital. I told him you'd come and stay with him. Here's the key to the flat."

Almost too choked up to speak, Shayna pushed away his hand. "I still have my key, unless you've changed the locks."

"I haven't."

"You've got your nerve, Yossi, taking me for granted like this."

Kishote looked around. "You're not planning to live here with these Americans, are you?"

"No, I've rented a flat near the Technion, starting next month, when I go back to work."

"Shayna, why didn't you come right home? You were there almost two years."

"I was stranded. I wouldn't accept their money, once Paul and I broke up. Not even for fare to Israel. I gave back the fur and the clothes, and I taught in a Hebrew school. To tell the truth, I also kept working on Paul. Maybe he was working on his mother too, I don't know. When he got engaged to a girl whose family had even more real estate, I bought my El Al ticket."

"Mrs. Rubinstein is my favorite Canadian," said Yossi, "and that Paul is a dish of noodles. I always knew it. I'm going." They both stood up. "About this baby, Shayna, I think Yael will take it to California and never come back."

"What do I care what she does?"

"You're beautiful, Shayna. A week at home and you're a mentsch. At the airport you looked awful."

"If you're going, *go* already."

"When Aryeh saw you he all but danced. Me, too."

He embraced and tried to kiss her, but she struggled free. "For God's sake, no crazy heroics at the Canal, now. You're a senior officer. Act responsibly."

"There are telephones at headquarters, Shayna. I'll call you at the flat when I can. I love you." He managed a swift kiss on her mouth, and he was gone.

In a heavy sweater and wool cap, for the weather at sea was predicted to be very cold and windy, Noah Barak was waiting for Daphna Luria at the bus stop near the base, when to his great disgust, far down the curving waterfront, the blue car came in sight. L'Azazel! It was bad enough that he had to call off their planned evening in Tel Aviv; dinner at Shaul's, the Joffrey Ballet, and then a whole night in the two-room flat on old Nakhmani Street, which she shared with another rebellious military daughter. Once she had acquired a place of her own Daphna had given Noah her all, and since then there had been many an exhausting roar of tempestuous marvellous sex in her narrow bed. Not, however, in the past three weeks of naval maneuvers, and Noah was on fire for more of that wild carrying-on. But now she would drive off with that pest Dzecki in his cursed Porsche, to do God knows what.

This nuisance had been dragging on and on while Dzecki took courses in Israeli law, then decided to serve his army sadir. Now and then when Noah was at sea or on duty at the base, Daphna had been dating his fool-headed American cousin, averring that it didn't mean a thing, that Dzecki was just fun and his car a convenience. That she would not consider marriage now — *"Look, I've just gotten my freedom, let me enjoy it a bit"* — was something else Noah had to put up with. Meantime what could he do about Dzecki? How could he show jealousy of a dizzy draftee, with the green passport that was his escape hatch from Israel anytime he wanted out; a garagenik with a knack for tinkering, for there was no other way to keep a Porsche running in Israel; a deliberate *rosh katan* (small head), choosing to remain a private, when with his education he should have applied for an officers' course?

"I do my three years and I'm out," Daphna had quoted Dzecki to Noah. "Rosh katan for me. Contracting is the thing here. These *kablanim* make fortunes. Look at Guli! A lowbrow, a boor, and a millionaire. The field's wide open, and once I make a bundle I'm getting into politics. This country is being run by old doctrinaire dumbbells, and it can't go on." Daphna had recounted this chatter with giggles, but Noah had not been amused. It was just like that American airhead to think he could run Israel better than the Israelis, even if the politicians were a sorry lot.

"No! I don't *believe* this," exclaimed Daphna, when she got out of the car and Noah told her their date was off. He saw his Uncle Michael sitting in the back of the Porsche, dressed much too lightly for the sea. What a mess, altogether! She was calling into the Porsche, "Dzecki, don't go yet . . . How come, Noah? Did you make a mistake? Aren't you off duty? Why didn't you CALL me?"

"*Hamoodah* [Darling], I'm sorry, I can't talk about it."

"Oh, you can't! Well, what about tonight?"

"I just don't know yet, Daphna." He led her aside by an elbow. "Look here. I got sudden orders, not two hours ago. Top secret, and I may be back tonight, I may not. It's one of those unpredictable things. I know it's rotten, but this could be important. Forgive me."

"Oh, to all the devils, I'm sure it's important. This country can drive you mad." She kissed him tenderly on the lips. "You're forgiven."

"What will you do, Daphna? Where will you be tonight, in case I do get back?"

"Forget about me, motek. I'll be fine." Daphna was cheering up a shade too quickly to suit Noah. "Let's talk on the phone whenever you return. Call me at the flat. If I'm not there, Donna will be. Leave a message." Her roommate Donna was usually at home, doggedly writing unproduced screenplays. Off rolled the

Porsche to deposit the professor at the base entrance, leaving Noah to trot after it, grinding his teeth. He helped his uncle get out of the car, and walked slowly with the limping scientist through the gate into the navy yard.

"Poor Noah!" Daphna settled back in the blue leather seat as they drove away. "And we were going to have such a big time in Tel Aviv. There's this ballet I'm dying to see, I've got the tickets and everything —"

"So? I'll take you there. No problem."

"Are you serious, Dzecki? You told me you intended to sleep for twenty-four hours."

"What else is there to do at home? I'll just grab a quick shower, put on some clothes, and we're off to the ballet."

"Dzecki, you'll fall asleep at the wheel and we'll both get killed."

"So you'll drive and I'll sleep. Just don't speed. If the Mekhess ever gets this car again, bye-bye."

"I won't speed, but are you sure the ballet won't bore you, motek?"

In a bleak corrugated iron hut, on the pier where the Cherbourg boats were berthed, Sam Pasternak, clad in a green waterproof parka and baggy pants, was drinking tea. A cold wind off the harbor whistled at the fogged window, and an electric heater by the tea urn gave off a red glow and not much else.

"Ah, there you are, Professor," Pasternak said, as Noah came in with his uncle. "Now all we need is the Treasury Minister. Everyone else is aboard the boat already. Get the professor some warm clothes, Lieutenant, or he'll freeze out there. For the Minister, too. He's very short and very fat. Professor, is the damn thing going to work?"

Michael Berkowitz limped to the urn, and as tea trickled from the spigot he said, "Can't say. My responsibility has been running checks on the computations. The aircraft people down in Lod built it, and I've contributed an idea or two. Live warheads are not my thing."

"You've seen the preliminary tests?"

Michael shook his head. "Just the designs. They're original and startling. These navy fellows are brilliant, but audacious. It's a whole new concept —"

"I know the concept, a sort of Tom Thumb battleship, no? A shallow-draft boat a hundred fifty feet long, with the punch of a heavy cruiser —"

"That's it, more or less."

"Michael, I'll ask a dumb army man's question. How can you throw such a punch from an eggshell boat hull?"

"Well, with a missile there's no recoil, of course. As for the deck guns —"

A telephone rang by the urn. Michael picked it up. "Yes . . . All right . . . The Minister's car just arrived, General."

"Then let's go."

At the gangway of his Saar (Storm) boat Noah helped the portly little Treasury Minister into foul-weather gear, while Pasternak assisted Michael. "Minister, do you get seasick?" Pasternak asked the cabinet member, an old friend. "I do."

"Just don't talk about it." The nervous politico wrestled a zipper over his bulging paunch, his white hair flying in the wind. "Just don't think about it. It'll all be over in a few hours. I sailed from Rumania in 1910, in a boat like a bathtub, and here I am."

Army and government observers crowded the deck and bridge of Noah's craft, but there were none on a similar vessel tied outboard, with two strange large gray housings on its deserted forecastle. "That's the Gabriel," said Pasternak to the Minister.

"Those two trash cans? Well, this test had better come off, that's all," said the Minister peevishly. "There's been much larceny going on in the defense budget, and Moshe Dayan will stand for no more of it."

The two boats left the harbor in a bright afternoon. Beyond the breakwater the swells from the west were smoothed out by an offshore wind, and Noah's craft moved steadily over a calm sea, but not steadily enough for the Treasury Minister, who within minutes was looking very green. The boat's captain brought him below to his cabin. "Just lie down, Minister, and you'll be all right. We'll call you topside for the test."

Collapsing on the dark bunk, the Treasury Minister groaned, "I was younger when I sailed from Rumania."

Michael Berkowitz was wedged in the captain's bridge chair, talking mathematical and ballistics jargon with the father of the missile boat project, Admiral Shlomo Erell, a wiry little man in a thick sweater and wool cap. Now retired, this former navy chief had been relieved early of his command, disgraced by the sinking of the *Eilat,* and the vanishing of the submarine *Dakar* on its maiden voyage. But nothing had stopped his indomitable pursuit of the "thumbnail battleship," and of all the people crowding the vessel, he seemed the calmest at this make-or-break point of his seven-year quest.

"Your nephew's a good officer," Erell remarked to Michael, as Noah executed a maneuvering order called down by the captain from gun control. "He should have been decorated for his action in the *Eilat* disaster, and he's going places."

"Can I tell my brother Zev you said that?"

"Why not? I just did."

"Target, Captain, one point on the starboard bow," Noah shouted up to gun control. "Range seven miles."

Visitors all over the small boat began saying, "What? Where? Who sees it?"

Noah passed Pasternak the binoculars. "Straight ahead, General, a little to the right."

"That hair on the horizon? That's the *Jaffa*?"

"That's her mast."

Noah gunned the motors, the boat leaped ahead, and the *Eilat*'s sister ship hove in plain view. With a pang, Noah remembered how glad he had been to espy it coming in sight over the horizon to relieve the *Eilat* on patrol. Now here was the moment of truth. After today Israel would either have a two-front navy in the Med and the Red Sea, of a strength that would astonish the world, or an insignificant coast guard, once for all.

Pasternak went below on a short steep ladder, and found the Treasury Minister supine on a bunk in a darkened cabin. "Are you all right, Minister?"

"As long as I lie flat," he moaned, snapping on a small bunk light and rolling over to face Pasternak. "Tell me again, Sam," he said hollowly, "why we have to sink the *Jaffa*."

"Nothing else to do with it. Its day is done. We'll have no more warships three hundred feet long, with two hundred sailors aboard."

"They could test the missile on a towed target."

"That's been done. The question is whether it can sink a vessel with a live warhead on the open sea."

"If it does, then what?"

"Then — and this is straight from Golda — the navy's got its twenty-five million dollars to finish and fit out those five Saar boats still stuck in Cherbourg. Otherwise that money will buy a lot of tanks, as you know."

"Sam, the French have embargoed those boats. We can't get them out."

Noah shouted down a speaking tube, "Preparing to fire, General."

"Minister, be a mentsch. This is why you're out here."

"I'm coming, I'm coming, Sam."

On the forecastle of the other Saar, about half a mile away, one gray pod now gaped open like a crocodile mouth. The Treasury Minister said in a dim voice, "Sam, wasn't it you who came with me to London when we bought the *Jaffa*?"

"Yes, it was."

"Then you know we paid spot cash for that destroyer. Spot cash! A check on the Barclay Bank in Tel Aviv! Now, only ten years later, I have to watch us try to sink her. Could anything be crazier?"

Over the wireless transmitter, the harsh voice of the captain of the other Saar: *"Cub One from Cub Two. Missile ready to launch."*

Admiral Erell, up in gun control with a microphone: *"This is Lion. ESH! [FIRE!]"*

Out of the gray pod a long dark projectile, with four large tail fins and a peculiarly bristly nose, whooshed skyward in a throbbing roar, trailing flame and black smoke. It flew in a long arc high, high into the blue, then suddenly nosed over and went diving toward the sea. All over the boat a general moan rose which changed to a cheer when the missile straightened out and went skimming over the surface toward the *Jaffa*. From his chair Michael was tracking the missile with binoculars, as it rose and fell just above the water, following the contours of the high long swells. "How to all the devils does it conform to the surface like that?" Pasternak asked him. "It's eerie!"

"Depth-finder principle, General, adapted to electronics," said Michael with growing excitement. "Flight path governed by constant rapid measuring of the distance to the surface. Inspired idea, though the mathematics were very complicated —"

"But look, isn't it off course, Professor? I'd say it'll miss by half a mile."

"Wait."

In a few moments the missile veered sharply, sailed upward, and then dived straight at the destroyer. Smoke, flame, and white water spurted up from the hull amidships, and a reverberating blast came rolling over the sea. Applause and loud cheers broke out from sailors and visitors alike. "By my life, sir," Noah blurted to his captain, as the splash subsided and the smoke drifted clear of the Jaffa, "she's listing already."

"ESH!"

The second missile sped over the sea, again wide of the mark, again turning toward it. Michael enthused to Pasternak, "How about that control, General? Did you see all that stuff on the nose? Special radar, a Jewish tchotchke. There was nothing that we could buy off the shelf, in Europe or America, to do the job."

The second missile "did the job" for fair, thunderously tearing another enormous black hole in the Jaffa, quite visible to the naked eye. A third Saar boat had been lying to, well clear of the test area, with the skeleton crew of the *Jaffa*'s last voyage aboard. As the three patrol boats slowly converged on the listing destroyer, a melancholy silence settled over the onlookers. Slowly, slowly, the dying *Jaffa* rolled over on its side, wallowed awash for long minutes, then lifted its Hebrew-lettered bow to the sky and slid down into the sea, leaving a boil of spume and a whirling slick on the blue water.

"Cubs One, Two, and Three from Lion," called Erell, *"last sa-*

lute." In column, the three patrol boats sailed round and round the bubbly slick in a tight circle, their sirens mournfully wailing. Then the column headed back toward Haifa under a sunset sky.

Admiral Erell approached Noah and handed him a small brown book. "When you get a chance, Lieutenant Commander, have a look at this."

"Sir, my rank is lieutenant."

"Not for long." The retired admiral dropped down the ladder. The book was Baedeker's *Guide to Cherbourg*.

7

The Shocks

"Yossi? It's Shayna."

Kishote sat up, wide awake at once. The window of his chilly bedroom in the ski lodge looked out on a vista of twilit Alps, where high snowy peaks were reddening in the dawn. "Is Aryeh all right?" he blurted.

"Aryeh's fine. Mazel tov, Yael just called, she had a nine-pound girl early this morning —"

"Oo-wah, nine pounds! A big, big girl! *Barukh ata . . .*" He rattled off the ancient blessing on good news.

"Amen," said Shayna, "and they're both doing well, she told me. Here, Aryeh wants to talk to you."

"*Abba!* I've got a baby sister! Aunt Shayna's taking me to the hospital today to see her!" The boy's voice was breaking with excitement. "I just talked to Imma, and she said it's all right, I could come. Isn't that great?"

"Beautiful, but go after school, hamood."

"B'seder, Abba. Oh, I'm so happy!"

"So am I. Kiss your little sister and Imma for me. Now let me talk to Aunt Shayna. . . . Look, Shayna, tell Yael I'll be back tonight or tomorrow, depending on the flights —"

"Yossi, she insisted you're not to break off your vacation, there's no need —"

"Doesn't she think I want to see my daughter?"

"I suppose she knows you pretty well."

The faintly tart, deeply sad tone scraped Don Kishote's nerves. A pause.

"How has Aryeh behaved?"

"His father's son."

"That bad?"

"Charged up with energy, that's all. Lovable anyway. I'm going back to Haifa after we see your daughter. May you raise her to Torah, marriage, and good deeds."

"Amen. Thanks, Shayna."

"For what? Goodbye, Kishote."

He was scheduled to go down a racing trail for expert skiers that morning. The instructor had warned him that pluck and skill were different things, that the trail was beyond him, and that he would be in a fair way to break a leg or his neck. He knew that if he went soon to the small local airport, he could make a connection to reach Tel Aviv that afternoon. He mulled it over, and got dressed for skiing, thinking that Shayna was right, Yael knew him pretty well.

Next day Kishote's driver met him at the bustling Lod terminal and brought him straight to the army hospital at Tel Hashomer, legs and neck intact. He had made it down the trail with only one spill in soft snow on a bad curve, and at the bottom the shaken French instructor had remarked that if all Israelis were that lucky, no wonder they won wars. He found Yael in a frilly pink bedjacket nursing the infant, who looked up blindly at her father with unblinking sky-blue eyes. "Isn't she cute?" said Yael, looking reasonably cute herself, her face made up, blond hair brushed out over her shoulders, eyes shining with tender pride.

"Not to be believed," said Don Kishote. They exchanged glances of rueful good will; no love here, but an undeniable new bond. "You have great babies, Yael."

"I've had help. See?" She caressed the baby's hair, dark like

Yossi's. "Aryeh was crazy about her, but Aunt Shayna upset him by bursting into tears. We had to explain that ladies sometimes cry for joy."

"Is there anything I can do for you?"

"Motek, I've arranged for a nurse, I go home Friday, and next week I'm back in the shop, which I bet is falling apart." The baby was making loud sucking noises. "Oof! Aren't you the hungry one? Yossi, I'd like to call her Chava [Eve], my grandma's name."

"Chava it is, then. She's a Chava, all right, Yael, fresh from the Garden of Eden."

"And in English, Eva," said Yael. " 'Eve' sounds sort of goyish. But what's the ceremony for naming a girl, Yossi? There's nothing to do, is there?" Yael made a wry face. "Nothing to cut off, you know."

"Ha! No, nothing. I just announce it at a Torah reading. I'll do that before I leave for the Sinai."

"Now listen, you take care of yourself. My brother Benny came in yesterday. He's been doing overflight photography at the Canal, and he says it's hell down there."

Yossi bent and kissed his daughter's forehead. "Goodbye, Chava. Elohim, those eyes. The first thing I ever noticed about you, Yael, so help me, was your eyes." She was removing her round pink breast from the sated baby's mouth. "Well, the second thing."

"Never mind," said Yael with a sour grin. "Ancient history."

Benny Luria had not exaggerated. Things were a lot hotter along the Suez Canal, Don Kishote soon found, than any Israeli who wasn't there could imagine.

In Tel Aviv, Haifa, and Jerusalem, the flush times of victory were going on and on. Jocund admiring tourists were flooding the big cities and the sightseeing spots, and new luxury hotels were springing up to accommodate them. Among the Israelis themselves, by and large, all was cheery confidence and mounting prosperity. They loved Golda, they trusted Moshe Dayan, and to them Nasser's one-sided War of Attrition was no more than a distant muttering futile nuisance. But at the front it was something quite different:

indeed, as the aviator had reported, an intermittent inferno for the few unlucky reserve soldiers manning the *maozim*, the strongpoints on the Bar-Lev Line.

To begin with, these fortified outposts were several miles apart; and though Kishote had known about this from maps, the reality of immense empty unprotected miles of sand, stretching as far as the eye could see along his sector of the front, came to him as a daunting shock. Tank units from his and other brigades were patrolling the huge gaps in the hundred-mile line; but the enemy, after laying down heavy artillery barrages, could send raider squads to cross the Canal almost at will, to ambush the patrols and mine the long military roads leading back to Israel. True, the tankists kept trapping and killing the raiders, but they kept coming, for Egypt's manpower and weaponry, compared to Israel's, were limitless. Kishote observed that the soldiers in the strongholds, fifteen or twenty to a post, could do little but crouch in their bunkers night and day, when the earsplitting deluges of shells came, and bear them as they might, for they were at a lopsided disadvantage in artillery.

Israeli combat doctrine of *"fire and movement"* assumed short conflicts, and turned on the air superiority and rapid massed tank thrusts which had won the Suez and Six-Day Wars, so artillery had been a poor third in planning and procurement. But now Egypt was forcing static warfare, in which artillery was the main arm, on Zahal, the Israel Defense Force. In plain sight on the other bank were heavy batteries of Soviet-made cannon, and aerial photography showed wheel-to-wheel mortars and howitzers positioned all along the hundred miles of ramparts from Port Said to the Gulf of Suez. For this formidable array of firepower, Israel's meager artillery was no match whatever, and making up such a dearth in a major branch of weaponry would take years and vast expense. Top-secret intelligence put the enemy artillery advantage at ten to one.

So perforce a new doctrine had been improvised, worded as *"flying artillery."* Mirages and Skyhawks had been pressed into use to pound the enemy batteries, and the tactic had in fact slowed the attacks. The air force was advocating an all-out campaign using the Phantoms, due to arrive in September, to strike back and once for all stamp out this War of Attrition. These were the most powerful combat aircraft in the world, and with the long reach and heavy punch of Phantoms — so the argument went — Israel could terrorize and if need be strangle Egypt; Phantoms over the Nile, sonic booms over Cairo, would teach the dictator an overpowering lesson, or perhaps even topple him. But Moshe Dayan was prudently dubious about the limits of the flying artillery concept, fearing on the one hand Russian intervention, on the other hand American delay or cancellation of Phantom deliveries if the air attacks were pressed too far.

How much longer, however, could Israel endure Nasser's one-sided voiding of the UN cease-fire resolution by exploiting his advantage in artillery? The UN itself of course was utterly indifferent, so long as Egypt was doing well. Casualties in the Bar-Lev Line were mounting. Either Israel had to leave the Canal, a policy unthinkable to Golda Meir and her worshipful public, or a decisive counterblow had to be struck to restore the cease-fire. So it was that in June, when Don Kishote had been in his new command two months, he received a terse secret order from the Minister of Defense: *Prepare and submit a plan to me for a raid into Egypt in force, using Soviet armor, as per your proposal in October 1967 after the* Eilat *sinking.*

About a month later Dayan's helicopter came thrashing down near Kishote's field headquarters, and they talked outside in the cold night while eager soldiers carried off the sacks of personal mail for the brigade which the helicopter had brought. Off to the west artillery thumped, flashes lit the sky, and drifting smoke half veiled the moon and the multitudinous desert stars.

"Is it like this every night, Yossi?"

"Much worse, before the raiders come over."

Dayan flung a hand toward the moon. "And can you believe — can you even begin to grasp — that this very minute two American guys are walking around up there on the moon? You know they've landed, of course?"

"Yes, we've been following that on the radio, Minister."

"Well, we've been seeing pictures on TV. Stunning! The greatest event in history since, I don't know, the discovery of America."

"Not the greatest, sir."

Dayan peered at him. "And the greatest?"

"That the Jews have come home."

With a somber nod, Dayan turned his face up to the moon. "You know about Green Island?"

"Yes, sir. My brigade's been giving them some logistical support. I'm still getting reports, but I gather it's a fantastic success."

"Fantastic, yes. Successful, yes." The Minister of Defense gestured at the moon. "No less than that feat, and those boys of ours would have flown to the moon, too, given the wherewithal and the orders. Nevertheless" — Dayan laid a hand on Kishote's arm, and looked him hard in the face, in the winking lights of the helicopter — "Israel's not America. We can't go to the moon, and we can't afford many more Green Islands. Let's have a look at your plan, Yossi."

Green Island was an Egyptian fortress in the sea, an artificial island with high vertical concrete walls rising from the waters of the Gulf of Suez; constructed as a radar warning station, manned by heavily armed defenders, and supposedly impregnable. Israeli frogmen swimming miles at night, much of the way underwater, had assaulted this island, together with elite commandos who came in rubber boats. They had all but wiped out the defenders, destroyed the radar, demolished the fortifications, and withdrawn. Though the objective was the radar, the purpose was *shock;* a demonstration to the Egyptians that if they persisted in violating the cease-fire, they too would be hit with punishing raids. When the cost in elite fighters killed or wounded came out, the brilliance of the feat was tarnished. Warriors of rare skill and heroism, some critics charged, had been expended for a political stunt. *Shanuy b'makhloket* is the old rabbinic phrase for unresolved Talmudic disputes; and remarkable as the Green Island raid was for audacity and success, that gallant feat of arms remained *shanuy b'makhloket*.

In the trailer where Yossi slept and worked, he showed Moshe Dayan a large hanging map gaudy with multicolored operational arrows and symbols. "There it is, Minister, the plan." As Dayan squinted at it in the harsh light of a naked bulb, an aide dropped two envelopes on Kishote's cot. Out of the corner of his eye Yossi recognized Shayna's pink stationery, and on the other letter Aryeh's writing.

Dayan gnawed a lip, shook his head, and rapped a knuckle on the map. "Green Island again, Yossi."

"With all respect, Minister, not so. It's not an elite coup, but an operation with combined regular forces."

"You've worked this up yourself?"

"I've consulted with Bren all the way, sir." Bren was Major General Avraham Adan, the austere able commander of the armored corps, who as OC Southern Command had built up much of the Sinai infrastructure.

"And he approves? He thinks you can get this kind of air and navy cooperation?"

"He believes it's feasible."

"I thought you'd plan a cross-Canal thrust, or a drive toward Port Said over the lagoons." Dayan rapped the map again. "But crossing the Gulf of Suez into *Africa*? Landing an armored force on an enemy shore? To be stranded and destroyed to the last man if things go wrong?"

"Minister, as you see" — Kishote ran a finger down a typed chart beside the map — "the plan calls for seven weeks of exercises and rehearsal, including several with air and sea forces, and —"

"All very fine in theory, but in the first place that African coast is solid coral reef. Ha? Thought of that? No opening for landing craft, and blasting openings will alert the enemy and kill surprise."

"Sir, there are creek and river mouths where silt has worn down and covered the coral. Reconnaissance patrols with frogmen have already been over there." Kishote hastily added as Dayan frowned, "Approved by Southern Command and General Adan."

"See here," Dayan pointed. "You'd land less than thirty miles south of Suez City. Powerful forces will come roaring down at the first alert and trap you. It can be a massacre."

"I believe not, sir. The road here, where we'll land" — Yossi slid a finger along the Egyptian coastline — "runs between steep cliffs and the water. Very, very narrow passage, just a few meters between a high rocky ridge and the sea. Once we're ashore sappers will dynamite the ridge, and create an impenetrable rock barrier —"

"Impenetrable? How can you be *sure*?" Yossi hesitated, and Dayan's tone sharpened. "Well? There's your fatal unknown, right there."

"Minister, I went over with the second patrol myself to reconnoiter that choke point, so I know —"

"You went *yourself* to Africa?" Moshe Dayan interrupted, glaring at him. "You, a brigade commander? Bren didn't approve that. He couldn't have."

"Sir, I just went and did it, so I know I can block that road." The telephone buzzed. Yossi pulled it from its bracket. "Yes. . . . L'Azazel! . . . One moment . . . Minister, raiders are attacking Matzmed outpost in force, and Amos Pasternak's tank patrol is counterattacking."

"Let's go there," said Dayan.

Taking off in a whirl of dust, they flew straight and low along the moonlit sand. Starshells were floating over the distant desert ahead, and the whole horizon was ablaze. The helicopter landed at the paved yard of an outpost dug into the rampart. A soldier on guard waved in welcome. Inside the yard lay many scattered weapons, two abandoned flamethrowers, and a sprawl of bodies in Egyptian uniform. Near the yard entrance an Israeli tank was on fire, pouring up flame and black smoke.

"That tank of ours got them all," said the soldier hoarsely, gesturing with his Uzi at the Egyptian corpses. He showed no deference whatever to the high brass. "But then it went out to fight the other raiders and it got hit by grenades." He jerked a thumb at the sandbagged doorway to the outpost. "The tank crew's inside. The driver got it bad, the others are okay."

Dayan and Kishote entered the stronghold, a bleak warren of low arched rooms of corrugated iron, smelling of cooking fumes, unwashed men, and tobacco smoke. In an alcove two soldiers were giving plasma to the groaning tank driver. The young lieutenant commanding the outpost, bewhiskered and shaky-voiced, said that Pasternak's patrol had arrived just in time to chase off the raiders. "A narrow escape, Minister! We aren't equipped to resist those bazookas and flamethrowers they brought. They'd have slaughtered us."

Dayan said he would climb out on the rampart and have a look at the Canal. "Minister," protested the lieutenant, "the Egyptian sharpshooters are very good at night. They're not two hundred meters away, and there's a moon."

"I know there's a moon."

The lieutenant went first, followed by Dayan and Kishote, who thought it a damn-fool exposure for the man next to Golda, but just like the Minister of Defense. The fortified roof was level with the sands of the rampart, only vents showing. Dayan wriggled on his belly to the edge, with Kishote beside him. There far below was the long ditch fading northward, and off to the south, the moonlit Great Bitter Lake stretching out of sight.

"Quiet now," said Dayan.

"They can open up at any moment, sir." The lieutenant was audibly nervous.

"Can you survive a direct hit?"

"We got one ten days ago. It was a mess. Even the overhead steel rails caved in." General Adan had reenforced the outpost roofs with torn-up steel rails from the coastal railroad. "We lost one dead, three wounded and evacuated. But we've repaired the damage."

"So I see. Very well, too."

"Minister, what else have we to do out here?"

At the bitter note, Dayan peered at the lieutenant, and slapped his shoulder. After a silence, he said to Yossi, "Well, as an obstacle, it's no Great Wall of China. Let's go and find Amos."

They took a jeep and set off northward on the road below and behind the rampart. A short drive brought them to three tanks sunk in muck, and two other free tanks chained in tandem, hauling one out with metallic groans and roars. On firm ground mucky soldiers were cleaning off a mud-coated tank. Dayan and Kishote did not recognize Amos Pasternak until he answered to his name. When he saluted, mud flew from his arm. "This is a great honor, Minister." Even in these straits he managed to sound cheeky. "Sorry I can't parade my unit for inspection."

"What happened here?"

"We were chasing the raiders, sir, and a half-track of ours went up on a mine. Nobody killed, but three guys in bad shape, so we got off the road to pursue, and that's how these tanks bogged down. It's swampy terrain. I went ahead with the other tanks and we caught and killed all the raiders. At least I think we killed them all. Now it's a question of pulling my tanks out of the mud, and it's a job —"

Like a thunder-and-lightning storm, the night suddenly erupted: distant artillery blasts, starshells floating down, and shells exploding around them, shaking the ground, deafening the ears, and throwing up sand, smoke, and fire. Arms akimbo, Dayan calmly watched the renewed barrage. It occurred to Yossi Nitzan that he looked happy. Pasternak went on extricating his bogged unit, the doubled-up tanks slowly dragging a muck-dripping tank onto dry ground.

Dayan shouted, "Amos, get in a tank and button up till it's over. Tell your soldiers to do the same."

"Is that an order, Minister?"

"It's ministerial advice, and very good advice."

"It's better to keep working, sir," yelled young Pasternak, his eyes reddened by the fire of a bursting shell. "My battalion has had thirty percent dead and wounded, and we're overdue for relief. But while we're out here, we'll get on with it." He bawled at the towing tanks, "All right, well done, hook up to the next one."

In the intermittent glare of the barrage, Dayan and Kishote drove back to the helicopter, and it returned them to brigade headquarters, skimming the sand. "You've got a good plan, Yossi," Dayan shouted as the machine settled down in a boil of dust. "Is Bren prepared to go with it?"

"Affirmative, sir. It's pretty much his plan, you know."

"You would lead it?"

"That's up to Bren, and to Southern Command."

"No, it's up to me, and you'll lead it." Dayan's good eye protruded in a stern stare. "It's on. En brera. We can't leave the Canal, not unless Golda jumps into some very cold political water. Militarily, the Canal isn't keeping out the Egyptians. As for the Bar-Lev Line," his voice went faintly sarcastic, for General Bar-Lev had been Golda's choice for Ramatkhal, not his, "it isn't delivering the goods, either. Until the politics change, the solution is force."

Kishote hurried to the trailer to read his mail. Aryeh's letter-writing was no longer boyish. He gave a clear spare account, in a neat hand, of his scout troop's visit to a snowbound army outpost on Mount Hermon.

> . . . They let us take turns at the periscopes, Abba. We could see Syrian soldiers moving around, and Syrian tanks and jeeps, too. They look so much like ours, it's strange. The outpost is very sad, just ten fellows up there by themselves in a hole, nothing to do but watch. Our leader asked what they would do if the Syrians attacked the outpost and they just looked at each other and didn't say anything.

Shayna's letter was a single pink sheet. She hoped he was safe, but reports of the Sinai fighting were disturbing. Aryeh's scout troop had passed through Haifa on the way to the Golan, and he had visited her with some nice friends. The stinger came on the other side of the pink sheet. Professor Berkowitz had asked her to marry him. His divorce was going through and Lena was already in Australia, having decided that Reuven should remain behind and grow up in Haifa with his father, among Israeli children.

An enclosed snapshot showed Shayna in a flowery park beside the pudgy professor, with the crippled boy in her arms. The picture told Kishote that this time if Shayna said yes, she would not back out. He had had a premonition that this might be coming, when he had first glimpsed her at the Barkowes' villa, holding the child. The penetrating pain he felt would have to be borne in silence. En brera.

So early in September 1969, an Israeli armored force using Soviet tanks and APCs, with Egyptian army markings, crossed the Gulf of Suez and landed at dawn under air cover. The ten-hour surprise operation, code-named REVIV, wreaked havoc along the enemy coast, destroying strongpoints, radar installations, and army camps, and leaving hundreds of dead and wounded. The force withdrew unscathed. On the Israeli side the sole loss was a fighter-bomber pilot who had to eject over the Gulf and was not found.

The raid caused an earthquake in Egypt. The army and navy

chiefs were dismissed, Colonel Nasser suffered a heart attack, and the War of Attrition died down, while the army coped with the shocking fact that Israeli armor could land in their country and operate freely. But as months passed the shock wore off, the Egyptians fortified the Gulf coast against another REVIV, and the War of Attrition went on.

8

Noah Departs

A sentinel with extended rifle halted Dzecki's dusty rain-spotted blue bombshell outside the gate of Tel Nof air base. Airmen loafing nearby, huddled in parkas against the chilly December drizzle, stared in wonder at the Porsche. Recognizing the daughter of the base commander beside the driver, the sentinel dropped the chain, and the car ran a gauntlet of raised eyebrows and dirty grins.

"By my life, Dzecki, you drove like a wild Indian. We're so early! Turn here, there's Abba's quarters. Hm! Noah isn't here yet, I don't see his jeep."

"Noah? *Noah's* coming? You told me months ago he was going to France."

"Well, his orders just came through, and of *course* I invited him. Are you out of your mind? How could I not invite Noah? Why can't you drive like him, anyhow? Now there's a careful driver." Dzecki ignored this devious Daphna talk. Whenever he let her drive he aged by the minute, and most Israeli drivers were like her or worse. If Noah Barak was really different, that figured. Straight arrow, son of straight arrow. "Park here," she said, outside a row of married officers' quarters, small semidetached cottages.

"So, this is the famous American with the Porsche." Her lean leathery mother, a moshavnik farm woman diverted into a life on air bases, looked out of the kitchen. "At last we see him! Does he speak Hebrew?"

"*Mama,* he's been here two years. He's in the army."

"So? He could be in intelligence."

"Well, he isn't. Dzecki Barkowe, meet my mother."

"I speak Hebrew, ma'am," said Dzecki, "and I'm very glad you invited me to come."

"Why, he speaks quite nicely," Irit Luria said to her daughter, not mentioning that she hadn't invited him, that it was strictly Daphna's doing.

"Well, since it's my birthday party, I guess I should put on a dress," said Daphna, who wore a dirty sweatshirt and dirtier jeans.

"Is this your brother Dov?" Dzecki peered closely at a framed picture of an aviator standing by a plane.

"That's Dov."

"Is he coming?"

The mother said, a shade too casually, "Dov is qualifying in the Skyhawk this week, so he couldn't get off."

"Too bad. Him, I'd love to meet. I'd rather have been a fighter pilot, Daphna, than anything in the world."

"Then why are you a rosh katan? You at least could have been an army officer by now."

Dzecki's answer was a shrug. "D'you suppose I could walk around the base, look at the planes?"

"Who'll stop you? You're in uniform. Just obey the signs, and stay away from jet engines, or you'll be deaf for a week."

Daphna went into her old room, which her younger brother Danny now occupied. Half the closet still contained clothes of hers, because in her flat she had only a tiny cardboard wardrobe. She doffed the sweatshirt and jeans and stood in peach panties and bra, contemplating her image in the closet mirror. Not bad, not bad at all. Look at those breasts! Why, she could compete with those *zonot* (whores) in the dirty American magazines the aviators passed around. Maybe she should try modelling. Oh, poor Dzecki, what he would give to be vouchsafed this sight, and what it promised. He had never gotten past a goodnight kiss, and never would. Noah had his drawbacks — a military right-winger, rigid in his doctrinaire

Zionism, scornful of her leftish Jericho Café set — but she couldn't help herself. He was a wondrous lover, that hot joy continued as gripping as ever, and he could be quietly sweet, too. Probably in time they would marry, because Daphna could not picture herself in any other man's arms, and she had fended off arms without number for years. But what was the rush?

The white woolen dress Aunt Yael had given her for her last birthday was nice, Noah liked the way it clung to her figure. She knew that Noah and her mother had been in touch, and that Imma was blatantly angling for a betrothal announcement with this party. But Daphna wasn't about to be pushed into anything, just because Noah was going off to France. She was drifting with the wind, so to say, her mind was quite unsettled, and bringing Dzecki uninvited to Tel Nof was her anchor to windward. Noah would be furious when he saw the parked Porsche, but too bad. She stripped and went to shower, happily singing an American rock-and-roll hit.

Meantime Dzecki was wandering through the air base, which was all a-rumble with planes taking off and landing. It was his first look at the Heyl Ha'avir (air force) from the inside. What a contrast to the army, especially his ordnance battalion on the Golan Heights: those dreary rows of patched tents, the rusty disabled tanks standing in puddles, tracks off, turrets removed, the muddy soldiers gabbling guttural slangy Hebrew laced with Arabic obscenities! Here was the Israel he had pictured when all the world rang with the Six-Day War, and when on impulse he had left his beginning law practice on Long Island and made aliya. Here all was order, all was clean, all radiated glory: spindly Skyhawks and Mirages in their earth-covered hangars, menacing as giant steel hornets, with hairy technicians in coveralls working them over or fueling them; and small older planes, and helicopters, and big transport planes, all in camouflage paint and marked with the Jewish star, all to be flown by Jewish guys his own age. Here at last was ISRAEL.

Dzecki was having a hard time in the army. The other recruits, mostly good-natured but coarse and ignorant, by and large seemed to think he was unbalanced. Why leave America to come here, when the dream of most of them was to go to America? And if his reason was Zionism, then he was exceptionally crazy. Zionism was for politicians' speeches, and for the sons and daughters of big shots who got into the elite services. At first he had been known as Porsh, till he sequestered the car in a Haifa garage. Only gradually had he become Dzecki to some, and Barkowe to others. The noncoms tended to go "BARKOWE!" at him like enraged watchdogs, not caring whether he was American or sabra, rich or poor, crazy or sane. He was in their power.

Arriving at his quarters in a flying suit, Benny Luria heard the birthday girl carolling in the shower, and found his wife in the kitchen, not at all in a party mood. "That fool daughter of ours," Irit snarled at him, squeezing a large crude blue 20 in icing on the white cake, "brought that fool American cousin of Noah's, with his fool Porsche."

"So I noticed. That's a nice new outfit, Irit. From Yael's shop?"

"You like it? Yes, I went to get a present for Daphna, and my dear sister-in-law let me have this for almost nothing. By the way, I saw the new baby, in a basket in her office."

"What did they end up calling her?"

"Eva," she snapped, with an acid side-glance.

Benny was silenced. Eva Sonshine supposedly did not exist, or at least the wife feigned to know nothing of the woman, though she had once been a runner-up for Miss Israel. Still, when occasion offered, Irit was not above such needling. After a long moment she went on, "So? You're wearing a flying suit to the party, are you?"

"I have a mission this afternoon." Irit threw down the icing scoop with a scowl. "Just more high-altitude photography, ha-moodah."

"Benny, this base command was supposed to be a rest."

Irit Luria had sweated out years of operations, hundreds of missions, several wars, and her nerves were still pretty strong, her husband knew. Something else must be eating at her, nor was it Eva. That was an old mess. In the synagogue at Danny's bar mitzvah he had half resolved to put an end to it. With one son qualifying in Skyhawks, and another burning to follow him, Benny Luria knew it behooved him to get on better terms with the old Jewish God. But such things took time.

"What's the matter? Noah's coming, isn't he?"

"Of course he is, but it's all ruined, ruined. I've been on the phone with him about the party, and I *smelled* an engagement announcement today. Not anymore. What an idiot! Will she ever do better than Noah Barak? Is she going to marry the Porsche?" That made Benny laugh, which only irked her.

"Irit, she's still a young girl —"

"Is she? In her own apartment with that fat nobody, that scribbler Donna, doing what with herself? Maybe ballet, maybe painting, maybe sculpture, and maybe I don't know what else! Where does she get all that? What was our mistake with her? That's probably Noah now." A motor was coughing and dying outside. Irit stalked off to the bedroom. "You talk to him."

In a blazer and turtleneck sweater Lieutenant Commander Barak was natty as ever, but down in the mouth. Obviously he had seen the Porsche. "So, it's France next," Benny greeted him cheerily. "Can you tell me about it?"

"Well, sir, it has to do with testing and maintenance of some new patrol boats in trial runs, that's all."

"I see." That was not all, if Benny Luria had any skill at reading young officers' faces and words. "Good luck."

Noah took an orange from a fruit bowl, peeled it neatly, and gestured at *Ha'aretz* lying on the table. "Did you read that editorial?"

"Which one?"

"The one about the 'flying artillery' policy?"

"No. Is it for or against?"

"Oh, against. What do you think of the policy, sir?"

"Think of it? I'm executing it."

"That's orders. The air force mission is *Clear skies over Israel,* right?

"Just so."

"Sir, is a dual mission good doctrine?"

Luria did not answer straight off. A sophisticated question, that one, much bandied about at air force headquarters. "En brera," he said.

"Why? Is the Bar-Lev Line really critical?" returned Noah, pulling the orange apart. "What about closing those miserable outposts and withdrawing our forces beyond artillery range?"

"Yes, so the Egyptians immediately cross the Canal with their artillery, occupy the ground we've yielded up, and dig in that much closer to the Sinai passes and to Tel Aviv. Then what?"

"Well, as soon as they start to cross, we've got them where we want them, haven't we?" Noah probed with this standard argument of the military journalists. "Our armor counterattacks and smashes them, and that restores the cease-fire —"

Clad in the white dress, all dimpling smiles, Daphna came swaying in. "Hello, motek," she purred, giving Noah a kiss and a hug.

"Happy birthday," he said, and her father left them together, noting that Noah's dark look did not lighten.

The party was a small one: Daphna's parents, her brother Danny, now a gangling redhead in tennis togs just past his bar mitzvah, and a few childhood friends from air force families, plus the glowering Noah and his bugbear Dzecki. As they sat around eating birthday cake and ice cream with tea or soda, the American with the Porsche was the center of attention, or at least curiosity. "But if your family isn't religious or Zionist, Dzecki, what made you come here?" Benny Luria inquired.

"Yes, good question. You didn't know me then," grinned Daphna. "Didn't you tell me it was because of the Six-Day War?" She enjoyed her American slave without too much curiosity about him. That the world owed her such an attendant, Porsche and all, was in the nature of things.

"Not entirely. I made some Israeli friends in high school, kids of your UN delegation people." Dzecki turned to Noah. "They knew I was related to your father, they were very impressed, and that made me feel good. What's more — and I've never told you this before, Noah — your father had a lot to do with my coming here."

"My father? How? Until you came here he'd never mentioned you."

"Well, he might not even remember. Our temple kids once

toured Washington. He was there on some mission. Two of the guys were Israeli friends of mine whose fathers knew him, and at the embassy they talked to him in Hebrew. He's kind of scary, your father, you know. Awesome, almost. I felt small and out of place. I didn't tell him we were related, I just kept my mouth shut. After that was when I started Hebrew lessons."

Danny was idly bouncing a tennis racket on his palm. "Why didn't you apply for the air force, Dzecki, once you got here? It's the only service."

"Eyes," said Dzecki. "Okay, but not good enough for a pilot."

"Well, you might have been a navigator."

"Not what I wanted. I swam for my college, so at first I wanted sea commandos, in the worst way. After I flunked the commando swimming test I figured okay, that's it, rosh katan, and I went for ordnance. I like machinery."

"Why not the paratroopers?" inquired Daphna.

"Infantry with red boots."

Noah growled, "Don't say that to a paratrooper."

"I won't, but there's nothing like the sea commandos. Colonel, what did you think of Green Island?"

"Bravest feat in our history," replied Luria.

A stumpy girl who was a squadron leader's daughter said, "My cousin in Holon had a boyfriend killed on Green Island."

Death was not a stranger at Tel Nof, but each mention was sobering. Dzecki said after a moment, "Sea commando, or frogman?"

"Neither. Special services."

"Brave, sure," Noah said to Colonel Luria. "Was it worth it?"

Benny was slow to answer. "Absolutely. The Egyptians learned that when it comes to commando raids, they're still outclassed. And knocking out that radar ripped a nice hole in their aircraft warning system —"

"Happy birthday, Daphna! Am I too late for cake and ice cream?" With a door-slam the aviator of the photograph strode into the living room, in a parka and slacks.

"Dov! Dov! You came!" His mother jumped up to embrace him, and a tumult of hugging, kissing, and handshaking ensued.

The father exclaimed, "So Dov, you've already qualified in the Skyhawk?"

"I soloed yesterday, Abba."

Amid more tumult of congratulation, his shiny-eyed brother eagerly asked, "How did it go, Dov, how did it go?"

"Well, I bounced so hard when I landed, the squadron leader told me to get my ass home for a day to calm down." Great laughter all around. "Say, is there a movie star visiting the base? I saw this Porsche outside."

Daphna said, "This is Dzecki Barkowe, Dov. It's his Porsche."

"Oh, you're her American guy. Hello." Dov coolly looked Dzecki in the eye and offered a callused hand. His smooth face was singularly pale, with hard lines around the mouth, and his smile was remote. He greatly resembled his father, and he made Dzecki feel very immature and very American. When Dov turned to Noah Barak his expression warmed. "What's this, Admiral? I hear you're off to romance all the oo-la-la girls in France. Such luck."

"L'Azazel, Dov," said Noah, glancing at his watch, and breaking out of his glum mood in a charming grin, "I should have left fifteen minutes ago, but I'm glad I didn't. At least I've had a glimpse of you. Kol ha'kavod on your solo. When I get back, we'll meet and talk about things."

"Definitely. You come to Hatzerim. We'll give you a decent air force lunch."

Noah laughed, and made brief goodbyes. Daphna walked out with him. A Mirage was howling off a nearby runway. "So, you're really going this time?" she screamed.

"Yes, you'll be rid of me at last," he yelled, as they passed the Porsche. "And vice versa."

"Don't be a pig, now. You know I hate the idea. I'll miss you. Write, you hear me? Write! How long will you be gone? Tell the truth." A whole unit of Mirages was taking off one by one, in an earsplitting racket. An aviator and a girl sergeant strolled past them deep in talk, from the way their lips and arms were moving.

"I love you," bellowed Noah in her ear, "but what's the point? We're not going anywhere. What does it matter how long I'll be gone? Feel free to do what you please, and finish."

"How dare you?" She whirled him around by an elbow, took him by the shoulders, and shook him. "How *dare* you, Noah Barak? Haven't I" — a shout in his face — "proved I love you? What more can I do? What more do you want?"

"You know! I want to get engaged."

"And I don't. Not yet. God knows what you're going to France for, or when you'll return. You won't tell me, and I'm not asking, but that doesn't mean —"

Noah roared, "I can't hear a word you're saying. Daphna. To all the devils, once for all why don't we get engaged? Let's go back right now and tell your parents."

"What?"

"LET'S TELL YOUR PARENTS."

"Tell them WHAT? About us? Have you lost your mind? My father will KILL me. *And* you."

"Your father will? I've heard things about your father, but never mind. Let's announce our ENGAGEMENT, I say. I bought this in Haifa." He took out a little purple box, and showed her a ring with a small sapphire.

Daphna opened huge eyes, glanced here and there, then passionately embraced and kissed him. "THERE. Enough. This is no way to do it. Keep that ring for now. We'll talk when you get back, and maybe then — but meantime, you stay away from those French girls! Those mademoiselles from Armentières! You're all mine, hear?"

Aroused and shaken by the kiss, he pulled her close. "You're impossible." He kissed her long and hard, then leaped into the jeep. "Sure, I'll write. But about the French girls — tough!" With that, he screeched into gear and drove off.

9

The Wild West Show

And he did find a French girl, if not exactly a mademoiselle from Armentières.

She was Mademoiselle Julie Levinson, the dark-haired daughter of Samuel Levinson, the president of the Jewish community and Cherbourg's most prosperous wholesale dealer in fresh fish. Julie was decidedly no oo-la-la girl, and no Daphna Luria, either. Businesslike and plump, she was dressed in a heavy old sweater and rubber boots when Noah first saw her, for she worked in her father's waterfront fish market. But that evening, when he came to the Levinsons' surprisingly large and elegant house for dinner, she had been at pains to beautify herself for the Israeli officer, and looked slimmer and prettier.

After dinner they walked out together. Nothing could come of the romancing that ensued, since he was in Cherbourg for only a few days and Julie was a nice Jewish girl, if not averse to limited carrying-on in the dark. But Daphna had wounded Noah with the damnable blue Porsche apparition at her birthday party, and her refusal to take his ring, so the quick-won affection of this warm-blooded French Jewish girl was very welcome. The eighty Israelis who had stolen into Cherbourg in small groups were under orders to lie low, but Noah managed to see a lot of Julie in that brief time he had.

On the morning of Christmas Eve they were walking along the windy quay, where gulls banked and screamed, and the oily harbor water slapped hard against the pilings. The weather forecast concerned Noah; it was bad and getting worse, especially down in the Bay of Biscay. "Julie, I won't be coming to dinner tonight." Noah's grade-school French was adequate for this friendship, and was even somewhat improving. "I'm sorry."

She swung his hand. "Oh, listen, Noah, I'll never see you again. This is the end. I realize that."

"What? Why?"

"My dear, Papa *knows*. People here know. Your supply officer has been buying up all the food in town, bit by bit. Forty more of you have arrived in the last three days, in civilian clothes, but of course they're sailors. The oil company knows, for sure, from the way you've been taking on fuel. Why, I'll bet the harbormaster knows. The only question is *when*." She looked at him with tearful eyes, and her hair blew around her sad face. "You're charming and I'll miss you terribly, but *c'est la vie*." In reply Noah just tightened his hand.

For a fact, the Israelis were counting heavily on the discretion and good will of Cherbourg's people. The town had decayed with the passing of the great ocean liners, and its brief glory as the pivot of D-Day was dusty history. The missile boat construction program had brought the somnolent port to life, creating hundreds of jobs for years. No less than the small Jewish community, the other townspeople thought the protracted embargo on the boats was an outrage. French honor was sullied, they maintained, by Pompidou's continued craven crawling to the Arabs after De Gaulle's resignation. Certainly in Cherbourg's officialdom, from the mayor and police chief down to the lookouts on the breakwater, Israel had only friends.

The fish market was crowded and clamorous with holiday buying and selling, when Julie's father came out in his proprietor's coat, tie, and wing collar to shake Noah's hand, his gray mustache aquiver with emotion. "Well, Noah, we're bound to come to Israel, my wife and I with Julie one of these days, now that we've got to know you. But just on a visit, my son, my business is here, and I'm too old to learn the new Hebrew. I can read the Bible, so can Julie, but I don't understand a word you boys say. God bless you. Good luck." He looked deep into the naval officer's eyes, leaving the rest unspoken, and walked off with bowed head.

Noah said, "Well, so there, you're coming to Israel. That's good news."

With a shrug more Gallic than Jewish, Julie said, "Oh, you'll be married to that Daphna by then."

When Noah returned to his Saar boat, the hard-bitten submariner commanding the Cherbourg operation, Hadar Kimche, was in the wardroom studying a weather chart. "Ah, there you are, Barak! What about the *certificat de visite*?" He was a dark lean officer who had already led an escape of two Saar boats months ago, and he was not popular with the French authorities.

"The customs agent will come aboard at two, sir, with the document. It's just a French formality."

"Yes, the final one, and it can stop us from going," snapped Kimche, "if the weather doesn't. Look here. Force nine gale expected in the Bay of Biscay! An American aircraft carrier wouldn't sortie in such weather."

But at half-past two in the morning, the five boats did sortie, navigation lights brightly burning. The good people of Cherbourg, all involved with Christmas festivity, failed to note the furious clangorous last-minute activity at the Israelis' dock, or their departure with loudly snorting diesels. At least, that would be their story later on. According to the legal papers, which Captain Kimche had in hand in case of challenge, down to the certificat de visite, the boats were bound for an oil-drilling company in Norway, which had bought them to run supplies to offshore oil rigs. Israel had waived title, the papers showed, for a refund of the money paid down. All true, if not the whole truth. But no French vessels were out in that wild dark night to challenge the flotilla's departure; and the lookout on the breakwater, who had been given several bottles of champagne to cheer his lonely Christmas vigil, somehow failed to see them go.

That same night Zev Barak left Washington for France. The call from Pasternak had come just as Nakhama was putting dinner on the table. The Norwegian cover story might unravel, Sam conveyed by hints, and Zev had better go at once to Paris. He could help the embassy manage the brouhaha; also, he was needed there for something even bigger.

"Are the boats all right?" Barak's query to Pasternak had reflected Nakhama's anxious stare when the phone rang. She had stood frozen, with a soup tureen in both hands.

"So far, fine, though they're running into a bad storm. Right now the problem is the media. There's a huge headline in tomorrow's London *Telegraph* — the whole front page, and it's already on the streets — '*FIVE ISRAELI GUNBOATS VANISH*.' "

"Oo-ah. Very bad."

"Could hardly be worse. Our London embassy is already being swamped by reporters and TV cameras. It's black midnight there, two o'clock here. The ambassador woke me up."

"How did the story get out?"

"God knows, but Golda's duty officer just turned down a call from the *New York Times*."

"Sam, I'm not in the picture anymore."

"Mocca Limon will give you an update in Paris." Admiral Limon, a former chief of the navy, had been in France for months masterminding the caper.

"What's my mission, exactly?"

"First, help Limon keep the Norway story going until the boats are through Gibraltar. Second, try to put out media fires, and stop the embassy people from idiotically starting more fires. Third, you've heard of Brigadier General Bradford Halliday?"

"Air chief of NATO?" Barak's pulse quickened. "Sure, sort of an acquaintance of mine."

"Right, right, I forgot you know his wife, Chris Cunningham's daughter." Ironic Pasternak overtones. "Well, he's over there in Belgium."

"I know he's in Belgium. What about him?"

"More later. You'll get a telex in the Paris code room."

"When do the boats transit Gibraltar?"

"Probably late tomorrow. That's a flash point. The British can halt them. The French fleet can even come out and block them. Have a nice flight."

It was not a nice flight. The plane ran into the huge storm system tossing the Cherbourg boats off Brittany, and it bucked, plunged, shuddered, and groaned to Paris. Barak arrived at the embassy bleary-eyed and fuzzy-headed. The European headlines on the press room table woke him up like a whiff of smelling salts.

OÙ SONT-ILS?
LE DINDON, C'EST POMPIDOU
JUDEN BESIEGEN FRANKREICH
PER POMPIDOU, LA PURGA

The British papers struck a note of sheer glee:

CHEEKY ISRAELI COUP!
BOATS, BOATS, WHO'S GOT THE BOATS?
ISRAEL 5, FRANCE 0

And so on.

The ambassador and the press secretary were ruefully contemplating the newspapers. With them was "Mocca" Limon, the tall balding Israeli admiral, a World War II French naval officer who had commanded the infant Jewish sea force in the early days and retired at thirty. "I can't put off the media any longer," mourned the ambassador.

Limon said, "Ambassador, we'll have to stage some kind of conference, the pressure is too great."

"Mocca, I can't face them. Maybe Avi can handle it."

"I can try," said Avi, the bearded young press secretary, "but what to all the devils do I tell them?"

"What do you know?" Barak inquired.

"Nothing," said Avi in an aggrieved tone. "Nobody tells me anything around here."

"That's just fine," said Barak. "How are you at acting stupid?"

"Not too bad, if it's called for."

"Actually Avi is pretty stupid," said Limon, patting his shoulder. "He's a political appointee."

"That's true," said Avi, more cheerfully. "Also I can't understand Parisian French. They talk too fast."

"You speak French?"

"Haltingly."

Zev asked Limon, "When will they transit Gibraltar?"

"Depending on how refueling goes, four or five this afternoon."

"Ambassador, I suggest you call it for seven tonight," said Barak. "The Frenchmen will all want their dinners. They may not show up in force."

"Good idea. Go ahead, Avi." The press officer left and the ambassador went on, "Golda summoned the cabinet at one o'clock this morning, Zev. She gave the green light to this thing very reluctantly, and now she's worried as the devil about our relations with France and Norway."

With great strain and half the crews seasick, Kimche's five storm-tossed boats made it through the heavy Bay of Biscay weather, but more trouble threatened the flotilla at its first fueling rendezvous.

The range of the missile boats was limited, and from Cherbourg to Haifa they had to sail more than three thousand miles; so the plan called for two fuelings at sea, since putting into a foreign port would risk seizure. In a secluded bay off the south Portugal coast, an Israeli freighter crudely modified as an oiler awaited them. The crews of three boats wrestled aboard the heavy flexible pipelines, and the freighter commenced pumping diesel oil. It was a slow tedious exceedingly risky business, for the boats were unarmed, and hour upon hour they lay dead in the water, exposed to detection or attack.

The last two boats were still fueling when a helicopter came buzzing at them over the distant wooded hills. Kimche and Noah uneasily tracked the aircraft with binoculars. Dropping down over a tiny fishing village, the only human habitation in the bay, it headed straight for them and hovered noisily above the freighter, not twenty feet in the air. Uniformed men inside were plain to see, making notes, talking into headphones, and plying cameras.

"We had better get out of here, Noah," said Kimche. He had been shrugging off coded warnings from Haifa about the media disclosure, preoccupied with surviving in the storm and then making rendezvous. Now he took alarm. "Signal *'Discontinue fueling.'* It's rough out there for hooking up again, but we must move to international waters."

"Captain, the boats can keep taking on oil as we move out."

"You're sure? Rupture those fuel lines and we're kaput."

"We rehearsed this off Ashdod for a week, sir. It works. It'll save hours."

"Let's do that, then."

The freighter weighed anchor and steamed seaward, trailing the two boats with the fuel lines. The helicopter followed for a while, then flew out of sight. Fueling completed, the five boats sped south and the slow freighter soon dropped out of sight astern. When the Cape of Trafalgar poked over the gray horizon, Kimche ordered the boats to close up, leave signalling to him, and prepare for radical evasive maneuvers in the Strait of Gibraltar.

"Well, hevra *[comrades], this is it,"* he said, speaking on the command circuit. *"It's forty miles through the Strait. Maybe the French have asked the British to stop and seize us. Maybe they've even sent warships or warplanes to turn us back. We'll find out in the next hour or so. We go through at thirty knots. Good luck."*

A stiff easterly wind was gusting in the Strait, and the gray swells were immense. The seasick sailors who had recovered during the fueling once more moaned in their bunks. Flying no flags, the flotilla ran in tight formation, a line of three by a line of two, overtaking here a freighter, there a tanker. The shores of the Strait kept narrowing like a funnel, until Gibraltar lay dead ahead. A high signal station on the Rock began blinking the international Morse challenge: *What ship?*

"No answer," Kimche told Noah.

The boats ploughed on.

What ship? What ship?

"Well, Noah" — Kimche's voice was tense and slightly

amused — "this blows the Norway story, anyhow, doesn't it? The Brits can count to five. They know who we are."

What ship? What ship? What ship?

The cloudy afternoon was fading to evening. The boats entered the narrows between the two continents, Africa to starboard, Europe to port, the headlands four miles on either beam. The Gibraltar light ceased its queries, and the Cherbourg boats sped into the Mediterranean Sea. Other vessels were slowly traversing the narrows, but no French warships were in sight.

"So far, so good," said Kimche, whereupon the Gibraltar light began blinking at the flotilla again. "Now what? Still *What ship?*"

"No, sir." Noah read the Morse code as it flickered in the gloom. *"Bon voyage. Bon voyage. Bon voyage."*

Kimche burst out laughing. "Translation," he said, switching to a burlesque British accent, *"Jolly good show, lads, fucking the French."*

At the embassy, Zev Barak was comparing notes with Pasternak in Jerusalem via scrambler telephone. The Arab governments and press were frothing at France and Norway. The French government was in an uproar, and certain high French officials, old acquaintances of Mocca Limon from World War II days, were discreetly keeping the Israelis posted. President Pompidou was on Christmas holiday, and when first informed that the boats had left for Norway, he had commented, "*Tant mieux!* If the papers were in order, good riddance!" But with the media explosion he was becoming concerned. His Defense Minister, in great rage, wanted to send the air force to sink the flotilla; the converted grandson of a rabbi, he was eager to make clear which side he was on. President Pompidou was not rushing into any action, but he was "requesting clarification" from Israel and Norway, and from Panama; because Norway, in assuring the Arabs that it was in no way involved, had disclosed that a Panamanian company was the purchaser, using a post office box in Oslo for reasons unknown.

At the press conference the French reporters, who had skipped their dinners en masse, fired hard questions about Norway's denial and the Panama development. Zev Barak, watching and taking notes, was delighted with Avi's dimwitted performance. The press secretary pointed out in somewhat floundering French that Israeli sources had never mentioned Norway. That was the doing of Cherbourg officials, who had revealed the contents of customs documents to the press. His understanding was that a Panamanian buyer had sent the boats to Norway for refitting, to service Alaskan oil rigs off the Canadian coast. Questions shot at him.

Why to Norway, of all places?

That was a question for the Panamanian embassy to answer.

Which Canadian and Alaskan companies were in the transaction?

The Canadian embassy might be helpful on that point.

Had Israel waived title and received repayment?

Israel was grieved by the unjust embargo, but financial details were not yet available. Israel was anxious to preserve cordial relations with Canada, Norway, Panama, and France, and had only admiration for Alaska.

Where were the boats?

Apparently not in Cherbourg, therefore apparently somewhere at sea.

So it went, and at the end of the conference the reporters left baffled and muttering. Barak heard one say, *"C'est tout une blague juive."* ("It's all a Jewish joke.") Avi had displayed such virtuoso stupidity, Barak later reported to Pasternak, that he might one day be the government spokesman in Jerusalem.

The tension in the embassy eased when the BBC announced the sighting by a Greek freighter of five small unidentified vessels heading east off the North African coast. "Well, then, they're *through,* anyway," the ambassador exulted.

"So am I," muttered Barak, and he curled up on the ambassador's couch and fell asleep. Not for long. When he opened his eyes, the ambassador was shaking his shoulder. "Zev, top-secret message for you in the code room." He stumbled down the corridor and knocked on a door marked with a red security warning. A yawning coding officer, crushing a cigarette into a tray full of butts, handed him a scrawled decode. By her smoke-shrouded lamp he read the message, and thrust it into the burn bag.

"You have the current NATO directory?" he asked the ambassador, who was in shirtsleeves in his office, shaking his head over huge headlines in three Paris evening papers.

LES BATEAUX ONT PASSÉ GIBRALTAR
POMPIDOU ENRAGÉ
LA NORVÈGE "NE SAIT RIEN"

"Shelf behind my desk."

Barak found a number for Brigadier General Halliday in the slender blue book. On second thought, he called Belgian information, and obtained the phone number of an address in the town of Casteau. Emily had been writing to him from there.

An embassy girl who had assured him she knew exactly where the restaurant was drove Barak round and round the dark maze of the Left Bank next night for an hour, chirping apologies. Our shlepper factor knows neither age nor sex, he thought, wishing Pasternak had found someone other than himself for this chore. Bradford Halliday was not a man he could enjoy meeting. The shadow of Emily lay across even their casual encounters. That Halliday was now her lord and master, so to say, and the father of her twin girls, would not much allay the awkwardness.

The American general sat at a rear table of the dim little restaurant in a tweed jacket and bow tie. He gestured a welcome, and Barak took a chair, saying, "Sorry I'm so late."

"Hello there. This is a good family place," said Halliday. "I think you'll enjoy the food."

"I appreciate your coming to Paris. I'd have gone to see you."

"Better this way." Brief look at Barak, cool and professional. "Quite a flap about those boats."

"Unfortunately, yes."

"Can you talk about them?"

Policy from Pasternak: be as open as possible with the guy, but use your head. "At last report they're being shadowed by a Russian spy ship."

"Trawler type?"

"Yes. They'll change the fueling rendezvous and alter course at midnight, to try to shake him."

A stout black-clad woman brought handwritten menus, with a smile at Halliday. *"Bon soir, Monsieur le General."*

"I recommend the veal here," said Halliday.

"You order for both of us. But you're my guest."

"Doesn't matter. Government business." After a brief colloquy over the menu, the proprietress brought a dusty bottle, and poured for them. "Try this wine," Halliday said, sniffing it and holding it to the light. "It's rather special."

"Very nice." Red wine like any other, to Barak's discernment. "Let me drink to the health of your little twins. Are they well?"

"Thank you. Emily is well, too."

(Try a smile.) "She writes that they're 'ugly as sin.' I don't believe a word of it."

No smile in return. "Yes, I know you correspond. Well, that's Emily, warding off bad luck, like the Chinese. They're very pretty girls. The Russians won't stop your boats, General, but what about the Egyptians?"

"We already have several missile boats in Haifa. Also Phantom air cover."

"Well, then the mission should succeed." Judicious pause. "A real coup."

"Much too much publicity."

"Yes, the press is a big pain in the ass."

"It sure is." *(He said "ass"! Progress. Human informality.)* Very long silence, the two generals looking at each other, Halliday evidently waiting for Barak to state his purpose. The proprietress brought warm crusty bread and a thick soup. They fell to. After a while Halliday said, "Incidentally, though it got no press, your waterborne armored raid across the Gulf of Suez, back in September, was a greater coup."

"As it happens, Colonel Luria's brother-in-law, Colonel Nitzan, led that raid."

"Is that so? Hmm. Well done. Our intelligence was that not only did Nasser fire his Chief of Staff and chief of the air force, but that it gave him a severe heart attack."

Barak's turn to nod without words. When they finished the soup he asked, "Do you know about Green Island, too?"

"Green Island?" Halliday wrinkled his broad brow. "Not offhand."

"There's a raid we didn't publicize at all." Barak described the operation in some detail, concluding, "We lost too many elite fighters, but that stopped Egyptian cease-fire violations for a while."

"When was this?"

"July."

"Your special units are first class. But the effect didn't last, did it?"

At this conversation-stopper the veal arrived, and they ate. "You're right," Barak said. "Good food."

Halliday put down his knife and fork and leaned back. "Well, General Barak, here I am, at your service."

"Okay." Barak glanced around the restaurant; a few elderly couples at other tables, none within earshot. Still, he dropped his voice. "This is about the Soviet P-12 radar."

"Yes?" Noncommittal as a computer response.

"I'm sure your intelligence on it is good." Not a word from Halliday. "But to be sure we'll be talking about the same thing — I mean the new low-level mobile system, range something like two hundred miles, top of the Soviet line."

"Very well. That's the P-12 radar."

"We have one."

"You have one *what*?"

"We have a P-12 radar. It's at an air base in Sinai. My government has instructed me to tell you this, and to invite a secret inspection. American inspection only, not NATO, no disclosure to the Europeans whatever."

Halliday took the wine bottle and poured for himself, since Barak's glass was still full. "Let me understand you, Barak. Are you telling me you people have captured a P-12 radar from the Egyptians?"

"Well, we have it, as I said."

"Now, we're not talking about a Green Island operation — or are we? Is this the wreckage of a destroyed radar?"

"No. The Green Island radar was a much older system. This is the P-12, the Soviets' newest and best. It's undamaged, intact, and complete. Except of course for the undercarriages. Those were just extra weight, and were detached."

"How in God's name did you get hold of a P-12 radar?"

"Well, that's pretty sensitive."

"I'll withdraw the question."

"You don't have to. The original plan was, in fact, to destroy the radar. It was interfering with our airborne response to the cease-fire violations. As you say, the Green Island effect didn't last. Nor did the armored raid shock. But the leader of the raiding force decided there was a chance to seize the equipment intact, and so they did."

"By what means, if you can tell me?"

"I can. Two of your Sikorsky CH-53D helicopters picked up and brought back the installation. Seven tons of Soviet high-technology air defense, General, in two sections. Barely made it, I may say. Complicated operation, some near-disasters, and some casualties, but we have the thing."

"By God, General Barak, you people are running a Wild West show out there."

"En brera, we say. No choice."

Halliday lit a cigar. "When did Israel acquire this radar?"

"Day before yesterday."

Heavy eyebrows raised high. "We don't rate our CH-53D with that lift capability."

"Now you know. One machine lifted four tons. Almost crashed in the sea, but didn't."

Puffing at the cigar, Halliday looked him in the eye. "How long will you be in Paris?"

"Until I hear from you."

"That will be soon." The proprietress brought him the check, and he paid it, waving off Barak. "Emily has told me your son is in the navy. Is he on one of those boats?"

"He is."

"God bring him safe to shore."

"Amen, and thank you."

They stood up. "Can I give you a lift, Barak? I have a car and driver."

"I'd better make my own way."

"Perhaps you'd better. Goodbye, then." A stiff handshake with a chilly hand.

10

Spécialité de la Maison

As the boats approached Haifa on New Year's Eve, with the whole world watching through circling airborne cameras, the embassy in Paris was a very busy place. But the Norway charade was over, so Barak was strolling the dazzlingly lit Champs Élysées, killing time before his appointment with Halliday, who had telephoned that he would meet him that night at the Hôtel Scribe. On impulse he turned off to the Hôtel George Cinq, where in the lobby and the bar numerous Americans were making an early start on their forlorn New Year's Eve roistering. He went up to the deserted mezzanine, and sank into an armchair.

If year-end melancholy was in order then let it be real melancholy, to all the devils! Ah, that skittish Sorbonne nineteen-year-old Emily, in a plaid skirt and fuzzy sweater, her hair a careless mop, with a bizarre crush on him which she had confessed right here so long ago; Mrs. Bradford Halliday now, mother of twins in her mid-thirties! The chandeliers, the wallpaper, the furniture, the very ashtray stands were the same. And he was almost all gray, much heavier, and stalled in his career near the top. Already he was thinking of where to look in civilian life.

"Hi. All that's missing is the woman feeding éclairs to her dog."

"Good God." He leaped up, looked around, and blurted the first thought that came to mind. "How the hell could you leave those twins? They aren't a year old."

She stood there in a red cloth coat with a gray fur collar, her hat stylishly tilted, grinning at his surprise. "Well, well, wouldn't you know. There speaks the paterfamilias. My Belgian nanny scolded me too for leaving them. It's only for overnight." She came to him, caressed his face with a curved palm, and lightly kissed his mouth. "Always in character, aren't you? Totally unromantic."

"Emily, where's your husband?"

"At the Scribe, of course."

He looked at his watch. "He wasn't getting there till seven, I thought."

"Urgent sudden schedule change. I heard him phoning your embassy. There must be a message."

"I'd better call." He strode off and found a phone booth on the mezzanine. The message was, *"Here early with Emily. How about dinner with us at the Scribe? Please meet me at six on our business."*

Barak returned to Emily, who sat in her coat on a sofa. "I'll be damned. Your hubby's invited me to dine with you."

"Why damned? Bud's a gent. Can we get a drink up here? That bar is a snake pit. More snakes than usual, writhing like mad. Maybe a few are mating. It wouldn't be noticed." Barak struck a bell on a serving table. "Bud has to fly to Rome tonight. No details. Maybe he'll tell you. We had tickets for *The Magic Flute*, dammit, and he's turning them in."

A withered white-headed waiter was tottering at them with a tray. *"Oui, monsieur? Madame?"*

"What were we drinking, old Wolf, that time aeons ago, in that sleazy bar near Union Station, when I was christened Queenie?"

"Who remembers?"

"Well, cognac then, to warm up. And Wolf, for Pete's sake, don't *stare* at me like that! I know I'm hideous."

"You're different, not hideous. Don't fish." She laughed out loud, a remembered lovely laugh. "God, Emily, my hair stood on end when I heard your voice."

"My love, like you I came looking for ghosts. And here we both are. Too too solid flesh."

"Your husband says the twins are very pretty. That you're just being a Chinese parent, running them down."

"Bud knows me pretty well." A deep sigh, an affectionate glance. "You're eating too many pistachio nuts, Wolf."

"Too many birthday cakes."

"Oh, hell, to me you look marvellous. It's so good, just setting eyes on you! It's true, my babies are beautiful." She rapped her knuckles on the table. "*Absit omen*. And I'm not hideous, hey? Tell me more about that." Barak glanced at his watch again. "None of that, I'll murder you, Wolf."

"Well, all right." He took a long look at her. Emily's hair was styled in current fashion, a careful coiffing with some feather touches in front. The once-prominent cheekbones were softened. It was a round face now. The big eyes, once so glittery and wild, were calmer, deeper, and a touch withdrawn. In short, crazy Emily had become a mother and a Washington wife. It wasn't in her letters, but in her looks. How tell her that?

The waiter brought the cognac. She seized a glass and drank. "Christ on a bicycle, toots, stop taking inventory. Just talk."

"Well, you were always too skinny, Em —"

"And now I'm a house," she flashed.

"Don't be absurd."

"I'll show you." She jumped up. "I am, I am."

"Don't take off your coat, we have to get out of here."

"If you do, I don't. I have plenty of time. I'm just shopping for stockings, if I can find an open store. I tore mine on the train. There!" She dropped the coat and whirled around. In a tailored black suit, she was now visibly endowed with bosom and hips. "Two-ton Tessie, queen of the freak show. What do I care? Bud likes them pleasingly plump. So he says. It happened when the twins came."

"All right, Emmy. Want me to say it? You're beautiful."

"Old gray fibber. Competition for Nakhama, you mean, in the curves department. Thank you, anyway. How is she?"

"All right. Look, I must check back at the embassy before I meet him. I've got to leave, Queenie —"

"Wait, wait. Drink your drink. There's so much to talk about! Why on *earth* did you stop writing all summer? You never explained. Three whole months, no letter. And me in Belgium going nuts with my two screamers!"

"Well, Nasser started his War of Attrition. You've heard about that?"

"Just vaguely."

"Tremendous resupply problems. My main job in Washington. Also, getting the Phantoms released was tough. The time slipped by." He took a gulp of cognac and set it down. "Look, when you had the babies I didn't hear from *you* for months. I'm off. See you for dinner, peculiar as it seems."

"Okay, okay. Go." She leaned to kiss him. Their mouths briefly clung. Her voice went husky. "Great balls of fire, this is an eerie encounter. For Bud, it didn't happen, you understand."

"Emily, did you will it with your occult powers?"

A wistful laugh. "Ha, my occult powers. So you remember! No, they failed so often that I quit. Go along to the embassy, let me enjoy a lone New Year's Eve wallow in memories. And not only of you, love, I spent *lots* of time in Paris, you know." She dinged the bell. "I do believe I'll have another cognac."

At six to the dot Barak was at the Scribe. Halliday opened the door of his suite in full uniform, with a rainbow bank of campaign ribbons. "Hello, there. Sorry about the switched times."

"Thanks for the dinner invitation. Accepted with pleasure."

"Fine, Emily will be pleased. I've got a hurry-up meeting in Rome late tonight. NATO flap, southern theater."

"Not about our boats, surely."

"Hardly. What'll you drink? I've got a cold bottle of Sancerre."

"Sounds fine." Barak did not know what Sancerre was. Halliday poured white wine which tasted to him like a mild cough medicine. The suite had very high dusty ceilings, tall windows, peeling wallpaper, and threadbare furniture. A black-and-white television flickered in a corner.

"That's about your boats." Halliday gestured with a thumb. "They're getting blanket media coverage. Sit down, General. Our NATO stations picked them up off Sicily. We've tracked them ever since. We've reported this to nobody outside NATO, but of course that includes France."

"That's okay. Pompidou told his cabinet today, '*We've been made to look ridiculous by the incompetence or conniving of our own officials. The less tumult we make, the better.*' That was the tenor, anyhow."

"And how do you know that?"

Barak shrugged. Halliday nodded. They both understood about talky French officials, and there was nothing more to say. "Seedy place," remarked Halliday, pointing to a dangling strip of wallpaper. "Hemingway would have been saddened. But the restaurant's held up well."

Emily bustled in with packages. "Hi, Zev, how nice to see you! Some shops are closed, Bud, but you'd be surprised how many are open for business."

"I'm never surprised, my dear, by French interest in *l'argent*. General Barak's joining us for dinner."

"Lovely."

"Now, can you make it a quarter to seven?"

"I'll be ready."

She closed the bedroom door. Halliday lit a cigar. "Barak, the Secretary of Defense thanks the Israeli government for the word on the P-12 radar. The State Department has been informed. My government's interested, but questions arise."

"Shoot." It was an American locution Barak liked.

"What are the conditions of the invitation?"

"No conditions beyond secrecy, General, that I'm aware of."

"Carte blanche for inspecting the equipment with a team of technicians?"

"Carte blanche."

"No quid pro quo?"

"None. Friendship."

"Will our inspection be disclosed to the media?"

"It's not in my country's interest to disclose it. Obviously."

"You have several parties in your unity government. Leaks are not unknown."

"Neither are they in Washington."

"Granted."

"The Israel Defense Force will be handling this, start to finish. It will be secure at our end. The Washington end is your problem."

"The State Department is anxious, you see, not to exacerbate Arab feelings. Especially after this affair of the boats."

"General Halliday, if your State Department can veto your inspection of top-secret Russian antiaircraft technology, out of concern for Arab feelings, that's that."

"Oh, don't misunderstand me. The offer is accepted, with appreciation."

"Well, good."

"Providing it remains, as you say, an army matter. No diplomatic exchanges, no formalities, no documents. A wholly informal visit of technicians, such as we frequently make to Arab countries."

"No paper trail," said Barak.

This struck a smile from Halliday like spark from flint. "You're picking up the lingo."

"I've been in Washington awhile."

"I'll head the team. Air defense electronics is more or less my bailiwick. One of them."

"That's why I was instructed to contact you."

"We'll come next month, at a date suitable to you." A roar on the television drew their attention. Halliday walked to the set, saying, "Are the boats arriving?"

"They can't be. They'll come in well after dark, so as not to exacerbate French feelings."

Halliday took the jibe with a side-glance. The TV showed Moshe Dayan addressing a crowd outside the Ministry of Defense in Jerusalem. The announcer said, *"Le Ministre Dayan dit que la France et la Norvège sont des bons amis d'Israël."*

"Ooser," said Barak.

"Ooser? What does that mean, Barak?"

"Untranslatable Yiddish, General."

"Something like 'in a pig's eye'?"

"That's not bad at all."

"Have some more Sancerre."

"Why not?"

"Look here," Halliday said as he poured. "I suppose you're all booked for tonight, it being New Year's Eve?"

"Not at all. In Israel we call it Sylvester. It's some Christian saint's day, and we don't do anything about it."

"Well, if you're an opera-goer, would you consider escorting Emily to *The Magic Flute*? We have reserved tickets, and she's very disappointed that we're not going."

Out of fashion for years, the Hôtel Scribe was quiet, the restaurant only half full. "Wouldn't know it was New Year's Eve," said Halliday. "Well, we'll have champagne at least."

A bald paunchy waiter in a black suit gone green at the elbows wheeled a four-tier hors d'oeuvre wagon to their table featuring, besides the usual tidbits, an array of multilegged or hairy little horrors quite new to Barak, in oil or sauce. "This is about what I'll eat," said Halliday, as the waiter served him what he selected, mainly horrors. "*Spécialité de la maison*. A French military plane leaves at nine and I have to be on it." Barak and Emily ordered Loire salmon. Halliday raised his glass. "Here's to your son's boats, General Barak, the talk of the world."

"Thank you. Only because of the embargo. If the French had delivered what we paid for, there'd be nothing to talk about."

"Here's to the landing on the moon," said Emily. "The one thing that redeems this wretched year we've lived through. That, and my babies."

They talked about the moon walks, the Mylai massacre, the Chappaquiddick scandal, and of course the Cherbourg boats. "Well, now," Halliday said, downing the last horror with relish, "I hope you enjoy *The Magic Flute*, Barak. My wife's a Mozart lover."

"So am I."

"Good. To me all Mozart sounds alike, just tinkly effete fiddle-faddle. She says I've got a tin ear. I do like Wagner."

"Naturally. Wagner wrote for tin ears," said Emily. "Will you call me from Rome?"

"First thing in the morning," said Halliday, getting up, and leaning over to kiss her. "Happy New Year, darling. And to you, General Barak," he added, as Barak rose to shake hands.

Barak and Emily looked after him as he left, and then into each other's eyes. At the same instant they burst out laughing. "You said our meeting in the mezzanine didn't happen, Queenie. I don't believe this is happening."

"But it is. Abélard and Héloïse actually get to see each other, instead of scribble, scribble, scribble."

"Emily, why did he bring you, once the opera was off?"

"Why? You don't know Bud Halliday. He said, 'Never mind. Wouldn't you enjoy dinner with your friend Barak anyway? Come along.' "

"I see," said Barak, although he didn't. "Very nice."

"Nice! Wolf, he's given us a whole evening together, a whole *night*! Bud's a prince . . . Wolf, you're making a funny face."

"Me? I am not."

"Oh, yes you are. When I said 'a whole night,' your mouth went *twitch, twitch*." She illustrated.

"I didn't twitch a single muscle."

"Now look, Zev dear. I'm a fat old mother. All that was in another country, and besides, the wench is dead. It's just not on, old thing. You understand that."

"Queenie."

"What?"

"Wait till you're asked."

Emily threw back her head and laughed. "Touché and double touché! How could I forget what you told me, the night we met at the Lincoln Memorial? You're impotent, right, Abélard? Good-o." She had been importuning him at that rendezvous, in a clumsy inexperienced way, to have an affair with her, and he had put her off with this thin pretense. "Hello, here's our salmon. I'm ravenous." She tossed off her wine, and dug into the fish.

"Em, when's the curtain at the opera?"

"I don't know. At the moment I don't much care. I know that overture by heart. I can whistle it. Shall I?"

"Have more champagne."

"Indeed I will. Are you really that eager for Mozart? Confound you, Zev Barak, *don't you look at your watch* again tonight, not if we stay up till dawn."

"Emily, the boats are entering Haifa. I'd like to glance at the TV before we go on to the opera. Okay?"

"Oh! By all means." She touched his hand. "Eat your salmon, Wolf, it's excellent."

The TV set in the suite ran streaks and flashes for half a minute, then a picture slowly faded in: all twelve Saar boats, tied up under floodlights in two rows of six. The scene switched to a large hall where, facing a horde of reporters in the glare of TV lights, Moshe Dayan stood at a microphone in a jacket and tie, with several unshaven men in rough work clothes. "Those are the navy's senior officers, Emily, who brought in the boats. And there, by my life, is my Noah." Behind the seniors stood younger men in a large ragged cluster, showing teeth in weary grins. His finger touched a small figure in a wool hat. "That's him. He looks so tired! They all do."

Emily put on glasses to peer at Noah. "I swear, he's the image of you, when you first came to our house. When I was all of twelve."

"Everybody says he looks like Nakhama."

"Nonsense. He's *you*."

The announcer was talking French, Dayan was talking Hebrew, and the reporters were shouting questions in several languages. Barak snapped off the set. "Well, they made it. On to *The Magic Flute*."

"God in heaven, how proud you must be. My father phoned me yesterday, you know. He said those boats have been on the *New York Times* front page all week. He's thrilled."

Barak looked out at the street. "Why are all those women lined up down there, Em? What's going on?"

"You poor innocent, don't you know? Those are *poules*."

"What?"

"Whores, dear, it's their street. It was that way, back in my Sorbonne days. Paris is very tradition-minded."

Barak stared, shaking his head. *"Vive la France."*

She twined fingers in his. "Quite. *Spécialité de la maison*. Let's get the hell out of here." In the cab she asked, "Was it so very important after all, Zev, the whole escapade? They're such small boats."

"With the stuff we're putting into them, they'll be very dangerous, and we needed every one. Now if we're attacked at sea on two fronts, the Red Sea and the Med, we can handle it. Yes, it was important."

"Your business with Bud is obviously important." Barak only nodded. "Whatever it is, thank God for it. And for *this*." She put her cheek to his.

When they came into the lobby at the opera house, they could hear the overture ending. Racing up the magnificent staircase, they got to their dress circle seats just before the curtain rose. "Darn good serpent," Emily panted, as the tenor bolted onto the stage, singing fortissimo as he fled a slithering green monster with flashing red eyes, and smoke jetting from its nostrils. Three magical ladies entered, causing the monster to recoil and crawl off. Emily barely whispered, as they sang a rousing trio, "This is real life, Zev. It's exactly this loony. Mozart knew that."

A blue-haired wizened woman in the next seat gave her a filthy look. Barak put a finger to his lips. She took his hand and dug sharp nails into his palm. Later when the Queen of the Night's coloratura pyrotechnics brought an ovation, she spoke through the applause. "*Nothing's* more loony than our just sitting here, you and I, unable to talk. Let's go."

He followed her out. Going down the deserted staircase he said, "I guess Mozart will understand."

"Mozart?" said Emily. "Mozart sits on the left hand of God, laughing and forgiving. Don't you worry about Mozart. Think about where we go next, what we do."

"It's your city, Paris."

"Yes, and it lies before us, doesn't it? Midnight mass at Notre Dame, *mon vieux,* in due course? Again, very traditional."

"I'm not for mass."

"Okay. Right. How religious are you, anyway, Wolf? We've never written or talked about that. I've seen you eat most things, for instance, if not Bud's creepy-crawlies." She clung to his arm.

"Heavy topic." They were idling along the boulevard in a fresh evening. The lights blotted out the stars, but a pallid half-moon barely showed over the buildings. The hurrying passersby were bundled up.

"Well, dear, let's drop it, then."

"No, I'll try to tell you. Why not? We Jews are unique in history, that's plain. We've lasted thirty centuries and more. Unless we're God's people, how come? But if we're God's people, why have we gone through such a thirty-century wringer of calamities? Have we really been all that sinful? And didn't He get badly absentminded or inattentive from 1941 to 1945? That's about where I bog down."

"So you're not a believer."

"Easy, now. I never said that, I said I bogged down. I just don't understand. I don't understand Mozart, either. How could a man born of woman do what he did? No, I don't understand God, but then, I don't understand much in this life. I don't understand, for instance, why your husband made me a present of this evening."

"It's a present to me, you fool. And I know what we're going to do. Flag down a cab."

They settled in a rear bench of a light-strung *bateau-mouche*, and it glided out on the breezy black Seine. On the half-empty benches ahead of them young couples were hugging and kissing. In the bow an old man was playing on a concertina things like "Autumn Leaves" and "La Vie en Rose". The river smell was pungent, the breeze was cold, and over the dark river he could see a few stars. Emily took his hand and prattled lightly about how different her twins already were, although only she could tell them apart. He could listen to her with half his mind, because she seemed to be talking with half her intelligence, a mere doting mother.

He sat trying to sort out the painful stirrings of this surprise encounter. Perhaps she was giving him a chance to do this, with her inconsequent chatter. He and Nakhama had been kids, after all, younger than Noah was now, when the flame had leaped between them. They had married, the children had come along, and that part of life had been wonderful, with its ups and downs. Nakhama was an irreproachable, all-embracing, lovable wife. Emily had broken into his life as a curiosity, then a diverting correspondent. He had ignited very, very slowly. Now she was in his life, an unforeseeable romantic passion which he wanted to hang on to, on paper or in rare encounters like this, as long as he lived.

"Penny for your thoughts," she threw at him.

He was startled into replying, "Just trying to figure out why I love you so much."

"Sure, sure."

"That's the truth, Emily."

She stared. "Oh, God, oh God, you're serious," she choked out. "Zev, you should not have said that."

"Why not? You asked me."

"Because this isn't working, that's why. Nothing works. I'm in deepest misery. When this thing docks we're going straight to the hotel." Barak felt a shock of pleasurable alarm. Of all things he wanted no lovemaking with Mrs. Bradford Halliday, but could he resist Queenie? She went on in flat nervous tones, "And I'm going to pack up that stuff I bought, and you'll take me to the Gare du Nord. I'm going back to my babies tonight, on the 12:22 milk train."

"Is there such a thing?"

"You bet your sweet life. When I had a Belgian boyfriend in the Sorbonne, it was the 12:29. All kinds of helling took place on the 12:29 to Brussels, kiddo! Now it's the 12:22."

"If that's what you want."

"What else? I can't stand the torment, Zev, I truly can't. Bud meant well, or maybe he's too clever for me. I still haven't figured him out. I know you much better than I do him. Don't, Wolf, *don't,* my darling, don't! *This* certainly won't work."

He was taking her in his arms. "Shut up for once, Emily." They kissed as they always had in the Growlery.

"Well, this is what they're all doing," she muttered, breaking away, and gesturing at the other couples. "But enough. To use Bud's favorite dismissive term, sex is a pain in the ass."

"Spécialité de la maison," he said, and she mournfully chuckled.

They did exactly as she said. When they arrived at the Gare du Nord, the huge clock over the terminal entrance and all the smaller clocks inside were inching up on midnight. While she bought her ticket horns blew, bells rang, and drunken Americans here and there in the terminal began bawling "Auld Lang Syne."

"He'll be calling the hotel from Rome in the morning," Barak said, trailing her with the bags.

"I left a message. No problem, he'll understand. Perhaps too well. It doesn't matter. Now I'm safe," she said as he set down the bags at the train gate. "So tell me, would you have asked?"

"How's that, Queenie?"

"You said, '*Wait till you're asked.*' I heard you. You had your chance, you know, old chum. There we were in the bedroom, while I packed. Just us two and a bed. Shades of the Growlery! And — nothing."

"Then there's your answer."

"Oh, yeah? Suppose I'd paused, just paused for a moment in that frantic nonstop packing, and given you a come-hither look? Just one?"

"Academic. You don't know how."

Clanging of train bell, hiss of steam, smell of the rolling vapor. *"Prenez vos places, mesdames et messieurs!"*

"Oh no? Watch me." She did an inviting leering slut, eyes almost closed, mouth salaciously curving.

"Okay, okay, I'll go with you to Brussels."

"How I wish it! Goodbye, my everlasting love."

"Goodbye, Queenie."

"You wretch, write more often."

He brought her bags aboard the train. There was nobody else in her compartment. They embraced and kissed until the bell clanged. He felt tears on her cheeks, and tried to brush them away. "Auld acquaintance," she gasped. "Go! Go! It was marvellous, delicious, and oh my love, a silver star for not asking. Happy New Year, and hooray for the Cherbourg boats!"

11

The Dogfight

In a sealed double envelope stamped TOP SECRET, the Secretary of Defense received at his house a thick mimeographed document from General Halliday, together with a memorandum written on long yellow sheets in a firm vertical hand. Halliday was regarded in the air force as something of an intellectual. A serious reader of political and military literature, he had served two years in the plans directorate, and the Secretary of Defense still called on him for informal analyses of current crises, and even for drafting an occasional presentation to Congress.

5 February 1970

Dear Mr. Secretary:

Herewith, as promised, an advance copy of my official report on the Soviet P-12 radar now in Israel's possession. My team of air force experts inspected and analyzed the equipment very thoroughly, as you'll gather from these 87 pages and four appendices.

My personal impression of Israel's strategic situation as it relates to our national interest, which you asked me to write in confidence on the basis of a first visit of five days, is also enclosed. I earnestly request that you consign it to a burn-basket once you've perused it. I've "told it like it is," kept no copy, and pulled no punches.

Respectfully,
Bud Halliday

MEMORANDUM

Personal & Top Secret

4 February 1970

Subject: Israel — strategic posture after Six-Day War

American policy in the Middle East has clearly been skewed toward the Jews, Mr. Secretary, partly out of sympathy for their ordeal under the Nazis, partly because of their domestic political clout. The Six-Day War established the Israelis as a nation of supermen, but that is media nonsense. I gathered in my visit, however, that too many of them, including senior army officers, believe it. That can prove dangerous. They achieved surprise with a professional preemptive strike, and fought well thereafter. Their air force in particular is first class. But the war's end left them in an overextended position. There is no basis for their occupation of Sinai except force of arms. Superior force can throw them out and Egypt is applying that force, increasingly aided and abetted by the Soviets. The Israelis are used to short wars of movement, but now have to hold a static front over 100 miles long at the end of very lengthy supply lines through the desert, while also guarding active fronts against Syria and Jordan. Colonel Nasser has large harassing forces right at the Canal, with no other front to worry about. The task is simply too much for the Jews. They are spread too thin.

Hence, shocking exploits like the radar capture, the Cherbourg boats, the Green Island feat, and the armored raid in September, all intended to paralyze Egypt. The Israelis are now playing their last card: deep air raids with the Phantoms. As a result, the CIA reports, Nasser went to Moscow last month to plead for Soviet intervention. Israeli intelligence, I was told, confirms that report. At this point Israel will be taking on a superpower! Such escalating military events cannot be indefinitely controlled. If the Jews find themselves fighting

Soviet forces in order to hang on to Sinai, Israel can become the Serbia of a third world war.

Israel has nobody to turn to but the United States, and its chances of survival will only improve when we manage, despite Jewish domestic pressure, to mend our fences with the Arabs. Views like these are more prevalent in the State Department, I realize, than in the Pentagon, where there is a tendency to admire and believe in Israel's invincibility. I too respect the doughty way the Jews have recovered from the Nazi massacre to create and defend their ministate. Like crows and coyotes, the Jews are an indestructible breed, a wonder of history, but for the narrow calculation of our own interest, something of a problem.

On this calculation, Mr. Secretary, I recommended over the telephone against accepting the Russian radar for transport to the United States, and I repeat the recommendation. My team's report contains all the useful intelligence that might be gleaned by stateside radar specialists, and should word leak out that we've acquired this hijacked equipment, our already strained relations with the Arabs would be much worsened. We truly don't need a snatched Soviet radar on American soil.

Respectfully,
Bradford Halliday

General Halliday's memorandum was disregarded. The radar was flown to the United States. In the months that ensued, CIA disclosures about the scope of Soviet intervention in Egypt amply confirmed his warning. By June 1970 some five squadrons of Russian-piloted MiG-21s were flying air cover over Cairo and major military targets; and a Soviet buildup of AA missile bases and systems, requiring thousands of military officers and technicians, was rapidly proceeding. As a result, murky diplomatic maneuvers were intensifying, to halt the War of Attrition and reinstate a cease-fire; and the State Department persuaded President Nixon to bring pressure on Israel by halting the delivery of Phantoms.

Then in July 1970 the Russian aviators began pursuing and even firing at Israeli aircraft, whose pilots were under strict orders to avoid combat with them, so that they had to flee with afterburners gulping fuel. Meantime Phantom losses to the new missiles kept increasing.

Eva Sonshine, runner-up for Miss Israel in 1968, was putting to rights her dishevelled long black hair when the telephone rang. "Benny," she shouted over the shower noise, "he's in the lobby."

"Already? Tell him, ten minutes."

"B'seder."

The aviator hurriedly dried himself with capacious Hilton towels, grateful to poor Eva for lifting him out of a mood of fearful gloom. He had had a harrowing morning, visiting the parents of Phantom airmen who had fallen to the sinister black "flying telephone poles," as the squadron was ruefully calling the missiles. What had made the visits especially difficult was that he really hardly knew the lost aviators, for the previous squadron leader had gone down only a few days ago. In this eerie new warfare between Phantoms and electronically guided Russian rockets, the air force was barely holding its own, and so Benny Luria, who had not yet qualified in Phantoms, had been commandeered to take over the squadron, and he was rushing through a Phantom course.

"Why are you so rough?" she grumbled when he came out, still drying his close-cropped head. "Look at my hair. Hopeless. Did you have to pick my lunch hour to fall in on me?"

"Motek, you've saved my life."

"Don't exaggerate. Listen, I'd like to meet this General Pasternak."

"You never have? Sure. Look for us in the lounge."

"I don't want to be that obvious."

"Nonsense. Do it."

A warm kiss, and he was gone. The runner-up to Miss Israel stared at the mirror, inventorying her slant eyes, smooth skin, and Greta Garbo cheekbones, as Benny called them. How much longer, really, should she put up with the man? This receptionist job he had gotten her was more secure than modelling, but so dull! And her looks would not last forever. Well, no matter, lovemaking in midday was something different, a bit wild, almost as in their early days. Back to the lobby then, to smile and smile at the stupid questions and angry squawks of rich Americans. It was a living for her and her bedridden mother.

Pasternak's eyes were bloodshot, shoulders sagging, head drooping from a three-day emergency trip to Washington. He and Luria sat in a far corner of the lounge, not crowded because the tourists were mostly out sightseeing. "Number one," Pasternak said hoarsely, sipping coffee, "they're going to resume sending the Phantoms."

"Hundred percent! It's definite?"

"Yes. On the quiet, so as not to step on Arab corns. Just the stuff they owe us that Nixon held up in March."

"Sam, what did it?" He looked here and there and dropped his voice to a murmur. "Habakkuk?"

This was the code name for intelligence from a deep source in Egypt, which revealed the reason for a sudden steep climb in Phantom losses; the Russians had equipped the SAM-3 missiles with advanced countermeasures to nullify the Phantom electronic shield.

"Habakkuk, plus the fact that the Russians weren't really bearing down on the Egyptians to consider a cease-fire." Pasternak heaved a thick weary sigh. "Nothing will ever stop the attrition but Soviet pressure on Nasser."

"But meantime, anyway, the Washington stick turns back into a carrot."

Pasternak's large head heavily nodded. "Yes, and if Golda would choke down the State Department's cease-fire plan, which is absolutely terrible, and which she's rejected so far, we'd get a bigger carrot than that. However —"

"Isn't that Colonel Benny Luria?" A lean very tan lady came striding through the lounge, followed by a bald man carrying a camera. On the general principle of being nice to Americans, Benny smiled and waved. She carolled, "Oh, so you *do* recognize me!"

As she came closer, he had a memory flare. "Why sure. Gloria. Los Angeles bonds dinner. You showed me how to do the frug."

"Well, bless your heart. Yes, I'm Gloria Freed. Julius, this is Colonel Luria, the air hero of the war."

"It's an honor," said the husband, whipping a camera to his eye. "By your leave, Colonel?"

"Why not?" The camera flashed.

"God, Colonel Luria, this *country,*" the woman exclaimed. "The places we've been! The Wailing Wall, Masada, Jericho, Hebron, Beersheba. We even climbed Mount Sinai for the sunrise."

"I have awesome pictures of everything," said her husband.

"Of course the red carpet is out for us," Mrs. Freed said. "Julius is the West Coast chairman of bonds. Otherwise, we'd never have gotten into this hotel. So *jammed.* The whole country is so *mobbed.* We even had to stand in line to visit that cave in Hebron. You know, where Abraham, Isaac, and Jacob are buried. Now I can't wait to read the Old Testament."

"Let me tell you, Colonel," said the husband, "you people have made me proud of being a Jew, and also humble. You're terrific."

The Freeds went off. The aviator grinned at Pasternak, who was sitting with his eyes almost shut, an insignificant pudgy man in a seersucker suit. "Benny, don't laugh," he said hoarsely, "the American Jews are our only sure ally on the face of the earth. Don't think we'd be getting the Phantoms otherwise."

"Wasn't I cordial enough?"

"I guess you were. I get tired, that's all, of the wise guys here who shit on these American Jews. They're wonderful. Now listen." Pasternak dropped one eyelid, and a dusky glint came and went in the other half-closed eye. "Number two, you've got the green light."

Luria sat up. "What? At last?"

"I've just come from Jerusalem. I reported to the cabinet, and maybe the news about getting the Phantoms put hair on their chests. Anyway, from now on your aircraft will fight Russians who pursue them."

"Thank God!" exclaimed Luria.

"Win one fight," said Pasternak, "just one, and I predict the Russians will make Nasser swallow a reasonable cease-fire."

Eva Sonshine was again at her desk near the hotel entrance in her blue silk uniform, well-groomed as ever, when Luria approached with a dumpy man in a wrinkled summer suit. Was this, she wondered, the shadowy Sam Pasternak, ultimate political insider and reputed womanizer? Nothing to look at, and his rare pictures in uniform made him out much younger. Luria said, "General Pasternak, Eva Sonshine."

"Hello," said Pasternak. "Who do I talk to in the hotel about a wedding?" When he smiled, showing big teeth and opening half-shut eyes, he was more formidable and interesting.

"To me, to start with." She gestured at a chair, and he sat down.

"Marrying off Amos, Sam?" Luria joshed.

"Amos? Ha! My daughter's serious about a guy."

"Daughters can fool you. Don't sign any contracts. Eva, I have to get back to base very fast. Take good care of General Pasternak."

"I'll do my best." As Luria hurried out she smiled at Pasternak. "What sort of wedding do you have in mind, General?"

"Not sure yet. Do you do Yemenite weddings? Her fellow's a Yemenite."

"We do almost anything, but don't Yemenites usually have those at home, or in a synagogue or something?"

"Possibly. Then again, it could all blow up. I'd like to take you to dinner, if you don't think Benny would mind."

Eva lost her breath for a moment. "Benny wouldn't mind, but what's the point?"

"I've been on the go, I'm low, and I'd enjoy dinner with a pretty woman. If you ran for Miss Israel this year, you'd win it."

"[illegible]-ah! That's a big lie, and I didn't think anybody remembered."

"Dinner, then?"

"What time, and where?"

As his driver went speeding through the lush farmlands south of Tel Aviv, Benny Luria's spirits were high. The melancholia of the morning had blown away like fog on a landing strip, and he was wondering what to do at last about Eva Sonshine.

In the early bravura days of the air force, wenching had been part of the game, with boozing, risky air acrobatics, and a pencil mustache, à la the movie image of the wartime RAF. Those days were gone. The newer pilots in Dov's age group were no monks, to be sure, but more down-to-earth, less given to playing Errol Flynn.

Eva was a cherished relic of that old way of life, and Benny's disapproval of Daphna, and his desire to be a model for his sons, did not exactly go with a girlfriend planted at the Tel Aviv Hilton.

Eva did not go with his religious stirrings, either. Benny Luria had been feeling these more and more, breaking through the flat concrete of a socialist upbringing. As the number of Phantom pilots dwindled, to the point where he had to get himself qualified in a hurry, and Dov too would soon have to fight, he was asking himself what all those marvellously accomplished Jewish boys were dying for. It had to be for something more than being an admired hotshot airman, and having an Eva Sonshine tucked away in a hotel for rich Americans.

Well, never mind, concentrate on business. Green fields and orchards flashed by as he thought about the coming air battle, working out the briefing in his head, selecting the men to fly the mission. Avi Bin Nun and Asher Snir would be leaders for sure, and he would consult them in picking the other pilots, the best of the best for a mission of missions, teaching a superpower a lesson. It would have to be a convincing clear victory, with no losses to the Heyl Ha'avir, and it could be done; man against man at last, not Jewish pilots against damned Soviet electronics and rocket warheads. . . .

Day of the sortie, July 30, 1970, 11 A.M.

"B'seder, let's fly."

So Luria winds up the briefing as usual, and the pilots hurry out through hot sunshine to their planes, carrying maps, photographs, helmets, and special cameras. No talk whatever about Russians as they pass among the ground crews, just the customary cheery give-and-take before they part into the revetments; Phantom pilots and navigators climbing into their American "wagons," clunky thunderous giants bristling with missiles and extra fuel tanks, the Mirage soloists like Colonel Luria mounting the ladders to their elegant French birds. These wonderful youngsters are not only unafraid, Benny senses, but eager to take on the foe that has been chasing them back over the Canal with impunity.

Coughing, rumbling, roaring of starting engines, rolling puffs of smoke, the screaming of compressors . . .

Luria pulls down the canopy of the Mirage, shutting himself into the quieter dark of the cockpit. Check every item in the scuffed manual. Ejection light on. Ease throttle forward. Ease on out, waiting his turn to taxi to the runway. He is not leading the Mirage foursome, younger fliers are running this show. But he is not about to miss it, either. Okay, second group to runway two.

Full throttle, shuddering howl of familiar engines. Into the air, off to the west and to a rendezvous with history, boys with names like Shmuel, Heshi, Moishe, shtetl-descended Jews versus the Red Air Force . . .

Crossing into Egypt, the Phantoms dive to skim the level sands, while the Mirages climb to thirty thousand feet. Luria expects a quick challenge, a hornet's nest of MiGs swarming to stop them. His squadron is again using the "Texas" tactic which all but grounded the Egyptian air force back in June. The Mirages penetrate five or six miles up, apparently on reconnaissance only; MiGs scramble up after them; Phantoms ambush the MiGs, roaring in from nowhere. It worked over and over, till the decimated Egyptians quit. About the MiGs' identity today there will be no doubt, for Russian-speaking Israeli intelligence officers will be monitoring their flight controllers. Anyway, Egyptian pilots are no longer engaging Israeli aircraft.

But where to all the devils are the Russians? Five minutes into the forbidden zone, and no action. Serene sky, serene earth far below, Mirages in air-show formation thrumming along deep into enemy air . . .

Ah, what confident young faces there were at that briefing! These boys hate the meat-grinder duty of bombing the missile sites. They have trained for air combat, and dodging those "flying telephone poles" instead is a dirty sickening business. When a pilot sees a missile lock in on the plane of a buddy and blow it up, the experience is horrible. The debriefings have been mournful, the losses appalling, yet their morale is still high.

Voice of the fighter director in Benny Luria's earphones. "No bandits on our screens yet. Keep going."

He strains his eyes ahead and above at blue sky, below at slow-moving farmland. So the Russians aren't on the fighter control radar scopes. So what? Could be atmospherics, could be new electronic countermeasures. Or have the Egyptians warned them about the Texas tactic? Again, so what? Russians afraid of Israelis? Unimaginable. And how will they come at us? No hard intelligence on Soviet air combat doctrine. Or for that matter, on their weapons. Something better than the Sidewinder?

Twelve minutes into the gut of Egypt, and still no Russians. Is it going to be an abort?

On and on, over ground almost as familiar as the Negev or the Galilee from many overflights. Tingling surge of elation in danger, the roaring vibrating Mirage part of his blood and bone. What a mission, the suspense, the unknowns . . .

Fighter control: "All right, here they come. Two foursomes taking off, from Kutma and Bani-Savif, MiG-21s."

Ahead and below, between eleven and one o'clock, moving dots climbing and expanding to sleek MiGs. Unmistakable nose cone, Egyptian markings. Eight, no, *twelve* of them, and the leading interceptor is flying straight up at the leading Mirage with a rattling stream of pale gunfire. Ho, that Russki picked a tough customer. Heshi's classy rolling maneuver puts him on the Russian's tail, and he shoots. Smoky trail of the missile, *BAM!* Billowing smoke and fire, out of which flies the Russian, by God, ejecting and parachuting. First victory over a Soviet pilot. Long float down from thirty thousand feet for Ivan Ivanovich, freeze his Russian balls off. Good luck, Ivan, you're too far from home, not your fight . . .

Aircraft crisscrossing, rolling, circling, zooming, diving all around in the wide sky, friendly and enemy, oo-wah, a regular Battle of Britain dogfight. And Benny Luria in the thick of it doing dizzy acrobatics, blue sky and green earth rotating around him, MiGs and Mirages shrinking to toys, then swelling to flash past his canopy . . .

The Phantoms!

Here they come, shooting almost straight up into the mass melee from their sneak approach along the ground, and far ahead a MiG blowing up in a globe of yellow smoky flame. No pilot ejecting, two victories in two minutes. Nothing so hot about the Russian combat tactics so far, sloppy random shooting of missiles, gunfire at extreme range, cautious flattish maneuvering. Oo-WAH, how about *that* stupid fool? Diving down on a discarded auxiliary tank . . . inexperienced, inexperienced . . . in Benny's earphones, calm Hebrew jargon, various pilot voices: *"Avi, check six, he's coming up on you . . . I've got this guy in my sights, Eli, break off, break off . . . Hertzel, I'm two kilometers west of the parachute guy, where are you? . . ."*

Voice of the fighter director, high-pitched: "MORE OF THEM COMING, LADS, TWELVE MORE HAVE TAKEN OFF, LOOK SHARP."

Luria makes a tight circle over the descending parachute, calling and calling his wingmate. "Dudu, Dudu, where are you? Over."

Fighting in pairs, looking out for each other, is the way to save your neck. Planes tumble and roar in the unquiet sky over peaceful greenery and glittering irrigation ditches. Wingmate, loud and harsh: *"Benny, Benny, break off, I'm coming in behind you, a thousand feet high. Break off, MiG on your tail. I'm going to shoot him with a missile, break off, break off."* Luria veers wide, looks up, sees a Sidewinder smoke past a MiG. Tough! Bad shooting? Malfunction? A Phantom blasts up from below at the MiG, shoots a smoking rigid metal cobra. Great explosion of orange-and-red fire, end of a third Russian.

Fighter control: "Russian transmissions are getting panicky, hevra. Cursing and babbling, reports of low fuel, one fellow swears they're fighting Americans, another yelling for reenforcements . . ."

This can't go on much longer. Fuel running out. Benny has one clear thought, get a MiG. Chance of a lifetime. Twenty or more targets out there, not putting up much of a fight, wandering around at sonic speed. Scared angry Russian youngsters, now that they're under fire. *"What the hell are we doing up here, risking our lives for the silly Egyptians?"*

"Dudu, Dudu, check six for me. I'm going after this fellow at twelve o'clock low."

Dive at full screaming throttle, G's building up, old painful pressure in stomach and balls, keep him in the scope. He's there, he's there. Wait for the whistle of the Sidewinder . . . there it sounds.

The Russian throws on his afterburner and dives straight down to escape. A Phantom comes zooming up after him, after *my* MiG! Release the Sidewinder quick, get him first . . . half a second of receding smoke trail. Hit, flame, spreading black smoke, pieces of the plane flying! But who got him, did the Phantom? Did I?

Returning to base with his fuel gauge needle trembling at zero, Benny does a quick victory roll over the field. Maybe I got that MiG, maybe not, wait for debriefing, meantime *roll!* Sky, landscape, hangars revolve in the canopy, then he levels off and lands, and as he steps to the tarmac, pails of chilly water drench his sweat-covered head and body. *Brrr!* Other victors are also doused by laughing ground crews. The pilots, dripping or dry, embrace, punch each other, shouting in jubilation, never mentioning Russians. Secrecy orders, highest stringency.

After the debriefing, wet and somewhat let down — there's no doubt that the Phantom got the MiG — Benny trots along the walkways of the married officers' quarters. Since taking squadron command he has avoided coming through here by daylight after a mission. He is the feared messenger, the Angel of Death. But today is different, not a single plane lost. He bangs on the door of his cottage, and out comes Irit in a shapeless housedress, a dust cloth on her hair. "So, back again. Benny, by your life, you're all wet, let me go!" As she yields to his sopping embrace with joy, he sees two women emerge on nearby porches to watch them, wives of aviators whose parents he visited yesterday; Uri, who spun down and may have been captured, and Mendel, who disappeared in a ball of flame.

"Got to get out of this suit, Irit. Good mission. All the boys came back."

"Thank God."

In a hot shower Luria's spirits revive, as a sober realization returns of what the day's work has been. *Shooting down Russians,* driving the Soviet Union out of the Egyptian skies! Well, that was the job, and the boys did it. Now let the politicians sort out the explosive politics.

12

Lost Victory

While the dogfight with the Soviet pilots was raging, Colonel Yossi Nitzan stood with a border patrol team on the Jordanian boundary south of the Dead Sea, peering at a trail of footprints leading through raked sand, severed rolls of barbed wire, and a dug-up patch of minefield. Evidently the infiltrators returning to their hideouts had passed through hours ago, for the prints were half-filled with grit blown by the hot wind. "A small gang, maybe half a dozen," he said.

From open-top command cars the trackers, heavily armed Bedouins in yellow kaffiyehs, were pulling their camels off dung-splattered wooden platforms amid much Arabic cursing and nasty camel noises and stink. One balky camel, spitting and roaring, caught his driver with a lashing kick that laid him out on the sand.

"New camel. Bad camel," the leader of the trackers, a master sergeant with an iron-gray mustache, observed to Kishote. These Bedouins, loyal to Israel, were invaluable for some army tasks.

Far down the ruler-straight tarred road that bisected the arid flat Arava to a shimmering horizon, a dust cloud was drawing near. It ground noisily to a halt and a bulky figure, tousle-headed and dust-covered, heaved out of a jeep. General Ariel Sharon, the new southern front commander, had recruited this camel corps and installed the hundred-mile barrier of minefields, barbed wire, and raked sand from the Dead Sea to the Red Sea. On his orders terrorists were now being tracked far inside Jordan, and killed in their mountain retreats.

"So, Kishote, what's the delay?"

The recalcitrant camel was bellowing and biting the air, as his bloodied rider tried to seize his bridle.

"Camel insubordination, General."

"L'Azazel, are you serious?" Sharon climbed up on the platform behind the plunging beast, and bellowing a foul Arabic curse he shoved it stumbling off the platform. The Bedouins yelled appreciation. "Get these trackers going," he said to Don Kishote, jumping down, "before the trail is stone cold."

"Sir, suppose I go along with them and see how they operate?"

"You?" Amusement sparkled in Sharon's eye. "Can you ride a camel?"

"How different is it from a horse?"

"Shh!" Scanning the sky with binoculars, Sharon held up a hand. Overhead sound of many jet engines, a throbbing rumble, the noise seeming to come from far behind the planes.

"Phantoms," said Kishote. "Lots of them. Returning home."

"Yes, but also Mirages. Something big went on over there."

Kishote shouted at the master sergeant, "Well, *yallah*!" The camels went striding through the wire and the minefield in single file, the yellow kaffiyehs of the drivers fluttering.

"Phantoms and camels," remarked Sharon. "Some war. Now listen, Kishote, you're an armor brigade commander, not a baby-faced paratrooper. No adventures on camels. Report to my headquarters at 2000, for some serious business, and by the way, I'm coming to your son's bar mitzvah."

"Marvellous, sir."

In the Hilton's lower lobby, under a wooden arch lettered in gilt NEW YORK DELI, Yael Nitzan and Lee Bloom walked in through the double doors. "Well! At least it's air-conditioned," said Lee. "I'm sweating buckets, and this is a tropical suit!"

Growl of a familiar voice. "Hello, there, Yael." Sam Pasternak sat in a booth with Eva Sonshine, who twiddled fingers at Yael with a bright smile. Obviously Sam had picked her up at her desk as she was: open-necked white shirtwaist, blue jacket with Hilton insignia, no makeup on that perfect pale skin of the professional beauty. Yael despised Eva for a lightweight, content to be her brother's longtime doxy. What was that confounded Pasternak doing with her? He said, "Say, isn't this Kishote's plutocrat brother from Los Angeles?" The men exchanged tart grins. "What brings you to Israel, Mr. Lee Bloom?"

"Actually, General, Aryeh's bar mitzvah."

"I see. Yael, did you get my message? I'm coming."

"Oh, you are! Lovely."

"D'you mind if I bring Eva along?"

Yael said to Eva, with shaded grace, "Well, how nice. By all means, you're invited."

"I'll have to change plans," said Eva. "But I'll try to come."

"Do. Eva, this is my brother-in-law."

"Oh, who doesn't know about Lee Bloom," smiled Eva, "and Sheva Leavis, the California real estate geniuses?"

Lee gave her an admiring grin, which irked Yael. Men were such idiots. The headwaiter greeted Yael by name, and scraped and bowed them through the clatter and spicy smells of the crowded deli to a rear booth. "A knockout, that receptionist," said Lee Bloom, with a humorous leer. "Think she'd like to work in Las Vegas? We could use her."

"You'd have to check with my brother Benny. She's his friend."

"No kidding, she is? Lucky him. I'm not starting up with the air force."

"Lee, you're sweet to have come so far for the bar mitzvah."

"Well, to be frank, Yael, I'm not here just for that. Sheva's been offered the President Hotel in Eilat. It's gone bankrupt, you know, and we have an idea about it." He waved for a waiter. "Let's order first. Will Joe find us back here?" Lee Bloom, and nobody else, called Yossi Nitzan "Joe."

"He'll find us."

Delicatessen smells made Yael ravenous, but after glimpsing Eva Sonshine she ordered cold sliced turkey breast, no mayonnaise.

Bloom, who was getting plumper and balder by the year, asked for a hot pastrami sandwich with double pastrami. "Now about that hotel." Bloom became all business. "You know how well Sheva and I have done in Las Vegas. A hotel with a casino is a money machine, Yael. Your best guess — chances of putting a casino in Eilat?"

"*Gambling*? Here?"

"Why not? It would bring in tons of foreign exchange."

"Dear, neon signs and naked showgirls in *Israel*? Unthinkable. The government would fall."

"Who says we do the glitz? Ever been to a Swiss casino? You could be in a Reform temple. Posh, mannerly, quiet, tasteful, the croupiers are like ushers or undertakers. Look, the country's swamped with tourists, and what's there to do here, once you've rushed around seeing all the holy places? Unless there's a fun reason to come again, Israel is a one-shot. The Swiss know that. When you've seen one Alp you've seen them all, and sooner or later all skiers just break their legs. Casinos, Yael! I tell you, Israel would never have to grow another orange." She burst out laughing. "Look, I'm serious. Now, Moshe Dayan runs the country, and you've known the guy forever —"

A hard hand gripped Lee Bloom's shoulder. "Leo, *ma nishma* [what's new]?"

"Joe!" He jumped up, and they embraced. "My God, how long has it been? Years and years."

There the brothers stood, arms around each other, the Israeli colonel and the Los Angeles real estate man, and Yael wondered that she had ever seen a resemblance between the sand-brown lean Kishote and the pale pudgy Lee. She said, "So, you wouldn't talk over the phone, but what's doing? Why have you left the Sinai?"

Slipping into the booth, Kishote ordered a beer from a hovering waiter. "Sharon has just made me his chief of staff for Southern Command, and —"

"Oo-wah!"

"Big promotion, eh?" said Lee. "Congratulations, Joe."

"It's not a promotion, Leo. I'll miss my brigade, I love those men. It's just more responsibility." He turned to Yael. "And we're meeting with the General Staff in an hour, about an outrageous violation of the cease-fire. That's why I'm here. We may have to go on to Jerusalem."

"What cease-fire?" Lee inquired. "Always something going on here, isn't there?"

Kishote did not know, for very few outside the air force did, about the victory of Luria's squadron. But a much improved American cease-fire plan had gone into effect right after the rout of the Soviet pilots, backed by a Russian guarantee of Egyptian compliance. He described how, in the sunrise that followed the agreed midnight cease-fire deadline, soldiers had come crawling out of the rampart bunkers on both sides of the Canal, waving at each other. This war was all news to him, Lee Bloom confessed, mixed up in his mind with the usual terrorist raids.

So with no trace of irony or impatience, Don Kishote sketched Nasser's War of Attrition for his brother in a few words. "We've licked him," he concluded. "After eighteen months, he's accepted a three-month standstill that restores the status quo ante. He lost half his air force and thousands of dead civilians and soldiers. Mortgaged his country to the Russians, and still he accomplished nothing. We gave up not one inch of the Sinai, and we never will except for a peace treaty. Maybe now he's got the idea —" He broke off. General Sharon was approaching. He wore a dark suit and blue tie, but there was no mistaking his massive swinging stride.

"Hello, Yael." A smile dissolved Sharon's formidable air to charming warmth. "I hate to disturb your lunch, but by your leave, I want a word with your Don Kishote."

"Of course."

Heads turned as Sharon and his new chief of staff started walking out. "By God there's Pasternak too," said Sharon. "Just our man." With the same warm smile he had shone on Yael, he borrowed Pasternak from Eva Sonshine. The three men sat down in a gloomy far corner of the lower lobby, on stiff brown leather furniture.

"Sam, is the intelligence conclusive on the missile batteries?" Sharon's inquiry was low and sharp.

"Oh, absolutely." A resigned shrug. "Right after the Egyptians signed the cease-fire, they and the Russians started moving them up to the Canal, working at night."

Sharon growled, "The terms of the cease-fire prohibited such an advance, no?"

"Why, that was the crux of the deal, Arik. The Americans accepted the Russian guarantee, so we had to, but Egypt and the Soviets have acted in total bad faith. The batteries are now lined up all along the waterline, and they're openly hardening up the sites by day."

"Sam Pasternak, are you saying," Sharon's voice dropped to an ominous rumble, "that we fight and win a long bloody war, and Nasser completely reverses the outcome with a sneaky ruse? Agrees to a standstill, then strikes a foul blow? And our government will stand for that?"

"What's there to do?"

"Cross the Canal in brigade force, *that's* what there is to do. Destroy as many of these moved-up batteries as we can, and hold the bridgehead till the rest are pulled back to the agreed-on fifty-kilometer line —"

"Reopen the war, you mean."

"Maybe, maybe not. That's up to the enemy. I mean a blow for a blow!"

"Look, Arik, the shooting has stopped." Pasternak sounded terribly weary. "The borders are unchanged. We stand on the Canal. The other Arabs are calling Nasser a betrayer and a coward for accepting the cease-fire. Our people are tired of war, those who've paid attention to it. Tired of lists of the dead. The government calls it a victory, and Nasser's moving up the missiles won't change that."

"Victory? Victory of an ostrich. Lost victory, unless we do something." Sharon stood up. "Kishote, you'll go straight to plans and operations section from here, to discuss the logistics for a brigade crossing at Kantara."

"Yes, General."

Pasternak said, "Arik, there's no heavy bridging equipment for such an assault —"

"We'll find bridging equipment," Sharon said, "or we'll cross in rubber boats, or we'll *swim* across, but by God, we'll cross. The surprise will shatter the Egyptians. They can't deal with the unforeseen. Before they recover we'll get the job done at Kantara. Then the Americans will have to come and verify the illicit advance of the missiles, and force their withdrawal. It will happen, and it will work. I'm off to meet with the General Staff." He lumbered away and up the staircase.

Pasternak and Yossi glanced wryly at each other. "Like your new job?" Pasternak inquired.

"You're right, bridging's the problem," said Kishote, half to himself. "And it's not the equipment, we could make do with what we've got. It's putting the bridges into place. Laying bridges with sharpshooters and machine gunners lining the ramparts on the other side at point-blank range, backed by heavy artillery, will call for a suicide squad of engineers. Lots of them, because they won't last long. Nor will the bridges."

"Put your mind at rest. Golda can read Nixon like a book. She never forgets the end of the Suez War, Soviets and Americans combining against us. The Americans are still up to their necks in Vietnam, Nixon's in a touchy mood, and he's claiming this ceasefire as his great achievement for peace and détente. A cross-canal attack would infuriate him, and it won't happen. Arik's butting a stone wall."

"Well, that's his career."

With a twisted grin Pasternak said, "And yours now, Don Kishote." He stood up. "See you at Aryeh's party."

The bar mitzvah reception on a lawn in Zahala was a buzzing social success despite the August sultriness. Army people, kibbutzniks, and Yael's political and business friends came. Presents for Aryeh piled up. Moshe Dayan appeared, a big triumph for the family. General Sharon showed up, too, a thundercloud in uniform. People hesitated to talk to him. "Kishote, our politicians are grasshoppers," he snarled, when Yossi offered him a drink. "That fine boy of yours will have to fight one day in a big new war, mark my words, and we may lose all we won in 1967, if in fact we survive."

"If Aryeh has to fight, he will."

Kishote glimpsed Shayna Matisdorf drifting here and there, with the bar mitzvah boy hanging close to her. She looked wan. He had no chance to talk to her. Yael was the queen of the day, magnificent in one of her original cocktail dresses, smiling and laughing with everybody, except when Shayna or Eva Sonshine crossed her line of vision.

Massive headlines broke out in September all over the world. On Christian Cunningham's hospital bed the *New York Times* and *Washington Post* shouted the news:

NASSER DIES OF HEART ATTACK;
BLOW TO PEACE EFFORTS SEEN;
NIXON CANCELS FLEET EXERCISE

PRESIDENT NASSER DIES, DEATH
ATTRIBUTED TO HEART ATTACK

Cunningham lay propped on pillows in a white gown, his face more gaunt and livid than ever. "I'm getting better," he said to Zev Barak in a weak voice. "At least I made it, and that poor fellow didn't." He gestured at the newspapers with a skeletal hand. "You'll miss him."

"Miss *Nasser*?" Barak sat in a folding chair by the bed. "Why? What do you know about this Anwar Sadat? Is he that much worse?"

"Hard to say yet. Dark-skinned mustached fellow, smokes a pipe. Minor nationalist hothead. Terrorist against the British in World War II, worked with the Germans. A Nasser shadow."

"More likely to renew the war, or less?"

"That's a tough one." The CIA man shook his head, wryly wrinkling his mouth. "Nasser sure snookered you on the cease-fire, didn't he, putting those SAM-3s along the Canal! Egypt's now got an air umbrella extending far into the Sinai, heck of an edge. Big temptation for the new fellow to go to bat and make himself a hero fast."

"Well, so you already have a visitor!" Emily entered flourishing a green bottle, followed by General Halliday in uniform. "Well, hi there, Zev. Chris, what do you think? Old Dr. Stein says a little crème de menthe might do you good."

Cunningham's sunken eyes lit up. "There are glasses in the bathroom."

"Not for me, thank you," said Barak. "I'm just going."

"Don't," Halliday said. "Like to talk to you."

"Sit down, Zev," said Cunningham.

As they chatted about his heart attack and convalescence, Emily sat holding her father's hand, glancing brightly at Barak. After a while Halliday extended a long leg to kick shut the door to the room. "Barak, you Israelis pull off one coup after another, don't you? Bagging five Russian pilots!"

"What? What's all this? Russians? An air battle?" Cunningham quavered, the glass of crème de menthe trembling in his hand. "How? When?"

"Right after you took sick, end of July," said Halliday, "and the day after the fracas the Soviet air chief of staff came roaring down to Cairo, and Nasser quit and accepted a standstill. The Russians must have twisted his arm real hard. Right, Barak?"

With a dull stare Barak said, "General, I have no idea what you're talking about."

Halliday grimly smiled. "Both sides are blacking out the story, Chris, for obvious reasons."

Straightening up in his droopy gown, which showed gray tufts on his chest, Cunningham said, "Then how do *you* know, Bud?"

"Never mind. I do. There was an Egyptian air officer right there in fighter control, filling in the Russian director about Israeli air tactics. When he saw how it was going, he advised the Russki to pull his MiGs out of the battle. The fellow said, '*We Russians don't run away.*' Direct quote. So five MiGs went down before they ran away." Halliday uttered a short cold laugh. "Happiest day for the Egyptian air force in years. Those Russian fighter controllers and airmen have been treating the Egyptians like dirt, like flies."

Barak realized that Halliday could only have gotten all this from the Egyptian air attaché, with whom he was too close for Israeli comfort.

Cunningham looked at Barak. "Come on, Zev. Talk."

Barak turned both palms upward.

"Proper response, Barak," said Halliday, "but please tell General Pasternak that we're urgently interested in that combat, and will keep top secret whatever intelligence we receive."

"At your service, of course."

"Thanks. It's interesting," said Halliday as he got up, "that the Russians blame the poor quality of the Egyptian pilots for their defeats. The Egyptians blame inferior Russian planes. They both ignore one other possibility. Namely, that your fighter pilots may be pretty damn good. Nice seeing you. Coming, Em?"

She pressed Barak's hand hard, and left. "Okay, Zev," said Cunningham. "What about the Soviet pilots?"

Barak did not hesitate. This was a friend, and nobody was better at keeping a secret. "It's quite true."

"Bravo!" Cunningham sank back on his pillows, and closed his eyes. "Don't go. I'm just a bit tired. My saying you'd miss Nasser puzzled you."

"Baffled me."

"Think, Zev! Think! Didn't Nasser frighten you quarrelsome Jews into hanging together? Otherwise the factions would have torn your fragile new country apart long ago." Cunningham opened his eyes to see how Barak was taking this. "But that's not all. By closing the Straits of Tiran in 1967, sending his army into the Sinai, whipping up the Arab masses into a televised blood frenzy, he made the world briefly sympathetic to Israel. And that gave you your chance in the Six-Day War."

Barak shook his head. "Nonsense. He was bent on our destruction, period."

"Zev, the God of history loves irony. Nasser kept you united and on your toes. When he found he couldn't beat you, he sold himself out to the Russians, and it was the Russians who killed him. Used him to penetrate the Arab world and flank NATO from the south. Made him send his people to die by the thousands, rode him to death like an overdriven horse. What will happen with this Sadat, I don't know. Watch out for him, and pour me some more crème de menthe, there's a good fellow."

Barak was walking out through the hospital lobby when a cockney streetwalker twang came from behind a post. "Hi sigh there, guv'nor, could you buy a girl a cup of coffee?" Hands on hips, Emily appeared with a sexy sway, grinning. "There's a ghastly canteen downstairs for the staff."

"Pleasure, Queenie. Lead on."

"Lovely. Then I've got to pick up my babies in McLean. First time you've seen Chris since he was felled?"

"Yes."

"What do you think?"

"Shockingly weak, but the mind's all there."

In the dismal cellar canteen there were only coin dispensers of hot drinks, soft drinks, and cakes in dusty cellophane. "We can just sit and talk, too," she said. "The coffee's vile."

"I'll have some anyway."

At a small plastic-topped table she put a hand over his. "Guess what? Old Queenie's pregnant again. Finally!"

"Em! That's wonderful."

"Yes, and it had better be a boy! This is *it*. I'm a drying-up hag."

"I agree."

"Curse you. How's Nakhama?"

Barak paused before answering, "Nakhama's not quite herself. She has these spells, and pulls out of them. I think she's homesick. What are the babies doing in McLean?"

"Nanny's straightening up Chris's house. Say, know what? Run me out there and see my girls. You never have done. Got the time?"

"By all means."

The Belgian nanny, a severe gray-headed woman in black, was feeding the twins in the kitchen. The girls were prattling, alike as mirror images. When Emily and Barak came in they fell silent, stopped eating, and regarded him with large solemn blue eyes.

"They freeze at strangers, like rabbits at headlights," said

Emily. "Kim's on the left, Sally on the right. I can tell them apart, but even Bud gets them wrong. Mind if I finish feeding them?"

"Of course not."

"Go down on the terrace, dear, and I'll join you."

Outside, the leaves on many trees were starting to turn, some were falling, and grandiose sunset clouds streaked the sky. Barak had not been on this leaf-strewn terrace in years, and bittersweet memories assailed him: Emily as a precocious twelve-year old, bringing him out here to see the fireflies and flirting girlishly with him; Emily on that November day many years later, which the smell of the leaves brought back poignantly, when their long correspondence had flashed into unwise compelling passion . . .

"Too windy out here, Zev?" She came trotting down the brick stairs. "Want a drink?"

"No, I'm fine, it's perfect."

"Not quite perfect. No fireflies."

"Too late. Firefly season's over, Queenie."

"Alas, yes. Nice while it lasted, hey old Wolf? And the leaves were further along the day Kennedy was killed."

"Oh-ho. Thinking of that, you too? Yes, the rain had pretty well beaten them off the trees."

"Do you like my girls?"

"Baby-food advertisements. Seraphs."

"Seraphs! They have their devilish moments, I assure you. How are your girls? All grown up, are they?"

"Galia's fifteen, and making problems. She rebelled at going back to the Hebrew high school here. Said the kids were all — I don't know — something not good. Schoolgirl term."

"Ah, my former specialty. Creeps? Twerps?" He shook his head. "Goons?"

"Not goons."

"Wimps? Clods? Geeks? Dorks? Nerds? Drips? Smears? Dweebs?"

"Slow down. Fourth from the last, again?"

"Nerds."

"That's it. Nerds. All nerds. So we put her in a private school.

Ruti's still at the Hebrew school, but Nakhama wants to take them both back to Israel."

Long pause. "I wish it were possible for me to be friends with Nakhama."

"It isn't."

"Will you go back soon?"

"I've begged for reassignment. For most jobs that are open, I'm too senior. For the General Staff, I'm not distinguished enough."

"I don't believe that."

"Well, what the army says is that I'm irreplaceable here."

"That sounds right."

"No. Nobody's irreplaceable."

He got up and sat beside her on the wrought-iron glider. They swung gently together. "It's such a strange kind of happiness," Emily said, her face pink with sunset glow.

"What is?"

"Oh, this surge of well-being, of rejoicing in existence, just because somebody's there with you."

"It's called love," said Barak.

She turned brilliant eyes at him. "Is that it? How dense of me."

The mood was glum in the Barak household at dinner. Galia sulked, eyes on her plate, mouth pulled down. "I can't stand liver," she said, then ate a lot of it. Ruti too was quiet. Usually vivacious, though still the ugly duckling at ten, she was chilled by her sister's ill humor. The girls cleared away the meal and disappeared into their rooms. Nakhama settled into an armchair, put on black-rimmed glasses, and read a Hebrew newspaper. Barak worked on industrial reports at a desk. The atmosphere seemed to him as heavy as in a buttoned-up tank. He laid aside an article on missile electronics. "Nakhama, what is it?"

She took off her glasses and beckoned him into their bedroom, where she pulled open a drawer. "I found this in Galia's room." It was an open pack of Kools.

Well, thought Barak, standard crisis, she's fifteen. "I'll speak to her. Or will you?" Nakhama did the feminine talking-to's, but this might call for fatherly gruffness.

"I'm not finished. Last week, when you were at Fort Knox, she went to the movies with that Freddie from her new school. Not even Jewish. With the long greasy hair in back, and the pimples. I woke up and went to the kitchen for a drink, and there they were on the parlor sofa, on top of each other."

After an embarrassed pause, Barak inquired, "Who was on top of whom?"

"What kind of question is *that*?" A ragged-nerved snap. "Does it matter? All right, she was on top."

"So this Freddie wasn't wholly to blame."

"Zev, you're being an animal. That school is full of degenerates. I'm not going on with this. The girls have learned English. They've learned altogether too much, to all the devils. God knows what else Galia has picked up in that school with no nerds! Ruti so far is fine. They have to go home, both of them."

"The Ramatkhal wants me here one more year."

"Then I'll take them home. Enough America for my girls! If you have to stay here, I don't."

"Nakhama, there are boys in Israel, and now and then they lie on top of the girls. Also the other way around."

Nakhama walked out of the bedroom. He gave her a few minutes to cool off, then went to the parlor. She was reading her paper again. "So, how's Emily Cunningham?" she said in a wholly pleasant tone.

He was startled into a witless echo. "Emily Cunningham? You mean Mrs. Halliday? Why?"

"Oh, yes, Mrs. Halliday. I visited Miriam Kress in the Georgetown Hospital, and I saw you both getting into your car. I waved, but you didn't wave back."

"I didn't see you, Nakhama. Her father's in that hospital, recovering from a bad heart attack. We happened to meet when I visited him."

"Ah."

"She's pregnant."

"Ah. That's nice."

"I gave her a lift to her father's house, where her kids were staying."

Nakhama nodded, and resumed reading. Heavy silence. When Barak could no longer stand it, he said, "Nakhama, I haven't seen Mrs. Halliday for months, or maybe a year, I don't even remember."

"Who asked you?" Nakhama removed her glasses and looked him straight in the face. "Zev, I'm not American, I'm not a shiksa, and my education is very limited. I'm not trying to make trouble. I just know that when I take the girls home, one way or another you won't be unbearably lonesome."

Within the week Nakhama and the girls were gone.

Emily Halliday had a boy, to the great rejoicing of her father and the marked approval of her husband. General Halliday was appointed commander of an air base in Florida, his wife and children went with him, and the Queenie-Wolf correspondence sporadically resumed. Barak talked now and then by telephone with Nakhama and the girls. He managed brief returns to Israel, always finding the people more prosperous, construction more hectic, automobile traffic more frightening, and tourism still on the rise. He came there with gladness and departed with an ache, trying each time for a transfer back home, but in the zigzags of internal army politics his chance at a sector command kept receding. When Dado Elazar became Ramatkhal he all but despaired; not that Dado had anything against him, but rather that he had been too long out of sight to ride the wave of new appointments.

Anwar Sadat came on as a weak colorless successor to the fire-eating Nasser, and a relaxed frame of mind began to prevail at the embassy. Announcing that 1971 would be "the year of decision," when Egypt would regain its honor and the Sinai by force of arms, the new fellow let the year go by with nothing happening. The superpowers kept pushing a wobbly UN peace initiative called the Jarring Mission, trying to get Israel to offer greater and greater slices of the Sinai in a peace settlement, and to persuade Egypt to talk to the Jews on any terms whatever; while quietly the Nixon administration let the Israelis know that keeping the Canal closed, thus denying the Russians a short sea route to Vietnam, was not the worst possible thing that could be happening in the Middle East.

Early in 1972 Barak began receiving increasingly urgent letters from the army engineering corps, asking for U.S. bids to supply a huge number of steel cylinders six feet in diameter and eighty feet long, with no hint of what they were for. The steel firms naturally wanted to know the purpose of these giant objects, advising Barak that they would have to be custom-made at high cost, and that even shipping would be a problem, but to his inquiries the army engineers remained mum. So the whole business was hanging fire, when a letter from Don Kishote shed some light.

SOUTHERN COMMAND

Chief of Staff
Top Secret

10 July 1972
By Pouch

Dear Zev:

Arik is after me about "the cylinders." They're not my job, but you know Arik. The bull charges and everyone runs for the fence.

I'm not surprised that Bethlehem Steel can't figure out the purpose, nor that the engineers won't tell you, but here goes. You know about our bridging problem. *Carry the battle to the enemy's territory* is doctrine, so to win any war Egypt starts we must cross the Canal. The bridging equipment we've got is from European junkyards. Trying to cross on those French amphibious rafts (crocodiles, we call them) or the British pontoons would be suicidal. As you've found out, the Americans won't sell us mobile bridges because they're not "defensive." We can forget the Europeans, Arab oil has them crawling.

Well, the cylinders are rollers for a bridge more than 600 feet long that will be towed to the Canal and pushed across by *tanks,* hence, no exposure of engineers to gunfire. Once in the water, the rollers become giant *pontoons*. That's the trick. Built in sections, it will be flexible enough to traverse the hills and dunes of Sinai. I recently watched a miniature prototype perform for the high brass on a sand table. Weird to see it crawling along on the level, humping itself over the obstacles, and slithering down into the mock-up Canal! The budget for the roller bridges means steep cuts in other hardware, and some muttering goes on in high places about "Tallik's monstrosity." But General Tal's number two to Dado, so several of these behemoths will be built. So please obtain a decent bid on those rollers and get Arik off my back. Producing them in Israel would strain our steelmaking capacity, though it's feasible. A few have been made here for a full-scale prototype of one section.

Arik assumes we'll have a war with Egypt as soon as Sadat is ready to go, and we've been extending the network of military roads in Sinai for a rapid war of movement. We keep hardening up the Bar-Lev Line too, though he questions the whole concept. He makes enemies the way a steamboat makes waves. I know how you feel about him, but the soldiers will follow him anywhere. That's something. His energy is awesome, and if war comes I'll not be sorry that he's OC Southern Command.

Yours,
Yossi

Barak was still working on the procurement of the cylinders and not getting far, when at last he was relieved of the extended attaché duty and ordered back to Israel for reassignment. At once he called his brother Michael in Haifa to say that he would be returning in time for his wedding to Shayna Matisdorf. He notified Nakhama, who sounded reasonably joyful, and he took bitter pleasure in packing up and getting out of the small furnished apartment off Wisconsin Avenue in which he had spent too much lonely and unrewarding time after his family's departure. Last-minute official duties delayed his detachment, forcing him to miss Michael's wedding, after all; a bleak end to a bleak tenure.

The morning of his departure was a whirl of trivia — landlord, bank, dentist, and so on. When he stopped his taxi at the embassy en route to the airport to make his farewells, Ambassador Rabin jolted him with a few slow dry words. "So, what do you think of Sadat now?"

"Sadat? What about Sadat? What's happened, Ambassador?"

"You haven't heard?" Rabin squinted at him, shook his head,

and a characteristic quick half-smile came and went. "Well, you're anxious to get home. It's the big news this morning. He's expelling the Russians, giving them a week to leave Egypt — all seventeen thousand of them — and he's nationalizing the Soviet installations and military equipment."

After a dumbfounded silence Barak said, "What do you make of it, sir?"

"I don't know."

From the ambassador down, Barak gathered as he said good-bye to the embassy staff, nobody knew quite what to make of this grand stroke, this international thunderclap, launched by a man rated low if not laughed at by experienced diplomats, Israeli and otherwise. The general sense was that the move was very good news, reducing the threat of war, for surely the Egyptians could not venture into battle against Israel without close Soviet guidance and support. Perhaps because of his chronic gloom at being marooned in Washington, Barak's first guess was that it could be an elaborate charade played by both Sadat and the Soviets, to lull Israel into exactly the sense of relief prevailing in the embassy. In any case it was not necessarily good news.

13

Shayna's Wedding

Daphna was puzzled by the invitation from Professor Berkowitz and Shayna Matisdorf to their wedding, but she knew her parents had been asked, so perhaps she was being included out of courtesy, or possibly Noah had seen to it, and was hoping to patch things up with her there. So she had accepted; but on the day, after a glance into her tiny closet, she decided to skip it. Three dresses, one tackier than the next. She and her roommate Donna, both being from military families and both, after their compulsory army service, in a state of anarchic revolt, wore only jeans day and night, preferably American jeans, preferably from San Francisco. Putting on a dress for a stupid wedding in Haifa was just too much. Besides, she had something better to do today.

A few nights ago, at a party of artists and writers at the Jericho Café, the haunt of Tel Aviv's bohemia, she had intrigued the famous ceramicist Shimon Shimon with bright questions about his art, and he had invited her to visit his studio. Since then she had been reading everything about ceramics she could find. Maybe that was a way to go, for the ballet dancing had long ago proved a dead end. Apparently she was too *zaftig* for ballet. She would have to starve down to stringiness, she had been told, and start in classes with twelve-year-olds and younger. Daphna had tried the starving, and the classes, too. But she loved to eat, and loathed the giggles of the bony little girls at the way her bosom bounced. So much for ballet. Now she was writing pieces for tourist handout magazines, which at least paid something. But ceramics seemed so exciting, molding works of art worth money out of muck! So she scrawled a note:

> Dear Dov — Sorry, I just can't face it. Shimon Shimon is showing me his studio this morning, and I may actually make a start at ceramics! He charges a fortune to teach, he's the best, but he said never mind money, let's find out first if you have talent. Nobody will miss me at that wedding. If they do say I dropped dead from boredom at the thought of it. Daff.

She crayoned a heavy red *DOV* on the envelope — he was supposed to pick her up and take her there — and jammed the disingenuous scribble into the crack of the door as she left. Daphna knew that two Berkowitz relatives would miss her badly, Noah and Dzecki, and she was just as glad not to be caught between them. She was especially sore at Noah, since their blowup at the Jericho Café over the Independence Day military parade.

It had been her mistake, perhaps, to take him after the parade to the night spot where her crowd hung out, drinking Gold Star beer and eating olives at a big wooden table. Donna had introduced her long since to these exciting people: long-haired bearded fellows, girls in jeans with crazy bouffant hairdos or unkempt heads, all-night smokers, talkers, and beer-sippers. They were *fun,* different, hip. Shouting over the rock group belting out American, Hebrew, European, and South American songs, they discussed writers like Camus, Sartre, Brecht, and Faulkner, they dissected the new Hebrew novels, films, and plays, they gossipped about painters and actors, they made acid jokes about Israeli politicians, and they were passionate on all sides of the Arab question.

Naturally, watching the evening news on the café's TV, they had made sarcastic cracks about the military parade. Noah had not been amused, countering with banalities about the danger Israel still was in despite the cease-fire. A real bore! He had even spouted some serious Zionism, a theme more old-hat, ridiculous, and taboo in this company than God. The scene had turned ugly when General Motta Gur appeared on the TV, and Yoram Sarak, the star of the Jericho Café crowd, exclaimed, "Ah, the Angel of Death!" A career cynic at thirty, with a lean choleric look, overgrown hair, and dark glasses to match, Sarak wrote an acerb column in a rowdy leftist weekly.

Noah spoke up sharply, "He's only the man who liberated Jerusalem."

"Yes, yes, '*The Temple Mount is in our hands,*' " Sarak sneered. "Thirty-six guys died on Ammunition Hill, my friend, and that battle should never have been fought. If Motta Gur hadn't been so hot to reach the Temple Mount first, Uri Ben Ari's tanks would have arrived from the north and wiped out the whole enemy force on the hill with cannon fire in ten minutes, and with no casualties."

"Is that so?" Noah barked. Ammunition Hill was an enshrined legend of Six-Day War heroism. "And how do you know all that?"

"Because I fought on Ammunition Hill, my friend, and two of my pals got killed. Paratroop Battalion Sixty-six." Noah was silenced. "And I'll tell you something else, Admiral." Sarak snapped open a beer can. "This whole country is one big Ammunition Hill."

"Yes? In what way?"

"A bloody story of futile deaths of too many great guys, for the glory of a lot of old fuckups and nonentities."

"Look here, Sarak, why don't you just pick up and go to Los Angeles?"

"And let the country fall into hands like yours, Admiral? I'm not that sour on it yet."

At that point Noah stood up and dragged Daphna protesting out of the Jericho Café, telling her as they went that if they remained he would have to knock Sarak on his ass. On a park bench under a lamp they had had the fight of their lives, and had not really reconciled since. She loved and admired him, but she was not letting him force her back into the old mode; not him, not her father, and not her go-go air force brothers, now that she had struggled free. Anyway, with Sadat throwing out the Russians, how important were the armed forces, really? How could there be another war?

Shortly after that fiasco, she had brought Dzecki to the Jericho as a sort of litmus test of his character. In uniform on a weekend pass, he came with her to the café willingly. Her friends rode him hard about leaving America for the glamorous life of an IDF draftee, and of course about the Porsche. He took it all with a good-humored grin and mild repartee in passable Hebrew slang. So they forgot him and went on with lively talk about new-wave movies ("the answer to Hollywood"), Leonard Bernstein ("a sentimental phony"), Günter Grass, Samuel Beckett, Arthur Miller, and so on, salted with inside talk on topics like the latest bank scandal and politicians' mistresses. Afterward Dzecki remarked, "They're okay, just ten or fifteen years behind New York." Understandable, coming from an American, if annoying. Dzecki was *in.* Her friends' needling was a rough well-deserved Israeli tribute. There was something to Dzecki! With three months to go in the army, he was already looking into real estate projects in Haifa. He had showed her an old Arab waterfront warehouse he and his father might buy and renovate. He even kept that battered Porsche going, though two Israeli drivers and an Egged bus had hit it. No garage in Israel could maintain a Porsche as he did.

And at least he did not consider her Jericho Café crowd traitors and scum, as Noah seemed to. Noah's attitude was intolerable. All her friends had served in the IDF. All still did their reserve duty. Most scrounged their livings by working at two or three jobs. Some had fought in the Six-Day War, several had been wounded. Daphna knew the military life all too well; knew pilots who had died, knew their widows and orphans. The air force was great, but so what? She had endured childhood nightmares of her father crashing in flames, and now she had to worry about Dov, and even her baby brother Danny was applying for flight training. Meantime the politicians schemed and lied to keep their jobs, wars broke out every few years, the generals screwed up, and the boys paid with their lives, or their legs, eyes, and arms. That was the plain Jericho Café truth about Israel, not the threadbare Zionist myth that Noah was still trying to live up to.

Such were Daphna's ruminations as she rode a bus to Rashi Street, and climbed dark creaky stairs to Shimon Shimon's studio.

A dirty skylight on the top floor showed the ceramic doorplate with his name, black flames on gold: SHIMON SHIMON. She tentatively knocked. No answer. Louder knock. Nothing. She pressed the doorbell, and its raucous ring made her jump. Heavy treads approaching, sliding of a lock, a muttered Arabic obscenity, door opening. In droopy underwear, the ceramicist peered at her, scratching his red beard with one hand and his hairy belly with the other.

"Hello. Am I early? I can come back later."

"You're who? Oh, yes, you're Daphna, aren't you? Right, right, Daphna. No, no, come right in." He grabbed a bathrobe from a hook. Daphna went inside, and Shimon Shimon closed the door.

Noah's missile boat was docking about then. He had been working since dawn on an automatic gun-loader that had jammed, for an exec had to be everywhere and do anything. He hurried to his quarters to get out of his greased-up coveralls, and dress for the wedding. At last a chance to see Daphna and smooth things over! He had not seen her since their quarrel. The navy had to keep constant watch for seaborne terrorists, and the nights on patrol were long and monotonous. Noah had much time to think, looking at the black waves, the crowding stars, and the lights of home sending up a glow on distant clouds. What to do about that provoking Daphna? In the draggy hours on watch, visions and sensations of their lovemaking haunted him, but she had drifted into that disgusting Jericho Café set. A vexing problem, for he remained infatuated with her.

A letter from Cherbourg lay on his cot. A picture of Julie Levinson slid out of the envelope, and to his surprise, the writing was in childish large-lettered Hebrew.

Dear Noah,

These are the first words I have ever written in Hebrew besides exercises!

You remember Shmulik Tannenbaum, your navy supply officer who came back to Cherbourg and married my friend Yvonne? They now have two babies, and Shmulik is giving Hebrew lessons to make extra money. Our class is small, five girls counting me, and two fellows. All the others plan to make aliya.

(It has taken me *half an hour* to write this much! I have to keep looking up words in my French-Hebrew dictionary, which is not very good.)

I and my parents will visit Israel right after Yom Kippur, only three months from now. I talk better than I write, so you can talk to me then in Hebrew to test me! (A joke.) You probably have forgotten how I look, so I enclose a picture (my verb forms are awful, I know).

We will only stay three weeks, but it will be nice to see you again. I have a boyfriend but he is not Jewish, he works in a bank. I think that is why my parents are taking me to Israel. But don't worry, they don't hope to match up you and me. Anyway by now you must have married Daphna! If so I hope you are happy and I would like to meet her.

Your friend,
Julie Levinson

P.S. — *Time, 2½ hours!*

In the picture she wore a jogging suit and a soft cap. Her face was thinner, hard to recognize. This was Julie's first letter in a long time. Noah could not write easily in French, he hated to make the slightest error, and once he saw Daphna again he had let the correspondence dwindle and lapse. He dropped the letter and picture in a drawer. Poor Julie!

As he dressed, Noah heard on the radio a roundtable of experts disputing about Sadat's move, mainly throwing up gassy clouds of bafflement and verbiage. He was baffled, too. L'Azazel! Could Egypt really be giving up the fight? Was Israel no longer in peril, after a quarter-century of cliff-hanging? Egypt was the powerhouse of Arab enmity. Without Egypt the front was broken, and without the Soviets the Egyptians were helpless. Chasing down those terrorists in rubber boats was no career for a man; would he never have a chance to fight in a war? He set out for the wedding in a fresh uniform, hoping he could take Daphna somewhere afterward. The damned Jericho Café was a good two hours away, thank God. Perhaps she would even come to the Dan Hotel for the night. *That* was the way of ways to put a fight behind them.

Daphna's Aunt Yael also ran a dissatisfied eye over her more extensive wardrobe, wondering what to wear for a mid-July strictly religious wedding; which, however, she was not about to miss. The sleeveless pink shantung would be coolest, but Elohim, no! The Ezrakh was officiating, the great Talmud scholar Benny so much admired, and to such holy men bare arms and bare breasts were all one. The blue pima cotton then, with sleeves below the elbow. If naked wrists were too immodest, haval! She was not coming to Shayna Matisdorf's nuptials looking like a pious frump. That was the bride's game.

Despite the hold she had on Yossi in their two children, Yael never quite shrugged off the sense of that religious old maid as a threat. Of course sneaked meetings with Kishote, even surreptitious telephone calls, were much beyond that goodie-goodie, though they were routine to the *shmatas* (loose women) he fooled with. But most men in the long run needed love, not shmatas, and that was the standing menace of Shayna. Yael was sleeping alone these days. The flame was out. She had not tricked him with Eva, and he knew that. Still, he clearly wanted no more children, at least with her, and he was employing the one unfailing contraceptive, cool distance. Otherwise she could hardly complain. He was good-humored, he seemed reconciled to things as they were, and how much time did other army wives get to spend with their husbands, anyway? Nevertheless, seeing with her own eyes Shayna Matisdorf removed from circulation was well worth killing a business day.

"Got to wash off the desert dust, first thing," Kishote said, coming in with a clatter of tankist black boots, as she was affixing a gold lion pin to the pima cotton. "How are you, Yael? You look elegant." He was unbuttoning his green blouse, omitting any kiss or hug, though he had not been home for weeks. "Where are the kids?"

"Aryeh's dressing up. Eva's in kindergarten. We won't bring her. There's a pressed uniform in your closet."

"I'll wear a shirt and slacks." He kicked off the boots.

"So, Shayna gets married at last," she ventured. He nodded without a word, stripping down to sweat-soaked briefs, a muscular glistening figure. "Yossi, what about Sadat?"

"Sadat? Good question." He ran a hand over his face. "I suppose I should shave."

"Have things changed at the Canal at all?"

"Dead quiet, but there's always plenty to do."

"Is it serious, his expelling the Russians?"

"Very serious." He went into the bathroom.

In the car heading up the coastal highway Aryeh, now a lanky fifteen but still beardless, sat beside the driver, turning around to look and listen as his parents discussed Sadat's move. "Sharon called a staff meeting that same night," his father said, "to exchange ideas about it. We were still talking when the sun came up. Five explanations emerged, or should I say survived."

"Let's hear."

"Well, *one,* the Russians were denying him first-line armaments, or charging too high a price."

"Oversimple."

"Maybe, but just like the Soviets. *Two,* the Egyptian people, especially the army, hate the Soviet presence. The crude Russians treat them like dirt, even their senior officers. We know that's true. *Three,* Sadat had to do something bold and popular after bluffing and doing nothing in 1971."

"That's more like it," said Yael. "It's what I think."

"Well, Sharon thinks it's none of those. The last two are bad, and one's worse than the other. *Four,* Sadat's decided to tilt his foreign policy to America, because Washington's where he can get the most leverage against Israel. *Five,* the Russians wouldn't let him plan to attack Israel, because that would end détente and might drag them into nuclear war with America. He kicked them out to free his hands for war."

At this Aryeh opened wide eyes.

"Oo-wah," exclaimed Yael. "Sharon's the pessimist, as usual."

"Abba, what do you think?" Aryeh said.

Kishote looked at him with affection. "Me, think? When I'm ordered, I fight."

The ceremony began as soon as Benny Luria arrived at Michael's apartment with the Ezrakh, the aged scholar famed for his grasp of Torah law, and for never having set foot outside the Holy Land; hence his sobriquet, which meant "the Native." Benny had met him years ago, through the bereaved parents of a pilot lost in a training accident, and they had struck up an unlikely but continuing friendship. Shayna had known the Ezrakh all her life, and that he would conduct her wedding was taken for granted.

Chanting the blessings under the canopy, the Ezrakh looked and sounded no older than he had five years ago at Reuven's circumcision in this same room, in the same rusty black hat and ankle-length threadbare black coat. His voice was weak, yet the hand that held the cup of wine was steady. Yael saw the ring go on Shayna's finger. Michael Berkowitz missed the glass on the first stamp, then *crunch*! The thing was done. "Mazel tov! Mazel tov!" cried the guests crowding the small flat.

But there was no outburst of song. Vibrations of romance or erotic excitement were not in the air of this stooped skullcapped professor's second marriage, to his associate in her thirties. Stepping out from under the canopy, Shayna embraced Reuven, leaning on his crutch nearby. She was adopting the crippled boy, Yael thought, and the handiest way to do it was to move in with the professor. Well, anyhow that was that, Shayna was locked away.

But the next thing Shayna did was to kiss Don Kishote! This struck Yael as not only unladylike, but against the religion. Shayna strode to Yossi through the relatives, neighbors, and friends in her plain gray dress, the white veil thrown back on her head, and planting a kiss on his lips, murmured something to him. Then she and her limping groom went off to a bedroom for the *yikhud*. Kishote looked after her with an expression that Yael had seen him direct at Aryeh in his baby years, and nowadays at little Eva, but never at her; a wistful tenderness that quite smoothed away his half-humorous half-menacing look. Shayna was disappearing into that bedroom and from his life, Yael perceived, but not to make room for her. The professor's wife would just leave a hole.

The yikhud custom required the bride and groom to absent themselves in a room, with witnesses to observe that they were sequestered inside long enough — in theory, of course — to consummate the marriage. Meanwhile, all in a congenial tumult, the guests divided for the wedding repast by generations; parents at one long table, sons and daughters at the other. "Where to all the devils is Daphna?" Noah asked Dov Luria, who had arrived in uniform just as the ceremony began. It was doctrine in the Luria household that Noah Barak remained the main hope to keep Daphna from going entirely to the dogs. Dov calmly lied that she had a cold. He meant to track Daphna down right after this dowdy affair, to give her hell; and that Shimon Shimon too, if any funny business was going on.

"She told me she was coming," said Dzecki, "but I figured she would duck out. Too many girls she knows are getting married. Weddings depress her."

Galia Barak spoke up. "I haven't seen Daphna Luria forever, not since I went to America. Is she still so beautiful?"

"You're the beauty now," said Dov. "My sister's a crone."

At this compliment from a Phantom pilot, Galia colored up. Shorter than his father, heavy-boned, with a flat Slavic face traceable to shtetl genes, Dov did not need good looks to fascinate a seventeen-year-old. Dov was now aiming for flight leader, with little spare energy for girls, but still he thought this black-eyed Galia Barak wasn't bad at all. He had last seen her years ago at some army gathering, a sullen plump kid with bad skin. Quite a change! And quite a family, these Baraks. Worth bearing in mind.

Aryeh had sat himself next to Dov. He was already the taller of the two and better-looking, with abundant blond curls and his mother's peachy skin. "Say, Dov, what does the air force think about Sadat kicking out the Russians?"

"I know what I think. A few will leave by air in front of the cameras, and sneak back by sea. It's a TV stunt to start another phony peace offensive."

"Well, I don't agree. I say the Russians wouldn't let Sadat plan to attack Israel, because that might drag them into nuclear war with America. He's getting rid of them to free his hands." Seeking attention from the pilot, Aryeh was citing the one reason his father had given that he clearly understood.

Noah, Dov, and Dzecki glanced at each other. Pretty good for fifteen! Over the noisy talk in the room, Don Kishote called, "Dzecki!" and beckoned him to a corner, where he spoke low. "Didn't I see you working on the roller bridge prototype, when I visited the Jeptha yards?"

"Yes, sir. I'm in Amos Pasternak's battalion."

"And you've made first sergeant, eh?" He tapped the insignia on Dzecki's uniform. "Isn't your draft service almost over?"

"I may sign up for another year. The bridge is a challenge, sir."

"Tell me about the bridge."

"Well, sir, there's not too much to tell yet. So far we've assembled only two sections. They say there will be eighty."

"Do the sections roll?"

"Like a dream. Linking them up is what's tricky. They tend to come apart."

"What's the problem, exactly?"

Dzecki started to talk jargon about joints and bearings, rigid and flexible elements. Kishote interrupted. "Did you go to engineering school in the States?"

"I graduated from law school, sir. But I like machinery."

When Shayna and her husband emerged from the bedroom the guests were in a jollier mood, having eaten and drunk. They all stood, clapped hands and sang. Her veil discarded, Shayna looked rosy and serene. From the round low table where the small children sat she plucked up Reuven, who wore a brace on a leg. Waving a camera, Nakhama Barak, who had been drinking a lot, pushed her closer to the limping Berkowitz. "A picture! A picture! Everybody stand back! Smile, bride and groom! Shayna, get Reuven to smile!"

She kissed the boy and said softly, "Well, Reuven? Aren't you happy?"

Reuven put both hands to her cheeks and smiled. "Perfect!" *Flash*. "One more!" *Flash*.

Dzecki Barkowe thought he must be mistaken, seeing a small

tear roll down Colonel Nitzan's brown cheek. Only women cried at weddings.

Daphna's visit to Shimon Shimon's studio started tamely with talk about the Sadat news. He showed her a *mizrakh* he was making for an Orthodox Belgian diamond dealer, a colorful ceramic of sunrise over the Temple Mount to be hung on an eastern wall; explaining like a university lecturer details of clays, glazes, and firing techniques, too fast for her to follow. Next he handed her a lump of raw red clay from a cluttered work stand. "Make something, motek." One of his cats, a big gray tom, was asleep on the stand, so she set about fashioning a slumbering cat. He watched with amusement for a while, then read Yoram Sarak's weekly, glancing now and then at her work as she intently molded and remolded the clay. "You're facile," he said, as the cat took form. "You have hands. That's something."

"All right, there it is," she said at last. "A cat."

She gave it to him, rather proud of it. He turned it here and there. "Hm. Proportions not too bad. Tail has a nice curve. Listen, it's not a dog or a monkey, it's a cat. Fine." He was setting out bread, cheese, and wine on a bare wooden table. "Let's have something to eat."

As they ate and drank he talked eloquently about the art and the marketing of ceramics. Once he jumped up to take a ball of clay and form it into a convincing turtle, giving her pointers on how to work the stuff. It was all fascinating, and when he sat down on the bench close beside her and clinked glasses to toast a budding artist, she saw nothing wrong with that. But on the refill he put an arm around her, and with the next glass he attempted a kiss, and Daphna was off and running.

The celebrated ceramicist came lumbering after her, exclaiming about her beauty, until he fell over another cat, a yellow-striped beast that let out a hair-raising yowl as Shimon Shimon thudded to the floor. Daphna halted, guffawing. The ceramicist weaved to his feet. "Laugh, will you, you little devil?" He lurched for her, and again she fled, not especially surprised or outraged, giggling as she kept her distance, and with it her virtue, such as it was. The wine slightly dizzied her, and made it all seem funny. But Shimon Shimon expertly closed in on her until he had her backed up to the worktable, where she seized the first thing that came to hand, a heavy red clay figure. "Please stop this foolishness, Shimon. By your life, I'm not interested."

"Girl, put that down," he panted. "That's a Moses, and I've sold it."

She glanced at it; Moses, all right, Ten Commandments, horns, and all, looking furious and raising the tablets high. "I wouldn't care if it was Jesus, just let me alone."

The ceramicist frowned, looking very offended. "I don't make Jesuses, girl," he panted. "I've never made a single Jesus, and there's money in them, too."

"Shimon, I'm engaged. All right?"

Reverberating knocks at the metal door.

"Who is it?" Shimon yelled.

"Is my sister in there? I'm Dov Luria."

He turned to her. "You have a brother?"

"I have two. This one's a Phantom pilot, and strong as a lion."

"She's coming," called the ceramicist, and he hissed at her, "You've still got my Moses, you idiot! Put it down. I'll let him in . . . Hello, there," he panted. "Yes, she's here."

Daphna, her chest heaving, was fooling with a red thing on a stand littered with tools and statuary. "What's that," said Dov, "a cat?"

"Not so bad for a first try, eh?"

"Is it such hard work?"

"Hard, no, why do you ask?"

"You're winded as if you'd just run a mile."

"Nonsense. How was the wedding?"

"Well, they got married. Noah wanted to know where the devil you were. That Dzecki was there, too." Dov was noting the broken bread and cheese on a small table, the bottle, and the two glasses, one empty and the other knocked over in a puddle of wine. "Come on, I'll drive you to your flat."

"I can get a bus. I'm in the middle of something."

"I gather that. Let's go."

Daphna put down the cat, quailing a bit under his eye. "Dov, I think I've got a career."

"So do I," said Shimon. "She has hands."

Dov said, "Whatever happened to the ballet?"

"I'm too zaftig."

The ceramic artist burst out in roars. They could hear him laughing as they went down the stairs.

"What's he laughing at?" said Dov. "That guy, talk about zaftig! Did he get fresh?"

"Him? He's as harmless as one of his cats."

"Don't be so sure. If he tries anything, Daphna, I'll zaftig him and his whole studio."

The Ezrakh slept all the way to Jerusalem, sitting beside Benny Luria's driver. In the back seat, Benny worried about Daphna's not showing up (that girl was going to lose Noah Barak, and serve her right); about his sister Yael's tense demeanor (that marriage seemed to be going down the drain); about the spectacle his wife and Nakhama Barak had made of themselves, passing a bottle of Carmel brandy back and forth and getting drunk; he knew Irit's problems, but what was bothering Nakhama? Most of all, he was worrying about Sadat.

The talk at the wedding had been a babble of guesswork. Benny had kept silent, for the air force intelligence was not reassuring. Sadat's missile wall at the Canal now included not only SAM-2s and SAM-3s, blocking the sky up to forty thousand feet, but the dreaded mysterious new SAM-6. It was mobile, therefore a difficult target, and it could pick up aircraft that skimmed the ground. So much was known. The sardonic word in the air force was that the SAM-6 could also make espresso and play "Hatikvah." It was, in any case, very bad news. Egyptians could not handle such world-class weaponry, and even if they could, the Russians would not trust them at the firing buttons, so the expulsion had to be at least in part a fake.

When Benny's driver stopped the car at the Ezrakh's cellar in an old stone Jerusalem house, the aged scholar opened his eyes.

"Thank you. A mitzvah, it was," he said, "gladdening the bride and groom, blessed be the Name."

"Rabbi, what do you make of what the Egyptian man has done?"

With a gentle gesture of a frail white hand, the Ezrakh said, "What happens behind the high windows, I don't understand."

"Is it good or bad?"

The Ezrakh looked at him with heavily pouched blue eyes sunk in deep sockets. "That young man at the wedding, in an air force uniform, was your son?"

"Yes."

"Is he a pilot like his father?"

"Yes. My other son is only sixteen, and talking about flying school."

Taking Benny's hand in his dry cool paw, the Ezrakh raised it to his lips and kissed it. This made Benny Luria very uncomfortable. "Let's part with a word of learning," the Ezrakh said in his feeble hoarse voice. "In Genesis, at the end of the sixth day it says, God saw everything that he had done, *'and behold, it was very good.'* You remember that?"

"Well, even in the moshav we learned Bible. Of course I remember it."

The Ezrakh nodded. "Rabbi Akiva commented, '*Good* is life. *Very good* is death.' He didn't explain. You ask about what the Egyptian man has done? It will be very bad and very good."

Like Akiva, he did not explain. He got out of the car and slowly trudged down into his dark dwelling.

14

The Raid

In the captain's cabin of the missile boat *Gaash*, tied up in Haifa, the second hand of the clock clicked to 5 P.M., whereupon Noah Barak spun the combination lock of his safe and took out a coarse brown envelope, rubber-stamped in red TOP SECRET. Opening the sealed inner envelope, he avidly read the blurry cover page of a mimeographed op order.

CHIEF OF GENERAL STAFF

April 2, 1973

TOP SECRET

OPERATION "SPRINGTIME OF YOUTH"

Sayeret Matkhal will conduct a seaborne raid into Beirut on the night of 9/10 April 1973, in a combined action with paratroopers, sea commandos, naval units, and air force rescue helicopters. The task group will execute the terrorists' leaders and demolish their headquarters, armament dumps, and weapons workshops. The task group will penetrate Beirut, carry out the mission, and withdraw by sea before the Lebanon police and army are alerted, so as to keep political repercussions to a minimum.

Sayeret Matkhal, General Staff Reconnaissance Force, was Amos Pasternak's elite group. Noah flipped the next two pages listing assignments of various units, and there it was: *Unit Amos embark in* Gaash. *Target Rue de Verdun apartment.* A list followed of the fighters and the details of their task, the killing of the terrorist chiefs.

Early that morning Amos Pasternak had already brought aboard his paratroopers and frogmen, with their clutter of weapons, walkie-talkies, signal gear, and rubber boats. This afternoon they were all down on the wharf, listening to the Ramatkhal, who had driven up from Tel Aviv to talk to the raiders. Noah yearned to go down to the dock and hear him, but he was too new a missile boat captain to allow himself that freedom. By chance, he commanded the same boat he had sailed in from Cherbourg, much upgraded in firepower and engine performance. He climbed to the bridge for a last-minute check on preparations for sea, and saw General Elazar ascend the gangplank, then come leaping up the bridge ladder like a boy. "You're Zev Barak's son, eh?" he said, returning Noah's salute. "Your father and I are old comrades in arms. Are you prepared in all respects for this mission?"

"Yes, sir."

"Any comments?"

"I wish I could go with them into Beirut."

Dado peered at him. "So do I, Captain, but we both must stick to our dull support jobs. I'll have a look around your boat."

"I'll come with you."

"Stay on your bridge."

The stocky Ramatkhal strode up and down the deck, dark curly hair stirring in the harbor breeze, talking to the raiders and to sailors at sea details, then he descended to the CIC and the engine rooms. Noah did not warn the watch below that Dado was coming. Surprise inspection, for good or ill, was salutary. Returning from below, Dado remarked, to Noah's considerable relief, "A smart boat. You'll do well."

As the Ramatkhal's car drove off the wharf, it passed two women approaching the *Gaash* in slovenly jeans. *What the devil?*

Noah thought, who are these civilians, and what are they doing here? He hurried to the gangplank, where sailors were gaping at them as they came aboard. The blonde was a stranger, but he recognized the beefy woman with the bouffant brunette hairdo at once. It was Amos Pasternak.

This raid had been a long time coming. Arab terrorism had been expanding into a fourth front against Israel, with the hijacking and blowing up of airliners, taking and killing of hostages, letter bombings, car bombings, and machine-gun and grenade attacks on airport terminals, synagogues, Israeli consulates and embassies, all planned, armed, and funded by PLO headquarters in Beirut. The seizure of Israeli athletes as hostages at the Olympic Games in Munich had achieved a peak of world attention. A bungled attempt at rescue by the German special services had resulted in the bound and helpless athletes being machine-gunned to death. Great were the media cries of outrage. Talk of actually calling off the Olympics lasted a day or two. Then, after suitable memorial ceremonies for the murdered Jewish competitors, the Games went on as before.

Within the Israeli government an exceedingly grim mood prevailed thereafter. At a meeting of the armed forces chiefs in the Prime Minister's residence, Sam Pasternak presented the picture of possible retaliation. "It comes to this, Madame Prime Minister. If it's to be a decisive blow, then the target is Beirut. Specifically, two buildings in the heart of Beirut — the PLO headquarters building, and the apartment house where the big shots have their fancy suites. We have the intelligence and forces to do that job. It's a political decision."

Drawn and sallow from her sleepless nights during the Munich hostage crisis, Golda asked, "Do it how?" She cut short discussion of a "surgical air strike" in a very tired voice down to a cigarette croak. " *'Surgical'* is a word, gentlemen. There would be civilian deaths, maybe many. The terrorists welcome headlines of death, the gorier the better. We have to consider world opinion."

From the long bitter colloquy the general decision emerged that something would have to be done, probably in Beirut, and that planning for various options should go forward. Six months later nothing had yet been done. Then the same terrorist group kidnapped two American diplomats in Sudan, and after some inconclusive negotiations with Washington, murdered them.

"Now we go," said Moshe Dayan, and Golda approved.

Sam Pasternak asked his son that morning, when he came to say goodbye, "You'll be wearing women's clothes? Why? They'll only trip you up, if things get warm."

His extended term in the Mossad ended, Sam now had a small office in Ramat Aviv, one secretary, and at the moment no income. Offers from industry and political parties were coming his way, including an invitation to run for mayor of Tel Aviv. In this courtship time he was going slow, being not coy but careful. Committing himself would be easy. Making a wrong move which he would regret for years might be even easier. At his age the margin for recovery from wrong moves was shrinking.

"I've trained and rehearsed in a dress. No problem," Amos said. "The target's a luxury high-rise, where ladies come and go. Some of those PLO big shots screw whores at all hours of the night. We strike at one in the morning. It makes sense."

"All right, you land on the beach. How do you get from there into Beirut?"

"Mossad guys, passing as rich European businessmen, will be waiting. They've rented cars."

"Let's say the cars aren't there."

"Then I guess we abort. They'll be there."

"Traffic in Beirut is a mess. How can you keep to a timetable? Moreover — what are you smiling at?"

"Dado called us in yesterday, and asked those same questions and plenty more. He's satisfied with the plan. So is Moshe Dayan, and he's been keeping track of our training for months. He kept postponing the raid until the American diplomats incident came along. Great instinct."

"But what about your tank battalion? How could you leave your command for this devilry?"

"They sent out the call for Sayeret Matkhal veterans months ago. I volunteered, and my brigade commander approved."

"Well, I hope this is the last time. You've done enough special jobs. You've got your decorations, Amos. Your future is in the tanks."

"You just don't want me to have a good time, Abba, the way you did."

The telephone rang. Pasternak grunted and pressed an intercom buzzer. "I told you, no telephone calls."

The secretary croaked in the box, "It's Mrs. Nitzan. She says it's important."

Sam glanced at his son, whose face went blank. "I'll call her back."

"Abba, this is an excellent plan," Amos said. "We've rehearsed it down to seconds."

"I've rehearsed many such plans. Some successful. Some not so successful."

"I know that. Dado said to us, *'The deeper you go behind the lines, the greater the surprise, and the better your chances for success.'* I believe he's right, and we'll soon see."

Pasternak's stern look faded in a laugh. "Okay, I've already studied the plan." Senior Israeli officers after retiring tended to stay in touch as consultants. "In fact I contributed a detail or two. I'm still welcome as a kibitzer at the Mossad. I'll probably be in the Pit to hear how it goes." He came out from behind the desk and they hugged each other. "One thing, Amos. Has Colonel Shaked drilled you to bring out not only the wounded but the dead, if there's trouble? *At all cost?*"

"That's doctrine, Abba."

"It's more than doctrine. Your raid may be a big success, but if the Fatah gets one Jewish boy's body, they'll claim a victory. They'll blackmail us to trade for his body all the terrorists we've got in jail, and for millions of dollars, too. They'll hang the body upside down in a public square. They'll stage dancing crowds for American television. They think that's good public relations."

"You exaggerate, but we'll bring out our casualties. I hope there won't be any." Another embrace, and the son left. Staring out the window, Sam returned Amos's wave from his car across the street.

Scratchy voice on the intercom: "General, Eva Sonshine called. Her mother's back in the hospital. Dinner is off. She'll phone you at home later and may come by."

"Anyone else?"

"Uzi Rubin. He wants you to return his call." This was the chairman of a heavy-industry conglomerate.

"Get Mrs. Nitzan."

Dead of night.

Three hundred yards from the landing beach, Noah's boat was barely moving on a black glassy sea. The city glow on low clouds shed a sort of artificial moonlight over sea and shore. The cluster lamps of the promenade lined the cliff above the beach, and neon signs glittered and jumped, blue, red, white, yellow. "Could almost be Tel Aviv," said Colonel Shaked, the raid commander. A lean bespectacled officer in uniform, Shaked was remaining aboard the boat to control the many-pronged operation by wireless network linked to the Pit, the underground command center in Tel Aviv.

"Engines stop," Noah ordered. "Prepare Zodiacs for launching. Raiding party prepare to disembark."

"There go the headlights," said Amos. The automobiles on the shore were blinking: two flashes, pause, two flashes, darkness. After a full minute, the signal repeated.

"So, Amos, you move," said Colonel Shaked.

Heavy splash of rubber boats. Lighter splashes of frogmen who would tow them in; silent approach, not even putt-putting of outboard motors. Noah shook hands with Amos, and Colonel Shaked accompanied the unit leader to the deck. The raiders, in shabby city clothes, went climbing down jingling chain ladders, Amos in a hiked-up red wool dress. Sea and wind conditions lucky, thought Noah. Gentle swell, light offshore breeze. In a fresh wind the frogmen would have had problems pulling in those high-riding Zodiacs, which now moved off smoothly and melted into the night. Colonel Shaked returned to the bridge and put on headphones. Side by side he and Noah watched the promenade with binoculars until the cars pulled away. "Unit Amos en route to target," Noah heard Shaked report to the Pit. The commander laughed and turned to him. "Dado says, 'Keep calm,' " he told Noah.

The phosphorescent bridge clock read a quarter to one. "What do you hear from the other units?" Noah ventured to ask Colonel Shaked.

"Holding to plan. So far, so good," said Shaked, and he dropped down the ladder to the control and communications center. Overhead Noah heard the thudding of a rescue helicopter showing no lights.

Under the bright globe of a promenade light, a man at the wheel of a Mercedes gave Amos a waggish greeting as he was sliding into the front seat. "*Giveret* [Madame], how's your father?" A woman made room for Amos, a real one, apparently a real blonde, and by the streetlights, quite attractive; especially compared to the phony blonde, a very tough-looking paratrooper under the wig, who was getting into the other car, a Buick.

"He's fine."

"Great gentleman, your father." The pudgy driver wore a dark Italian-cut suit and several gold rings. He had the beautifully waved gray hair of a European man of affairs, maybe an importer or a banker; much too soft and sleek a fellow, one would have thought, to be anything else. Amos glanced over to the other car, where all his paratroopers were now inside. The blond-wigged one gave a thumbs-up.

"Yallah," Amos said.

The Mercedes drove out into a boulevard jammed with traffic, much resembling Hayarkon Road on the Tel Aviv beachfront. Altogether Beirut was an Arab Tel Aviv: squat old structures and towering new office buildings, shabby shops, fancy shops, and brightly lit cafés lined higgledy-piggledy along the avenues. In the dark narrow side streets the buildings were tumbledown, the pavements full of potholes. Just like home! The driver led the other car in a zigzag route through the city, getting directions in French at each turn from the blond woman. Amos broke his silence to say in French, "You know this city pretty well."

"Born and raised in Beirut. In the good old days, Papa was in business here." She smiled at Amos. "You look very pretty."

"Sorry I'm getting you all wet." The Zodiac had shipped much water, soaking Amos's shoes and nylons and bedraggling his dress.

"Let that be my worst problem tonight."

This was his first reprisal raid scented with costly French perfume, thought Amos, quite a change from helicopter drops near terrorist bases, or stealthy night crossings of borders in the wilds. Northwest Beirut was a neighborhood of imposing walled villas, and high-rise flats with large corner balconies, very much like the wealthy district of north Tel Aviv where they had rehearsed every move of this raid. The car halted for a moment in the Rue de Verdun at a darkened two-story villa, with tall palms poking over the high garden wall, before going on. "This is where we'll be posted," said the woman, "until you come out."

The Buick went by with the squad that would provide cover for Amos's attack on the apartment house. Another assault unit had turned off in different cars to hit the headquarters building. Amos's eye was on his wristwatch, for the two strikes had to be simultaneous. "B'seder, we go," he said. Across the street from the apartment house, two Arabs, guns slung on their shoulders, were talking and smoking cigarettes. They quite ignored the Mercedes as it drove up and stopped; obviously, as intelligence had reported, such posh cars came and went here all the time.

"Bonne chance," murmured the woman as the car drove off.

Amos and his three companions strolled nonchalantly into the house under the eyes of the guards. Toughest moment. Pounding heart. Okay, all the way in, beyond the streetlight. One remained in the dim lobby, Amos and the other two bounded upstairs, each to his assigned floor. *Deep penetration, total surprise.* So it was working out. Behind this third-floor door, Amos's target, was Abu Youssef, the planner of the Munich massacre, and the real brains of the Arab terror network strewing death worldwide. Silencer on the gun. Shoot off the locks and hinges. No misfire of the silencer, thank God, no gunshot, just crunches of metal. Through the doorway! A light snapped on far inside the flat. Amos raced to that room. There naked under a blanket was the black-bearded Abu Youssef, unmistakable from his photographs, beside a naked woman, both staring at him in sleepy shock. Rotten job, but this was it, and he killed them both with four shots, mere muffled thumps; they scarcely moved as they moaned and bled and died. In a smell of gun smoke, he hurried through the flat looking for documents and record books, swept whatever he found into a suitcase from which he dumped a woman's clothes, and went out to the landing.

There he waited and listened. Eerie quiet on this staircase! What was going on above? Amos leaped up three flights, saw an open door, and sidled inside with gun at the ready. On a rich carpet in the large front room a clothed mustached man lay dead, blood pooling in his long black hair. A broken venetian blind dangled in the window, and beside it was one of his men, Yoni, pulling documents from a bookcase. "Amos, this stuff is gold," he said in a conversational tone, riffling the papers. He gestured at books, pamphlets, and documents he was piling on a chair. "Take a look."

"Listen, take what you can grab and let's go."

"*En lahatz* [No pressure], don't rush." Yoni glanced at his watch. "This is a rare opportunity." He took down more papers and rapidly scanned them.

Amos Pasternak prided himself on keeping his head in tough spots, and he had proved himself often. But in some ways, this old friend was beyond him. Yoni Netanyahu had served with him in Sayeret Matkhal years ago, then had left the army to study at Harvard. Now he was back without having completed his degree; a small guy with a slight physique hardened by exercise and willpower to iron and wire, and kept so despite a grave wound in the Six-Day War. His coolness now was infectious. Certainly he was right, this intelligence bonanza could save hundreds of lives. It could even crack the whole terror network. "Okay, but be quick about it —"

BRATATAT, BANG, BANG! Amos jumped to the open window. Machine-gun bursts outside, cracks of rifles. "It's the headquarters building, Yoni. I see the flashes. Trouble. Yallah!"

"Sure. What can I carry this stuff in?" Yoni looked here and there. "A pillowcase, maybe. Just a second."

In the Pit, the cigarette smoke as always was thick and foul. Senior officers paced the enormous map-lined room, Sam Pasternak among them. At a table with a microphone General Elazar and Moshe Dayan sat side by side. "Mano Shaked, Mano Shaked, this is Dado. Say again, what has gone wrong?"

Reply from an overhead loudspeaker, harsh with static but understandable. *"This is Mano. The boys killed the guards outside the headquarters, according to plan. But a machine gun has just opened up from across the street, from some kind of truck or van, and — wait, I'm getting another report."*

Deep silence in the room. Crackling of static. Rasp and flaming of cigarette lighters.

"Okay, this is Mano. Five of our guys are down. The van has been silenced, but more guards are coming and firing. The demolition squad inquires whether to go into the building or abort."

The Ramatkhal and Dayan looked at each other. Dayan shrugged. Dado said briskly, "He's the guy on the spot," and spoke into the microphone. "Mano, this is Dado. What do you recommend?"

"I say proceed with demolition. We have good supporting fire. I'll send reenforcements to cover withdrawal."

"Approved."

As the most iron-nerved airline pilot agonizes through a storm when he is only a passenger, because he knows the hazards and cannot act, so Sam Pasternak was shaken by this turn. Amos was attacking a different building, but still the whole raid was already compromised. The gun battle was bound to alert the lax Lebanese police, and army units too might roll. A fast withdrawal to the beach was the raiders' best chance. Once trapped in Beirut, they would be overwhelmed and captured, if not gunned down forthwith.

Sayeret Matkhal in Arab hands! Blindfolded and chained prisoners on world television, a mockery of Israel's prowess, an ineradicable disgrace! Moreover high Lebanese politicians were hand in glove with the terrorists, that was known, and prison in Lebanon was no haven. Lynching, kidnapping, vanishing, death by mutilation — all real possibilities. An interminable tumble of army jargon on the signal channel, but from the demolition unit no further word. Since the landing, nothing at all from Amos. Sharp voice of Colonel Shaked cutting through, ordering all units to clear the channel.

"Dado from Mano. No word from apartment unit. Headquarters unit has fought its way out against police and terrorist fire and is heading for the beach, bringing out all casualties."

Dayan leaned to the microphone and pressed the button. "Mano, this is Dayan. Was the demolition carried out?"

"Minister, they set the explosives, but they've been in a running gunfight, shooting from their cars. They don't know."

With a headshake at Dado, Dayan let him have the microphone.

"Mano from Dado. What casualties?"

"This is Mano. Two lightly wounded, one severely." Somber looks around the room. Pause. Mano's voice again: *"Two dead. Hagai Ma'ayan and Avida Shor."*

Crackling of static. With a noisy scrape of his chair, Dayan got to his feet. "*Fashla* [Fuckup]," he said drily, and walked out. Some officers drifted after him. Dado slumped at the microphone, his rugged face a tragic mask in the bleak fluorescent light. Reports kept trickling in. Pasternak's pulse thumped to hear, *"This is Mano. Apartment Unit Amos now safe on board* Gaash. *Mission carried out, three terrorist chiefs killed, two boys lightly wounded."* Dado managed a wan smile at Pasternak.

Within an hour the picture was clear. The entire raiding force, with the Mossad agents who had met them in the cars, were aboard the boats and heading home. At Haifa's Maimonides Hospital the helicopter had unloaded the wounded and the dead. The high wall clock showed a few minutes past three. Dado stretched, yawned, and spoke after a long wordless time. "Well, Sam, your Amos did valiantly. All the boys did. Still, Moshe's right. Fashla."

"Dado, they got the leaders."

Dado leaned his head in his hands. "Two of our boys, just for those three murdering bastards?" The telephone at his elbow rang. He picked it up. "Dado here. What?" His face brightened. "Well, did you record all that? . . . Excellent, rush the tape over to my office. . . . Look, Sam Pasternak's here, tell him." Dado handed him the phone. "In America the raid's on the evening news." He went striding out to the steep staircase.

Slow deep voice of the new Mossad chief. "Sam? The raid is the big news on American TV and radio. They're interrupting regular programs. The story's already coming out of Beirut, uncensored. First of all, the terrorist headquarters building was totally demolished —"

"Aha! That's definite?"

"Blown to a big pile of rubble."

"What's the American reaction so far?"

"Positive, admiring, and they're all citing the Munich massacre of our athletes, and the murder of their two diplomats in Sudan."

The big surprise so far, the Mossad chief went on, was the candor of the Lebanese authorities. They had immediately disclosed the name of the chief terrorists who had been killed, and were allowing cameras at the headquarters building, where rescuers were digging for PLO personnel who might be buried in the flattened ruins. No neighboring structures had been damaged.

Sam broke in, "You're sure of that? Amos told me there was a big dispute over the exact weight of explosives they would need, so as not to injure civilians."

"Somebody guessed right. The building's a wreck, nothing else touched. That's what our consul saw on New York TV. I just got off the phone with him. Sam, it's an international success, a masterstroke."

"Two boys died," Pasternak said.

"I know, I know. Avida Shor and Hagai Ma'ayan, kibbutznik volunteers, just kids. The cost, always the cost! But go and listen to Naftali's tapes, Sam, those boys died for something great."

Mediterranean weather can change fast. At sunrise the wind was whipping up whitecaps, and even entering Haifa harbor the *Gaash* was rolling and pitching. On the unsteady bridge Amos and

Noah were peering through binoculars toward the pier. "Quite a welcoming party out there," Noah said. "The Defense Minister, the admiral —"

Amos exclaimed, "There's my father, by my life! Why the devil did he drag himself to Haifa?"

The blond woman, climbing the ladder to the bridge in a white sweater and tan slacks, overheard this. "*Bonjour*. Which one is your father?"

"Ah, *bonjour*." Amos handed her the binoculars. "He's the short man on Dayan's left."

"So, that's General Pasternak." The wind tossed her loose yellow hair and the pink scarf flung around her neck. In strong morning sunlight she still looked fetching, though decidedly older than Amos; slim, heavily tanned, her bony face alive with excitement. "Hm, quite a resemblance. *Ai!*" She fell sideways against him, and he steadied her with an arm. "*Merci, monsieur.*"

Amos was bleary from writing up his report in the wobbly wardroom, and also bone-tired, but not too tired to feel a stir in his loins. His smile, as the woman returned the glasses, was more than polite. "Did you get any sleep?"

"*Ah, oui!* That cosy cabin of yours! Rocked like a baby. *Ai!*" Another cry as the wind snatched at her scarf, tore it from her neck, and fluttered it aft, out of sight.

Amos said, "The Israeli government owes you a scarf."

"Most assuredly."

When the *Gaash* tied up, the raiders were all on deck, a ragtag unshaven lot, and the crew was mustered at attention. Assorted high brass who were in on the secret operation came aboard and went shaking the hand of every raider, one by one.

"For victory, many fathers," laughed the blonde, leaving the bridge. Sam Pasternak stood aside from the ladder to let her pass, then came up and bear-hugged his son. "Go shake hands with the big shots, my boy."

"Abba, you look awful. When did you sleep last?"

"Well, now I'll sleep."

Amos saw the Frenchwoman descending the gangplank with the Mossad men from Beirut. "Excuse me, Abba." He hurried after them, and intercepted the woman as she was about to get into a car.

"Goodbye," he said to her, "and many thanks."

"Mais pourquoi? Au revoir."

"Look, how do I get in touch with you?" She faintly smiled. "I mean it. What's your name?"

"Ah, Major, it's all over, but I won't forget the pretty lady with the cold clammy stockings and the wet clothes. What was her name, by the way?"

"Her name?" He laughed. "She didn't exist."

"*Justement*. Neither do I, Pasternak *fils*."

As he stared after the departing car, his father came beside him. "Abba, who was she?"

"Nobody. A volunteer, recruited for the purpose. Amos, it was a great coup, it's the talk of the media. Of the world. Well done."

"We had losses, Abba."

Pasternak nodded. "I heard. Now you had better get back to your battalion."

"Why? Something doing down south?" Amos asked wearily.

"Heavy enemy troop movements, Amos, on the Sinai and Syrian fronts. Supposedly war games, but the estimate is that these may not be games."

"Let them start something," said Amos, aroused out of his fatigue. "It'll be a slaughter, and then maybe there'll be peace."

Pasternak kept to himself, secrecy being second nature to him, that in the innermost government circle a state of highest alert already prevailed for a possible enemy surprise attack on May fifteenth during the Independence Day parade; code name for the crisis, BLUE/WHITE.

15

The Big Parade

Amos and Noah snapped to attention with the other raid leaders and missile boat captains, all in dress uniform, as the Prime Minister entered an anteroom of her office where a few select onlookers waited, including the Minister of Defense and the Ramatkhal, who had just concluded with her an urgent conference on BLUE/WHITE. Sam Pasternak had been invited to see his son honored, and Zev Barak came in with Golda, for he was now her military secretary, probably his last army assignment.

When upon his return, she had asked him face to face to take it on, he realized that sector command had gone glimmering. He had been away too long. So close to power, though wielding none, he figured that he could at least speak the plain truth to Golda Meir whenever asked, and that too would serve the Jewish State. For from his Washington-acquired perspective, the truth about his euphoric country's situation was somber. Perhaps that was why she had chosen him. She had already dubbed him Reb Ma'azik, Mr. Alarmist. Anyway, how could he have refused the Prime Minister?

On his visits home during his attaché years it had sometimes struck Zev Barak that Israel was a sort of asteroid, floating somewhere near the earth but not quite of it. Now that he was back from America for good he was recovering his roots, sinking into the

Israeli frame of mind, enjoying the sense of being truly home at last, but the outlook of his Viennese boyhood still caused him to look about askance at the complacency prevailing in the little land. When all was said and done, he was a transplant, and perhaps that had given him his fatal skill at "handling Americans"; if there really was anything to that image, which had shaped and in effect closed down his army career. Still, he was back in the bosom of the family he loved, walking the soil of Zion he loved, and there stood his son, a hero among heroes, about to be honored by the Prime Minister of the Jewish State. Good enough. He had no complaints against the old Jewish God.

"It's a hard thing, my dear young heroes," Golda was beginning hoarsely, "that the brave achievements of the elite services can't be publicly recognized. Some of your boldest feats may have to go unsung for a hundred years. By then my generation and yours will all be dead, and forgotten from men's hearts."

The stately sentences rolled as though they had been written out for her. But Zev Barak, whose eyes moistened at seeing Noah in his dress whites, knew that the words were extemporaneous, since he now drafted most of her written utterances.

"However, when the records are opened at last, the world will learn what great deeds young Jewish fighters like you performed in the early years of our struggle to survive. Then with God's help we will be living at peace with our Arab neighbors. Perhaps then, even they will join the world in saying, *'This was a Jewish generation like Joshua's.'* For now, speaking for the Jewish people, I can only humbly thank and bless you." One by one she shook hands with all of them and trudged off into her office, followed by the ministers and generals.

Zev Barak stopped to shake his son's hand. "Kol ha'kavod."

"Abba, all I did was run a ferryboat."

"You brought them there and back. The operation was a great gamble. The navy gave us an extra dimension of capability. Well done. Do you have time to see your mother?"

"I will, Abba."

"Good, good. She hasn't been too well."

Sam Pasternak left with Amos to drive him to the Sde Dov

airfield. His ancient Peugeot twice stalled on the way, causing angry honking from the heavy traffic, already much thickened by the rental cars of tourists who were piling into Israel for the big military parade celebrating the Twenty-fifth Independence Day. "Time you got yourself a new machine," said Amos, "and a driver."

"I can't afford either. Yonatan wants to come and work for me." Yonatan had been his army and Mossad driver for seventeen years. "When somebody hires me, I'll hire him. I'm still looking around."

"I'd like to see you in politics."

"What, and be a *kabtzan* [beggar] the rest of my life? I'm already having a taste of it, and I don't like it."

"Well, this rotten political system can't go on, Abba. It's a worse danger to our survival than the Arabs."

"So everyone's been saying since 1948, and here we are." Pasternak abruptly changed the subject. "Now, what about that bridge project? Are you really involved with it?"

"Well, one of my companies will be doing the towing, yes."

"Isn't the thing a monstrosity? A fashla? So I've heard."

"Not at all. The idea is a stroke of genius. Whether it will work —"

"*What* is the idea? Why, to all the devils, a giant mobile bridge, a thousand feet long and weighing seven hundred insane tons, that travels on rollers?"

"Those aren't the figures. How much do you know about it?"

Maneuvering the car past a pileup of snorting busses, Pasternak almost shouted, "Not much, not my field."

Amos described the concept, and the present state of the incomplete bridge. His father nodded as he listened, pursing his lips in disapproval. "No wonder it's eaten such a hole in the army budget."

"Well, it's a colossal job, but it may indeed win a war, if we have one. *'Carry the war to the enemy!'* Not that I think the Arabs are really about to start anything." He looked keenly at his father, who returned not a word.

Driving through the guarded airfield gate, Pasternak saw Yael Nitzan's red Oldsmobile parked, and her son Aryeh nosing around a small army transport plane, recognizable mainly by his blond curls, tall as he now was. He came loping toward Amos in the long effortless leaps of a cheetah, as Sam Pasternak entered the terminal hut. "Amos! Ma nishma? I ran ten miles yesterday with some Gadna guys." Gadna was a paramilitary youth troop.

"Don't push yourself too much. You're still growing."

"It was easy." Aryeh's eyes shone, and he laid a hand on Amos's arm. "Oo-wah, that Beirut raid. I bet you were in it. Were you?"

Amos's face stiffened. "Learn not to ask childish questions."

Aryeh said meekly, "Sorry."

"Okay. I'm a tank battalion commander in Sinai, and whoever did that raid won't talk about it, maybe not for years. Ten miles, eh? With a sand pack?"

"The Gadna guys wore packs. I didn't."

"That was sensible."

Sam Pasternak found the Nitzans inside the hut. "Yossi, your battalion commander's outside with Aryeh," Pasternak said, drawing lukewarm coffee from an urn, "ready to return to Sinai."

"No rush. Sharon's not here yet." Yossi Nitzan looked a lot older to Pasternak these days. The antic Don Kishote was metamorphosing into a hard-driving colonel, sure to make brigadier and a front-runner for higher posts.

"Well, Sam, how are you?" said Yael. "What are you doing with yourself?"

"Collecting unemployment insurance, Yael, and looking for work."

"Oh, you," she laughed. "You'll land on your feet, I bet, if you haven't already."

The sharpest Mossad agent, thought Pasternak, could not detect that she was faking, that in recent weeks they had been talking long, earnestly, and often on the phone. In her fashion Yael was unbeatable.

General Sharon ambled in. "Sam, good to see you." He took a coffee cake from the plate by the urn and wolfed it, smiling at Yael. "Hello, darling. I've eaten nothing all day." His ogre reputation made the pleasantry very engaging. Yael said her goodbyes and walked out. On the instant Sharon's smile changed to a glare.

"Kishote, you know who they've picked to relieve me? Gorodish. *Gorodish*!" He turned on Pasternak. "Do you believe it? Gorodish, commanding the southern sector? Gorodish, versus the Egyptian army? *Gorodish*?"

Pasternak was in fact surprised. Shmuel "Gorodish" Gonen was a good armor officer and a Dado favorite, but junior to other qualified generals. A clash of cliques in the army, complicated by civilian party politics, must have brought this about. "Well, Arik, Shmuel's a tough field commander."

"He is that," said Yossi. "I was his number two in the Six-Day War."

"I know you were," Sharon snapped. "But you've been observing those Egyptians across the Canal, Kishote. It's a different army today. Their uniforms, their maneuvers, their discipline, their *numbers*."

Pasternak said, "Well, to be frank, I'd be happier if you were remaining in the south, Arik, at least until they stand down from those war games. They and the Syrians."

Sharon threw up meaty hands. "Sam, the cabal has done its job, and I'm out. A farmer I was, a farmer I've always wanted to be again. If there's a war, and to me it looks like fifty-fifty right now — I can't tell those Arab war games from a mobilization, myself — it'll all be up to the brigade and battalion commanders, and to you, Don Kishote, to you. *Gorodish!* Let's go."

As Barak drove home, gloomy sentences and paragraphs were forming in his mind. Golda had asked him for a written comment on the BLUE/WHITE alert.

On every side he saw preparations for the big Independence Day parade: banners, bunting, flags, placards, bleachers, grandstands. All Jerusalem was breaking out in festive blue and white to hail the *"great march of the New Jew,"* as the exultant newspaper rhetoric went; the Jew of the straight back, the Jew who had risen like the phoenix from the fires of Nazi Europe to go home again and reclaim the Holy Land. And this display of Israel's armed forces, which for twenty-five years had beaten off Arab attempts to wipe out the new Zion, would be a simple peaceful warning, *"Don't tread on me."* Some politicians were decrying the expense of the martial extravaganza, and some academics and editorial writers were clucking at such arrogant un-Jewish imagery, but their spoilsport voices were few and lost.

Ever since coming home, Zev Barak had felt out of step with this exultant mood. Had he been away too long, after all? The giant United States was in a morass of worry and self-doubt over Vietnam, a war ten thousand miles away; and miniscule Israel, with huge enemy forces maneuvering at its very borders, was acting cock-of-the-walk. Like their idol, the Minister of Defense, most Israelis these days seemed to be seeing things through one eye.

He found Nakhama busy in the kitchen, where there was an appetizing smell of roast lamb. She flashed her old smile, which he had not been seeing of late. "Galia is bringing Dov Luria to dinner."

"Oo-wah, so she's caught herself a Phantom pilot. Not bad."

"Well, let's say he's circling her. And Noah came by. So handsome! Why was he called to the Prime Minister? Can you say?"

He shook his head. As he bent to kiss her, she turned her cheek, her usual way since his homecoming. With a shrug he went to his den, took a writing pad to the armchair, and began scrawling.

April 18, 1973

My dear Madame Prime Minister:

As your Reb Alarmist I am against the very grave decision not to go public with the Blue/White alert. General Zeira states that the Arabs now can strike heavy blows on both borders but that the chance of their doing it is "very low." That is his estimate as chief of military intelligence, but he is one man, calculating *intentions*. I reply that it is irrelevant whether the enemy maneuvers are innocuous war games, or another Sadat cry of "wolf," or a political nudge to the superpowers. They can also be a start toward a war. The *capability* exists. That is what matters.

I know something about the Americans. Most Israelis, including you, Madame Prime Minister, can't quite fathom what the Watergate fuss is all about, but believe me, the Nixon presidency is disintegrating. An Arab offensive now would jeopardize the détente with the Soviet Union, with which a desperate Nixon hopes to revitalize his wounded image. Our going public with Blue/White would if anything galvanize him into warning the Arabs to cut out the troublemaking. That's my estimate.

Madame Prime Minister, you will bear a ghastly historical responsibility if, knowing the threat, you fail to share the truth with the people, and then a war ensues. Why not consider, at least, calling off the big parade? What clearer signal could be sent to our enemies and to the superpowers that we are on guard and mean business? Tourism must take second place to security, surely.

The Arabs will keep trying war until they are convinced that the price for land is a treaty of peace, and nothing else. They are now in all respects ready to try war once more. Blue/White should become an alert of the nation, not just of your kitchen cabinet. To do otherwise, given the facts at our borders, gambles with the survival of the Jewish State —

He was trying to think of a less apocalyptic way to finish when his daughter Ruti looked in. "Galia's here with Dov. Dinner is ready."

"I'm coming."

"Dov's brought a nice present. And Mama told me to give you this." She dropped on the desk a gray envelope with a red-white-and-blue airmail stripe, and no return address. Emily? Had it crossed his letter, asking her to write no more? He had done this hoping to pull Nakhama out of the dumps, for something was clearly amiss. He closed the door, ripped open the envelope, and found two handwritten lines on a plain white sheet.

Wolf dearest,

I completely understand. Until I hear otherwise from you, mum's the word. I love you always.

Queenie

He shredded the letter into the wastebasket and went into the dining room, where the girls and Nakhama were admiring a small glazed statuette of a stout woman in biblical robes, dancing with a tambourine. The name scratched on the base was MIRIAM, but the gnarled face was clearly Golda Meir's.

"My sister's getting pretty good at this," Dov said. "She's even sold a few things. Cats. Americans buy cats. Cats and menorahs."

"I think it's wonderful," said Galia, looking radiantly at the Phantom pilot, who wore faded jeans and a short-sleeved white shirt. He kept a modest mien at dinner, praising Nakhama's lamb and rice, eating heartily, and scarcely looking at the girl he was visiting. He opened up only when Ruti asked if the air force would be in the parade.

"Oh, sure, we'll do a flyover. We rehearsed it this morning, in fact." He turned to Barak with a grin. "Just before Golda makes her speech, sir, the Phantoms will pass over Jerusalem in a Star of David formation. It was mighty ragged today, but we'll get it right."

"The people will go wild!" exclaimed Galia.

"Look here, Dov," said Barak. "Suppose the Arabs take it into their heads, while you're flying your Star of David over Golda, to launch attacks at the Canal and on the Golan Heights?"

"We have a contingency plan for that," Dov returned, with a short nod. "If they're interested in committing suicide, we can accommodate them."

From all over the world, in trains, planes, and ships, more than a hundred thousand tourists were converging to watch and to cheer the great military parade in Jerusalem marking Israel's twenty-fifth Independence Day. In Southampton the *Queen Elizabeth II*, about to sail on a gala Passover cruise to Haifa, was chockablock with happy Jews booked to celebrate the festival at sea en route, and last-minute arrivals were hurrying up the gangways. Among them were the tanned blond lady of the Beirut raid and her natty little husband, who as they came aboard gave their names to the first-class steward as Armand and Irene Fleg.

"I had better check in the dining salon, my dear," said her husband, as they unpacked in a luxury suite, "to make sure all is in order. As you know, matzo disagrees with me, binds me up like concrete."

He had arranged for seating at the captain's table, where he would be sure of eating British cuisine, bread included. They were travelling by ship because he hated to fly, especially with terrorists machine-gunning airports and hijacking planes. The rumors of a possible submarine attack on the great ship, M. Fleg shrugged off. A third-generation Parisian Jew, he was quite indifferent to Passover rules and customs, but the *Queen Elizabeth II* had ten rabbis aboard to conduct seders and services for seven hundred passengers, and the cruise was billed as strictly kosher, which, if serious, meant matzo instead of bread for Jewish passengers.

"Yes, dear, you —" Three thunderous blasts of the foghorn drowned her out. "Yes, you do that, my dear," she said, her ears ringing. "I'll go up on deck."

RAF fighters were snarling overhead as the great liner backed out of the berth and a brass band blared "Rule, Britannia" and then "Hatikvah." On the crowded promenade deck, unmindful of a gray drizzle, passengers laughed, cheered, and wept, throwing colored streamers and confetti to the shouting well-wishers on shore. The blond lady went climbing up and up to the deserted rainy boat deck, where she leaned on the rail to watch the shore slip away as the *Queen* speeded up, heading out to sea in thickening rain. The tumult on the promenade deck below died down, the deck trembled, and the blond lady's spirits lifted.

Israel ahead! Lovely, lively, grubby, parochial, claustrophobic Israel, no place for anyone used to elegance or even comfort; but the place where one saw those bronzed young men in field-green uniforms, and the army girls in perky black caps and beige miniskirts; quite a change from the pale timorous Jewish youngsters of her own childhood and youth in Beirut and Paris. It did one's heart good to glimpse them now and then. Staring out at mounting waves, gray-green as Zahal uniforms, the lady idly wondered whether by chance in the big parade she would catch sight of that interesting Pasternak *fils*.

Irene Fleg's recruitment for the Beirut raid had been a bizarre series of chances that in retrospect made her wonder at herself, and to thank God that she had emerged safe. To this day her husband knew nothing about it, and almost it seemed like a dream. That young Pasternak, at first in his preposterous female disguise, and next morning as a brawny round-faced soldier in a green army sweater and woolen cap, was a dream figure, and he was haunting her here on the weather deck of the *Queen Elizabeth II*. The rain on her face and the gusty sea wind were conducive to romantic thoughts. It was a good while before she reluctantly went below.

At the captain's table that night, as the *Queen* majestically rolled in a storm, the stout gray-haired captain steered the talk away from Middle East politics to the far-off Vietnam war, the latest movies, and the snowballing scandals of Watergate. While a jocund Hebraic tumult of Passover songs and chants resounded from three enormous horseshoe-shaped seder tables, he maintained a tolerant Christian beam, and over the dessert wine he disclosed half-humorously to his table guests, mainly journalists and broadcasters, that there were fifty security agents aboard. "That is, British agents whom we know about. Perhaps the Israelis have booked on a few as well, and if so more power to them. They're very capable." His eyes twinkled. "I've even been told that one of the rabbis is a Mossad man. That would be a most effective disguise." Chuckles from the guests. "At any rate, we can all sleep soundly on this voyage. Weather permitting — and we'll soon be through this bit of weather — I will myself."

Barak's forebodings continued to plague him at the parade rehearsal which Golda sent him to observe. As the masses of machines went clanking and snorting through flag-lined streets of East Jerusalem, all shut up and silent but for swarthy Arab urchins running about, and old men glowering from doorways, it more and more seemed to him a costly thunderous mistake, as well as an invitation for an onslaught at the borders. Of the BLUE/WHITE alert, the jocund Israeli public was utterly unaware.

But the real parade on Independence Day, as it rolled before the reviewing stand, at last broke through the thick crust of his detached pessimism. The bands marching past played the great songs of the old days — "Shoshanna," "Finjan," "Sycamore Garden," "Eretz Eretz" — and despite himself his spine thrilled. As the orderly hordes of war machines growled through the cheering sidewalk crowds, where children on their fathers' shoulders were waving thousands of little blue-and-white paper flags, the machines themselves were incongruously festooned with flowers, as though to say, *We look and sound terrifying but we mean peace.* Primitive 1948 weapons and captured Soviet machines headed each section. Ahead of the huge self-propelled cannon pottered the ludicrous little Davidka and Napoleonchik; ahead of the Centurion and Sherman battalions and the giant T-55s, a few toylike Hotchkiss and Cromwell tanks; ahead of the armored personnel carriers, the crude "sandwiches," the steel-plated old busses that had run the blockade of Jerusalem. He remembered riding up that perilous road through shellfire in those creeping groaning sandwiches; he remembered wondering, as he drove out to Latrun, whether Ben Gurion's "state" would last a month.

The female soldiers marching like men, the navy in dazzling white, the red-beret paratroopers with rigid backs and faultless ranks and files — the cumulative power of these stirring shows was too much even for Mr. Alarmist. Through the cracks in his skepticism gushed old old feelings and memories, a freshet of Zionist enthusiasm, of youthful joy in the birth of the Jewish State, in fighting for it, in winning the Independence War, in being a New Jew, free of the terrors of Europe. Cheers and applause louder than ever rose from the thronged Israelis as the air force planes appeared in the distance. The Phantoms came roaring overhead, a vast perfect six-pointed star in the clear blue Jerusalem heavens. Golda Meir, sitting in the row in front of him, between President Shazar and Moshe Dayan, turned around and caught Zev Barak's eye.

"Nu, Mr. Alarmist?" he heard her say over the Phantom roar, and he was able to laugh with her at himself. He had been wrong, General Zeira right. Whether there had never been a real danger, or whether Dado's vigorous quiet preparations had discouraged Sadat — speed-up of road-building and fortification construction, establishment of vast emergency stores and ammunition dumps near the fronts, and forward positioning of masses of tanks — the borders were quiet. No whisper of danger dimmed the glory of the big parade.

Michael and Shayna Berkowitz came with Dzecki's parents from Haifa for the parade, so they all dined afterward with the Baraks, and Nakhama served cold dishes of vegetables and fish on paper plates. Michael was pale and thinner, and Shayna seemed low. They had been trying in vain, Barak knew, to have a child. When Shayna asked Barak in an aside how Don Kishote was doing in the Sinai, and he said Yossi was an ever-rising army star, she briefly glowed as Galia had at her Phantom pilot, and he felt very sorry for her.

Dzecki's father said that the parade had been an eye-opener. At last he understood why Dzecki had made aliya. He balanced this concession with pungent stories of the troubles he was encountering in his Haifa real estate deals with slippery sellers, lying contractors, obfuscating lawyers and immovable Haifa *pakkidim* (bureaucrats). "All the same," he said, "Dzecki and I have acquired some great properties, and we've found a real friend in a Mr. Gulinkoff, a reliable wealthy individual, and a very disinterested adviser. We're going to show these people the American way to make money. Dzecki's Hebrew is my ace in the hole. Nothing gets past him on paper or in a meeting."

Mrs. Barkowe said, "It's a pity he had to miss that wonderful parade."

"Somebody has to stand guard in Sinai," said Shayna. "I admire your son."

"He didn't have to reenlist," complained Mrs. Barkowe. "I tried to press him about that, but he only mumbled nonsense about some stupid bridge. I'll never agree with my husband. Jack's crazy. He wouldn't be missed if he'd go home, and then we all could."

Irene and Armand Fleg watched the parade in a small section of the main grandstand reserved for the Alliance Israelite Universelle. Glancing around during Golda's sonorous speech after the Phantom flypast, she caught sight of General Pasternak in a top row. When the ceremonies ended and the government leaders left, people came pouring out of the stand, behind the mounted policemen who brought up the rear of the parade; and Irene Fleg managed to meet Pasternak as he came down the tiers, escorting a dark-haired woman who had the sheen of an actress or model.

"Why, hello, General Pasternak. A memorable parade, eh?"

Astonished and nonplussed, then recognizing her from the brief brush on the missile boat, he grunted a hello.

"How is your son?"

"Quite all right."

She said hurriedly, "Do you have a card?"

Wordlessly he took one from his wallet. She appeared next day at his shabby little office, and when the secretary asked her business, she just gave her the card. Pasternak rose at his desk, and gestured her to a chair. "What can I do for you?" He had no idea who she was, but at a glance he got the picture: married, from the ring; decidedly well-off, from the clothes; clever and bold, from her direct approach, and the way she looked him in the eye and remained standing. A volunteer just for that one job, he was sure.

"Thank you. You must be extremely busy." She pulled a sealed envelope from a chic suede purse. "Your son is a brave young man, and he was kind to me. This is a letter of thanks. Will you oblige me by giving it to him? No reply needed."

He took the letter, and she offered him a bony little hand. "*Merci, monsieur*. I'll trouble you no further." With that she left. He scrutinized the square blue monogrammed envelope, then pulled out a desk drawer. He kept a file labelled *Soon,* and he dropped the blond lady's letter into that file.

16

The *Concepzia*

"There it comes!"

A general shout of the Prime Minister's entourage greeted the sight of the roller bridge, looking like nothing so much as a gigantic mutant out of the horror films, a black millipede hundreds of feet long crawling on the white Sinai sands. It hove in view humping itself over a high dune, slithered down, and headed toward the viewing stand where Golda Meir, an age-spotted hand shading her eyes from the blazing sun, watched with incredulity. It dwarfed the tanks that towed it, and absolutely looked to be on the move by itself, a flexible living steel nightmare.

"Jewish heads," exclaimed Golda in Yiddish to Dado and Dayan. *"Yiddishe kep!"*

The wooden platform stood on an embankment overlooking a huge ditch for practicing crossings, a mock-up of the Suez Canal which Dado had ordered dug in the desert below a dam near Refidim. The flooded trench in the rubbly landscape conformed strictly to the Canal as a water obstacle, in width, depth, and slope of the banks. If this rolling monster could really bridge it without mishap, and a waiting column of Centurion tanks could then cross to the other side, not only would the tactics of a war with Egypt be affected, but the army budget, too.

For May, June, and July had gone by, and the threat at the borders had faded away. The Arabs had marched up the hill and marched down again. They had not dared. General Zeira had triumphed. In the inner command circles the BLUE/WHITE alert, never made public, was being called off. *Time* magazine quoted Moshe Dayan as stating, *"There will be no major war in the Middle East for ten years."* A wave of defense cost-cutting was on, of retrenchment, of plans to cut down the regular army and even the term of reserve duty, so the building of more such bridges was much in question. For the participants in the test, and for the bridge's inventors, there was the tension of an opening night in the theater. After much rehearsal, would everything go right? Or would one of a hundred possible hitches make a fatal fashla under the eyes of the big decision makers?

Clanking and squealing past the stand, the giant millipede plunged into the water with a towering muddy splash. It seemed to be going straight down, down, down! Fiasco already? But no, the hollow rollers performed as planned, the bridge heaved to the surface and, with one tank riding it, eerily swam straight across. As it struck the far side this tank rolled to the front, pushed over a flexible ramp curled like a scorpion's tail, and climbed up the sandy slope into "Egypt." Some onlookers applauded. All this time not one soldier had been visible in the exercise, only the machines.

Next the long column of tanks, their motors running and warmed up, headed for the bridge in an enormous noise, raising plumes of dust mingled with dirty exhaust. One by one they nosed down the embankment and groaned out on the steel surface, and the onlookers saw a sight certainly not before observed on earth. Under the weight of each tank, sixty tons or more, the bridge sagged deeply. Between the tanks, however, the very buoyant rollers popped upward. Soon the tanks filled the bridge a few yards apart, forcing it into the strangest shape, a series of curves that travelled along between the tanks like the wavy lines on an oscilloscope. It seemed impossible that this weirdly wiggly bridge would not come apart, one way or another, under such peculiar stresses. Tank after tank after tank, the column streamed across the preposterous contraption and mounted to the far side. When all had passed over, the bridge straightened itself out, floating with a gentle up-and-down motion.

Golda turned to Moshe Dayan. "Unbelievable. Wonderful." The inventors, Generals Laskov and Tal, breathed easier and beamed. The tank column that had crossed the bridge began heading back westward to the Canal. The soldiers of the bridge demonstration lined up for a cooked meal at a field kitchen, while jeeps brought the VIP observer party to a luncheon tent nearby.

At the command truck under a canvas awning, where Yossi Nitzan was barking orders and assistants were making colored scrawls on transparencies over maps, Barak jumped from the jeep, strode to him and grasped his hand. "Kol ha'kavod, Don Kishote. Kol ha'kavod."

Army insiders kept score on front-running officers like Yossi Nitzan, and Barak knew that this morning he had scored high. Such an unwieldy ballet of complicated machines and experimental tactics, performed under the eyes of the biggest of big brass, did not come off without superb planning, command, and control. Not bad for a refugee lad from Cyprus who had showed up twenty-five years ago at Latrun on a mule, at the height of a battle going very badly, and had plunged into the thick of it like a lunatic; in fact, like Don Kishote.

Yossi's hard businesslike look relaxed in a puckish grin. "Hi! How did they like it?"

"Outstanding success."

"Great. I've been fired."

"What!"

"Talk about it later."

In the breezy tent Golda put Gorodish, the new Southern Commander, on her right hand; a bullet-headed thickset general, radiating pleasure in the exalted company and the morning's success. Dayan sat on her left with Dado. The others took folding chairs at random at the long plank table, and all fell to. "Madame Prime Minister, this is Colonel Nitzan," said Barak, entering the tent with Yossi, "the commander of the exercise."

"Ah. Well done, Colonel. I know they call you Don Kishote," said Golda, "but if you're crazy, I need more crazy officers like you."

"Kishote is crazy only during full moon," said Dado. "Or when a girl goes by."

"A fine officer," said Gorodish stiffly. "I'm sorry to be losing him."

Amos Pasternak came in with Dzecki Barkowe, for Golda had asked to meet soldiers from the bridge project. Both were so sweaty and dust-covered that it was hard to tell the major from the sergeant. "And who are these?" inquired Golda. She peered at Amos and smiled. "Hmm, I seem to have met this one recently."

Barak said, "Major Pasternak, commanding Armor Battalion Seventy-seven. A company of his tanks moves the bridge."

"Amos, how do you manage not to pull it apart," Dayan put in, "with ten tanks hauling at it this way and that?"

"They're all on one wireless network, Minister, and they move only on signal."

"And this young fellow?" Dado asked. Dzecki was standing at rigid attention.

"A sergeant on the bridge, General," Amos said.

Golda asked, "Did you have problems, Sergeant?"

"Nothing we couldn't handle, Prime Minister," said Dzecki.

Her heavy eyebrows shot up at the accent. "By my life, an American. Like me."

"Member of my family," said Barak. "Long Island branch."

"I'm from Milwaukee, myself," she said to Dzecki, holding out her hand to him. He showed her his own, black with grease, and she laughed. Soldiers were bringing in platters of schnitzel and steak. Golda invited Kishote to join them for lunch.

"A great honor, Prime Minister, but the cooks know I eat with the men."

She nodded and smiled. "Smart."

Barak said, "Yossi, I want Dzecki to show me around the bridge afterward."

"Why not?"

"It looks better from a distance, sir," Dzecki said, "and climbing down on it will be slippery."

"Okay," said Barak.

After the exciting show the mood at the table was jovial. The desert air had made everyone hungry for a field luncheon, and the VIP fare was lavish, Kishote had seen to that. "Tell me something, Mr. Defense Minister, will you?" Golda said to Dayan. "That was a fine show, but if we're not going to have a war for ten years, why do we need more of these bridges now?"

She was taking a rare bantering tone with Moshe Dayan, for her usual dry courtesy masked deep political discord. Dayan had once bolted the Labor Party with the Rafi splinter, and Golda never forgot anything.

"I said a *major* war, Madame Prime Minister," Dayan coolly replied to this needle about the *Time* interview captioned "Waiting in the Wings," which had strongly implied that Dayan aimed to succeed Golda. "I spoke of a general conception. I wasn't prophesying. Reporters oversimplify, as you know."

"*Oy vay*, do I know! Well, so what is your conception?" She spoke the Hebrew word *concepzia* with faint irony.

"My chief of military intelligence should be here," said Dayan. "It's his estimate, which I fully accept, and he has it at his fingertips."

"He isn't here," said Golda.

Dayan nodded and took up the challenge. Neither Egypt nor Syria would start a major war alone, he said. Intelligence had established this. Syria was the weaker power, so everything depended on when Egypt would feel ready to start a war. After the air pounding by Phantoms that they had endured in 1970, this was out of the question, until they had acquired airplanes and missiles that could strike deep enough into Israel to deter or neutralize the air force. That was now basic Egyptian doctrine, and they could not achieve it before 1975 at the earliest.

"That's two years away," Golda observed. "You said ten years."

"We won't be standing still meantime, Madame Prime Minister. Our qualitative edge will keep increasing. Incidents can occur, possibly serious incidents. Not a major war. It's a complex analysis, but that's it in a nutshell."

Golda nodded and looked around, causing a lull in the clatter of cutlery. "I call on my Reb Alarmist," she said, "to oppose the estimate of the chief of military intelligence, as the Minister puts it in a nutshell."

All eyes shifted to Barak, with some smiles. He shrugged, and spoke slowly. "General Zeira's judgment was proven spectacularly correct in BLUE/WHITE. I don't presume to challenge it. I'm sure his concepzia is based on hard intelligence, and draws its conclusions with hard logic. My concern is that the enemy's logic may not work quite like ours."

Golda turned to Dayan, who smiled pleasantly at Barak. "Well said, Zev. But fear is human, and the logic of fear is much the same for Arab and infidel."

Chuckles around the table. "Very good," Golda said. "Anyhow, I'll settle for 1975, then we'll see."

"And returning to your question, Madame Prime Minister," said Dayan, "we can use more such bridges, because 1975 will come around before we know it, and ten years will also pass."

"Those are reliable predictions," replied Golda drily.

When command cars took the VIPs off to the Beersheba airport, Barak remained behind. What struck him most, as he inched down the greasy steel sections of the bridge toward the muddy water, was the gargantuan size of the thing. If he had not seen it scuttling over the sands, he would not have imagined it was movable. Mechanics and engineers swarmed on it, hammering, tinkering, dragging hoses and heavy equipment here and there. Guiding him through the mess, Dzecki said, "Plenty went wrong this morning, sir, but God was good, and we made it."

"Indeed you did. The Prime Minister was dumbfounded. So was I. Why, this monster is as flexible as a snake."

"Not really. A snake can wiggle this way and that," Dzecki illustrated with gestures, "and go around corners. The bridge is flexible only up and down. It will need a straight road to the Canal."

"And if there's no road?"

"There is one, and they're building others."

"Dzecki, you're a long way from Great Neck."

Showing white teeth in a grease-blackened face, Dzecki said, "I'm where I belong, sir."

Don Kishote appeared on the embankment, waving. "The helicopter's in sight, Zev," he shouted, "to take us to the Bar-Lev Line."

Barak inquired as they walked out to the landing place, "What's all this about your being fired, Yossi?"

"Well, Gorodish wants his own deputy, not a Sharon man, so I'm out," said Kishote. "Arik got thrown a bone, command of a reserve armor division. He wants me as his deputy."

"Careful, Yossi. Arik's retired and jumping into the October election. The division will be entirely on your back."

"I look forward to that."

"Can I give you advice?"

"You're my army father."

"When Golda discusses appointments, she always asks, *'Is he one of ours?'* That's what has finished Sharon. If you play along with Sharon's game you're finished too."

"I don't play anybody's game. And if that's the criterion for army advancement — *'Is he one of ours?'* — too bad." The helicopter was slanting down to them. "Here we go. What can I show you in the Bar-Lev Line, and why?"

"When Golda visits it the press and the brass are there. She can't really find out anything. Arguments about it keep buzzing around her like bees. Is it an effective deterrent? Should it be held in war, or abandoned?" He glanced at Kishote. "You've had to think a lot about that."

"I have. The Prime Minister is wise to send you on a surprise inspection."

The helicopter took the Mitla Pass westward. When it began its descent to the glittering blue Canal, Barak touched Kishote's shoulder, pointed forward, and bawled into his headset phone, "When to all the devils did the Egyptians build those ramparts? They're higher than ours!"

Kishote's voice gargled in the headphones. "They started it long ago. So we went higher. Then they went higher. Both sides are up to about sixty feet now. They never stop, though."

The helicopter jolted to a dusty landing. Across the Canal a fortified tower like a truncated pyramid rose above the Egyptians' sand wall, and the two prodigious earthworks stretched far out of sight to the north. "Where exactly are we?" Barak asked, as they both got out, faced downwind, and pissed on the sand.

"Deversoir. A likely crossing point, for them or for us."

"Why?"

Kishote gestured southward at a broad shimmer of water. "Great Bitter Lake protects one flank."

Emerging from a sandbagged concrete entrance under layers of rock and iron, a lieutenant was buttoning his uniform. "Not expecting visitors, Colonel Nitzan," he said, saluting.

"That's the idea," said Kishote.

Most of the soldiers in the bunker were in undershirts or stripped to the waist. One shaggy bearded soldier was giving another a haircut. The outpost was spacious and well lit as Zahal burrows went, only steamy-hot, not like the cramped chilly observation bunkers on the Golan. There was the usual underground smell of earth, sweat, cigarette smoke, and cooking. Tunnels led off the main bunker to pillboxes where half-dressed soldiers on duty lolled at their guns, some wearing slippers instead of boots; reading, smoking, talking, or listening to rock-and-roll music. An air of dreary boredom reigned, and Barak thought, Why not? For three whole years this front had not been under fire, not since the War of Attrition ended, and the worrisome Egyptian maneuvers always subsided without incident.

"These maozim are pretty much alike," said Kishote when they left, "but this one is special, and I'll show you why." He brought Barak out to the back of the rampart, where the packed sand sloped away at an angle that tanks could climb. But here the slope had been excavated, except for a thin bit on the Canal side, to make space for an enormous red-brick-paved yard. "Here's where a crossing will probably happen if war comes," said Kishote. "Bulldozers will knock out what's left of the rampart in minutes, a bridge will be rammed through, and attack forces will head across the Canal. Did you manage to read the DOVECOTE plan on the way?"

"Some of it," said Barak. "I'd like to see another one or two maozim, Yossi. They're how far apart?"

"Seven miles, more or less."

"Seven-mile gaps? Then in what sense is it a line at all?"

"Well, there are observation posts and tank emplacements in between. You'll see them. It's a thinly manned line, sure. Mobile armor brigades and the air force are supposed to crush any assault force, once across and detected."

"Then what you've got here is an early-warning system."

"Yes, also what the deep newspaper brains call *'a political presence on the Canal.'* "

They were walking back to the helicopter. "But what can the air force do at the Canal," persisted Barak, "with all those SAM batteries lined up right behind that rampart wall?"

Yossi gave a sad headshake. "Look, when they sneaked those SAMs up to the Canal, Arik screamed for weeks for orders to cross and destroy them. Golda and Dayan said no. The air force has updated its countermissile doctrine and equipment, and its number-one priority in case of war is *'Knock out the missile screen,'* as they knocked out the airfields in '67."

After hops to two more outposts the helicopter landed back at the Beersheba airport, where Kishote's driver was waiting with an army car to run them to Tel Aviv. As they rode Kishote began cracking and consuming sunflower seeds at a great rate, dropping handfuls of shells out of the window. From Beersheba to Tel Aviv, he said, was a three-sack drive.

"All right, Yossi," said Barak, accepting a sack from him, but eating few, "give me your own judgment on the Bar-Lev Line."

Kishote finished a handful of seeds before replying. "I'm a fighting man with a reputation for being crazy, which even the Prime Minister knows about. You really want my crazy opinion? Nobody planned the Bar-Lev Line. It grew like a weed in the sand."

Barak blinked. "How do you mean?"

"Why, I mean that when Nasser broke the truce, sank the *Eilat*, and started shooting at our Canal patrols, the engineers had to dig fortified holes for the boys to hide in like rats. Then the thinkers started thinking about those holes, and in a way they worked out something. Strongpoints seven miles apart don't give observational cross-coverage or mutual supporting fire, but with the smaller outposts you do have an early warning system of sorts.

At least it makes some sense of the holes. The thing took form while Bar-Lev was Ramatkhal and by the time Dado relieved him it was a fait accompli, the Bar-Lev Line."

"Good or bad?"

"According to our national defense doctrine, all wrong. '*Movement and fire!*' '*Carry the battle to the enemy!*' Our boys are sitting down in those maozim, fifteen or twenty to a hole, year in and year out like a lot of Frenchmen. Did you see their appearance? Their manner, even when two senior officers came in?" The car was winding up a hilly road offering vistas of the Dead Sea with its white salt flats and the red-gray mountains of Moab. Kishote scattered a handful of shells through the window. "Still, it's there now. It's an obstacle, a deterrent. The enemy will have to plan to breach the line, and by the Soviet book they'll assign to it tremendous effort and much time. Time we'll need to mobilize the reserves. If the Arabs ever dare to go, that time will be precious."

"Will they go? What's your estimate?"

Yossi crumpled an empty bag, threw it out, and ate seeds from a fresh bag. "First you ask me to think, now you want me to prophesy? No, thank you."

"Don't clown with me, Kishote."

With a glance at his swarthy young driver, Yossi abruptly shifted to English. "Look, Zev, when Dayan tells a *Time* reporter we'll have no major war for ten years, what can make him so sure? '*Qualitative gap*'? Ha! Will Sadat dare an attack, fearing that we can bomb him back to the Stone Age? Who knows? If I were Sadat, I'd pick my time and go, and figure to lose and still come out ahead politically, once the superpowers intervened. But then, I'm crazy."

Barak's laugh was melancholy. "You're not far off from Dado's analysis, and he's not crazy."

"Really? He's a great leader, so I'm complimented." Kishote reverted to Hebrew. "I'm on my way to say goodbye to my wife."

"Oh? Where's Yael off to now?"

"Back to Los Angeles, where else? And she's taking our little girl."

"Yossi, are you getting a divorce?"

"In those rabbinic courts?" Kishote hoisted his shoulders. "That's a big nuisance, and neither of us wants to marry somebody else, so why bother?"

"I'm sorry about this. Yael's a great woman."

"Zev, there's nothing I don't know about Yael. The lack of feeling is mutual. I thought she might stay on in the flat for Aryeh's sake, make a home for him until he finishes school. But he's almost a soldier now, he'll be okay, and so will I. She made a lot of money in California, and Lee has been after her to come back. Him and that Iraqi moneybags, Sheva Leavis." A pause. Kishote stopped cracking seeds, staring out of the window at the Dead Sea far below. "She may also figure that by taking up with Sharon, as you say, my career is finished. In any case, she's going."

"Yossi, lately you haven't given her much reason to stay."

"Oh, I am what I am. I'll say this for her, she does feel a bit guilty. When she broke it to me, she brought up that *Time* article. It's not desertion anymore to leave Israel, and what Dayan said proves it."

A white Mercedes was weaving and slipping through downtown Tel Aviv in the worst of the early evening traffic. "It rides like a cloud," Yael said to Pasternak, "and Yonatan is a hero at the wheel. He hasn't changed."

The driver turned to smile at her, showing stained broken teeth. Long, long ago she herself had recruited him for Pasternak during the Sinai campaign, a skinny Tunisian corporal of nineteen with perfect teeth. But the years had been hard on Yonatan; he was stout and getting bald, and had seven children to support. So he was joyous at being back at his lifework, driving Sam Pasternak.

"Excuse me, Giveret," he said, "but you're as beautiful as always. It's you who haven't changed."

"If I weren't leaving," Yael said to Pasternak, "I would steal Yonatan."

"Only you could do it, Giveret," said the driver, "except I love this car too much."

"I don't, but it's the company car for the chief executive," Pasternak said. "It's too rich for my blood."

"Oh, you'll get used to it." Her white hand patted Pasternak's brown hairy paw. "Real fast, too, Sam."

What had not changed was Shimshon's. Once Yonatan had driven them there through the dark crooked Jaffa streets for a certain memorable dinner. When Pasternak had asked her now where she wanted to eat, she had shot back, "Where else? Shimshon's." They passed through the crowded street-level eatery — bright lights, tile floor, Formica tables, popular prices — and descended to the costly gloomy nook of ornamented dark wood booths for American tourists and high-flying Israelis. "No appetizers," she said as they sat down, "and right away, red wine. Not Avdat. Vegetable soup, and of course *kevess b'tanur*."

"You know what you want," said Pasternak.

"I usually do, though I can't always get it."

A waiter in Yemenite costume — nevertheless a real Yemenite — took their orders. The wine came at once. "Well, I invited myself to dinner," she said, raising her glass, "and you're sweet to put up with me, Sam. *L'hayim*."

"L'hayim. It's a pleasure, but your leaving is a shock."

"Not to Kishote." Head archly aslant, she said, "A last chance for some frank talk, old sweetheart, before we part?"

"Why not? Let me say I'm with Yonatan. You look marvellous, and you don't change."

"Charming of you, dear, but it's partly the dim lights, and partly the memories, hey? Why do you suppose I suggested Shimshon's? I was in uniform then, that's a change right there, and twenty, that's *another* change, what? Ah, well." She drank with the old mannerism. Yael did not just lift wine to her lips, she brought up the glass with a zestful little flourish; and she was smiling at him in the old alluring way. Eva had a far prettier mouth, she still picked up money doing head shots in candy and toothpaste ads, but Yael's full mouth, when it stretched in a smile, had a tangy unexpected sweetness, as though a leopard were showing a house cat's affection.

"Enough about that," said Pasternak. "I avoid looking in mirrors these days. How are your kids?"

"The baby's an angel. I'm taking her. As for Aryeh, he's a

young lion, and he hero-worships your Amos, with good reason. He lives in our flat and goes to school nearby. Quite self-sufficient. Please give me more wine . . . Thanks. About Aryeh, now." A long leisurely sip. That seductive mouth twisted in a sly grin. "Let me take you back a few years, old dear. All right? Suez crisis, Ben Gurion and Dayan in Paris. Kishote's brother Lee has a suite in the Hôtel George Cinq, and Kishote comes out of the bedroom wearing a towel —"

Pasternak took her up. "And tells me he has a French *zonah* in there, and you've gone out shopping." A pause, eyes meeting. "The rest I guessed long ago, Yael."

"No doubt. But look, love, *you* brought a Hollywood *kurva* to that suite. What for? To discuss Suez?"

He held up a flat palm. "We all have a green light for whatever we did then. We were young and liberated, and life was tough."

"Ah, but sweet, no?"

"I said, we were young."

"You should have divorced Ruth then." Yael turned sharp and abrupt. "And married me. I tried my best. We were so much in love, Sammy —"

"Yael, enough. I was Dayan's runner. There was crisis after crisis, and who had time for haggling with the rabbis? Anyway, at that time she'd have given me nothing but *tzoress,* and no divorce."

"So in the end she left you high and dry for a goy. And I had Aryeh. And here we are." Yael's voice slightly shook.

"And here's the soup."

"Lovely! I'm starved."

They ate for a while in silence. Since he had plunged into an alien bewildering world of corporate business, Pasternak's private life had been, as it were, on hold. Still, his recent phone talks with Yael had intrigued him. He had been thinking much about her. After all, they were both in middle years, both more or less free, though she was not divorced. With this dinner at Shimshon's and her bolt to California, was Yael trying to force an issue? So she had tried to force it years ago — in essence the same issue — by breezing off to Paris with Yossi Nitzan, in place of that shy religious girl who had backed out. Yael was Yael.

People really did not change much in their natures, he reflected, admiring this old love opposite him. And in Sam Pasternak's eyes tonight, after more wine than he usually drank, it seemed that Yael had not physically changed much, either. This was still pretty much First Sergeant Luria, the shapely blonde from Dayan's moshav, whom Dayan himself had recommended as an aide. There had been nothing in Sam's life, before or since, like the passionate explosion of the encounter with the girl Yael Luria. He could feel the radiant warmth yet when he was with her, especially in Shimshon's, alone together over wine.

"Good as ever, the soup," she said.

"Everything's as good as ever," he was startled into replying. At the lightning flash in Yael's eyes he added, "Which could be the stupidest remark I've ever made, but at the moment I mean it, so let it stand."

"Sam, what about Kivshan?" Very casual shift of subject. "Are you happy with your decision?"

"Not sure yet, Yael. I'm still turning over rocks, and Histadrut shleppers keep scuttling away from the light. It's alarming, I tell you. On the research and development levels, I find something like genius. Managerial and production levels, I'd call acceptable. At the top — the decision makers, the moneymen, the powers — a tangle of political worms."

"Israel!" she exclaimed. "Any wonder that it stifles me, and I keep running away? I wish you'd gone into politics. You could change this hopeless system. You, yourself! You've got the strength and the brains. You'd make a great Prime Minister."

"The politicos would cut off my balls the first day," he said, "before I'd hung up my hat and coat."

"Really? Well then, dear," she said, and the mouth widened in the leopard smile, "by all means let's keep you at Kivshan, what? We can't have that, can we?"

"Kevess b'tanur," said the waiter, setting down a large savory lamb roast on a board.

While they ate it with rice, pita, and more wine, he talked about the ramified industries of Kivshan. He was uncovering more each day, he said, a mess of bad administration and tottery finance in Israel's biggest government-owned manufacturing complex. "I'll tell you what," she remarked when he paused. "They got you in not because of your ability — what do they know or care about that? — but because you are who you are, with a big reputation and a spotless name, so you keep them kosher. For a while longer, anyway." And as he went on, all her comments were informed and keen. Unlike Eva Sonshine, she knew everybody in high circles, up to Dode Moshe, and also knew nearly everything that was going on. After a while they were talking about Dayan and the *Time* article.

"Do you agree with him?" she asked.

"Yes, I agree, and in a way because of Moshe himself. Dayan's image is awe-inspiring, Yael, more so among the Arabs even than here. The one-eyed Samson, the giant-killer. I suspect they won't dare to move while he's alive. And who knows, if he lasts long enough, the status quo could come to seem normal."

"Will the new wife change him?"

"Oh, that's been going on for years. Finally his marriage broke up, so he could marry the lady. That's all."

"Sammy, the same woman as a girlfriend and as a wife are very, very, *very* different persons." Over his wineglass he gave her a rueful look. She added, "I speak with some authority."

"Confirmed, with equal authority."

She took a half-joking tone. "Well, then, are you going to try me as a wife, or not?" He did not answer. "I'm serious, Sammy."

"It's all talk. I don't really believe you."

"Why not? You know about my marriage. Last chance, hamood! Kind of late, twenty years later, but why not?"

"Want to take me with you to California, Yael? Big charge for excess baggage."

"Oh, talk sense. I have things to do there and almost nothing here, it's just too empty, small, and boring. But darling, at Kivshan or in politics — and don't wave off politics yet, Sammy — you can use me, in fact you *need* me. Now let me tell you something that may sound very peculiar, but it's absolutely true. In the army and in the Mossad, you've led a sheltered life."

"*Sheltered?* In the Mossad?"

"Sheltered, I say! I know all about the dangers you went through as you advanced, the difficulties, but you gave orders, and things happened. You're just now finding out at Kivshan what the outside is like, and your head is spinning. Isn't it? And you're right, politics is even more slippery and booby-trapped."

"Sheltered," muttered Pasternak. "Now there's a thought."

"It's a fact. Yossi Nitzan is an army star, he's the father of my kids, but to me he still seems a big tough boy scout. He hardly seems older than Aryeh. Maybe that's why we've never hit it off — though, again, I've tried my best."

"You're divorcing him?"

"If there's a reason to, I will. He knows that."

He reached across the table and took her hand. "What a piece you are, First Sergeant Luria."

"Such compliments." She gave his hand a small squeeze. "Now then, tell me about Eva Sonshine."

"Tell you what?"

"My brother's girlfriend! Surely you're not *sharing*? That's not you. Not Benny, I'd swear. And from the little I know of her, not her either."

"No."

"What, then?"

A heavy sigh. "I doubt you'll believe me."

"I'll know if you're lying, Sam."

That made him laugh. "All right. She's nice. I like her. She's no shmata. Between the hotel and the modelling she scratches a living and supports her sick mother. Every fellow who comes along tries to screw her, especially the wiseguy Americans at the Hilton. It's her looks."

"And you don't, Mr. Innocence? Is that what you're telling me?"

"Just that. At first I amazed her. She thought I had an original approach. But I enjoyed talking to her, and I sort of felt sorry for her. I still do. Of course to her I'm Dayan, Ben Gurion, and I don't know, Humphrey Bogart or somebody, rolled into one. It's ridiculous, but it's nice. If it got into screwing — anyway, I wouldn't do that to Benny, she's straight with him — all that would be gone like smoke. It's just something pleasant that's happened. She makes me feel good. That's it."

"By my life, I believe you. You're a very lonesome man, Sammy."

The half-closed eyes peered at her. "No more than I want to be."

"She's no threat, then?"

"To what?"

Yael picked up her purse and took out a mirror. "Hm. No wonder you think I look passable. Good old Shimshon's! I can hardly see myself. And oo-ah, my head! I've drunk more wine than I've had in years. It's been a marvellous dinner, and God help me, I love you."

He took a while to answer. "Well, I guess I believe you at that."

"Such a pretty speech! Let's get out of here. Yonatan can take me home. Kishote and Aryeh are helping me pack."

"You leave when?"

"Monday."

"Yonatan will take you to the airport."

"Accepted! Exit Mrs. Nitzan in style."

They kissed a lot in the car, much to Yonatan's discreet delight and hope. But Yael left for America on schedule, much to his sadness.

17

Rumbles

Pasternak was at his Swedish modern desk one morning in late September, in a big office with picture windows looking out over uptown Tel Aviv and the sunny sea, when a building guard rang from the lobby, reporting that an army major wanted to see him, claiming to be his son.

Amos not in Sinai? Now what? "Tell him to come up."

"Only the service elevator is running, sir."

"So let him use that."

Like the government and most Tel Aviv businesses, the Kivshan Building was shut down. The season of holy days was upon Israel; tonight at sundown Rosh Hashanah, ten days later Yom Kippur, then Sukkot — the annual three-week lull of rituals for pious Jews, and beachgoing or travel for others. Pasternak was alone on the executive top floor, no secretaries, not even a cleaning woman. In field uniform, briefcase in hand, Amos walked in and dropped letters on the desk. "Your mail, I stopped at the flat first. I've been ordered to the north. Why are you working today?"

Pasternak recognized Yael's handwriting on the top letter. High time. "To the north? That's sudden. What's happening?"

"The Golan's getting warm. I'm bringing up two companies and my command HQ. Know anything about it, Abba?"

Pasternak's response was guarded. It was still inside intelligence that the Arabs were massing and maneuvering again, north and south, in a virtual replay of BLUE/WHITE. "Well, after shooting down all those planes of theirs we had to expect some kind of reaction." In mid-September Syrian MiGs had scrambled to pursue an Israeli reconnaissance flight, and in an extended dogfight with its air cover had lost twelve aircraft to Israel's none.

"Abba, that was an encounter that got out of hand on both sides."

"I know. Still, they ended up with a big public black eye. Some sort of limited reprisal may well be in the wind."

"No, Yanosh thinks it's a lot more serious than that." Colonel Yanosh Ben Gal, Amos's hawk-faced brigade commander, in peace was something of a cynical womanizer, which to Pasternak was no great black mark against him, and in war he was a resourceful stubborn fighting man. "Yanosh expects the whole brigade will be moved up. There are seven Syrian divisions on the Golan by now, and we have only one brigade there, he says."

"Probably right," said the father wryly. "Peacetime deployment."

"Well, that's a monstrous asymmetry, Abba, twenty-one brigades to one! It's been a balagan, calling my troops back from holiday leave, deciding who goes north and who stays in Sinai. Come on. Will there really be war this time? Do you know? Maybe we should get it over with. All these false alarms —"

"Yanosh is wrong. They won't dare, Amos. It's more of the old bluff to keep us on edge. Not pleasant, of course, while it lasts." Pasternak felt a stir of disquiet. He was sure that the concepzia was sound, and that it was just a BLUE/WHITE feint again. Yet, if a Syrian reprisal for the air incident did occur, his son would be in the hot spot. "Good luck, son."

"I need luck at the supply depot up there," Amos grinned. "They're fighting with my deputy about releasing the reserve tanks."

Pasternak pulled open a drawer and fished a letter from his *Soon* file. "I don't think this is important, but here it is. Some lady brought it, I think a Frenchwoman, on the day of the parade. It got buried, what with moving my office and all." The father saw no point in mentioning that the woman was the elusive blonde of the Beirut raid. Let her stay elusive.

"Thanks." Amos slipped the blue envelope into his briefcase. *Frenchwoman! Hmm.* "Well, if things cool down, maybe Yanosh will let me come and join you for Yom Kippur."

"Sounds good. Now what about that rolling bridge? If your brigade's in the north and there's trouble down south, how does it get to the Canal?"

"Not up to me, Abba. I hope somebody's thought about that."

Pasternak resisted the notion of embracing Amos; too heavy a gesture for what was happening, so far. "Okay. If you can get to a telephone up there, call me. *Shana tova* [A good New Year], Amos."

"Shana tova, Abba." Amos threw him an ironic salute and left. The desk drawer was still open. It occurred to Pasternak that the best place for Yael's letter was the *Soon* file. The intense mood of the dinner at Shimshon's was fading, after weeks of searching his mail for word from her, and waiting for a phone call, at least. Nothing. Nothing! Who could tell, with First Sergeant Luria? To the *Soon* file with her! So he thought. But he reached for the paper cutter and slit open the letter. What to all the devils was she up to now?

No way of knowing, from the single sheet of warm bright chatter; the sound of Los Angeles and of pure devious Yael. He dashed off one rapid sheet in reply.

KIVSHAN
TEL AVIV

26 September 1973
Erev Rosh Hashanah

Dear First Sergeant —

Amos just brought your letter, which is three weeks old. He picked it up at the flat on his way to the Golan Heights. His battalion has been transferred there from Sinai, a funny business. Our air force tangled with the Syrians two weeks ago and shot down twelve planes, so Dode Moshe may anticipate a reprisal attack.

I was giving up on you when our post office snails finally crawled up with your short billet-doux. So you're busy now with that film foolishness and happy to be back in the expatriate paradise.

Good luck to you. I envy Sheva Leavis your services as adviser and troubleshooter. I could use them. Business is bound to bring me to the USA one of these days. I'll let you know when I come, and maybe we can pick up where we left off at Shimshon's. Meantime enjoy Eden, don't eat the wrong apples, and shana tova.

Avoiding the Rosh Hashanah eve highway traffic, Amos's driver tried to speed north through shortcuts and byways, but it was slow going here, too. Vehicles were few on the farmland back roads, but people cluttered them in holiday best, walking to the villages or to relatives' homes. Up on the wild green Heights the Rosh Hashanah feeling dimmed in the ambience of crossroads guarded by bored soldiers, fenced-off Zahal camps flying the Star of David, and many armed jeep patrols. At the local brigade headquarters Colonel Ben Shoham greeted him with something like wartime briskness. "Pasternak, as soon as you've drawn your tanks and supplies put your battalion here." He fingered a red circle on a wall map. "Be ready by morning for all eventualities. You'll be my counterstrike force."

"What's the situation, sir?"

"Not clear. Not so good." The bushy-haired officer sounded unafraid, but he had the grim weary look of a field commander with a single brigade, holding a front against seven enemy divisions.

"My deputy's been having trouble drawing tanks."

"That's all cleared up. Yanosh's troops have top priority on everything."

Near sunset the bulk of Amos's men arrived in a long convoy of busses. They swarmed into the supply depot to draw tanks out of storage; to test engines, bore-sight guns, load shells, magazines, and signal equipment, and grab up the thousand items of tank kits, all in a great noisy chaos. Here Rosh Hashanah ceased to exist, except for a small knot of soldiers in knitted skullcaps off in a corner of the depot with prayer books, rushing through a New Year service. Amos and his junior officers kept watching and checking far into the night, to ensure having at sunrise a counterstrike force of thirty-five working tanks. At 3 A.M. he went to snatch a little sleep in a bleak tin-roofed officers' hut. Piling coarse blankets on a cot, for it was very cold, he pulled off his boots, and glanced again at his orders. The envelope his father had given him fell out of his despatch case: square, pale blue, no stamp. Inside was a single sheet.

> *Mon cher* Pasternak *fils*:
>
> My husband and I are here for the Independence Day Parade. I have been troubled to think that in our recent adventure I may have been unnecessarily rude or evasive. You asked my name. It is Irene Fleg. In "real life" I am a happily married woman living in Paris, the mother of three children. My husband is M. Armand Fleg, a businessman active in the Alliance. If you happen to be in Paris one day, we will be pleased to see you. Meantime let me thank with less coyness the brave lady with the wet stockings who brought off a great exploit for Israel, and made me feel safe in a very foolhardy escapade. I was approached, felt challenged, and volunteered. Thanks in part to your cool courage, I came out with a whole skin. Never again!
>
> Irene Fleg

Pasternak *fils* had more pressing things on his mind now than the tanned blond lady, but he had been long in the field and he had no steady girlfriend. As he slipped under the blankets in his heavy tank coveralls he was reflecting that this was an oblique sort of come-on letter. A Parisienne with three children and a husband active in the Alliance, therefore probably rich; out of the question, and not his style anyway. Still, how peculiarly seductive she had seemed. . . . Maybe one day when all this cooled down . . . He fell asleep indulging in these weary fantasies.

Dov Luria had a very different Rosh Hashanah eve. At midday he was flying at forty thousand feet over the Golan, photographing Syrian tanks and artillery, massed for miles on miles right up to the Purple Line of the cease-fire; and before sundown, dressed in a stiff new civilian suit, he was walking arm in arm with Galia Barak to the Ezrakh's synagogue in Jerusalem. A bizarre transition, but such was an aviator's life. The Baraks had invited him and his parents for holiday dinner, and his father had told him to bring

Galia to the Ezrakh's services first. Dov was mildly tolerant of his father's drift to religion, and Galia was not about to object to anything suggested by Dov's famous father. She was dizzy with tension, awaiting a serious word from Dov. She wore a costly red wool dress bought for her in Tel Aviv by her mother, just for this dinner, after they had shopped vainly for two days in Jerusalem.

As for Dov, he was more than ready to speak the serious word, but this fighter pilot was plain scared. Galia Barak baffled him. Did she really like him? She now seemed to him the unmatchable girl among girls, her dark eyes a fathomless mystery, her body a tall sweet flame, her every word charming and witty, her every motion full of grace, her relatively shy and chaste kisses the tantalizing essence of undeclared love. He hoped she cared for him, but on the other hand he had heard she was also seeing a very tall paratrooper. Dov was uncomfortable about his short stature, for Galia was half an inch taller. Girls! Suppose she turned him down?

They were walking in the pedestrian stream filling the street, for in the Holy City, auto traffic was down to zero. Friends greeted her and gave Dov sharp-eyed looks which warmed her heart. That Galia was going with a Phantom pilot was known all through Jerusalem's teenage set, though at the moment he was in mufti and complaining about it. "The tie chokes me," he said. "My father had this religious grandmother. She once told him that in the old country a new suit for Rosh Hashanah was a must. So last week he dragged me out and bought me this getup."

"I love it," said Galia. It was a checkered brown suit which the Hebrew label called "Scotch tweed," and for Israeli ersatz it fit well enough. Services were already droning inside the Ezrakh's little synagogue on a side street, and Benny Luria was waiting by an open worm-eaten wooden door hanging askew on its hinges.

"You go in the women's section," he said to Galia.

"I know, I know." She slipped away, laughing. A bearded *gabbai* led them to reserved front seats in the packed plaster-walled shul. Deep in prayer by the Holy Ark, the Ezrakh did not glance around at them, though General Luria's uniform was causing a stir. Without explanation, the Ezrakh had told him to wear it.

For Dov the service was a bore. The standings, sittings, and chantings confused him, and he passed the time reading the quaint Hebrew of the liturgy, all new to him. When the Ezrakh gave a brief talk, Dov was surprised at his clear colloquial Hebrew. He was half expecting Yiddish.

"K'tiva v'hateema tova!" the Ezrakh began in his high weak voice. ("A good decree, written and sealed, to you all!") "This greeting, dear friends, should not be used at services tomorrow, on the second night of our holiday. Tonight, as we are taught, the righteous and the wicked receive their final decree. But *bainonim* [mediocrities] have the ten days until Yom Kippur to review their deeds, and true remorse can still change the outcome." He stroked his long white beard, glancing around with a little smile. "So you see, if *tomorrow* night you wish your neighbor a good decree, you imply he is not righteous, but a mediocrity! Yet how can you be sure? We must judge every man on the side of merit. All the same, my friends, I give you permission to wish *me* a good decree tomorrow night, because to my pain, I am a mediocrity of mediocrities, and I thank the Creator for the Ten Days of Repentance."

Dov asked Galia, when they came out amid the chattering congregants, "How was it in purdah?" The women were all staring at his father.

"Oh, b'seder, but I sure got funny looks. Mostly old ladies in there. I guess the young ones are home making dinner." The first stars were out in the clear violet Jerusalem sky, and a cool breeze was blowing. "General, I told Mama that Dov and I would walk to the Wall after services. So enjoy dinner, and we'll be back later."

"Shana tova," he said, with a paternal wistful smile. Those two could skip dinner or do what they pleased. The world was theirs.

Hand in hand they walked downhill, across a valley and up the slope to the Old City. More tense than he had been while flying over Syria, Dov wondered how to speak a serious word, meantime telling Galia about a tank column that had broken through here to the Jaffa Gate in the Six-Day War. He had learned this in an army tour of battle sites for recruits. The route was unmarked, just so many hilly streets and vacant weed-choked lots.

"We were in Washington then," she said. "We missed it all."

"I was here, all right. My father led the air strike that won the war."

"Oh, who doesn't know that? He's a great hero."

"Well, he heard Dayan say that your father was more important to the war in Washington than two brigades on the battlefield."

"I was twelve," Galia said. "What did I know? I just knew I didn't like America. I missed my friends."

"As soon as the war was over," Dov said, "my father brought us to the Wall. All this here" — he gestured back at the valley — "was no-man's-land. Ruins, barbed wire, minefields, booby traps. It's hard to imagine now." They walked in silence, intertwined fingers tightening. After a while he said, "Could you hear the Ezrakh?"

"Barely. Why?"

"Are we supposed to believe all that? Decrees, repentance? A book in heaven where everybody's deeds are recorded, and a judgment is written down for next year — who lives, who dies, who by fire, who by water, and so on? I figure it's all metaphorical, don't you? My father's going in for religion lately."

"My mother's getting back to it, too."

"You know, Galia, I talked to the pilots who knocked down the Syrians in that dogfight. They say that going into battle you're too busy to pray, but coming out of it you sure thank God, whether you're religious or not."

Once inside the Old City walls, Galia led him by the hand through gloomy narrow alleys and deserted little streets, moving always downhill. "You're at home here, aren't you?" he said.

"Oh, there's nothing to do in Jerusalem on Shabbat, so we come here, my friends and I. You can explore the Old City forever. There's good shopping, too."

"And the Arabs?"

"Some are nice, others not so nice. Naturally they all wish we'd drop dead."

They came out on a terrace above a wide plaza, where the floodlit Wall was mobbed by turbulent worshippers. "There's always a huge crowd on holidays," she said.

Dov said, "You know, the Wall used to be in a long dark alley.

You couldn't see it till you got right up to it. That's how I first saw it."

"It already looked like this," she said, "when we came home."

Descending a long flight of stone steps to the plaza, they could hear discordant chants rising from half a dozen services going on at once, clustered around different reading stands and prayer leaders. "This section's for the men," she said. "Want to push in, up to the Wall? Some people make a point to kiss the stones."

"No thanks." He was staring over the people's heads at the Wall. "This makes me think, though."

"Of what?"

"Abba brought us here right after the war. Me, Daphna, Danny. He told us Jews used to spend their life savings, just to travel to see the Wall once before they died. Some even came on foot, thousands of miles. Galia, in six years this is the second time I've been here."

"It's too easy now," said Galia. She added with a laugh, "See? We girls have to watch out for that."

Dov did not react to her teasing at all. "You know something? From the air at reconnaissance altitude, Galia, you're looking down, through the clouds, at mountains, valleys, rivers, lakes, farmland, and the sea. Just the earth as it is — brown, green, gray, and then the big blue stretch of the Mediterranean. There's no Syria, no Iraq, no Jordan, no Egypt, no Israel. It's all of a piece, all the same. No Promised Land. Zionism looks a lot different from up there." He grunted. "Still, returning to base, you sure look for that little Promised Land."

"Come."

"Where to?"

"You'll see." She led him through more alleys, up dark staircases, along stone parapets, and under ancient arches. They climbed and climbed, and arrived atop a rough windswept stone tower under black sky crowded with stars. Below, lights twinkled on all sides, as far as they could see. "Now here's a view of Jerusalem few people know about," said Galia, leaning against him. "Three hundred sixty degrees. Chilly, though."

He put an arm around her. "I'm not cold. I've got on my Rosh Hashanah suit."

"So you have. It feels rough, but nice."

They were both oddly short of breath. "Who wants to kiss stones?" the Phantom pilot said, and he seized her and went to full throttle, which had been Galia's idea, conceivably.

Israelis seldom run out of conversation, but after dinner at the Baraks' the talk was halting, as the four parents avoided the question in all their minds: namely, what to all the devils was happening with Dov and Galia? Nor did the men want to involve the wives in war talk. The November election was a safe topic. Barak feared, so he said, that Sharon's attempt to form a "Likud" bloc to challenge Labor would give the religious splinter parties leverage to force through more blue laws. Luria argued that no political price was too high to get rid of Labor's arteriosclerotic socialism.

"Come on, Benny," said Barak, "can you picture that crazy Begin as our head of government?"

"This is a crazy country," said Luria, "and crazier developments have turned out well."

The opening of the outside door put an end to all this. Galia sailed in dishevelled and radiant, Dov close behind. "We have two announcements," she carolled. "First, we're starved. Second —" her sparkling glance invited Dov to speak.

"We're engaged," he said. "Shana tova!"

The day after Rosh Hashanah, Noah telephoned his father from Haifa to hint at ominous new naval intelligence. Barak responded, "Drive down here, let's not talk on the phone about it," and Noah soon arrived in coveralls, obviously having broken all speed limits. They sat down to lunch on what remained of Nakhama's New Year kreplach soup, and Barak told him about the engagement.

"Engaged? Look, Abba, I like Dov, he's first class, but she's only seventeen —"

"Well, she'll do her sadir service first. That's another long time of growing up. Right now they're planning to go skiing in Switzerland after Yom Kippur, if he can get a three-day leave. It's Benny's engagement present to them."

"A three-day leave?" Noah stopped eating. "Elohim, hasn't the air force gone on alert?"

"Not unless I haven't been told, and that's most unlikely."

Noah dropped his spoon with a clank. "Okay. I may be stepping out of line to say this, Abba, but I came down here to say it. In the name of God, the Arabs are about to go to war! Doesn't the air force know that? Doesn't the Prime Minister? Doesn't the Defense Ministry? Don't *you*?"

"You're talking about your naval intelligence reports."

"Exactly, and it's war this time, believe me."

Noah reeled off the preparations for combat that naval intelligence was tracking in the Syrian and Egyptian fleets. Barak nodded and nodded, regarding his son with a glum mien. "Noah, your admiral and his chief intelligence officer were here for hours yesterday, arguing with General Zeira. He knows those facts, and a lot more they don't know. His assessment remains *'very low probability.'* "

Noah gnawed his lips. "And is Golda Meir actually going to France, as the papers say?"

"She is."

"To address some stupid socialist convention?"

"No, the Council of Europe."

"What's that? Does it have any military power? Is it part of NATO?"

"NATO? No, it's a forum for talk about political unity and human rights." Barak pushed back his plate, and looked his son in the eye. "I'll trust you with a confidence. I objected forcibly to her leaving Israel now."

"Good for you, Abba! And what did she say?"

"Well, I'll tell you, pretty exactly. She said: 'The world's greatest soldier is my Minister of Defense, and he has great generals under him — Dado, Tallik, Bren, Arik, Raful, you know them all. Do those warriors need an old lady nursemaiding them and second-guessing them?' "

Noah broke in mulishly, "Maybe they do —"

"Listen! She went on, 'It's an important honor for Israel that I address that council. Cancelling would play right into Arab hands. Their game is to paralyze us, to keep Israel from functioning like a normal country. Anyway, I'll be back the next day, and at worst I can return in five hours.' " Barak shrugged. "That's what she said."

"B'seder, Abba. So that's that. I guess I had my nerve coming here. But I'll tell you this. When it starts — and it's going to, very soon — the navy will be stripped for action, with warmed-up engines."

"That's fine for the navy, Noah. It's not the same as alarming our people and the superpowers by mobilizing the reserves, and giving the Arabs just the excuse they may seek to attack."

"Be straight with me, Abba. Do *you* think the reserves should be mobilized?"

They stared hard at each other. "Noah, I've been disgracefully wrong on that question before. I'm not the chief of military intelligence."

After an awkward moment, Noah spoke with a complete change of tone. "Have I ever told you about the French girl I met in Cherbourg?"

"Yes. Julie something, father in the fish business?"

"Good memory. Julie Levinson. She's here, and she's got herself a job in the French Embassy. Keen girl."

Barak smiled. "Chasing you down, is she?"

Not returning the smile, Noah said a shade stiffly, "Julie's here for real. She knows all about Daphna, and she's not chasing me. Lovely girl, though. Sweet, stable, intelligent."

"Well, with all these engagements going on, what about Daphna?"

"I'm going now to her studio, as she calls it."

"Will you come home for Yom Kippur?"

"Not in our state of alert, not unless our admiral relaxes a lot."

"Well, if not, have an easy fast."

"You too, Abba."

Noah had to ring several times before Daphna in a smeary smock opened the door of her dingy cellar room in Jaffa. "Oh, it's only you," she said, wiping her hands on a rag. "Come in. It's a frightful mess."

"What does that mean, *'only you'*?"

"Oh, just that I'm expecting a guy from the Mekhess. Tax problem. What are you doing here?"

For answer he took her in his arms. "Oo-ah," she said between kisses, "how ardent! You're almost as grimy as I am, so — No, no! Hey, hands off! Easy, motek!" She broke free. "Why aren't you in Haifa?"

"I had to see my father in Jerusalem. I'm on my way back, but I wanted to talk to you, hamoodah. There's going to be a war."

"What? A *war*?" She gestured at a radio murmuring American rock-and-roll. "Is there news I missed?"

"Daphna, take my word for it —"

"Noah, did you fall on your head? Things couldn't be more peaceful. I delivered a menorah this morning to a Canadian client at the Sheraton. Mobs! This city is bubbling like New York. A war?"

He was glancing around at the worktables piled with tools, clay lumps, unfinished ceramics, stained cloths, and dirty dishes. "What kind of tax trouble? You really make that kind of money?"

"Oh, *prutot* [pennies]. But they're after me all the same. God, there's no place to sit down, is there?"

She cleared a skirt, sweater, and frilly underwear off a cot. He pulled her down beside him and asked, "Are you going home to Tel Nof base for Yom Kippur?"

"By your life, no! My father's importing Hassidim to conduct services at the base. He's getting real strange. I'll stay right here, I have work to do."

"On Yom Kippur?"

"Noah, you know me. Why pretend?"

"Well, come to Haifa, at least. We'll be in port, for sure —" He was fondling her hand. He stopped and pointed to her wristwatch. "What's this?"

"Oh, that. Dzecki gave it to me."

"A *Rolex*?"

"I tried to refuse it, motek. He insisted, the fool. He was just too sweet about it."

"Yes, and he can afford it."

"Oh, don't be like that, why shouldn't I have it? Dzecki's matured a lot, you know. He's staying on in the army. I admire him."

This visit was not going at all as Noah had intended. He had come to snatch a last sweet tumble before the battle, but romance was clearly not on Daphna's agenda. Not yet. A change of mood called for, alcohol indicated. "Let's have a beer, Daph. What are you working on now?"

"Oh, menorahs, menorahs. What else?" She went and took a bottle from a rusty icebox. "But at last through Dzecki I've got one decent commission, Samson killing a lion, for a hotel lobby. There's this rich kablan in Haifa, Avram Gulinkoff, he builds hotels and such. Dzecki and his father have formed a company with him, and —"

"What, with Guli? They're in business with Guli Gulinkoff? Why, Guli is a gorilla, the biggest crook in Haifa! He'll eat the flesh off those Americans' bones. Then he'll use their bones for soup. For Guli you're making a Samson? And what's this, am I drinking alone?"

"When the Mekhess gets here I have to be sharp. It'll be any minute. Drink up, motek." Daphna paced the little room. "Okay, Dzecki says Guli is sort of gross, but why a gorilla? Apparently he knows a lot about art. He owns a Degas and a Miró."

"Did he hang them in his jail cell?"

"Ha, you're in a sour mood. You *know* the indictment was dropped, and he never spent an hour in jail. Dzecki says the politicians eat out of Guli's hand. Guli gets permits, clearances, variances in a day that for other kablans can take a year — What time is it?"

"Daphna, come here. Sit down."

"Well, the thing is —"

The doorbell rang. With an exasperated shrug, she answered it, and Yoram Sarak came in, carrying two falafels in paper napkins. The apparition of this hairy iconoclast in dark glasses was a most disagreeable surprise to Noah. "I know I'm early, Daph, but — By my life, it's Horatio Hornblower," exclaimed Sarak. "Daphna didn't tell me, Admiral, or I'd have brought another falafel. No problem, you can have mine, I'm getting over a spastic colon. Ma nishma?"

"So you work for the Mekhess now?" Noah said.

"Me? The Mekhess? Are you crazy?"

"My mistake." Noah looked at Daphna, who seemed quite at her ease, except that her ears were going pink.

"Say, Admiral, do you happen to know a navy officer, Ben-Ami Bernstein?"

"What about Ben-Ami?"

"He says that there'll be a war any day, hard navy intelligence. This is serious. I'm all set to hop to Athens after Yom Kippur, I've bought tickets for me and a friend. Isn't Ben-Ami out of his mind?"

"Ben-Ami's mouth works with no connection to his mind."

"That's reassuring." Sarak glanced from Daphna to Noah. "Well, you've got company, Daphna, and I've got a column to write. Sure you won't have my falafel, Admiral?"

"Enjoy it, and take care of your colon."

As Sarak closed the door Noah said, "Are you going to Athens with that bedbug?"

"Noah, you're so cranky, and who are you, anyway, to call such a brilliant writer a bedbug? Why did you come here in such a rotten mood?"

"I came here because the navy's on full war alert, and God knows when I'll see you again —"

"Navy and war, navy and war, that's your whole world. It isn't mine. I have my own friends, I go my own way, and —"

"To Athens, for instance?"

Daphna flung out at him, "All *right*, to Athens. There! How often do I get to see you? What am I supposed to do with myself? If you're jealous, for God's sake, don't be. As far as all *that* goes, I think Yoram's despicable, why, he's got a friend of mine pregnant right now. He's an utter lowlife and to me not attractive in the least, not in that way, but he's fun, *fun*. You don't know what fun means, except in bed."

These two had once broken up for almost a year, and Noah felt that another break might well be imminent. Let it come, he thought. Slavery to a girl, any girl, even Daphna Luria, was not for Noah Barak. *Showdown*. "You're not going to Athens, Daphna."

"Oh, no?"

"You won't be able to, for one thing. The war will break out first, so —"

"Foolishness." She glanced at the Rolex. "Listen, enough of this, it's no good. You're going back to Haifa now, aren't you? I have to see Guli with some sketches. Drive me there."

"My Porsche is in the repair shop."

She looked startled, then said slowly and coldly, "Dzecki is younger than you, darling, and he's more of a mentsch. I like him. My friends like him. He amuses Yoram like anything. Dzecki's witty, good-humored, broad-minded, he's not demanding like you —"

"He's rich."

"You want a fight, don't you? Have it, then. You may become chief of operations one day, Noah, you're very smart, you come from a wonderful family, but you're as narrow as this finger." She flourished it in his face. "And with a father like Zev Barak! How is it possible? I've wondered for years."

"Athens is off, Daphna, do you hear?"

"Oh, go to the devil."

Noah strode out of the flat, started off in his car with a squeal and a roar, and squealed and roared to the French Embassy.

The corridor of the Defense Ministry was lined with blown-up photographs of former ministers — Ben Gurion, Lavon, Eshkol, all canny old Labor politicians — and finally the incumbent, the world-renowned warrior with the eye patch, in suit and tie. Usually Zev Barak walked by the pictures unseeing, but today the seamed stern faces of the departed ministers seemed to be warning him that Israel's survival was now partly on his shoulders. From behind a big desk in the office next to Dayan's, Pasternak greeted him with the old sardonic grin. Barak asked as he sat down, "What's your position here, Sam, exactly?"

"The minister's still figuring that out. Meantime I'm here, on leave from Kivshan."

"Well, thank God you're here."

"Thank Dayan. Not quite the same, except in this building.

He kicks off Labor's election campaign tomorrow, so I'm keeping abreast of field reports of the Arab buildup while he politicks. Same drill as when he used to skitter around the fighting fronts. He's in there right now" — a thumb toward a side door — "working on a speech." He fixed a heavy-lidded glance on Barak. "What do you hear from Golda? How did they like her speech in Strasbourg?"

"Sam, that's why I'm here. Now she's decided to go on from there to Vienna."

"L'Azazel, she has? Why?"

"To get Kreisky to reopen the transit camp."

"That won't take long. She'll accomplish nothing, he'll just shit on her, that apostate dog. His knees tremble at the sound of Arabic."

Chancellor Kreisky had recently closed Israel's only transit camp in Europe for the few Jews trickling out of the Soviet Union. Arab gunners had seized seven of these emigrants on a train and threatened to murder them all and explode terror all over Austria unless the Schonau Castle camp was shut down. Kreisky had at once complied and provided the terrorists air passage to Libya.

"I've been on the phone with her," Barak said, "arguing against her going to Vienna. It's an idiocy —"

"Well, listen, I can understand her. The election's a month away, and she's a politician. Our media are screaming Schonau, terrorists, Soviet Jews, and Kreisky. Biggest tumult in years, and she's showing action."

"Sam, would Dayan consider telephoning Golda to come straight home?"

"Ask him," Pasternak said, as the side door opened and Moshe Dayan walked in.

Totally ignoring Barak, he handed Pasternak several sheets. "This is a passage I just dictated. Verify any fact you're not sure of. Glance at the last paragraphs right now."

Dayan's demeanor was different here than in Golda's office, Barak observed. Here he was the most powerful man in Israel, with a budget as large as all the other ministries put together; also the master of a million Arabs in the territories. But when he was in her presence she was the boss, and Dayan knew it and showed it. It also struck Barak that Dayan was looking much happier, better groomed, and thicker in the middle since marrying again.

"I would cut this part, Minister," said Pasternak, pointing. "Too complicated."

"That stays. It's her policy and mine. The Galili Document in a few words." This was a Labor Party manifesto waffling on the issue of the settlements. Dayan went out with an unsmiling nod at Barak.

"Well, why didn't you ask him?" inquired Pasternak.

"Ha!"

"Listen, Zev, what'll you accomplish by hurrying her back? It's one more day. The facts in the field are threatening, but that's happened before."

"Not this threatening."

"Well, if a blow does come, we're ready to absorb it. We spent millions during BLUE/WHITE, remember, on the new roads and the forward depots of ammunition, tanks, and supply reserves. That stuff's all in place now."

"Golda has a nose, Sam. If she were here, she'd *know* whether to mobilize."

"A nose is fine. So's our military intelligence, and she'll get seventy-two hours' warning of any turn toward war."

"Yes, we've heard that from Zeira over and over. You believe it?"

"I know it." Their eyes locked in confrontation. Pasternak repeated, "Seventy-two hours. I know it." The tone was hard, and the look said, *Don't press me further*.

"Okay, Sam, you know it."

Utterly exhausted, her face dead-gray, Golda arrived at the airport next night in a drenching rainstorm. Barak held his tongue, riding with her to her Ramat Aviv home. The rain lashed the car, the windshield wipers danced, and neither spoke. At last the Prime Minister growled, *"Ayzeh davar akher!"* ["What an unmentionable thing!" — i.e., a hog.] To my *face*, he turned me down. So cold, so deaf, so indifferent. Only interested in crawling to the Arabs. *'We live in different worlds,'* he said. Different worlds! He'll learn one day, that apostate davar akher, that for Jews it's all one world." Both she and Pasternak were rather hard on Kreisky, Barak thought. The Austrian was frankly anti-Zionist, true, yet at times he had secretly intervened to help Jews in mortal danger. In Golda's present mood, of course, she wasn't to be argued with. Her anger once vented, her tone lightened. "Nu, Zev, so we meet tomorrow morning. It's serious?"

"Prime Minister, Zeira's assessment stands. *'Very low probability.'* But Dayan asked for this meeting."

"To share the responsibility of not mobilizing, I'm sure." Golda's weary voice shaded into heavy irony. "Well, he's right. Let's hear what our best minds have to say." She peered at him. "Alarmed, are you?"

"Less so, Prime Minister, now that you're back."

"What a nice compliment."

The morning meeting in Golda's office of the inner cabinet and army chiefs was calm, the intelligence briefing spare, the comments matter-of-fact, the mood unworried. Nobody questioned that the Arab armies were on full war alert, massed at the borders, and capable of immediate all-out attack. Israel's two most eminent soldiers, Dayan and Yigal Allon, now both ministers, flanked Golda. With them was the white-haired old Yisrael Galili, her stone-bottomed Labor cohort. They all took in stride the dark picture and heard without demur the ongoing assessment, *"Still very low probability,"* by Zeira's head of research, a quiet-spoken general who gave the briefing since the chief of military intelligence was ill. The Prime Minister interrupted with only one edgy question, when he said, "At all events, if there's a change on the other side to a decision for war, we'll know seventy-two hours beforehand."

"One moment." She lifted a rigid finger. "Seventy-two hours? Tell me, how will we know? By some unusual preparations?"

"Prime Minister, we will know. With seventy-two hours' warning." He glanced at Dayan. So did Golda. Dayan gave her a nod and a subtle smile. She shrugged and asked no more.

As the meeting was ending she asked the Ramatkhal abruptly, "Dado, two questions. Do you accept this evaluation? And in any case are we ready?"

Elazar expressed dour confidence in his military intelligence chief, and in Zahal's readiness if the unlikely happened. "The trouble is, Madame Prime Minister, a lot is expected of us," he said wryly. "Unless we win in three days this time, we'll catch a lot of flak."

Thereafter Zev Barak decided to suppress his anxiety, or paranoia, or whatever it was. Who was he to be alarmed, if even Golda with her "nose" accepted composedly these dire facts? Sabras like Allon and Dayan tended to hint that a "*galutnik* mentality" haunted those who feared war. Was it so, and was he after all at bottom a Viennese galutnik? Had the iron of Europe's anti-Semitism really entered his soul, or the American Jews' way of looking over their shoulders at the goyim? Or had he simply been out of the field and behind a desk too long? *No more,* Zev Barak resolved. *This time I will shut up.*

The resolve cleared his mind, and for the next two nights he slept well. He cheered up so much that Nakhama, recently pensive and withdrawn, reflected his mood with smiles, jokes, and little affectionate ways that he thought she had forgotten. "So where will we hear Kol Nidrei?" she said over their morning coffee, very early on Yom Kippur eve. "Just the two of us, ha? Something new!" Galia was going to Tel Nof to be with Dov, Ruti was staying at a kibbutz, and Noah's vessel would be in port on high alert, unless he went out on patrol.

"Well, we could walk to the Wall. How about that? Nice effect it had on Dov and Galia."

Nakhama bridled, laughed, and said, "Hm! We'll see."

He drove to Tel Aviv that morning in his happiest frame of mind since the start of the crisis. On his desk he found a sealed despatch in a pale green military intelligence envelope, stamped URGENT. He tore it open:

> ALL SOVIET DIPLOMATS LEAVING EGYPT AND SYRIA TODAY WITH FAMILIES BY AEROFLOT PLANES. MEETING AT 8:30 A.M., OFFICE OF DEFENSE MINISTER.

The date was Friday, October 5, Yom Kippur eve.

PART TWO

The Awakening

WHAT IS IT WITH THEE, O SLEEPER?
RISE AND CALL UPON THY GOD . . .

Jonah I:6

18

Earthquake

Yom Kippur eve, sundown. The voice of the young black-bearded Hassidic rabbi throbs through the crowded Tel Nof assembly hall, transformed to a synagogue with a Holy Ark, Torah reading platform, and even latticework to partition off the female soldiers; "the works," as Benny Luria has promised the rabbi. Everyone is standing for the ancient solemn melody . . .

Kol Nidrei, v'esorei . . .

Never has there been such a Yom Kippur at Tel Nof. All the pilots, instructors, ground crews, clerks, mechanics, and cooks in the male section wear the white shawls and yarmulkes furnished by the Hassidim. The base kitchens are shut down. The streets and walks are deserted. No war warning has come down from the Chief of Staff to the Air Force Command. No machine moves except the ever-rotating radar on the control tower.

Proud and pleased with what he has wrought, Benny Luria stands between his Dov and Danny in a front row. Even the Ezrakh, he is thinking, might approve of his improvised shul. And when all is said and done, this Tel Nof base, the air force, Zahal, and Israel are more about Kol Nidrei than about the Mapam socialism in which he was raised; and that is true whether Golda Meir is also hearing Kol Nidrei tonight, or smoking cigarettes and drinking tea in her Ramat Aviv home.

"Good cantor," murmurs Danny, the yarmulke precarious on his mop of red hair, as they sit down amid a noisy scraping of chairs. He is now the tallest of the three. "I liked that, but it wasn't Hebrew, was it, Abba?"

"Aramaic," says his father. "Talmud language. There's a translation in the prayer book."

"Poor Galia, behind that fence," says Dov.

"Your mother's taking good care of Galia, don't worry."

Next morning when the telephone rings by Zev Barak's bedside, he wakes disoriented, peering at his illuminated clock. Four-thirty? On Yom Kippur Day? Hearing Golda Meir's voice, he thinks at first it must be a bad dream, like others he has been having. "Zev, come to Tel Aviv." The tone is harsh, tired, level. "Be at my office by seven. Zeira just called me. The war will start at six this evening."

His throat contracts, his spine coldly prickles. It is no dream.

Dawn streaks the sky outside the windows of the Tel Nof commander's office. The young lieutenant with the duty watch has gone all night without food or drink and is in a foggy state. "Yom Kippur is cancelled." Benny Luria startles him, coming in clad in a G suit.

"Cancelled, sir?"

"Cancelled. Call the cooks. Kitchens will be activated at once, full breakfasts prepared for the whole base. All gates of the base to be closed. Returning personnel may be admitted. Nobody leaves Tel Nof."

"Yes, sir." The duty officer cannot resist. "Is it war, General?"

Luria ignores the query. "All sections go to Aleph Alert. Meeting of squadron leaders and deputies in fifteen minutes."

He returns to his quarters, where Irit meets him with a cup of steaming coffee. In the kitchen Dov is having coffee and cake, also in his G suit. Galia in Irit's red bathrobe sits blinking and yawning. "I'm still fasting," she says. "I'm not air force personnel."

"It's foolish," says Irit. "Have coffee. Who knows what the day will bring?"

"Suit yourself, Galia," says Luria.

"Benny, is it the Six-Day War again?" Irit wants to know. "We're attacking?"

"Can't discuss it. I have to talk to those poor Hassidim. I've housed them near the kitchen. They'll go crazy when they pick up cooking smells."

In the Prime Minister's office, as Barak listens in silence to the sobered talk about what steps to take next, Yom Kippur does not have to be cancelled, it does not exist. Pastry, tea, coffee, cigarette smoking, business as usual; same room, same faces, same calm tones, with this difference, that catastrophe now appears to be thundering down on Israel. Zeira and Dayan are maintaining, though a shade forlornly, that it may still be a false alarm. After all, Zeira's ultrasecret special source has only raised the probability overnight from *"very low"* to *"eighty percent sure."* And what about the guaranteed seventy-two-hour warning? No explanation, and Dado and Golda are now assuming the worst, war at sundown. Her words are coming back to Barak: *"Do those great warriors need an old lady to nursemaid and second-guess them?"* The appalling answer seems to be yes.

For Dayan and Dado are at loggerheads. The Ramatkhal wants immediate drastic moves to head off the surprise. The Defense Minister urges prudence, with minimum hue and cry. A strange debate this, between the rugged handsome Elazar in field uniform, his square face wrinkling in worry under his thick curly hair, and the world-famed balding general with the eye patch, dressed like a civilian but bearing himself like a composed super–Chief of Staff. *How many reserves to mobilize?* That is the question, and to cut the argument short, Golda decides: less than Dado wants, more than Dayan thinks necessary. And what about the air force, the great winner of the Six-Day War? Dado is for a preemptive strike against Syria, but Dayan opposes it. After much talk she goes with Dayan.

The hurried meeting at last ends. When Barak is left alone

with her, she turns to him a face of white stone, deeply scored with tragic lines. "Nu, Mr. Alarmist? Go ahead, say, 'I told you so.' "

"But I didn't this time, Madame Prime Minister. And it's not war yet." She dismisses this with a hand-wave, as though brushing away a fly. He adds, "The American ambassador is waiting in the next room."

"I know that. So, Zev? What do I say to him? Do I tell him" — she falls into Talmudic singsong — "to tell *Nixon* to tell the *Russians* to tell the *Arabs* that we won't shoot first? Will that stop them? Or will it only encourage them?"

"For the Americans it'll establish your bona fides."

"Bona fides, shmona fides! They've sent me messages all week while the Arabs were massing, *'Don't preempt. Don't preempt.'* Like De Gaulle before the Six-Day War, *'Ne faites pas la guerre!'* " As she chain-lights a cigarette the stone face melts into the concerned countenance of a grandmother. "Your children, where are they?"

"The girls are too young to serve. My son Noah commands a Saar boat."

"Ah, the navy." She nods. "Well, it's a nice navy, but what can the navy accomplish? Now it's all up to the boys at the Canal and on the Golan. They'll have to hold and fight while we mobilize." She rests her head in her hand. "Seventy-two hours. We were promised seventy-two hours."

Zev Barak has a strong urge to plead for immediate total mobilization. It might still give the country some precious hours to gear up for war. Dado as army chief could demand it. Dayan as Defense Minister could recommend it. Why has the idea already been discussed and dismissed? Various reasons. Panicking the country on this holiest of days might prove needless, after all; a warlike move might trigger a still-doubtful Arab attack; and again, *always*, *always*, how will the Americans react? From the CIA as yet, there has been no warning at all. So who is Zev Barak to raise his squeaky voice? And what is wisdom now, with all Israel observing the Day of Atonement, and tank forces as numerous as Hitler's at his peak, poised north and south to close on the oblivious little Jewish State like the jaws of a nutcracker?

Golda lifts her head and stares at him, her eyes reddened.

"Yesterday, the minute I heard about the Soviet diplomats, I *knew*. I thought the great generals must know better. Maybe they did. Maybe they still do. Maybe it's not going to happen. But if it does, I'll be beating my breast till I die because I didn't act yesterday, and go to full mobilization." She bitterly smiles. "Some Yom Kippur, ha, Zev? I see you're still fasting, you've put nothing in your mouth. Eat something. Drink something. You'll need your strength."

Barak pours himself a glass of water and drinks it.

"That's the way." She looks down at her gray dress and straightens the skirt. "Call in the American ambassador."

In Haifa's main synagogue, Professor Berkowitz as a trustee rates a seat by the chief rabbi near the Holy Ark, but Shayna prefers the overflow Yom Kippur service in the downstairs social hall, so that is where they are this morning. The rabbi's son, an old beau of hers, officiates here and gives no sermon, in itself an attraction; and through gaps in the cheesecloth partition she can peek at her menfolk, Michael and Reuven, with Noah Barak, Don Kishote, and Aryeh, who all ate the last meal before the fast at her flat.

Kishote has come to Haifa after conferring with Arik Sharon at their division headquarters about the latest air photographs and intelligence maps of Egyptian dispositions. "It's war, all right," Sharon said. "But Gorodish has three hundred tanks in Sinai. That's enough to hold them while we mobilize, once we get the warning. I'll try to spend Yom Kippur at my farm. . . . Haifa? Why not? Go ahead. Have a light fast." With his deceptively gentle grin, Sharon then added, "Wear a uniform and boots. Just in case." So Kishote has come here with Aryeh, who is still desolate because his Gadna youth group was ordered off the Golan Heights, where they were visiting the outposts.

What an awesome view from Mount Hermon, Aryeh enthused to his father as they were driving to Haifa; Syrian tanks, howitzers, APCs, thousands of war machines stretching far, far out of sight, beyond the antitank ditch on the plain below. At the outpost, a narrow crowded hole in the ground, everything was thrilling: the telescopes, the guns, the military talk, the patches of snow, the army food, the crude bunks like shelves, everything! But all leaves were abruptly cancelled, and the Gadna youths sent home. No reason given. By chance he had encountered Amos Pasternak at a crossroads, directing groups of clattering tanks here and there. Amos gave him a hasty hug, but no information. "No, no war, Aryeh. Not that I know about. We're just here to discourage them from trying anything." Aryeh yearns for that smelly dugout on the Hermon, and the terrific view of the Syrians. However, spending Yom Kippur with his father and Aunt Shayna is nice, too.

Next to Shayna sits Hedva, a deeply pious friend who snagged the rabbi's son when Shayna broke up with him. Hedva now has three children and a barrel figure. Whenever Shayna peeks at the men Hedva frowns, but so what? Looking at Kishote and Aryeh does her heart good. Shayna does not envy Hedva Poupko the bewhiskered Chaim and her kids. Everyone's life is different. She has Michael and Reuven, and in a bizarre way she has Yossi and Aryeh, too. Cooking for them all before Kol Nidrei, especially for the Nitzans senior and junior, filled her with a unique precious emotion, an obscure deep joy tinged with pain, such as her friend Hedva would never know.

But odd things are going on beyond the cheesecloth. A paratrooper in uniform is making his way through the rows of chairs and taps the shoulder of a bearded youngster, who gets up and goes out, folding his prayer shawl. Moving here and there, the soldier hands worshippers slips of paper, and one by one they leave. Kishote and Noah too drop shawls on their chairs and depart. Shayna hurries to intercept them in the lobby.

"Yossi, what is it?"

"Reserve call-up. It may not mean much. Still, I'd better get back to headquarters. Keep Aryeh with you for the holidays, will you? I'll telephone tonight if I can."

Behind the offhand manner Shayna can discern an abstracted brain turning over contingencies, options, plans. "Come on, Yossi."

He smiles, life flows into his face, and the eyes twinkle behind the glasses. "Wonderful last meal, Shayna. Being with you is heaven for Aryeh. I don't mind it, either. Is the fast bothering you?"

"Kishote, is it war?"

"Not right now. If it comes, we'll win. Shayna, I love you. Get back behind the curtain, and" — he lapses into Yiddish — "*davan gut* [pray well]!"

On the chance that some plane, military or civilian, will be flying south, Noah Barak drives him to the airport. Moving automobiles all have their headlights on, signalling respect for the national fast day while driving on official duty. Reservists are hurrying this way and that in the streets in holiday clothes, some still wearing prayer shawls. At the airfield planes are being dragged by tractors from hangars. "Well, good luck in Sinai, General. An attack on Yom Kippur!" says Noah. "Makes sense from their viewpoint, I guess, the bastards."

"Easy, Noah. So far this is a limited mobilization. Yom Kippur's not such a bad day for us to go to war, anyway. Empty roads, and I know where most of my reserves are, they're either at home or in synagogue. . . . Hold on, that looks like my ride." He jumps from the car and trots after a tall striding figure in slacks and a sweater. "General, are you going south?"

The former air chief, Ezer Weizman, turns. "Don Kishote! Come along. How's Yael?"

"She's in Los Angeles."

"Ha! At the moment, a pretty good place to be."

Climbing into the Piper Cub, Yossi waves at Noah, who speeds off.

The navy base, when Noah gets there, is busier than he has ever seen it: fuel and ammunition trucks rumbling about, working parties loading every vessel in sight, boat engines snarling and coughing as they warm up. He parks the car with the headlights ablaze, then remembers and goes back to snap them off. With that he snaps off all awareness of Yom Kippur.

The flotilla commander, a small dark man named Barkai, with a tough face and a disposition to match, is leaning over a chart on the desk in his map-lined office, under a majestic picture of Golda Meir. "Ah, you're here, Barak. Good. So much for army intelligence, hah? You sail in the second group. The word is, the Arabs will launch all-out war at six tonight. By then we'll be off Cyprus with five boats, out of Syrian radar range. We'll penetrate Latakia harbor after dark and sink the Syrian fleet. Surprise the surprisers. Any questions? My staff and I will ride in your boat."

Noah's heart thumps. He does indeed have questions, for the Syrian fleet is armed with the Styx missiles which sank the *Eilat*. The Cherbourg boats, and the new boats constructed in Haifa, have the Gabriel missile, but its range is less than half that of the Styx: twelve miles, against twenty-eight miles. The Syrians can stand off and fire Styxes with impunity, unless the Israelis can somehow close the range and survive to fight. What about the newest countermeasures from Rafael, the armament authority, he asks, is there still time to install them?

"No, no. Look, we're already loaded up with countermeasures. If one won't work maybe another will. Anyway, we've drilled and drilled at missile-evading maneuvers, and to Azazel with the Styxes. We're going after the Syrian navy."

General Luria has to brief a crowd of nonplussed Phantom pilots, all suited up and ready to go, on a last-minute change of targets. If war actually breaks out now, he explains, the reserves will need two or three days to mobilize. Meantime the small regular forces will have to hold off the Arabs north and south. The Egyptians are two hundred miles from Israel, whereas Syrian tanks are just a fifteen-minute run from some Jewish settlements on the Golan. Egypt remains the chief target, and the air force will certainly smash that missile screen along the Canal, which by doctrine has been first priority for any outbreak of war; but now, with the short warning time, crushing the Syrians' offensive capability becomes more urgent. New target for the first strike, therefore: the Soviet missile batteries covering the Golan front.

Eagerly the pilots man their planes. Dov Luria runs through the checklist strapped to his knee, jet engines roaring all around him, his nerves taut. Like his father he is at last being locked into the cockpit by his ground crew to take off for a preemptive strike! He has been drilling for this since getting his wings, and he is hot to take off. But it turns out that the strike will hit Syria, not Egypt, and for that there have been no drills, unfortunately, and the intelligence map is sketchy, the weather report vague. He is exchanging final instructions with his radar man when — *"Attention! All aircraft! Attention!"* The controller's voice in his earphones, agitated and urgent. *"Abort, I say again, abort. Operation cancelled. Acknowledge and return for further briefing."*

What a rotten letdown!

Back in the briefing room his squadron leader explains that reports of bad weather over the Golan have caused the abort. While new intelligence maps and an op plan are improvised, the fliers wait a whole hour; then they return to their planes, digesting the information thrust at them, and much less eager. Change of target yet again; instead of the missile batteries, some airfields deep inside Syria, where skies are clearer. Trundling his huge howling machine out to the runway in a lineup of Phantoms and Skyhawks, Dov is rattled by these sudden alterations in long-laid, well-rehearsed plans. Once more ready to take off, he hears a sudden sharp call from the controller *"Abort, abort! Return to hangars!"*

WHAT TO ALL THE DEVILS IS GOING ON?

Not only Dov is thinking this. So is his father, shouting at a hapless army telephone girl to connect him to General Peled, the new air force chief. Luria knows that Peled will level with him, if only he can get through! This on-and-off pushing around of nervy fighter pilots is horrible, and surely not Peled's idea. At this rate the air force will start the war, if one is about to break out, not with another glorious MOKADE, but a bloody fashla.

"You're through, sir!" exclaims the girl.

"Luria?" Peled comes on with a note of gruff affection.

"Sir, I called off the preemptive strike on the airfields, but barely, let me tell you. They were warming engines on the runway."

"And you're not happy."

"Not dancing with joy."

"Luria, Dado ordered the scrub at the last second, and he didn't dance with joy, either. Golda and Dayan made a political decision not to strike the first blow."

"But why? Why?"

"You know why — *'What would the Americans think?'* "

"So what's the mission, if it's war?"

"The mission? We absorb the first blow, to satisfy Mr. Nixon and Mr. Kissinger. What we do next depends on how the attack unfolds."

"Maybe it's not war, sir."

"Well, we'll know by six tonight."

They know earlier, because the sirens sound all over Tel Nof shortly after two. Within minutes the first wave of Phantoms and Skyhawks is in the air heading southwest: back to the original plan! Five successive strikes, north to south, to destroy Egypt's missile batteries at the Canal. Dov Luria, in the second wave, rolls his Phantom out to the runway, heart beating fast and mouth dry, ready to take off against the flying telephone poles, about which he has heard a bit too much.

From Weizman's Piper Cub thrumming south above the seacoast at five thousand feet, Kishote can see Yom Kippur dissolving all over the sunlit Jewish State. When they took off, the roads outside Haifa were almost empty, but more and more vehicles keep streaming into sight, and by the time the gray spiky blotch of Tel Aviv looms ahead, the thoroughfares are becoming clogged. "Look, I'll fly you down to your division," Weizman says.

"You don't have to do that, sir. Plenty of cars heading south now."

"Well, I will. I shouldn't be in the air anyway, I might as well be useful." The plane banks steeply, bumping in air currents. "You have to fight. I'm out to grass. All I'll do is kibitz in the Pit."

"It's not war yet, sir."

The ex–air force chief, his hatchet features half-hidden by helmet and headphones, makes a face. "This is it, Yossi."

When Kishote arrives at the frantic division HQ, the duty officer tells him that General Sharon has checked in, looked around, and then driven off to Gorodish's command HQ in Beersheba. *Arik and Gorodish!* thinks Kishote. *A small war starting before the big one.*

Though General Sharon has charged off into Israeli politics like a rhinoceros, he has never lost touch with the troops. A month ago he ordered an exercise in countering a surprise attack, and Kishote staged two days of drills, complete with a mock battle and live fire. Today he finds the headquarters staff repeating these drills in high spirits. He makes a jeep tour of the sprawling camp. Order is emerging from chaos in a cheery if horrendous racket, as thousands of lawyers, teachers, garage mechanics, shopkeepers, and other assorted civilians go about forming up into an armored division of two hundred tanks. In fact an air of make-believe pervades the camp, because it is all so much like the recent drills. The threat of war seems very remote here. Many soldiers are still fasting.

In his office in the command hut he finds on his desk the latest intelligence summaries of Egyptian tank and troop movements; veiled jargon, full of unit names and coded locations. Having followed these reports for two weeks — especially of the positioning of new Soviet bridging equipment all along the Canal, and the visible massing of huge water cannon and motorized rafts — Kishote has long since guessed that this is to be an attack, astutely planned to look like training maneuvers to the last moment, so that a preemptive strike by Israel will raise a world howl of *"Aggressor!"* But intelligence is not his job. One thing is evident: for this round of war, if it breaks out, better brains, Arab or Russian, are at work in Egypt than in 1967.

"Well, the top brass have royally fucked it up again." A recognizable abrasive voice speaks behind a thin plywood wall. *"And so our asses are back on the line."*

"Exactly so." Another familiar voice. *"And they'll be shot off on day one if it's up to Sharon. Tough to be a Jew."*

First voice: *"Well, at least that fat son of a whore knows what he's doing. Not like those fuck-headed politicians of ours."* Crash of falling signal equipment. *"Hey, easy! That receiver's not one of your shitty ceramics, it's valuable."*

"No harm done, you can drop this thing off a cliff. You're right about the politicians. Golda's been a major disaster."

"In what way?" Yossi inquires, walking into the signal room next door.

Unshaven, in ill-fitting uniforms, the two reservists get to their feet; Shimon Shimon and Yoram Sarak, pals in the army as at the Jericho Café. Equipment is piled in disorder around them for transfer to field HQ signal cars, and coffee cups and remnants of sandwiches litter a table. Though still fasting, Yossi is not offended or surprised at this pair of scoffers. They are both keen signal operators, which is all that concerns him, *rosh katan* enlisted men who ducked officer training during compulsory service; better at the job than the kids in the regular army, but with other things to do except in war.

"Is it the real thing, sir?" inquires Sarak, with a nice mix of deference and friendliness. From his viewpoint, Brigadier General Nitzan is a good reserve boss. Some officers enjoy lording it over well-known civilians doing their *miluim* (reserve duty), but this Don Kishote is all business, very sharp, now and then slipping into tart humor with the journalist under him. Also Sarak, a notorious skirt-chaser, can respect Nitzan's rumored success at that game.

Without replying, Yossi looks to Shimon Shimon. "In what way has Golda been a disaster?"

"Sir, that's a large subject," says the ceramicist. "I don't want to commit treason while on active duty."

"Frank talk isn't treason," says Kishote. "Go ahead."

Shimon glances at Sarak, who grins and shrugs. "B'seder, sir. I think she's weakened Israel, if not destroyed it. From 1948 on we lived by a consensus just to survive, and to convince the Arabs to let us live in peace. But she and her gang — that foul Galili and the rest — decided after the Six-Day War to be a *big* little country, and hang on forever to the Sinai, the Golan, and all the rest. The national consensus is kaput. We're split down the middle. Frankly a lot of us sympathize with the Arabs, sir — me included — and if this is a war, we may be too divided to win it."

"I could hardly say it better myself," says Sarak, "though in fact I have. I wrote that column six months ago, Shimon."

"Well, are you two guys ready to fight?"

They look at each other. "What's that got to do with it?" says Sarak. "En brera."

"Good enough," says Kishote, and he goes out to an orders group of brigade and battalion commanders. He is still addressing them in bright sunshine about plans for a night advance to the Canal in case of war, when at 2 P.M. the sirens go off.

In the smoky gloom of the Tel Nof fighter control center, operators closely watch the radar scopes for the approach of enemy aircraft, while noncoms wearing headphones mark the progress of the war on the big table map, and others chalk Hebrew cabalisms on blackboards and Plexiglas panels. Benny Luria paces amid busy officers, awaiting word on the effectiveness of Egyptian antiaircraft against the first wave. A girl brings him a phone on a long cord. "For you, General."

"Luria?" Peled sounds hoarse. "Pick up the red telephone." He dashes up two flights of stairs, down a long corridor, and through the side door of his inner office. "Luria here," he says, out of breath from tension, not exertion.

"Trouble, Benny. OC North is asking Dado for close air support *at once and at all cost*. The Syrians threw a giant artillery barrage for an hour, and now they're clearing the minefields and bridging the antitank ditch. They have eight hundred tanks in the jump-off zone. We have about eighty there to stop them till reenforcements and reserves arrive."

"Rough."

"Very rough. In a few hours their armor can be running all over the Golan and down into the Galilee. What planes do you have ready to go?"

"Six units of four, set for the second strike against the Canal missile batteries."

"Wrong armament. Switch them to antitank and strafing ordnance."

"Sir, unloading those heavy bombs has got to take a lot of time."

"You're right. Send those aircraft to drop their bombs in the sea, and return to rearm."

Luria is taken aback. It is an emergency procedure for a plane in trouble, otherwise unprecedented. "Sir, are you seriously telling me to order my pilots to jettison their weapons?"

"Luria, Dado has ordered *immediate* air support in the north. Immediate is immediate. Last time we surprised them, now they've surprised us. That's how it is. En brera. Central Command will give you latest enemy movements and weather in the north."

With heavy foreboding Benny Luria issues the order: *Urgent. Second wave jettison all armament at sea and rearm for close air support north.*

Of all commands Dov Luria could receive, even *Proceed alone to bomb Cairo* might be more welcome. He takes off sick at heart. Jettison his bombs! What a contrast to MOKADE, the great triumph his father led six short years ago! But he does as he has been told, roaring with Major Goldstein's unit of four out over a blue sea wrinkled by a strong offshore wind; and as his first act of war, with a sense of nightmare, he drops into the water weapons worth millions of American dollars. His radarman, a dour young moshavnik planning to go back to dairy farming, says as the bombs splash far below, "Well, sir, don't feel bad. Maybe some Arabs are swimming around down there."

Circling to land at Tel Nof, Dov sees ground crews waiting beside bombs all laid out in the well-drilled pattern for rearming planes fast. Here at least is an echo of MOKADE! Armorers and mechanics swarm over his plane as he climbs out. At the coffee urn in the hangar he finds Itzik Brenner, number three in the four-plane unit, a dark big lieutenant with a huge nose and a black beard.

"I thought I'd make it through the fast," says Itzik with a guilty grin over his coffee cup. Though from a religious kibbutz, Itzik is no longer very observant. "But I want to be sharp for the Syrians. I owe them."

Dov knows what that means. Itzik grew up within artillery range of the Golan Heights. When he was four a direct hit collapsed the kibbutz shelter, killing two kindergarten friends and breaking his arm, which is still crooked. But the kibbutz has hung on, though since the Six-Day War the young people have been drifting away to the cities.

Amid the racket of the reloading and the roar of patrol planes landing and taking off, the pilots are briefed on the field by the squadron leader. General Luria is there, noting the strain on his son's pale young face as he listens to late fragmentary intelligence. But such were the briefings in the turnarounds of the Six-Day War, too. This has been something like Dov's bar mitzvah as an Israeli pilot, the father wryly thinks. Passing the course, getting the wings, earning praise for high performance in training — all very well! Now the enemy waits in the north. As he watches the quartet take off, and Dov's plane leap into the air and dwindle away, he mutters a prayer.

Flying up the Jordan Valley in cloudless sunlight over familiar terrain, Dov feels his mood clearing. This was something he has also trained for, after all, close air support, and he feels ready. Those poor tank guys on the Golan are catching the heat, so the mission is a necessary one. Ahead and to the right of him roar three aircraft, Major Eli Goldstein in the lead. Dov's fit of nerves is gone, his head is cool, and his heart soars to be flying to a real fight in the world's best fighter-bomber, with these familiar dials, the familiar cockpit smell of fuel and electronic ozone, the familiar reassuring engine roar . . . but damn, the weather reports are not wrong. Ahead over the Golan Heights clouds are piled, dark and multilayered from the horizon to the zenith.

19

Fathers and Sons

About the time Dov is taking off, Arik Sharon is returning to his division. He finds Kishote at the optical gear depot, in a dusty field overgrown with rank-smelling weeds and crowded with a vast jumble of private cars, delivery trucks, ice cream wagons, moving vans, taxicabs, even one cement-mixer, the motley vehicles by which the ten thousand reservists of the division are solving the Yom Kippur dearth of busses. Kishote is quelling an angry dispute between the quartermasters and a besieging mob of tank commanders. The hubbub dies when Arik appears in his blue leather jacket, gray-blond hair windblown, the most recognizable man in Israel after Moshe Dayan. "What's all this?" he demands.

The supply of binoculars and periscopes is short, Kishote explains, since many were drawn for peacetime war games and never returned. Now the quartermasters are requiring forms filled out for each instrument. Sharon shouts to the quartermasters, "The forms are waived! First come, first served!" Cheers from the sergeants commanding the tanks, ranging from youths who have barely finished their draft service to middle-aged reservists. Sharon again. "If the supply runs out, there will be more down at Tasa, don't worry! First come, first served, I say, and make ready to move, all of you.

Nitzan, call an orders group for section heads and brigade commanders."

Around a long narrow conference table, some fifteen senior officers gather to hear the few reliable facts that Sharon has learned from the confused first reports at Gorodish's HQ. Without question, he says, the Egyptians have achieved complete strategic and tactical surprise. This is not the time to ask why and how. One day soon the people will call the government to account, no fear! *(There speaks the politician still, thinks Kishote.)* Now there is a war to win.

The bitter truth is that Egyptian forces are crossing the Canal on motorized rafts in at least five major thrusts, bypassing the Bar-Lev maozim, which they stunned and silenced with an hour-long rain of murderous artillery fire. Already they have gained several shallow lodgments — he raps a pointer at the locations on a large Sinai wall map — and are now blasting breaches in the ramparts with water pumps of fantastic power, and starting to lay pontoon bridges. General Mandler's three regular brigades, with less than two hundred tanks, face an Egyptian onslaught of seven divisions and at least a thousand tanks! The position accordingly is very dangerous.

Having poured on the gloom, Sharon turns brisk and optimistic. The Arab is a good soldier and a brave enemy, *so long as he fights on a set plan.* So far Egypt appears to be doing things by the Soviet book, planned and drilled to the last detail. The way to reverse this initial success is to break up the enemy timetable. The two reserve Sinai divisions — this one, and one under General Adan coming from the north — have to race down the peninsula and counterattack to contain the invaders' bridgehead, then cross the Canal and cut them off from the rear. With this the entire Egyptian front in Sinai can falter and collapse in three days. But meantime it will be very hard going all the way.

"The bottleneck right now is tank transporters." Sharon slaps his pointer on a wall photograph of a monstrous low-bed trailer truck carrying a sixty-ton Centurion. "General Adan has requested priority on these. I didn't argue. He has farther to go. I don't know how long it'll take to round some up for us, and so, gentlemen, I mean to run south all night on our treads." Troubled glances around the table. Sharon turns to Kishote, sitting near him at the map. "What about it, Nitzan?"

"That will grind down the tanks, sir," says Kishote drily, "before they ever fire a shot. It's a hundred thirty miles. It'll push the crews to the fatigue limit. A lot of breakdowns en route are inevitable. Traffic will pile up in the passes and the high dunes. Tanks will bog down getting off the roads. A total mess."

"So you're against this?" The tone is calm, but Sharon's eyes narrow.

"I'm saying what to expect, sir, but we have the best repair gang in Zahal. Our garageniks can take apart and put together a Centurion in the dark like an Uzi. What's more, transporter drivers can't be controlled. They can wander off or be commandeered. Our own tanks we can control. We'll get there worn out, sir, but we'll get there as a division, ready to fight. Let's do it."

Among the officers, a rueful murmur and nodding of heads. Sharon dismisses the meeting, and when he is alone with Yossi he slaps his shoulder, "Well done, Kishote, stating all the objections before they could. I'll lead the first company that gets on the road. You come along with command headquarters, and check at Point Yukon yourself in the morning, to make sure that Tal's brainchild, that confounded roller bridge, is ready to go. I intend to cross into Egypt day after tomorrow."

"What! *Monday?*" Kishote blinks. "Does Gorodish agree?"

"Gorodish is out of his head. The roof has fallen in on him. He's issuing orders that make no sense, and he's very self-conscious and touchy about taking advice. He served under both Bren Adan and me in this very command, and now he has to command us. He's well aware that Bren created the Bar-Lev Line, that I built up the Sinai infrastructure and road system, and that we both know ten times as much as he does about all this. *Zeh mah she'yaish*, Kishote. But Bren's the greatest tank man in Israel, and between us and Mandler's brigades we'll win Gorodish's campaign for him."

Droning over the white-capped Sea of Galilee, Dov's plane and the three other Phantoms are bumping into the dense murk over Syria. Now Dov is locked to the dead reckoning of Major Goldstein, once his navigation instructor. Their target is a large Syrian tank force, and as Dov is figuring it the objective has to be ahead at about five miles, when Goldstein's voice breaks radio silence with one word: *"Nered."* ("Let's go down.") The air becomes rougher, the cloud layer thicker and darker, as they descend. At moments Dov can see only Itzik's wing ahead and to his right. Two thousand feet, fifteen hundred. Dirty mist, rain hammering on the canopy. Okay, there is the ground, glimpsed through thinning wisps of cloud and drifting rain curtains.

Nothing there.

Not a thing. Broken rock, greenish scrub, here and there a shallow conical hill, not a sign of war in the two-mile circle of hazy visibility. Nothing! Old intelligence? Wrong intelligence? Or has there been a sudden breakthrough, and are those Syrian tanks already rolling westward over the Purple Line forts into the Golan?

Straight ahead a jagged ridge of low hills, vague in the mist. Goldstein: *"That ridge is not on the map. The target may be on the far side of it. Forward, then."*

As they are arching over the ridge, antiaircraft fire ignites the air all around them; sudden hell of fireworks, ground twinkling below, colored balls rising up, flames exploding all over the murky sky.

Wow, the real thing! Change altitude, jink like mad, evade, evade, evade . . .

Oh God, oh God, ITZIK! No!

It happens so close to Dov that the blast rocks his aircraft. One moment Itzik is zooming to evade, and the next second he is vanishing in a dirty billowing expanding globe of flame, with black ragged pieces tumbling away. Blown to bits! Red and yellow explosions flaring everywhere in the gray sky, over the canopy, across the windshield. Oh, *Itzik!*

Now Goldstein, level-voiced. *"I'm hit, but I have power. I'll try to eject over our territory. Abort, abort, return to base. God rest poor Itzik. Abort! Dov, Avrash, acknowledge."*

"Avrash here." Very shaky tones. *"Acknowledged."*

"Dov here. Acknowledged. Major, Avrash and I can still try to find that tank force. It's our mission."

"Shlilee, shlilee! [Negative, negative!] Abort. Go home. That's an order. I'm turning west. Out." Dov reverses course and roars full throttle skyward, for the antiaircraft is obviously locked in on their altitude. In seconds he is over the ridge, climbing into thick clouds. He can't see Avrash. Has he too fallen?

Whirling thoughts. Sickly urge to urinate, never mind that. Flying by instinct and by drilled-in responses. Compass course west by south and climb, climb, to get out of the overcast. Hang on to yourself. Itzik is gone, you have to fight all the harder, fly more missions. What a pitiful start for a combat career! What a difference from the Six-Day War . . . what a defeat . . . one pilot out of four surely dead. Maybe two, maybe three. Benny Luria's son fleeing for his life. How can he face his father and Itzik's ground crew? And Itzik's pregnant wife, Ida, from the same kibbutz, nineteen years old, a religious girl, no television on Shabbat . . . After the debriefing he'll have to walk past the apartment of big-bellied little Ida, a widow and not yet aware of it. Dov's father has talked much about the sad side of being a tayass, but not until you've seen a wonderful guy like Itzik die instantly in a midair explosion . . . Why not me? Just crazy luck . . .

Out of the clouds. Ahead the Sea of Galilee, the ribbon of the Jordan, and there is a Phantom in front at eleven o'clock low, on the same course. Avrash! So he'll be breaking the terrible news first. . . .

At Tel Nof, when Dov releases the drag parachute and rolls to a stop, he can see Itzik's crew huddled on the runway and Avrash walking away head down, helmet dangling from his hand. Itzik's plane captain calls as Dov climbs out of the cockpit, "Any chance he made it? Ejected? Got captured?"

"Itzik is gone. We'll never see him again." Their stricken looks spur him to add, "It was over in a second. He went out in fire."

Among the somber faces is his own plane captain. "Major Goldstein is safe, sir, behind our lines," he says.

"Thank God."

In the briefing room, his father is waiting with the squadron commander and Avrash. Dov does his best to return professional answers to the questions, to show no trace of feeling. That rule he has breathed in with the air of his family. "In your judgment, what went wrong," asks the debriefer routinely toward the end, "and what can be corrected?"

Avrash and Dov look at each other. Though Avrash is senior, he gestures to Dov, the base commander's son, to speak. Maybe Avrash just isn't up to it.

"What went wrong, sir? Bad weather, poor intelligence, very bad luck. What I really think is, sir, we lost two Phantoms on a wild goose chase." Dov glances at his impassive father, and regrets the escape of the angry words. Unprofessional. But he blurts on, "How can it be corrected? Well, I don't know exactly how Itzik can be brought back. Sorry, sir."

On the grass-lined path to the quarters Benny Luria puts an arm around his son's shoulders. "Itzik was a superb aviator."

Dov chokes out, "I guess you're glad to see me."

"Don't talk about it. I'm going back to fighter control."

"What's happening in the war?"

"Terrible confusion, no solid information. We seem to be holding them, north and south, but the air force is mostly responding to howls for help. No coherent new battle plan yet."

"I have to walk past poor Ida's porch."

"You won't see her."

Dov does not. The shades are drawn. When he enters the family quarters he smells frying meat, Yom Kippur quite forgotten. Galia springs at him to embrace him, and her face is wet. He has to clear his throat. "So you know about Itzik."

She leans away in his arms, staring at him with tearstained dark eyes. "And about Major Goldstein."

"Well, Goldstein's fine. Listen, so is Itzik. Is it so bad to die fighting for your country? It's bad for his wife." He gives her a squeeze and a kiss. "Something to think about, motek."

That night Zev Barak works his way through corridors of the labyrinthine Pit far below central Tel Aviv, where there is no night or day, and officers hurry here and there with harassed pallid faces. He finds Sam Pasternak in the Defense Minister's cubicle, morosely writing on a pad. "Can we talk, Sam?"

"Make it fast. Dayan wants a sitrep for the cabinet meeting at ten."

"That's exactly what Golda wants — some solid facts going into the meeting." Barak takes the hard chair facing the desk. "The telephone reports are making her head swim. She told me to question Dado, but his room is so jammed with ex-Ramatkhals and major generals, you can't see him for the uniforms and the smoke."

"Ask me the questions."

"Aleph, is the news really that bad?"

"Not that good." Pasternak's head sinks between his shoulders. "When the sirens sounded this afternoon, Zev — and it seems a week ago — I estimated that if the Egyptians sleep tonight on this side of the Canal in substantial force, they'll have won the war. Politically, which is what counts in the long run. I hope I was wrong, because it's happening, and the north is worse." He peered blearily at Barak. "Amos is up there, though I don't know just where. The Syrians are overrunning or bypassing our fortified points all along the Purple Line. They have night-vision equipment, we don't have any, and they have ten tanks to our one. The Mount Hermon outpost has already fallen, with all our ultrasecret stuff. Small but terrible disaster right there."

"In short," Barak says, his heart cold, "no good news on any front?"

"Well, the mobilization is way ahead of schedule. At this rate we'll be up to strength north and south by tomorrow night. Amazing job. And of course the Jordanians haven't attacked yet. Still, they're massing troops, and two Iraqi formations are reported on the way. Now, Zev, what about the politics? The UN? What does Golda hear? The Arabs blatantly broke the UN cease-fire, no? Fired the first shot, no? So? No action in New York?"

"Oh, yes, the Egyptians claim *we* started it. Our navy shelled them, so they're simply defending themselves, and the Syrians are coming to their aid as allies. The UN is studying this grave charge of Israeli aggression."

Pasternak stares at him and grunts, "Are you joking?"

"I swear it's true."

"And Washington?"

"Vague noise. The State Department won't say who fired the first shot. I have to get a navy statement right now on that nonsense."

"Good luck." Pasternak shakes his head and resumes quick scrawling.

Barak threads through the fluorescent-lit corridors, where air vents hum and rattle without seeming to remove the smoke or bring fresh air; past the huge main war room with its three-story operational maps, crowded by gloomy junior officers wearing earphones, to the navy's area in the Pit. Much against their will, Navy Command has been moved here from Haifa because — so the Supreme Command has decided — in their eyrie on Mount Carmel they have been too independent and detached. But even here underground the navy HQ is as different as though it were still on Mount Carmel. The officers appear cheerful, the young female sailors perky and pretty, all in a milieu of excited optimism. Even the air seems more breathable.

"Ah, Zev," says the *Mahi* (chief of naval operations), a good-looking big-jawed man, who like Barak was brought to Palestine as a child to escape the Nazis. "Just in time." He gestures at the table map, where the girls are moving boat emblems eastward. "The flotilla has been lying off Cyprus, and now they're heading full speed toward Latakia. The flag is in your son's boat."

"What's the plan, Binny?"

The CNO taps the map at the Syrian shore. "Their coastal radars are bound to pick up our boys any minute, so we assume their missile boats will sortie to challenge. What's coming up, my friend, is the first missile-to-missile battle in naval history" — he rolls off an orotund phrase with relish — "a Mediterranean Coral Sea!"

Barak knows the exact ranges of the Styx and the Gabriel. His smile at the hyperbole is strained. "And suppose the Syrians don't come out, what then?"

"Barkai will enter Latakia port and engage by gunfire."

"And the coastal artillery? The minefields?"

"Intelligence got us the minefield charts. As for the coastal batteries, well, you know Barkai. He'll say 'L'Azazel,' and go in."

Barak's voice drops. "Look, Binny, we both know how far the Styx outranges the Gabriel."

The CNO matches the lowered voice, not the anxious tone. The big jaw thrusts out, the eyes are hard. "The Styxes were able to sink the *Eilat* for two reasons — surprise, and size of target. A Saar is a water bug, and the Styx is a fire-and-forget weapon, no operator guidance. Electronics can fool it. Smart ship-handling can dodge it. As for the Gabriel, wait and see."

"Binny, what about that Egyptian fabrication that your ships shelled them?"

The CNO promises to provide him with a full factual refutation within the hour. Barak returns to Golda's conference room, above in the main army building, where the cabinet members are gathering, some in shirtsleeves, others tieless in wrinkled suits; the big fish in Israel's small pond, the usually complacent faces now showing uncertainty and shock. The few who matter like Dayan, Galili, Sapir, Allon, are not among them. So well known because politics is Israel's chief spectator sport, endlessly interviewed, pictured, caricatured, they are self-important strutters all, in Barak's opinion, but tonight, what a deflated lot of middle-aged worriers!

Golda takes him into her inner office. "Let's hear." She listens with half-closed reddened eyes, nodding and smoking, to his report. "A bad picture. But all this is from Pasternak? Not Dado himself?"

"Prime Minister, Sam is there for Dayan, and he gets whatever information Dado does, and at the same time. Dado is three-deep in generals."

She sourly smiles. "I can picture it. Dado's coming to talk to the cabinet soon, so that's all right."

"Madame Prime Minister, I have to return to the Pit for the navy's answer to the Egyptian fakery. Also, a sea battle is shaping up off Syria, and my son's missile boat is in it."

"A sea battle?" With a bleak nod, brushing ashes off her bodice, she says, "Go ahead, Mr. Alarmist, by all means, stay with the navy till it's over. God guard your son in the sea battle. What concerns me right now is the land, our land. God guard our sons in *that* battle."

"*Target dead in the water.*" Zev hears those words as he returns to the navy war room. What a contrast to the long faces elsewhere in the Pit, and the deep dejection at the Prime Minister's offices! Smiles and handshakes all around here, and the CNO raising a hand for silence. Loudspeaker voice again: *"Large silhouette on fire and listing. Probably a minesweeper. Over."*

"Minesweeper?" says the CNO into the portable mike. "What's a minesweeper doing out in five hundred fathoms of water, Barkai? Over."

"Picket duty, like that torpedo boat we hit. I've detached Motti to sink both cripples with his guns, and am running ahead with four boats to Latakia. Over."

"Ah, Zev, look here." The CNO takes him by the elbow to the big map table. "First they got a torpedo boat picket with their three-inch, then this big radar blip showed up, so Barkai closed and launched Gabriels over the horizon. Two big flashes, and now he's confirmed it — a large vessel aflame and disabled, huge holes blasted in the hull —"

"Not a neutral? You're sure?"

"Not a chance! A picket. Saw our boats on radar and ran. Something to tell Golda, hey? The Arabs need Russian missiles, but we Jews make our own, and —"

"TEEL . . . TEEL . . . TEEL." The flotilla commander again on the loudspeaker, his voice calm and unchanged. Startled faces in the room. Sudden silence, but for the whirring of the air vents. *"I say again, TEEL . . . TEEL . . . TEEL. Urgent. Activate all countermeasures. All boats commence evasive action, maneuver at discretion . . ."*

Wind and spray blow hard in Noah's face as he comes scrambling topside. Yes, there those things are again to the southeast, the yellow moons of the horrible *Eilat* night and of his nightmares ever since, hanging among the stars, growing larger and drifting to the right. The two Saar boats far up ahead are turning sharply this way and that, firing off their countermeasures. Noah's own rockets of chaff and decoys go hissing and blazing into the night sky, making slashes and zigzags of red, yellow, white, against the darkness.

Barkai's voice on the bridge speaker: "Noah, ninety seconds to impact." Below at the command console Barkai is watching the pips of the missiles in flight, and of the enemy boats which have suddenly emerged from the radar shadow of the land for this surprise launch.

"Acknowledged, sir. . . . Hard right rudder! Engines ahead flank speed." If all the electronic countermeasures fail to work, he can still try to dodge those evil globes. The six years since he went down with the *Eilat* melt away and the fright is on him again. But now he is not helpless, he is captain of this feisty little vessel, and he can do radical evasive maneuvers. "Hard left rudder. Left engine stop." Those lights are swelling in the sky, showing dark smoke trails. But will the ECMs work? Does Israel have a sea defense, or are those damned things homing on him, and is he about to go down in enemy waters, this time probably forever?

"Rudder amidships! Flank speed." The boat sways and shudders, smashing at the waves, throwing spray high as the bridge. "All engines stop. . . . All engines back full."

The lights are sinking, the Styxes are going into their dive at the boats ahead — no, also at him, *at him*. Noah is feeling the fear now in his stomach and his balls.

Underground in Tel Aviv, frozen attitudes in the navy pit. Eyes on the clock, time of Styx flight about two minutes, almost over. Second hand clicking loudly from mark to mark.

Barkai's voice a shade above his usual calm. *"Five splashes."*

Outbursts of joy: kisses, hugs, dancing, jumping, one man spinning insanely round and round and round the room and cheering. Zev shouts at the CNO, "Who is he and what's the matter with him?"

"That's Zemakh and the matter with him is, he created the countermeasures. All of them. *Magiya lo* [He's entitled]! Now we know we can beat the Styx, and it's all Zemakh's doing."

Barak catches the spinning man in his arms and kisses his bristly cheek. "I salute you, my son's out there."

Barkai's voice, everybody quickly silent. *"Three enemy boats now retiring at high speed. I will pursue and destroy them. To Zemakh, a salute and the thanks of my crews. And of the Jewish people. Over."*

The CNO thrusts the microphone at Zemakh, who says hoarsely, "Hello, Zemakh here. Acknowledged. Go get them. Over."

"I intend to. Out."

A radarman says to Noah as he drops back down into the CIC, a large smoky room amidships crowded with electronic equipment and operators, "Captain, target number two seems to be reversing course." Noah peers at the screen. Yes, clearly the middle green blip is moving away from the other two, toward the flotilla.

"Kol ha'kavod, one of them turning to fight," grates Barkai. He seizes the microphone and addresses the flotilla. "All boats, prepare to launch missiles."

Tense quiet in the CIC. Soon the radarman calls over his shoulder, "Enemy missile launched, Captain."

"I see it." Small new green blip on the screen.

Almost at once another radarman. "Captain, Gabriel launched by our lead boat." Noah clambers topside, and glimpses something he will never forget: amid the decoy trails in the starry sky a white light soaring over a larger golden light, the missiles crossing in midflight; then the Styx light falling into the black sea, the white trail disappearing, and after a tense minute, a great *FLASH* on the horizon. He tramples back down the ladder. Barkai exults, "Noah, one enemy missile boat sunk, it's disappeared off the radar."

"I saw the flash, sir."

"B'seder. Now we're closing the range on the nearer one. Go ahead and shoot him."

"Ken, ha'm'faked." ("Aye aye, sir.") The radar blip shows the Styx boat nineteen thousand yards ahead. Noah has often scored hits in the simulator at that range, but this will be his first actual Gabriel launch. "Prepare missile for firing."

"Captain, missile ready."

"Very well." Rapid orders, lights flashing white and green on the consoles, quick back-and-forth jargon among Noah, the weapons officer, the radarmen, the missile men. Flotilla commander silent, watching.

"Captain, system on target."

Waves are crashing and sloshing against the heaving hull, just as in the endless simulator exercises, complete with rolling and pitching, only now the sea is doing it, not a mechanical rocker, and a real missile topside is primed to go, and a real Syrian Styx boat is trying to run away. With a last glance over the consoles, Noah presses an isolated white button labelled PERMISSION TO FIRE. *GHRANG, GHRANG, GHRANG!* Alarm all through the boat, all lights on consoles turning red. Silence. THUD. The boat shakes, the Gabriel is in the air.

Though shorter in range, the Gabriel is more advanced than the Styx. Like the Styx, it homes with a nose radar; but an operator on the bridge controls it with a joystick, locking it to ride on the boat's radar beam until the missile itself sends the electronic signal saying *"Okay, I'm in charge."* It is then so close to striking that no evasive tactics will avail.

"Takeover signal from missile, Captain."

"Very well. Over to missile."

Pause, all eyes on the radar consoles. Radarman drone. "Missile blip merging with target, sir." A break of his voice to boyish glee. "Captain, the target's gone from the screen."

A yell over the loudspeaker from the missile operator on the bridge. "Huge explosion ahead, sir, enormous flare on the horizon."

Barkai at the central console: "Noah, you've blown him up. He's gone."

"All hands," Noah announces on the PA system, "scratch a Styx boat."

The vessel rings with cheers. Barkai, his eyes agleam, throws him a salute. Revenge for the *Eilat*, and not the last of it. The remaining Syrian captain appears to be running his vessel up on the nearest beach, despairing of making good his escape to Latakia. "Noah, go in and destroy him with gunfire," says Barkai.

As Noah's vessel races landward to within a hundred yards of the beached boat, coastal batteries light up the sea with green floating flares. Shells begin to straddle his vessel, throwing up towering splashes. The stranded Syrian boat is a wreck, half out of the water and steeply canted on the beach. Roaring back and forth through the shellfire, Noah rakes it again and again with all guns. From the dark derelict some sporadic shooting back, as it absorbs the rain of shots for a long minute or two, then it explodes in heavy smoke and bright flame.

Zev Barak drives as fast as he can through blacked-out streets jammed with army vehicles chugging and rumbling into and out of Tel Aviv, repeating Barkai's dry victory report under his breath, for he means to quote it to Golda word for word. *"Five enemy vessels encountered. Four sunk, one stranded and set ablaze. No damage or casualties to the flotilla. Returning to base."* This battle off Latakia, though small in scale, has surely been a turn of naval history; the first missile-to-missile sea fight, and a victory of little Israel over the Soviet Union. Vindication of the navy, of the Gabriel, and of electronic know-how in the Jewish State.

Wrapped in an old black shawl, Golda is drinking coffee and smoking on a worn sofa in her Ramat Aviv home. "So?" she asks in a rheumy voice, setting aside a wire basket of despatches. "Your son is all right?"

The way she brightens at his account of the battle does his heart good. "Wonderful boys," she exclaims. "Those missiles, those electronic gadgets, fine. A victory, a ray of light."

He produces a sheaf of navy papers and photostats. "Absolute proof the Egyptians invented that pretext, Madame Prime Minister. Location of all our war vessels at the time, impossibly distant from the scene."

Nodding and sighing, she says, "The Americans at least will believe us. That's good. The cabinet meeting, Zev, was not so good."

"Dado's pessimistic?"

"Dado was all right. He cheered them up. He said this is the containment phase, very hard, but the war will turn around. It was Dayan. He wants to pull back already in the Sinai, to a line twelve miles from the Canal and try to build up our strength there. Retreat, retreat, shorten lines, fighting withdrawal." Golda raises pouched sleepless eyes to Barak.

Barak's exultant mood fades, the Latakia fight shrinking to the marginal event it really is on this shattering first night of war. "Was that the decision? Was there a vote?"

"There was no vote. Dado said he would hold on both fronts and fight back. The cabinet went with him and I went with him, although the news is very bad from the Golan. Even Dado said he might have to order a retreat there, but not yet." She sourly smiles. "So, how alarmed are you now?"

"Madame Prime Minister, we're going to win this war."

"From your mouth in God's ears, that's what I believe, but we won't win it on the sea. And if God forbid we lose it, it will be on the Golan."

20

The Third Temple Is Falling

Golda speaks true. In a melee of clanking snorting war machines, thundering guns, and lurid fire, Israeli and Syrian forces are tangled together on the Golan Heights. Amos Pasternak's sector is on a slight rise facing the valley where the Syrians have been massing for weeks, and more and more tanks keep coming at him. Over and over he shouts on the battalion network, *"Identify before shooting! Identify before shooting!"* Any tank that comes in sight through the darkness, the smoke, and the dust is probably an enemy, but above all he can't afford losses to friendly fire.

Shaken and bruised by the violent maneuvers and half-deafened by the gun blasts of his own tank, Amos nevertheless is in fighting rage. His boys are picking off Syrian tanks one after another in bursts of flame, but agonized cries and death reports fill his earphones. Night fighting, once a prowess of Zahal, is a weakness this time because the Syrian tanks have infrared headlights and see the battlefield almost as in broad day, while the Israelis are fighting blind. Amos has been calling and pleading and yelling for starshells. The artillery officer has returned soothing promises but as yet no light.

Venturing high up in the turret with a special infrascope to glimpse the battle, which to the naked eye is all black night and stinking combat haze, Amos is horror-stricken to find himself square in the beam of an infrared projector, in effect a brilliant searchlight. *"Driver, driver, full speed reverse,"* he bawls. The driver down in the tank's belly sends it jolting and rumbling backward. *"Now sharp left."* Amos swivels the turret gun as they lurch and crunch over rocks, intending to fire at that projector, when a crash hurls him against the hatch cover. They have backed into another tank. Friendly or enemy? *"Forward and turn right."* He risks switching on his searchlight. A head and shoulders emerge from the other turret. L'Azazel! Dark, mustached, a young Syrian, looking as scared as he himself probably looked in the infrared glare. Point-blank range, not twenty feet. An instant of pity for the youngster with the round frightened eyes. *"Fire."* Roar of cannon, BAAM! Ringing in his ears, choking smoke. The tank aflame, the Syrian's uniform on fire, the poor guy clawing at himself and at the turret, trying to jump out.

"Driver, left turn and stop." He trains the gun back toward the Syrian lines, and clicks the mike button to the battalion circuit: *"Yardstick commander here. All Yardsticks make reports."*

Strung out across the sector, some tanks answer up, but too many remain silent. Sector barely covered, gaping holes. Falling back is unthinkable, yet if some reserves don't show up soon there will be no defense line blocking this valley, the main northern corridor into Israel.

Amos's father is dozing off at his underground desk. When the telephone startles him awake he is not sure whether it is night or day, or what day. Dayan sounds refreshed and chipper. "Sam, I'm going to the Golan at first light. Pick me up and run me to Sde Dov, just the two of us, no driver. Organize a helicopter."

Suppressed yawn. "Yes, Minister."

Gray-faced and red-eyed, Dado Elazar nods and tiredly smiles when Pasternak tells him about this. "Well, of course. The Minister wants to smell powder. Talk to air operations." No wonder the Ramatkhal is wide awake, Pasternak thinks; on the wall map of the Golan, heavy crimson arrows slash almost to the command HQ at Nafekh, scarily close to the Jordan bridges. The Sinai transparency tells just as grim a story; the Egyptians are across the Canal from end to end, still advancing.

In a brightening dawn Dayan waits on the street outside his Zahala home in a field uniform, red paratrooper boots, and a crumpled U.S. Army cap he acquired visiting Vietnam. They drive through streets streaming with heavy army transport. "Dado wouldn't come with me," says Dayan. "I asked him. He's wrong, Sam. A commander-in-chief should see the battlefield with his own eyes. The dead, the wounded, the burned-out machines, the way the men look and talk. That's how you get the feel of what's really going on. How do you read the battle so far?"

"Minister, the Golan is the worst, it's critical today."

"That's why I'm going there. Syrian tanks looking down the chimneys of Tiberias! A nightmare, who could have believed it? At least the women and children are off the Golan, thank God. I saw to that. But we can't possibly evacuate the Galilee. It would panic the nation." A pause. Abruptly, "Sam, how did we ever get into this fix?"

"Sir? You mean the surprise?"

"No, we war-gamed for surprises." Dayan's enigmatic probes are often rhetorical, but now the good eye is staring at Pasternak for an answer.

Pasternak ventures a guarded comment. "Well, Minister, doesn't it go back to the military budget cuts? Dado warned the government that he would no longer be able to fight a war on two fronts. That he'd have to defeat them one at a time, shuttling our forces. Those cuts were political decisions by the cabinet."

"Right! It was the politicians, and I told them the same thing then. Last night I also told them the hard truth. The enemy's seized the initiative, and now we have to think in strictly military, not political terms. Fall back to lines matched to our strength, survive until a cease-fire, and live to fight another day. That's what we did in 1949, and that first truce saved us. But Dado was all optimism, promised to counterattack in the next few days and turn the war around. It was what they wanted to hear, and I was the bearer of bad news, so I was ignored."

The helicopter is coming down as the car pulls into the airfield.

Dayan shouts over the noise, getting out of the car, "I'll try to see your Amos."

After the all-night fighting Amos and the driver are having their turn at a nap, while the loader and gunner stand guard. Opening his eyes, he feels rested and famished. He climbs up in the turret with binoculars for a look-around in the early sunlight. By God, his battered battalion and the rest of Seventh Brigade did a job. Scattered far and wide on the brown valley floor below are burned-out Syrian tanks, APCs, and other vehicles, many still flaming or smoking, and dead Syrians too. A few shadowy figures skulk among the wrecks. Several Soviet T-62s are undamaged, evidently abandoned, valuable booty to be towed in when the chance comes.

"Yanosh here, calling Amos." In the helmet earphones the brigade commander sounds hoarse and fagged out.

"Pasternak here."

"Ammunition and fuel now available at the crossroads. Replenish by platoons. Meet me there."

"Pasternak here. I expect another attack soon."

"So do I."

High time to replenish, at that. Amos's surviving tanks look much the worse for wear; outside equipment boxes ripped, one tank still smoldering, another on its side with its gun pointed at the sky; and on the battalion circuit the talk is nervous and sad — many wounded and dead, supplies almost gone. Upright in the turret, Amos leads his battalion into the dense pack of tanks and trucks at the crossroads depot, where unshaven soldiers are noisily prying open ammo crates and passing shells, and the smell of diesel oil is rank in the air from all the pumping. Colonel Yanosh Ben Gal stands by his signal jeep, a helmet clamped on his hawk face and wild long hair. The tubby man beside him in a cloth cap is nobody but the Minister of Defense! Dayan inquires without ado, "Amos, what's been happening in your sector?"

Amos collects his thoughts and begins an account of the night battle, insofar as he can reconstruct it. His crew feverishly takes on shells and a fuel truck is pumping away, when he hears, "*Planes.* Planes, coming in low. Take cover!" The shouts send him diving under his tank. A fusillade of low-aimed AA fire breaks out, bullets whizzing and whining close by. He sees the Minister of Defense standing there with hands on his hips, watching two gaudily-painted MiGs fly past a few yards overhead as though he were at an air show. Amos wonders, peering up at the famed warrior, whether he has no nerves or a death wish. The bombs explode without damage, throwing up splashes of earth and smoke far beyond the depot, and the planes dwindle away.

"From what Yanosh tells me, Amos," says Dayan, resuming their conversation as if the interruption were a telephone call, "you've got a battalion of heroes out there."

"Many, many casualties, Minister. It was a hard night."

Amos's loader pokes up in the turret. "Sir, Yair reports Syrian tanks coming up the valley, distance four miles."

"Here we go," says Amos.

"Good luck," says the Minister of Defense. "Reserves are coming, Amos."

"One moment," says Yanosh, his bristly face worried and drawn. "Amos, look here." He produces a scrawled-over Golan map, holds it against the tank hull, and marks it with quick swooping pencil lines. "Their artillery is beginning to zero in on the ramps." These are the slanting earthworks where the tanks are positioned. "On my signal, move your tanks to back off and deploy here instead. Got it?"

"Yes, sir." Amos climbs up on the tank, and plugs in his headset. "All Yardsticks, return to sector. Minister, please tell my father I'm okay."

"I'll tell him more than that."

Nakhama moans as the bedside telephone rings. "My God, how long have you been asleep? An hour?" Barak came home to tell her about Latakia and cheer her up, and he has managed to sleep a little, for the sun is high.

"Barak here. Yes? . . . B'seder, I'm on my way."

Nakhama buries her head in the pillow. He dresses quickly, worried about her shot nerves as well as the war. Far from rejoicing over Noah's victory, she has been whimpering about it. Suppose those countermeasure gimmicks don't work next time? It'll only take one failure! Why did he make Noah stay in the navy? The sea is worse than the air. A pilot can parachute from a burning plane, but if Noah's boat is sunk in Arab waters he can only drown, or get captured and murdered. Wars! Wars! The wars will never end until the Arabs have cut every Jewish throat, if it takes a hundred years. Such is Nakhama's tune these days. When he bends over her to kiss her neck and say goodbye, her response is a gruff sound into the pillow.

In Dado's crowded underground command cubicle a commotion is going on, when Golda Meir and Barak arrive. The Chief of Staff hangs up the telephone and jumps to his feet. "Is there a problem?" she coolly inquires.

"We're handling it, Madame Prime Minister." Dayan is on the Golan Heights, he tells her, giving direct orders to the air force. Only immediate massive air strikes, Dayan is insisting, can stop the Syrians from overrunning the Galilee. "But Madame Prime Minister, that is a judgment for me to make," Dado says in level firm tones. "I don't yet believe things are that bad, and I know the Golan. I captured it in 1967. And even if the Minister is right, my air weapon is my decisive reserve, and only I must control it."

The new air force chief, General Peled, stands at Dado's elbow, a short dapper aviator with a keen aspect and the obligatory pencil mustache; a test pilot, a combat hero, and unlike most pilots an intellectual with an engineering degree. Golda shifts a questioning glance to him. "It's being straightened out, Madame Prime Minister." Peled's speech is brisk and clipped, as in an RAF movie. "Motti Hod is landing there now as my deputy. The chain of command will be respected."

Golda sits down and takes a cigarette pack from her capacious white purse. "Dado, I must talk to the people today. I'm working on the speech, and I want to give the truth as far as I can, without aiding our enemies or depressing our soldiers and their families. So tell me — what's actually happening? What can we expect today? How is the war going, in your judgment?"

Passing from map to map with a pointer, General Elazar gives her as frank and full a picture as he can, dark but far from hopeless. "The truth is, Madame Prime Minister, it's not the enemy attacks that trouble me most right now, it's the unreliable reports. That's inevitable, the war's just starting."

"Can we rescue those boys in the Bar-Lev Line?"

"We'll try. I'll soon ask the war cabinet's permission to counterattack in Sinai tomorrow. Arik Sharon and Bren Adan will be arriving down there in force today, so we'll have better than six hundred tanks in the area. That's a lot of strength."

"But if the air force is busy in the north, that counterattack will have no air support."

Glances pass among the generals crowding the room. "By then, Prime Minister, the picture may be different in the north."

"Also, won't the missiles make air support at the Canal too costly?"

Dado looks at General Peled, who says, "We have a plan to take out those missiles, Prime Minister. We've been diverted to the Golan, but we'll do it."

When she and Barak are returning to her office, she says to him, "So, Mr. Alarmist, you heard all that. How bad d'you judge it is on the Golan?"

"Madame Prime Minister, the one sure fact about war is the fog it raises. It's very difficult up there now, that's clear. Catastrophic? Not that bad yet. Not from Dado's summary."

She chain-lights a cigarette, smokes in silence, then shoots a question at him. "Then who can I send up there to have a look?"

A shock. Moshe Dayan is there now, and he is her military brain. This gnarled old woman is in the crisis of her life, she thinks in black and white, and her weakness is military ignorance. *For or against us? Good or bad news? Winning or losing?* B.G. at least studied strategy; Eshkol built the army and was an underground fighter. If she is losing confidence in Dayan's judgment, in a war not yet one day old, that is a very bad turn. Before he can reply she goes on. "Maybe Dado should go. But then again he has the whole war to attend to, and things change by the hour. So he has to sit in that hole, like a spider in the middle of a web, waiting for vibrations. I don't envy him. He looks bad."

"He's a strong guy, Madame Prime Minister. He'll pace himself."

"I'm thinking of sending Bar-Lev. What do you say?"

Haim Bar-Lev! Ex-Ramatkhal, advocate of the crumbled line, retired general, now Minister of Trade and Industry. Not Barak's first choice, but a simon-pure Mapai Party man, and by Golda's political standards, *"one of ours."*

"There would be complications. He's a civilian."

"So is the Minister of Defense, no? See to it, Zev."

"Yes, Madame Prime Minister."

It has been a hard night in the Sinai, too, for the one regular armor division of less than two hundred tanks trying to hold back the enemy surge across the entire hundred-mile Canal front. From some bypassed and surrounded maozim have come desperate appeals for rescue; from others, bold bloody breakouts at night through their Egyptian besiegers, twenty and more soldiers clustering on a single tank.

Strung out for many miles on narrow Sinai roads are the reserve divisions of Adan and Sharon, two immense convoys far apart, some four hundred tanks in all with their long support trains, crawling to the rescue all night in rolling fogs of diesel fumes and dust at about twelve miles an hour; the best speed they can make through the rocky passes and steep sand dunes, what with the traffic jams and breakdowns of all manner of vehicles, from giant transporters to old sedans. Don Kishote has been cruising back and forth along his convoy in a signal jeep, keeping track of stalled units by wireless network, urging on the laggards, getting cripples dragged aside for repairs, and clearing bottlenecks. On a hot sunny morning the great convoy at last rolls into Tasa, Sharon's central sector command base several miles east of the Canal; worn down and with many stragglers, but an intact fighting force. Over the tumult of the traffic, the thump and grunt of big guns are sounding from the west, though in the sunlight the flashes cannot be seen.

The command bunker underneath the sprawling racketing depot is narrow, gloomy, and quiet except for the staff conversation and sporadic bursts of loudspeaker jargon. Someone is saying as

Yossi comes down the stairs, "Yes, and what will the Labor Party do now about all those posters and billboards, *'The Bar-Lev Line Is Ours'?*" Barks of derisive laughter. The politics go on, he thinks, even within sound of the guns. Down in this hole there is loyalty only to Arik Sharon, verging on adoration. It has now and then seemed to Don Kishote that Israel is not a serious place, a parody of a country, but the day after the Yom Kippur attack he is not amused. "Where is Arik?"

"He's lying down." The operations officer gestures at a tacked-up wall map of the Sinai, under a transparency thick with colored military symbols, arrows, and code names. "We were having an orders group, and he fell asleep standing up."

The talk continues about the grim fiasco at the Bar-Lev Line. The trapped boys, reservists who replaced the regular troops for the Yom Kippur holiday, are still begging or screaming for help. Several strongpoints have gone silent, probably fallen. During the night tank platoons audaciously charging to the rescue were mowed down by Egyptian tank-killer guns and the fearsome new Sagger wire-guided missiles; and Sagger teams are now emplaced right on the Bar-Lev rampart. These advanced Soviet rocket weapons are fired with a wire attached, along which an observer sends signals directing the shell from launcher to impact. The accuracy is frightening. Spent wires crisscross the sands this morning amid burned-out and blasted tank hulls, and Sharon is infuriated, the officers tell Yossi, by this futile frittering away of tanks. He intends to gather every available tank in Sinai for one quick mighty smash across the Canal tomorrow, the third day of war, to save the boys and turn the war around.

Kishote is at a narrow desk glancing through despatches, when Arik Sharon strides in, his face damp from a wash, his manner rested and alert. "Ah, so you're here at last, Yossi," Sharon says. "I don't know yet how I can talk the General Staff and Gorodish into crossing the Canal tomorrow, but it *must* be done. The Egyptians are dancing with victory. They've never beaten the Jews before. Their tails are up. They've got the momentum now and they're very very dangerous. They need a swift hard shock. *Tomorrow!* Bren Adan and I can do it. Are you very tired?"

"Sir, I'm at your command."

"That's my Kishote. Number one, run right down to Point Yukon, or wherever that roller bridge is by now, and see what shape it's actually in. I can't get a straight report out of anyone."

"I'll leave now."

"B'seder. By the time you're back I'll have an operational plan for the crossing, with a detailed map. You'll take it to Gorodish, not me. He loves you. You'll report how he responds, and then my fight with him starts."

The sun is blazing by the time Yossi's signal jeep, with Sarak and Shimon at the voice transmitters and receivers, reaches an outpost in the desert where he comes upon the famous roller bridge, which he has not seen since the summer demonstration. It lies broken apart in several gigantic sections on the white sand, and helmeted soldiers are fussing at it. Nearby in a tent camp more soldiers move about, and smoke rises from a field kitchen.

"What to all the devils is this?" Kishote asks a bespectacled lieutenant with hands jammed in a parka, watching a snorting bulldozer tug at a bridge section.

"Balagan, sir."

Seeing Dzecki Barkowe on top of a nearby roller section, banging with a wrench, Kishote shouts, "Dzecki! Come down here!" He turns on the lieutenant. "We cross the Canal tomorrow. Will this bridge be ready?"

"I'm only a supply officer, sir."

His face masked by grease and sand, Dzecki climbs down and salutes. "What's happened to this bridge?" Yossi demands.

Dzecki explains that Amos Pasternak's battalion went to the Golan with the tanks trained for towing the monster. Another company was assigned to practice towing the bridge, and on the first try they pulled it all apart. Then they were ordered to forget the bridge and return to the Canal to fight. Somebody, Dzecki didn't know who, sent the bulldozer, which just arrived.

"Can the bridge be towed by bulldozers?" inquires Kishote.

"Oh, no, sir. Coordination by tank network signals is vital."

"Then why the bulldozer?"

"En lee musag." (Universal Israeli reply; roughly, "Haven't the foggiest.")

Kishote ruefully contemplates the dismembered bridge. The bulldozer is dragging a section with snorts, squeals, and clankings, amid confused shouts by soldiers running here and there. "How is it," he asks Dzecki, "that you didn't go north with your battalion?"

"Sir, Major Pasternak left a small party of us to guard the bridge."

"Who's in charge here, and where is he?"

"The new chief engineer is around somewhere, sir. Maybe in the latrine. He just got here and he has the runs bad."

"What's to be done, Dzecki?"

"It's not nearly as tough as it looks, sir, to put it back together. If ten tanks get here today, the bridge can still go tomorrow. The main thing is getting the signals straight among the tanks. That's what went wrong. It's a network control problem. They all must pull at once. It's crucial."

Yoram Sarak and Shimon Shimon are both dead asleep in Kishote's jeep, with headphones on their ears. "Come with me, Dzecki. . . . Wake up, you!" He prods Shimon Shimon. "You're staying here. This is Master Sergeant Dzecki Barkowe. He'll explain." To Dzecki he says, "Ever heard of Shimon Shimon?"

"The ceramicist?" Dzecki's grimace conveys eloquent dislike. "I've heard of him."

"By my life!" exclaims Shimon Shimon, yawning. "Yoram, it's the kid who gave Daphna the Rolex, the goofy American. Ma nishma, Dzecki?"

"Ten tanks will come here this afternoon, Shimon," says Kishote, "to tow this thing. Dzecki here knows the drill. The signal arrangements are crucial. You will take charge and arrange them."

"When do I rejoin you, sir?"

"When this bridge is across the Canal."

Yoram Sarak peers at the huge scattered sections. "This is a bridge? It looks like a train wreck. Is this the thing that won the Israel Prize?"

"Shimon is your man, Dzecki," says Kishote. "Tell your chief that he not only makes menorahs, he's a master of circuitry and networks."

"Keep your head down, Yoram," calls Shimon, standing by the broken bridge as the jeep heads back to Tasa. There Kishote picks up Sharon's plan and map, and drives at top speed on the military road through the desert to Southern Command advance headquarters at Umm Hashiba, on a high bluff near the Gidi Pass, forty miles from the Canal. Knowing Gorodish well, he expects to find him shouting at somebody about something while staff officers scurry frantically about. The sedate calm in the expansive HQ puzzles him until he comes on Moshe Dayan in Gorodish's inner office. They are drinking coffee and seem pleased to see him.

"So, Arik wants to cross the Canal tomorrow." Gorodish's tone borders on sarcasm. "Fine idea. You brought a map?" Yossi pulls it from the briefcase and unfolds it over a larger map on the desk. Gorodish puts on thick black glasses to glance at it, and shakes his head. "There are no Egyptian bridges in that area. How will he get across?"

"The roller bridge."

"It's in pieces, and don't tell me it can be repaired by tomorrow! It's a big nonsense, that Tallik patent, that Israel Prize contraption. I'll cross on captured Egyptian bridges when I'm good and ready. It's the only way now."

"Remember, they're pontoon bridges, Shmulik," says Dayan. "One artillery hit can finish a bridge."

"That's what engineers are for, Minister, to repair them."

Arik Sharon has sent Yossi to soften up Gorodish, knowing that, insofar as the prickly OC Southern Command allows himself to like anyone junior to him, he likes Don Kishote. But the presence of Dayan queers the game at the start. Brusquely Gorodish hands Arik's map back to Yossi, and resumes describing to Dayan his own attack plan for the morrow. It is a strangely unreal scheme, Kishote thinks, like a sand-table war game, complicated and overambitious. To Dayan's questions Gorodish responds airily, shifting his eyes to Kishote now and then, and calling in staff officers to explain details of logistics and intelligence.

"Well, I'm just a minister," Dayan says at last, getting to his feet, "all this is up to the Ramatkhal."

"My plan will work, Minister, I promise you," says Gorodish. "I've talked to Dado about it, we're in constant touch."

"Kishote, walk out with me," says Dayan. He speaks no more until they are at the helicopter. He looks very pale, and his good eye bulges white. "By my life, I wanted Shaika Gavish in this post," he exclaims. "What a fashla! When war came, the DOVECOTE deployment we drilled and drilled was never executed. Those reservists were out there in the forts without tank support, with no warning, on holiday routine —"

"What about Arik's plan, Minister?"

"Yes, yes, he's been pestering me about that. Arik's a stallion, but he hasn't the wherewithal. A Canal crossing that fails will lose the war, will lose everything. The Golan may be lost already." He strikes Kishote's shoulder, and painfully smiles. "Just do your job. We'll get through this. You're *amitz* [courageous], Yossi." There is no higher praise in Zahal than that.

When Yossi walks back into the commander's office, Gorodish breaks off a howling rebuke to a meek logistics officer and dismisses the man with a rough gesture. "So, what did Dayan say? It's a great plan, isn't it, Yossi? It'll win the war. It's my plan, my G-3 just put in the details."

"Well, it's clear he's not for Arik's plan, sir."

"Oh, that! Sorry, Kishote, your boss is out of his mind. You be sure to tell him that if he tries his old trick of turning off the volume" — an armor force euphemism for ignoring orders — "I'll have him relieved!"

Dayan's helicopter whirs down in the Sde Dov airfield, where Sam Pasternak waits beside his car. "What's the latest from the Golan?" Dayan calls as he jumps out of the aircraft.

"Hard day so far, Minister." Pasternak keeps his voice low, for several officers are nearby. "Syrian tanks overran division HQ at Nafekh. Raful had to pull his command staff out into the field. Ben Shoham was killed an hour ago."

"Ah, my God, no!"

"I'm sorry, he's gone. The Syrian columns in his sector have halted, but we don't know why. The way seems wide open for them down into the Galilee."

"The air attacks have stopped them, for the time being," says Dayan. "I knew they would. We were overextended and unprepared, Sam, on both fronts, and we were taken by surprise. If Golda and the war cabinet will only listen to me, we may yet pull off a miracle. That's what we're talking about now, a miracle to save the country."

Riding back to the Pit, Dayan paints a black picture of the southern front. Bad as things stand, Gorodish is bent on something worse, a plan that will destroy half the meager forces he has. "It's a historic calamity that Gorodish is down there, Sam. A fine armor man, Gorodish, but he can't command a front. I knew that. I *told* Dado that. He wouldn't listen. Well, I fought for years to get a withdrawal from Sinai, didn't I? Remember my speech about *'jumping into the cold water of negotiation'*? I even called for a unilateral pullback, to let the Egyptians operate the Canal and give them a stake in peace. But that's all in the past. Sam, the Third Temple is falling."

"Minister, it hasn't come to that," says Pasternak, with a terrible chill at heart. This, from *Moshe Dayan*?

"You're sitting in the Pit, Sam. I've now been to both fronts, I've seen the field hospitals full of broken bloody boys. Whole battalions in retreat, with shocked and frightened faces. My Zahal warriors! Our tanks smashed and burned by the dozens, all over the Lexicon Road and the Tapline Road in the south, and the Purple Line in the north. We don't have much time to save the situation, and the Gorodishes and Dados can't do it. It's up to the platoon leaders, the company commanders, the battalion commanders like your Amos. They preserved Israel in 1949, and they can again, but the leadership has to give them a fighting chance."

The air in the Pit, on this second night of the war, is exceptionally hazy and foul. Pasternak has to elbow a way for Dayan through the backs of generals bunched in Dado's office. "Gentlemen, the Minister." They all make room, and the Ramatkhal gets to his feet.

Dayan says, "Dado, I'm about to report to the Prime Minister what I've seen so far today on both fronts, and the conclusions I've drawn. I'm telling you first, so that if you disagree, you can come with me to make your views known."

"Please, sir!" Dado politely waves a hand at the wall maps.

Moshe Dayan gives his blunt views to this crowd of army seniors, the military elite of Israel, including several former Ramatkhals and most of the General Staff. As though to an orders group, he delivers an apocalyptic vision with his usual quick-witted incisiveness; and his magic aura of martial authority, built up over a quarter of a century, lends his words fearful force. Pasternak can see consternation taking hold of these poker-faced officers, all Dayan-approved appointees, old acquaintances of his, disciples, even worshippers, as they find themselves facing a choice of calamities: the collapse of Israel, or of Moshe Dayan.

For with these judgments which the Minister of Defense is laying on the line, either the Ramatkhal has to order precipitate retreats in Sinai and on the Golan, which will trumpet to the Arabs and the whole world that Israel is falling back, on the second day of war, to a last-ditch fight for its very existence; or if Golda does not accept Dayan's view, and the army then stands its ground and in the end wins out, the credibility of the one-eyed military genius will be destroyed, his aura gone, his image shattered.

When Dayan finishes, David Elazar's face is calm, his tone professional, as he responds that he fully agrees a fallback in Sinai is an urgent matter to consider. He has already ordered Gorodish to work on this. The question of where to draw the line remains open. Meantime, holding the forward positions will preserve the various options of counterattack tomorrow, if Adan and Sharon can deploy in time. The Egyptians themselves might try to attack, for instance, and smash themselves against these powerful tank forces. As for the Golan, the latest reports suggest that the situation has somewhat stabilized and —

At this point a message is brought in for Dayan, a summons from Golda. "Come with me, Dado," he says.

"There's much for me to do here, Minister, on tomorrow's operations."

"I understand." Dayan walks out.

At once the atmosphere changes. Officers start pelting Dado with reactions and suggestions, ranging from agreement with Dayan's doomsday view to assertive optimism that Arab weakness and Israeli strength will soon surface and reverse the picture.

"I'm for Arik's plan," speaks up one venerable ex-Ramatkhal. "He's right, Dado! Cross the Canal tomorrow with the force you've got there. Throw the enemy off balance and into disarray. The Soviet doctrine they've been taught allows no improvisation. Our strength is in just that! In movement, in daring, in doing the unexpected."

Murmurs of agreement.

Dado nods. "I've considered it, and as a rule I'm all for the bold immediate gamble. You know that. But those two divisions are all I have between the Canal and Tel Aviv. That gamble I won't take."

"Arik would say," the elder returns, "that you're being absurd. That the Egyptian objective isn't Tel Aviv, but a big political victory; the capture of a limited chunk of Sinai under their missile umbrella, and then a Soviet-sponsored cease-fire."

"Possibly, but once the road is open to Tel Aviv, as it hasn't been since 1949, it might look rather inviting to the Egyptian Chief of Staff. No?"

Murmurs of agreement.

21

We'll Break Their Bones

The folds in Golda's face deepen and the skin goes livid as Dayan gives his report to the inner cabinet. She is close to paralysis by bewilderment, Zev Barak senses, and also by fear, insofar as fear can break through that iron will. She keeps looking to General Allon and to Galili, her old bone-tough socialist cohort, the two advisers on whom she most relies: Allon for his army savvy, the other for his political horse sense. She sees no comfort in their faces, nor do they interrupt Dayan. But when he says that if the Arabs offer a cease-fire in place right now he would accept, Galili passes both hands through his graying hair, scribbles on a scrap of paper, and passes it to Barak:

Get Dado here at once.

The ministers are sharply cross-examining Dayan when Barak returns from making the call. How can he consider retreating to the mountain passes, Allon demands, giving up without a fight advance bases that are the keys to the Sinai Peninsula, built with the finest technology at vast cost? Galili just as bitterly challenges the notion of abandoning the oil fields at Ras Sudar and Abu Rodeis, which in themselves have repaid the cost of the Six-Day War, made Israel energy-independent, and gone a long way to balancing the budget. Golda sits smoking with abrupt gestures, sucking hard on the cigarettes and stubbing out just the cork tips.

Dayan fights back coolly. He is being pragmatic, he claims. The successful surprise has overturned all Israel's security estimates and doctrines. The initiative, Zahal's customary edge, is gone. The Canal line is gone. The remaining boys in the moazim will have to fight their way out at night, with perhaps some help from a few tanks, though the Sagger wire-guided missiles are proving to be deadly tank killers. The Arabs can draw on endless resources of manpower and Soviet arms, while Israel may literally, and soon, come to the end of fighting men and weaponry, feeding them into the meat grinder of frontline battle. The only hope is to retreat, dig in on the mountains, and make a desperate effort at once to get more planes, tanks, and arms from America, and even from Europe, to carry on the fight.

"Moshe, what fight?" Golda breaks a long silence in a harsh voice. "Are we going to throw the Egyptians back to the other side of the Canal?"

"No, Madame Prime Minister, not now."

Dado comes in, his heavy brows beetling, his square jaw set. "Madame Prime Minister," he says at once, "we are still in a down, but I can report that on the Golan the Syrians have been driven back out of the Nafekh command camp. Also, the air force has destroyed a large number of Syrian missile batteries, and also several Egyptian bridges across the Canal in the south."

Her grave expression lightens. "So, there's some good news. Now, you've already heard the proposals of the Minister of Defense?"

"Yes."

"What do you say to them?"

"They are realistic and wise. They must be seriously considered, along with other options."

"Let us hear the options."

He begins to lay out Arik Sharon's crossing plan, but before long Allon interrupts him. "Forget Arik's brainstorms, what else?"

"Gorodish has a plan for a limited counterattack tomorrow.

Phase one, attack the lodgments on the flanks and throw those Egyptians back across the Canal." Golda's drawn face lights up as Dado describes that action in some detail. "Phase two, if he succeeds, send an advance force across captured bridges, and exploit the success to sow maximum panic and confusion in the main army over in Egypt."

"He's dreaming," snaps Dayan. "I discussed the plan with him thoroughly just a few hours ago. It bears no resemblance to the military realities on the ground."

"Agreed," says Dado. "The crossing is not yet in the cards. However, his scheme of a flank assault along the Canal from north to south by Bren Adan — with Sharon in reserve — might just catch the enemy lodgments by surprise and roll them up. That would be a start toward counterattack."

Golda looks to Allon and Galili. They are silent, thinking hard. Zev Barak admires the way Dado is handling this. After Dayan's cataclysmic fallback plan, and Sharon's radical attack proposal, Gorodish's operation as he is modifying it seems the sound compromise. Barak has not credited David Elazar with the adroitness he is now displaying, in putting off Dayan's pleas for a major retreat.

"Well, it's not my view that three options exist," says Dayan. "Gonen's plan, even scaled back, risks unendurable losses, and in our situation the Arik plan is madness."

"Prime Minister, I will fly to Southern headquarters tonight," says Dado, "and thrash out Gonen's operation with him. The war rolls on. We must do something, and one way or another a decision must be made by tonight. I'll probe the facts before I approve *preparations* for a limited attack. I won't signal a final go-ahead till the morning, depending on the situation."

Golda glances to Dayan, who barely nods his head. She stubs out a last cigarette with a sweep of her hand. "We'll see each other in the full cabinet in fifteen minutes." She gets to her feet, and the ministers stand up as she trudges to the door of her inner office. Dado, Allon, and Galili go out. Barak starts to follow the Prime Minister as usual after a meeting, but Dayan stops him with a tap on his arm, enters her office instead, and closes the door.

Barak is glad of a moment to catch his breath. Despite his

pallor and tension, Moshe Dayan is looking more like himself again. The ministerial suit and tie are gone. In his improvised field garb he is every inch the super-Ramatkhal, guardian of Israel's security, with Dado as sub-Ramatkhal, a sort of deputy, entitled to state alternate views to the boss's judgment. But in this disagreement of deputy and boss there is a final arbiter, Golda. That is why Dayan is in there.

The door opens. Out strides Dayan, the good eye sparkling, and with a rare warm smile at Barak, he darts a thumb at the door and leaves. Barak finds Golda Meir hunched over the desk, head in hands. He can see only gray hair between knobby brown fingers. She does not look up at the sound of the door closing. "Madame Prime Minister?" he says softly.

She raises her head. Barak thinks this woman incapable of tears, and she is not crying now, but her bloodshot eyes are filmy and moist. She lights a cigarette with unsteady hands. "He came in to resign."

"What!" The thunderstruck reaction bursts from him.

"That's right. He said, *'Without your confidence I can't go on. I'm offering my resignation.'* " Golda straightens up in her chair. "Can you imagine?" Her voice grows stronger. "Can you picture the effect on our people? On the world? On the *Arabs*? The great Moshe Dayan resigning after one day of war? The next thing to a white flag! Yes or no, Zev?"

"It's absolutely unthinkable, Madame Prime Minister."

"Just so. I refused to accept. I did my best to cheer him up. I assured him that of course I believed in him, I took his warnings to heart, he must go to the full cabinet with his views, he was the greatest general and military mind we had, the greatest maybe in the world. There was nobody who could possibly replace him. I guess he heard what he wanted to hear, because he retracted."

"Madame Prime Minister, you worked wonders. He came out a changed man."

"You think he did? Then that's that. So, now I go to the full cabinet, and I'll have to sit through all that again." As she pushes herself up with both arms on the desk, she manages a fatigued mournful grin at him. "You're no longer my Mr. Alarmist. You've been relieved."

At one in the morning of October 8, the third day of the war, returning from a meeting with Gorodish, Sharon glances up at a red streak crossing the starry sky and growls to Kishote, "Frog missiles still coming, eh?"

"They haven't stopped, sir."

"Well, now at least I know Gorodish's plan, as Dado has modified it. We're to sit here and do nothing while Bren Adan attacks north to south. I could make a more idiotic plan, but it would be a strain."

They are standing outside the command bunker at Tasa. Off to the west, the thumping and flashes of heavy artillery go on and on like a distant thunder-and-lightning storm. "Those poor lads in the moazim, no respite. Well, no help for it. Orders group in half an hour, Kishote. All officers, battalion commanders and up."

A map-festooned tent, stretching between two trucks and illuminated by jeep headlights, is the field war room. Sharon's manner at the maps shows no trace of anger or doubt. He is brisk, clear, and soldierly, laying out Gorodish's plan for the weary young officers, who in a few hours may have to lead their men to fight and perhaps die by it.

"We face two enemy lodgments north and south of the Great Bitter Lake," he says, rapping the map with a pointer. "The Second Army to the north, the Third Army to the south. General Adan will attack the Second from the north, driving southward toward us. We'll be his reserve, containing any enemy counterthrusts here in the center. When he has completed his mission — which should be by midmorning — we'll run south to smash the Third Army and exploit the breakthroughs. This day can be the turn of the war, the saving of our homeland. If it's a go, and we win this day's fight, we'll also save those boys in the moazim. So be strong and of good courage. General Nitzan, take over." He lumbers off to sleep in a command car.

On his feet to explain sector assignments and logistics, Kishote hopes he is being coherent. The maps and faces swim before his burning eyes. With the responsibility for ten thousand men plus their vehicles, now lined up along the desert ridge or on the Artillery Road below, he has been too keyed up for two days and nights to nap, too busy making notes, thinking ahead, handling foul-ups and crises. Now he is done in. Meeting over, he gives night orders to his operations officer, stumbles to his command APC and is asleep as he falls on the bunk.

Heralded by a great plume of dust rising in the morning sun, Bren Adan's division comes in sight about nine o'clock rolling southward. Even the Sinai's high dunes and great rocky ridges cannot dwarf the grandeur of the miles-long columns of machines. For Kishote it is a scene out of his favorite Walter Scott, regiments of steel-clad Crusaders advancing to fight the paynim. He says this to Sharon.

"Agreed. It's just as well war is so terrible," says Arik Sharon, peering through binoculars, "or we would become too fond of it." He turns to Kishote, his hair tousled by the wind. They stand on a high ridge overlooking the slope of the desert to the Canal six miles away, where dust clouds show that the enemy is also on the move. "Do you know who said that?"

"Napoleon, sir?" Negative smiling headshake. "Caesar? General Patton?"

"Close! General Robert E. Lee. Have you studied Lee's campaigns?"

"No, sir. In armor school we started with World War One, then Guderian, Rommel, and so on."

"A mistake. Lee was a genius. The art of war doesn't change, Yossi, just the tools — but where the devil is Bren Adan going? He should be heading far to the west of us, toward the Canal —"

Bursts of loudspeaker chatter from Kishote's signal jeep. "Message for General Sharon, General," Yoram Sarak calls to Kishote. "From Southern Command headquarters. *'Proceed south with your division according to plan.'* "

"Proceed *south*?" Sharon bellows, lunging toward the jeep. "Now? Is Gorodish crazy? What has Adan accomplished so far? We have to hold the center while he carries out his attack. Keep Southern Command on the line. I want to speak to General Gonen."

In the Pit, after two ghastly days and nights, upbeat reports are at last trickling in from both north and south fronts, so Pasternak declines Dayan's suggestion that he go home to bathe and rest. Since the war started he has not been out of his uniform or even his shoes, and his head throbs from breathing the stale Pit air, but even Dayan is seesawing to good cheer, advocating a possible quick crossing of the Canal, just a token lodgment in "Africa." For if the balance tips toward Israel the UN Security Council may well impose a speedy cease-fire, and Israel needs facts on the ground to trade off for an Egyptian withdrawal.

The Ramatkhal is as high as anybody at the apparent turn. His outward calm is unchanged, but he is saying things like, "We're past the critical point. . . . The surprise has worn off. . . . We're starting to counterattack on both fronts with mobilized reserves, this is more like it." His mood spreads through the subterranean warren like a dawn breeze. The public above is rife with anxious rumors after Golda's vague somber speech, so the Pit's inside knowledge of the counterattacks is all the more cheering. Pasternak joins a mock pool on when the war will end, as he will later wince to recall. His guess is four days.

At the morning cabinet meeting Dado's optimistic summary delights Zev Barak too, in his newfound respect for the Ramatkhal. Phone calls from the Pit reinforce his report: a breakthrough on the Golan to the Purple Line, an Adan battalion reaching the Canal and capturing a bridge, sixteen Egyptian planes knocked down. Though praising Dado for the swift turnaround, Golda remains impassive. Afterward she tells Barak that Dayan so froze her blood yesterday it will be a long time thawing and circulating again.

On his return to the Pit, Dado encounters pleas that he talk to the press. The favorable news is snowballing. Despite battle confusion, enemy jamming, and distance distortions, signal officers monitoring the command networks keep passing on fragmentary information from both fronts, all almost too good to be true. Long experience in intelligence warns Pasternak that they may be listening for what they want to hear, and he is for putting off the press until the evening. After all, the battles are still going on. Dado accepts this cautious view, orders a press conference for 6 P.M., and goes off for a tour of the Syrian front.

Yoram Sarak's bristly face pokes out of the signal vehicle rolling alongside Kishote's half-track at the rear of the southbound column. "Sir, General Sharon wants you to report to him, highest urgency."

Shifting to the jeep, Kishote speeds along the clanking column through a curtain of diesel fumes and whirling dust, and comes on Sharon leaning against a Centurion tank, rapidly making notes on a writing pad. "What took you so long, Kishote? Halt the division and turn it around. Bren is in desperate trouble. We must go to his rescue, back to exactly where we were."

Yossi Nitzan is more or less inured to battlefield shocks, but his mouth literally falls open. The forward elements have been running south for four hours, and the division is strung out for miles along the Lateral Road. A glance at the sun; no way to get back to help Bren before dark. "Unbelievable, hey?" snarls Sharon. "Get them going the other way, I tell you, then I'm sending you to Tel Aviv." He gestures at a helicopter landed nearby on the sand, its rotor slowly turning. "En brera. We are in extremis here. You can go there and be back by the time we reach Hamadia."

Kishote issues orders on the brigade network, whereby the rear of the giant metal snake becomes the head, and the thousand machines of the tank division clumsily turn around where they stand; time enough to redeploy, he decides, on the move. Sharon is still scribbling as tanks begin to pass them heading north.

"Well done, Yossi." Sharon hands him several sheets flapping in the wind. "Now then. Commit this to memory as you go, then *destroy the papers*! Understand? You'll have to tell it all to Dado face to face. He knows and esteems you, and he also knows you have my confidence. Who can figure what nonsense Gorodish is reporting to the High Command? It could even be that they think we're winning. Read this over, and ask any questions."

"Yes, sir."

Arik to Dado. Gorodish is endangering the nation's survival. Another day like today, and we will be pleading for terms. What has happened to Bren's division I don't yet know, but I am en route to help him. I suspect he received confused and contradictory orders. The order I received this morning at 1100 was lunacy. While Bren was still fighting his way south, Gorodish ordered me to abandon the central sector, and head toward Suez City! I pointed out that he was abandoning vital high ground and depriving Bren of his reserve. He shouted at me to obey or consider myself relieved, so I obeyed.

My division has yet to fight. It ran a whole night on its tracks just to get to the front, and now at Gorodish's orders it will have spent a whole day running south and north in the desert like a chicken without a head. This cannot go on. Kishote will verify every word. I still believe Bren and I can combine forces tomorrow for a winning smash across the Canal.

"No questions," says Don Kishote. "But will this helicopter pilot wait there to bring me back?"

"He will, because I told him to," says Sharon, with the sudden hard smile that probably overcame the pilot. "On your way."

Pasternak and Barak are standing in the lobby of Beit Sokolow, the Journalists' Hall, talking somberly about the afternoon reports that have now sent the mood in the Pit plummeting. Dado has remained levelheaded. "War is ups and downs, gentlemen," he comments. "The important thing is, we're turning the corner."

Among the journalists streaming through the lobby comes hustling a figure in uniform; Don Kishote, unshaven, unkempt, dusty, hollow-eyed. Barak hails him in astonishment. These are two men with whom Yossi can be frank, so in a few words he tells them his purpose and his news. They exchange appalled glances, and Pasternak says, "Look, Yossi, Dado makes his opening statement in ten minutes. He's with the army spokesman now. You'll have to see him afterward." The three are walking into the packed hall, which resounds with excited talk in a babel of languages.

"Sam, are you sure? Maybe Dado should first hear all this,"

Zev Barak argues. "We can still get Kishote through to him. Let these curs wait a few minutes more."

"Don't worry. Dado's no fool, he's read all the reports, he'll handle this thing. Anyway, it's too late, there's the spokesman now."

A youngish officer comes to the microphone and reads off the latest veiled army communiqué. During the English translation the noise level keeps rising in the hall, but when Dado strides to the rostrum there is silence. In a fresh uniform, shaved and well groomed, Dado makes a noble figure: his color good, his frame erect, his bearing exuding modest authority. He reads a statement in Hebrew about the day's developments on the battlefield, illustrating at a map with a pointer. To the relief of Barak and Pasternak, his words are cautious. But when he puts aside the written statement and the pointer he puts aside caution, and speaks with the fighting spirit of the battlefield: of counterattacks on both fronts, of dogfight victories in the air, of full coordination of air and ground forces. "We have the upper hand now," he concludes. "This is a grave battle, a serious war, but we are at the turning point, and on the advance. I'll take questions."

Hands go up all over the hall. Sharp queries shoot at him about the delay in counterattacking, about the failure to mobilize, about the extent of losses, about the Arab victory claims. He fields these well, but with an edge of growing weariness. One Hebrew journalist in front persists with a single question: "Dado, how long will the war last?" Though Dado repeatedly turns him off, the reporter insists and nags that he at least make a forecast. "Forecast? All right, I'll forecast one thing," the badgered Ramatkhal retorts. "We'll continue striking back at them, and we'll break their bones."

This brings a burst of applause, and a small groan from Barak. "There's tomorrow's headline," he says. " *'We'll break their bones.'* "

Pasternak makes his way into the tumultuous anteroom where Dado is taking the plaudits of generals and senior journalists, while Barak brings Yossi through the gloom outside to the Ramatkhal's flagged car. After a while Dado appears at the car, and his careworn face lights up. "So, Don Kishote, here you are. Ride with me."

He leans back in the rear seat, nodding and nodding at Sharon's message. An audible sigh. "Well, Yossi, I approved Gorodish's order for Arik to go south. I acted on the information I was given, and it's my responsibility. Dayan and I will fly down there around midnight to confer about what is happening in Sinai. Tell Arik I guarantee he'll take part in that meeting. B'seder? My car will take you back to the helicopter."

"Thank you, sir."

"I'm glad you're with Arik." Dado grips Yossi's shoulder. "He needs you. Logistics never mattered for Rommel, either. He would seize the moment, his staff would go crazy, and the logistics one way or another would follow." Dado grunts. "That is, usually! And so to Rommel his superiors were sluggish fools who didn't get the picture. Tell Arik I *know* we have to cross the Canal to win the war, and I *know* there are problems with Gorodish. Stand by him. Cool him down when he boils over. He's a fighter, and it will be all right."

22

The Black Panther

October 9.

The newspapers are spread on Golda Meir's desk, as her haggard war cabinet hears Dayan holding forth. On this morning of the fourth day of the war, the Minister of Defense is calling not only for retreat to the mountains, but the mobilizing of seventeen-year-olds, overage citizens, and the physically exempt, to be armed with antitank weapons against a surge of Arab forces into Israel's heartland. Only an immediate huge American airlift, he warns Golda Meir, will enable Israel to fight on. Golda's sadly ironic glance goes from Zev Barak to the streamer headlines:

DADO: "WE WILL BREAK THEIR BONES"
WAR HAS TURNED THE CORNER — RAMATKHAL

On the front page of one paper is a grimly smiling picture of David Elazar. She speaks with slow gravity, "It's so serious, Moshe? So urgent? Overnight? Nixon has already promised to make good our losses. Are you saying I should fly to Washington?"

"Absolutely, Madame Prime Minister, today, if you can."

"Moshe, what's happened to you?" Allon exclaims. "Mobilize

teenagers, elderly, sickly? Is the enemy at the gate? A *levée en masse*? We had a bad day in Sinai yesterday, sure. We had bad weeks, bad months in 1948. You drove on like a lion. So did we all, and it never came to a *levée en masse*."

"I was right yesterday about the Sinai, Yigal," returns Dayan, "and with a heavy heart I tell you I'm right today."

Golda picks up her telephone. "Get me our ambassador in Washington. . . . Gentlemen, we'll meet again at the full cabinet." Zev Barak stays behind as the others leave, still disputing.

"Hello, Simcha? Sorry to wake you. Call Kissinger, and . . . I *know* it's midnight there in Washington. Now you listen to me." In brief harsh words she recounts what Dayan has been saying. "Call Kissinger," she repeats, and hangs up. "Nu, Zev, why the long face? We've been through worse."

"Madame Prime Minister, Kissinger won't agree to your flying there."

"I'll handle Henry Kissinger."

"May I speak my mind?"

"That's your job."

"I understand the Defense Minister's concern, but don't act on it. You'd be running up the white flag for the world to see. Even more than his resigning would have done."

Golda scowls. "Why? I can go incognito."

"Pardon me, Madame Prime Minister, you can't. It's bound to become known. Golda flying to Washington! The Arabs will gloat on TV that Israel is collapsing. What's worse, they'll believe it. It'll pump them up to drive for the kill. Jordan will move in to grab its share, across a border we've stripped of forces to stem the Syrians on the Golan. In the UN the Soviets will call for a quick cease-fire, and Nixon will be in a dangerous corner."

"Dangerous how? To us?"

"To us, exactly. Remember Eisenhower and Dulles after Suez? *'Gentlemen, be good enough to give up everything you've won, or else!'* "

"Remember? How could I forget?"

"Madame Prime Minister, that's your exposure if you fly to Washington. Between Watergate and his crooked Vice President,

Nixon is in crisis. A foreign policy success like ending a war will be a godsend to him. Give him this opening and he can make snap judgments that will be our sorrow for centuries."

"Don't exaggerate."

"I don't. You may hand him a knife to cut our throats with."

"Hm! You're still Mr. Alarmist, after all."

The telephone rings. "Simcha? What already? Nu, what did he say?" She turns on her rare angry voice. " '*Sort it out in the morning*'? What's the MATTER with you? . . . Well, we *also* thought it was going well, but the situation has changed. Why does he think I want to fly there, because I like the food on El Al? If America lets us run out of weapons she'll face her first big defeat by the Soviet Union on the world stage! You tell Kissinger that, and tell him *right now*!" She slams down the receiver. A total change of voice, a genial smile: "Simcha Dinitz is a good ambassador."

"Madame Prime Minister, can you afford to leave the war for two days?"

She lights a cigarette with an odd sidewise glance at him, eyes half-closed, mouth corners wrinkling. "Isn't it fighting the war to get an airlift from Nixon? Simcha can't do that. I can."

It strikes him that this is now the woman talking. Her coquettish manner should be grotesque in the grim chunky old lady, but it is not. It brings to his mind Golda Meyerson's legendary love life among the Zionist founding fathers. She used her charm in those long-gone days, some people say, as a political blunt instrument. Perhaps! At any rate she can still flash that charm from her ruined body and timeworn face.

"And if you hear from the President that you're not welcome, then what?"

"Then I'll send you, so be prepared. Why the smile, Mr. Alarmist? Think it's a joke? Simcha is fine, so is Motta Gur, but I remember what you accomplished there in the Six-Day War." She picks up a paper on her desk. "The man on the military side handling resupply is one Halliday, Brigadier General Halliday. You had dealings with Halliday, I suppose?"

"I had dealings with him."

"Is he our friend?"

"No."

"Did you get results?"

"Yes."

"How?"

"Americans like winners. But they don't like whiners."

The wisp of femininity fades. She looks affronted.

"One more point, Madame Prime Minister."

Cold nod.

"I beseech you to ask Dado under four eyes how urgent an airlift is. He's the one who knows best. He may not agree with Moshe Dayan."

"Moshe Dayan." Leaning her elbow on the desk, she holds her arm up and stiffly fans it back and forth. "One day like this, one day like that. The great Moshe Dayan!" She clumsily gets up. "Time for the cabinet. Is your navy son all right?"

"So far, fine."

"Good. So far, the navy's our one pleasant surprise."

Noah Barak is leaping from his boat to the sunlit wharf in high spirits, though his eyes smart from lack of sleep after another long night battle, this time off Port Said. Result, three Egyptian Styx boats sunk, one escaped, and to the Jewish flotilla no damage. Latakia all over again. On the Syrian coast oil-tank farms flame from offshore bombardments, and the Wasp patrol boats in the Red Sea report knocking out numbers of Egyptian landing craft. In short, success after success at sea.

He has no inkling, strangely, that Israel is not winning just as handily on land. The army communiqués of the first three days have been vague, of course, as they were in the Six-Day War. Now as then the Arab broadcasts boast of huge successes, and now as then, the noncommittal Israeli reports are a strategic deception, he is certain, to stave off a UN cease-fire while Zahal mops up the enemy. From a booth on the dock he telephones the French Embassy in Tel Aviv, and learns that Julie Levinson has volunteered to work in Haifa's Rambam Hospital. Great news, she is just ten minutes away. He stops the jeep at a kiosk to pick up a morning paper.

DADO: "WE WILL BREAK THEIR BONES"

Fine, situation normal. In the hospital's crowded entrance hall, he comes upon his Aunt Shayna, pale and sad, who tells him that Uncle Michael had a stroke two days ago. "It happened during Golda's speech on television," she says, "of all times."

"Will he be all right?"

"I don't know yet. I must wait and see."

"What did the Prime Minister say, Aunt Shayna?"

"Nothing so shocking, I thought, simply realistic, but he took it very hard. He was saying she looked terrible and didn't sound like herself, then he sounded awful himself and fell over on the couch."

"I'm very sorry."

Shayna wanly smiles. "Well, God will help. How is it going at sea?"

"Not too badly." Obligatory Israeli taciturnity. But Noah is young at the game, he is fresh from a triumph, and a few words break through. "So far, clean sweep! Can't say much more."

"Good for the navy."

He goes looking for Julie in the wards, where bloodily messed-up soldiers fill the long rows of jammed-together cots. More are arriving on stretchers or wheeled tables, with hurrying medics dripping plasma into their veins. "The French girl?" says the harassed head nurse. "Try the nurses' lounge, green door down the hall."

Julie is alone in the narrow windowless room, crouched on a cot and crying. She springs up and embraces him. *"Oh, Noah, Noah! Mon Dieu, c'est toi! Tout est perdu! Les Arabes nous ont vaincus! La guerre est finie! Que ferons-nous, chéri?"*

He can barely follow this rapid-fire outburst of anguished French. "*Doucement*. I thought we agreed to speak Hebrew."

"Yes, yes, I'm sorry." She dashes a hand across her eyes. "It's so frightful! I worked in a hospital in Cherbourg, but I never saw such ghastly things. The boys — the wounds —" She chokes. "I can't talk about it. Oh, Noah, the hospital is overwhelmed, and still the wounded pile in. The terrible stories from the Golan! We've lost the war."

"Nonsense! What stories?"

"Ten of our tanks against a hundred, fighting day and night without stopping. A tank driver from Kfar Blum with both legs smashed told me it's all over, the government's lying, the Syrians and the Iraqis will be in Haifa tomorrow, and it'll be a big massacre. That's when I broke down and started to bawl. He said we've lost nearly all our tanks, there are no more reserves, nothing to stop them, and —"

Noah is flabbergasted. "Battle-shock talk. Not a word like that on the radio. And look!" He shows her the newspaper. "Our army tells the truth, you know that."

"Is that the commander-in-chief? He looks cheerful enough."

"Can you get off duty?"

"I'm dismissed for the day." Her eyes fill with tears again. "I'm so ashamed —"

"Come. You've got to get out of here."

In a sidewalk café with a view of the harbor, over cake and coffee, he tells her of the victories at sea and she begins to cheer up. "I promise you we'll win on land too, Julie. The Ramatkhal says it's a hard war, and it is. The country was caught by surprise. Only the navy wasn't. But those regulars on the Golan and in Sinai are great fighters. They'll hold till the reserves come up, and then we'll drive out the enemy, you'll see."

She is eating her flaky pastry, and he is thinking how pretty she looks in her rumpled nurse's uniform; no Daphna, of course, but with beautiful honest brown eyes, a creamy skin, and a promising bosom he has yet to explore. "Oh, Noah, everything's so different out here in the sunshine. That hospital is hell."

"It was good of you to volunteer."

"I'll stick to it. I just fell apart today."

"Great! And your job at the French Embassy?"

"After the war I can have it back. Meantime I've rented a room here."

"You have? Julie, on the first date we had in Cherbourg, you said nice French girls didn't go out with sailors. Not seriously."

"I know." She manages a weak laugh.

"Do they go out seriously with naval officers?"

"Why do you ask?"

"Well, do they?"

The large brown eyes widen, and she is a girl on instant alert. Her reply in Hebrew is slow and arch. "Well, *chéri,* nice Jewish girls certainly don't. Not with the gentiles, and if there are Jewish officers in the French navy, I've never met one. *L'Affaire Dreyfus,* you know."

He said, "Lots of them in the Israeli navy. No Dreyfus problem."

"So! What's all this about, *chéri*?"

He leans over to embrace and kiss her. At the other tables, drinking coffee and sunning themselves, old people observe this light moment of the war with amused nudges. She murmurs, her mouth against his, "Well, well. My parents have been on the telephone every day, begging me to come home. I truly don't know why I haven't gone —"

"Where's your room?"

"My ROOM? *Doucement, doucement*!" A wise wary enchanting smile, a new gleam in rounded eyes. "Why, what do you have in mind? What about this Daphna? I never have met her yet."

"Over. Forgotten. Never worked out. Couldn't. She likes leftists, and she smells of clay."

"*Vraiment? Vois-tu,*" she lapses into evasive French chatter, "a leftist proposed marriage to me just before I came here. I should have accepted, what's more. He's Cherbourg's supervisor of sewage disposal. A nice Jewish fellow. Civil service, very reliable income."

"Hebrew, lady!"

"Ah, yes, yes. Sorry."

"Where did you say your room was?"

She blinks. "I didn't say. What does clay smell like?"

"Mud. Drying mud."

"Don't you have to go back to your boat?"

"My crew's taking on missiles, ammo, and fuel." He glances at his watch. "An hour and a half."

"Actually, it's just around the corner, but it's a dismal hole."

He jumps up, beckoning to the waiter. "*Doucement,*" she says, seizing his fingers. "Can't I finish my coffee?"

"*Panter Shakhor!*"

A few hours earlier, in the bone-chilling starless gloom and clanging racket of the replenishment area, Amos Pasternak has encountered another battalion commander and impulsively embraced him, exclaiming again, "Panter Shakhor!" ("Black Panther!") Short, squat, with a bristly growth of black beard, and thick unkempt hair hanging below his helmet, Major Kahalani, like Amos, has been fighting for three nights and two days, and he is acquiring a Neanderthal look. Between them these two battalion commanders hold a crucial stretch of the front, a low saddle in the ridge that blocks the enemy advance into Israel.

"Some panther!" Kahalani's voice is hoarse and cracked from shouting over the combat networks. "No claws left, hardly."

"Black Panther" is a bitter joke Kahalani made over the brigade network at his own expense, during the worst of yesterday's Syrian onslaught. *"Don't worry, Yanosh, I'm a Black Panther. They won't get past me."* Actually the Black Panthers in Israel are Tel Aviv street toughs, Moroccans and other dark-skinned Jews of the so-called Eastern community, or "Second Israel," from Arab countries. But Kahalani is a Yemenite, a proud different group of ancient lineage, which nevertheless endures similar disadvantages in Israeli society, and in the army too. In the heat of battle fury Kahalani lashed out with that defiant jape, and Amos loves him for it.

"How long does this go on, Avi?" Amos says. "How can the Syrians keep it up?"

Except for a few gun flashes to the east, the third night battle has at last died off. Tanks are parked higgledy-piggledy at the ammunition trucks, and unshaven crews stumbling with fatigue are loading shells by the glare of headlights. All night the embattled defenders of the saddle were unable to drop back and replenish, and some tanks have shot off their last shells and held their ground with machine guns and grenades. En brera! If the Syrians once break through this gap they cannot be stopped short of the main Golan roads, and the highway to Haifa. In the terror-stricken stories Julie

Levinson has heard from the wounded soldiers, that much is grimly accurate.

"As long as they keep coming, we hold!" says the Panther. "You're doing brave work over there on Booster, Amos." Booster is the southern hill of the saddle. Kahalani holds the commanding northern Hermonit Hill, the highest ground, which has been taking the brunt of the artillery and tank assaults.

"But where are the reserves, Avi, to all the devils?"

"Raful must be sending them all to the other sector to protect Tiberias." General Raful Eitan is commanding the Golan battle. "It's a shambles down there, Amos. Colonel Ben Shoham's dead."

"My God, Ben Shoham!"

"Yes, and God knows what else is happening. For all we know the Syrians are in Tiberias already."

Miraculously, the Syrians are not in Tiberias.

On the first night and the first full day of war, the brigade defending the southern Golan Heights was shattered by two Syrian divisions, the commander, Yitzhak Ben Shoham, was killed, and the way down the escarpment into the Galilee — and on to Tel Aviv, for that matter — lay open to a large unopposed Syrian armored force. Why that force halted remains a mystery to this day. Granted this marvellous respite, General Raful Eitan has been throwing all the reservists as they arrive straight into the worst gaps in the southern Golan. That is why Yanosh, defending the northern sector, has had to fight with the troops and tanks on hand. Drastically decimated, his Seventh Brigade is barely hanging on, and its weakest point is the saddle between Hermonit and Booster, manned by Kahalani and Pasternak.

"Look, *havivi* [my friend]," Kahalani tells Pasternak as they part, "when the battle's hard for us, it's hard for the enemy, too. We're fighting for our homes and families. For our land. What are they fighting for? Just obeying orders. They'll break first."

"Besides," says Amos, "we've got a Black Panther on our side." Kahalani's teeth gleam through his whiskers in a big smile, and his tank snorts away, leading his column of Centurions.

Sinking into battle exhaustion as the first streaks of dawn show ahead, Amos leads his depleted force, now down to eleven tanks in all, back toward Booster. His ears are still half-deafened by gun blasts, his whole body is sore from getting thrown around as his tank pounds over bad terrain, his spirit is darkened by what he has seen of dead and wounded friends — guys with shell splinters stuck in their faces, gushing blood, guys disoriented with shock and pain, guys weeping from exhaustion and fear, guys sprawled in pallid death. As he rides erect in his turret, scarcely awake, Amos Pasternak now has an experience he will never forget.

He is all at once overcome by a weird feeling of disembodiment. It is as though he is rested, happy, well, and floating ten or fifteen feet above the rumbling Centurion, above his own physical self that is standing in the turret and peering through the darkness, with the persisting battle stink of gunpowder and burning in his nose.

He is down there, yes. But he is also up here, thinking calmly and philosophically about the Yemenite Black Panther, and about the way Jews have returned home from all over the world in response to the colossal German slaughter, and have tightened themselves into the hard fist that is Israel. Amos's own parents are from Czechoslovakia and Germany. His gunner is a South African, the driver a Persian, the loader-radioman an Iraqi. Yanosh is a Pole, the division commander Raful a native-born sabra, the Ramatkhal himself a Yugoslavian. Even the Prime Minister was born in the Ukraine and grew up in Milwaukee. What a country, what a people, what a fantastic Return, how good it is to be fighting this battle! It is all he wants of life, right now. If he has to die doing it, why not?

So he floats in hallucinatory exaltation, all the while conscious and giving orders to the driver, far below in the tank. The mood, or feeling, or waking dream, whatever it is, begins to fade when his tank arrives at the ramp, and he sees again the flaming town of Kuneitra, and the fires of burning tanks and APCs winking all over the *Emek Habokha,* Vale of Tears, as the Israelis are already calling it. He descends into his body, as it were, and is himself again. But the memory of that disembodiment keeps haunting him as his tanks range along the ramps, and he recalls where each tank captain comes from: Rumania, Iran, Hungary, Canada, Tunis . . .

"Kahalani, Yanosh here."

"Kahalani here. Good morning."

The words break the silence in Amos's headset and jerk him out of a doze. He climbs up in his turret. The east is growing light. The wind is brisk and frigid. Yanosh is ordering Kahalani to move from a reserve position back to the Hermonit, for the Syrians are coming. The sky brightens, the nerve-shaking artillery salvos resume; fire flashes far off, *CRUMP!* of guns, shells exploding all along the saddle. In Amos's binoculars long columns of tanks come crawling forward, bumper to bumper, winding around and through the hundreds of wrecked smoking machines in the valley. For the third straight day, more of the same, more than ever. God in heaven, how many tanks do they have? Or are these now the Iraqis? A blinding sun is rising over the Damascus Plain, and the defenders must wait until it climbs high enough so that they can see to fight. Dark glasses are no help, nothing blots out the glare that doesn't blot out the enemy as well. Heart-pounding wait, then after a while he sees a crowd of tanks looming through the dust and glare nearby, on the long shallow slope up to the saddle.

Battalion network: *"Kahalani to all units, keep the battle thrifty. Short ranges. No spotting shots. Fire to hit."*

Amos to his tanks: *"Pick your targets and shoot."* He seizes his turret handle and swivels it at a monstrous approaching tank, massive and ugly in Soviet style, must be a T-62. First encounter with one of those. A shout to his gunner: *"Fire, point-blank range."*

BAMM! Heavy jolt of the recoil. The T-62 bursts into flame, and the crew comes jumping out and scurrying down the slope. So, the Russians can build them bigger, but they are still firetraps. Across the saddle Amos sees that the Panther is already in trouble. The enemy columns are pouring toward the Hermonit. Kahalani's tanks are backing off from their hull-down positions on the ramps, for the Syrian artillery has them pinpointed, blasting fountains of dirt and fire among the machines. Kahalani can only retreat, let the enemy come over the ramps, and try to pick off tanks as they appear.

But this time there are just too many. Groggily Amos surmises that an entire fresh armored division must be pouring into the narrow gap. Almost too bleary to think, firing and firing again, he sees many many tanks aflame below and Syrians scurrying among them, yet on and on the machines come.

"Yanosh to Raful. I am withdrawing Kahalani's battalion before I lose it. En brera."

Amos does not know whether to cheer or cry. That Kahalani's battalion is crumbling he can see for himself. Another half hour of this battering and it will cease to exist, like the brigade in the south. He himself will soon be overrun at this rate, but for the Black Panther to be pulled out of action, after three nights and a third day of such a stand . . . !

"Raful to Yanosh. Can Kahalani hold on for fifteen more minutes? Help is on its way."

A new voice on the brigade circuit: *"Kahalani, Wake Up here. I'm coming with forty tanks. I'm now at Point Rambam. Yanosh, where do you want me?"*

Amos wonders whether he is falling into the dream state again. It is the voice of an old friend, a battalion commander of Ben Shoham's destroyed brigade, but he knows that that commander, Major Ben Hanan, is in Nepal on his honeymoon. Ben Hanan? Forty tanks?

"Yanosh here. Wake Up, come over Booster and attack the left flank of the enemy."

"Wake Up here. Coming."

It has to be Ben Hanan. His father does a morning exercise show called "Wake Up." How the devil has he gotten here from Nepal? Amazing, but Syrian tanks are breaking through all around the Black Panther, and his few tanks are firing in every direction. Amos himself is in a frenzy of shooting to hold his own ground against the swarming enemy tanks. And here by God comes Wake Up rolling over the hill, not forty tanks but a dozen or so, advancing abreast and firing. That *"forty"* was surely a deception meant for the Syrians, who copy all the Hebrew signals.

Now Amos hears Yanosh hoarsely telling Raful unbelievable good news. An outpost on the Purple Line, besieged far behind the front, reports that the Syrian supply train stretching many miles eastward into the valley *has started to turn back.* If true, then Kahalani was right, they are actually breaking first, but is it possible? Below, the hordes of machines are also starting to churn into disarray. Over on the Hermonit, Kahalani's dwindled force is charging back up on the ramps to blast away at the disorderly tanks milling below in a confused stampede of steel, fire, and smoke.

"Fire! . . . Fire! . . . Fire!" Amos keeps shouting at his gunner. There are so many targets down there it is impossible to miss. Before his eyes the chaotic Syrian tank masses are beginning to crowd eastward toward a high sun obscured by haze and smoke, their guns trained backward to fire, and a shell bursts deafeningly close by. He sees zigzag colors and lights, feels piercing burning in his left arm, and his forehead drips warm blood into his eyes. He cannot see. He drops down in the tank, and as the loader and gunner are dressing his wounds he hears on the brigade circuit:

"Yanosh here. Raful says our brigade has saved Israel. Kol ha'kavod, Kahalani."

"Kahalani here." Exhausted croak. *"Maybe we've stopped a massacre. We still have to win a war."*

Zev Barak accompanies Golda to the Pit, extremely uneasy about her planned flight to Washington. The Mossad has declared the incognito precautions airtight, and the negative reactions in Washington are not changing her mind.

For this meeting with Golda, Dado has cleared his underground office of ex-Ramatkhals and assorted high brass. Only his quartermaster general is there, with the array of supply charts Barak knows well. From Phantoms and Centurions to rocket-propelled grenades and small arms ammunition, they are all broken down on the same pattern, *Stocks on hand before the war, Average daily depletion, Estimated days of war, Stocks on hand now.*

The Ramatkhal offers Golda a chair. Pasty-faced and hoarse, he is all business and does not act downhearted. "I understand you want answers to two questions: what is our supply situation, and how urgent is an airlift?"

"Yes. Let's hear." She lights a cigarette, smooths her dress, and regards the Ramatkhal with keen remote eyes in a mottled dour face.

"Madame Prime Minister, the surprise attack has cost us very, very heavily. The quartermaster general's figures are plain to see." Dado gestures at the charts, then clasps his hands on the desk, leaning toward her. "The consumption of ammunition is many times our prewar estimates. There's never been such density of fire in any war on any front, not even in World War Two. It's a new factor. Tank and airplane losses have been extremely severe. Our armorers are marvellous at sending damaged tanks back into action, but as for Phantoms, when a plane's gone it's gone. The air force reports that at the present rate of loss, we're three or four days away from the red line."

She looks grave. "Go on."

"I come to the urgency of an airlift. We can and must counterattack to survive and win this war, and I estimate we can do it with stocks on hand if necessary, depending mainly on how heavily the Russians resupply the enemy."

Golda Meir raises her thick eyebrows, glancing at Barak. "The Minister of Defense thinks differently."

"Madame Prime Minister, he bears a heavy responsibility and his worry is understandable. I've lived this war in my mind for nearly two years. We've thoroughly war-gamed it. It's a hard war. We're having painful disappointments, but not to a catastrophic degree."

"Dado, you say it depends in part on the amount of Soviet resupply. Our intelligence says they're already starting to resupply by air and sea."

Dado grimly shakes his head. "Yes. Do the Americans want Russia ruling the Middle East? That's the real question. An airlift will be insurance for them, as well as for us, so I'm all for it. And as I say, we do need replenishment of unforeseen burn-up of consumables. So far, mainly ammunition."

The quartermaster general answers some penetrating questions by Golda, then she leaves with Barak. In the car driving back to her office, she sits in a brown study, saying not a word.

"Zev, are my flight arrangements all set?" she says as she sits down at her desk.

"In every respect."

"And yours?"

"Is that settled? Am I to accompany you, Madame Prime Minister?"

"You're going. I'm not." She takes in with sour amusement his nonplussed look. "Do we need a big airlift immediately? I *still* don't know. Dado doesn't like to admit he may run short. Naturally! But I can't face that risk. And the air force must have planes. I've been on the phone to Washington, and you're right, I'd better stay here. You take the next flight out."

"My instructions?"

"Get an airlift."

He ventures a light tone. " 'Piece of cake,' the Brits say."

Golda echoes it. " 'Duck soup,' the Americans say. For diplomacy I have Dinitz and Eban, but when it comes to *takhlis* [brass tacks] I want a military man who can talk to Americans. Specifically, to this General Halliday, and those other Pentagon fellows nobody's heard of, who get things done. You have access, you've done it before. Motta Gur's a fine attaché, work closely with him. Pleasant journey!"

The long lounge beyond passport control at Ben Gurion airport is dark except at one gate. Amid a huddle of passengers Zev Barak sits in a tweed jacket, tie, slacks, and the old Aquascutum topcoat he picked up while at staff and command college at Sandhurst. As he reviews papers from his despatch case, late summaries of the supply situation, there echo in his mind Emily Halliday's excited tones and happy laugh on the telephone. Unable to resist, he has just called her to say he is coming. Her joy at the surprise call and his own pleasure at hearing her voice, have lifted his spirit. Their romance, whatever its strange origin and fleeting time of passion, is a hopeless thing, yet a fugitive but durable grace of the years and a match flare in the present gloom.

"I'll meet you at the airport," were almost her first words. "When do you arrive, and on what flight?"

"Emily, that's absurd. I'm hoping to make the first shuttle in the morning, but who knows? The weather report isn't good, and —"

"I'll be there. If you don't show up, I'll go home. Nothing hard about that, love."

"Okay, I'll look for you, and thanks."

"Marvellous. I won't sleep all night."

What a contrast to his parting with Nakhama! Her first comment, when he told her he was going, was, "Well, I guess you'll see Emily Halliday"; all the more rasping for its penetration. He had let it pass, told her what he could of the mission, and packed a carry-on bag while she fretted about the war, the children, and his leaving her. Nakhama's once hearty good nature is much altered, especially since a bad hepatitis which she picked up on a holiday in Greece. That is why he called off the correspondence with Emily.

Sam Pasternak is approaching him across the nearly empty lounge. All shops and restaurants are closed, and his footfalls echo hollowly. "Ever since you called me I've been exploring landing rights for an airlift," Pasternak says. "It doesn't look good. Once the Arabs scream 'oil,' those European politicians will all fall down *kohrim* [prostrate]. Even if an airlift goes, the Americans may have to refuel in the air."

"That's a fighter plane maneuver. Can they do it with big transports?"

"You'll have to find that out. Meantime France hasn't said a flat no, so I may go to Paris. I still have connections there from the old days. If the Americans can land in France we're all set — if we get the airlift."

They are sitting in a dark row of empty seats. "Sam, tell me, what has happened to Moshe Dayan? Nobody's closer to him than you. What is it? Shock? Guilt about failed responsibility? This man is not Dayan."

"Isn't he?" Pasternak's big oval face, hardly visible in the shadows, settles in sad lines. "You tell me, was Dayan ever Dayan?"

"I don't understand that."

"The most famous Jew in the world after Einstein? The one-eyed military genius? The New Jew incarnate? On Yom Kippur afternoon that image was smashed. If he had died a year ago he'd be our Robert E. Lee, our Lincoln, our Roosevelt, but now he feels his place in Jewish history is gone and he'll die despised. Maybe I exaggerate, but I believe he'd welcome a stray bullet that would kill him."

"I've seen him in good moods, Sam, since Yom Kippur."

"Of course. He goes way up or way down, depending on the despatches. He changes twice a day."

"This is the final boarding call for El Al flight number 001 for New York . . ."

"Well, here I go," says Barak.

"Look up Chris Cunningham," says Pasternak. "He's still as smart and knowledgeable as they come, over there."

"Of course I'll see him."

Pasternak adds, "And the Hallidays, naturally." Barak picks up his hand luggage without a word. "Zev, General Halliday is crucial."

"Is he? Just where did Golda get that idea, Sam? From you? From the Mossad? Is that why I'm going? Bradford Halliday only obeys orders."

"He has plenty to say about the orders he gets."

The passengers are crowding toward the gate: late-departing tourists, black-clad Hassidim who come and go on El Al no matter what, youngsters summoned home by worried parents, businessmen, couriers, a lugubrious lot, not a smile among them and not much talk. Pasternak gives Barak a rough hug. "Have success, Zev."

An old pious response comes to Barak's lips, only half-ironic. "If the Name wills."

23

Kissinger

Emily is not at the plane gate, and outside the terminal he does not at first recognize her, in a gray tailored suit with a skirt much longer than the fashion, and her hair pulled back in a flat plain style. But when she smiles, it is Emily, all right. He makes his way to her, and she grips his hand. "Oh my God, I can't believe this. You're *here*." She kisses him and peers at him with shiny eyes in shadowed hollows, with some new lines at the corners. "Yes, it's you. After three years. You're the same, only you're getting sort of *white* now, hey kiddo? Very premature, aren't you still in your forties?"

"Barely, Em."

"Oh, listen, it looks fine, with your young strong face. Wisdom plus everlasting youth, Israel to the life."

"Don't pile it on, Emily, you don't have to. Seeing you is joy enough."

She squeezes his hand hard. "Where do I take you? Can we sit down for a cup of coffee? Bud told me you're coming, by the way. I tried my best to act surprised. He said, 'No doubt you'll see him.' I replied, 'My God, I hope so.' He expects to meet with you today."

"He does? I'd better go straight to the embassy, Queenie."

"Come along, old Wolf Lightning."

"How's your father?"

"Chris is all right." Her ebullience dims. "He's very alarmed, though, about what the Russians are up to in this war."

"I have to see him."

"Great. Just tell me when."

She is anxious to know about Noah. Barak's account of his victories amazes her. "Imagine! That's all news to me." She is driving one-handed, fingers linked in his, now and then touching his hand to her cheek. "The media coverage is sure fouled up this time. They're all confused, they expected you'd beat the Arabs overnight. So did nearly everyone. Not Bud, I must say, and not my father. Chris thinks this war is Armageddon."

"Well, old Chris tends to take a messianic line about Israel." Tired as Barak is, and with desperate deep war worries, he feels all the old sweetness in being with this one woman, of all the women in the world besides Nakhama. His body is warm with the delight of it. "But the Messiah didn't bring the Jews back to the Promised Land, Emily, a few crazy irreligious socialists started it, and what with two world wars and Hitler, the thing came to pass. That's the mundane view, anyway."

"If you say so, honey. Just don't argue with my father about it."

Pulling up the car at the embassy she asks, "Now then, how do we work this? Don't burden yourself with me, but my God, any moment we can have together —"

"I'll call you. Thanks for the lift."

"Anytime, Whitey."

And so he trudges into the embassy, and back into the war. There are doubled security guards at the entrance, and more bustle than usual in the halls. Where Eshkol's picture hung in the lobby, there is a solemn Golda portrait. But the main change is in the faces of the hurrying embassy people, many of whom he knows. The very air of the building is thick with foreboding and shock.

"So you're here, Zev." The ambassador greets him with a wave of his pipe at a citron and palm branch on his desk. "*Hag samayakh.* [Joyous holiday.] A thoughtful rabbi just brought these." So Barak is reminded that today is indeed the eve of Sukkot, the harvest festival. For a week, war or no war, many Israelis will be eating in palm-roofed booths, even agnostic kibbutzniks, even soldiers in the field. But neither the ambassador nor the military attaché, General Gur, looks festive.

"I sent Mendel with the limousine to get you," says Motta Gur, his round face impassive, "but he saw you go off with some lady."

"Yes, an old friend gave me a lift. What's happening?"

Gur gestures at a clipboard of despatches. "On the Golan, Raful's counterattacking, that's the best news, and we're more or less back on the Purple Line. Did you hear how Ben Hanan flew in from Nepal and showed up with a pickup force of tanks to reenforce Yanosh?"

Nodding as he leafs through the despatches, Barak exclaims, "What's this? Dado's put Bar-Lev over Gorodish?"

"Well, *with* Gorodish," says Gur, "and Sharon's in a big rage because he can't get either of them to approve a crossing."

The ambassador answers his telephone. "Dinitz. . . . Yes, General, he just arrived. One moment . . . Zev, it's General Bradford Halliday. He got word from the American Embassy in Tel Aviv about your trip."

Barak takes the phone. Halliday's office voice, dry and formal. "Ah, General Barak. How was your flight? . . . Good. If you're not too jet-lagged, how about dropping over here now?"

"I will, General. Thank you." Hanging up, Barak says, "Can Mendel take me to the Pentagon?"

"No problem," says Gur. "That Halliday is a tough nut, to all the devils."

"Where do we stand with the airlift, Motta?"

"At the moment, simple. No airlift."

"*What?* None?"

The ambassador puts in, "Not in American transport planes, Zev," and he quickly sketches the situation; a meager offer to replenish combat losses, all matériel to be picked up at obscure airfields, either by El Al planes with the markings painted out, or by planes under Israeli charter. "The idea, you see," says Dinitz, "is not to upset the Arabs."

The tough nut's office is on the outermost ring, on a high floor overlooking a river lined with trees in autumn flame. On the broad desk are pictures of Emily, the twin daughters, and the problem son; on the walls, portraits of Nixon and Agnew. Halliday is slender and black-haired as ever, though his face is becoming a bit seamed.

"We're still wrestling with the insurance problem," he says. "Seems to be an impasse."

"I can understand," Barak says, "that El Al planes, or local planes chartered by Israel, are a very poor risk. Why do you require us to use such means?"

"Coffee?"

"Please."

Halliday presses a buzzer and leans back in his blue leather swivel chair, dancing ten lean fingers together. "We're old acquaintances. Can we talk with our hair down?"

"That's why I'm here, General."

Halliday swivels to face the trees and the river. Fingers together, not looking at Barak at all, he says, "Why charters? Because an airlift by our transport command to a country at war would be an act of military intervention against the other side. Charters by us would be a mere transparent subterfuge."

"The Soviets are intervening."

"A trickle. Anyway, the Soviets don't care a hoot about world opinion. The United States must." Halliday turns to Barak with a squeak of the chair. "Look, Barak, here it is straight. Until yesterday the word from all your people here was that the attack was being contained. All was well. The tide would turn in a day or two. It would all be over by Friday or Saturday. The President promised to replenish what you'd expend in the war, and there was great mutual satisfaction. Overnight comes this anguished cry for an immediate airlift of a mountain of weapons, plus a cloud of Phantoms. That's asking for an instant radical shift in American foreign policy. How come?"

"The war situation shifted, General."

"Isn't that Israel's problem? This President's a beleaguered man. His ace in the hole is his success in foreign policy, especially détente. To ask him to change it at a snap of Mrs. Meir's fingers is preposterous."

"What's friendship for, if not for a time of need?"

Halliday takes a paper from his desk, scans it with head aslant, and hands it to Barak. "Okay. The Secretary asked me and a few other senior officers for an urgent estimate *'on one sheet of paper'* of the airlift problem. Go ahead, read mine."

Barak rapidly scans the carbon copy on onionskin paper.

10 October 1973

From: Brig. General Bradford S. Halliday, USAF

To: The Secretary of Defense

Subject: Airlift to Israel: Military Estimate

The Israelis have already lost the war. Egypt and Syria have dispelled the illusion of their invincibility. Their fine air force is stymied by walls of Soviet missiles effective to almost ten miles altitude. They are badly deficient in artillery and mechanized infantry, and their prowess in tank warfare has been neutralized by huge losses. The Arabs are in a position to accept a UN cease-fire anytime as victors. The war will soon end, probably through a UN cease-fire backed by both superpowers.

So why an airlift? Organizing a significant effort, assembling the aircraft, filling the domestic pipeline, setting up refueling sites, loading and despatching the planes, might take as much as a week while the war winds down. We can assume that the Soviet Union is geared up for a major airlift, though the Arabs are winning without that, no doubt to the Kremlin's great glee. But the start of an open U.S.A. airlift could provoke an equivalent Soviet response, which would only prolong the war; and Israel would suffer immensely more than the Arabs from such attrition.

Moreover an oil embargo might well ensue, a grave development for the security of the United States and for NATO. In short the best option for the Israelis and for everybody is an immediate cease-fire in place. A clear defeat, but being surprised in war is costly, and an airlift cannot now save them from the consequences.

Bradford S. Halliday

"Cream or sugar?" speaks a charming voice.

Barak looks up from the document. As in Israel, the air force has the prettiest girls. The black sergeant who brings the coffee tray looks like a model in Nakhama's favorite *Paris Match*.

"Sugar, please."

Halliday moves spread fingers at the memo. "Any comment?"

Barak waits until the sergeant goes out. "Hair down, General Halliday?"

"Shoot."

"That's a political estimate, start to finish. There's no hard military information in it. It reads like a State Department paper, of which I saw enough as an attaché. Same preconceptions and bias."

After a long silent moment, Halliday laughs. "Hair down to your shoulders, eh?"

"Your rule, sir. I wonder at your going out on a limb, predicting — in writing — the length and outcome of the war. Suppose you're wrong?"

"Barak, I'm a hero around here because when the war broke out I said in writing that you wouldn't win in three days, and would never push the Egyptians back across the Canal. I was a lonely voice in this building five days ago." He gets up to pour more coffee for Barak. "Political estimate? Yes, crystal-gazing is what SecDef really wants. Still —"

The black sergeant knocks and enters. "General, pardon me. There is a call for General Barak from his embassy."

Halliday gestures at his desk telephone. Barak takes it and Motta Gur comes on. "Listen carefully, Zev. Some intelligence just in can change the whole tenor of your meeting. A Soviet airlift has begun for real. Twenty-five Antonov transports are heading for Syria via Hungary and Yugoslavia. The CIA's bound to confirm it, and those monsters are comparable to the C-5A Galaxy. First flight of eleven, second flight of fourteen. Don't tell him the rest, but the war cabinet has already approved bombing the Syrian runways."

"Understood, Motta." He is talking Hebrew. "Can I tell this tough nut that we're back at the Purple Line on the Golan?"

"Just a second." Murmured talk. "Simcha says, 'Why not? If it won't depress him too much.' "

"B'seder." Barak hangs up. First he reports the Russian airlift, at which Halliday soberly nods. "Now, about your paper, you may want to modify it. As of now the Syrians are pushed back to the armistice line, and our offensive will continue."

"For that disclosure I'm grateful. What about the Egyptians?"

"Just wait."

Halliday stares at him with a glint of wary appreciation. "Like to hear some other opinions floating around this building, about a hurry-up airlift? The Israelis are doing fine, but they're just singing the blues so as to alarm Congress and the American Jews, and acquire all the aircraft and tanks they can, to hoard for the next war. Also, you want to throw the onus of your early reverses on us, for warning you not to preempt, and it's just a maneuver to lock America in on your side."

"Hostile nonsense," says Barak, "not worthy of discussion."

Halliday gets up. "The Secretary should be told at once about those Antonovs." He holds out his hand. "Stay in touch."

"I'm here for that."

"Perhaps you'll have time for a drink with us, out at the house. Emily would like that, I know. You'd see our son."

"Well, thank you. My instructions are, 'Get an airlift.' It seems I'll be here a little while."

For the second time, Halliday laughs. "That's a political decision. I'm just an airplane jockey who obeys orders."

Dinitz and Gur are impressed by Barak's inside glimpse of negative Pentagon thinking, and highly curious about the frosty general's candor with Barak, so he describes the business of the captured Soviet P-12 radar, and their contacts since the Six-Day War. That they have been in love with the same woman for years, which conduces to some informality, he does not mention. They are all for his going for a drink at the Halliday home. "Just stay in touch," says Dinitz. "The situation keeps changing."

"And the more you drink, the better," says Gur. "The only trouble is, they know how to drink and we don't."

"You learn here, Motta," says Barak.

He betakes himself to a second-rate hotel near the embassy to rest. Utterly disoriented by the wake-up call a couple of hours later, he has to pull together the threads of his existence. He is lying on a bed in a small shabby hotel room. He is in civilian clothes. He is in America. There is a war on at home, and Israel is losing. It is Wednesday, October 10, 1973, Sukkot eve. He is due at Emily Halliday's home shortly. Weird.

A cold shower restores an everyday mood. On the long taxi ride, Zev Barak's musings stray to comparing himself to Napoleon. This peculiar train of thought begins with a trace of guilt over his happiness at the prospect of an hour or so with Emily before Halliday gets home. How come? What about the war? What about his grim mission? Does the gorgeous Virginia foliage of October, and the bright vision of Emily Halliday, blot out the fierce reality of Israel's peril? Well, didn't Napoleon write many a billet-doux to his inamorata from the bloody battlefield, with the dead still strewn outside his candle-lit tent? And come to think of it, didn't Wellington after winning at Waterloo sit right down and dash off a famous letter to a lady in Brussels? Pretty good company in a human weakness, Napoleon and Wellington both. War puts an aureate edge on love for women, and there you are. Enjoy it. Barak fully intends to clasp Emily Halliday in his arms, if only at the moment she opens the door. Some golden moments weigh against gray years.

It does not quite work that way. Emily greets him at the door with a brilliant bewitching smile. He holds out his arms, and she sways toward him. But a small shape brushes past them and goes down the porch steps, and her smile vanishes in a yell. "Oh, Christ, there he goes again! Zev, stop him!" He turns and sees a very little boy toddling rapidly down a lawn sloping to bracken. "And oh God, there goes Merlin!" A huge black Labrador comes bounding through the door after the boy. "Zev, there's a goddamn skunk and four baby skunks down there. Oh, Christ." They both run in pursuit. He catches the boy and Emily seizes the dog's collar.

"Would this be the famous Chris?" inquires Barak, trying to pinion the boy's arms as he wriggles and kicks, protesting in shrill gibberish.

"That's Chris. My father wanted a grandson and he's goddamn got one. Haul him inside, don't let him get away. He's mad for the skunk, and so's that damn dog." Barak catches a whiff of the pungent odor as he drags Chris Halliday, struggling like a captured alligator, up the slope and into the house, followed by Emily with the dog.

Once released the boy turns tractable, and Emily leads him and the dog off to a nursery, where Barak can hear her rattling in French with the nanny she has brought back from Belgium. Soon she returns to the sitting room, looking out on a garden carpeted with fallen leaves. She still wears the gray suit in which she met him at the airport. Now he embraces and kisses her, but the afterscent of skunk in his nostrils somewhat shades his Napoleonic pleasure. "That kid," she mutters. "That perisher. He can be an angel, but oh God what a problem. Here, I've got martinis mixed." She goes to a portable bar. "Oh God, Wolf, I'd think this was a dream, one of many I've had, if not for Chris and the skunks. All too real! How did it go with Bud?"

"Very well. Your boy still doesn't talk?"

"Not a word. It bothers the hell out of Bud. He hasn't got around to baby talk on schedule, so Bud worries he won't get into the Air Force Academy. But the doctors say don't worry, so I don't. I *know* one day he'll burst out with whole paragraphs, probably obscene."

They sit down on a wicker couch, clink glasses, and drink. She says, looking out at the green-and-gold trees, "Early fall this year. Bud bought this place right after the war, seven acres and the house, for next to nothing. Mostly he's left it wild. Now the developers are crowding us. The land's worth a mint, but he chases real estate agents off the grounds like vagrants." She sips her drink. "Okay, now straight off, what's Nakhama's trouble? Why on earth did you black out our correspondence? That was a blow, honey, believe me."

He describes his wife's changed behavior and erratic health; and how, during the high-fever phase of hepatitis, she talked incoherently and angrily about Emily. "Israeli army wives learn to be good sports, Queenie, or at least to act that way. But it was all there inside, and it came out."

Emily finishes the drink at a gulp. "God, I'm for Nakhama myself. I feel wretched."

"Queenie, all we do is write."

"Oh, you — you MAN, all we do is *love each other.*" She cocks her head, listening. "Shoot, I have a lot to tell you about me and Bud, a hell of a lot, but I hear tires on the driveway. It has to be Bud, and he's bringing my father. Another time."

"Emily, I'd better check in with my embassy."

She gestures at a small wood-panelled room. "Bud's den. You won't be disturbed."

The desk is bare except for the telephone, a blotter, a clock, and a writing board with a clean yellow pad. Motta Gur's direct line is busy. So are all the embassy numbers. So are Dinitz's three lines. Something going on! At last he gets through to Gur. "Zev! L'Azazel, high time you called. Another tremendous development —"

Barak blurts, "Good or bad?"

"Couldn't be worse. Half an hour ago Brezhnev proposed to Nixon, over the telephone, that the two superpowers sponsor a cease-fire resolution at once in the Security Council."

With a very sick qualm at heart, Barak says, "Golda must reject it."

"We all know that, but will she have the option if Nixon goes along? Kissinger called Dinitz and he called Golda." Motta Gur sounds as exercised as Barak has ever heard him. "She was in an all-night conference on where to counterattack, our biggest decision of this war — whether to hold on the Golan and try to cross the Canal, or hold in Sinai and drive toward Damascus. Dinitz's bombshell blew that conference wide open. The phone lines and teleprinters to Tel Aviv are burning up."

"Motta, it's unthinkable, a cease-fire now freezes us in a defeat."

"Well, the next move is up to the White House. Is General Halliday there?"

Barak can hear Halliday and Cunningham talking in the living room. "He just got here."

"Let us know anything he says that bears on this. He may not even know about it yet."

"Will do."

Christian Cunningham's appearance surprises Barak. He last saw the CIA man wasted, white, and feeble in a hospital gown, recovering from a heart attack. Cunningham is himself again, erect in his customary impeccable gray suit, gray vest, gold watch chain, with the old secretive sly look behind thick glasses. Only, he is skeletally lean. His shirt and suit collars stand away from a neck of cords and bones. His handshake is dank and hard. "Hello, Barak. Your country is in bad, bad trouble. Emily, where's my grandson?"

"I'll fetch him. Bud, there's lots of martini there."

"I've got news, Barak," says Halliday, pouring drinks. "We may charter some aircraft, after all. A response to the Soviet airlift, which is confirmed, though so far going only to Syria." Halliday glances at Barak's unsmiling face. "Not what you're here for exactly, but it'll speed up the shortfall items. Motta Gur is pleased, or says he is."

"Well, it's a start." Not much of a start, Barak thinks, against twenty-five Antonovs.

Emily leads the boy in by the hand, shining clean, hair brushed, clothes neat. Halliday's face lights up as Chris runs to him. "Say hello to your grandfather, son."

The boy approaches Cunningham, babbles happy nonsense, and kisses him. The beaming CIA man takes him on his lap.

"He has to eat, father. The girls are at the table."

"In a minute," says her father, and Emily goes out.

"You know," Halliday says to Barak, "that the Vice President resigned at last this afternoon? The media are all in a tizzy. You'd hardly know there's a war in the Middle East."

"How will that affect policy?"

"Well, the President will be preoccupied, picking a successor. I'd guess he's out of the equation, more than ever."

"That leaves Kissinger in charge," says Cunningham. "Worse yet for the Jews."

"My other news, and I don't think the media have it yet," says Halliday, "is that Brezhnev wants Russia and the U.S. to cosponsor an immediate cease-fire."

"Good grief, Bud, when did that happen?" Cunningham exclaims. "It's unthinkable. That sells the Israelis out before they can counterattack."

Halliday asks Barak, "How will your government react?"

"Depends on the terms. We've craved real peace since 1948, on almost any terms."

"Don't talk diplomatic boilerplate," snaps Cunningham. "You're in a private house. The Arabs have you on the run right now, and they'll force you back behind the 1949 lines. In those boundaries your country will wither and collapse in ten years, if another attack doesn't finish you off sooner."

Emily comes in. "All right, Grandpa, give up the boy genius."

"He is one, you'll see," says Cunningham, putting little Chris off his lap.

"Why doesn't he talk, then?" says Halliday.

"Well, Einstein didn't talk until he was four."

"That's all malarkey," says Emily, "people kidding themselves about their slow darlings. I bet when Einstein was born and the doctor slapped his little bloody behind, he yelled, *'E equals mc squared!'* In high German, yet." She takes the boy's hand. "Come eat your mush, Einstein."

Halliday pours himself another martini, his third, and offers the large sweating pitcher to Barak, who waves it off with a murmur of thanks. "I tell you what, Barak, if you people are wise you'll grab this cease-fire. I was thinking about your recovery on the Golan. You've got brave soldiers, and they've bought you a chance to quit with honor, if Brezhnev can deliver the Arabs. That's what's dubious, and you'd better hope he does. Why should they let you off? They've got you on the ropes."

"You think so?"

"Do you mind my speaking freely? We're not in the office."

"Hair down," says Barak. "Go on."

Cunningham is looking from one to the other with a crafty expression.

"Just so." Halliday drinks. "Well, the Arabs fight by the Soviet book. That's how come you've recovered on the Golan. Soviet doctrine doesn't permit initiative to exploit. Your enemies achieved surprise and had the war won in two days, but they *stopped*. Stopped, north and south, to bring up forces according to plan and await further orders. They could have finished you off, but they have no Rommels or Pattons, so they lost some time. All the same they've got you on this round."

"Is that your view, or the Pentagon's?"

Cunningham strikes in as Halliday hesitates. "That's so much poppycock, Bud. Those Israelis can overcome prohibitive odds in the field. What they need now is *time*. Their greatest danger isn't in the field but right here on the Potomac. I mean this détente President and his détente Secretary of State, with their détente openings to China and Russia." The old CIA man all but spits out the word *détente*. Emily has written Barak long ago that her father's views on the spirit of détente may cost him his CIA job. Cunningham growls on. "Watergate and Agnew are just symptoms of the fog the President's in. If not for détente, d'you suppose Sadat would have dared to start this war? We've been snookered, so has Israel, and its fate now hangs on that court Jew, Kissinger. I've never been more alarmed."

"Easy, Chris," says Halliday, with a side-glance at Barak.

"By George, the jigsaw puzzle falls together, doesn't it?" the CIA man rasps. "Those malignant scoundrels mean to nail down a decisive Soviet victory in the Middle East, with those Antonovs plus a quick cease-fire. They're more cautious as a rule, this huge airlift is pretty adventurous, but they're counting on the President's weakness and Kissinger's rubber conscience."

Emily enters, wiping her hands. "Einstein picked up his dish and splatted corn mush all over his puss. Relativity. Relatively speaking, he's a fiend. Dinner in fifteen minutes, gents."

"I should have told you, Em," says Halliday, looking at his watch, "I won't be here. Sorry. In fact, I have to go in a minute."

"Too bad." A shadow flits across her face. "Lamb roast."

Cunningham gets up. "I'll now have a chat with my genius grandson about mass and energy, until dinner."

Halliday holds out his hand to Barak. "Look, I admire you people. You understand that." They shake hands. "I really hope your government goes for the cease-fire. As my history prof at the academy pointed out, Thermopylae was magnificent, but nobody survived." He kisses Emily's cheek, says, "Sorry about the lamb roast, dear," and leaves.

"I know what *he's* going for," says Emily, "and it's no goddamn lamb roast. Not that I have much right to grouse, with you here. Any booze left? Ah, yes. Lovely."

"He's a very able man."

"Bradford Halliday is an exceptional man, and a good father," says Emily, drinking, "and I won't let the louse into my bed."

Startled, Barak asks, "Why? If it's none of my business, say so."

"Indeed it is. If you hadn't shut off my letters, I'd have written a ream —"

A telephone rings in the den. Emily answers it and calls, "Zev, a woman for General Barak."

He jumps up. "The embassy. Thanks." Emily closes the door behind him as he goes in.

A cultivated woman's voice, faintly British, quite goyish, nobody in the embassy: "General Barak? Please hold for the Secretary of State." Barak waits for a long minute.

A deep Germanic voice, the most recognizable in the world. "Hello, General, Simcha Dinitz gave me this number. I hope my call is not inconvenient."

"Not at all, Mr. Secretary." *(This cannot be!)*

"Vell, how fortunate. I vould like very much to see you, General Barak, as soon as possible."

"I'm at your disposal right now, sir."

"Excellent. Ve'll send a car."

"That'll be fine. The address —"

"Ve have the address. The car vill leave now to pick you up."

Barak walks into the living room and says, "Guess what? I'm going to see Kissinger."

She opens saucer eyes. "Wow, you clannish Jews. You sure stick together, don't you?"

Wrong bridge, thinks Barak as the limousine crosses the Potomac in purple lamp-lit twilight, *if we're going to the State Department.* But they are not. The black-uniformed driver turns into the back gate of the White House, passes through with a few quick words to the sentry, and parks the car. In the entrance lobby he hands a brown paper bag to the gorgeously uniformed young Marine orderly, asking, "Has he arrived?"

"Yes, he's in the Map Room. Follow me, General."

The awe of the White House is on the Israeli, though in his attaché years he often walked these august halls. The orderly knocks at a door. Unmistakable voice: "Yes, come in." Kissinger sits alone at a long polished table, tubby and rumpled in a dinner jacket, black tie askew, looking through a pile of documents. The orderly hands him the paper bag and leaves.

"Please sit down, General. Ve meet here for privacy," Kissinger rumbles, waving at a chair. "The State Department is a goldfish bowl." He opens the bag, peers into it, and sniffs it. "You know, Abba Eban vunce told me that General de Gaulle's first vords to him, ven he received him before the Six-Day War, were, '*Ne faites pas la guerre!*' But I say to you — and your Prime Minister has told me to talk to you exactly as I vould to her — *Faites la guerre!* Fight! Fight as hard and as fast as you can, because as things stand on the battlefield you're in terrible trouble, and so are ve, vit the Soviet cease-fire proposal."

He extracts and unwraps a sandwich from the bag, and sighs with pleasure over it. "Roquefort on rye. Food of the gods. My fiancée has put me on a starvation diet. But I'm about to host a banquet for the President of Zaire. Banquet food isn't food. I had no lunch. Forgive me if I eat vile ve talk. Vot's really happening over there, General? Who's vinning the war?"

"I wish I could say we are, Mr. Secretary."

The Secretary bites into the sandwich with gusto, and gives him a sharp look. "Do you vish that? But vouldn't that undercut your mission? Mrs. Meir mentioned half-jokingly that she vould send her military secretary to 'get an airlift,' after I urged her not to come herself. I told her Dinitz and Gur are doing nobly. But she sends you, so — fine." He eats, and says after a moment, "My God, what a hideous notion, for her to fly here. Not like her at all, to go into such hysterics." The heavy German accent seems to fade away after a while, or rather Barak stops hearing it.

"Mr. Secretary, she is cool as can be. It was Moshe Dayan's idea, and she thought better of it."

"Thank God. You know what they were saying in the Pentagon? If Golda Meir could come here during a war, that showed the Israelis must be winning and didn't really need any help." With a glance through thick glasses over the sandwich, he says in an offhand way, "You've been at the Pentagon today. What's your impression?"

"That all your Arabists have been lend-leased to Defense, Mr. Secretary, and are making policy."

"Hm! Not bad." Kissinger glances around at the handsomely furnished room, which looks out through bushes at a floodlit brownish lawn. "You know, this is where Franklin Roosevelt conducted World War Two? The Map Room, he named it. He got the idea from the war room Churchill had aboard the *Prince of Wales,* at the Argentia conference. A lucky room." After a pause while he eats, Kissinger says, "All right, on Golda's say-so I'll talk to you as I would to her in private. No diplomatics, nothing on the record. I'll discuss two things, the cease-fire and the airlift."

"Yes, Mr. Secretary."

"Cease-fire first. The Egyptians will want you to first agree to withdraw to the pre-1967 lines. Just for starters. That you won't do, I realize. You'll want a return to the lines that existed right before Yom Kippur. Forget it. Over, dead, gone. In the Pentagon they say, *'How can we make the Arabs give back to Israel their own land that they've recaptured?'* What lies ahead as things stand now is a cease-fire in place, a disaster for you, then a tortuous political process which will not help and may harm you. So, I say again, *Faites la guerre!* Change the picture on the battlefield!"

"We're trying, Mr. Secretary."

Kissinger nods. "The Russians won't move for the cease-fire at the UN without us, not for a few more days. That much, détente has accomplished. It's no small thing. But we can stall only so long."

"How long?"

"By Saturday, General, the United States will be in a very awkward spot. If the Russians move the cease-fire and everybody else votes for it — which of course you can count on — how can we veto a unanimous resolution for peace?"

"Do the Arabs want a cease-fire, Mr. Secretary?"

"The Russians want it, that we know. As to the Arabs, we have to wait and see." He seems about to say more, then eats, and goes on abruptly. "Now, about an airlift. I've pressed since day one for expediting the items you're short of. Dinitz will confirm that. But until last night, I tell you man to man that I understood transport in Israeli aircraft was all you wanted. Now things have changed. Journalists and congressmen, of course, will start howling for an immediate colossal airlift by the United States Air Force. They think those things happen like turning on a faucet. I expect more realism from Golda Meir, and less dramatics."

"She will be happy, sir, if she has your word that an urgent airlift is in the works with your backing."

The Secretary gives him a long solemn look. "General, the President has told me, *'Israel mustn't be allowed to lose.'* That's why the Sixth Fleet has sailed east and taken station off Crete. It's a signal the Soviets understand. He may be very distracted, but his instinct for foreign policy is still keen. The President knows that if you're defeated the Russians will dominate the Middle East, the Arabs will be impossible to deal with, and the world balance will tilt against the United States. I don't know why the Pentagon doesn't share that view, but I assure you I do."

"Then am I to tell my Prime Minister, Mr. Secretary, this: that you yourself recognize the need for the airlift, that resistance within your government, specifically at the Pentagon, is causing delay, but that the President and you will ensure that the airlift flies by Saturday?"

Staring at him, the Secretary of State finishes the sandwich and brushes crumbs from his dinner jacket. "I begin to see why Golda sent you."

"Am I mistaken, sir?"

An impatient shrug. "General, the airlift is a problem for the Pentagon and the Department of Transportation. I'm lost in all this talk about civilian charters, painted-out military markings, and so on —"

"You said Israel must achieve a military success by Saturday, Mr. Secretary, or the U.S. may face a dilemma at the UN. In my country it's already Thursday. An immediate all-out battle, very costly in weaponry and blood, is the task you're laying on us."

"I'm not. For your own preservation you must do it."

"Yes, but how do we fight on after that, Mr. Secretary, if all-out resupply is not in the air by then? If we're overwhelmed, no matter how well we fight, by the sheer weight of Soviet metal?"

In slow, heavy, irritated tones, the Secretary says, "Listen, General, our national concern is not just the predicament of our good friend Israel. Mrs. Meir understandably thinks of nothing else, but we must also consider the welfare of our European allies and Japan, and our détente with the Soviet Union, the one present ray of light in world affairs. This war must lead to a peaceful long-range settlement in that vital oil region. There are those in the Pentagon who cry that if we now give Israel any help at all, we *'blow our role as honest broker.'* Those are the elements we deal with, hour by hour."

"Mr. Secretary, what would you say to my Prime Minister, if in fact she had flown here and was now sitting in this chair?"

"Well put." The anger dims from the Secretary's face and voice. "Number one, *for God's sake keep me accurately informed of the battlefield situation*. If I'm in the dark about that, how can I be a useful friend in negotiations? Second, don't talk or even *think* cease-fire anymore, while you're losing in the field. The other side is brutally quick to sense weakness. They'll just keep upping the price. Third, the status quo ante is *gone*. For good! It was always an unstable stalemate. It couldn't have lasted. Mr. Sadat fooled you by crying wolf for years and then launching a war that looked unwinnable, just to break up the political ice. I'm sure his success has amazed him. He's proved himself a statesman, and you may hate him now, but with such an astute personality you may in time do business." The Secretary glances at his watch. "As for the airlift, I would emphasize the President's resolve that Israel must not lose the war, and ask her patience. And please, no dramatics."

"Mr. Secretary, I've read your work on Metternich, *A World Restored.*"

"You have?" Kissinger looks surprised and pleased. "Was it all right?"

"Outstanding. In one passage you call a statement of Castlereagh's *'thin gruel.'* "

This surprises a hearty laugh from Kissinger. "I must go. I would tell Mrs. Meir one thing more. She's thrown her voice very effectively across the ocean. But I'd hasten to add, General Barak is no dummy."

"You're a flatterer, Mr. Secretary."

24

The Fork in the Road

In Jerusalem, for some time before the alarming Brezhnev cease-fire proposal reaches Nixon and is relayed to Dinitz, a fateful strategy conference has been going on in Golda Meir's office. More senior officers are crowded into the Prime Minister's conference room than Sam Pasternak can remember from his days in the Mossad; and since then, this is the first time he has been included in such a meeting. Out of the government for nearly a year, Sam has been keeping his mouth shut and scribbling notes on the different viewpoints:

Allon: Transfer all available forces south and cross the Canal at any cost, because hitting Syria won't end the war . . .
Dado: No, Syria now. The world's waiting for Israel to do something, and we can move tomorrow only in the north . . .
Benny Peled: Agrees. Air Force almost down to the red line, can operate for three or four more days, wants quick action, hit Syria now . . .
Dayan: Neither option viable. No decision can be forced on either front, we lack the strength. Retreat and dig in north and south, harden up defensive positions — the Purple Line and the Sinai mountain passes — and regroup to fight another day . . .

Pasternak is thinking that Dado long ago foresaw this dilemma and warned the politicians that, with the cuts in the military budget, he could not wage all-out war on two fronts. The question now is, which way to hit out? At which front to throw all strength to seek a decision in the war? Round and round the arguments have gone while Golda Meir sits silent at the head of a long table, yellow-faced with fatigue and concern; almost like a wax museum effigy of herself, which puffs smoke and brings cigarettes to its mouth with one movable arm.

Pasternak is startled by a woman's voice cutting through all the guttural army Hebrew: "Nu, Sam, no opinion?"

"Madame Prime Minister, I'm with Yigal Allon. Attack in the south."

"Why?"

"Clausewitz principle, *'Strike for the heart.'* If you knock out your strongest enemy, you win the war."

Dado speaks up briskly. "Sam, we've all studied Clausewitz. That rule is modified in our case by geography, time, and the position of the forces. In the north we can act tomorrow at dawn. It'll take us four or five days just to move our forces south. And suppose meantime that the UN votes a cease-fire, on lines that seal the enemy's surprise success?" He turns to Golda. "Madame Prime Minister, I say again — and I can't emphasize it enough — *at least two Egyptian armored divisions are still west of the Canal, where I can't get at them. Nor can the air force, because of the missiles.* A premature crossing against such power is a reckless gamble —"

"Sooner or later, Dado, you'll have to fight them," says Allon, "to end the war —"

"I know that. But the time may come when —"

It is at that moment that a red telephone rings at Golda's elbow. Sudden ominous silence, for only emergency news can break into this meeting. Golda takes the call and listens poker-faced for long minutes, with now and then a gruff "Ken," and finally, "B'seder, Simcha." She hangs up. "Gentlemen, Brezhnev has telephoned President Nixon, to propose an immediate joint cease-fire resolution in the Security Council."

Grim prolonged stillness, grave faces turning to each other;

then the strategy debate starts up again with added urgency and heat. Pasternak is shaken. Clausewitz is all very fine, but Dado is right, unless Israel hits out at once, this cease-fire will clamp her in defeat.

"Enough, gentlemen." Golda raises her hand and speaks heavy slow words. "If I had the option to strike north or south tomorrow, it would still be a difficult choice. Now I have no choice. Henry Kissinger has told me, over and over, *'You have to start winning on the battlefield.'* Sound advice. He has neglected to mention how. He leaves those details to me."

A mutter of bitter amusement around the table.

"So it must be the Syrians, gentlemen. If we have a success and hold territory beyond the Purple Line at the cease-fire, the outcome at least will be unbalanced. The Egyptians lodged in Sinai, but our forces deep in Syria and heading for Damascus. That's already a negotiation."

Earlier on this same fifth day of the war, Yael Nitzan sets out to fly home. Like most people, she thought when it started that the Arabs were committing suicide, but day by day she has become more and more concerned, and her Leavis involvements have seemed to matter less and less. So after an all-night session on paperwork with her secretary she blearily boards a plane to New York, masks her eyes, and falls fast asleep in her first-class seat well before takeoff. When she awakens the plane is thrumming along high above sunlit clouds, and in the seat beside her a man is reading a book in Arabic. But except for a few words she recognizes, this is like no Arabic she has ever read or heard spoken, though she can read a newspaper or magazine and converse in a simple fashion.

He is a strange man with strange mannerisms, probably in his mid-fifties, with curly black hair streaked gray, and a long dark Spanish sort of face. He is pleasantly scented or pomaded. His very wrinkled black suit is of fine material, and the gray pullover under the jacket looks like cashmere. As he reads he pencils notes, not on the margins of the pages, which have the marbled edges of an old library volume, but in a pocket notebook, pushing his glasses up on his forehead, and holding notebook and pencil nearly to his nose.

Boredom plus curiosity make her say at last, "I beg your pardon, are you an Arab?"

He peers at her. "Do you know Yiddish?"

Taken aback, she says, "A little. Why?"

"Very old joke. In the New York subway a black man sits reading a Yiddish newspaper. Man beside him can't resist. 'Pardon me, sir,' he asks, 'are you Jewish?' The black replies, '*Nor doss felt mir oiss* [That's all I need].' "

"Ha! I deserve that for disturbing you."

"You read Arabic?"

"Not *that* Arabic. It's Chinese to me."

"Ah well." He closes the volume. "It would be to many Arabs. And are you an Israeli going home because of the war?"

"Just so. And you?"

"I live in New York. A few days ago I lectured on 'Vico and Heroic Islam' at a university to a small comatose audience. Tonight I repeat it in a very grand Manhattan temple. Now that this war is on, I shall be hooted at and possibly stoned by anxious New York Jews. That is, if anybody comes." He speaks in rapid bursts of words, punctuated by breaths like gasps. "Though if one pays attention, what I have to say isn't too bad from the Jewish viewpoint. I gave a similar talk at Tel Aviv University last summer. It was well received." The flight attendants are approaching with the bar cart. "Join me in a glass of sherry."

"I'd better not. I've interrupted your work."

"Nonsense, my eyes are tired, do drink with me." The attendant pours for them. "Tell me about yourself and your family."

"My husband is an army general. I have a business in Los Angeles. We have two children. My name is Yael Nitzan."

"Nitzan?" He shifts in his seat to stare. "Is your husband the one they call Don Quixote?"

"You know him?"

"He was at my lecture in Tel Aviv. Forced his way to me afterward, captured me and took me to eat Yemenite food in Jaffa and explain my lecture."

"That's my husband."

"Well, here's to Don Quixote. May he emerge safe and victorious from this wretched war."

"Amen." She drinks. He gives her a smudged card.

DR. MAX ROWEH
DEPARTMENT OF PHILOSOPHY
COLUMBIA UNIVERSITY

"Roweh? Didn't a book of yours just get a rave in the *Los Angeles Times*? In fact, I bought it."

"*Vico and Descartes: The Fork in the Road,*" he says. "You truly bought a copy? How lovely of you. Heavy going, isn't it?"

She is embarrassed. Yael follows the book reviews, sniffing for novels that may make movies. On impulse now and then she buys highly praised nonfiction to improve her mind, which however resists improvement as a mackintosh resists rain. "Frankly, I'd never heard of Vico. I didn't reach the fork. Maybe I will."

He smiles. "A-plus for honesty. That first chapter is a sinker. Vico is not easy. This is dreadful sherry. Have you spoken to your husband since the war began? Inevitable, the war, but good may yet come of it." She is about to ask him to explain, but in his voluble way he runs on. "Vico's theory of history has been badly vulgarized — in the unscholarly vogue he's been having lately — to a cyclical view of civilizations, which would not be original with him, it's in Aristotle. James Joyce made Vico modish after he'd been neglected for centuries, by supposedly basing *Finnegans Wake* on his theories. So an academic cottage industry is springing up, and small journals are breaking out in a Vico rash. Look, wouldn't you rather have a nap, or read your *Vogue*?"

"What I'd like to do is hear your lecture. I have to stop in New York overnight."

"Bless me!" He looks astounded and delighted. "Would you really? How brave. Well, nothing easier! My car is meeting me. We'll just drop off my bags at my flat and take you on to the lecture. Afterward, where are you staying?"

"Airport Hilton."

"You'll be driven there. In fact" — he glances at his watch —

"we might still have a decent glass of sherry in my flat before the lecture. Small courtesy to the wife of a true hero. I've heard much about your Don Quixote."

"Where is your flat?"

"River House. Midtown, east side."

"I know where River House is." Yael tries not to sound bowled over. "Will your wife be there?"

"Alas, I'm a widower. I lost her four years ago to cancer."

"I'm very sorry."

"Thank you. She was a great lady, enormously active in good causes, Israeli and otherwise. I've had to carry on much of her work in endowments and foundations, and I'm quite unsuited to such things. But one must be true to her memory, and her family expects it."

"She wasn't an Israeli, was she?"

"Oh, no, no. On her mother's side, she was a Rothschild, British branch." Roweh glances sidewise at her. "The impecunious cousins. It's decided then? You'll come to my lecture."

"I will indeed, and thank you."

"Splendid." He opens his book.

"Now, what is that you're reading?"

"Ibn Khaldun."

"Should I have heard of him?"

"No. Academic subject. He's the Arab Thucydides, a great historian, fourteenth century. Not quite as great as Toynbee says, but then, Toynbee mainly cribs from Khaldun. I've come to Arab thought late, but it's very important."

Yael is in far over her head, she thinks, as Roweh immerses himself again in Ibn Khaldun. But sherry in River House with the widower of a Rothschild of sorts ought to be nice, though beyond it glooms a lecture about Vico. She'll have plenty to tell Sam Pasternak when they meet in Paris.

And indeed the River House apartment stuns her: opulent furnishings, fairyland night view of downtown Manhattan and the bridges, walnut-walled library massed with books floor to ceiling, and on the living room walls, among other paintings, a Degas dancer and a Corot river scene. A fussy Irish cook-maid serves finger sandwiches of smoked salmon with the sherry. Yael is used to Sheva Leavis's moneyed luxury, but Max Roweh is a highly novel meld of intellect, wealth, and class; yet after all just an untidy middle-aged scholar, with his mind off on the moon. The whole encounter is dreamlike. She likes him.

A peculiar scholar though, taking her in his own chauffeur-driven Lincoln to hear him lecture! His rapid-fire talk traces stages in the "civilization of Islam" according to Vico's scheme of history, and what she can understand, before she dozes off, is all new to her. Roweh appears to admire greatly Mohammed and the Koran, and to see virtues in Islam which have never crossed her mind. His lecture style is much like his talk in the airplane, rat-tat-tat sprays of words with glints of irony and humor; hard to follow and much too much for the postprandial audience in the majestic Reform temple. She is not the first one to fall asleep. As they drive away from the temple he explains that he has been paid a large honorarium, which will go to one of his wife's foundations. "There is no such thing as enough money in philanthropy. They were unwise enough to invite me. I did my act. Remaining conscious was their lookout."

Next day Yael carries aboard the Air France plane a new copy of *Vico and Descartes: The Fork in the Road,* inscribed

For Israel's Don Quixote,
and his charming Dulcinea,
Yael Nitzan,
with the author's best wishes
for health and victory
M. Roweh

Again the first chapter defeats her, inducing a long restful nap, which with a movie and a good French dinner makes the flight pass quickly. She means to keep at the book and worm through it, no matter what. She wants to understand Roweh if she can. His erudition awes her. He learned Arabic in a year, he told her, in order to read the Koran and Ibn Khaldun in the original. Besides Russian, Yiddish, and Hebrew, which he absorbed in Kiev as a child, he knows five European languages. The mere list of titles of his books is scary. All the same, she has a handle on him as just another lonesome man who has taken to her. About that she knows she is not mistaken. She glances often at his formal stern photograph on the book jacket, with a wall of books behind him. That isn't the whole picture of Max Roweh. Not half!

And now for a rendezvous with Sam Pasternak, a very different sort of lonesome man. Unlike the brush with the wealthy philosophy professor, it will lack the edge of the unexpected, but she is very glad it's on. When she called from Los Angeles before leaving, he told her that Amos was in the Rambam Hospital, badly wounded, and a warm impulse to console him flooded her. "Look, darling, you say you'll be in Paris tomorrow? I'm coming home via Air France. I don't want Aryeh lying about his age and volunteering for something crazy. Where will you be in Paris? Let's meet." And it is still something to look forward to. After all, that moment at Shimshon's . . .

Sam Pasternak finds two messages at the desk of his Paris hotel.

> *Plane delayed two hours by fog in JFK airport. But I'm coming, patience! Love, Yael.*
>
> *Am in the bar. Uri.*

Uri is the military attaché in the Paris embassy. Pasternak attended the circumcision of Uri, son of a Palmakh buddy, and remembers the wild wail Uri raised, spitting out the soothing wine. Now Uri is a lieutenant colonel with a neat black beard. Sam finds him drinking wine in the bar and looking pained, as though the taste subliminally reminds him of the covenant of Abraham.

"Is there any hope?" he greets Pasternak, who drops beside him in a leather-lined booth.

"Hardly any. And what's your news?"

"All negative so far," says Uri. "We expected the British to refuse, of course. But the Italians, the Belgians, the Dutch, the Spanish, the Greeks — *Lo b'alef raboti!* [No with a capital N!] You were hoping for some results with the French, Sam."

"Near zero."

"Well, I'm not greatly surprised. Say *'oil'* to a French politician and he goes catatonic. But what to all the devils ever made you hopeful?"

"I know the Minister of Transportation from the Resistance days. Actually I once saved his life. We've remained in touch, and he even stayed in my home in Ramat Gan. When I talked to him on the phone, he thought landing rights might be arranged, so I came. There's a lot of public sympathy for Israel here."

"That, I know. It stops at the third bureaucratic level. That's the snow line, and above is ice and stone."

"Look, Uri, I'm dead tired. Tell the ambassador that Corsica is still a possibility, the minister's working on it. I'll report the minute I hear anything."

"B'seder. You realize, Sam, today makes six days? A bit different this time."

"Yes, well I guess repetition would be boring."

In his room Sam is about to lie down when a bellboy brings a card engraved in small neat script, *Mme. Armand Fleg*. On the back a few French words in a hurried hand: *M. Pasternak. Am in the lobby and would much appreciate a word with you*. He recognizes the husband's name, a very wealthy unobtrusive Jewish leader. When he steps out of the elevator, there stands a blond woman with the tanned skin and lean figure of a skier, dressed with killing Parisienne chic, complete to the off-white silk stockings that are now the rage. She is the lady of the Beirut raid, no doubt of it. She smiles and comes to meet him. "So good of you! The minister mentioned to my husband that you are in Paris. Has your trip been successful?"

"Can't say yet."

She gestures at a couch, and they sit down. "We're terribly worried here about the war."

"It has started off badly, that's true."

"My husband has already raised a large sum to purchase urgent matériel on the embargo list." In a lower tone: "Illegally of course. A shipment will go by sea tomorrow. That's terribly slow, but air freight is out of the question. The airports are under wartime surveillance." Pasternak does not comment, regarding her with weary watchful eyes. "Your son is in combat?" He nods. "Of course he would be. Where?"

"The Golan."

"Is he all right?"

Expelling a heavy breath, Pasternak says, "He's been wounded."

"Badly?"

"He'll have a full recovery, I'm told. At least ninety percent. Shrapnel hits in face and arm."

"Your son's a brave young man. I'm glad about the full recovery. I'm sure he's distinguished himself."

"Your husband, Madame Fleg, has distinguished himself as a friend to Israel. You, too."

"Me? If you mean my adventure with your son," she replies with nervous haste, "I grew up in Beirut, and your Mossad has persuasive recruiters. It was no business for a mother of children to get into. Crazy. Once it was over and a success, I was naturally pleased with my tiny part in it."

"And your husband must have been proud of you."

"Armand? *Mon Dieu,* he hasn't the remotest notion that I did — or would ever do — such a thing. Never mention it! I'll take chances on the ski slopes, that's my amusement, in fact I met your Mossad recruiter there. Otherwise I'm a very conservative person, like Armand." Pause. "Not that it's important, but did your son ever receive my little note?"

"Oh, that. My fault. I moved my office, and it was misplaced. I did give it to him just before the war, when he was on his way to the Golan."

"I see. I thought perhaps he didn't bother to reply to a foolish matron, which would have been quite right." In a sinuous unmatronly motion she gets up and holds out her hand. "*Bonne chance.* My husband and I are at your disposal, if in the slightest way we can be of any help to you here in Paris."

Pasternak wakes from a nap thinking about First Sergeant Luria. Maybe it's not too late, after all, to pick up the pieces, and what better setting than Paris? In the long hours of bombinating nightmare in the Pit he has thought a lot about Yael. Getting out into the light of day, catching some sleep on a plane, taxiing around in Paris, have somewhat brought him to earth, and French official frostiness and haunting worry about Amos have further dimmed anticipation. In a way, so has Madame Fleg. The woman exuded romance like a flower scent. On the Haifa wharf he saw that his son had fallen for her. Such a flare of the real thing can hardly be blown into life in the embers of the old, old Yael Nitzan affair. Or can it yet?

"Avar zmano, batul karbano." It was a favorite phrase of a learned uncle of his on the kibbutz. *"Time past, sacrifice cancelled."* Talmudic rule about temple ritual: if the daily or holiday offering is not brought at the appointed hour, there is no making it up. It is gone. Ah, First Sergeant Luria! It did not seem so at Shimshon's, over the second bottle of Golan red wine . . .

"Well, here's where it all happened, isn't it?" Yael says. They are walking past the Hôtel George Cinq to a small three-star restaurant, in a windy night of falling leaves. "Four lives messed up for good by one crazy afternoon, eh?"

Pasternak thinks for a moment. "I count three."

"Shayna Berkowitz, hamood, Professor Berkowitz's wife, have you forgotten? Kishote was mad for her. What's more, I'm pretty sure they still love each other, poor dears." She takes his hand. "And *you*! You, with that Hollywood kurva!"

"I don't remember her name, Yael."

"You're a shocking lowlife. Always have been."

It is a suitable restaurant for a rendezvous: dim lights, partitioned booths, candles and roses on the table. They talk about the war, and about Amos. He tells her what he knows of Kishote: unhurt, much commended by Sharon, and by the Ramatkhal, too. "I heard Dado say Kishote's coming into his own in this war. However it ends, your hubby's going places afterward."

"Not with me."

It is an opening. Pasternak lets it go by, and Yael is not offended. Sam must be several years younger than Professor Roweh and seems older. But then, is that fair? Sam has carried much responsibility for Israel's fate for years, while Roweh has picked up languages and dug through obscure philosophers like Vico. Anyway, Sam is still an attractive old dog.

Pasternak for his part well knows he has declined a gambit, though nothing changes in Yael's look or manner. Over the years Yael has played the old girlfriend on amiable terms with him, but that is all off since the dinner at Shimshon's. This is their first time face to face since then, following a very sweet intimate transatlantic telephone talk, when she comforted him about Amos and he responded with much of the old affection.

Now there Yael sits, still lushly seductive in her middle forties, her yellow hair pulled back and parted, Beverly Hills smart in a dark green wool suit and a pearl choker, with a turtle pin of pearls on one shoulder. If she is travel-weary she doesn't show it. Her eyes are glowing at him, her smile is inviting, or so it seems. That she is legally Mrs. Nitzan is almost a technicality. Yael acts as though she is free, and no doubt she can be when she wishes.

Falling silent as they eat grilled sole and drink Chablis, they hear a couple talking in the next booth about the war, the woman maintaining in a piercing Parisian soprano that it is high time *les Juifs* get it in the neck, even Hitler didn't teach them their lesson, they are still out to rule the world. Not too remote, Pasternak thinks, from the sentiment he has encountered all day in the French bureaucracy.

Yael says with an acid smile and a nod toward the voice, "A long way from Shimshon's, eh, hamood?"

"The other pole," he says.

She lays a hand on his and says softly, "Sam."

"Yes." Here comes the Shimshon approach again, he thinks, and how do we deal with it this time?

"Sam, forget it."

"What?"

"You're too nice to say that the clock of love doesn't run backwards, chickens don't turn into eggs, and in short there's no going back. I'm too proud and vain to admit it was a stupid idea, so let's just leave it all unsaid. B'seder?"

When he recovers from his surprise, he bursts out laughing, and she chimes in. "Oo-ah, I don't think I've laughed since Yom

Kippur," he gasps, and they laugh more and more. Then he says, gesturing at the next booth, "Easy, our friends will think we're Arab sympathizers rejoicing."

"Relieved, my dear?" she says.

"First Sergeant, I'll never stop loving you."

"Fine. Let's enjoy our dinner. I met an interesting man on the plane to New York. Ever hear of Max Roweh?"

"Sure, an author. Very rich wife, very charitable woman. As a matter of fact" — from habit he drops his voice — "we have a Mossad fund for the widows and families of guys lost on assignment. She endowed that fund."

"You know she's dead."

"Oh, yes, unfortunately."

Yael tells him about the River House apartment, and the lecture at the Reform temple. Over brandy she tries to recount Roweh's ideas. Pasternak's brow begins to wrinkle and his eyes to cloud. "Yael, that's one obscure gent, that Max Roweh. He wrote a book called *Heine and Hegel.* I like Heine's poetry, so I tried to read it. Heavy, heavy highbrow stuff! I've never met the man. Is he saying Islam is a primitive society? That's not a world-shaking new idea, motek."

"No, no, that's exactly what he was *denying,* Sam. He calls Islam a great civilization, advancing through history at its own pace. It would help if I hadn't fallen asleep. I just can't put it the way he did, but to me it seemed promising for Israel and for peace. It's all tied up with Ibn Khaldun and Vico. Ever hear of Vico?"

"A Greek, like Plato?"

"God, no, a modern Italian. Or of Ibn Khaldun, the Arab historian?"

"Ibn Khaldun, yes, vaguely. Anyhow, you like this Roweh, ha?"

"To all the devils, Sam, not like *that*! He's an ancient professor. But interesting."

"Your plane leaves when, Yael?"

"Half-past midnight."

"Well, drink up, and let's get back to my hotel."

"Whatever for?"

"You dropped your bags in my room, remember? You have to pick them up."

"It isn't nine-thirty."

"Well, you don't want to miss your plane." He gives her a wise ogle.

"Why, you horrible old rogue, what are you suggesting?"

"Punctuality."

"Don't rush me. I'll have another brandy."

They are back in his room at ten. He puts a call in to a number in Israel, reading it from a message he picked up, then tries to take her in his arms.

"Sam, by my life, you're not a serious person. Never have been." She fends him off. "It's a real character flaw. Who did you call?"

"Dayan, in fact."

"What about?"

"I guess he'll tell me."

"Hey! General Pasternak, hands off! What is this? Are you being polite? Reassuring me that I'm still a hot piece? It's not necessary, believe me."

"Old times' sake," he mumbles into her neck.

In his familiar embrace, somewhat cushioned by both midriffs, Yael does a lightning review of options. After two brandies and much wine she is feeling kindly to Pasternak and sorry for him. What then, laugh him out of it? Bring up Eva Sonshine? Or after all, what the hell?

He lets her go to pick up the ringing telephone. The conversation is very short, and all on Dayan's end. As Pasternak listens, his face settles into the hard wartime lines Yael knows well. "Yes, Minister, at once. . . . Well, that's it, Yael. Come with me to the embassy." He slings a small bag and a despatch case on the bed. "I have to call him on the secure telephone. You and I will be going back on the same plane."

"Can you tell me what it's about?"

"After I find out myself, maybe."

Not until they sit side by side in the half-empty plane does he talk, and then in low, almost whispering tones. Dayan believes the war is suddenly at its absolute crunch. By all intelligence from Washington, New York, and London, a cease-fire is rapidly coming on, and the race against the political stopwatch will brook no more delay. Not only have the Golan forces been ordered to advance into Syria, but the desperate expedient of sending the Sinai forces across the Canal at once is up for decision. The cabinet has met to discuss crossing the Canal, and after putting Dado through hours of grilling, the ministers have decided to meet again next day and vote the crossing up or down.

"Only the Jews could figure out such a chain of command, Yael. Such a vital military decision must be made by the full cabinet, you understand. Each minister with one vote! Transportation, Health, Religious Affairs, Housing, Justice, that whole sorry political mishmash, some of whom don't know which end of a rifle shoots, that's our many-headed commander-in-chief. By your life, that's the way it works. The cabinet authorizes Golda, she authorizes Dayan, he authorizes Dado, *he* authorizes Southern Command, *they* authorize Sharon and Adan, they give orders, and somebody finally shoots a gun."

She laughs.

"It's no joke, Yael. Or rather, it's a sick Jewish joke, the whole system."

"Kishote never described it to me that way, and he can be scathing about the army."

"It's the view from the top. One day, he'll see it for himself. Good luck to him."

He folds *Le Soir* to a war analysis with maps, and Yael pulls Roweh's book out of her leather carry-on bag. "*Vico and Descartes*," Pasternak reads aloud, glancing at the jacket. "*The Fork in the Road.* What fork? What road?"

"I'm trying to find out."

She shows him the inscription. "Dulcinea, hey?" Pasternak grins. "Don Kishote's lady fair. It was all a delusion, you know. In reality she was just a farm wench, fat, ugly, and stupid."

"Thanks, Sam."

"My pleasure, motek. Let's see his picture . . . hm. Too old."

"You're an idiot. Read your paper."

She opens the book to the first chapter. Before Pasternak finishes the lucid, meticulously technical, and totally mistaken battle analysis of both fronts by a retired French general, Yael is out cold, her head to a side, the book fallen in her lap. She looks pretty and young. "Dulcinea," he murmurs, laying a blanket over her, "at least I never bored you like that. And you were no delusion. Sleep well."

Avar zmano, batul karbano . . .

In the dark morning hours on that same sixth day, Yanosh summons his battalion and platoon commanders to his HQ tent for a briefing. A ghastly-looking lot they are, Yanosh included: hollow-eyed, stubble-cheeked, dust-covered, sooty, bandaged, patched, drooping, dozing, altogether played out. Colonel Yanosh Ben Gal, who came to Israel through India in a shipment of rescued European children, is a natural and ferocious field tactician. He stands at a large map of Syrian terrain, notebook in hand, stooped over because he is too tall for the tent height, running his bloodshot gaze around the group. Many are new to him, soldiers pressed into leadership because their commanders are wounded or dead.

"Kahalani, where's Pasternak?"

"Evacuated, sir." Kahalani sits cross-legged on the ground, map in his lap, trying to keep his eyes open.

"To all the devils. How bad?"

"Not sure, sir." He describes how Pasternak's crew turned him over to the medics bloody and barely conscious.

With a sad shrug, Yanosh begins the briefing by telling these battle-worn troops that they will have to launch a counterattack in a few hours. They take it with dulled disbelief, and the order goes much against Yanosh's military grain. After five days of hot and sanguinary head-to-head combat, the enemy has at last slacked off, and these troops urgently need to rest and regroup. Yet he not only has to give the order to go on fighting, but he must inspire them to carry it out.

The high politics that call for the counterattack — *"change the battlefield picture, forestall a cease-fire"* — would make no impact on these soldiers. Yanosh speaks straight hard words. He tells them they have broken the Syrian attack, taken the worst the enemy can do, and sent him reeling back home. One more blow can knock Syria out of the war. Then it will probably end, and Israel will be safe again thanks to the heroes of the Golan Heights campaign. So the cry is *"On to Damascus!"* The exhortation works. The young men perk up and start bandying about possible names for the new push, a code word for this thrust into Syria. Suggestions ranging from comic to obscene bring laughs and groans.

A voice at the tent flap speaks up. "Call it 'Black Panther.' "

Amos Pasternak stands just inside, his face and arm bandaged, his tone buoyant. Kahalani jumps up and hugs him amid a chorus of welcome. "You escaped from Rambam, maniac?" asks Yanosh.

"No, sir. The doctor told me if I was fool enough to want to come back, he wouldn't stop me."

Amos's coup de théâtre sticks, and when the Seventh Brigade crosses into the Syrian minefields behind the roller-flail tanks at eleven o'clock that morning, the signal is *"Black Panther."* And Amos stands in his turret leading nine tanks, all that is left of his battalion.

By the time Sam Pasternak lands at the blacked-out Ben Gurion airport his son is deep in Syria, advancing through burning abandoned tanks and vehicles under a shell-streaked sky. When Friday, October twelfth, dawns, his tanks are a third of the way to Damascus, under heavy fire from entrenched defenders; and the whole attack all along the front is slowing down, for a fresh Iraqi armored division has rolled into the battle.

The rising sun of the seventh day, October 12, shines through the trees into the garden of Dayan's Zahala villa, where he sits with Pasternak. Around them are Canaanite antiquities, some of them almost priceless, which Dayan has acquired, one way or another. A few he has restored with his own hands.

"I'm going to the north, Sam. That's where this war is being decided. I'll find out what I can about Amos."

"Why, Amos is in the hospital, Minister. It's such a balagan there, they couldn't tell me anything more, but —"

With his old crooked grin, Dayan says, "No, no. He's back with his battalion. Yanosh himself told me. Like father like son."

"If you mean we're both crazy, b'seder. He can't be too badly injured, then. That's a relief."

"Now listen, Sam. Here's my view of crossing the Canal at this juncture. I want you to attend the meetings in my place, and speak for me."

"At your orders, Minister."

With his customary clipped authority but in a new faintly doleful tone — the downswing of Dayan's "yo-yo syndrome," as the Pit has begun to call it — he tears apart the crossing proposal. The air force is the limiting factor. It is near the red line on planes and pilots, American plane shipments are still almost nil, and the Soviet missile wall at the Canal is unbreached. So a crossing will have no air support to speak of.

Moreover, no adequate bridging equipment is on hand. Tal's rolling monster is an unknown quantity, subject to breakdowns. Pontoon rafts and rubber boats, at best too slow and vulnerable, can only trickle across a small bridgehead. Egyptian armor will snuff out such a weak effort in a shattering final catastrophe. Better a cease-fire than that! He has made these points over and over ad nauseam in several forums, and his position is on record. "Sam, you know I can't stand committee drivel. There will be long meetings all day about this thing before the cabinet votes. First in the Pit. Then with Golda's war cabinet. Finally with the full cabinet. *That* one I must attend as Defense Minister. For the rest, you sit in for me, b'seder? Say I'm coming, and call me if there's any crisis."

Though Pasternak doesn't like this, he only repeats, "At your orders, Minister."

But the crisis comes soon. The Ramatkhal is at a far reach of exhaustion and nerve strain, and when Pasternak tries to explain Dayan's absence in these crucial talks the result is a rare terrifying explosion of Dado wrath. Hurriedly summoned, Dayan returns from the Syrian front to the Pit, and then goes with Dado and the staff to the inner war cabinet meeting.

The red-hot but unmentioned issue of the day, Pasternak well knows, is RESPONSIBILITY. Only the full cabinet can make this decision on which may turn the future of the nation. In Israel's governance the army, as the "military echelon," has to look for orders to the "political echelon." Dayan himself as Ramatkhal often ignored or bypassed this rickety scheme, which dates back to the coalition schemes of Ben Gurion. It has survived, with all the fuzzy compromises that govern Israel, because no party will risk its seats to upset the balance. Now, however, the fate of Israel hangs on how the makeshift system will work. The political echelon has so far ducked a decision on crossing the Canal, so the military echelon has been paralyzed.

In Golda's office, where the few members of the war cabinet are meeting, the talk drags on and on. Nobody seems eager for the responsibility of this move, but Dado is adamant. Enough words! He will not go to the full cabinet, the political echelon, without a clear-cut decision by this inner cabinet in hand. He is patiently describing once more to them how a proposed crossing on Saturday night will go — emphasizing the high risk, refusing to guarantee success — when an aide comes in with a despatch for the Prime Minister. She scans it and calmly hands it to Dado, asking him to read it aloud.

It is hard ultrasecret intelligence that Anwar Sadat *has once for all declined a cease-fire, and has ordered his armored divisions still in Egypt to cross the Canal into Sinai on Saturday or Sunday for an all-out attack toward the mountain passes.* In the smoky room an almost prayerful silence falls. For if this is true, an awesome miracle may be in the making.

These few insiders and the army staff have long been speculating how to tempt Sadat to send his armored divisions across the Canal and out from under the missile umbrella. The Israeli forces in Sinai are now dug in after a four-day lull, rested and in good fighting trim. By the rules of modern war, the strength of the defense is as four to one against the offense; so if Sadat's armor divisions do attack, they will be smashing themselves against these hardened-up defense lines, and all the while Peled's air force will also be punishing them. Thereafter an Israeli crossing of the Canal, instead of being an almost incalculable risk, can become at last a feasible if bloody way to win the war.

Golda speaks first. "Gentlemen, it appears events have made

the decision for us." She looks around with sunken old eyes in which hope and humor glitter. "The full cabinet meeting is cancelled."

Pasternak glances to the dour Dayan, who slightly shrugs as though to say, *"Fine, Sadat has shouldered the responsibility."*

25

Everything That Can Fly

"*There* you are! Quick, before the fuzz runs me in," Emily calls, throwing open her car door as Barak emerges from the Senate Office Building, into a chilly wind whirling leaves along Constitution Avenue. A policeman is glowering at her from the intersection. "I told him I was waiting for my father, the senior senator from South Dakota, and you don't fit either description." She rockets away from the curb while behind them a whistle angrily blows. "Where to, Wolf? Is lunch on?"

"Lunch, sure, but brief, Em. Embassy first."

"Right." She jerks a thumb at a large basket on the back seat. "I packed a picnic, to hell with restaurants and waiters. Christ, what delayed you in there?"

"Henry Jackson's just a mighty busy senator. I shouldn't have asked you to pick me up —"

"No, no, this is perfect, I've snagged you at last. Did you accomplish anything?"

"Yes."

"Tell me about it. I never talk, you know that."

"Okay."

She listens with lips compressed, shooting a keen side-glance at him now and then in her father's manner. "Fascinating. How do you know him so well?"

"From my attaché years. He didn't understand much about the Middle East then — still doesn't, really — and he used to ask me lots of questions. Maybe the chairman of the Foreign Relations Committee should be more informed, but men like that are so beset, Queenie, they have to rely in the end on staff, or on people they trust."

"How did he know you weren't just feeding him propaganda?"

"Because I wasn't. Those guys do have a nose for the truth, and he's exceptionally smart." Barak pauses. "Also — though this may not be relevant — we'd run into the Jacksons socially now and then, and Nakhama really charmed him."

"Aha. Relevant as hell! Two powerful lubricants in this town, reliability and charm." She lightly touches a fist to his chin. "Reliability is much scarcer, friend, I'll tell you that."

Under the loudly flapping blue-and-white flag of the embassy, where policemen and Israeli security officers are standing guard, a few quick Hebrew words pass between Barak and the Israelis. "Emily, they'll let you park behind that TV truck for fifteen minutes. I'll be out by then."

"Here I'll be."

He finds the ambassador still on the telephone. Nobody has refused Dinitz's calls all morning as he drums up support for an airlift. Governors, senators, columnists, TV anchormen, editors, have all been coming right on the line, and in this Barak detects a grassroots surge. The American people have grasped that Israel is in great danger, if the administration hasn't yet.

"Your column is brilliant, Scotty," Dinitz is saying to the almighty James Reston of the *New York Times*. "Cuts right to the bone. Sure, the Soviet SAM-6s have played hell with our Phantoms. It's been a shock, I don't deny it. And we were caught off guard by the attack. All true, but . . . No, no, I make no accusations, God forbid. My country still counts on America's good faith. But in war timing is everything, and so far, I regret to tell you, the aid we've been promised isn't forthcoming. . . . Thanks, Scotty, I appreciate that. General Gur's office will furnish you all details. From you, no secrets whatever."

Dinitz hangs up with a flourish, swivelling his chair to Barak. Sleepless for days, he rides a crest of exhilaration. Not always do the powerful take his calls, or respond with such readiness to help. "Nu, any luck with Scoop?"

"He'll call the Secretary of Defense."

"He will?" Dinitz sits erect. "Not maybe? He will?"

"He will. *Gemacht* [Done deal]."

"Thank God. When?"

"Right after lunch."

"Great. All I got from him was a vague promise to look into it. Zev, well done. You've earned your place in the Garden of Eden."

"How about a place on the next plane home?"

"That's more difficult. You stay here until an airlift flies. Golda's instructions."

When Barak returns to the car Emily asks, "How much time have we got?"

"Say an hour."

"An hour? A whole hour with you alone? My God, half a lifetime. We're off. Listen, do you know there's talk starting up about you in the Defense Department?"

"About me? Why? I'm nobody."

"Ho! This white-haired shadowy figure who's flown here from Israel on a mystery errand. Right out of the Protocols of the Elders of Zion." She is zipping riskily through the heavy Massachusetts Avenue traffic. "Damn, I'm not about to spend our precious hour in this bloody car. Wolf, so help me, I find it hard to sleep, just knowing you're here. It's unbelievable. I'm haunted. How about your son? Have you heard anything more?"

"Well, the navy's still doing wonders, and so far he's unscathed."

"Nakhama must be happy about that."

"Nakhama isn't happy about anything."

Conversation-stopper. They do not talk again until she parks the car by a brown deserted lawn. "Grab the basket, darling, and follow me." They make their way through tangled shrubbery to the curving deserted walk around the Tidal Basin lined with leafless Japanese cherry trees, where the shallow blue water ripples in sharp gusts of wind. "I love these poor out-of-season trees. *'Bare ruined choirs, where late the sweet birds sang.'* Here's a good bench."

" *'Bare ruined choirs'* — is that Emily Dickinson?"

"Zev, for Christ's sake, Shakespeare!" She begins unpacking the basket. "About the way true love hangs on, no matter how old and unattractive one gets. Reassuring, what? I'm going to divorce Bud." She hands him a sandwich. "That's turkey, okay? Not much mayonnaise."

"*What?* Say that again."

"Turkey, easy on the mayonnaise. Or would you prefer egg salad? I brought both —"

"For God's sake, Queenie, did you just say you're going to divorce your husband?"

"Bud doesn't know it yet. Neither does Chris. You're the first one I've told." He stares at her, dumbstruck, as she placidly unwraps a sandwich and takes a bite. "Well? Don't goggle at me like a fish, there's this woman, Elsa. A Norwegian. It's been going on for a while, a torrid thing. I was going to write you all about it, cry on your shoulder. Lord, when I got your last letter I thought I'd die! Old Wolf, you're my anchor in sanity, you always have been. Now more than ever. Why did you do it? What did Nakhama say? After all these years!"

"Tell me about the Norwegian."

"Oh, Elsa. Must I? Okay, where shall I start?"

"Well, is she pretty?"

"Spoken like a man. I've seen her only once, and a cover girl she ain't. She does have these fine blue eyes. Ice and fire, sapphire eyes. I'll give her that. Spiffy eyes. And she's tall, almost as tall as Bud. Maybe that's the attraction. Who knows?"

"How did you find out?"

"How do you think? He told me. Ever the officer and gentleman, Bradford Halliday. One evening over the martinis he just up and let me know, all square and upright. The woman works for an old friend, a retired colonel, Jack Smith —"

"I know Smith."

"So you do. Well, he's now a consultant on defense contracts, and that's how Bud got to know Elsa. Anything else?"

"What did you do when he told you?"

"Oh, I was adult and modern about it, of course. No choice really, is there? I took off a shoe, threw it at his face, and called him a fucking son of a bitch. Well, he caught the shoe and brought it back to me. I couldn't help saying, 'Speaking of sons of bitches, at least you retrieve, it's more than Merlin does.' And that's about where it stands."

"Emily, seriously —"

"Don't, Zev, *don't* talk seriously. It's too serious for that, and I feel too good sitting on the same bench with you. For the moment I'm in heaven. I ask no more. I've never loved Bud. He and I both know that. We've jog-trotted along, but now there's this goddamn Elsa, and to top it off *you* show up, and I realize all over again what love is. Bud's treated me well, put me on some kind of pedestal, but I'm going to climb down and let him have his love. Everybody should try it once, I say."

A stiff gust across the water stirs the cherry branches, withered leaves tumble past the bench, and it seems to him that this whole scene — Emily sitting there in a red cloth coat with a gray fur collar, the scuttering leaves, the taste of turkey, the shock of her disclosure — all has happened before in exactly this way. Never has this sort of delusive dreamlike memory slippage hit him so strongly. He *knows* she will next say, as she does, "All I brought to drink is a thermos of coffee. Here." She pours coffee into the white plastic cap and offers it to him.

He says, "You drink it."

"Not on your life, I've got the shakes as it is."

"Emily, if you want my opinion about this divorce notion —"

"Skip it." Anger flashes across her face. "Last advice I had from you, kiddo, was to get married. I've taken it from there, okay?"

"Okay, toots."

She manages a smile, and her tone softens. "Sorry, Zev. I'm awfully unhappy. It's not an affair, puss, it's *love.* He loves her. And he loves the girls and adores little Einstein. Who, by the bye, has yet to say 'Mama,' even. So it's one big fat Gordian knot, calling for a sharp sword stroke —"

"Queenie, listen to me —"

"I won't, and keep it light, lover boy, for God's sake. It's not something Bud'll get out of his system. It's what his system is starved for. More coffee? No? Well, don't look so down in the mouth. I'll survive, believe me. I sure as hell will need to see more of you, though. Say once a year, for a few days, and strictly on the up-and-up. Would that be utterly out of the question, if for instance I go and live in Paris? Would it?"

"Nothing's utterly out of the question. Still —"

"Stop right there." She puts cold fingers on his mouth. "Let me have something to hang my hat on, old darling. The kids would grow up bilingual like me, that would be nice, and there wouldn't be an ocean between us."

"The Med's no fishpond, Queenie."

"Oh, it's a hop, by comparison. I still hear from André, you know. He won the Goncourt Prize, can you imagine? With a novel called *The Bad Breath of the Gorgon*, which nobody understands. I've always loved Paris."

"I've always loved you," says Barak without thinking.

"Not so," she says, her lips quivering, her eyes moist and brilliant as she repacks the basket. "I had to convince you, and it took forever. In your heart I'm still the twelve-year-old minx you snubbed, for being snotty about chemistry. But God knows I've always loved you. Back to the car, there's a war on, you know."

They embrace in the gloom of the bushes. She kisses him at first in her usual hesitant, almost girlish way, then with passion, clinging tight to him. "My God, how I want to be held by you," she chokes. "Will I see you again before you vanish?"

"I'll talk to you, no matter what."

"All right. And one day, one way or another, if I have to come to Israel to do it, I'm going to have it out with Nakhama. I *need* your letters, Zev."

Ambassador Dinitz is pacing, red in the face, his pipe clenched in his teeth, puffing gray smoke like a train going uphill.

General Gur in spic-and-span uniform sits watching him with concern. "Simcha, don't have a stroke," he says. "It's only a war."

"He'll see me today," says Dinitz, "*today,* or he'll find out what a war with the Jews is like."

"What now?" Barak asks.

With choppy angry gestures, Dinitz replies, "The Secretary of Defense did return my call, thanks no doubt to you and Scoop Jackson. He offered to meet me tomorrow sometime. Not today, busy all day. The war news gets worse by the hour. Kissinger assures me that Defense will increase and speed up delivery of Phantoms and all supplies, but when Motta calls the Pentagon, they don't know of any increase or speedup. I just rang Scoop and he's phoning SecDef again. The runaround stops this afternoon, by my life!"

"Motta, what bad news?" Barak asks.

The attaché heavily sighs. "Well, let's see. Two more Iraqi armored divisions coming into Syria. Jordan sending in a brigade. The Russians publicly urging Algeria to get into the war. By last count *seventy-three* Antonov planeloads of weapons landing in Damascus and Cairo, mainly tanks and antiair missiles. Thousands of tons more coming by ship, a short run from the Black Sea." Gur pauses. "Bad enough?"

Dinitz says, "So why did you leave out the three Soviet airborne divisions? They don't count?" The telephone rings. "Dinitz here. . . . Yes, yes, put him on." Grim smile, hand over the mouthpiece. " *'Hold for the Secretary of Defense.'* "

"Russian airborne divisions?" Barak is shocked and incredulous. "Rumor, Motta? Fact? What?"

"Fact. I saved the worst for last," Gur replies gloomily. "Our own army intelligence, and CIA confirms. They're on highest alert, ready to go."

"Hello, Mr. Secretary. . . . Thank you, that's good of you . . . Well, I wish we could be that optimistic. I'll be glad to give you the full picture." A long pause. Dinitz's glasses glitter as he turns to Barak and Gur and nods. "Six o'clock. Can't it be earlier, sir? . . . Well then, six it is. Much obliged."

"You're getting your meeting," says Gur.

"Not only with him, but with every top *mamzer* over there. What will come of it I don't know, but it'll be a real Litvak wedding. Motta, you'll come with me. Zev, contact this Halliday, and see him right away."

"What about?"

"Just tell him it's urgent and secret." The ambassador gets up, closes his office door, and drops his voice. "Here is what you must convey."

Halliday is reading the *Washington Post* on a lobby couch in the Army & Navy Club. He stands up, a long lithe figure in brown tweed and gray flannel. "Hi."

"Hi. I'm afraid I gave you very short notice."

"No problem, you said urgent. Come in here, it's quiet."

Barak tries in vain to picture the tall blue-eyed Elsa, as he follows the aviator into a large writing room with nobody in it. Meeting him like this is disconcerting, so soon after the picnic disclosures. This is not a man one can imagine consumed by ardor. In a remote corner they sit down in black leather armchairs, near a loudly ticking old grandfather clock. Halliday looks to the Israeli to begin. No offer of a drink, and no smile.

"General Halliday, you're aware that my ambassador is meeting with your secretary, and that a diplomat can only give hints sometimes in formal meetings."

"Whereas you can talk plainly to me off the record. Well, fire away." Halliday folds his long arms, stretches out his long legs, and fixes Barak with a steady eye.

"Thank you. As things now stand, the United States is reneging on its commitments to Israel — some of long standing, some made when the Arabs attacked my country." Halliday takes this stiff start with a slight widening of his eyes. Barak goes on, "Your government has yet even to admit publicly that the Arabs started the war. Israel is in grave danger because of apparent American bad faith."

"General Barak, Israel is in grave danger — if it is — because your people were caught flat-footed, due to overconfidence and unwise contempt for the enemy."

"As you were at Pearl Harbor."

"Just so." Halliday's eyes go opaque, then clear. "Proceed."

"I said 'apparent' bad faith, General. My government prefers to believe that, at a time of our greatest peril, your bureaucratic wheels are unfortunately stuck. You know about the alert of three Russian airborne divisions?"

"We do. Routine Soviet practice in crises. Like replacing the tattletale merchant ships, which tail our carrier groups in the Med, with tattletale warships. One learns to live with these political signals. That's all they are. Translation, *'You stay out and we'll stay out.'* "

"General, the Russians are not staying out. Their airlift is public and massive, and an immense sealift has left port —"

Halliday holds up a hand. "Look here, Barak, you asked for a secret urgent meeting. My department knows all this." He glances at his watch. "What exactly can I do for you?"

"At noon tomorrow, General, Saturday the thirteenth — that's a little less than nineteen hours from now — if the bureaucratic wheels have not come unstuck, Israel will go public to express dismay at your government's deserting an ally in her hour of need. Golda Meir will probably do this herself on television."

Long, long silence. Clock ticking, ticking, then striking the half hour with a groan and a sonorous BONG.

Halliday says, "Is that it? Your ambassador can get that across to the Secretary, surely."

"Wrapped in cotton, yes. That's it straight."

"And what good will such dramatics do your country? It will cause the Arabs great joy, that's for sure. What else can you hope for?"

"We think the outcry in this country from the people, the media, and the Congress will either force swift action, or come close to bringing down a shaken administration."

Halliday utters an incredulous grunt of "Really!"

"Really. That's our judgment. Foreign policy is this President's one remaining high card. Such a firestorm would destroy that card, and we believe he won't let it happen. Heads will roll, and those wheels will turn."

Another silence. Halliday purses thin lips, and cracks interlaced knuckles. "You're talking about cranking up the Jewish lobby, aren't you? There are more broadly based American interests, General Barak, that take a very different view of all this."

"Saturday at noon, General Halliday."

"I hear you. General Barak, you're an Israeli. I understand you, and your loyalty to the Jewish State. No problem. These people in the Jewish lobby — are they Jews or Americans? Where's their ultimate loyalty? If they question the good faith of my superiors, is their good faith beyond question?"

Barak has heard this jab often enough as a military attaché, and has often riposted. "You're quite right, there are more powerful interests at work here, General, the oil interest for one. Its power is truly awesome. As for the so-called Jewish lobby, it can accomplish nothing in this town, unless the American people are already for a given policy. In this case, your people have clearly decided that Israel should get aid at once to match the Soviet aid to the Arabs. You've seen the polls? ABC, *Time,* and this morning's *Washington Post*?"

Halliday takes a while to answer. He stands up, with a brisk oddly light, "Okay, got you," and another glance at his watch. They leave the club and part on the breezy sidewalk with no more words.

In the cubicle between the double security doors of the embassy, the guard speaks from behind glass on a microphone. "Sir, General Gur wants to see you the moment you return."

"B'seder."

The attaché is working at a piled-up desk under a handsome photograph of Dayan in coat and tie. He hands Barak a pencilled decode form. "What do you make of this?"

> TOP SECRET URGENT PRIME MINISTER TO DINITZ GUR HARD INTELLIGENCE TWO ARMORED DIVISIONS WILL CROSS CANAL INTO SINAI SATURDAY THIRTEENTH TELL KISSINGER.

Barak takes a moment to answer. "Could be good or bad."

"How, good?"

"If Sadat's gotten cocky and decided to attack and finish us off, it would be a bloody business, but our position could improve."

"Or he could be hardening up his lodgments in Sinai," says Gur, "to prevent our crossing before a cease-fire. That would do it, too."

"Is Dinitz back from the Pentagon?"

"No, he went from there to the White House. Nixon's about to announce his new Vice President. Big secret still. How did the meeting with Halliday go?"

"Frank and open." At this diplomatic jargon for a nasty encounter, the attaché sourly laughs.

When Dinitz returns to his office, yanking off his topcoat, Barak is there, waiting. The ambassador is very pale, and his brow is deeply creased. "Looks like another long night, Zev. I have to talk to Golda right away."

"Three in the morning there, Simcha."

"I doubt she's asleep." Dinitz drops exhausted in his chair, buzzes the coding officer and orders the call put through on the scrambler. "But I tell you, I nearly fell asleep on my feet at the White House. The new man is Congressman Gerald Ford, not bad for us. What a weird business! TV cameras and lights, a big crowd, applause, Nixon all smiles, not a care in the world, you'd think." He lights his pipe and vigorously puffs. "Kissinger was off in a corner talking with Ambassador Dobrynin. Afterward he told me what it was about. Very, very bad. He'll receive a cable from Moscow tonight, accusing Israel of all sorts of crimes and atrocities, and saying, '*The Soviet Union cannot remain indifferent to such barbaric conduct.*' Words to that effect. The message is that either Israel accepts a cease-fire *at once,* or those airborne divisions will go."

Quelling his own pulse of alarm, Barak says calmly, "But the Arabs haven't yet accepted."

"I'm telling you what Dobrynin's threat is."

Desk voice box: "Mr. Ambassador, your call's going through."

At almost the same moment the telephone rings. "Yes? . . . By all means, put him on. . . . Zev, it's Reston of the *Times.* Take that scrambler call and tell Golda about Dobrynin. I'll be along."

Golda sounds wide awake and reasonably cheerful. "Oh, it's you, Zev. Nu? Something good for the Jews?"

"Simcha will be right with you, Madame Prime Minister. He's talking to the *New York Times*."

"Fine. That's more important. Me he can talk to anytime."

Barak is baldly describing the Dobrynin threat and the way it was conveyed at the White House, when Dinitz comes in and takes the scrambler phone. "Sorry, Madame Prime Minister — What? Yes, Kissinger thinks it's serious. Deadly serious." Long pause. "No, the Pentagon meeting was terrible. Flat denial of broken promises or slowdown. They'll speed up Phantom delivery to two planes every three days." Another pause. Dinitz rolls his eyes at Barak. "Golda, I *told* them we need forty at once. Impossible. Out of the question. Meantime I'm meeting Kissinger in an hour and I must have instructions. . . . Yes . . . Yes . . . Yes, I understand." He turns to Barak. "Write this down, Zev, word for word. *'If the Secretary thinks it wise to proceed with negotiations — for a cease-fire cosponsored by the Soviet Union and the United States — Israel will interpose no objection.'* "

From the scrap of paper on which Barak has scrawled, Dinitz slowly reads the words back to her. "Very well, Madame Prime Minister. . . . Yes, I understand. . . . Of course, no matter what time, I'll call you." He hangs up and regards Barak with heavy sad eyes. "By my life, that's a rotten message for me to bring to the American Secretary of State."

"Why? Listen, Simcha, it's a smart shifty message," Barak says forcibly. "Now Kissinger can parley and stall, and she knows he *wants* to stall until the battlefield picture changes. As long as there's talk of a cease-fire, those airborne divisions won't go, will they?"

"Probably not." The ambassador brightens. "As usual, she may be two steps ahead of all of us. Henry Kissinger included."

It is in fact a long night. Barak's head has hardly hit the pillow in his hotel room, so it seems, when the telephone rings. The sun is blazing through a dirty window. What now? Has the stall worked? *Or are those Soviet troops landing?* He grabs the telephone.

"Morning, Bradford Halliday here. Are you a jogger?"

"What? Ah, why?"

"I run a few miles before work. Maybe you could join me, and we could talk. Things are happening."

Barak blinks at his watch. Half past eight. "General, I'll walk as far as you like. Running, no."

"Good enough. At the corner of M and Thirty-third there's a parking lot. Meet me there at nine."

Merlin comes bounding out of the car ahead of the general, and makes friendly leaps and licks at Barak's face. Halliday, in a fuzzy purple running suit, says, "Merlin, stop." The dog desists, and trots at his heel down to the towpath, where fallen leaves carpet the packed black earth with random color, and float all over the muddy canal. Broad and blue, the Potomac glitters through the barren trees of the embankment.

"Good place to run, except for the traffic fumes," says Halliday, striding off at a fast pace. "You people have won your little game, you know."

"Eh? How's that?"

"You haven't heard? You will, soon enough." His long steps are hard to keep up with. He looks straight ahead as he speaks. "I don't know how much will be made public, just yet. What I tell you now is secret, for your ambassador only. You Israelis have gotten a very distorted picture of this entire airlift business."

"I'm all ears, General."

"Very well. Early this morning Dr. Kissinger told the President that Defense has located three C-5As which could fly at once on an airlift, if that is his desire. Those are our giant transports, you know, matching the Antonovs. The President told him, and this is a pretty direct quote, '*Hell, the Arabs will hate us as much for three planes as for three hundred. Put everything in the air that can fly.*'" Halliday glances at Barak. "'*Everything in the air that can fly.*' How about that from President Nixon, whom the Jews have never supported?"

"To be honest, I'm stunned."

"Okay. Now let me speak frankly about Dr. Kissinger, meaning no slur on a co-religionist of yours. The President has been up to his chin in hot water trying to survive, and your war has been low on his agenda. He's been leaving that policy to Dr. Kissinger, probably figuring you'd smash the Arabs in a few days. I guess Dr. Kissinger thought so, too. Our department's directive from Kissinger was crystal-clear." Halliday's voice slows to a deliberate quoting pace. " 'No need to rush matériel to Israel and anger the Arabs. This war is our opportunity to break the political stalemate. Our aim is to play honest broker. Decisions about filling the Israelis' supply demands are left to the Defense Department's judgment of their actual needs.' Then on Tuesday, four days into the war, Mrs. Meir hits the panic button, wanting to fly here and talk to the President. Mind you, the night before we were assured by your attaché, General Gur, that Israel would be ending the whole thing any day."

"We had a disastrous couple of days, October seventh and eighth."

"No doubt. My point is that Defense has been carrying out State policy all along — go slow, don't irritate the Arabs, preserve our neutral-broker status, avoid an oil embargo. That was behind the whole charter idea, which is now up the flume. The air force will start today on an all-out airlift, refueling in the Azores." Halliday throws him a look of glittery pride. "And now that we have our orders, Barak, I assure you military transport command will out-deliver the Russians two to one, though it's five times the distance, and none of our European allies and friends except Portugal will let us land."

"It's terrific news, General."

"Not to me. The cease-fire will be voted in the UN anyway in a day or so, but this futile airlift gesture will finish us with the Arabs. An oil embargo's inevitable, and for the next twenty years the Soviet Union will be calling the shots in the Middle East. That's not good for us or for you."

"Well, I don't quite share your pessimism." Barak is warming up and recovering stride, taking deep breaths of the sweet autumn-smelling Washington air, tainted by the blue haze of the morning traffic on the Key Bridge. "I think I'd better hurry on to my embassy."

"Right. I'll walk back a ways with you and then have my run. Come on, Merlin."

As they pass through a stream of chattering teenage girls on bicycles, Halliday says, "Dr. Kissinger's a historian, and one hell of a shrewd article. The way he wants it to come out, the Pentagon's been the foot-dragger, he's been your advocate, and now he's won. The truth as I see it is otherwise."

"What's the truth, General Halliday?"

"The truth is, the President's waked up to the war, however late, and *he's* ordering the airlift. Maybe to rescue an ally. Maybe to stand up to the Russians for prestige reasons. Maybe Congress and the media have gotten to him. Maybe even to hold off Mrs. Meir going on TV! His reasons are none of our business. He's the commander-in-chief, and you've got your airlift, but not because Dr. Kissinger has ridden to your rescue, and not over my secretary's dead body. Okay?"

"Okay," says Barak. The silence between them grows long as they stride back toward Key Bridge. Barak's mind is already on his return home, and on the possible effect on the war of Nixon's belated move. *Everything that can fly!* Astounding, historic, but can it still make a difference? A squirrel runs across the path. With a yearning backward look at it, Merlin trots straight on. "I have to compliment you on that dog, General."

"He does heel, but that's about it." Halliday points ahead. "You can take that crosswalk over the canal. At the top of the hill there'll be cabs, no problem."

As they shake hands, Halliday appears to relax, though not to smile. "Israel is very highly respected at the Pentagon. That hasn't changed."

"Good to know, sir."

"A lot of people here forgot, I think, that Superman is a comic strip. Some of yours, too, maybe."

"Maybe. On a personal note, if you'll allow me, my son Noah didn't talk till he was three, and was a total wild devil. He's an outstanding naval officer."

"Well, the trouble is, by contrast my girls seem to have been born talking a blue streak."

Barak can't resist saying, "Mother's genes."

"Obviously." Halliday still does not smile. "You knew her long before I did, and she values your friendship and your correspondence." Barak thinks that the eyes faintly warm in the general's long sober face, and that he is going to say more. "Come on, Merlin, boathouse and back, five miles. Goodbye, Barak."

Amid much scurrying about of excited aides in a din of Hebrew, Motta Gur is on the phone, shouting army acronyms. "B'seder, check again, I'll stay on the line . . ." Covering the mouthpiece, he snaps to Barak, "When you get home tell Nehemiah to find his head and screw it back on." He is referring to the army's quartermaster general.

"What's Nehemiah's problem?"

"The Pentagon's suddenly offering us *ten C-130 transports* for immediate airlift as well as three C-5As, and wants to know what we need most. Nehemiah is all excited, and right away he says shells, shells. Zev, I know we've got enough shells to fight till Hanukkah. We manufacture them ourselves! They're piled up in depots or loaded on trains, or coming to the front in trucks, but they're somewhere. Helicopters, tanks, howitzers, air-to-air missiles, antitank missiles, *those* we need . . . Yes, Nehemiah? . . . So? What did I tell you? And it's the same story with armor-piercing, you'll see —"

Barak retrieves his document case and waves a farewell to Gur, who returns a harried gesture. Dinitz's secretary meets him in the corridor. "There you are, General. The ambassador's waiting for you. I'm still working on getting you out today."

Dinitz's color is better, though the eye-hollows are deeper and purpler. "So? Halliday's turned friendly, has he, like the rest of the Pentagon?"

"Not exactly. That man's viewpoint doesn't shift with the wind."

"Let's hear." Dinitz cuts off his calls, lights his pipe, and listens with an intent air and an infrequent nod. "Yes, there's always another side, and he's a pretty shrewd article himself, that Halliday," he says when Barak finishes. "He makes a case. But you weren't there last night in the Pentagon, when I sat for two hours, banging my head against that blank wall of frozen faces."

"They were acting on Kissinger policy, he claims."

"Yes, so he says. Zev, ask yourself one thing. If John Foster Dulles or William Rogers were sitting in Henry Kissinger's chair today, would this airlift be going? Not a chance in hell, I say —"

His secretary looks in. "General Barak, there's a Laker flight from New York to London that you can catch at JFK, and in Heathrow you can connect to El Al. I've booked you through, and a driver's waiting downstairs."

"B'seder."

"So, Zev, you're off? I wish I were going with you. Well done."

"Well done? I haven't done a damned thing."

"How can you say that? You know what the Secretary of Defense said to me, at the end of that miserable meeting? He said, 'Who exactly is that white-headed fellow? What's his job?' When I told him you were Golda's military secretary, he looked skeptical. If I'd said, 'He's Nixon's Jewish cousin from Tiberias,' he'd have believed me. Pleasant journey."

At Kennedy airport Barak dives for the one unoccupied telephone in the long row near the plane gate, where people gabble in several languages.

Emily's voice: "Of course, operator, I'll take the call — Wolf! Where *are* you? The embassy said you'd already left for Israel."

"I'm at JFK, and I had only one quarter, so I'm calling collect —"

"Great, scrumptious, a bargain. Listen, got time to talk to my father? He's here, playing with Chris."

"A little. My plane's posted a delay."

"Jehosephat, were we ever snookered!" Cunningham's reedy voice, as he comes on, is high with indignation. "Détente this, détente that, and meanwhile those Russians turned the Arabs loose on you and beefed them up with fleets of Antonovs while we sat idle, letting you and our whole Middle East position go down the tubes! The airlift probably comes too late, but it'll sober up the other side at least, show them America isn't sleeping straight through this big disaster. . . . What, Emily? Yes, by God. Right! Barak, Chris spoke his first word this morning, and you know what it was? *Grandpa!* Grandpa, loud and clear. Five by five! Have a good trip, and remember Ezekiel: '*I am against you, Gog, saith the Lord* . . .' Even if there's a cease-fire, the Arabs will blow it. There's a miracle in the making. Don't despair."

"Me again, Wolf."

"Em, did he really say '*Grandpa*' ?"

"He sure said something. It might have been '*sandbar*,' or '*ham hocks*.' Anyhow, his grandpa is delighted, he's been dancing the kid around on his shoulders. Zev, whatever you do, keep writing to me, won't you? These few days have been a blood transfusion, my darling. I've come out of a coma. I'll handle my troubles, one way or another, but I have to know you're there. You're my anchor."

"I'll write, Queenie."

"Lovely. Will you ever forget the picnic? I keep reliving it. Imagine, a white-headed soldier and an air-headed ex-schoolmarm, smooching in the bushes! Who would believe it? How beautiful it was!"

"My plane's being called. I love you, Emily. Goodbye."

"Goodbye, my sweet. Go to victory! See you in Paris someday."

Victory, thinks Barak as he hangs up, depends on the next Egyptian move, which may well happen while he is en route. It is a correct surmise. While he is in the air and out of touch, Anwar Sadat formally notifies London, Moscow, and Washington that he is rejecting the cease-fire.

26

That Crazy Bridge

Still panting a bit from the steep climb, Don Kishote stands on a windswept sandy ledge where a Centurion tank lurks, only the turret poking up behind fresh earthworks. In the weak red light of the sun just rising over the mountains behind him, the Egyptian tanks in his binoculars remind him of a Soviet war movie about the Battle of Kursk: long green-brown lines on the gray sand advancing all across the horizon out of a dust cloud, a crawling lava tide of machines, unreal and beautiful. Shells are exploding thunderously here and there among the dunes, artillery salvos hurled randomly by the enemy into the desert wastes.

No surprise this time! Intelligence has come in during the night on the size, scope, time, and direction of the attack. And no zeroing in of the heavy Russian-made artillery, either, days before any fighting, on big static targets like the Bar-Lev Line outposts. This sector, the central thirty miles of Zahal's hundred-mile Canal front, is now battle-ready; Sharon's three hundred tanks dug in hull down on the dunes and ledges, virtually invisible; ten to a mile, five hundred feet apart, interspersed with antitank guns and missile launchers. The thirty-mile zigzag of open *V*'s facing the enemy will become a killing ground, even if their units penetrate to the defense line. Tank maintenance is high, fuel and ammo depots are stocked, armor repair and medical units are at the ready. Above all, the soldiers are rested, well fed, and cheery; mostly cynical and bored as always, some shaken by the recent fighting, but Zahal troops again, not reservists disoriented and disheartened by the surprise wrench out of their civilian lives.

The tank captain in his open turret, binoculars to his eyes, says, "Well, General, here the bastards come." This freckled-faced redheaded company commander, one of his best reserve officers, is a high school mathematics teacher, whom he has tried in vain to talk into staying in the army.

"Ready for them, Heshi?"

"More than ready, sir." An edge of anger in the voice. "My brother Romi was caught in a maoz. I still don't know whether he's dead or alive."

A flaming shell-burst on the slope below sends rocks flying high, and sand and smoke blow toward them. Heshi drops out of sight, shouting as he closes the hatch, "This will be our day, General."

As the earsplitting barrage continues, the foremost enemy tanks come within gun range, and red tracer shells begin to fly, whining and crisscrossing. The advantage is all with the defenders; they pop up to fire and disappear, while the enemy must plod closer over open desert. No air action so far; the Egyptians are wary of the superior Israeli air force, while Israeli aviators are stymied by the SAM-6 missiles with their slant range reaching far into Sinai air space. Kishote sees enemy tanks already bursting into flame, while along the defense line there is no sign of fire or smoke from a hit. Heshi may be right, the day is starting off as a gift from the Lord of battles.

A yell from below: "Ha'm'faked!" It is Yoram Sarak at the wheel of Kishote's signal command car, monitoring the brigade and division networks. "General Sharon's orders, sir. Report to him at once."

He scrambles down through the rocks to the dirt road below and gets into the car, which buzzes with harsh signalling on three receivers. "Lot of shooting out there, sir," says Sarak with a friendly grin and no trace of deference. The journalist looks more hirsute than in peacetime, with a week's growth of bristles, and long hair falling into his dark glasses. "How are we doing?"

"It's just starting."

As the command car bumps along the flinty unmarked back road, Kishote wonders how Sharon is taking all this. He has been vociferously pushing for an immediate Canal crossing ever since the disastrous October eighth. The very next day he led a reconnaissance in force all the way to the Canal, disobeying direct orders at the risk of being relieved or even court-martialled. From there he signalled that he was discovering an undefended "seam" at the northern end of the Great Bitter Lake, between the two Egyptian armies. "I am dipping my toes in the Canal," he exulted to the high command, "and there's no enemy in sight. In the name of God, let's cross at once and end this war." Turned down and reprimanded, he has since taken his case to the newspapers; Zahal has to plunge across now, *now,* NOW, to cut off the enemy before he can harden up the Sinai lodgments. But Dado has stuck to his decision; in the north attack, in the south dig in, calculating that Sadat may send his armor over into Sinai, where Zahal can cut it up. After the tense lull which has enabled the defenders to set up their formidable line, the event seems to be proving the Ramatkhal right.

"What a sight, Kishote, what a battle!" Sharon hails him on high ground looking out over the entire smoky battlefield, where numerous fires now flare. His white-blond hair flying, his eyes agleam, Sharon looks years younger and full of the joy of life as he sweeps an arm around at the panorama. "The Lord is delivering them into our hands. No more foot-dragging. Tomorrow we cross."

This is pure Arik; never mind yesterday, on with the action. Yossi's blood is up too, at the sight of all those burning tanks. "By my life, sir, I hope you're right."

"Yossi, your defense line is a brilliant job. Highest commendation. Now I want you to proceed to Tasa and let me know what's happening on the other sectors, and also in Syria."

"Yes, sir."

"Then when the action wanes, start marshalling the crossing equipment. First check on that roller bridge, make sure it will be at the Canal by tomorrow. Locate all the other stuff, the rubber dinghies for the paratroopers, the pontoon rafts, the crocodiles" — he is referring to amphibious wheeled rafts, discarded for combat use by the French — "and boot all the butts you have to, but get everything *moving*. Understood?"

"Understood, sir."

With a wolfish smile and a gesture toward the burning tanks, Sharon says, "Sorry to send you from the battlefield."

"At your command, sir."

In the cement bunker under Tasa headquarters, Yossi can see the entire Egyptian attack on the big wall maps, kept up to the minute by clamorous signalling and the moving of colored tokens. A textbook Soviet-style operation is unfolding, heavy forces pushing out in at least six prongs toward the passes, a hydraulic press of war rather than one concentrated thrust. But massive though it is, the attack looks to him somewhat irresolute. Not all the heavy armored forces that crossed the Canal have been committed, not by any means. Why not? Perhaps staff arguments have produced a compromise attack, such as disagreeing Israeli generals sometimes launch, usually to their regret. At any rate there remains, in Kishote's view, more than enough power in the lodgments on either side of the Great Bitter Lake to choke off a crossing, though Arik will probably disagree. And on the Syrian front also, disquieting news: Jordanians and Iraqis moving in to join a counterattack in force.

All the same what is taking shape before his eyes is a historic head-to-head tank battle, which may open the way to a victorious if bloody cease-fire. Gleeful reports are pouring in of the numbers of enemy tanks destroyed on all three sectors of the Sinai front; and an end run toward the Mitla Pass by an Egyptian brigade, venturing out beyond the missile umbrella, is being crushed by the air force. All in all, the best day yet of a hard war.

"*Blessed are you, Lord God, King of the Universe!*" Straightening up in his wheelchair, Professor Berkowitz weakly but joyously blurts the benediction on good news. *"For keeping us alive, and sustaining us, and bringing us to this moment."*

"Amen" from Shayna, little Reuven, Aryeh Nitzan, and even

Dzecki's irreligious parents. On the black-and-white TV the first airlift C-5A is just touching down at Lod airport, army trucks are rolling out in a column toward the behemoth aircraft, an army band plays a rousing welcome song, and a crowd of onlookers cheer and dance.

"My brother Zev made this happen," says Michael, tears in his eyes. His face is gray, and he looks shrunken in a heavy gray bathrobe, but he exudes hectic high spirits. "He'll never say so, but I'm sure of it. Now we're going to win this terrible war, against all the odds. Come, let's rejoice at lunch in the sukkah, with an extra glass of wine to toast the Americans!"

They all crowd into the small palm-roofed booth on the chilly balcony of the Berkowitzes' Haifa apartment. Aryeh brings along his shortwave radio, obsessively following the war news. At sixteen he is acquiring his father's muscular frame and is the biggest person in the sukkah. Professor Berkowitz rolls the wheelchair as close to the table as he can, and glancing up at the palm fronds, he says, "*Roshi v'rovi,* my head and most of me are inside. Kosher!"

On the hour, as they are eating cabbage soup, the cool dry voice of the BBC newscaster comes on.

"Here are the headlines. In the Middle East the greatest tank battle in world history has been raging since dawn . . ."

They look at each other in dismay, and Michael waves a limp hand at Shayna, saying, "I'm fine, don't fuss."

". . . in Washington the crisis heightens as President Nixon offers to let a senior senator listen to the White House tapes, and in Chile, student riots oust the military government.

"Now for the news. Radio Cairo reports that more than a thousand Egyptian tanks are advancing deep into the Sinai, while simultaneously two Iraqi armored divisions and a Jordanian brigade have joined the Syrian army in an offensive against the Israeli lines. According to a highly placed official at Whitehall, Israel can oppose no more than eight hundred tanks in all to at least fifteen hundred tanks now attacking on two fronts . . ."

"Arab lies!" A hoarse cry from Michael. "Aryeh, switch to Kol Yisroel."

Dzecki's father, togged Great Neck style in blue blazer, striped tie, and button-down white shirt, says to Michael, "I'm afraid the airlift comes too late."

"Oh, God, Leon, where did Jack say his unit was?" the mother frets.

"He didn't say, dear, but he can't be too far from the Canal."

The radio is rattling rapid Hebrew. The professor holds up a hand. "Here comes the army communiqué." He nods and nods, then translates for the Barkowes. " *'Major enemy tank attacks in the north and in Sinai are being successfully resisted by our forces —'* "

"Halevai!" exclaims Shayna. She says to the Barkowes, "That means, 'It should only be so.' "

"I know what *halevai* means, dear," says Mrs. Barkowe tartly. "I've been living here awhile. Halevai the plumber will come, the fifth time he promises. Halevai the landlord will turn on the heat before January. Halevai my husband's next partner won't embezzle their joint bank account and fly off to Buenos Aires. Israel is the land of halevai." With a sharper note in her voice, "Halevai my son will come back alive from this damned war, which is none of his business."

Aryeh says, "Look, Uncle Michael, suppose that for once Radio Cairo is telling the truth?"

Dzecki's mother bursts out, "Oh, they are, they are, but Kol Yisroel isn't. This government isn't. Why, they didn't announce casualties for a whole week! My neighbor found out only yesterday that her son was badly wounded on the second day. Is she ever bitter! She said to me, 'The Arabs have learned from us how to fight, and we've learned from them how to lie.' "

The festive spirit in the sukkah is extinguished. When Shayna brings a carved-up chicken from the kitchen, her husband is slumping in his wheelchair, talking disconsolately about a cease-fire.

"Where's Aryeh?" she asks. His chair is empty.

Mrs. Barkowe says, "He just got up and left."

Shayna finds him in the spare room packing a duffel bag. He has been living with them while he attends a pre-army school in Haifa. "What is all this, now?"

"Maybe the war isn't Dzecki Barkowe's business, but it's mine. I'm going to enlist."

"Are you crazy? They won't take you."

"Why won't they? I'll lie, the way Abba did when he was my age." He runs a hand over his clean-shaven jaws. "They'll believe me, all right."

"Don't be a fool. This isn't 1948. Your age is on a computer, with everything about you."

"Yes? Then it shows that I'm checked out on machine guns, howitzers, and antiaircraft guns. We learned all that in Gadna." He is stuffing clothes, sneakers, books, and boots into the bag. "There's already talk of drafting seventeen-year-olds, anyway."

"Aryeh, you're not going."

"Yes, I am. Sorry, Aunt Shayna."

"Your father told you to obey me." She pulls the bag from his hands.

"We weren't losing a war."

Mrs. Barkowe comes into the bedroom. "Here's a surprise, Aryeh."

Yael Nitzan appears in the doorway, elegant as ever in her California tailored suit and a Paris hat, smiling and holding out her arms to her son. "Imma!" Two strides, and he embraces her in long powerful arms.

"By my life," Yael exclaims, "is this really you, Aryeh? Look at you, a big gorilla! Aunt Shayna is really feeding you up. Thank you, Shayna."

When Yael suddenly returned like this during the Six-Day War Shayna was devastated, but this time the sight of her is welcome. With a despairing gesture at the duffel bag, Shayna says, "Yael, thank God you're here, maybe this idiot will listen to you. He wants to go and enlist."

"Enlist? Nonsense, Aryeh, wait for the next war, don't worry, it'll come along."

"Imma, you didn't hear the BBC." He seizes the bag from Shayna. "Kol Yisroel is hiding the truth. We're under attack by nearly two thousand tanks! At least I can go and fight."

"The BBC! Ha! Let go! Let go, I say." She pries the bag from his hands. "You're getting more and more like your crazy father. Don't go imitating him. There's only one Don Kishote, and he's more than enough." She turns to Shayna. "What's the matter with your husband? Why the wheelchair?"

"He's had a stroke. It's the war, I'm sure, the war! Worrying him sick —"

"Then Shayna, he's going to get better. Right now we're winning the biggest battle of the war, or we've already won it."

Astounded exclamations from Shayna and Dzecki's mother. Aryeh takes her by the shoulders. "By your life, Imma, are you serious?"

"Is that something to joke about? I tell you, Zahal has been smashing a huge Egyptian tank attack all morning, and throwing back the Syrians, too. It's the turnaround at last. This morning I called General Pasternak at the Defense Ministry and he told me all about it. In the Sinai alone —"

"Shayna, you'd better come." Dzecki's father is in the doorway. He says no more, but the look on his face makes her dash out. "You too, Aryeh. She'll need your help."

Yael follows them and sees the wheelchair overturned, Professor Berkowitz on the floor, Shayna kneeling beside him, clutching his hand and frantically calling his name. The little boy Reuven is crying as Mrs. Barkowe hugs him close. Leon Barkowe says shakily to Yael, "I don't know, he just tried to get out of the wheelchair, babbling something, and he keeled over before I could do anything."

Yael cannot help the way her mind works, and two thoughts flash through it: that Shayna may well be free one of these days, and that her dark beauty has persisted through all her misfortunes.

Returning to Tasa in the light of a full moon, Kishote finds the staff officers passing around a whiskey bottle to toast the "greatest tank victory since Kursk." It is a mood he does not entirely share, though the victory is now a fact. Arik is in his caravan, they tell him, working on his plan for the crossing attack.

Sharon welcomes him with the joviality of a winner, which fades as Kishote makes his report: roller bridge stalled, the other equipment scattered and moving sluggishly all over the desert; dinghies held up here, crocodiles immobilized there, some pontoon rafts untraceable. Traffic jams in the rear area block and disperse the stuff, slackness and unconcern prevail, and there is little genuine belief that Zahal is actually going to cross the Canal.

His aspect altering to dangerous pugnacity, Sharon growls, "To all the devils, those crocodiles at least can move on their own power. Until Tallik's monster arrives they can be linked up as a temporary bridge. Where exactly are they?"

"Sir, I've located every one, but they're huge and they're mostly stuck at one bottleneck or another —"

"Well, and those British pontoon cubes? We have mountains of them, they can be assembled into rafts, even bridges —"

"I found them all still stacked in warehouses at Baluza and Refidim, sir. I ordered them loaded on trailer trucks and I stayed and saw the job started myself —"

"No belief that we'll cross, eh? Wrong, Kishote, wrong. Southern Command doesn't *want* to cross. They want no part of it or of me. That attitude's seeped all down the line. *'Arik . . . wishes . . . to . . . hang . . . himself . . . so . . . let . . . him . . . go . . . ahead.'* " He is crudely caricaturing Bar-Lev's drawl. "But I'll blast Bar-Lev and Gorodish about traffic control and I'll get the jam-ups moving, believe me. Now then, have a look at my crossing plan." He beckons him to the map on his desk. "You weren't with me at Abu Agheila in '67, but —"

"Sir, I know the Abu Agheila battle by heart."

Sharon gives him a brief gratified grin. "B'seder. Same principle. Surprise night attack on a major hardened defense position from three directions. Look here . . ."

Dzecki Barkowe's anxious mother would not recognize her boy under the layers of sandy grime and the sprouting blond whiskers. The gargantuan steel structure on which he is perched stretches away from him on the open desert for some six hundred feet, with engineers banging at it all along its complicated length. Beyond the far end Lieutenant Colonel Lauterman, the Jeptha* officer who has

* Jeptha: special unit of army engineers who design and build matériel for Zahal's unique needs.

just arrived, is supervising frantic activity around some disconnected rollers. Daphna's letter, written on the back of a creased beer-stained cardboard menu, is not easy to read.

Dear Jackie:

Here I am in the Jericho Café, of all places! After eight straight days and nights in Fighter Control at Ramat David, my CO finally took pity on me and gave me a 12-hour *after*. So I headed for the Jericho and who is here but Lieutenant Colonel Lauterman, playing his clarinet. He's great pals with Yoram Sarak and Shimon Shimon, so I know him pretty well. When he mentioned where he was going, I begged him to bring you a word from me. That's how come I'm writing on this menu, and I'm sure you won't mind my "stationery." Hah!

Now about this lieutenant colonel, he's a strange guy, and whatever you do, don't refer to him as Yo-yo Lauterman! Behind his back people do, and it annoys him. He's a mad genius like many of those Jeptha fellows. He's also a big peacenik. He's been for giving back all the territories right along. My father might kill me, but I'm beginning to agree with him. Anyhow, he doesn't pull rank, and he was nice about bringing you this scrawl.

I hope you're all right! I'm fine, only *dead* tired. The air force has been having a very tough war, I guess you know that. Thank God my father and Dov are still okay. Dov's bound to get a commendation, the things he's been doing.

Now guess what? Noah Barak has got himself engaged! There's this girl he met in Cherbourg when they liberated the boats, she's made aliya and she works in the French Embassy. I guess she pursued him here. I've heard she isn't very pretty, sort of pudgy, but she has something, so bye-bye Noah! The truth is Noah and I never really were compatible. It was one of those things, we fought all the time, and I finally had to tell him off. I hope he'll be happy, and I mean that.

Incidentally, my Rolex makes eyes bulge out here at the Jericho, and at the air base even more. When people get nosy I say casually, "Oh, it's from an American admirer." That explains it, since all Americans are millionaires. It keeps marvellous time. Sometimes the Fighter Director even checks with *me.* Noah gave me the devil for accepting it, but I'm glad I did. You were terribly sweet, and I was deeply touched. I don't have to tell you how much I admire you. Fellows like Noah and my brothers are born into this everlasting mess and have to do their part, but you came here and made it your fight as a Jew. I love you for it, and I hope you return safe to your worried parents. And to me.

Yours,
Daph.

I love you! Return to me! New words from Daphna Luria, after keeping him at arm's length for years, with an occasional goodnight kiss or a very rare laughing fumble in the dark. Poor Dzecki is dazed and exalted as he reads the blurry words over and over.

"Dzecki!" Unmistakable command timbre of Brigadier General Nitzan, at the wheel of a jeep below. Dzecki leaps to his feet and salutes. Kishote calls, "Has the Jeptha officer showed up yet?"

"Sir, he's down at the other end," Dzecki gestures, folding the menu into his coveralls.

"Come down." Dzecki obeys. "What's the problem with those scattered rollers back there? Did the bridge break?"

"Oh, no, sir, the bridge is fine. Those are spares. There's no crane to handle them, and no big trucks to take them to the Canal, but we need them for emergencies, so it's a real problem."

"Get in."

"Yes, sir."

Kishote's jeep speeds over the sand to the back end of the bridge, where tanks and a bulldozer are hauling the loose rollers about in a great racket. A red-bearded officer in fresh coveralls salutes him awkwardly. "General Nitzan? Haim Lauterman, sir. I believe, sir, you ran the bridge demonstration for the Prime Minister."

"Right. What's going on here? Can't you go to the Canal without the spares?"

"Inadvisable, sir, so I've ordered them linked up, sort of like a short roller bridge, and one bulldozer can just tow them along."

"It's a great solution," an ordnance major says, "and we all feel like idiots not to have thought of it ourselves."

"Otherwise, is the bridge ready to go?" Kishote asks Lauterman, whose sharp blue eyes twinkle through very thick glasses, as though he is having fun or is otherwise amused.

"Well, General, I just got here, you know. Suppose we talk about it in my tent?"

"Fine."

Lauterman says, "Dzecki, find a cook to make some sandwiches."

"Yes, sir." Dzecki jumps from the jeep and trots off.

"I recommend that American," says Kishote, "if you need an aide."

"Yes, his girlfriend told me he's b'seder."

In the hot sagging tent, the colonel has hung up over the plank table a mechanical drawing of the rig; the gigantic bridge blue, the tiny tanks red. Kishote glances at it, nods, and unfolds a map to show Lauterman the route to the crossing point. "Bridge in the water by tomorrow morning," he says. Lauterman blinks and whistles.

"You have a problem with that?" inquires Kishote.

"As I say, I just got here, General."

"Lauterman, the bridge can move at five or six miles an hour, right?"

"We've often done that in test drills, yes, sir."

"All right. Today you move it five miles or so southwest to the Tirtur Road. From there it's some ten miles west to the Canal via that road. Starting at dusk, moving at night, you've got twelve hours to go ten miles."

"Then we should make it, if all goes well."

"Bear in mind that you'll be seen by air recon, and helicopter commandos may land to try to stop you. What do you do?"

"Sir, no problem. The tanks can shed the towing cables in seconds by blowing pyrotechnical links. Ten tanks can operate fast to destroy any commando unit that lands." A shy grin. "Fact is, for designing those links I received a commendation."

"Then what's your hesitation about tomorrow?"

Lauterman gestures at the bridge diagram. "Sir, I'm sure you know the tactical concept of this design." He plunges a hand into his windbreaker, pulls out a green yo-yo, and begins spinning it up and down.

Kishote tries to ignore the toy, no doubt a nervous tic of some kind. "Certainly, to put across a preconstructed heavy bridge, without exposing sappers and engineers to enemy fire."

"Not one bridge, sir. *Five* bridges. Positioned all along the Artillery Road. And at the seventy-two-hour warning — before a shot's ever fired in the war — all five are supposed to advance to the waterline. That was the plan."

"Yes, well, the seventy-two-hour warning we never got, of course, and there's just this one bridge available. So?"

"Sir, is Zahal going to cross into Egypt on this one bridge?"

"Of course not. To start with we'll also use pontoon structures and rafts. Maybe we can capture some Egyptian bridges. Once the bridgehead's secure we'll lay down a solid earth bridge. But for the first few days, we must have this bridge, to move the really heavy stuff across at the required volume and speed."

Lauterman stares at the map, and returns the yo-yo to his pocket. "Now just suppose, sir, this bridge gets bombed out en route?"

"The marksmanship of Egyptian pilots isn't that good. Also, you'll have AA protection."

"And if the bridge breaks down?"

"That's why you're here."

"Just so. I understood my mission was mechanical troubleshooting. Now you say it's up to me to get the bridge to the Canal by tomorrow morning, with winning or losing the war maybe hanging in the balance. Is that about right?"

"The idea bothers you?"

"General, I'm a design engineer. That's more responsibility than I'm used to."

"Shall we ask Jeptha for a replacement?"

"Well, no, but one thing you must do."

"Which is?"

"Sir, I gather you made Shimon Shimon coordinator of the towing tanks."

"I did."

"Well, Shimon tells me that no sooner does a tank company get used to doing this job than it gets pulled away to fight. Then another unit comes that knows nothing about it. This tank company I've got now *must* stay with the bridge or we'll never get there."

Nodding, Kishote says, "Good point. I'll designate a senior officer to come and help you keep moving, and make sure you hang on to your tanks."

Dzecki appears with a suitcase, a duffel bag, and a long black leather case. "Here's your gear, Colonel, from the helicopter."

"Put the stuff down anywhere. That's my clarinet," Lauterman says to Kishote. "Maybe I'm a damn fool to have brought it."

"If you have time to play it, Lauterman, that will be a good sign." The two officers salute, and Kishote leaves.

"Dzecki, I need an aide," says Lauterman. "You're it."

"Honored, sir."

"Pass the word, towing drill at 1100, and we move out at noon."

"Yes, sir. Cook bringing sandwiches, sir."

Left alone, Lauterman absently takes out the yo-yo and spins it up and down, contemplating the map, tracing with a finger the course of the bridge from Point Yukon and along the Tirtur Road to the crossing point north of the Great Bitter Lake.

When Yossi returns Sharon is addressing his senior officers outside the Tasa command bunker, at a giant operational map garish with colored arrows, circles, boxes, and unit emblems. Pointer in hand, his hair stirring in the wind, Sharon radiates zest for imminent action. Kishote can see in these old reserve soldiers — old in battle, though probably none is over forty — a reflection of Arik's glow. Since Yom Kippur they have been eating the ash of defeat. Yesterday they tasted the success of former wars, and now Arik is telling them that the time has come to win this war, and the way to do it. Weary and saddened as they were by the first bloody shocking week, they look ready to try.

"Yossi Nitzan will carry on," Sharon concludes, putting aside the pointer. "We don't have approval of the plan yet from headquarters, but I'll get it. Gentlemen, prepare to go to Africa tonight." A smile charged with the old rough charm, and off he goes into the bunker.

Kishote steps up to face Sharon's senior cadre in their wrinkled dusty field uniforms and windbreakers, some bearded, some unshaven, all looking rather stunned by the daring, complex, and very dangerous plan. After a silence he says, "Nu?"

It breaks the mood and brings uneasy laughs.

"It's Abu Agheila," says one brigade commander, "with horns on."

Another: "It's insane," but this goes with a resolute grin.

A third, soberly, "We can do it. But bones will be broken."

Kishote beckons to the intelligence officer, who comes forward with a bulging portfolio. "Most of the broken bones will be Egyptian. Kobi will give the latest enemy dispositions."

All that morning the sprawling depot is alive with the clamorous chaos and billowing dust of a division preparing to move out — more than ten thousand men hurrying among the buildings and shouting, hundreds of tanks, self-propelled guns, APCs, and "soft" vehicles, rumbling, honking, crisscrossing — a kicked-over anthill, but these are army ants, forming up to march. The question is whether and when the command to march will come. Between his rounds to observe the progress toward readiness, Sharon is incessantly on the telephone to southern headquarters or to the Pit, trying to get an official go-ahead. At last word comes that General Bar-Lev is on his way, without his co-commander Gonen, for a final review of Sharon's plan to seize a bridgehead on both sides of the Canal.

"Yossi, I want you to be present," says Sharon, "when Bar-Lev comes."

"Yes, sir."

Sharon showers and shaves. He is on record expressing harsh

contempt for Bar-Lev's decisions and abilities. Kishote guesses that he means to show relaxed confidence in his plan, to this old-boy Palmakhnik who for better or worse has the ear of Dado, Dayan, and Golda Meir. Bar-Lev cannot veto a crossing, for Golda and the cabinet have voted it, but he can certainly snarl Sharon's bridgehead assault scheme. When Bar-Lev arrives, a trim lieutenant general of few slow words and reserved opinions, he welcomes Kishote's presence in the caravan with a cool smile and no more.

After brief chitchat about the Syrian front and the Security Council intrigues, Sharon turns to a map of his assault plan. Bar-Lev absorbs with silent nods the bold picture of Sharon's night attack to open the way, cross the Canal, and seize a bridgehead. The concept is simple enough. A powerful frontal attack on the Second Army, which is entrenched north of the Great Bitter Lake, will actually be a massive diversion; while another force will slip southwest into Sharon's "seam" to capture Deversoir, and then drive northward along the Sinai bank of the Canal to strike the Egyptians from behind, *from the Canal direction*. This is to be the shattering surprise. Other forces will meantime clear the roads to the Deversoir area so that the boats, rafts, and bridges can get to the Canal. By morning at least two bridges will be in place, and the main invasion will be on.

"There's the crux, isn't it, Arik?" This is Bar-Lev's first comment. "The bridges?"

"Absolutely."

"And will they be there, when and as planned?"

"Of course."

"Which ones?"

"The roller bridge and the crocodiles."

Bar-Lev sits silent, staring at the map, nodding and nodding.

Kishote knows, and Sharon knows — and they can figure that Bar-Lev knows — that there is the weak point in the entire scheme. Sharon himself has been raising hell about the traffic on the roads which blocks the movement of the crossing equipment. Now there sits Bar-Lev weighing Sharon's master plan to win the war, and putting his finger right where disaster lurks. Not two weeks ago Sharon, the founder of the Likud Party, was publicly berating Golda

Meir, Bar-Lev, and the entire Labor Party as incompetent and corrupt. Twice in the past week Bar-Lev has backed Gorodish in trying to get Sharon relieved. Now Haim Bar-Lev is to pass a detached judgment on Sharon's great bid for glory and victory! A grotesque situation but there it is, Yossi is thinking, when Bar-Lev abruptly turns on him. "Nitzan, you've been monitoring this matter of the bridges and the rafts, haven't you?"

"It's been one of my assigned duties, yes, sir."

"Will those bridges be there tomorrow as scheduled?" One lean hand darts an accusing finger at the map. "In other words, as matters now stand, is this whole scheme realistic and responsible?" Kishote glances at Sharon, to whom Bar-Lev turns, speeding up his drawl a bit. "Do you mind my asking Nitzan? This is serious business. Dado considers Yossi Nitzan an outstandingly reliable officer."

At once Sharon says, "Kishote, tell General Bar-Lev exactly what you know and what you think. Pull no punches. That's an order."

Don Kishote looks Bar-Lev in the eye. "The bridges will be there in the morning, sir," he says with soldierly calm.

Bar-Lev returns the look and after a moment says, "Good enough. Good luck, Arik. God keep our fighters who have to carry out this murderous plan of yours."

Kishote remains in the caravan while Sharon accompanies Bar-Lev to his helicopter. Returning, Sharon punches his shoulder. "Well done."

"What's the use of a reputation for reliability," says Kishote, "if you can't lie when it matters?"

"When I'm Prime Minister, Don Kishote, you'll be my Minister of Defense."

"Sir, I'd better get out and crack some heads on the roads."

"One moment." Sharon drops into a chair. His genial confident look fades into stony concern. "Yossi, will the bridges really be there at *some* time tomorrow? And what about the rafts for the tanks tonight? Without tank support I can't send Danny over. You know that." Colonel Danny Matt commands the paratrooper infantry brigade.

"Sir, I'll have another look at the roller bridge first, then I'll follow up on the rafts."

"B'seder. If I'm going to attack at dusk, remember, the division has to start out no later than three o'clock."

"Understood, sir."

27

The Crossing

Kishote wonders, espying the bridge far off on the move, whether he may not inadvertently have told Bar-Lev the truth. It is creeping steadily over the wide empty desert in the noonday sun trailed by its supply vehicles, fuel trucks, and AA half-tracks, with the "short bridge" of spare rollers bringing up the rear; and when it comes to a rise in the ground it goes straight ahead, humping itself over like a vast caterpillar over a rock, and continues on its way.

"Sir, that has got to be the weirdest thing I've ever seen," says Sarak, staring in disbelief. They are approaching the bridge in the signal jeep. "Shimon's told me about it, but hearing isn't like seeing."

"That weird thing won the Israel Prize," says Kishote. "Pull alongside the half-track."

"It should win the Nobel Prize," says Sarak, "if they give one for lunacy."

Accompanying the bridge in a half-track are Haim Lauterman and the newly assigned colonel, a stumpy desert-dried ordnance officer named Yehiel. The moving colossus raises a considerable tumult as it labors along; snorts and rumbles of the ten tanks, nine towing and one braking; clanks, screeches, hollow booms, and some up-and-down writhing with great groans. The smooth movement is an illusion of distance. Up close the bridge is a protesting tortured Frankenstein of steel, doing its masters' will but screaming to the sky that it should never have been created.

"How's it going?" Kishote shouts at Lauterman.

"Slick as water, sir," the Jeptha man calls back. "We'll be at Tirtur at three o'clock, no problem."

"Kishote, what the hell am I doing here?" bawls Yehiel. He is an old friend, a reliable hard-charging commander. "This bridge is okay. I've got a lot of urgent things to do at Tasa."

"Get the bridge to the Canal, Yehiel. Nothing's more urgent."

"If you say so, Yossi."

Yehiel waves as Kishote's jeep drives ahead; an unlucky guy, that Yehiel, slated for brigadier general until his secretary accused him of raping her. In the ensuing mess, though not officially penalized — Yehiel claimed it was a mutual attraction, and that she proved to be a mental case — he lost all advancement prospects. The woman emigrated to Los Angeles, and still writes him love letters, or so he says. Anyway, Yehiel is now just serving out his time, much embittered.

Straight ahead a high white dune stretches east to west for perhaps a quarter of a mile without a break; impossible to go around, for the bridge is not built for turns, so it will have to climb over the obstacle.

"Sarak, drive up on that dune. I want to watch this."

"B'seder."

As the jeep mounts the hard-packed slope, the wireless receiver squawks, *"Flagpole Central to Yossi."*

"Yossi here."

"Flagpole wants to know where you are."

"Tell him I'm observing Snake, heading for Tirtur, ETA 1400, all normal."

"And what about crocodiles?"

"Proceeding next to check crocodiles."

"Hundred percent. Out."

With nine tanks hauling it up the slope — three yoked in front, three more pulling on each side, and the braking tank trailing behind on an extra-thick cable — the bridge slowly, slowly crawls up the dune, amid showers of sand from the tank tracks, savage engine roars, and great clouds of dirty blue exhaust. The three leading tanks pass the crest and start down. The first rollers follow over the top, and the bridge begins to move more easily and a little faster, as the drag of gravity behind decreases. What happens after that goes very quickly, and Kishote does not understand it at first, or quite believe his eyes. As though coming alive and revenging itself on its tormentors, the bridge takes off, scampers down the hill with great squeals and clanks, and leaps up on a leading tank with a hellish colliding crash and a shower of sparks. There it stops, its huge length stretching back almost to the crest of the dune in a boil of dust and smoke.

"God in heaven, I hope nobody's killed," Kishote exclaims. "Let's get down there, Sarak."

"By my life, I think Shimon is in that tank." Sarak throws the jeep into gear and hurtles down the slope.

When they reach the scene Yehiel is pounding at the tank hull with a wrench, and getting answering bangs from inside. Yehiel exclaims to Kishote, "They're responding in there, anyway. What a fashla! Who ever dreamed up this rolling nightmare?"

"Can you get them out?"

"Sure, but it'll take a while."

Lauterman is peering up at the rollers that mounted the tank. "That first roller is kaput," he says to Kishote. "We'll have to replace it, and I guess we'll need another tank."

Trotting around to the other side of the wreckage, Kishote crawls under a giant roller hanging askew, and manages to pry loose the tank's hull telephone. "Hello, in there! Brigadier General Nitzan here. Are you all right?"

"Hi, General. Shimon Shimon here." The ceramicist sounds very hoarse and trembly. "All right? We're pretty shaken up. It sounded like the end of the world in here. The loader is bleeding, he fell, nothing serious. How can we get out, sir? Both turret hatches are jammed."

"They're working on it now."

"Well, the sooner the better. Not to put too fine a point on it, sir, one of us has shit in his pants. It's a bit stuffy in here."

"Open any vents you can. You're not in danger. The bridge got away and ran up on you, that's all."

"Sir, I *warned* the idiot commander of the brake tank about just that! He must have been asleep, or jerking off. He's from Savayon, the jerk-off capital of Israel." Savayon is a wealthy suburb, much abused by people who don't live there.

Yehiel is discussing with the tank commanders gathered around him how to pull the bridge off the tank. The Jeptha man stands by listening. Yossi says, "Lauterman, any ideas?"

"Uncouple the first two rollers, I'd say, sir. Back up the bridge and they'll probably just fall off the tank. Maybe it's even usable. These cylinders are hollow, and that Patton has a strong hull."

Yehiel overhears him, and glances at him with a trace of respect. "Excellent. That's it. Get your engineers to do the disconnecting, and we'll free the tank."

As Lauterman goes off, Yehiel takes Kishote aside and says in a guttural whisper, "Kishote, that fellow plays with a yo-yo."

"Well, he knows his stuff. We all do strange things."

"To the devil, that's true enough. If I'd had a yo-yo, and a different secretary, I might be a brigadier general."

"How long a delay, Yehiel?"

The colonel squints at the bizarre pileup of rollers on the tank, then at the bridge stretching far up the slope, the tanks stalled with limp cables dangling from them, and the soldiers swarming out of the personnel carriers to work on the wreck. "I'd guess two to four hours."

The Jeptha colonel is already giving instructions to a knot of grease-streaked sappers. "A word with you," Kishote says to him.

"Certainly, sir. Dzecki!" Lauterman calls. "Come along here."

"Yes, sir."

The three walk a little way up the slope, amid settling dust and pungent drifting smoke. "Is this going to happen again, Lauterman? Or anything like it?"

"General, this bridge traversed such obstacles with ease — bigger ones too — when Major Pasternak's tanks towed it. Dzecki, confirm that."

"That's right, sir. Any number of times, before they got sent off to the north."

"There you are," says the Jeptha man defensively. "You can't blame the bridge, sir. It's an inspired, beautiful construction. A work of genius! But it's meant for trained handling."

"You're not answering my question. Will it happen again?"

Lauterman brings out the yo-yo, and absently spins it. "Sir, I'd ride in that braking tank myself, but frankly I get claustrophobia in a tank. Even with both turrets open, I want to puke or scream. I've done both. My hat's off to these tank fellows, I tell you."

"Colonel, may I suggest something?" says Dzecki.

"Yes?"

"Why not put Shimon Shimon in that rear tank, sir, instead of in the lead? He's very familiar with all this. He can control the braking better than anyone else."

"Elohim, a good idea," says the Jeptha man.

"Hundred percent, Dzecki," says Kishote. "Lauterman, you do just that."

As he leaves the bridge, Yossi is unworried. Yehiel is a tough man who gets things done. In his bizarre way Lauterman is impressive, too. The bridge will reach the water by morning. Meantime he must make sure that enough rubber dinghies and other equipment are on the move to carry out the paratrooper crossing at Deversoir *tonight*. It is one thing to fib to Bar-Lev, so as to counter his hostility to Sharon's plan which, risky as it is, seems to Kishote the best chance to end the war in Israel's favor. It is another to commit two divisions to a terrible firefight, in an operation that can't be supported logistically and is likely to collapse.

What he sees on the narrow black ribbons of road twisting through the high dunes and ridges discourages and confounds him. Long long lines of machines are still backed up for miles, clear out of sight, where a sharp turn, or a crossroads, or a broken-down heavy vehicle has halted traffic both ways. At these ganglions of delay traffic-control officers are now posted, trying hard to unsnarl the massive blockages. But General Adan's division has been rolling down from the northern sector to its assembly point for crossing after Sharon; nearly three hundred tanks, with hundreds of APCs and supply vehicles. The situation is actually worsening.

"I'll take the wheel, Sarak."

Kishote goes tearing back to Tasa, at some points climbing up high dunes and plunging down them at roller-coaster angles, cutting off long stretches of blocked traffic and giving the journalist stomach butterflies. Yoram Sarak has learned to be silent as he rides with Brigadier General Nitzan, who can be genial one moment and frighteningly stern the next. Sarak is keeping a daily war diary which he counts on publishing in magazine installments, and afterward as a book. In his job as driver-signalman for Nitzan, he is getting a valuable inside view of Sharon's campaign.

But after a very long silence, as they speed back to base, Sarak cannot hold his peace. "Sir, it isn't going to happen."

Not looking at him, his face abstracted and gloomy behind dust goggles, Kishote says, "What isn't?"

"The crossing. Not tonight." Nitzan is silent. The jeep jolts speedily along. "Sir, I wrote an article about the crossing problem back in May for *Yediot*. It's not just that bridge. They'll probably get it repaired. It's the crocodiles and pontoon rafts. There's no way in the world they can get to Deversoir tonight."

Nitzan's silence chills the journalist, and he regrets opening his mouth, a rare feeling.

At Tasa, the division is already drawn up in hot afternoon sunshine for the night assault; three brigades of about a hundred tanks each, stretching far and wide over the sands with their APCs, half-tracks, self-propelled artillery, AA guns, and support trucks and busses. Surveying the panorama, hands on hips, Sharon sees Kishote and beckons. "Quite a sight, Kishote, eh?"

"Yes, sir. Quite a sight."

At the sober tone Sharon gives him a sharp look. "Well, come along." Back in the caravan he slices some yellow cheese, and with it eats dried apricots from a bowl. "So? Your report." Tersely Kishote gives him the picture. Silent moments pass before Sharon speaks. "The crocodiles are the critical element, Yossi. I know the pontoon rafts are hard to move on those enormous transporters, but the crocodiles run on their own wheels. Why can't they make it?"

"Sir, I know the location of all the crocodiles. You can't hold to your timetable. None of them will be here by midnight."

"No? How about by dawn?" Kishote shakes his head. "By mid-morning, then?"

"Half a dozen or so, possibly. Most of them later."

Sharon picks up the telephone. "Connect me with General Bar-Lev . . . Yossi, three crocodiles lashed together can ferry a tank. We've done it in exercises."

"Yes, sir. In exercises. If the landing is a surprise, well and good. In an opposed landing if a shell or even shrapnel hits a crocodile's rubber float, down it goes, and the tank with it."

"Bar-Lev? Sharon here. I'm reporting with regret that the timetable I gave you for the crossing tonight turns out a little optimistic . . . Yes, I know. But Yossi Nitzan himself has been out on the roads, and the bottlenecks that have since developed, what with Adan's division . . . The roller bridge? Minor breakdown. It's being repaired. But the traffic problem . . ." A long pause. Sharon darts a glance at Kishote. "I see. Let me give that some thought. I'll ring you back shortly." He hangs up. "Predictable, that Bar-Lev! He says Southern Command recognizes the problems and is sympathetic. If I request a postponement for twenty-four hours, it will be approved. He didn't say *'I told you so,'* but it was in his voice. The cat that ate the bird." Sharon regards his deputy through half-closed eyes. "What do you think?"

Don Kishote is slow to answer. "Sir, today you have a green light. Tomorrow there may be a red light, from the UN, or Southern Command, or Kissinger. If you go tonight, the army will follow. You can commit this army to a crossing, nobody else."

"It's not necessarily true that the army will follow me." Sharon's ebullience is all gone. His face is graven with heavy lines. "The army may follow, and it may not. The operation may never get a chance. If things go badly in the first few hours — and that's a fifty-fifty shot — Gonen or Bar-Lev or even Dayan may get cold feet and abort it. Just another Arik Sharon brainstorm, that killed a lot of Jewish boys to no purpose."

"Sir, there's no way to win this war except to cross the Canal."

"Yes, I've pointed that out once or twice. You're right that after tonight the light can suddenly turn red. Yet you've just told me that I don't have the means to cross tonight."

"Maybe postponement is the answer, then, sir. En brera."

"It's no answer." Sharon shakes his head brusquely. "The whole operation turns on surprise. Our preparations are already visible. A day's delay, an alerted enemy, and the bridgehead may not be an achievable objective." He leans his face on a hand over his eyes.

On impulse Don Kishote says, "General Sharon, release me from other duties and let me go out on the roads tonight and stay there, all night if I have to. I'll commandeer tanks and bulldozers. I'll shove vehicles off the asphalt into the sand. I'll order every kind of unit, including General Adan's tanks, to make way for the crocodiles and rafts. I'll threaten court-martials. I'll draw my gun, if I must. It requires a general, sir, to get this thing unsnarled, and I'll do it."

Sharon looks up. "And if so, what result can I count on?"

His mind running back over the bottlenecks he has seen, Kishote replies — with a very strong sense of jumping off into the unknown, and perhaps taking Sharon's ten thousand men with him — "Sir, six crocodiles in the water at dawn. More at midday, with the first pontoon rafts."

"I said *count on,* Kishote."

"I heard you, sir."

Grasping the telephone with a swoop of a thick hand, not taking his eyes off Kishote, Sharon calls General Bar-Lev.

"*Acapulco!*"

In Kishote's headphones, at two o'clock in the morning, the long-awaited signal from the paratroop leader; the first unit has gone over in rubber dinghies and landed on the other side. Near his jeep a bulldozer is pushing a stalled empty tank transporter off the Refidim road in bright moonlight, to break a mile-long traffic jam. Three and a half hours behind schedule, the thing is happening, the Canal has been crossed.

Sharon on the command network, calm and cheery: *"Well done, Danny. What's the situation over there?"*

Easygoing tones of Colonel Danny Matt: *"So far, so good. We're cutting the wire fences. Very quiet here. Not so quiet over on your side to the north, I see. Plenty of trouble at the Chinese Farm."* Toward midnight the so-called Chinese Farm has erupted like a volcano, and it has been flaming and thumping ever since.

This abandoned Egyptian agricultural station partly blocks the roads on the way to the Canal, so Sharon's forces are battling to clear the entrenched enemy out of the "Farm," where several square miles are crisscrossed with embankments and irrigation ditches, perfect cover for concealed defenders. "Chinese Farm" is a complete misnomer. After the Six-Day War the army found rusting machinery there, with Oriental lettering, probably Japanese. The soldiers dubbed it "the Chinese Farm" and the name has stuck to this widespread and very formidable military obstacle.

From twelve miles away, Kishote can see the fire flashes and starshell glare all over the sky above that area. Sharon's plan is clearly working, for Danny Matt's paratroopers had to run right past the Chinese Farm en route to Deversoir, and the dinghies with their engineer personnel also had to get by there, to ferry them across the Canal. But the laconic reports of the brigade commanders fighting to clear the Farm are grim: many tanks burning, heavy casualties, major withdrawals to regroup.

Sarak says, "Sir, Flagpole is calling you." He flips switches on the receiver. Sharon, level and unhurried: *"Yossi, what is your situation?"*

"Four crocodiles free, sir, and well along toward the Canal. Now freeing two more. The bridge is on the move. Several pontoon rafts are on their way as well."

"Good. Find a senior officer and delegate that job. I need you at the Yard right away."

"Yes, sir."

Nobody better than Yehiel, thinks Kishote, if all is well with the bridge. He has no trouble finding it in the bright moonlight, a black giant horror acrawl over level sands.

"Got it!" Yehiel bares his teeth in a cruel moonlit grin. "On your way, Kishote. Lauterman has this baby under control now, and it's on schedule. The crocodiles will be there by dawn, I promise you, and I'll deliver some pontoon rafts, too. I'm the man for this. You're a gentleman, I'm not. I fuck secretaries. The one officer in this army who does such a horrid thing."

The gunfire at the Chinese Farm battlefield is growing thunderous as Yossi speeds his jeep along the sands, bypassing bumper-to-bumper road traffic. The sky is slashed with all manner of colored streaks and flashes, a colossal fireworks display paling the moon and betokening fearsome carnage below. At a main road junction the fat lieutenant controlling traffic shouts to Kishote, over the vehicle racket and the booming of the guns, that he is diverting movement southward, because the tank battle at the Farm has spilled over across the roads to Deversoir. Evil tidings! The junction is cluttered with ambulance busses heading the other way; wounded being evacuated already, a disheartening sight.

Kishote goes jouncing across the open desert, a very rough ride, but this is terrain he knows well, and finding his way through the seam is not hard. He comes on Sharon standing amid the half-tracks and APCs of his mobile headquarters. Alone among the officers and soldiers he wears no helmet, and his white-blond hair identifies him from far off. He points to the flaring sky over the Chinese Farm battleground. "Picturesque, yes? Our battalions are fighting like lions. It'll be all right." But Kishote knows the man and hears undertones of deep worry in the tranquil words. "Yossi, go over in the next dinghy to the other side, have a look around and bring back a report."

Astonished, Yossi blurts, "Sir, have you lost contact with Danny Matt?"

"Certainly not, all's well over there. I'd go myself but I must stay close to this fight." He gestures at the flame and tumult to the north, takes Kishote aside by the elbow, and speaks hard quick words. "We're at a crisis. It's happening early. Southern Command considers me a liar or a simpleton, and their yellow streak is showing already. They claim we're cut off and surrounded! I assure them over and over that the Chinese Farm battle is difficult but going well, and that Danny Matt is securing his beachhead. Nothing doing. I'm in extremis, they say, and can lose Danny's brigade as we lost the boys in the maozim. Yossi, we've got a triumph developing here, and they're on the verge of cancelling it. Dayan's already suggested pulling Danny back. Call it a night raid, he says, and let it go at that. God knows what's happened to Moshe Dayan."

"Sir, why should Dayan believe me more than you?"

"Dayan told me to send Yossi Nitzan over. Understand? Now get going."

Kishote goes and returns, a brief eerie excursion to Egyptian soil, where Matt's paratroopers are methodically digging in and deploying a perimeter defense in predawn twilight, as though on a night exercise in the Negev. Of the enemy, no sign there, while the inferno blazes to the north. When he gets back the sun is coming up and the Chinese Farm has at last become quiet, no more rattle and crash of guns, and no strange lights tearing the pale sky. At Deversoir tanks and APCs are crowding into the Yard, the enormous brick-paved parking area which Sharon ordered dug into the rampart years ago. Bulldozers are tearing away at the thin sand-and-brick wall which was left after the hollowing-out of the Yard, and Kishote is not surprised to find Sharon driving one of two bulldozers. "I know exactly where to dig," Sharon bellows at him, "and I have to show these shleppers!" As he speaks, another bulldozer breaks through the wall. A cheer goes up from the tank crews, for there across the Canal, misty green in the morning sun, is Egypt, a vision of Eden from the dead Sinai sands.

Sharon wallows down from the bulldozer, and shouts to his operations officer, "Get all those tanks to move aside, so we can launch the crocodiles."

"They're here?" Kishote exclaims.

"Six of them, and more on the way. That Colonel Yehiel is a man of valor. So, what did you see over there? Is Danny Matt being too optimistic? Are we in extremis?"

"By no means. We walked the whole perimeter. There's just no sign of the enemy, sir. Total surprise so far, in fact Danny's begging for tanks, he says with tanks he can roll to Cairo."

"Then it's *working*. Thank God. That's what matters." Sharon grasps his arm, and his voice falls. "It's been a terrible, terrible night at the Chinese Farm, Yossi. They're still taking out the dead and wounded. Hundreds of casualties, whole companies of tanks destroyed. Terrible. Fearful." He stares at his deputy, hollow-eyed and sunken-cheeked. "A horrible price, but it's *working*. Now we ferry the tanks over until the bridge comes. Once it's in place Bren Adan and I can pile all our power across, and panic the enemy into collapse. We can still win this war *today,* Yossi. I'm going to call Southern Command. Come with me, and stand by to report on what you saw over there. Bar-Lev is waiting."

Outside the Yard the crocodiles, ungainly wheeled boats with puffed-up floats along their hulls, are lined up in column. Kishote strides to Yehiel, all covered with dust, and embraces him. "Yehiel, by your life, Sharon calls you a man of valor."

Hoarsely Yehiel replies, "Let him tell that to the promotion board. Maybe they'll listen to Arik Sharon."

In Jerusalem Zev Barak is putting on a dress uniform as he listens to the 6 A.M. news. Top story Syrian front, next item American airlift; about the Canal crossing not a word. Good, security is holding. He is bleary from sitting up with Golda most of the night, until Dado's report that the beachhead has been taken, the paratroopers are digging in; and by Sharon's account, while there has been something of a problem in keeping the roads clear past the Chinese Farm, the situation is well under control.

Nakhama is at a mirror in the foyer, clad in a suit she bought in Washington and seldom wears. Fussing with her hair, she says, "You're *sure* now, Zevvy? Why do I belong at a ceremony honoring the airlift?"

"Golda asked me to bring you, motek. All right?"

As they drive to Lod airport, Nakhama chatters in rare good spirits. Noah's sudden engagement to the French girl has cheered her. They hardly know Julie, but Nakhama has come to dislike Daphna Luria, of elite family but a maddening fickle girl. Also, in the few days since his return from Washington she has been warmer to him, he is not sure why, and as for trying to figure her out, he has given that up long ago.

Parking at the terminal, they can see out on the sunny tarmac a double line of troops drawn up, an honor guard with four large flapping flags: the Stars and Stripes, the Star of David, and the banners of both air forces. In the office of the airport director, Golda is drinking tea as she smokes. "Hello, my dear," she says to Nakhama. "So glad you could come. This is your husband's doing, he performed marvels in Washington."

"I did nothing, Nakhama," says Barak, "but this is the last time I'll deny it."

"How are your girls, dear, and your navy captain? How proud you must be of him!"

An aide looks in. "Madame Prime Minister, the tower reports the C-5A will be landing in two minutes."

Brushing ashes from her skirt, Golda Meir walks out with Barak, Nakhama, and her small entourage to the microphones on the tarmac, where the American ambassador and his military aide already stand. Shouts arise from spectators lining the fences and terminal roof. *"There it comes!"* The dot in the hazy morning sky over the Mediterranean is swelling into a giant aircraft. "Look at that, will you?" Nakhama cries. "A flying Empire State Building." Golda smiles indulgently at her. As the Galaxy touches down and taxis to the terminal, and the army band strikes up "The Star-Spangled Banner," the Prime Minister draws herself up stiffly. "Thank God, thank God we did not launch a preemptive strike," she says to Barak when the music ends, loud enough for the American ambassador to hear. "If we had done it, this would not be happening. We would be friendless in the world. We have kept the faith, and so has the American President."

The ambassador edges toward her. "Madame Prime Minister, I should tell you that through some slipup the pilot has not been notified that there's a ceremony scheduled. I'm sorry."

"So what? Don't worry, he'll handle it."

The Galaxy stops, the nose and tail ramps open out, the spectators cheer. Flatbed trucks roll up the ramps followed by swarming cargo handlers, and the pilot, a gangling blond young man in blue coveralls, emerges from the plane. The ambassador goes to meet him, and escorts him to Golda Meir. "Madame Prime Minister, allow me to present Major Tom Robinson, United States Air Force."

"Major Robinson, welcome to Israel. I'm sure you're tired and I won't keep you long." Her amplified voice reverberates over the field. "I said to my daughter yesterday, 'I could kiss the pilots of these planes,' and she said, 'Well, then do it.' That's why we're having this little ceremony." Rising on tiptoe, she kisses the pilot on the cheek. From the crowd, laughter and cheers. Flashbulbs pop, and portable TV cameras move in.

The pilot steps up to the microphone. "Ah, uh, Madame Prime Minister, this is mah first flight here," he says, his voice booming from the loudspeakers, the southern accent plainly coming through. "The fellers who've already done it told me they were greeted bah beautiful women with flowers and kisses. Mah question is, where are yo' flowers?"

The crowd applauds. Golda laughs to the ambassador, "Nu? Did I say he'd handle it?" Walking off the field, she touches Nakhama's arm. "Will you have lunch with me, my dear, or are you busy?"

Nakhama happily gasps acceptance, and Golda draws Barak aside. "Now listen, Mr. Alarmist," she grates, her genial manner vanishing, "order a helicopter at once, go down south, and for God's sake find out what's really happening in that crossing. Don't come back without *facts*. Getting information out of the military, and I include Dado and Dayan, is hopeless. In all my life I've never been more uncertain and on edge."

"Madame Prime Minister, when an attack is just starting it's hard —"

She rides over him. "I tell you, Zev, I'm starting to feel the way I did the day before Yom Kippur. In the dark, sick at heart, frustrated. How are the troops and tanks getting across? *Are* they still crossing? What's happening to that bridge of Tallik's? Is fighting going on, and if so, where, and how serious? Is this airlift all for nothing? Suppose a cease-fire proposal comes in today? I must *know*!"

"But even the commanders on the spot won't know all, Madame Prime Minister. Reports come in slowly and —"

"They know something. I know *nothing*. Nobody wants to say anything to me, because I might hold them to account for it. Zev, my nose tells me there's trouble. Get down there."

Gorodish's advance headquarters at Umm Hashiba remind Barak of the Pit on Yom Kippur; anxious officers and secretaries rushing around, clamor of loudspeakers, clatter of teleprinters, a general air of discombobulation. In the war room the huge floor-to-ceiling maps show an alarming picture. The supply corridor to Deversoir is a hairline of blue through the two thick red enemy lodgments in Sinai, and across the Canal Danny Matt's bridgehead makes a tiny blue wart on the vast red expanse of Egypt. That is exactly how things stand, Bar-Lev and Gorodish angrily tell him. Sharon has plunged masses of troops into futile all-night butchery at the Chinese Farm. The losses in men and machines have been frightful, yet none of his promises have been fulfilled. The roads are still virtually impassable, and there are no bridges. What is worse, he is still sending forces across in rubber dinghies and a few old crocodiles, and proposes to go right on with this foolhardy ferrying of his own and Adan's division this morning.

"Can anything be more irresponsible?" cries Gorodish. "Lodging two divisions in enemy territory, their backs to a water obstacle, with no secure supply line, and not one bridge in place? Is he insane? They can run out of fuel and ammunition in a few hours of combat! Then what?"

"He has no sense of military realities." Bar-Lev speaks like a judge passing sentence. "His supposed brilliance is adventurousness. He takes rash plunges that others have to make good, to save the soldiers' lives he gambles with."

"En brera, the responsibility is ours," says Gorodish, "and I'm about to order a halt, Zev. I'll instruct Sharon, straight out, *No more forces crossing the Canal until a bridge is in place*. And if in thirty-six hours we have no bridge, I'm bringing back Danny Matt's brigade, by God, while I still can."

"Where exactly is the roller bridge, Gorodish? What shape is it in? Golda keeps asking about that bridge."

"It broke down yesterday. Sharon claims it's repaired and on the move west of Yukon. But who knows? Between Tallik's *meshugas* and Sharon's *meshugas,* God help the Jewish State."

"With your permission I'll go and see for myself."

"By all means," says Gorodish.

Bar-Lev dourly nods.

28

Sharon Halted

Viewed from the air, the blocked roads in Sinai appall Barak. Most war games involving Egypt have ended in a Canal crossing, but no "worst scenario" has ever contemplated such stupendous traffic jams. A paralyzing sight, those serpentine miles and miles of unmoving war machines, supply lorries, ambulances, and miscellaneous vehicles; lucky it is that Golda has not made this foray herself. What targets for strafing! With a little courage the Egyptian air force could create ghastly ruin here. Reenforcements and supplies for the crossing are piling up, backing up, choking the accesses because they have nowhere to go. If Tallik's Israel Prize could only get to the Canal and provide a broad stable sluice the traffic would start to flow, and the crossing might have a chance. Otherwise, the pessimism at Southern Command makes frightening sense.

"Could that be it, sir?" Speaking in the headphones over the helicopter noise, the pilot points to a dark line ahead on the sands.

"Probably. It's got AA escort, remember."

"No problem." The helicopter tilts in a slow wide curve. Harsh coded AA challenge in the headset. Pilot's calm coded reply.

"Okay. Good morning, helicopter," says the challenging voice. *"Welcome to the bridge."*

"By my life, sir," says the pilot, looking through his side window, "I thought you were joking. That bridge does crawl."

"Well, tanks are towing it."

"I realize that, sir. Even so." As they descend, the bridge is traversing a gully, and the head is climbing up one side while the tail is still going down the other. "I'll be seeing that thing in my dreams, sir," says the pilot. "It's a horror, sir."

On the ground Lauterman, Yehiel, and Kishote are riding in a half-track ahead of the bridge. "Who can that be?" says Kishote, squinting up at the helicopter. "Nobody from Southern Command, surely. To them this bridge is a big creeping leprosy."

"Then they should all be ashamed," says Lauterman. "The bridge is an engineering marvel, like the Eiffel Tower. It'll become a legend."

"Legend, ha," says Yehiel. "Let's just get this *verkakteh* [shitty] monstrosity to the Canal."

The helicopter settles down in a boil of flying sand and Barak jumps out, happy to see the bridge so smoothly on the move.

Kishote hails him from the half-track. "Welcome, Zev, hop in."

"Thanks, I hear you've been having problems."

"All solved. See that big dune ahead? Just wait."

"How far are we from the crossing area here, Yossi?"

"Nine miles, maybe less."

"Then the bridge should be across the Canal by midday, no?"

"It should. The real question is the Tirtur Road, you know, as it goes past the Chinese Farm," says Kishote. "It's not altogether secure, but — well, we'll talk about that. Now just watch. You're about to witness something impressive."

As the half-track jolts up the dune, Lauterman explains the towing team's braking technique to Barak. He has to raise his voice because the tanks are making their usual climbing tumult, and the bridge is clanking, squealing, and groaning in its unique Frankenstein voice. The brilliance of the design, he says, is that a single tank in the rear can brake the whole six-hundred-ton structure. Everything depends on coordinating the signals among the towing tanks;

a simple question of balancing the nudging of the tanks and the power of gravity, to ease the bridge over the top. With practice, this company of tanks is getting very good at it.

"There it goes," says Lauterman, as the lead tanks top the crest and head down, followed by the first rollers. "Now watch! It's a tug-of-war, you see, the nine towing tanks versus the braking tank. That's where the coordination comes in."

"To all the devils," says Barak, "that braking cable is going to part. It has to."

The thick cable looks in fact as rigid as a telephone pole under the strain, as the braking tank resists the pull from above.

"Not a chance," says Lauterman. "That cable can tow an aircraft carrier."

Slowly the tug-of-war begins to favor the towing side, as more of the bridge passes over the crest. The braking tank, dug in like a mule on the up-slope, barely moves. It seems utterly incredible to Barak that the cable does not snap, but in fact it does not. What happens instead is that the bridge, with a sudden startling scream and clang of shearing steel, breaks apart. One half rolls down behind the towing tanks, while the other half sits where it is, draped over the top of the dune, with the cable to the braking tank gone slack. Colonel Yehiel explodes in a stream of very filthy Arabic curses, all directed at General Tal, the bridge, and the art of ceramics, as near as Barak can make out.

"You're quite right to be annoyed, Yehiel," says Lauterman, shaking his head sadly. "Now why the devil did Shimon Shimon do that?"

"Shimon Shimon?" exclaims Barak. "The artist? What's he got to do with it?"

"He's in the braking tank," says Kishote.

"*Shimon* is?"

"Yes, and what could you expect?" rages Yehiel. "Didn't I *say* we should put in an ordnance officer, not a verkakteh menorah maker?"

Barak asks, "How long a delay does this mean?"

Yehiel looks at the Jeptha man, who says, "Not long, sir. I

worked on the design of those links. They're made for quick replacement. Three hours, maximum."

"I'm riding in that braking tank," says Colonel Yehiel, "from here to the Canal."

"You're upset, Yehiel," says Lauterman. "I don't blame you. Well, back to work." He walks toward the broken bridge, spinning his yo-yo. Repair personnel are already trudging up the dune, as the tank crews climb out of the turrets to see what is going on.

Staring after Lauterman and the jumping yo-yo, Barak says to Kishote, "Sanity has no place in this project, has it?"

"Well, I'll tell you, General Barak," Yehiel puts in, calming down, "that yo-yo guy does know what he's doing. We'll be moving again by midday."

"Just an eccentricity," adds Kishote. "Engineers tend to be odd. Say, there's that young relative of yours, Zev." He calls to a figure running by, all sand and grease from head to foot. "Dzecki, come over here. Yehiel, let's have a look at that break."

Dzecki trots up to Barak and salutes. "Hi, Uncle Zev. What a surprise. Sorry you have to see such a balagan."

"Well, it was spectacular."

"Look, sir, *please* report to the Prime Minister that this bridge is working. Because it really is." At Barak's ironic glance toward the wreck, Dzecki bristles. "Okay, what about the space program back in the States? One fashla after another, no? But they got to the moon, didn't they? And this bridge will get to the Canal."

"It had better."

"I get so sick and tired," exclaims Dzecki, "of all the jokes about the bridge. The Egyptians put seven Soviet bridges across the Canal, latest equipment. No country would sell us anything but old junk like crocodiles and pontoon cubes. We *had* to invent something."

Barak smiles and clasps his shoulder. "You're quite right, and I admire you. Get back to your job."

"Yes, sir. Please phone my folks, tell them I'm okay." Dzecki runs off.

"A mess, but it'll be all right," says Kishote, returning. "Want to come to the Yard at Deversoir with me? That's where the crossing is happening."

"Good enough."

The half-track goes bumping down the dune. "Well, Zev, what do you think of the great roller bridge?"

"That bridge is Zionism," Barak says.

Kishote looks blankly at him, then a rueful smile wrinkles his broad mouth. "Just so, and it's going to work. The waters won't part, but we'll pass over them."

"Halevai."

The helicopter pilot stands by his machine, watching open-mouthed the tanks struggling with the broken bridge, and soldiers climbing all over the two pieces. Kishote asks him, "What are your orders?"

"To take General Barak wherever he says, sir, except into combat areas."

"Very well," says Kishote. "Let's go."

"Sir, I circled for an hour with General Adan yesterday, waiting for air force permission to land at Point Kishuf. I never got it."

"Right. I understand. Yallah."

"B'seder, sir." As they lift off Kishote radios for a jeep to meet them at Deversoir, outside the direct fire zone. "Deversoir? I have to report this flight, sir," says the pilot in the headphones. "Shall I say General Nitzan is ordering me to do it?"

"No, no. I'm threatening you, scaring you, and ordering you *not* to report it. My responsibility. I'll tell your superiors that. We'll sort it all out after the war."

"That's fine," says the pilot dubiously. "Thank you, sir."

Through Kishote's binoculars Barak gets a horrifying, gut-churning view of the Chinese Farm battlefield. *"Something of a problem"!* In this gruesome aftermath of the night battle, smashed and burned-out tanks and APCs dot the rough terrain as far as he can see, some still smoldering. There must be hundreds of destroyed machines; he cannot identify them from this height, but a large number must be Israeli. A lot of Jewish boys, too, must be lying killed among all those pitiful tiny sprawled bodies, though most probably have been removed with the wounded in the darkness.

"The Valley of Death," he says to Kishote.

Kishote nods, his face empty of its usual humor, a sad unshaven mask. As the helicopter comes down Barak can see two-way ferry traffic crossing the Canal, and the paratroopers and tanks busily moving here and there on the other side. A jeep speeds them to the Yard, where Arik Sharon stands bareheaded, waiting. "Well, Zev Barak!" He looks terribly haggard, but his hearty handshake and tough grin are undaunted. "By my life, you're a welcome sight. Imagine, we're winning a great battle, and you're the first general who's showed up to see what's actually going on."

In Barak's opinion there are only two ways with Ariel Sharon, you are for him or against him. They are almost of an age. Early on Barak saw himself in a race with Sharon and others for army advancement, but Arik has long since charged ahead into his controversial star role, by many distrusted, by some adulated. Without rancor or envy Zev Barak is on the whole against him, for his cruel Bonapartist streak. Israel is too small for a Napoleon, and too Jewish. He can't help acknowledging Sharon's ruthless resolve and military know-how, and this crossing so far has mainly been his doing, but that Chinese Farm shambles! Also his doing . . .

"I hope we're winning, Arik."

"Well, maybe I should have said that we *were* winning." The magnetic mien flashes into rage. "I've just received the most incredible, inept, destructive, defeatist order of my career from Gorodish. '*Halt all crossing activity*'! Zev, look here."

Spreading a map on the jeep hood, Sharon argues fiercely for continuing the attack. Surprise is a great but fleeting advantage. His deceptive stroke, a frontal attack on the Second Army, worked out well, convincing the enemy that the Chinese Farm fight was only a diversion, whereas it was the main thrust. Those valorous boys shielded the way of the paratroopers and their boats to the crossing. "Zev, *seizing the moment* is all of generalship, you know that, and there's no generalship at Southern Command. *Now* is the time to throw our strength across the Canal. Not thirty-six hours from now. Now. Today! We can ferry a tank across in seven minutes, and we have four ferries going. Bren Adan and I can be across with two divisions before the Egyptians know what's happening and —"

"Arik, you'll need fuel, ammunition —"

"We can ferry those too until a bridge is up. The momentum, the *momentum* is everything. We've *got* it now. Gorodish is squandering it, throwing it away, throwing away the campaign and the war."

"But lacking even one bridge —"

"Zev, I swear to you the Egyptian front will collapse, if we cross in strength today and start to cut them off from behind. They'll be pulling back their armor in panic, and, Zev, once they start retreating across the Canal they're finished. They've been coasting on their amazing success of the first two days. If only —"

"Arik, can I get over to Africa?"

Sharon brightens. "You want to do that? Kol ha'kavod! But if anything should happen to you —"

"Golda ordered me to see what's going on."

"Yossi, get him a helmet and take him over."

Led by Kishote through racketing tanks, APCs, and half-tracks, Barak jumps after him onto a pontoon raft, where a Centurion is rolling aboard with a deafening clank of iron on iron. The propelling unit snorts, the raft moves off over still water, and Zev Barak's blood stirs. Seventeen years since his last combat, the march on Sharm el Sheikh in the Suez War . . . The Chinese Farm carnage is hideous, but what alternative is there to fighting, as long as the Arabs keep trying "the military option"?

"Yossi, man to man, can this crossing continue?"

"Zev, it must."

"No bridges? The main roads blocked? A single weak supply line with heavy enemy armor choking it north and south?"

"Yes, it's so audacious the enemy can't believe we're trying it." Kishote's tone is hard and positive. "They think it's an empty feint. That's our big chance. The Jewish God is throwing a deep sleep on them."

Egypt under my boots, by God! What a contrast to the tobacco-poisoned tension and boredom of the Pit, the nervous tirades at Southern Command!

Here at last is Zahal of Barak's young years. Alert confident helmeted Jewish boys ride fast-moving machines through a beautiful green watered setting like a field exercise in the Jezreel Valley; all the more like an exercise in that the enemy is — at least here in Africa — almost an abstraction. No gunfire at all, only sporadic sputters to the north over in Sinai. The commandeered half-track crosses a narrow freshwater irrigation canal and rolls through palm trees, lush orchards, and cultivated fields to Danny Matt's signal truck, where a hefty tank brigade commander, Colonel Haim, is just back from a reconnaissance in force. Aglow with success, Haim reports destroying several missile batteries with a ten-tank company, and sending a mobile SAM-6 unit running off toward Cairo. "They were totally surprised, Danny, no opposition but feeble machine-gun fire."

"But the surprise is over now," says Barak.

"Not necessarily, sir," says Danny Matt, a tall colonel with a black Theodor Herzl beard. "Thank God, they still seem to think we're a diversion. But, Yossi, Yossi, when are the rest of Haim's tanks coming? And what about the timetable? What about Adan's division?"

Kishote says little, and nothing about the halt order. As he and Barak return on an empty raft, three crocodile ferries go by the other way, each carrying a tank. They find Sharon haranguing two very grim and grimy brigade commanders, one of them bloodily bandaged. "Well," he says to Barak, "so did you see a defeat? A disaster? Are we surrounded? Is it a Sharon catastrophe?"

"It's a courageous start, Arik, very risky but very powerful. I'll tell Golda that."

Sharon brightens. "That's all I ask. Meantime these fellows here have cleared the Tirtur and Akavish Roads alongside the Chinese Farm. There's still gunfire going on, and I'm not saying we won't have to keep fighting, but we've secured our supply line."

"We have," croaks one of them. "And it wasn't easy."

"Those tanks that just went over, Arik — what about the order to halt?"

"Why, I wouldn't dream of disobeying Gorodish, that would

be insubordination," says Sharon with a crafty grin. "I'd already ordered those three tanks of Haim's to cross, you see, and I couldn't break the crews' hearts."

"Ah. Are there many more hearts not to be broken?"

"Look, Zev, I'm grateful that you came. You've seen it with your own eyes now. For God's sake just tell Golda and Dado they've got a great victory in the making here, if only they'll get Bar-Lev and Gorodish off my back!"

Golda Meir greets Barak when he comes into her office by flinging both arms in the air. "Kosygin is in Cairo. How about that? The Premier of the Soviet Union! Can you imagine Nixon flying here, to tell me how to conduct policy? We're fighting the Russians, plain and simple. Sit down, Zev, you look tired. Did you hear Sadat's big parliament speech?"

"No, Madame Prime Minister, I've been on the move."

"Well, nothing new. He'll consider a cease-fire if we'll just go back behind the old armistice lines and so on. Generous. Your wife's a charming lady, my grandchildren loved her. So, what did you see? The military's been opening up a bit, but you're an eyewitness. What's going on down there?"

He does not mince words about the traffic jams and the Chinese Farm havoc. Her face falls. "I knew it. I *knew* there was trouble. They're still soft-pedalling it for me." But at his picture of Zahal in Egypt she turns radiant. "Why, Zev, that's what matters. We're carrying the fight to them. We're back to being ourselves. A week ago who would have predicted this?" When he starts the topic of the halted crossing she holds up a flat palm. "Zev, Dado is fighting this war, he's doing a good job, and I won't second-guess him. Now the bridge. What about the bridge?"

She cannot help a painful smile at his account, shaking her head. "Tallik's patents."

"It will get there, Madame Prime Minister. Meantime they're putting over a bridge of pontoons."

She stands up heavily. "I'm very glad I sent you. Come along now, I have to respond to Sadat in the Knesset."

When she mounts the podium with a proud look and a fighting face, the buzz subsides in the Knesset chamber and the galleries, usually half-empty but now crowded wall to wall. Her first words are an apology for the delay in disclosing casualties. She accepts full responsibility. Enemies were listening, and the news of the first days' losses would have given them aid and cheer. The whole country's grief has weighed on her heart for a week. Now she is sharing it with the families of the fallen and the wounded, who bore the brunt of the surprise assault and saved Israel.

"Some nations fault us for *'inflexibility'* " — a bitter smile — "in insisting on peace treaties as the price for returning territories our enemies lost in the Six-Day War. But we remember all too well how Nasser, when we stood on the old armistice lines, announced that the Arabs were going to wipe out the *'Zionist entity'* once and for all. Now suppose this new unprovoked attack, on our holiest day, had struck at those same lines? We who lived through the dread weeks of May 1967 can easily imagine, and we will never never take that risk again. Let our enemies know that."

Well, there's her answer to Sadat, and plain enough, thinks Barak.

"Some of these very nations that deplore our *'inflexibility'* have declared a hypocritical *'embargo'* on our region," Golda's voice rises in anger, "which only means they won't have to deliver defense materials we've bought and paid for, while the Soviet Union is flooding the most advanced munitions to our foes. Fortunately, to redress this unjust imbalance, the United States of America alone has stepped in with an airlift —" A standing ovation drowns her out and sweeps the chamber, and also the whole gallery except for the diplomatic section. "An airlift, I say, that will have the everlasting gratitude of the Jewish people.

"Moreover, not only have Egypt and Syria, outnumbering us more than twenty to one in manpower, been waging all-out war on us, with massive resupply and expert guidance of the Soviet Union, they have been openly joined by the armed forces of Iraq, Morocco, Jordan, and Libya. Yes, we too are now getting help from America," she looks straight up at the diplomatic section, "but in fighting to survive *we are doing it ourselves.*" In this round of applause Barak sees a few diplomats furtively clap.

"How well we're doing, I'm not prepared to reveal. As I say, the enemy is listening. But we have pushed back the enemy in the north, in the south our forces are operating on both sides of the Suez Canal, and further disclosures —" She has to stop as a ripple of noise spreads through the chamber. "Further disclosures will come as appropriate, from our gallant army leadership.

"I turn now to the domestic tasks that lie before us . . ."

She has not proceeded far when Barak feels a tap on his shoulder. At the whispered word, "Telephone call from the Ramatkhal," he hurries to a corridor telephone. Dado comes on with a roar of anger. "By my life, Barak, has she lost her wits? The grossest breach of security! Places in danger the lives of all my soldiers in Africa! Compromises the operation! Why to all the devils did she do it?"

"Sir, after all the bad news I guess she wanted to say something uplifting —"

"Any uplifting event in the field was for the military to disclose!"

"Also, sir" — Barak is doing his best to sound calm, for Dado in a rage is unnerving — "if Kosygin's pressing Sadat for a ceasefire, this may give us more time to carry the fight into Egypt. Now that the world will know we've crossed the Canal, Sadat may well dig in so he won't seem to be collapsing."

Tense pause. "She doesn't think that way," growls the Ramatkhal. "It's too subtle. Anyhow, Zev, you just convey to her in no uncertain terms that I'm furious, and that she has harmed our chances of winning the war."

Crash of receiver.

Early next morning heads turn as the most recognizable Israeli of all strides into the bustling Tel Aviv Hilton in army fatigues and Vietnam cap. Israel's plushiest hotel is full up, though not with tourists. Those birds of passage have long since taken flight, and birds of another feather have wheeled and alighted; foreign correspondents, radio commentators, TV anchormen, film crews, combat photographers, and the like. The compound bird's-eye of the media is ever cocked for a fresh episode of the perils of Israel. Dayan joins Sam Pasternak and Eva Sonshine at a coffee table in the lounge, looking around at the journalists with one reddened eye. "So, Eva, what are the vultures croaking about today?"

"They smell blood, Minister."

"Whose blood? Mine?"

"To tell the truth, Dado's. He had a bad press conference after Golda's speech."

"Well, he was caught unawares. So was I, God knows."

"Eva tells me," Pasternak says, "of all kinds of rumors going around here. Our bridgehead's been smashed, Dado's had a heart attack, you've fired Arik Sharon —"

Dayan's sallow face freezes. Quickly Eva stands up, saying, "I have to get back to my desk," and hurries away.

Rubbing his eye, Dayan mutters, "Still another disaster at the Chinese Farm last night, Sam. Word just coming in."

"Elohim, what now?"

"A paratroop brigade from the south sector was thrown into a night fight without briefing, to help clear the road for Tallik's bridge. They were stopped cold, pinned down in the ditches. Tanks had to go in to rescue them and take out their dead and wounded. Second terrible fiasco there. Ready to go? Come along."

Outside beyond the portico it is raining hard. Dayan's dripping car drives up, the doorman salutes him, and people waiting for taxis stare at the famous one-eyed hero. "Amos is all right?" Dayan asks as they get in.

"Well, he's still out there in Syria with his battalion."

"A son of his father. My God, Sam, the price, the price of this war. Already nearly a thousand dead, and no end in sight. My telephone never stops ringing, my closest friends have lost sons or they're missing." He leans on an elbow, glumly looking out at the drumming rain.

"Where are we going, Minister?"

"Dado has called a meeting of senior officers down south at Kishuf, to decide how to continue the war, now that Golda has cut off our retreat."

Gloomy silence, slap-slap of windshield wipers.

"Minister, the airlift news this morning is great."

"Yes?" Dayan rouses himself. "What's the latest?"

"Eleven Phantoms coming today, *eleven* more, on top of the fourteen that have arrived. Twenty-six Skyhawks due tomorrow. Tanks rolling off the Galaxies like an Independence Day parade."

"And I had to push Golda on the airlift!" Dayan shakes his head in wonder. "Where would we be otherwise?"

"Minister, most of the stuff won't reach the front before it's all over. This is mainly resupply —"

"Nonsense. The Phantoms can fly tomorrow, and we're right at the red line on them. Those fighter-bombers refuel in the air, you know. American carriers are strung across the Mediterranean to protect them. All organized in five days, Saturday to Wednesday. They're phenomenal, the Americans, once they get going."

"Moshe, they simply woke up to their own national interest, and high time," the hardened Mossad skeptic retorts. "They can't let the Russians win a surrogate war here —"

"Easy to say! Shallow! This will cost them a damaging oil embargo, and who can say whether their 'surrogate,' as you put it, will win? Can you? Can I? They're being magnificent."

Two Phantoms are overflying the Suez Canal more than sixty thousand feet up, on a mission rendered urgent by Golda Meir's disclosure. Benny Luria in the lead plane has already heard on the morning news Cairo's dismissal of the *"token raid for television."* Aerial reconnaissance of Egyptian troop movements is now mandatory, and the flight is testing a gap reportedly blasted in the missile wall by Sharon's tanks. The pilots and navigators in oxygen masks are peering down tensely for the flash of a missile launch. So far, as the Canal and its lakes slide slowly under their wings, nothing. Thrumming engines, azure peace of the stratosphere.

Benny Luria is courting disciplinary action, for base commanders have now been forbidden to fly missions. But Dov is in the other plane, and on hearing of this he preempted the lead plane. Let come what may! He has been drilling hard with Dov on an anti-missile tactic he read about in an American air force journal, developed in Vietnam. Benny knows it works, because earlier in the war he saved his own life with it.

Five minutes into Egypt air space, and still nothing. Breathing easier, Benny wigwags his wings to signal *Commence photography*. He and Dov fly flat ever-widening circles over the assigned areas, while automatic cameras capture copious photographs. The landscape below is blotchy with the shadows of drifting clouds, and from this altitude, troop concentrations are only more vague blotches. But the pictures taken by these CIA supercameras will show the hairs on the mustaches of the Egyptian tank commanders.

"All right, we've done it, Dov. Let's go home."

Rattling roar of the jets, heavy vibration of the plane as it accelerates to Mach 2. Thrust of helmet against headrest, a hard blow. Far ahead the thread of the Canal sparkles, the low sun glares. Watching for landmarks of Sharon's missile gap, Benny Luria spots a pale flash.

"Missile, Dov, eleven o'clock."

"I see it."

The spurt of flame climbs and seems to be locking on Dov's plane. He jinks and it is after him, veering as he veers, straightening as he straightens, steadily ascending toward him, a visible missile now. *L'Azazel,* Dov has fought a good war, made a fine record, three confirmed MiGs downed. God help him to evade. Drilling is one thing, staring down at climbing death is another, as Benny too well knows.

That evasive maneuver he taught Dov is simple but tricky, and the timing is everything. At the last possible moment, you flip over and break downward; a few seconds too soon, and the missile will detect the move and change course to hit. A second too late, goodbye! But if you time it just right, the plane will fall off so fast in the thin air that the rocket, unable to alter its course in time, will fly past harmlessly. No way to help Dov now, either he will save himself or not . . .

Now, Dov, NOW, BY YOUR LIFE, over and down.

Aircraft and fire-spurting pole still converging.

Dov, Dov, *Dov, GO* . . .

The other plane flips and drops like a stone. The missile flames past it and up into the fathomless blue.

In Benny's earphones, his navigator: *"He did it, sir, hundred percent."*

Calm voice of Dov as he straightens out far below: *"How was that, Abba?"*

"B-plus. You waited too long," Benny Luria replies through a choked throat. He hears his son laugh, and feels for the first time the trickling sweat that has broken out all over his body inside the G suit.

A few minutes before the Ramatkhal takes off for the decisive strategic meeting in the south, the developed Luria photographs are delivered to his helicopter.

29

Goodbye to Glory

Shells are now falling all around Deversoir. In the enormous brick-paved Yard the tanks and APCs are battened down, in the Canal below an occasional explosive splash drenches the pontoon bridge engineers, and everywhere stinking gunpowder smoke swirls and stings the eyes. Don Kishote is supervising traffic himself, keeping access clear for the nine pontoon rafts rumbling in on huge transporters. Defying the whistling shells and the flying shrapnel, the engineers down at the waterline are linking up several of these rafts into the stub of a bridge, already projecting a third of the way across.

"Arik, it's Arik, sir." A dirty bloody soldier runs up to Kishote. "Arik's been hit!" Kishote follows him through the crowding machines and sees Sharon down on the bricks, his back to a tank track, bright blood welling into a bandage around his temples. He looks slack-jawed and vacant. Pushing through the anxious officers around him, Kishote asks the medical orderly, "How bad is it?"

"He'll be all right, sir. Shrapnel wound, but it's not lodged in his head. He's just dazed."

"I'm not dazed," says Sharon irritably. "Kishote, they're finding the range, the bastards. Pull all the command vehicles out of the Yard right away, before the antennas get knocked off and we lose communications. Then go back outside and keep those pontoon rafts coming, whatever you do."

In a little while he emerges from the Yard, his hair blowing over the stained bandage, his stride somewhat shaky. "B'seder, Yossi, tell Ezra to take over command here, and let's go to Kishuf."

Half an hour later, unshaven and very dirty, Sharon and Kishote mount the path to General Adan's advance command post, their boots sinking in the yellow sand. As they go up, a grand Sinai panorama unfolds, full of sights and sounds of war; from the Canal direction the pale flashes, delayed thumps, and rising smoke of Egyptian heavy artillery; closer by, in the enemy's Sinai lodgments north and south as far as the eye can see, broad dust plumes of brigade-scale movements. Directly below the winding path, Bren's armored division is arrayed on the level desert, a textbook diagram drawn by a thousand machines.

Yossi is not looking forward to an encounter with Major General Bren Adan, a soldier's soldier, all business and sparing of talk. Bren must still be smarting under his disaster on October eighth, caused in part by Gorodish's sending Sharon uselessly south and back north; and he has smarted over the years at being in the everlasting shadow of the flamboyant Sharon. Bren Adan is certainly entitled to be distant and crusty with Sharon's deputy, but he is no fun. At the top of the path, to Kishote's delight, he is hailed by Colonel Natke Nir, one of Bren's brigade commanders, sitting on the sand with two other colonels at a large map. "Kishote, to all the devils!" Kishote springs to seize the extended horny hand and pull Colonel Nir erect, for he cannot get to his feet by himself. The old friends embrace and pound each other, making rough banter.

Kishote knows nobody quite like Natke Nir, who once served under him. The man seems to be made of pig iron for indestructibility, and in fact has much metal in him. Both his legs were all but blown off in the Six-Day War. Many operations and a lot of artificial patching have restored his locomotion, but he cannot get in or out of a tank. Yet he has waived total disability pay and risen to lead an armor brigade, always assisted into and out of his command machines. Natke, as everyone calls him, has been in the thick of the Canal fighting from the start.

"So, what devilry are you fellows up to?" Kishote greets the other two colonels, both as sandy and whiskery as Natke, with a gesture at the map.

"As a matter of fact, Yossi," says Nir, "it's exciting, though it's probably just a dream. Look here." Kishote helps him kneel down at the map, and he hoarsely expounds Bren Adan's op plan in rough army jargon, a forefinger skimming the map and making a quick sketch now and then in the sand.

"By your life, Natke," Kishote interrupts him, "it's Hannibal, that's what it is."

Nir blinks at him. "Hannibal? With the elephants? Why Hannibal?"

Military history of ancient times is Don Kishote's hobby, and the great battles are at his fingertips. Crouching at the map, he describes how Hannibal ambushed and annihilated a Roman army in 217 B.C., at the Battle of Lake Trasimene. "Its a classic, Natke, and Bren's concept here is pretty much the same. The key is the lake. In Italy it was Trasimene, here it's Great Bitter Lake. An impassable water obstacle traps your enemy when you hit him head-on and from the flanks. He has no room to maneuver, and he's in a killing ground."

From a slumping bald colonel, a dubious grumble. "217 B.C., eh? Quite a while ago."

"Bren didn't mention Hannibal," remarks the other colonel.

"No, and maybe he never heard of that lake or that battle," exclaims Natke, "but we've got the code name for the plan, gentlemen, it's 'Hannibal.' I'll tell Bren. Thanks, Yossi, that's really interesting."

"It'll never happen," says the bald colonel. "The Egyptians aren't that stupid, to march a brigade into such a trap."

"We'll see," says Natke. "They could be as stupid as the Romans."

On the flat summit of the high dune Sharon has meantime joined the top brass. Around a large tactical map Bar-Lev reclines on an elbow, smoking a cigar, Adan sits cross-legged, and Dayan and Pasternak squat on their knees. It occurs to Sam Pasternak, as Sharon approaches with heavy swinging tread, tousled white-blond hair showing above the bloody bandage, that if the crossing succeeds, Sharon and his bandage may become a trademark of the war, as the Six-Day War's symbol was Dayan and his eye patch. Sharon kneels to peer at the map. Nobody speaks a word to him until Dayan at last says, "Shalom, Arik."

"Shalom, Minister."

Very long silence, then Bar-Lev utters his first words, slowly and tonelessly. "The distance between what you promised to do and what you have done is very great."

Sharon's reply is composed. "How so?"

"What can I say? No enemy collapse. No secure bridgehead. No secure supply corridor. And no bridges."

"I don't agree with that judgment. We are across and winning."

Bren Adan, his rugged features set in stern lines, jumps to his feet as a helicopter buzzes far to the east. "There comes Dado now." He goes off to greet the Ramatkhal, and the others walk about and stretch, talking in low tones.

When the meeting begins Kishote squats by Sharon. The noonday desert sun is scorching, and orderlies bring cold orangeade while Dado passes around the aerial photographs, which clearly show large Egyptian reserve forces forming up, and advance units on the move toward the bridgehead. Sharon plunges to talk first, vehemently pressing for immediate attack, and Dado listens without comment. Half his force is already over in Africa, Sharon argues, so it makes sense for him to ferry the rest across at once, and smash north to Ismailia or south to Suez; objective, to panic the enemy into pulling his armor back into Egypt, which may trigger a general collapse.

General Adan coldly objects. The original plan calls for *him* to cross while Sharon seizes and holds the bridgehead on both banks. Why change? The photographs only confirm the urgent need for Sharon to secure the bridgehead before anyone sallies out on the offensive. After almost an hour of abrasive talk — which to Sam Pasternak is obviously all about who will lead the assault into Egypt — Bar-Lev proposes a compromise: a brigade each of Sharon's and Adan's should start the breakout together.

Now Dado takes charge. His bloodshot eyes are puffed half-shut, the heavy brows contracted in dogged resolve. His deeply lined face is gray from the days of unrelieved tension, sleeplessness, and polluted underground air. Among these desert-bronzed officers his pallor is almost pathetic, yet he speaks with all his accustomed clarity and authority. No compromise with the original plan. It is all right. Once the bridgehead is secure, Adan will cross. After that Sharon will bring over the rest of his forces, and the two divisions will exploit north and south to force a decision. "The only real question that's open," says Dado, "is whether to resume crossing at once with pontoon rafts and crocodiles, as Arik suggests, or wait until the roller bridge arrives, or at least until one pontoon bridge is up, before we commit major forces." He looks around at the others.

"Wait," says Bar-Lev.

"Wait," says Adan.

Dado glances to Dayan, who waves a hand to pass the question. "Sam, what do you think?" Dado says to Pasternak, who sits beside Dayan on the sand.

"I'm not entirely in the picture down here, sir," Pasternak replies.

"I'd like your view, all the same."

"Then, I say, *im kvar az kvar* [if we go, we go]! Those photographs show the Egyptians still off balance but starting to react to the crossing. Let's send everything over now, by any and all means."

Dado peers around, polling staff officers and deputies and getting varying views, until he comes to Don Kishote. "So, Yossi? Let's hear from you."

Kishote hesitates, glances at the poker-faced Sharon, then around the senior circle. General Bren Adan is regarding him fixedly and skeptically.

"Sir, yesterday General Pasternak would certainly have been right, but the situation has changed, hasn't it? The surprise has been blown" — he leaves unspoken *by Madame Prime Minister,* but their faces show they understand and agree — "and today the Egyptians are alerted. We're being heavily shelled at Deversoir, and we can see big movement in the lodgments. If they try an attack on this side today, we'll crush them as we did on Saturday, providing we still have the forces here. But if they engage us on the other side, we'll need assured fuel and ammunition resupply over there. Therefore the factors —"

"Plain language, Kishote," Bar-Lev cuts in. "Go or wait?"

Pasternak is watching Sharon, who shows no tension or concern in the momentary pause. In such Zahal discussions juniors are allowed to speak up with candor, though the yes-men play it safe. Don Kishote is not one of those, yet the stakes here are very high.

"Wait."

Pasternak's are not the only eyebrows raised at Yossi's temerity.

The talk continues round and round until Natke Nir comes hobbling up to Bren Adan and speaks in low rapid tones. "Well, there it is," Adan says to the others. "Scouts report a tank brigade from the south heading along the lake toward my sector." He turns to Dado. "With your permission, sir, I should attend to this."

"Go ahead, Bren, the meeting is over," says Dado. "We wait for a bridge. Good luck."

Natke Nir stumps by Kishote, and punches his shoulder. "Hannibal," he says and goes off, his eyes agleam.

Pasternak comes to Kishote and mutters, "You had your nerve."

"Dado asked me, so I spoke my mind."

"Kol ha'kavod. Yael keeps calling, to find out how you are."

"Yes, I managed to talk to her once. She had to stop Aryeh from lying about his age and enlisting. Amos's influence. Hero worship."

"Father worship," says Pasternak.

"Is Amos okay?"

"Still fighting."

"Good."

In the seven-mile drive back to Deversoir across sunbaked wastes, Sharon says not a word to Kishote. Dayan rides with them in the command car, also silent. At the Yard there is a lull in the shelling, but the stump of pontoon rafts has not progressed far. A shell-hit damaged it, the chief engineering officer explains, killing two of his men, but it will be ready by four o'clock. Dayan walks out among the machines, talking to the amazed and awed crews.

"There's Dayan at his best," Sharon says to Kishote. "Seeing for himself, sensing the mood of the men, reading the battle on the field. Not like those map room generals."

The words are innocuous, but Don Kishote hears a new distance in Sharon's tone.

"Sir, I've never forgotten the lesson I learned in the last war, at the Jeradi Pass." Sharon's response is a bleak quizzical look. "Just smashing ahead isn't always the answer, sir, is it? If the enemy has the forces to close up behind you, you can lose all your men in a big disaster."

"But you didn't, at the Jeradi Pass."

"I was lucky."

"Doesn't luck count in war? You learned exactly the wrong lesson in the Jeradi Pass." Sharon's voice and expression harden. "You reached El Arish the first day. I took Abu Agheila the first night. With their two anchors in the north gone, the Egyptians panicked and collapsed all over Sinai. Right or wrong?"

"That's what happened, sir."

"Yes, and we could have won this war by crossing in force two days ago. *Attack, and the logistics follow, Yossi, because they must.* But Gorodish has lost us a day and a half, and now Dado's written off the edge of surprise we've still got. It'll be a bloody long slog to victory. Not very sound, your opinion, and not very collegial." Sharon pauses, regarding his deputy with a stony eye. "I'll be taking my headquarters over to Africa now. Moshe Dayan is coming with me. You will remain in Sinai, get Tallik's bridge at all cost to the Canal, and keep this yard functioning no matter what, until a cease-fire comes. Understood?"

"Understood, sir." Kishote understands perfectly. Sharon is sentencing him to share none of the glory and career value of combat in Africa.

So be it! His own view, which he has kept strictly to himself, is that neither Arik nor Dado was the right decision maker for the crossing into Egypt, but in tandem they have been perfect. The decision called for a warrior burning to charge across the Canal against all odds, and for a calculating superior to rein him in until the right moment. In this great gamble with Israel's fate Sharon might have gone too soon or too far, as he did in the Suez War back in '56, at the Mitla Pass. On the other hand Dado, not dragged by Sharon, might not have seized the fleeting moment when it came. God or luck has placed Elazar and Sharon in the right niches in Jewish history to fight this war. God or luck has put Yossi Nitzan on the wrong side of the Canal for glory.

So be it.

Hannibal happens.

The Egyptian armored brigade, coming up from the south to close a vise on Deversoir, rolls blindly into gun range of Natke Nir's brigade, concealed on its right flank in the high dunes. Nir opens up and blasts it as he closes in, while Bren Adan sends in other forces north and south of the Egyptians. They are caught under heavy fire front, rear, and flank. Their left flank is trapped against Great Bitter Lake, and there is no escape. The entire brigade is annihilated, with all its APCs and supply trains, an enormous smoking mass of ruined war machines spread over many square miles of desert. Only a few tanks escape to tell the tale of Bren Adan's obscure victory, which protects Arik Sharon's celebrated crossing.

"To all the devils, where is Adan? *Where is Adan?*" Messages from Arik Sharon in Africa begin blistering the air at Southern Command headquarters that afternoon. "The pontoon bridge has been up since four o'clock. Why doesn't he cross?" General Adan at the time is regrouping and reloading his tanks and APCs, almost depleted of fuel and ammunition by the battle. "*Where* is Adan? The Minister of Defense is standing right beside me and he also wants to know. Why the delay? What to all the devils is he waiting for?"

Only half-replenished, Adan's division begins crossing after nightfall. By now the Deversoir Yard is a nightmare of red flame, choking smoke, shattering explosions; and rows of dead and wounded lie on the sand, under the ghastly light of starshells drifting in the sky. Natke Nir's jeep comes rolling into the Yard. "Yossi!" he bellows, holding out his arms. His driver stops the jeep and Kishote trots up to embrace him. Nir roars over the tumult, "Hannibal went a hundred percent, everything but elephants. A great battle. It's our turn now, and why aren't you over in Africa with Arik?"

"Too much fun still on this side," shouts Don Kishote, and with a wave Natke Nir goes bouncing off into the smoke and the flaring crimson gloom.

All night long Don Kishote is too busy to feel deprived of his chance to win glory in Africa. He is well aware that the lifeblood of battle is logistics, a sort of colorless lifeblood noticeable only if it stops flowing, whereupon the gangrene of nonsupply can be quickly fatal. His job now is of the highest urgency, and in its shadowy way exalting; to remain quite unnoticed and inglorious so as to make glory possible for Zahal in Egypt.

By daybreak he feels on top of the job. Traffic is streaming across the rough pontoon bridge, and more traffic that has been stalled in the Sinai is loosening up and arriving. Three full divisions — twenty-five thousand men, more than three hundred tanks, a thousand other vehicles — are over in Africa, regrouping or fighting. The pontoon bridge is bumper to bumper, the ferries are ceaselessly plying back and forth, yet the clamor for resupply is on. Clearly it will be up to the great roller bridge to solve the shortfall. This it can easily do, for compared to the pontoon makeshift it is a broad highway, and after a variety of technical snags reported by Yehiel during the night, it is smoothly on its way, due at noon. Meantime the pipeline is open, the crossing so far is a success, and as the sun rises white, warm, and dazzling over the eastern crags, Don Kishote can draw breath.

He does something he has been putting off for days. In a corner of the Yard religious soldiers have put up a makeshift sukkah of ammunition boxes and packing crates, roofed with scrubby desert vegetation. He takes his morning coffee and roll inside the narrow space to breakfast at a plank over two oil drums. Sukkot is past, today is Rejoicing of the Law, but he makes the sukkah blessing anyway. The frail booth represents the precariousness of the Jews' existence, and their ultimate dependence on God for survival. On this touch-and-go day of Jewish history, what could be more to the point? So he is thinking, while downing the hot coffee and the army roll with appetite, when his signal officer pokes his head in.

"Sir, Colonel Yehiel calling."

"L'Azazel." This cannot be good. Yossi bolts the rest of the roll with a swallow of coffee and hastens to the signal jeep. "Nitzan here."

"Yehiel here. We're under attack by eleven tanks that were lying in ambush, here in the dunes." Yehiel's battleground voice is terse and cool. "My tanks have cut loose from the bridge and are engaging them."

"Any damage to the bridge?"

"Negative, not yet."

"Can I send help?"

"We could use air support, but there's no time to call it in. I think we'll be all right, but there'll be a delay. Over."

"Understood. Keep in touch. Out."

"Yehiel out."

30

The Bridge Arrives

Earsplitting concussions resume all around Deversoir, the inevitable sunrise barrage as October 18 begins. Silencing that heavy artillery is supposed to be a high priority for the forces in Africa, but obviously no luck yet. Huge splashes in the Canal, bricks jumping as a shell bursts at the far end of the Yard, and to all the devils, there go pontoons, flying from a square hit on the bridge. Engineers start to swarm over the partial gap torn near the Egyptian side. Kishote orders all traffic halted, and the Yard is again becoming choked up and smoky when Yehiel once more calls.

"Well, it's over, Yossi. A hard fight. I'm looking at eight burning Egyptian tanks. The crews of the other three jumped out and ran off into the dunes."

"How about our tanks?"

"Bad shape. We were surprised, so it was fighting at close range. The bridge is all right, but this unit has sustained too much damage, and too many casualties, to tow it any farther."

There is no arguing with a seasoned officer like Yehiel. "Where are you?" Yehiel gives him the grid coordinates. "B'seder, Yehiel. All tanks here have been fighting day and night at the Chinese Farm, you know. They're beat."

"If you need the bridge send ten tanks, Yossi. We'll rehearse them and get going again."

"You'll have them inside of an hour."

"If so I'll be at the water at four o'clock."

The pontoon bridge traffic is once more on the move by the time Yossi locates a ten-tank company to despatch to Yehiel. Meantime the jam outside the Yard has gotten much worse, and urgent calls for supplies are increasing. Arik himself comes on the radiophone, sounding exhilarated and friendly but frantic for fuel. The news about the roller bridge sobers him. "Well, these things happen. The battle's on your shoulders now, Kishote. I'm very glad you're over there in charge."

The barrage subsides, but shrapnel has ripped open the float on a ferry raft. It slowly sinks under the light blue waters, and Yossi is watching the rescue of the crew, when he notices that all the pontoon bridge traffic is halted yet again, this time behind one small automobile around which soldiers mill. He strides out on the bridge, and a lieutenant tells him that the rusty black Volkswagen tore up its underside bouncing over the pontoons, and cannot get going. "What to all the devils is a tin can like this doing on the bridge?" Yossi snaps. "It should have gone over on a raft."

"Sir, the driver was told that. He just ignored us and ran out here, so —"

"Throw it in the Canal."

"General, General, I'm the driver," a paunchy gray civilian standing by loudly protests, "I volunteered this car, it's my car, and —"

"Nobody's stealing it. After the war, fish it out of the Canal. Or take your ownership papers and sue the State of Israel." Six men pick up the Volkswagen and give it a heave. It makes a tremendous splash. The traffic resumes running, shaking the bridge, while the car fills and submerges, and the driver, ownership papers in hand, laments that it has four new tires and new upholstery, and the general is a maniac.

At noon Kishote calls Yehiel. The ten tanks have arrived, the colonel confirms cheerily, and are hooking up to the towlines now. "Beat is no word for these fellows, Yossi. Most of them haven't slept for seventy-two hours. Still, they're strong kids, good boys, and they'll be all right."

But Shimon Shimon calls an hour later, sounding lugubrious. Lauterman is repairing a new break in the bridge. "Sir, those tank men were just too tired. The rehearsal went well, and when I asked on the network, '*Ready to go?*' they all answered up by the numbers. So I ordered '*Go,*' but in those few seconds one tank captain had fallen asleep. He didn't pull, all the others did, and the bridge cracked."

Yossi's number-one priority is now that bridge, and he decides to go and see for himself exactly how things stand. He turns over the Yard and the traffic-control network to his deputy, Ezra, an overworked lieutenant colonel from Raanana who is holding up under the strain of recent days and nights by gobbling sugar cubes. Ezra is reliable, and the news from Africa is good except for the rising howl about shortages. The answer to that is the bridge, *the bridge*.

"Elohim, Yehiel, what happened now?"

"Verkakteh air attack, Yossi, right after Shimon talked to you. That's what happened."

Yehiel is lying on a stretcher, his left leg in a splint and a thick bloodstained dressing. The desert around the stalled bridge is pitted with shell holes, and corpsmen are working on several other soldiers down on the sand. A cool afternoon breeze is springing up. The bridge makes a long shallow *V* on the desert, the break hardly visible. Tanks are pushing and pulling at it, combat engineers are climbing all over it in a great noise of tools and yells, and Lieutenant Colonel Lauterman stands at the break, flipping his yo-yo. Three low-flying Egyptian aircraft attacked the bridge shortly after it broke, Yehiel tells Kishote. The bombs missed, but though he dove for cover under a truck, shrapnel got his leg. A medical helicopter is on its way to evacuate the casualties. Fortunately, nobody has been killed.

"My mistake of course was to take cover," says Yehiel, with a groan. "With Egyptian marksmanship, the safest place was right on the bridge."

"Yehiel, three divisions are now operating in Africa. The pontoon bridge and the ferries can't supply such a force, and besides, they're very vulnerable. This structure must reach the Canal tonight."

"I'm out of it. Good luck to you," groans Yehiel. "I don't know what else can go wrong, but I tell you that this bridge is alive, it's vicious, and it doesn't want to cross the Suez Canal. I need more morphine."

When the corpsmen are about to load him on the helicopter, Yehiel reaches out a hand to Yossi Nitzan, and pulls him close. "You won't forget, will you, Kishote," he gasps, "to make sure Arik talks to the promotion board?"

"I'll do it, I promise."

"Yossi, I'm not religious, but I do fear God. I'll hold a Torah and swear I didn't rape that woman. In fact it was all her idea. She had disgusting legs." He catches his breath and groans. "Damn, I hurt. Goodbye, Yossi."

As the helicopter departs, Lauterman stands by Kishote, watching it go. "A fine officer," he says. "He'd have gotten us there. I'm not sure I can, sir. But I'll try, and I'll be ready to move before nightfall."

"I'll take it to the Canal," says Don Kishote.

Peering at him to make sure he is serious, Lauterman exclaims, "Hundred percent, sir!"

The sun is setting when the repairs are done. The tank crews, forty yawning disheveled green-clad youngsters, are sitting on the sand as Kishote briefs them, hands on hips, squinting into the red sunset glare. "Soldiers, once we start going, we GO. Only one signal will halt this bridge, a word from me. *Atzor* [Stop]. Understood?"

Murmurs and tired nods from the soldiers. He has in mind to give them a fighting talk about the life-or-death necessity for the bridge in the next crucial hours of the war, but looking at these Zahal tank men, he cuts it down to, "Soldiers, nothing is more important to our victory than getting this bridge to the Canal before midnight. I tell you this as Arik's second-in-command. *Yallah*." They jump up and run to their tanks.

A long uneventful crawl ensues.

Darkness has fallen and the crowded desert stars are shining bright when they reach the Tirtur Road, a straight run to the Canal laid down long ago for this bridge. Hardly has the whole majestic structure rolled onto the road, however, when shellfire engulfs it from "Missouri," high ground that the Egyptians still cling to, despite repeated attacks, so as to interdict Tirtur traffic. Moving steadily ahead, the ten towing tanks return fire with all guns, and for some minutes the air is filled with red tracer streaks and the booming of the salvos. But it is all noise and flame. Undamaged, the bridge passes beyond gun range of Missouri, and emerges from smoke into starlight. Riding in a lead tank, Kishote sees that the road ahead is cut clear across by a dark hole.

"*Atzor!*"

He and Lauterman leave their vehicles and peer down into a deep wide freshly dug trench. "The bridge can cross this," says Lauterman. "No problem."

"The tanks can't," Kishote says. "It's a standard antitank ditch."

He orders the tanks to unhook from the bridge, attach bulldozer blades, and set about filling up the hole. In a wild tumult of tumbling earth and snorting engines, they comply. When the hole is almost level ground again, Shimon Shimon appears out of the gloom. "Sir, there's a call for you from Deversoir."

"Very well."

"Sir, how's Yoram? Not wounded, is he?"

"He's over in Africa with General Sharon's signal crew, at his own request. Looking for material for his book, I suppose."

"No doubt." The ceramicist wearily laughs.

It is now eleven o'clock, and off to the south the bombardment of Deversoir is lighting up the sky. All is going well, Ezra reports, though casualties are mounting, and the demands for fuel, food, and ammunition are overwhelming the signal channels. He is calling to warn Kishote that eyewitnesses have seen the Egyptians laying a minefield in the Tirtur Road.

Cursing under his breath but exhibiting calm good cheer, Kishote orders sappers to clear the mines. He and Lauterman walk behind them, as the bridge ponderously follows with its accustomed clanks, squeals, and rumbles. The night is turning bitter cold, too cold for the slow plod behind the line of sappers, who advance step by step, poking very cautiously into the sand with long slender flexible steel probes. So far, nothing. This can take till morning, thinks Kishote, and further delay menaces the lives of the fighters in Egypt. He has a memory flash of Yehuda Kan-Dror, driving through the Mitla Pass to draw the enemy's fire. "I tell you what, Lauterman," he says. "The battle's been going back and forth across this road for days. I'll bet there's no minefield here. I'll run a jeep to the Canal and see."

"Sir, that's committing suicide. The eyewitness report said —"

"I know, I know. Half the time, on the battlefield, such reports are nonsense."

The sappers stare open-mouthed when he drives past them. "Keep searching," he shouts. The jeep wheelbase is a fraction of the roller width, so he zigzags as he drives down the Tirtur Road. After five very long hairy minutes of bouncing westward under the stars in a chilly wind, and praying from the heart not to get blown up, he sees the moonlit Canal through a gap in the rampart. So much for eyewitness reports! Catching sight of him returning, the sappers cease their prodding to cheer.

"Lauterman, we roll."

"Sir, I salute you."

And that does it. All the fight is out of the bridge. It moves with tamed docility and no further balking to the brink of the Suez Canal, and soon engineers and tanks are easing it into the water a short distance north of Deversoir. The first rollers slide down the embankment, hit with a towering splash, and float. Heavy as the steel colossus is, the huge cylinders give it all the buoyancy it needs. Slowly it is pushed across to where paratroopers await with signal flares, and tanks start hauling it up on the embankment.

Kishote gets on the radiophone. "Ezra, Nitzan here. The bridge has arrived."

"Beautiful. Hundred percent, sir."

"What's your situation at the Yard?"

"Further bombardment casualties, not too bad. Bridge traffic and ferries going strong, but supply problem truly getting out of hand."

"It'll improve now. Out."

Lauterman approaches him, flipping the yo-yo up and down. "Ah, sir, we encounter a problem."

"Problem? What problem? It's across, isn't it?"

"Yes, sir, but as it turns out, the bridge is too long."

"Too long? *Too long?*" Kishote cannot believe his ears. "Lauterman, how to all the devils can a bridge be too long? It can be too *short*. Is that what you mean? Too short?"

"No, sir. Too long. You see, sir, the Canal is only a hundred eighty meters wide, and the bridge is two hundred meters long. That's creating a very steep slope on both sides. Tanks can manage it, but supply trucks won't be able to."

Don Kishote stares at the Jeptha colonel, and at the spinning yo-yo, and at the bridge floating gently on the Canal. There certainly is a very long tail draped over the rampart and out on the road.

"I see. Got any ideas?"

"Oh, yes, sir. It's simply a matter of removing two rollers. We should have the bridge ready by dawn."

"Just tell me this, Lauterman. Everybody — but *everybody* — knows the width of the Suez Canal. It's a world statistic. How is it that Jepthah made a bridge seventy feet too long?"

"I would have to call it an oversight, sir."

"I see. That explains it. Remove the two rollers, then. I'm going to check things at Deversoir, and I'll be back before dawn."

The bridge has yielded, Kishote muses as he drives south, it is spanning the Canal, but it has had the last laugh.

By the glare of starshells and the glow of guide flares, a very strange sight greets him at the pontoon bridge. Vehicles are rolling across as before — tanks, busses, APCs, self-propelled guns, fuel trucks — but near the middle, on one side, stands a stark naked stout man, fighting with soldiers. As Kishote hurries out on the bridge the naked man breaks free and dives. "What in God's name is this?" Kishote shouts.

The soldiers bawl above the clanking of caterpillar tracks on the pontoons that a few minutes ago a shell hit a tank and made it veer off the bridge. It has gone down like a rock with all hatches shut and no hope that the crew can escape. The naked man, a relief driver on a fuel truck, knows his son is in that tank. He jumped off his truck, stripped, and dived. He has been diving ever since. He is exhausted and out of his mind, and they are afraid he is going to drown himself. As they yell all this the man surfaces, choking and sobbing.

"Get him out," Kishote orders. Two soldiers grab him and pull him up, soaking themselves.

"Let me go! He's down there. I was banging on the tank. I swear I heard them banging. Why doesn't somebody help me? You're all cowards," he gasps, his gray hair streaming. When he tries to stand up to dive again, he slips and collapses on the greasy pontoon.

"Keep him here," says Kishote, "and no matter what, restrain him." He threads through the traffic to get off the bridge, and sends orderlies with a stretcher to sedate the man and put him with the injured.

To give Ezra a breather he takes over Yard and traffic control. The dark morning hours go by, the east grows pink, and most of the stars are gone. The bombardment is letting up, though to the north red arcs of artillery tracers still rise from Missouri. Time to make sure the roller bridge is in use, something Kishote can still hardly believe. He calls Lauterman on the radio telephone. The two rollers have been detached, Lauterman briskly reports. The bridge is firmly anchored on both banks, level and ready for traffic. A few shells have been landing in the area without doing damage, nothing like the fiery all-night spectacle at Deversoir.

"Now Lauterman, what I really have to know is, can I start rerouting traffic to that bridge?"

"Absolutely. Some trucks are crossing already, sir."

"No more surprises or oversights?"

"Inconceivable. That's all over. Thanks to you, sir, we've done it at last."

"Thanks to you, Lauterman. You're not a normal soldier exactly, but you were the man for that bridge."

"Thank you, General."

"I mean it. Kol ha'kavod, and if I have anything to say, you'll get decorated for this."

"Send on your traffic, sir."

Kishote issues instructions on the traffic-control network, splitting the flow of vehicles down the Sinai roads between Deversoir and the roller bridge. He orders a rearguard artillery battalion to keep bombarding Missouri, and he stirs up Ezra to resume command of the Yard. Then he takes a jeep and drives north on the sand alongside a lateral road, where dense traffic is now wheeling slowly but freely. The jeep comes over a rise, and there ahead is the bridge, with a solid train of shadowy shapes moving across it westward into Africa. Seen through the ground mist the whole picture is vague and dreamy, almost like a mirage. It is happening! Despite all, the bridge is across the Canal, with the lifeblood of victory flowing over it. He can hear the distant drumming of heavy traffic on the sturdy steel roadbed as the jeep draws closer.

Attack, and the logistics follow, Yossi, because they must!

At the rampart by the head of the bridge, to his astonishment, all is shouting and calamity: medical orderlies running with stretchers or kneeling by groaning men, others helping bandaged soldiers into a hospital bus, and here and there on the sand, green greatcoats covering a few bodies. A corpsman tells him that a random salvo fell on the bridge personnel only minutes ago.

"Where's Lieutenant Colonel Lauterman?"

The corpsman points to a greatcoat and hurries away. Beside the coat lies a yo-yo and a crumpled string. Lifting the coat, Kishote sees that Lauterman's head has a catastrophic hole in the back, oozing blood into a broad pool. The string is still attached to his finger. His hand is warm as Kishote detaches the string, rolls up the yo-yo, and puts it in his pocket. *"Blessed be the True Judge,"* he murmurs, closing the engineer's staring eyes, and he covers him with the coat.

A soldier in a parka approaches him, carrying a long black case. "Sir, this is Colonel Lauterman's clarinet. I'm putting together his stuff to send back, but I'm afraid it's the kind of thing that can get lost."

"I'll take it." Kishote peers at the soldier. He is short, roly-poly, very young and very unshaven. "Who are you?"

"I was his runner, sir. Mostly I worked for his aide, Sergeant Barkowe."

"And where is he?" The soldier does not answer, but his sad face grows sadder. "What, is Dzecki dead, too?"

"He's not dead, sir." The sergeant points at a parked yellow hospital bus. "They're taking him to the dressing station, where the helicopters come."

Kishote boards the bus. The wounded lie in two tiers, some moaning or crying, several with needles and tubes stuck in them. The smell of blood, antiseptic, and rank bodies is strong. He comes on Dzecki in a lower tier, where a corpsman is holding a plasma jar over him. His uniform is blood-soaked, and Kishote's stomach turns at seeing most of his right arm gone. The stump is heavily bandaged and very bloody.

Dzecki is conscious, and even manages a smile. "Hi, General," he says in English. "I was lucky, I'm left-handed. They say Colonel Lauterman's dead."

"I know, Dzecki. This is his clarinet. Your runner brought it to me."

"Good. He's a nice boy." Dzecki sounds weak but peculiarly cheery. Kishote has observed this before, in soldiers in shock from terrible wounds. "Yo-yo actually played the clarinet one night at Yukon, you know. Played Benny Goodman and then Mozart. Not bad, in fact. He said his son played better than he did. You should give it to his son."

"I'll be sure to."

The corpsman says, "General, I think the bus will be starting."

"It's my mother I'm worried about," says Dzecki. "She'll be mad as hell, and the trouble is she'll blame the Israelis, not the Egyptians."

"She'll be great. Don't worry."

"Sir, will you give me a kiss?"

Kishote kneels and puts his lips to the bristly face bathed in cool perspiration. "God bless you, Dzecki, and send you a quick healing."

"Thanks. The guys are always saying I was crazy to come here from America" — Dzecki's voice is fading, and his eyelids droop — "but I helped get the bridge to the Suez Canal, didn't I?"

"You're a lion, Dzecki." Don Kishote kisses him again, presses his sweaty hand, and leaves the bus. A glittery edge of sun is just creeping up over a distant Sinai ridge, glorious and blinding. It warms his tearstained face, and strikes the steady stream of thunderous traffic on the roller bridge with a blaze of light.

31

Golda and Kissinger

On this day, Friday, October 19, thirteen days after Yom Kippur, with the Israeli army starting a three-pronged rampage into Egypt and the American airlift coming to flood, Anwar Sadat yields to Russian insistence and accepts the proposal of a cease-fire in place. At once Brezhnev cables President Nixon, urging that he send Kissinger to Moscow to negotiate the cease-fire terms, and Air Force One leaves Washington at 2 A.M. with the Secretary and his entourage.

Now unfolds a rapid-fire international comedy-drama such as the world has never seen, nor indeed is likely to see again. For it takes place in the shuddery Cold War era of Mutually Assured Deterrence, or MAD, the quite serious acronym of the time for the nuclear stalemate, when people are living with the half-buried awareness that if one superpower leader makes an imbecilic misjudgment, or a supposed fail-safe military control mechanism malfunctions, much of the world can be cremated or fatally irradiated in a few hours. It is in this frame of reality that Dr. Kissinger, who has just received the Nobel Peace Prize for his Vietnam War negotiations, wings off to Moscow.

Once he gets there, cables, telephone calls, letters, despatches, threats, pleas, cajoleries, snarls and counter-snarls spark at all hours of the day and night among five points on the globe: Washington, Moscow, Cairo, Jerusalem, and New York, where the Security Council keeps convening at very short notice and very odd times. Meanwhile in "Africa" the Israeli attack rolls on: General Adan's division, with Natke Nir in the van, driving southward toward Suez City to entrap the Third Army lodged on the Sinai side of the Canal; Sharon pushing north to Ismailia to cut off the Second Army; and a third division battling westward on the main road to Cairo.

At the height of the frenzied diplomatic signalling, Golda Meir sends for the Ramatkhal and puts a blunt question. "Dado, how much time do you need?"

"For a decisive result, Prime Minister, three more days."

"All right, I'll do what I can. But with Kissinger in Moscow," she raises her hands and her eyes to heaven, "who knows? Who knows?"

Monday, October 22. To the cease-fire negotiated in Moscow, Israel has agreed; Egypt, not yet. In bright sunshine the unmistakable Air Force One, with its immense Stars and Stripes and THE UNITED STATES OF AMERICA painted on the gleaming white fuselage, taxis to a stop in Lod airport, and out steps the Secretary of State in a very creased gray suit. He appears nonplussed, not to say startled, at his reception by the Israelis: sightseers at the terminal, cargo handlers swarming at the big airlift transports, and soldiers guarding those planes are all cheering. Descending the ramp, he holds out his hand to Zev Barak, who awaits him in dress uniform. "Ah, the vite eminence again. General Barak, is it?"

With a polite smile at the pleasantry, Barak says, "Correct, sir. Welcome to Israel. The Prime Minister is eager to see you."

"Is she? I hope so." The visitor uncertainly waves at the Israelis applauding him, as he walks from Air Force One to a waiting limousine.

"Congratulations, Mr. Secretary," Barak says, opening the car door, "on your Nobel Peace Prize."

"Aren't you nice. Thank you." He settles into the back seat and makes an inquiring gesture toward the driver.

Barak mutters, "English is all right, sir."

"Vat is Golda's mood?"

"She's furious."

"Oh? Tell me vy."

"We'll be in Herzliyya shortly, sir. She'll do that better than I can."

An owlish look through thick glasses. "No doubt. So, vat's the schedule?"

"She'll meet with you alone first, sir, for forty-five minutes, before lunch with ministers and army leaders."

"Very good. And after that? I must take off again at five o'clock."

"After that, sir, General Elazar will brief you on the military picture."

"Ah. Now *that* will be damned helpful. I kept begging Dinitz from Moscow for a battlefield update. Nothing! I had to negotiate in the dark. Under the circumstances, I've truly done my best for you." Kissinger looks at him earnestly and touches his arm. "As you see, at Golda's insistence, I even changed my return route in order to stop here. It meant clearing a new flight plan over the Soviet Union, and arranging an escort by our carrier fighters through the war zone. It wasn't easy."

"Sir, I know the Prime Minister appreciates that."

"She does? Good. Anyway, here I am."

At a bleak villa on a knoll surrounded by barbed wire, Barak escorts him through a side entrance to a glass-enclosed porch where Golda waits alone. Stubbing out a cigarette, she rises to greet Kissinger, and they sit down side by side on a threadbare red couch. Her subtle eye-signal tells Barak to remain. After chitchat about the flight from Moscow she abruptly turns harsh. "Mr. Secretary, why on earth did you rocket off to Moscow at two in the morning on Saturday? What was the big rush? Why not take at least a day or two to prepare for such a momentous meeting? Wouldn't that have been more reasonable? And much more helpful?"

"I couldn't. It was a forced move, believe me. Sadat was in great distress." Kissinger adopts a placating tone. "At any moment, Madame Prime Minister, the Soviet Union might have put a resolution to the Security Council, ordering you to withdraw to the pre-1967 lines under threat of sanctions. Except for us, it probably would have had unanimous support." Kissinger lifts his thick eyebrows and peers at Golda Meir. "Do you understand? Where would that have left you? And for my government it would have posed a grave dilemma. If we'd vetoed it we'd be kaput with the Arabs. If we abstained or supported it we'd be betraying you. I forestalled all that, you see, by hurrying to Moscow."

"What you forestalled was our victory." She brandishes a paper at him. "This despatch you sent me from Moscow is not a communication between allies. It's an ultimatum."

"An ultimatum!" He looks pained. "Nothing of the kind, Madame Prime Minister, I assure you."

"What else can I call it? It arrives at eleven last night, just before the Security Council goes into session to take up the deal you made in Moscow. And simultaneously I receive a cable letter from your President, warning us to accept your terms for a cease-fire immediately or face an end to the airlift, and no U.S. support in the Security Council vote. Not an ultimatum?"

"Forgive me, Madame Prime Minister, but you must have misconstrued the President's letter."

Barak has read it and thinks it is probably Kissinger in style, but it is not his place to put in a word.

"I did not, it was in plain English. Too plain. Our cabinet had to stay up all night figuring out exactly what your terms cabled from Moscow implied, while the Security Council debate was already going on. You'll meet some frazzled people at lunch."

"I'm very sorry. You'd have received the terms at seven o'clock, not eleven, but there was a communications disaster. For four hours we couldn't get messages out." Kissinger's German accent seems to thicken with fatigue. "Maybe the Soviets jammed us. The result may have been a discourtesy, vich I deeply regret, but it was certainly not an ultimatum."

"And the President's letter?"

"He wasn't threatening you. If the phrasing was unfortunate —"

She interrupts, "Mr. Secretary, why did you agree to an urgent night session of the Security Council, altogether? Why a midnight vote on a cease-fire resolution? Why couldn't they have met today? Wasn't that soon enough?"

With a sharp satiric look from under drooping lids, Kissinger says, "Yes, while your army kept advancing and advancing, eh? Brezhnev was in such a sweat to put the deal through that we wrapped it up in four hours. His hurry proved greatly to Israel's benefit, as you're bound to agree when I give you the details."

He glances at Barak, and she gestures at her military secretary to leave. In a big room cloudy with cigarette smoke, various cabinet members and generals sitting around on motel-style furniture begin to fire questions at him as soon as he appears. Moshe Dayan holds up a hand. "Let him talk. What happened at the airport, Zev?"

"Minister, they cheered him."

"*Cheered* Kissinger?"

"Yes. He seemed surprised."

"He should be," says a bitter voice out of the smoke, "after selling us out."

Another bitter voice. "The people are tired of the war, and they don't know the cease-fire terms."

"What's his demeanor?" Dayan asks. "What did he say?"

After a moment, Barak replies, "He says it's the best deal he could get for us. And that he detoured here with much difficulty."

"Ha! He had to come," says old Yisrael Galili, and it occurs to Barak that here is Golda's true white eminence, with snowy thick hair suited to his years. "It was getting close to a vote in the Security Council, and she wouldn't knuckle down to his terms, not until he promised to come straight here from Moscow and explain himself. He was worried enough to do as she insisted. I predicted that he would."

Later the bigwigs are lunching at a large U-shaped table with Golda at the head, Kissinger on her right, and Dayan on her left. At the foot of the table sits Barak, convenient to the orderly who brings him a despatch as he eats a compote dessert. One glance and he hurries it to Golda. She peers at it and passes it to Kissinger. He clinks a glass with a fork. "Gentlemen, I have the pleasure to tell you," he says, "that Egypt accepts the cease-fire terms."

The hand-clapping is temperate. "Interesting, isn't it, Mr. Secretary?" observes Dayan, with a shade of sarcasm. "They were pressing for the cease-fire, not us. Yet we accepted it the moment the Security Council voted it, ten hours ago, and they've waited until the very last minute to agree."

Kissinger says in his slow accented rumble, "Conceivably that has been done for domestic political reasons. In any case, it's a great relief."

"Your time is short, Mr. Secretary," says Golda aridly, "so let's go on to the military briefing."

"By all means."

In a smaller room lined with rows of chairs, Dado describes at a blown-up army map how Adan's division is about to cut off the Third Army at Suez, while Sharon, with smaller forces in worse terrain, is well on his way to Ismailia. It is a deliberate disclosure of top-secret battle intelligence, for Golda has ordered Dado to tell Kissinger everything.

"I thank you, General," he says to Dado. "You must understand that I was getting none of this information — none — in Moscow, though I pleaded and pleaded for it."

"Anyway, now you know," says Golda. "Can't you see what a difference a few hours would have made? In fact, would *still* make? And it would only strengthen your hand with the Soviets, Mr. Secretary. Against them, we've been fighting America's battle in the Middle East. You and I both know that."

"Well, anything that's really a matter of a few hours, Madame Prime Minister, can hardly be prevented by a cease-fire. There's always a little slippage in cease-fires, such as we encountered in Vietnam." He smiles ingenuously at her. "And now I really should be going, or my staff will be wondering whether I've decided to make aliya and stay here."

This unexpected sally about his own Jewishness brings a burst of relieving laughter from the Israelis. Dayan escorts him from the room and Golda says to the others, " '*Slippage*'! How do you like that? '*Slippage*'!"

Galili says, "No doubt Mr. Sadat knows all about slippage too."

"Well, if he tries it, we'll show him slippage," she says. "Excuse me, gentlemen, while I see our Jewish friend off."

In a mud-splattered uniform, rifle slung on her shoulder, Galia Barak stands by a runway watching dark shadows flit roaring across the faded orange streaks of sunset; Phantoms returning to Tel Nof, releasing their drogue parachutes as they land. Among the pilots leaving their planes she recognizes Dov Luria, shorter than the others and walking with his own jaunty spring, swinging his helmet. But Dov does not notice her, absorbed as he is in thinking ahead to this last debriefing (so it seems) of the war. Are the great scary days really over? He feels exhilarated at having survived, yet strangely let down. Much later, emerging from the squadron room, he halts amazed. "Galia! How did you manage this?"

"Glad to see me?" The demure smile is somewhat marred by the mud streaks on her face.

"Why, sure, but what to all the devils happened to you? You're red mud from head to foot."

"Oh, a stupid lorry went splashing through a puddle on the road and got me."

The bulky G suit makes their brief embrace awkward. As they walk to the base commander's quarters she tells him how, on hearing that Egypt accepted the cease-fire, she wheedled a twelve-hour leave from her supply depot supervisor. She laughs, hugging his arm. "It helped to tell him that my fiancé flies a Phantom."

"Syria still hasn't accepted," he says soberly, "and I'm sorry Egypt did. We'll soon see —"

"You're *sorry*? By your life, Dov, haven't you had enough of this rotten war?"

"Hamoodah, we had them on the run. We should have smashed them so they wouldn't try it again for twenty-five years. All this cease-fire does is throw a spanner in the works and save them. Damn Kissinger."

"Leave it to Golda. She knows what she's doing."

"Ha, en brera, poor Golda. What does your father say? Have you talked to him?"

"Not in days. Even my mother hasn't. He's never home."

Tea and cakes are on the table, where his parents and brother sit waiting for him. They greet Galia with warm badinage about her muddy state, and as she goes off to clean up, Danny presses Dov to describe his last strike. With the usual hand gestures and aviator jargon, Dov holds forth to the shiny-eyed redhead, now much taller than he is, while the parents exchange wry glances. "Anyway, it's stopping," says his mother, "and thank God for that! Now let the politicians pick up the pieces. A fine fashla they made of it."

"It isn't over, I bet," says Danny.

"It's over," says the base commander flatly. "I have no air operations scheduled for tomorrow. It's over, and none too soon." Both parents are relieved to their very souls that Dov has come through safe, though neither has said a word about it.

"We were told at the debriefing," says Dov, "that we remain on Aleph Alert."

"Of course," says his father. "That'll go on for a week, Dov, till we're sure the truce holds. Golda's broadcasting at eight, and we'll learn more then, but it's over."

"Well, then off with this suit for a while, eh?" He jumps up to kiss Galia with unabashed ardor as she returns, freshly washed and combed. "Motek, did I mention that your coming here was a great, great idea? I love you." The words and the kiss make her visit worthwhile. The suit smells of fuel and sweat. She adores the smell, the coarse suit, and the aviator inside it.

Coming on the air Golda Meir sounds exhausted and far from triumphant. Dr. Kissinger's visit has been reassuring. Positive developments are occurring in the direction of peace. The government has reason to believe that Syria will soon accept the cease-fire. Lasting good is bound to come out of the enormous sacrifices and brilliant victories of this hard war. The Jewish people owe eternal gratitude to the fighters who threw back the enemy, above all to the heroes who fell. So she concludes. As the Israel Philharmonic recording of "Hatikvah" follows, throbbing and melancholy, Dov drops his head on an arm. Over the music, he says in a muffled voice, "*Itzik . . . Eric . . . Heshi . . .* it stopped too soon. Too soon."

Galia puts an arm around him, and his father says huskily, "You did more than enough."

That night the engaged couple are in Dov's room, listening to a Mozart piano concerto. At least, that is what his father hears through the door when he knocks, several times. "Dov? Dov?"

A pause, then a hoarse reply. "Yes, Abba?"

"Can I talk to you?"

"Well, in a moment." It is quite a long moment. "Sure, come in."

Galia and Dov are fully clothed, if somewhat intertwined, and they both look amused and a bit sheepish. "Want to hear some Mozart?" says Dov. "Sit down and join us, Abba."

"I think you'd better get some sleep, hamood. I'll have Galia driven to the bus stop."

Dov extricates himself and sits up straight. "What's happening?"

"The cease-fire is being violated right and left." Benny Luria's face is set in his hard wartime look. "Base is back on red alert. Word from central headquarters, *'Prepare for strikes at dawn.'* "

Galia clutches Dov's hand hard.

"So it's on with the suit," he says. "Big surprise."

After managing an uneasy doze of a few hours, Dov walks to the revetments in early twilight. "Well, Yaakov," he says to his plane captain, with a slap on the Phantom fuselage, "Is G'mali ready to ride again?" "Camel, My Camel" is a popular Yemenite song, and Dov has long since dubbed his aircraft G'mali, My Camel.

The dark-skinned sergeant grins. "G'mali ready and eager, sir."

As Dov settles into his ejection seat and Yaakov hooks him up, a familiar unwelcome thought recurs. *Of all things, let me not have to eject over Egypt.* To be transformed in an instant from a winged warrior, crossing the sky at twice the speed of sound, to a pathetic dangler on parachute cords, falling into angry probably murderous hands . . . *Shut it out, shut it out.* One more ride, maybe a few more, and back to Galia.

Ignition!

Four Phantoms howl into the upper air, where the sunrise of October 23 glints on their wings. An hour later, as the base commander waits at the runway, peering into the sky, three return from that flight. Benny Luria waits and waits. Only three.

In two days of continuing "slippage" on both sides, a superpower confrontation unmatched since the Cuban missile crisis now blows up. Amid all the recriminations only one battlefield fact is clear: the Egyptian Third Army is trapped in the Sinai desert, south of the Great Bitter Lake. Its repeated efforts to break out have failed. Some forty-five thousand battle-worn soldiers and two hundred fifty tanks are cut off from water, food, fuel, and medical supplies in the barren sandy wastes, with nothing to save them but intervention by outside forces.

Anwar Sadat's demands for succor increase in stridency by the day, until General Secretary Brezhnev himself warns President Nixon that unless the United States will agree to joint military action to relieve the Third Army, the Soviet Union may unilaterally intervene. This kicks off a high state of alarm in Washington. Chilling CIA reports confirm that seven Russian airborne divisions are now on full alert, a Soviet flotilla is moving through the Dardanelles with detectable nuclear cargo on two of the ships, and most ominous of all, the Soviet airlift in the huge Antonov transports *has ceased*. Those are the planes that take airborne troops into combat.

During a long night while Richard Nixon, beset by eight separate Senate impeachment motions over Watergate, is trying to get some sleep, the crisis mounts. An emergency meeting at the White House of military and cabinet leaders, chaired by Secretary of State Kissinger, takes some tough steps: the return of B-52 bombers from Guam, the despatch of more aircraft carriers to the eastern Mediterranean, and in Germany the Eighty-second Airborne Division called to the highest state of readiness. Most drastic of all, an urgent warning flashes to American forces worldwide of a preliminary nuclear alert, *DEFCON THREE*.

Toward dawn, when Soviet intelligence is bound to have picked up all these signals, President Nixon's reply goes to Brezhnev, cautioning that unilateral action by the Soviet Union will bring "incalculable consequences"; and a few hours later at a Security Council meeting Egypt withdraws the request for joint superpower action. With this the Soviet Union is off the hook, and the crisis abates. The Russian trump card of unilateral intervention, whether bluff or threat, has been called, and it has failed to relieve the Third Army.

That same morning a wild hullabaloo ensues in the United States over the short-lived nuclear alert, with angry hints in Congress and the media that the President faked the entire emergency as a distraction from Watergate. The whole world is in shock from the brief bloodcurdling doomsday moment. The Security Council is paralyzed. In a sudden reversal, the Americans find that the plight of the Third Army is now on their hands, the Russians having been foiled as rescuers, and Dr. Kissinger's role shifts to an all-out clash with Golda Meir over a UN proposal to send a "humanitarian convoy" with nonmilitary supplies to the Third Army. Golda demands, as a quid pro quo, that Egypt not only agree to return all prisoners swiftly, but to negotiate face to face with Israel the terms of a genuine cease-fire.

At this Sadat balks, bound by the Khartoum pledge, *No recognition of Israel, no peace with Israel, no negotiation with Israel.* But Golda too holds firm, under heavy American pressure; face-to-face dealing, or no convoy! Near midnight Friday, October 26, Kissinger warns Ambassador Dinitz that if Israel prefers to be raped, very well, she will be forced to yield. The Security Council is meeting in about nine hours, and if by then Golda has not given in on the convoy, the United States will not oppose whatever action is voted to relieve the Third Army; possibly including sanctions against Israel as well as the landing in Egypt of Soviet troops! "You are committing suicide," he admonishes the ambassador.

At that moment Saturday the twenty-seventh has already dawned in Cairo and Jerusalem. The sun comes up, baking the besieged, waterless, and foodless Third Army. In Washington in the dark of night, Kissinger waits. Two hours later Golda cables a reply which Kissinger himself in exasperation calls a great stall. "I HAVE NO ILLUSION BUT THAT EVERYTHING WILL BE IMPOSED ON US BY THE TWO BIG POWERS. . . . JUST TELL US PRECISELY WHAT WE MUST DO IN ORDER THAT EGYPT MAY ANNOUNCE A VICTORY OF HER AGGRESSION." To this masterful vagueness, which the sleepless Kissinger receives in Washington at 2:10 A.M., he never manages to reply, because within the half-hour *Sadat agrees to open direct talks with Israel.*

Golda takes Dinitz's call with this news in her small inner office. As the ambassador slowly dictates the Egyptian message relayed via Kissinger, Zev Barak, listening on an extension line, copies it down. President Sadat proposes a meeting of generals at Kilometer 101 on the road to Cairo, well inside Zahal-held territory, at three that very afternoon.

When they hang up, Prime Minister and military secretary look at each other for long seconds without words. "Note the time, Zev," she says.

"I have, Madame Prime Minister, *ten-sixteen A.M., Saturday, October 27, 1973.*"

"And when is that hangman Security Council meeting scheduled to begin?"

"In New York, eight A.M. Less than five hours from now."

"So, it's been close. Close." With a deep noisy sigh she leans back in her chair and stretches out thick brown-clad ankles.

"Madame Prime Minister, I didn't think I'd live to see this day." Zev Barak is shaken with relief, astonishment, and exaltation. "The Khartoum pledge is dead. Egypt originated it, and now Egypt has voided it. The Third Army's situation must be desperate."

"Well, Sadat's evidently is."

"Will he survive this, Madame Prime Minister?"

"Survive?" Her voice takes on a metallic timbre. "Survive? Sadat is the hero of this war. He dared."

"And you? You've beaten Egypt, Syria, Russia, and Henry Kissinger, Madame Prime Minister, and you've won the war."

"Don't exaggerate." She wearily wags a reproving finger at him. Then she telephones the Minister of Defense to set up the meeting of generals in Africa at Kilometer 101. "Moshe Dayan is surprised and impressed," she says, hanging up. "Now listen, Zev, Kissinger isn't an enemy. He has just been doing his job." With a faint grin she adds, "He did get a bit annoyed with me. As for winning the war, let's wait and see if those Egyptian generals show up at Kilometer 101, and if they do, let's hear what they have to say." Lighting a cigarette she inquires, squinting, "So is there any news of Benny Luria's son?"

"Thank you for asking. Galia tells me a pilot from another flight believes he saw Dov eject as his plane went down. So now we wait for the prisoner exchange, and she's feeling more cheerful."

Grim folds deepen on Golda's face. "The prisoners. That will be the real test. In Moscow the Russians promised Kissinger swift return of the prisoners as part of the cease-fire deal. But can they make Sadat deliver?"

The wind is the worst. It has sprung up about midnight at Kilometer 101, blowing sand that obscures the stars, whipping and whining through the open tent, swaying the portable lamps to make leaping shadows, covering the tacked-down maps on the field tables with fine sand, and chilling to the bone the four sleepy Israeli generals.

"Enough," says Sam Pasternak to Major General Aharon Yariv, a short sharp-faced former chief of military intelligence. "I'm putting on my Hermonit, and —"

"Wait!" Yariv covers the mouthpiece of the field telephone. "They're really coming now, Sam. They've been held up at the Kilometer 85 outpost. . . . Very good," he says into the telephone, "we're ready for them, and waiting."

"What a balagan," groans a black-bearded paratroop general, who has been asleep with his head on the table. "How late are they now? Eleven hours?"

"It's the communications," says Yariv. "Terrible. The latest thing was, at Kilometer 85 the UN man had to telephone his superior in New York, about arranging for an Israeli patrol to escort them behind our front lines."

"Most diplomatic," says Pasternak, "since it might be indelicate to suggest a white flag."

"So?" asks the paratrooper. "How long did that have to take?"

"Well, New York had to contact Washington to clear the idea with Cairo. Before calling Cairo, Washington had to speak to Jerusalem. All this took about an hour and a half. Otherwise, from

Kilometer 85 those Egyptians could have driven here in ten minutes."

"Through Zahal-held territory," says the bald corpulent armor general, munching on a sandwich. "That UN man was prudent."

"I'm famished," says the paratrooper.

"Have some more turkey salami, there's plenty," says Yariv.

"To the devil with this wind," says Pasternak. He pulls a small bottle from a pocket. "Who else will have brandy?"

"Easy," says Yariv. "You're representing Israel."

"I didn't ask for the great honor." Pasternak throws coffee dregs out of a paper cup and pours it full.

He was in fact selected somewhat casually. Encountering him outside the Kirya that morning, Yariv said, "Good. You're coming with me to Africa."

"What for?"

"To negotiate with the Egyptians at Kilometer 101."

"Why me?"

"You're a major general, and you're around."

Pasternak tosses down the brandy and coughs. "Ah. That helps, but I'm still getting into my Hermonit." He goes out to the helicopter, leaning against the wind. Throwing the air force jacket inside the aircraft, he takes out and puts on a quilted jumpsuit, the kind worn on Mount Hermon by snowbound soldiers. When he returns to the tent Yariv and the others are brushing sand off the maps, to review the disputed cease-fire lines and the proposed route of the UN–Red Cross convoy.

"What do we do when those Egyptians show up?" asks the armor general. "Shake hands? Offer them folding chairs? Do we do the whole thing standing up? Are we cordial? Do we offer them turkey salami?"

The paratrooper, who is eating several slices of it on bread, begins to gobble. The armor man chimes in. "Look, we're all tired," expostulates Yariv, "and put out by waiting here so long in the wind and the cold. But we're making history, and let's be equal to the occasion."

The sense of making history does steal over Pasternak when he hears the vehicles approach and stop. The Jewish generals line themselves up on one side of the table, and in walk four erect unsmiling Egyptians in full faultless uniform with medals; a decided contrast to the Jews, three of them bareheaded in bulky air force jackets, the plump Pasternak in his jumpsuit and fur hood.

"Major General Aharon Yariv?" inquires a stiffly straight Egyptian in a deep voice.

"I am Yariv."

"I am Gamasy, my delegation's leader." The Egyptian salutes. This is the Chief of Staff of the Egyptian army.

Yariv returns the salute, and a round of salutes and introductions follows. There are no handshakes. An orderly brings chairs, the eight major generals sit down facing each other, and the parley begins as the wind whistles and the sand blows. The Egyptians unfold maps to compare with those on the table. The talk is in English. At first it is about matching place names, but soon the Egyptian leader switches to the convoy route. That has to be settled at once.

"A concurrent topic," Yariv replies, "has to be the immediate exchange of prisoners."

"On that I have no instructions."

"I do. The convoy passes when arrangements for the prisoner exchange are confirmed. Not before."

"But that is a political, not a military, matter."

The officer facing Pasternak is shaking all over. Pasternak inquires in an undertone, "Are you ill, General?"

"General, I was sent out here without warning, except to put on full dress uniform. As the Americans say, I am freezing my balls off."

Pasternak jumps up, leaves the tent, and comes back with an air force jacket. "Wear this, General."

The Egyptian glances at his leader, who nods. He pulls it on and zips it up. Yariv says to General Gamasy, "Perhaps that's a good idea for all of you, General."

"We accept," says the leader with a sudden charming smile. When the talk resumes, there are seven officers at the table in Israeli Air Force jackets, and one in a Hermonit. The parley lasts about an hour. As the Egyptians are folding up their maps, Yariv says, "Everything we have discussed, General, is conditional on satisfactory arrangements for a prisoner exchange."

"I will bring an answer to our next meeting."

The paratrooper general speaks up. "Sir, a nephew of mine was captured in the Quay stronghold of the Bar-Lev Line. Can you get word about him? I'd be very grateful."

"I can try. Please write down his name and rank."

Pasternak says to Gamasy, "General, I'd be grateful if you could bring word about another prisoner, a Phantom pilot." He scrawls *Captain Dov Luria* on a chit.

The general opposite him, to whom he first offered a jacket, holds out his hand. "Let me see to that. A relative of yours?"

"Son of a close friend."

The Egyptian tucks away the chit and unzips the air force jacket. "Many thanks for this."

"Gentlemen," Yariv says, "it will be a cold ride back to Cairo. Accept the jackets with Israel's good will."

The Egyptian leader removes his jacket and folds it on the table. The others follow suit, salute, and walk out, leaving four jackets lying across the cease-fire maps.

Arik Sharon and Don Kishote are lunching in the shade of the lush green mango orchard where Sharon's command APCs have halted near Ismailia, amid an array of field tents, and scores of tanks undergoing noisy maintenance. On the high Egyptian ramparts off to the east, large Israeli flags wave in the strong wind.

"Politics, Kishote. Politics. In the middle of a war, with boys dying, politics to the end." Sharon appears much rested, if no less angry and bellicose; unshaven and shaggy-haired, but with bright eyes and good color. The bandage is gone, leaving a red scar on his temple. He slices a thick piece of yellow cheese and lays it on fresh bread. "But that gang has not heard the last of Arik Sharon."

"Arik, you sent for me urgently?"

"Absolutely." Sharon's anger fades into a cold professional tone. "You know about the meeting at Kilometer 101? A huge convoy — a '*humanitarian*' convoy" — the sarcasm is as thick as the cheese slice — "is en route from Cairo to Suez."

"So I've heard."

"It's true. Hundreds of trucks, enough to keep the Third Army alive for weeks. I want you to be there when the stuff arrives at the Canal, and keep a sharp eye on the search and transfer procedures."

"At your orders, sir."

"Medical supplies!" Sharon's eyes slyly narrow at Yossi. "Remember when the British were searching our convoys to Jerusalem?"

"I came from Cyprus after the British left, Arik, when the war was on."

"So? Well, I tell you, our nurses were carrying grenades in their brassieres and by your life, in their crotches! We found plenty of ways to smuggle in arms and ammunition. Now, you report to me by telephone, and if there's the slightest funny business, I'll raise a howl with Dayan that you'll hear down there in Suez."

"Arik, it's a UN and Red Cross convoy. I don't know the Security Council's stand on searching brassieres." Sharon grunts a laugh. Kishote adds, "Not to mention more restricted areas."

"I leave it to you. Dayan was here yesterday, Kishote, and commended your performance at Deversoir. I'm sure you'd rather have been up front." With a savage grin he adds, "Next war."

"I hope there won't be one, sir."

"Well, if we throw out that Labor gang and get some real leadership, maybe not. Our enemies will remember this beating for a good while, anyway."

Driving along and behind the front lines, checking the supply depots as he wends south to Suez, Yossi sees evidence everywhere that Zahal is near the end of its rope. The tragic backwash of the crossing — the streams of vehicles heading east with dead and wounded, the disabled tanks, wrecked APCs, and self-propelled guns being towed back for salvage — all that gives him a dark view of the victory. So have the final orders from Tel Aviv to the advancing brigades: *"Charge ahead carefully . . . we don't want any Stalingrads . . ."* Here in Africa he sees no exulting victors, but bewhiskered hollow-eyed youngsters, sunk in deep fatigue and on a nervous edge. If the war starts again tomorrow — and the Arabs will certainly go if they see any hope of gain — these boys will certainly get back into the tanks, the APCs, the command cars, and fight again. With the air support they now can count on, they might well cut off more Egyptian forces. But to what end? Cairo declared an open city, and occupied by Jewish soldiers? Then what?

With such dismal musings, Don Kishote stands beside Natke Nir in the break of the rampart where the convoy vehicles are unloading. The line of Red Cross trucks flying blue UN banners and gaudy Egyptian flags stretches out of sight along the narrow road to Suez City, which still smokes on the horizon from Bren Adan's assault.

"Look at them, Kishote," growls the gnarled little brigade commander, limping forward for a better look at the Israeli pontoon boats being loaded up by Egyptian soldiers. Several boats are already on the other side, where Third Army soldiers have lined up in human chains, singing and cheering as they pass crates and barrels. "Look at them! For three weeks they've been killing my men, and now we're saving their lives. Yesterday we sent over five tons of our own medical supplies, and eight tank trucks of water. For what? Why? Because of Kissinger. That Jew Kissinger, who stopped us from crushing them once for all. I swear, Yossi, if Kissinger were standing where you are —" Natke draws his pistol, brandishes it, and grinds his teeth. "By my life, I'd shoot him through the heart. God damn Kissinger."

"Natke, you're wrong," says Don Kishote. "Thank God for Kissinger."

Natke Nir stares at him in stupefaction, as the Egyptians sing and cheer on both sides of the Canal.

32

Nakhama and Emily

Emily Halliday has not been in the King David Hotel in seventeen years, and like an old love song the unchanged lobby wakes poignant memories. She remembers her thunderstruck surprise when Zev Barak came through that revolving door, she remembers the small shabby room where they listened to Ben Gurion's speech, she remembers that first kiss which ran through her body like a live-wire shock and made her cry with joy. And here comes General Barak through that same revolving door, white-haired but otherwise hardly changed. "Welcome, delighted to see you both." Same deep warm voice and slight charming accent. "My car is just outside."

General Halliday insists on putting her beside Barak in the front seat, asking as he gets in the back, "How's your navy son, Barak?"

"Still at sea with his flotilla, thank you."

"We've had good reports about your navy's role in the war."

"It did well. You and I will visit the base in Haifa, and the CNO will brief you on the sea campaign. The battle off Latakia has interesting aspects. Yes, you might say our navy found itself in this war. And you might say we almost lost ourselves."

"It came out all right," says the American.

"Not at that cost. But the bill was presented, so we paid it."

Sitting beside Barak, hearing his voice, her senses stirring with the King David remembrances, Emily feels nineteen years old and vibrantly alive, and at the same time all too weighted with the years.

Nakhama opens the door in a plain pink housedress and a white apron. "Hello, welcome."

In all that thick black hair Emily sees not one silver thread. She has hundreds. Thousands. "Nakhama, this is my husband, Bradford Halliday."

Zev's wife gives Halliday a warm smile and a firm handshake. "Well, Zev's told me a lot about you, General."

"How are your girls?" Emily asks when they are at table, and Nakhama is serving a spicy-smelling soup. "They must be young women, both of them."

"Ruti is still in high school. Galia's engaged, but her fiancé's missing in action, Phantom pilot."

Halliday perks up. "F-4? He must be good. Was he hit by a missile? Was he seen to eject?"

Barak tells him what he knows of Dov's disappearance. Halliday soberly nods. "I was in the F-4 for years. It's a tough workhorse, it can take a lot and keep going. In Vietnam we rescued many a Phantom pilot who crash-landed and was missing for a while. Tell your daughter not to lose hope."

"I will," says Nakhama. "Coming from you, it'll mean a lot."

The men talk about the war, and Barak almost ignores Emily — which is all right with her — describing how the navy's electronic countermeasures outclassed the opposing Soviet equipment. "We take some pride in that," he says. "Product of Israel, all of it."

"You should. We were disappointed that the stuff we sent to shield your Phantoms didn't do the job."

"So were we. It took combat testing to find that out, and some losses."

Halliday looks rueful. "We sent the best we had."

"I'm sure of that. We're still analyzing the data from two aircraft that went down, and one that got through. It's voluminous."

"We'll be grateful to see that material."

"Of course you'll see it all."

The telephone rings. Barak talks Hebrew in low tones, then inquires, holding the phone, "General, are you very tired?"

"Not in the least. Why?"

"General Elazar can meet you this evening, after all. Change of plans. He's here in Jerusalem, and he's free right now. Otherwise day after tomorrow as scheduled, in Tel Aviv."

"Let's go now, by all means."

"Very good. The army is sending a car, and the driver will take Emily back to the hotel."

Nakhama interjects, "Why? I can do that."

"Or I'll walk. It's not far," says Emily. Here is a chance to have it out with Zev's wife.

When the men have left, Nakhama asks, pouring tea, "So, how long will you be in Israel?"

"Not as long as Bud. I'll be off to Paris day after tomorrow."

"Paris. I've yet to see Paris," Nakhama sighs. "Can you imagine? We've been to Athens, Rome, even London. He's been to Paris, but I haven't."

Remembering well her Paris times with Wolf, Emily holds her tongue and drinks tea. Nakhama rambles on. "Well, I can't blame you for cutting short your visit here. Israel's a sad place these days. We're still very shaken up by the war. Zev was surprised to hear that General Halliday was bringing you."

"I asked to come, and Bud was nice about it. Sort of a going-away present."

"Going away? I don't understand."

"We're getting divorced."

Nakhama opens great eyes. "You're serious?"

"Oh, quite. I'll be looking for a flat in Paris. Let me help you clear those dishes."

"Sit where you are, it won't take a minute and we'll go."

"If you're like me," Emily says, getting up and collecting plates, "you can't walk out the door leaving dishes unwashed."

Nakhama laughs. "Well, you're very nice. Don't stain that lovely suit."

In the breakfast alcove near the sink, Emily sits down, saying,

"I don't find Israel a sad place. Lively traffic, people going about their business. Things seem back to normal here, pretty much."

Nakhama shakes her head as she rinses dishes. "Not so. Not at the borders, and certainly not in our spirits. Listen, you amaze me. Why the divorce? Or would you rather not talk about it?"

"I don't mind. It's simple enough. Bud found himself a great love, which I never was, truth to tell. He's been open and honest about it, and he's made very decent arrangements for me and the children. I don't complain."

"A great love, you say?"

"Secretary of a friend. A beautiful Norwegian. At least he finds her beautiful."

"You don't?"

"Far from it. But you know how that is."

Nakhama dries her hands. "I suppose I'm lucky."

"How so?"

"Well, Zev found a great love, but he stuck to me."

The two women's eyes meet. "Good God, Nakhama," Emily chokes out.

Nakhama shrugs. "It's true, isn't it?"

"Christ almighty! Are all Israeli women like you? You're the damnedest woman I've ever known." Unable to help it, Emily wipes her eyes.

"Why do you say that? Look, how about a glass of wine before we go?"

"If you have whiskey, better yet."

Nakhama goes out and comes back with a dusty brown bottle. "Canadian Club, is that whiskey?"

"That's fine, thanks."

"We have no soda. Will it go with Pepsi-Cola?"

"Nakhama, just pour it in a glass, will you? No ice, no water, nothing."

"Right. I'll keep you company with a little wine."

Emily gulps the whiskey. "Ahhh. Best medicine for jet lag. Or for practically anything."

"Have more."

"Yes, please."

"Let me tell you something," says Nakhama, pouring red wine for herself. "I've been jealous of you for years. Any Israeli woman would be. Sometimes so jealous it made me nasty and sick, not a good wife. But lately I had a real deep change of heart, when Zev went off to Washington to try to get an airlift. The war was so terrible, and my son was fighting out at sea, and Dov — that's Galia's intended — was flying against those missiles, and there went my husband on such a vital mission, and I thought, so what if he sees Emily Halliday? So *what*? For *what,* all these years, have I been eating out my kishkas? Kishkas are intestines."

"I gather that." Emily holds out her glass.

Nakhama fills it again. "The truth is, we married too young. I was a very, very pretty girl, Emily, but I never was a book reader, I'm not an intellectual, not really a match for Zev —"

"Balderdash, he adores you."

"I said I'm lucky, and I know it. But your letters mean the world to him, and so do you, and I can understand why. But it hasn't been easy for me, and —"

"He's stopped writing."

Nakhama blinks. "I didn't know that."

"He thinks it annoys or upsets you."

"Should I talk to him about that? I'll be glad to. What's wrong with letters?"

Emily is speechless. All the way to Israel she has been marshalling arguments to convince the wife that the correspondence is innocuous. The wind is knocked out of her.

"You know," Nakhama goes on, pouring still more Canadian Club for her, "we've had this old bottle here for years. I forget who gave it to us. I've never tasted the stuff. Is it good?"

"It's strong."

"I'll try it." She puts some into her empty wineglass. "Oo-ah. Burns going down, doesn't it? Where was I? Well, what's more, Zev is an Ashkenazi, you see, and I'm a Sephardi. Both my parents were Moroccan immigrants. He's from an old Zionist family, originally Polish, later Viennese. We're the black Jews, the *'second Israel,'* they're the whites, and believe me, his mother let me know it. To her dying day she didn't let me forget it, and —"

"Truly? Among Jews, race distinctions?"

"Oh, yes, yes. Now remember that time in that cottage of yours in Middleburg, when you were so embarrassed about the pistachio nuts?"

Emily feels a flush from her toes to her scalp. It remains a horrible if buried memory, when Nakhama came to the Growlery and caught sight of the pistachios she kept set out for Zev.

"I remember," she manages to say.

Nakhama says matter-of-factly, "It almost killed me."

"You never turned a hair."

"What was I to do? Remember I said then that it was all right? It cost me blood but I said it. You gave him something I couldn't, and I realized that. I still do, and I say it again, it's all right."

"Nakhama, for God's sake, let's go."

"B'seder. Oo-ah, that Canadian Club. I'll talk to Zev about the letters. Really, it's all right."

As they come outside Nakhama is weaving along the sidewalk, and Emily is not too steady herself. Muttering in Hebrew, Nakhama has trouble fitting the key into the Peugeot's ignition.

"Nakhama, are you up to driving?"

"Well, we'll soon know, won't we?" She runs Emily to the King David in minutes, stopping for red lights and doing nothing bizarre, except turning too wide on one curve and mounting a sidewalk, causing pedestrians to dodge and yell in Hebrew. "Oo-ah, that's hard on the tires," she remarks. She sweeps up the driveway of the hotel and squeals to a stop. "Here we are."

"Thank you for everything."

"For what? Listen, Emily, if I were you I wouldn't give up on a man like General Halliday. He's very impressive. I'd fight that Swede."

"She's Norwegian."

"Sorry, Norwegian. Here we get these blond women coming down after our men, and mostly they're Swedes. Give her a battle."

"Good night, Nakhama."

"Well, I know I should mind my own business. Good night, then. I'll talk to Zevvy about the letters."

Sandbagged, thinks Emily, walking back into the memory-haunted lobby. Sandbagged again by Nakhama, the nonintellectual. Gone, the comforting fantasy of eventual romantic interludes in Paris with the White Wolf, once she is free. It's all right with Nakhama, so it's impossible.

Zevvy!

"Come on up, Barak," says Halliday on the house phone, two days later. The clock over the King David reception desk reads 8 A.M. "Suite 708."

"Hi." Emily opens the door in the dark gray pantsuit she wore to the Israel Philharmonic concert, where as usual Nakhama fell asleep.

"Hi, still here? I thought you'd be off at the crack of dawn." Beige leather suitcases and a hatbox are stacked near the door.

"My doing," says Halliday. In a golf sweater and an open shirt, he is rapidly writing on a yellow legal pad. "She's taking a later plane. Look, can you and I put off leaving for Haifa till about ten?"

"No problem."

Emily asks, "Is the Wailing Wall far from here? I seem to have a couple of hours to kill."

"Twenty minutes or so by foot. Five minutes by car. I'll take you there."

"Lovely. I'll put on walking shoes."

Halliday says as she goes out, "Thanks, Barak. She's a mite annoyed."

"My pleasure."

Left alone, General Halliday writes busily for half an hour, then stretches, and rereads:

King David Hotel
Jerusalem, Israel
2 November 1973

Personal and Secret

Dear Mr. Secretary:

My mission in Israel is to report to you on one question: *what will be the effect here if the United States relieves the Third Army with an airlift?* Herewith I offer my best judgment, responding to your urgent telephone call at three o'clock this morning, local time. I met with the Chief of Staff, Lieutenant General David Elazar, the first night I got here, for a long frank talk. When I mentioned the possibility of an American airlift for those besieged Egyptians, his answer was a poker-faced shrug. Elazar is a hardbitten man who fought a tough war and wants a viable end to hostilities, so his reaction was predictable.

The Prime Minister's military secretary, Major General Barak (the white-haired gent who recently came to Washington), suggested a helicopter tour of the combat theater, and I accepted. From the air, the Jews and Arabs at first seem to have fought a Disneyland war in a tiny mock-up of a war zone. But by the figures Barak provided, the tank battles rivaled Kursk and El Alamein in real numbers of tanks involved, and total war deaths were comparable to World War II, in percentage of population. The Israelis are consequently in a state of shocked gloom. There is a general sense here that they lost the war, whereas they won a most remarkable comeback victory, or we wouldn't be planning an airlift to save an entire Egyptian army from destruction.

Flying over the Golan Heights and the Suez Canal, one sees two extensive blasted battlefields where the Jews took the worst the Syrians and Egyptians could throw at them. They won both battles by a whisker. These two Middle East Verduns, which they call the Valley of Tears and the Valley of Death, saved them from losing the war; and then they forced President Sadat to cry uncle with the audacious crossing of the Canal by General Sharon, and the cutting off of the Third Army by the lesser-known but very able General Adan. We flew over the Second Army's lodgment north of the Great Bitter Lake, which the Israelis did not quite succeed in cutting off, so its supply lines seem to be functioning, though it's immobilized. But looking down on the Third Army lodgment, I could understand Mrs. Meir's intransigence. Over many square miles of barren wasteland, thousands of machines and tens of thousands of soldiers are languishing in a sunbaked death trap. That's her ace in the hole in negotiating a disengagement.

We lunched with General Sharon at his field headquarters in an

Egyptian orchard, and afterward his deputy, Brigadier General Nitzan, took me by jeep to the Canal. At a paratroop battalion camp in a melon field he stopped, summoned the men into a big semicircle, and talked in Hebrew. Looking at those unshaven haggard frontline troops, I almost felt myself back in Vietnam. They broke into applause when he said that I was an American Air Force general. We crossed the Canal on a giant prefabricated steel structure floating on rollers, and Nitzan told me how its construction was forced on Israel because they couldn't buy mobile bridges from us or anyone else. This bizarre Jewish improvisation may well have saved the Sharon attack. Nitzan spread a map on his jeep hood to argue that if the Third Army were set free to fight again, the Israeli forces now in Egypt could find themselves trapped in turn. That was pretty much General Elazar's contention, but out there in the field it made hard sense.

When the helicopter got back to Tel Aviv, Barak had not yet mentioned the airlift to the Third Army, so I put the question to him again. "I've answered you," he said, "as well as I can."

Now for my own view. Operationally the airlift will be simple. Landing rights in Europe will of course be no problem. It will certainly sour our relationship with the Jews, and this is something to think about. I opposed the airlift to Israel, yet I have to say we're getting value received. We now have access to the entire spectrum of captured Russian war matériel, of which they showed me vast arrays. They are compiling and offering us vital data about all that booty, and a serious study mission should come here as soon as possible.

Mr. Secretary, one can sit in Washington and hold to George Marshall's judgment that the Jewish State is a historical mistake and anomaly, but on the ground here this view seems overtaken by events. I was sobered by seeing those two battlefields and those paratroopers. I remain an advocate of the proposed airlift as a major gesture to Arab pride and welfare, and a probable end to the oil embargo, which threatens the security of NATO. As De Gaulle said, nations are cold monsters, and the United States must act in its own national interest. Yet writing from Jerusalem, to be quite frank, it becomes a close call. These people won't shoot down our C-5As, but I doubt Mrs. Meir will bend.

My wife is leaving for Paris this morning, and she will deliver this report to the embassy there (possibly more secure than the one in Tel Aviv) for the diplomatic pouch.

Respectfully,
Bradford Halliday

When Barak and Emily emerge from the hotel into a breezy sunny morning, she exclaims, "God, two whole hours with you. Am I dreaming? Look, we don't have to walk to the Wall, I just said the first thing that came into my head."

"Emily, why the delay?"

"I don't ask Bud questions. When I woke up he was changing my reservation."

"Have you ever seen the Wall?"

"No, but I'm not in a wailing mood. Except at parting from you. But that's our thing, isn't it, sweetie? Snatched hours and hurried farewells."

"Nobody wails at the Wall anymore, Queenie. We call it the Western Wall. It's a nice walk. Come."

"Say, Zev, who is this Don Quixote?" They are passing the old windmill at the head of a steep stone staircase to the valley.

"Eh? Oh, that's Sharon's deputy. Hang on, Queenie!"

She is stumbling on the rough stones, going down. "Wow! I sure will. Why Quixote? Is he a little nuts?"

"Far from it. Nicknames just catch on sometimes. Why do you ask about him?"

"He intrigued Bud."

"Understandable. He's a brigadier general, very able." He makes her laugh, describing how Yossi at sixteen showed up at Latrun on a mule, a long skinny figure in a tin hat with a broomstick, and went galloping onto the battlefield. Then he asks abruptly, "Em, did you tell Nakhama that I had stopped writing?" He glances at her and Emily says nothing. "I gather you and Nakhama had quite a talk."

"We yatted a bit, yes."

"What about?"

"Oh, girl stuff." Crossing the valley bridge they have to dart through the heavy traffic grinding up and down the Jaffa Gate road. "Ye gods, last time I was here this was all no-man's-land, Wolf. Barbed wire, sandbags, machine-gun nests, and the road was deserted, quiet as death."

"Never again. Now let's see. The short way is through Zion Gate, but let's do Jaffa Gate. Arab market, more colorful."

"Lead on. No problems with the Arabs?"

"Not now."

They trudge up the steep hill, where busses, trucks, and cars go by in a great racket, belching fumes. "You know," he raises his voice, "if King Hussein hadn't attacked us in the Six-Day War, all this would still be quiet as death. Two weeks ago, when we were in very deep trouble, he could have walked in and taken back all he lost. But he sat on his hands."

"Timing is everything in love and war, eh, old White Wolf? And mine's even lousier than King Hussein's."

"Poor, poor Queenie." He takes her hand and kisses it.

"Yowie, bingo! When in doubt, turn on the self-pity. The men are suckers for it."

Rifle-toting soldiers in the arch of the Jaffa Gate stare at the brigadier general and the fancy foreign lady in the pantsuit. At the shops in the arcades, merchants are setting out their wares. Emily gives a huge sniff as they pass a fragrant bakery. "Know what? I'm absolutely starving. I've had one cup of coffee today."

"Okay, this way." He leads her into a crooked stone byway. "I have three vices, Queenie. Two you know about, pistachios and yourself. I'll now disclose the third."

Inside the small dark shop, Arabs in work clothes are eating at bare Formica tables, and older men in long robes sit around a hookah smoking through long coiling tubes, amid pleasant smells of coffee, fresh-baked bread, and aromatic tobacco. A stout black-mustached shopkeeper welcomes Barak with a gold-toothed smile, and they chat in Arabic. The other customers ignore the uniformed Israeli officer and the foreign woman.

"Is your Arabic really good?" she asks, over fine thick coffee.

"Well, when I served in Central Command I spent much time with Arabs."

"You get along with them?"

"I like them." She raises her eyebrows. "I do, Em. Mind you, theirs is another world, and always will be. They're bitter, angry, and miserable — and that's partly our doing — ah, here we are." An urchin brings two round pans full of a brownish pastry. "Try this. It's rather sweet."

After one warm mouthful she gasps, "*Rather* sweet? Yikes, what is this stuff? I've just swallowed four thousand calories."

"Klafi. This place is my opium den."

"Can I have one of those flat breads instead?"

The proprietor himself brings it to her with a courtly bow. "This is more like it," she says, tearing and eating the bread with gusto. "My God, *look* at you. How can you choke that gunk down?"

"I sneak over here once in a great while. I'm a klafi fiend."

Afterward they traverse stone arcades, always going downhill, until the wide plaza comes in sight. Emily halts to scan the scene below; the wheeling crying birds, the green plants growing high up among the great stones, the soldiers on nearby roofs standing guard with guns at the ready, while knots of worshippers are at their prayers all along the Wall. "So that's it," she says. "That's what's left of your Temple."

"That's just the retaining wall. The Temple was on the Mount above, where the mosques are now. So the archaeologists say."

"My father told me that the Wailing Wall was in a squalid dark blind alley."

"It was. No more. We'll taxi back to the hotel. Your time's short."

"With you when isn't it short?"

In the cab she lightly kisses his mouth. "There, old Wolf. For auld lang syne."

"Queenie, why were you so hesitant to come? I telephoned you the minute I heard Halliday would head the mission. Why did you just hem and haw?"

"Dearest, how could I know how he'd react? But he was as nice as pie about bringing me. Maybe he's working off his guilt this way. Speaking of which —" She has to catch her breath as he seizes her and kisses her hard. "Back off, back off. I'll be goddamned if I'll take on any more guilt about foolery like this. It's hopeless and futile. Your Nakhama is a world genius at making me feel like a dog caught stealing a steak."

"Stealing a bone, you once put it."

"Whatever."

"Come on, Emily, what did she say about the letters? What went on between you two?"

"Not a bloody thing you'll know about, except that it's okay for you to write. And you'd better, do you hear? Hey, there's the hotel across the ravine. Just hold me, darling. We'll be there in an eye-blink."

The cab swerves sharply to cross the valley bridge and her body is pressed against his. She murmurs, lifting his hand against her mouth, her breath warm on his skin, "I'll tell you one more thing she said. She's never been to Paris. How's that possible?"

"Well, somehow it's never happened."

"If I find a flat in Paris, you'll come there, won't you, every now and then? With her, natch. Just so we'll see each other, my love."

"That's on, Queenie."

As the cab nears the hotel he releases her to touch a handkerchief to her wet face. "Holy cats, tears?" she mutters. "I didn't even know. Something in the Jerusalem air, no doubt."

Halliday is waiting in the lobby in uniform with Emily's luggage. He takes her aside and with a few low cautious words hands her a thick envelope. She nods slowly, slips it into her leather shoulder bag, zips and locks the bag. "All set, Barak," Halliday says.

"Fine. The navy car is waiting outside."

The bellboys are busy with a huge tourist group, so they both help Emily into a cab with her luggage. She kisses her husband, and waves a casual goodbye to Barak.

"I suppose I should see the Wailing Wall, too," says Halliday, as they get into a waiting navy car, "and the Via Dolorosa, and so on. There's more to your country than war, war, war."

"General, when is your airlift to the Third Army supposed to go?"

For once Halliday's impassive face shows a flicker of surprise. "Unlike Sharon you do believe it's serious?"

"I believe the Pentagon gentlemen who are for it are all too serious."

Halliday regards him for a long moment. "Okay. Next Thursday Dr. Kissinger is scheduled to visit Cairo. First time for an American Secretary of State since Dulles in 1953. Big breakthrough in American-Arab relations. Unless your people at Kilometer 101 show some flexibility soon, the airlift may well go by Thursday."

"Flexibility? Sure, when we hear some sense about prisoners and disengagement. Sadat's counting on a bailout by you without any of that, so that he can trade our prisoners of war for the whole Sinai Peninsula. About his own prisoners — we've got thousands — he obviously doesn't give a damn."

"Sounds like the airlift will fly, Barak."

"Maybe. On the other hand, your President may have reasons to think twice about it. On our left here, General, is the new campus of Hebrew University."

"Handsome buildings."

33

Beaten-Out Willows

On a cold windy noonday late in November, Galia Barak and Daphna Luria stand side by side gripping hands as Dov Luria's coffin sinks into a pit of reddish earth in the military burial ground on Mount Herzl, ringed by the sunlit Jerusalem hills. Family, friends, and Tel Nof aviators cluster around the grave, the mother bowed but dry-eyed, Benny Luria and Danny standing rigid in black skullcaps. The Ezrakh, thin and frail, conducts a short burial service, then Air Force Chief Peled begins to eulogize "a fallen eagle from a family of eagles," his usual forceful voice faltering. Galia breaks into sobs, and Daphna puts an arm around her.

Across the open pit Daphna can see among the mourners Noah Barak in white uniform beside a plumpish dark girl in a heavy brown sweater; no doubt his French fiancée, at first glance quite as plain as Daphna has heard. An unworthy thought at her brother's open grave, and she tries to pay attention to the air force chief's words, but he is just spouting straight Zionism, flyboy style, such as she has heard all her life. Maybe the familiar phrases, like rote prayers, are making her parents feel better. No words can console poor Galia or herself, brimful as she is of Jericho Café bitterness about the war. Dov died because the lying old politicians and the puffed-up old generals, now so busy covering their asses, were caught asleep. The kids had to save Israel, kids like Dov and like pitiful maimed Dzecki, already showing off how he can drive his Porsche with one arm. She feels guilty about not seeing more of Dzecki, but that stump gives her the horrors. Yet at least he is alive.

Never will Daphna forget those long weeks of waiting for news of her brother, the high hopes for the prisoner exchange, the agonizing moment when the whole family came with Galia to Lod airport and he failed to appear among the gaunt shaven-headed figures in pajamas descending from the Red Cross plane; then hard upon that the crushing news from the search team, the shattered body found in a dense mango grove, miles from the charred wreckage of his Phantom near the Canal. Evidently Dov tried to the last for a crash landing in Sinai, and ejected too late for the parachute to save him. Her parents have been as stoical as she expected. Galia has surprised her. After all, Galia is a soldier herself, from an army family, but she is so broken up that she has been granted hardship leave. She cries all through Peled's talk while Daphna's eyes are quite dry.

The ceremony ends. The mourners disperse with few words along the rows of the dead. Daphna does not leave the hillside cemetery with her family, wandering instead among the terraces, her hands jammed in her pockets, the cold wind blowing her hair. Of the hundreds of new graves dug here when the war began, nearly all are now filled, with metal name markers stuck in mounds of fresh dirt; and she comes on one grave after another of friends from school or her scout troop or the army. As she walks, she hears on the wind an incongruous sound in this place of the fallen. It is a clarinet. Too far off to be recognized, a soldier stands on a knoll beside a pile of earth, playing a Mozart air. She realizes at once that this has to be Colonel Lauterman's son. She heard him play at the Jericho Café, she knows his father was killed, and it can be nobody else. She stands listening to the piercing slow music, and now she starts to cry, warm tears rolling down her cold cheeks. She turns and hurries away toward the cemetery entrance.

Yo-yo Lauterman, too. That poor talented son! What a catastrophe, that war! Dov gone, Dzecki crippled, Noah slipped away, no other men worth bothering with in her life, and what of her family? She had never believed Dov could go down. Like her father, he had been to her an invulnerable air warrior. And now Danny is talking with scary intensity about qualifying for Phantoms, and her father, never once mentioning his dead son's name, is sitting and reading the Bible till all hours, night after night. Only with her mother, who loves to reminisce about Dov, is Daphna at all comfortable.

She does not notice the man on crutches bowed over a grave, until he says, "Hello, Daphna. I'm sorry about your brother."

"Hello, Shimon."

The ceramicist is clean-shaven and much thinner. "Today's a month since Yoram died." His touch on the grave marker is like a rough caress. "I felt like visiting him."

"What happened, exactly, Shimon? I heard he got killed in a tank. How come?"

"Oh, it's a story. Yoram once qualified in tanks, you know. Hated the army, liked the tanks. This tank captain over in Africa got blinded by shrapnel, and the crew shifted up as usual — gunner to captain, loader to gunner, driver to loader. So they needed a driver, and Yoram just jumped in that tank and drove. It hit a mine. Bad news for a tank driver, mines."

The ceramicist puts on a skullcap, rattles off a liturgy passage about the resurrection of the dead, and recites two short psalms. "Well, goodbye, Yoram," he says, taking off the skullcap. "I'm sorry you had to die in that shitty war. We'll miss you. We need you. Now more than ever. Haval!" He turns moist eyes to Daphna, and blows his nose. "Can you imagine how Yoram would be roasting the irresponsible idiots who got us into it, if he were alive? There's nobody left like Yoram."

"There's plenty of roasting going on."

"Not enough."

She says as they start to walk out, "Shimon, you're not getting religion, are you?"

"I had religion as a kid, motek. It hangs on like malaria, and breaks out now and then. I see you're still in uniform. When do they let you out?"

"Who knows? With all the Syrian violations, the air force remains on high alert. Are you back at work?"

"Absolutely. In fact" — his mournful manner changes to sudden good cheer — "I've had a big break, Daphna. A Reform temple in Houston, Texas, wants me to do a lobby wall ceramic. David slaying Goliath, six by ten, real money."

"Well, that's great, Shimon."

"Isn't it? I may get out of the menorah business yet. Listen, call me when you have an *after,* and we'll go to the Jericho and raise a glass for poor Yoram."

"Lovely. I'll do it."

At the central bus-ticket office, Daphna hesitates. Straight to Afula and the base, or via Haifa and Dzecki? Well, it has been two weeks now. So — dutifully — Dzecki.

Yael Nitzan murmurs to Kishote, as they walk out the cemetery gate, "A nephew I really loved, gone! I remember Dov the day he was born, Yossi, blue-eyed, sweet, yawning, a perfect baby, and now —" She breaks off, for Sam Pasternak is walking by arm in arm with Eva Sonshine, and he nods unsmiling. Through the pall of death, life obtrudes upon Yael in a pulse of disapproval. That woman should not have come, and Pasternak is a thick-skinned fool to have brought her.

"When is your appointment with Dado?" she asks, starting up her rented Mercedes in the cemetery parking lot.

"One-thirty. After that a condolence call on Shayna in Haifa. Come along, Yael. It's a mitzvah."

"Well, maybe," says Yael dubiously. The widowed Shayna is not likely to be much consoled, she figures, at the sight of her. As they drive down the broad boulevard to the Tel Aviv highway, she asks, "Yossi, will there be peace now?"

"Hard to say."

He talks about the shaky cease-fire while the Mercedes winds down the mountain road in thick army and civilian traffic. The enemy has been trying attrition again; shooting incidents on the Sharon perimeter, Sadat threatening to renew the war, the Syrians resuming their harassing actions. The Arab standing armies can maintain this pressure indefinitely while their civilian life goes back to normal, he explains, but all Israel has to stay on war alert. The personal lives of the reserve troops are being disrupted, national morale is sinking, the economy is running down; still, the siege of the Third Army has to go on. It is Golda's sole leverage for some kind of real move to peace.

"There were rumors for a while of an American airlift to that army," says Yael. "What happened?"

"The Egyptians sent our prisoners home, and Golda let one more supply convoy through."

When the Tel Aviv skyline comes hazily in sight, Yael says, "Listen, Yossi, I'm off to Los Angeles next Monday. I've been away from Eva for over a month. Also, Sheva Leavis wants me back."

"Do you have any more pictures of Eva?"

"Always. In my purse here. Yellow envelope."

He shuffles the pictures. "She's becoming so beautiful."

"Yes. Also developing an iron will and a fierce temper, and she's the worst flirt I've ever seen. She's ahead of Aryeh at this age in talking English and Hebrew. You should come and see her."

"If only I could." He stares with longing at the fair-haired little girl, laughing on a rocking horse.

Yael pulls up at the curb outside the Kirya and turns off the ignition. "I have something to tell you. Sheva Leavis is interested in your future once you leave the army."

"My future?" Kishote pushes his glasses up on his nose and peers at her. "In what way?"

"His business base is in the Far East, always has been. Your brother Lee has never taken to that side of Sheva's interests, he's all for real estate, casinos, films, and so on. Sheva has to travel months on end, it's all face-to-face handshake business in Asia, with very big money involved. He's getting old for it, and he believes you could handle it."

"Me? All I know is the army."

"How much longer can you stay in the army? Three years? Four? Ramatkhal you won't be. You're that good, but you're not in the running, not in the club. What will you do once you get out?"

"Who knows? Go around the world, for a change. Then maybe sweep the Jerusalem streets, and keep an eye on Aryeh. Tell me about Max Roweh."

"Who? Professor Roweh?" Slight pause. "Why, I met him on a plane, and I heard him give a soporific lecture. What about him?"

"He heads a fund to help war widows."

"Yes, his wife established it."

"Right. I'm trying to get money for some real distress cases in my division. The tea-drinking shleppers who run that fund just drivel and don't pay. A word from you to him might help."

"I don't know him that well, but I'll do what I can."

"Great."

The Ramatkhal stands up behind the desk to hold out his hand. A small courtesy, but that's Dado. A mentsch. The yellow-gray color is gone and his eyes are less puffy, but he still has the war-harried look and the harsh cough. The maps on his walls show green cease-fire lines slashed across Syria and Egypt, with red marks and dates noting cease-fire violations.

"So, Yossi, what's been happening in Africa?"

Kishote summarizes the picture in the north sector he now commands while Sharon electioneers. Dado asks sharp questions about the weaker units, naming commanders down to the company level.

"Well, you've been doing a good job," he says at last. A girl soldier brings in pitted dates, which Dado eats as he talks, now and then coughing. "It was a very hard war, Kishote. You know, of course, about this Agranat Commission?"

"I heard the news last night on Army Radio." The uproar about the surprise attack has led to the appointment of an inquiry panel: two Supreme Court justices, two former Ramatkhals, and the state comptroller. "Isn't it a premature step, sir? An internal army inquiry should come first."

"Well, a public circus was probably inevitable with an election coming on. Maybe it'll clear the air a bit." He looks keenly at Kishote from under his heavy brows. "I have good legal advice, but I may want to talk out some military aspects with you now and then."

"With me, sir?"

"I trust you. You're a truth teller."

The words and the tone give Yossi a strong sense of how lonely a Chief of Staff must be, ever surrounded with intrigue and pressures; Dado more than any before him, perhaps. Formality discarded, the Ramatkhal leans back in his chair with a friendly smile. "You mamzer, you had your nerve, disagreeing with Arik that day at Kishuf. You paid dearly for it, too." *(Not much escapes him!)* "But you told the truth. Yossi, I have you in mind for Deputy Chief of Staff for operations. The slot is occupied, but I'm thinking ahead."

This dreamlike turn confounds Kishote. He has assumed that Dado summoned him to explain a fatal mishap in his sector; and as for advancement to such a central post, he has despaired of it. He blurts without thinking, "Sir, about that tank accident, I visited the parents of the driver and loader this morning. The captain was a concentration camp survivor, so no parents. I'll see the gunner's family in Haifa later today."

Dado does not blink at the non sequitur. "What happened, exactly, and how?"

"Sir, we've lost so many tank crews, we've had to qualify more of them in a big hurry. One of the new tank commanders bypassed an electronic safety lock, his gunner fired off a shell and blew up a tank ten feet away. Killed the crew, all four of them."

Dado listens with a scowl. "A rotten business. Bad enough when the boys die fighting Arabs. But listen, this was a war casualty, too. We have to man the perimeters until we disengage. We lost forty percent in tanks, and accidents with green crews will happen. The whole armored force should get a warning despatch about this incident."

"I've drafted one, sir, for Chief, Armor Command."

"Kishote, what do I say to the Agranat Commission when they ask, '*Why were we surprised?*' "

To this abrupt probe, Kishote slowly returns, "First and foremost, sir, an intelligence failure. Who could anticipate and plan for a warning of only eight hours?"

"No good. I'm responsible for the state of our military intelligence. Intelligence guessed wrong on the probability of war, and on the seventy-two-hour warning. I didn't have to accept those guesses."

"The Minister of Defense accepted them."

"He's a civilian."

Stung, Kishote bursts out, "Dado, the enemy started with every possible military advantage — strategic and tactical surprise on two fronts, lopsided edge in weapons and numbers, resupply and backing from day one by a superpower — all that, and under your command we still beat them. Can the Agranat Commission ignore that?"

Dado smiles at Kishote's vehemence. "Their writ only runs to what went wrong militarily in the first three days."

"What went wrong was that everyone lost their heads except you and Golda."

"We'll see. There's credit and there's blame for me, Yossi. A Ramatkhal should resign if he disagrees strongly enough with government policy, that's his way to yell, *'The house is on fire!'* I never felt that way in the months before the war. Maybe I should have." Dado stands up with a cheery smile. "So tell me, how is that handsome son of yours? That Aryeh?"

"He goes to the army next year. His ideal is Amos Pasternak, so his goal is Sayeret Matkhal."

Dado's heavy eyebrows go far up. "Can he do it?"

"Well, I'm not sure. He already wears glasses."

"You haven't done badly with glasses." As Dado walks Kishote to the door, taking his elbow, he whimsically inquires, "How will your boss make out in the election, Yossi?"

"I don't know, but I wish he'd drop the hindsight noise he's making about the war."

"Well, Arik is Arik. One thing is sure, Golda will lose a lot of ground. The people want a scapegoat, and heads must roll."

Daphna has to admire the deftness with which Dzecki parks the Porsche in a narrow curb space between two cars, using the stump in a pinned-up sleeve to steady the wheel while his left hand shifts gears. But the performance is freakish and repellent to her. That, she cannot help.

"Well, well, old Guli is here," says Dzecki. "Nice of him."

"How do you know he's here?"

"There's only one silver Lincoln in all of Israel." Dzecki gestures at the huge gleaming car in front of them. "He owns this building and forty others in Haifa."

"So, I get to meet Guli again. According to Noah Guli's a jailbird, a crook, a gorilla who'll strip you and your father down to your underwear."

"That's Noah's opinion. So far we've made money with Guli. I'll tell you this about Guli, his AA unit on the Golan was overrun, the captain was killed, and Guli took over and they shot their way out, back to our lines." As they climb the stairs to the Berkowitz apartment on the fifth floor, they hear several voices above, men and women, one louder than the rest. "That's Guli now," says Dzecki, "coming down."

Daphna has been picturing the kablan, since she first glimpsed him years ago, as something like an Israeli King Kong, but today he is a reasonably well-groomed businessman, beefy and blue-jowled, dressed in a dark suit and tie for a condolence visit. He stops on the landing and exclaims with a bear hug, "Dzecki! Your mother and father are up there. Shayna's a strong lady, she's bearing up well."

"This is Daphna Luria, Guli."

"Ah yes, Shimon's protégée. Hello there, where's my Samson?" he inquires with mock gruffness.

"It's the war, sir. As soon as they let me out of this uniform —"

"Well, no hurry, but that spot in the hotel lobby is empty and waiting."

"So that's Guli," says Daphna, as he tramples downstairs. "Not such a monster, after all. Was one of those ladies his wife?"

"His wife died last year. They didn't get along. Guli once told me that he's slept with more women than he has hairs on his head. I believe him."

"Ugh," says Daphna.

Through the open door to the apartment comes the sound of

lively talk. "These are mostly university people," says Dzecki as they walk in. "Friends of Professor Berkowitz, or else members of his synagogue. We won't stay long, just pay our respects to Shayna —"

"Why, there's General Barak," says Daphna, discerning him sitting in uniform on a low stool. Another mourning stool beside him is empty. "He was just at Dov's funeral." She makes her way to him. "Sir, accept my condolences about your brother Michael."

"Thank you. A day for mourning brothers, isn't it?" he says. "You were very good with Galia, Daphna. She was more grateful than she could say."

Words about Dov stick in Zev Barak's throat. His own brother has been a casualty of the war, but in a different way. Barak has attended too many funerals of his friends' sons, each interment a new agonizing laceration. The visits to the badly wounded, like Dzecki Barkowe there near the door, talking to his mother and father, are in a way even more harrowing; less final, less black, but harder to endure because of the glaring disfigurement and the pain. Alas for those poor stunned Berkowitz-Barkowe parents and their one-armed son, maimed in a Jewish war so far from Great Neck, Long Island!

Dzecki comes to him and gestures at the vacant stool. "Where's Shayna, sir?"

"She's packing up for Reuven in the back bedroom. His mother has come from Australia to take him."

"Haval. That's very sad. Very hard on Aunt Shayna."

Dzecki goes off with Daphna to the back room. Other consolers approach the general, and some try to engage him in talk about the Agranat Commission, but he makes no response. Yossi Nitzan shows up, and sits down on the low stool beside Barak.

"That's not necessary, Yossi. Family only. Get yourself a chair."

"In a minute. Zev, what's going to happen with this Agranat Commission? Whose heads will roll?"

"That's what they're ordered to decide."

"How does Golda feel about this?"

Barak shakes his head. "I don't know. She's inside a thick shell these days."

"Well, let me tell you, I see Dayan as the prime target. All the big political and military decisions — size of army, length of reserve service, weapons budget, projecting of strategy and tactics in case of war — all back up to him, don't they? And it was Dayan who said there'd be no major war for ten years. He didn't change his mind until the Egyptian and Syrian artillery opened up."

With a melancholy smile Barak inquires, "Working up Dado's defense, Kishote?"

Shayna appears and takes her place on the stool that Kishote vacates. Visitors form a line to step up and console Professor Berkowitz's wife and his brother with the ancient formula, *"May the Name comfort you, in the midst of the mourners for Zion and Jerusalem."* It is late in the day and all but a few leave, though a few remain to consume cakes, coffee, and wine set out on a table.

"Where's Reuven?" Kishote asks Shayna, when the line has gone by, and Zev Barak has left.

"Taking a nap. Lena will be here any minute. It'll be a long tiring trip for him."

"You look well, Shayna."

She does. Kishote has expected to find her woebegone, incoherent, perhaps unkempt, but her black dress is neat, her hair carefully parted and braided, and if anything, some lines in her very pale face have smoothed away and she seems younger. "You're being kind, as usual," she says.

"Appalling that you have to give up Reuven."

"Oh, Yossi, she's his mother. It's only right." She shrugs and spreads her hands. "I really have nobody now, I guess. An orphan, a widow. I have my work, and I had a few beautiful years."

He says with low intensity, "Shayna, you'll have many beautiful years."

Her response is a grieving glance, and an affectionate flash of reddened glistening eyes. She jumps up. "There's Lena now."

A stoutish woman in a tailored red suit and a gaily feathered red hat is coming toward her. "Pardon my travelling clothes, Shayna. Where's Reuven?"

"Ready to go, Lena," Shayna says. "Come and get him."

"I'll help," says Kishote.

Reuven is sitting up on the bed, reading a picture book.

Dressed in a suit and tie, he looks older than his six years and not very comfortable, but he smiles and holds out his arms to Lena. "Imma, are we going to ride on the airplane now?"

"Yes, darling. All the way to Australia. A nice long ride."

When she tries to pick him up, he protests. "I go myself." Slipping off the bed, he tucks a crutch under one arm and limps to the door, glancing at her for approval. "Myself," he repeats.

"Very good, Reuven."

He also insists on going down the four flights of stairs himself, hanging onto a bannister and carrying the crutch. It is a slow business. He clearly takes pride in it, and the adults do not hurry him. Lena murmurs in English, "You and Michael have brought him up right."

"He's brought himself up," says Shayna. "We just had the joy of it. He's advanced in every way, and he's a good boy."

A taxi is waiting. Reuven allows Shayna to help him in, and kisses her. "Goodbye, Shayna," he says cheerfully. "Come on an airplane and visit me in Australia."

"It's a long way for Shayna," says his mother. "Goodbye, Shayna. Goodbye, General Nitzan, and thank you."

The boy waves as the taxi pulls away. Kishote puts his arm around Shayna. She leans against him, watching the car until it disappears around a corner. "A good boy," she repeats in a steady voice. "Come up and eat something with me, Yossi. I've eaten nothing all day."

"This is a complete Israeli victory," says General Gamasy, leafing the disengagement document with a sour look. The tent at Kilometer 101 now has transparent plastic curtains, also electric heaters to combat the January cold. But a few feet from the red-glowing coils the tent is chilly, and the atmosphere between the two warmly clad negotiating teams is as frosty as the desert air.

"A victory? General, this is a unilateral pullback by Israel, our first since 1956." Aharon Yariv's riposte pleases Sam Pasternak, huddled in his Hermonit. He would have said as much himself.

Gamasy angrily shakes his head. "Our President Sadat, I say frankly to you, has made a wretched bargain."

"And I say to you, General, that for us it's bitter medicine prescribed by Dr. Kissinger, and forced down our throats by President Nixon. There are long lines at American filling stations, and Mr. Nixon wants to end the oil embargo and maybe hold off his impeachment. So your Third Army is marching home in honor with all its arms, instead of being starved out or destroyed as the situation in the field dictated."

"Not so, the Third Army was ready to fight its way out!" Gamasy strikes the table. "Only Dr. Kissinger stopped it with this one-sided deal."

Yariv throws up his hands. "Let's say it's a hard bargain on both sides. Are you ready to sign?"

Journalists come into the tent for the grim short signing ceremony, enlivened mainly by the popping of flashbulbs.

Afterward Sam Pasternak drives from Kilometer 101 to Kishote's headquarters. "Get ready to take your boys home, Kishote," he says, coming into the command caravan. "It's done."

"So, we win a war with Egypt," Kishote says, "and they stay put while we retreat from the Canal to the Gidi and the Mitla Passes, without another shot being fired. A funny victory."

"How will your boys take it?"

"They'll be glad it's over, that's all. After they get home, they may start wondering what the devil it was all about, and why their friends got killed."

"Is that how you feel about this deal?"

Kishote takes a while to answer. "It can be one more Arab trick to make us drop our guard. If this man Sadat means peace it's a miracle, but we have to try it."

Pasternak says, "Good, I agree. Look, if Ben Gurion had lived one more month, he'd have certainly called it a miracle. That's how I felt, there in that tent. A face-to-face deal with Egypt! Messiah's time."

"Halevai," says Don Kishote.

The long withdrawing columns of rumbling machines are halted at the Canal and backed up for miles, waiting for passage over the bridges. Kishote mounts an Egyptian rampart from which the Israeli flags are gone, to watch his troops crossing the Canal the other way. On the bridges the traffic is now all eastward. To the north and south he can see in the Egyptian lodgments the dust plumes of moving vehicles and the smoke of field-kitchen fires. Out of regard for tender Arab honor, the Israelis are backing out first. Only then will the Egyptians get out of Sinai. The bridges will be left behind like the evacuated Bar-Lev Line; or will Zahal engineers try to salvage them? Kishote doesn't know. He does know that those pontoon bridges, and the solid earth bridge, and the roller bridge itself, are relics of the past. A phrase of his childhood leaps to mind: *Opge-shluggeneh hoyshainess!* (Beaten-out willows!). He speaks the Yiddish words aloud to nobody, "Opge-shluggeneh hoyshainess!"

Once a year, on the day called the Great Hosannah, worshippers beat willow stalks on the synagogue floor to knock off the leaves. The meaning of this ancient custom is obscure, something to do with bringing rain. On Great Hosannah day before morning prayers the willow stalks, hoyshainess, are at a premium in Jewish neighborhoods, eagerly sought after, never enough to go around. Afterward they lie scattered around the synagogue, broken and half-denuded, for the shammas to sweep up and burn. Beaten-out willows . . .

Beaten-out willows, these bridges.

He crosses the roller bridge in his command car. Most of his division is already over in Sinai by now, wending eastward on roads chewed to bits by tank treads and already drifted over by the blowing sand, mere vague tracks on the desert floor. Kishote stops at the Sinai end, walks out on the greasy steel-netting surface against the booming clanking traffic, and in mid-Canal murmurs a prayer for the boys in his division who fell.

The weeks that follow are hectic for Don Kishote. Demobilizing ten thousand men, coating and storing hundreds of tanks, inventorying and warehousing mountains of weaponry, make for incessant work. The time races by for him, while Dr. Kissinger is doing his picturesque shuttling around the Arab capitals, trying for an armistice on the still-smoldering Syrian front. From Don Kishote's viewpoint the world news continues bad for Israel. Mr. Nixon has his big success, the oil embargo is lifted in March, so the gasoline lines in America evaporate. But the drive to impeach him does not, and the price of oil stays at the new sky-high level, since the European governments, not daring to unite against the cartel of Arab oil producers, are making shifty individual deals with them. That is the one clear outcome of the war. The Arabs have learned that they have Europe over an oil barrel.

Dado talks often to Kishote before and after he testifies to the Agranat panel. He returns from these sessions confident that he has done well, and Kishote is dumbstruck when early in April the newspapers explode with gigantic headlines. The Agranat Commission in a "partial finding" has not only cleared but praised Moshe Dayan, and has recommended that General David Elazar be relieved. Golda Meir has already requested and received Dado's resignation.

The next morning a public commotion starts to boil up, and in the army there are angry mutterings of resignations. Don Kishote goes very early, uninvited, to see Dado. An unprecedented hush lies over the entire Kirya. The female soldiers in the outer offices are as silent as at a funeral. When the Ramatkhal arrives and sees Don Kishote, he holds up a hand, says, "Another time, Yossi," and goes inside. In all the years he has known David Elazar, Don Kishote has never seen him like this, bowed, stunned, unmanned.

A beaten-out willow.

PART THREE

The Peace

THE LORD WILL GIVE HIS PEOPLE VALOR,
THE LORD WILL BLESS HIS PEOPLE WITH PEACE.

Psalm 29:11

34

Amos and Madame Fleg

Madame Irene Fleg could dawdle for hours in bathing and dressing, or, like an actress making a quick change backstage, she could get herself dried, combed, made up, costumed and out the door in minutes, as she did now in her Tel Aviv Hilton suite. She rode down by herself in the large ornate elevator, for all the journalists had long since flown, and tourism was still at a jittery ebb. Into the almost-deserted lobby she strode, hoping the pink wool dress snatched at random from the closet was on straight. There stood a robust fellow in a green uniform, grinning.

"Oo-ah, quick work!" he said. "Sorry I got you out of a bath. You're sure you're dry?"

"Am I dripping?" The hand that shook hers in a firm grip felt callused and scarred. She peered at his face. "So you're Pasternak *fils*! I hardly remembered what you looked like, to tell the truth. I thought you were taller."

"Disappointed?"

"How on earth did you find out I was here?"

"Julie Levinson told me."

"You know Julie?"

"I know her bridegroom, very well."

"I see. Well, let's sit down." On the long curving lobby couch, which in good times was crowded, they were the sole occupants. "My husband's in an Alliance Israelite Universelle meeting here. He'll be out soon. My children should be showing up, too. They're going on a day trip with a group."

"All three of them?"

She laughed. "The two oldest."

"Madame Fleg, will you be in Israel for a while? I have to return to my battalion right after the wedding."

"I'm afraid we leave Sunday."

"Oh. Too bad. You came for the wedding?"

"Not exactly. Julie's parents scheduled it for this week, so that their Alliance friends could attend. Monsieur Levinson is on the board."

They sat smiling at each other. "I can't stay now for long," he said. "Some angry army officers, including me, are meeting at headquarters to discuss what to do about the Agranat Report."

"What's it all about, Amos? The whole country seems to be up in arms, mostly against Moshe Dayan, and now Golda is resigning! Why? And Armand's board is meeting with her today. That'll be embarrassing, won't it?"

The smile faded from Amos Pasternak's round full face. He looked grimly businesslike, as he had in the Beirut limousine and on the boat. "The country's in a very bad mood, Irene, if I may call you that."

"That's my name, Amos."

"Okay. We're still mourning the dead. Israel's a small place, everyone knows a family that had someone killed or wounded, and —"

With a pleasant cheery noise, children came trooping through the lobby, rattling in French. "There are my kids," she interrupted him. "They're going to Masada." She waved and beckoned. "Anatole! Rachel! *Venez-ici! Voici un vrai héros de la guerre, mes enfants,* Lieutenant Colonel Pasternak."

They were tidy, well-groomed youngsters, dressed for hiking. The boy solemnly saluted. *"Un vrai héros! Formidable."* Amos returned the gesture just as solemnly, and they scampered away to rejoin their group.

"You know, seeing you again is disorienting," Irene Fleg said. "That Beirut business seems like a dream, almost. I've done scuba-diving and rock-climbing, but that was different. Maybe it was the only worthwhile thing I've ever done. To you, I suppose, it was routine."

"On the contrary, just as scary for us as for someone like you. Maybe more so. Such operations are intensely rehearsed, and we're extremely aware of all the things that can go wrong. Whoever recruited you probably glossed over those."

"No, I was fairly warned. Why I made such a scatterbrained commitment I'm still not sure. How is your father? We saw in *Time* magazine his picture at Kilometer 101."

"He's back in business, all the excitement over."

"I saw him in Paris during the war."

"Oh? He didn't mention that."

"Well, it was just for a minute. He did say you got my little thank-you note, after a delay."

"Yes, just when the war was breaking out. I still have it."

Brief silence. "So! Will you be coming to the wedding alone?"

"I'm not bringing a girlfriend, if that's what you mean."

"No, of course that's not what I mean. I mean we have a car and driver, and you can ride with us to Jerusalem, if you like. There's room."

"Great, I accept."

"But don't tell me you have no girlfriends."

"Did I say that?"

A dozen men were coming from the elevator, speaking French with Gallic gestures. "*Bien*, there's Armand." Her husband saw her and approached, a thin man with curly gray-blond hair, in a perfectly cut pin-striped suit. "My dear, this is Sam Pasternak's son."

"Ah yes, Amos." Brief handshake with a slim small manicured hand. "I sit on the board of Kivshan, Colonel, so I know your father. One hears you're to receive a medal for heroism."

"Unthinkable, sir. I did nothing to warrant it."

"I've invited Amos to ride with us to the wedding," said Madame Fleg. "He's a friend of Julie's groom."

"Merveilleux!" Fleg nodded at Amos. "We leave from here at

noon. Perhaps on the way you can explain about Golda's fall. It's all very perplexing, you know, very damaging to Israel's image."

"I can try." Across the lobby he could see Eva Sonshine returning to her desk, a sheaf of air tickets in hand. "I'll be back well before noon, sir, and very glad to ride with you."

Behind the receptionist's desk, the arcade shops that Amos could see were all shut and dark, except for the El Al office. "Eva, ma nishma? My father said you were quitting your job."

"I'm finishing out the month. You finally found your French friends, I see. She's pretty."

"Yes, for a lady with three kids, not bad."

"Lucky lady."

He caught the wistful note. His father had told him that Eva wanted children. Amos was still unused to the notion that Eva Sonshine, the longtime girlfriend of Benny Luria, might become his stepmother. Eva's good name was reasonably intact, for in the tight terrain of Israel, by general courtesy, such discreet liaisons were known but overlooked. If his father wanted a marriage instead of his customary casual romances — or in addition to them — that was his business. He said, "You're coming to the wedding?"

"Sam won't hear of skipping it, so I'll go." It was Eva's way of saying that she could do without encountering the Lurias, who were bound to be there.

The only silver Lincoln in Israel pulled up to the Barkowe home on Mount Carmel. "There he is," Dzecki said to Daphna at the window, "right on the dot. Say what you will about Guli, he's punctual. Let's go, Mom, Dad."

Guli was no relative to bride or groom, and Noah, who knew what went on in Haifa, utterly despised him, yet he was coming to Noah's wedding. Guli had worked this through Dzecki. He was fond of these American associates of his, though he was well along in a complicated scheme to plunder them. Guli had a special regard for the bright young Dzecki, was honestly saddened by his mutilation, and had often visited him in the hospital and at home. So it was that he had heard about Noah's nuptials, and about the Alliance executives who would be there. This intelligence alerted Guli as the scent of a banana, or more accurately of a female, would a true gorilla. Guli was on a perpetual hunt for real estate investors, on the prudent rule that only an amateur or a fool, and he was neither, would invest his own money in such a chancy business.

"Dzecki, by my life, there are no richer Jews than those Frenchies," he had exclaimed on hearing of the wedding, "especially the ones from Iraq and Syria. And from Egypt, Egypt! By my life, those Egyptian Jews, the ones who got out before Nasser, have money. And they're very Zionistic, very idealistic, all these rich Frenchies. What we have to do, Dzecki, is bring some of them into our waterfront project." Thus Guli, wangling the invitation. Guli particularly loved Zionistic investors, because they risked great sums in Israel, and lost them with reasonable good cheer as a sort of involuntary UJA contribution.

Dzecki was resolutely blocking out the depression of his maiming by a plunge into business, and Guli kept him distracted by bringing projects to him and discussing them quite seriously. He thought Dzecki had a pretty good head for business, though not good enough to escape being fleeced in due course. For his part Dzecki had a fair idea of what Noah thought of Guli, so he called Julie Levinson, and Julie, feeling sorry for Dzecki as everyone did, said of course he could bring his friend. When Noah found out that Dzecki Barkowe was bringing Guli Gulinkoff, his first reaction was, "Let's call it off and get married in Cyprus." But he simmered down, sharing his bride's sympathy for poor Dzecki.

The Lincoln snaked down the Mount Carmel hairpin turns, and soon was zooming south on Haifa Way. An ordinary Israeli driver had to figure two hours between Haifa and Jerusalem. Guli's best time was one hour and thirty-eight minutes, and he kept trying to beat it. Speed limits and solid dividing lines were not for Guli. The Barkowes in the back seat had driven often with him and had learned to relax, as a wise rider will on a runaway horse. But Daphna was wincing so visibly, as Guli whipped around trailer trucks into the other lane where like as not a car was coming, that he had to pat her silk-clad knee now and then with a hairy gold-ringed hand.

The kablan was astonished at how elegant and beautiful Dzecki's girlfriend looked. When he had last encountered her, on the stairs to Shayna's apartment, he had seen a tired female soldier in wrinkled uniform and no makeup. This was a different creature, fresh out of a beauty parlor, dressed to kill in a beige suede outfit made for export and bought cheap after much wear by models. Daphna's idea in attending the wedding was to tear Noah Barak's heart with vain regret. She had no notion of captivating the gorilla, but seemed to be doing so, as the Lincoln careered through dense traffic as though travelling at midnight on an empty road. Guli's hand was now resting steadily on her knee, with an occasional squeeze by way of calming her nerves.

"Guli, don't you ever get arrested?" she asked.

From the back seat Dzecki said, "Arrest Guli? All the cops in Israel know this car. It's worth their job to pull him over."

"Foolishness," said Guli. "Don't believe him. I respect the police. I'm a trustee of the national policemen's benevolent association."

As he spoke, he was overtaking a roaring convoy of army trucks, and heading straight for a hay wagon drawn by a mule team. Darting between two trucks to the derisive yells of the soldiers in them, Guli said, "Those wagons are a hazard. There ought to be a law to make them stay on back roads." He passed the entire convoy and was bowling along at his usual 150 kilometers an hour when a patrol car drew up behind him, red light revolving and siren wailing.

"Oo-ah," said Daphna.

"No problem," said Guli. "He must be new."

The patrolman was very dark and very young. As the Sephardim, the "second Israel" from the Arab countries, were gaining political clout, their employment in the lower government jobs was increasing.

"I'm Guli," said the kablan genially, opening a wallet that displayed various cards and badges.

"I recognized your car, sir," said the patrolman. "License and registration, please."

"Certainly. What's the problem, officer?"

"You almost covered the highway with mule meat, sir."

Guli did not argue, and the ticket was soon issued. He said, as he drove on, "He'll learn. He's a nice kid." After going a mile or so he tore up the ticket and scattered it out the window.

Dzecki's mother was scandalized. "Guli, for heaven's sake! Don't they have those tickets on computers in Israel?"

"Of course, but someone has to read the computer, and do something about it. No problem. Now, Dzecki, where do we pick up that Porsche of yours?"

"It's far out of the way, Guli, in a body shop in Netanya. Let me off at the Netanya exit, and I'll catch a hitch or a bus —"

"Let you off? Foolishness. Five minutes, no problem."

The Zion Gardens restaurant in Jerusalem offered modest weddings on a trellis-bordered lawn. Julie's parents had wanted to stage a big affair at the Hilton, but had yielded to the Baraks' advice that the somber mood in the country called for austerity. In the bride's retiring room Daphna came upon a grand to-do around Julie Levinson, who sat on an elevated thronelike chair radiating joy. Galia, Nakhama, Ruti, Shayna, and a portly woman who had to be Julie's mother were all giggling wildly as they fussed at her gown. "Hi, Daphna." Julie guffawed. "Delighted you could come."

The others all turned to Daphna, still laughing, and she felt like the butt of a joke she hadn't heard. The radiance of bridal white haloed the French girl. There was no outshining her today, alas. "Julie, you won't believe the present Avram Gulinkoff has brought," Daphna blurted. "A Mondrian! Not a big one, but it's real. Everyone out there is admiring it."

"Mon Dieu, un Mondrian, Julie," exclaimed the mother. *"Quel bon ami!"*

Galia said, going out, "Oo-ah, I want to see that Mondrian. You look marvellous, Daphna."

"So do you, dear." For a fact Galia was not withdrawn and sad today, and her frock was a cheerful flowered yellow.

The little painting was propped on a round table. Galia edged herself into the crowd around it, naval officers, army officers, older couples chattering in French, and many young people she didn't know. She found herself beside Dzecki Barkowe, whom she had not seen since the war. "Hello, Galia," he said. "My God, I'm sorry about Dov."

"Thanks. I'm sorry about — " she clumsily indicated the pinned-up sleeve in his blue blazer jacket.

He shrugged, and gestured at the painting. "What do you make of that? To me it's like a square of kitchen linoleum. Guli says it's worth a lot of money."

She slipped her fingers into the fingers of his left hand. "Listen, Dzecki, will you tell me all about that bridge sometime? What I've heard and read is unbelievable."

Dzecki grinned. "How about right now? Let's find something to drink."

Daphna came back to the group around the Mondrian as Guli was introducing Dzecki's father to the Alliance guests as "my American partner, the prominent Long Island lawyer and developer, Mr. Barkowe," by way of extolling the golden opportunities in Haifa real estate. His French was fluent. The Mondrian gave him instant credibility. Clever guy, she thought. Guli's background was murky. Unfriendly word had it that he was a camp survivor with a dubious record. He lived part-time in Paris, and he owned a home in Geneva which he rented out. So much she had learned from Dzecki. Now she perceived that the wily gorilla could put on smooth manners and even a certain jolly charm. As for Dzecki, he was off at the bar talking with Galia Barak, which Daphna did not mind at all.

"Shayna, Shayna!" At the door of the bride's room, Don Kishote appeared and beckoned. She came out exclaiming anxiously, "Well? What did Dado say about your resigning?"

"He calls it a futile gesture that would make no difference. Your opinion almost word for word."

"And Zev Barak? Did you talk to him?"

"Just now. I told him I honestly couldn't go on now in the army, I'm sick to my gut at what's happened to Dado. Zev says I shouldn't quit, I might be sorry. If I ask for a year's leave or even longer, it'll probably be granted."

"That makes a lot more sense than resigning. But —"

He interrupted. "Shayna, there's Dayan."

The Minister of Defense was hesitating at the flower-decked archway into the lawn. He had a wan look and his shirt collar seemed a size too big. Zev Barak brought the bride's father to him for an introduction. They shook hands, and Levinson proudly led the Minister to meet his Alliance friends.

Shayna said, "My God, is he sick?"

"Heartsick maybe," said Kishote, and he acidly quoted the Book of Numbers, " '*A land that eats its inhabitants.*' They're trampling him in the mud. Why? He didn't write the Agranat Report."

"God bless you, Kishote," remarked Sam Pasternak, who had come up beside Yossi and heard him. "He's still a great man, and they're hounding him to death. He and I were walking down Ben Yehuda yesterday, and a woman spat at him, screaming, 'You murdered my son,' and ran off. He turned dead white. It happens to him often, things like that. God pity anyone who's ever led the Jews! From Moses onward."

Noah Barak appeared in a new blue suit, accompanied by a fat French-speaking rabbi with a square red beard, engaged by his parents because of the Alliance guests who would be baffled by a harangue in Hebrew. Passing the table of presents, Noah saw the people gawking at the painting and halted. "What is *that*?" he asked his father, who was showing it to Dayan.

"It seems to be a Mondrian, son," said Barak, "and it seems Guli brought it."

"Guli, eh? It goes back to him tomorrow."

"The Levinsons are thrilled by it, Noah. Better ask Julie."

"I don't have to ask her. I'll tell her."

The two musicians furnished by Zion Gardens began to play an old wedding tune on loud electronic instruments. "It's starting, Yossi," said Pasternak, and he walked off toward Amos, deep in converse at a side table with Irene Fleg.

Abruptly Shayna said to Kishote, "I may go to Australia, you know."

"What!" Yossi pushed up his glasses and stared.

"Just to see Reuven. Lena writes that he isn't eating, and doesn't like it there. She's invited me to come and cheer him up."

"Well, Shayna, I may be going to Los Angeles myself." At the dark look crossing Shayna's face he hastily added, "Listen, I want to see my daughter, and there's business I can look into."

"By your life, Don Kishote, California? Whatever you do, come back."

"Do you imagine I won't? There's the bride. The ceremony's on."

In a buzz of admiring comment among the guests seated in rows of gilt chairs, Julie was entering the lawn on her father's arm, and she came to Noah's side under a permanent canopy adorned with fresh flowers. The French-speaking rabbi was expansive. He was a Rumanian refugee from Hitler, he said, and he had lived in France before making aliya. How heartwarming to be marrying a Jewish girl from France to an officer of the Jewish navy, the first since the reign of Solomon! France had been Israel's greatest friend in her struggle to survive, and one day would be again. Young people like this happy couple could not conceive how Jews had been regarded in his own youth; a cowardly, weak, helpless, victimized race, surviving only by cunning, like rats. He still thanked God every day that he had lived to see the rebirth of a strong free Jewish people in the Holy Land, with powerful armed forces. And so on and so forth, at passionate length.

Standing with Nakhama at Noah's side, Zev Barak was very ill at ease with all this galutnik effusiveness, but looking around he could see that the Alliance people were eating it up, while the Israelis who knew no French were fidgeting, and those who understood exchanged cynical smiles. What surprised him was that Moshe Dayan, half-hidden in the crowd, was listening with enthralled attention, his pallid face lit with something like its vivacity of former days.

Noah crushed the glass with his heel, the musicians struck up a gay tune, and nearly all the men took off the skullcaps supplied by Zion Gardens. Dayan came to Zev Barak, grasped his hand, and with his one eye agleam, looked him in the face. "Thank you for inviting me, Zev. Beautiful bride, splendid son." He walked out without another word to anybody.

Amos was helping himself to chicken salad when his father came beside him. "So, when do I celebrate yours?"

"When I meet the right girl."

"You fancy that blond French lady, eh? You won't find one like that in Israel."

"I'm not looking for one, Abba."

"Well, just watch yourself. A lady like that, Amos, can eat you for breakfast, and you won't even know it until she shits you out."

Amos screwed up his face. "To all the devils, Abba, that's crude. That's disgusting."

With a heavy-lidded look, his father put a hand on his shoulder. "I see a great future for you, but not as a Parisienne's poodle."

After a buffet lunch the wedding guests left Zion Gardens with the customary extravagant compliments to the Levinsons and the Baraks, who stood at the archway making farewells. Soon they were all gone, and waiters were dismantling the table and cleaning up the littered lawn.

"Alors, c'était très joli," sighed Julie's mother.

"Well, it was in good taste," said Mr. Levinson, "and considering the country's mood, the Hilton might have been too elegant at that. With whom do I settle, Zev?"

"I'll take care of it and let you know."

"Now, I'm the father of the bride. This was at my expense, everything."

"Most generous of you."

When Nakhama and Zev were left alone amid the debris and the gossiping cleaners, she said, "So, Noah goes first, not Galia. The war, the war! Poor Galia."

He put his arm around her. "They say married people get to think alike, Nakhama. There's an instance for you."

She laid her head on his shoulder. "Oh, what a fool that Daphna Luria was, what a stupid fool, with her stupid ceramics. But Julie's nice, and they're decent people, they'll be nice in-laws."

"Especially living in Cherbourg," said Barak. It made her giggle. "Nakhama, where are the girls?"

"Waiting in the car, I guess."

Ruti was, but Galia sat with Dzecki Barkowe in his newly repainted gleaming blue Porsche, parked behind their car in the street. "If it's all right with you," Galia called to her parents, "I'd like to drive out with Dzecki for a while."

"Why not?" said Barak. Nakhama clutched at his arm as the Porsche rocketed off.

The brisk woman behind the Air France counter in the Athens airport cast an admiring eye at the broad-shouldered man in brown tweed who handed her an Israeli passport with his ticket. "All the way to California today, Monsieur?"

"Yes, land of dreams." She laughed and checked the bags through.

"Kishote!" Amos Pasternak exclaimed, as Yossi dropped beside him in the tourist section of the Air Bus. "What were you doing in Athens?"

"Knocked around Greece for a week. Very educational. And you?"

"Going to Paris on a five-day leave."

"No place better, but you should have a girl along."

"You're going there too?"

"Just to change planes, then on to Los Angeles."

"You haven't resigned, have you, Yossi? There's been talk —"

"I know. Motta Gur agreed to my going inactive for at least a year, possibly two. I'll spend some time with Yael and my daughter in L.A., do some travelling, and then — what's the matter?" Pasternak was staring at a black-mustached swarthy man arguing with the stewardess at the front of the section.

"Nothing. How will Motta do as Ramatkhal, do you think?"

"Motta was lucky. He was in Washington, so he made no mistakes in the war and he starts clean."

Amos put a hand on his arm, as the stewardess wrested a large bag away from the man and stowed it. The man passed down the aisle, muttering. Amos whispered, "You remember the Sabena plane?"

"Who doesn't?" Sayeret Matkhal had stormed the hijacked aircraft at Lod airport and gunned down all the terrorists.

"That guy is the twin of a hijacker I killed. This sure is the airport for them, it's a security sieve. They shot up the TWA counter here, you know, a bloody massacre."

"I know." Kishote spoke low. "Well, are you concerned?"

"No, no. TWA had a flight going to Tel Aviv, so they were killing Jews and Americans, fair game. Air France isn't a terrorist target, Yossi, no government crawls to the Arabs like the French."

"Amos, will my son make Sayeret Matkhal?"

"He'll just have to apply, when the time comes."

"You put the idea in his head."

"I did."

"Now he'll be heartbroken if he can't get in."

"Look, he's courageous and physically he excels. He'll get his chance."

At takeoff Amos passed the *International Herald Tribune* to Kishote. "Seen this?" he shouted over the jet roar. A cartoon reprinted from the *Los Angeles Times* showed Kissinger trying to drag a balky mule with a Golda Meir face to a wagon labelled "Peace Process," where a Sadat-featured mule stood smiling in the traces, ready to pull. On the ground lay a wooden plank, lettered NO MORE AID. The caption read, *"To reason with a mule, use a two-by-four."*

"I've seen worse in our own press," said Kishote. "The country's in a total funk. In the army, in the government, in the people, I see nothing but decay and collapse."

Amos argued against Kishote's gloom. The war-weariness in the country was a natural thing, he said, but in fact the future looked good. The Arabs had blown their one shot at a decisive surprise assault, Israel had passed an ultimate test of fire, and Zahal now controlled more Arab territory than it had before the war. The enemy had learned once for all that the military option led nowhere. Egypt had broken the united Arab front with the face-to-face disengagement talks at Kilometer 101. If the national objective was peace, it was coming closer.

"Well, I like your attitude, young fellow," Kishote said, "but we don't hold the cards we held, our image is badly damaged, and to me the crime against Dado is a symptom of deep rot."

The stewardess brought lunch trays. Amos bantered with her in French, her replies were perky, and when she swayed away Kishote said, "There's a girl you might have fun with in Paris."

"More trouble than it would be worth," Amos said.

Kishote recalled seeing him hanging around one of the French wives at the Barak wedding. Was she awaiting him in Paris? *That* could prove far more trouble than it was worth. But the young man was not asking his advice. Yossi settled back in his chair and slept like a soldier in the field. In the airport he hurried off to make his Los Angeles connection, and Amos passed through customs behind the twin of the hijacker, who now seemed harmless enough, juggling luggage like everyone else.

At the front of the crowd outside the plane gate, Madame Fleg gave Amos a shy little wave. She wore a pale blue suit with a crisp white collar, a lily of diamonds as a shoulder pin, and a small gray hat and veil.

"Hi. This is for you, Irene."

"*Tiens!* A present!" She began tearing the duty-free shop wrapping off the package.

"Wait, wait till you get home."

"I never can . . . Oh, Amos!"

"It's nothing. Just to replace the one that blew overboard."

She whipped the pink chiffon scarf around her neck and kissed him, a quick cool brush of thin lips on his mouth. *"Merci!"*

"Where do we get a cab?"

"Come along."

"My reservation is at the Hôtel Feydeau."

"Yes, you told me." She led him deftly through the terminal throng, and out into a warm rainy afternoon. "Here we are." To a wizened old chauffeur at a black Jaguar she said, "Take monsieur's bags, Theodor. Hop in, Amos."

In the back seat, while Theodor stowed the bags, Amos swept an arm around her. She pulled away with a warning smile, pointing at the chauffeur. As the car left the airport, she squeezed his hand hard against her wool-clad thigh. Amos kept wondering why to all the devils she had brought this decrepit driver. Couldn't she drive a Jaguar herself? Puzzling lady, but fascinating, that bony face, those high cheeks. A few wrinkles at those slanted clever eyes, so what? He knew a dozen smooth-skinned prettier girls who bored him.

They turned into a dead-end alley in an old section of Paris and stopped. "Where are we, Irene? This isn't the Feydeau."

"This is our garage, *chéri*," she said, as Theodor got out and opened a double wooden door. "The fact is, Armand insists that you stay with us."

"Armand? You said he'd be in Italy."

"Well, he got back early."

"Look, it's absurd, Irene, out of the question."

"It's done, *chéri*. Armand is a quiet man, but what he says, goes."

They entered from the back a narrow town house, where children's voices resounded as they went up many stairs. "We have a modest guest room for those who can climb three flights," she said, panting a little.

"Call this modest?" There was a four-poster bed, hunting prints on the walls, and a red leather armchair and ottoman by a brick fireplace. He dropped the bags, seized the slender body of Irene Fleg and gave her a hungry kiss. "Look, Irene, I can't stay in your house, you know it's preposterous —"

She slipped from his arms, whispering, "*Doucement*, here's Madeline." In walked a tall uniformed maid with a square hairy face, carrying towels and bed linen. Behind her came the son wearing a natty school uniform, who snapped to attention and saluted. *"Bonjour, le vrai héros!"*

"Bonjour!" Saluting, Amos racked his brain for a way to get out of this trap. He had not flown to Paris for five days of bourgeois hospitality, to all the devils. Romance under the Fleg roof, with three children racketing around and servants popping in and out, was not to be thought of.

"Come, Anatole," said Irene Fleg, "we'll let the hero rest before dinner, and I'll help you with your English lessons."

In her son's room she coached him through Poe's "The Raven," smiling about poor Amos up there in comic discomfiture. She had been unable to resist his telephoned offer to come to Paris. He would expect her to make love, she realized, *vite, vite,* on his arrival, no doubt in his hotel room; not her style, but she had agreed to his visit, leaving all to chance and impulse. Her husband's early return had gotten her out of an awkward spot. End of problem, Amos was here for five days under her roof. Why look beyond that?

The dinner with the Flegs that night was not a comfortable experience for Amos. The salmon and the duck were delicious, the wines better than any he had yet tasted, the attentions of the gliding blank-faced manservant somewhat unnerving. The three children sat silent, eating with neat manners until Monsieur Fleg asked them questions about their schoolwork, when they answered up to his satisfaction, judging by his faint smiles and nods. Irene sat silent. Evidently the dinner table was Fleg's domain. He talked about Israel's economic problems with a grasp beyond Amos, sharp-focussed as Amos was on warfare, security, and his own advancement. And the pictures on the walls looked like a real Renoir and a real Modigliani, and the furniture was massive and gleaming, and the dishes and silver were obviously very costly, and it was all too much for Amos Pasternak. He was not intimidated, nothing could do that, but he felt at Monsieur Fleg's table like a tamed bear sitting upright.

"I haven't asked you to talk about the war, Amos," said Fleg over a green cream dessert. "You didn't come to Paris for that. Having you with us is an honor, and the house is yours."

For the first time, the boy Anatole spoke without being spoken to. "I should like to talk to the hero about the war."

"We will talk," said Amos. "Maybe tomorrow."

That night came a tap on his door, and Irene Fleg entered in a silvery silk robe over a white negligee. He was already in bed, wearing only shorts. He leaped out and embraced her, but she pushed him off. "*Doucement*," she said, "go back to your bed and let me tell you something."

The command was gentle but serious. He obeyed. She sat down in the armchair and lit a cigarette. "Armand is not here tonight. He is undoubtedly with his mistress of some years, a dancer at the Opera, a Polish woman, pleasant enough. Since Françoise, my third child, was born we have slept in separate rooms."

Pause, a long drag on the cigarette.

"I have no arrangement, so to say, with any gentleman, and I'm quite content with that state of things. That is, I was content until I agreed like a madwoman to go to Beirut. Since then I have been discontented. *Stay where you are.* You would be a very great fool, Amos Pasternak, to become involved with me in any way. I would be even sillier to allow it. It's no good. I did agree to your coming to Paris, and that was as impulsive and foolish as my going to Beirut. Now be wise and send me back to my room."

Amos got off the bed and pulled her to her feet. She touched his bare brown skin here and there. "Ah, such scars, such scars. Some not yet really healed —"

The robe slipped off.

"By God, you have an exquisite body, Irene."

"Not since my childbearing. Useful mainly for skiing, for a long time now. Leave it at that, Amos, I advise you, I *beg* you."

He did not, of course.

What followed were five days and nights not entirely of bourgeois hospitality. Amos Pasternak was no newcomer to lovemaking, nor to romantic passion, but those days and nights marked a sharp turn in his life. Although she never said so in her whispered endearments, he surmised that she was snared like himself in something powerful, that this was not an older woman merely enjoying herself with a young buck. Encountering Armand Fleg during those days, usually at dinner but twice at morning coffee, was very awkward for Amos. The free and easy ways of Israelis did not stretch to this sort of thing. But Monsieur Fleg was ever the genial bourgeois host, entertaining a war hero under his roof and considering it a privilege. He did convey to his guest, in a way too subtle for definition, that he was well aware of how far his hospitality was extending, and that it was quite all right with him. In short, Amos was in civilized Europe.

On their last night together, their passion took on an edge of poignancy that forced from him, in the early hours of the morning, a cry from the heart. Was it unthinkable to Irene that she leave her husband and marry him? It would be difficult, but he was ready to do it, and how could they live without each other, after this? How could they endure long separations?

Irene Fleg was absolutely horrified. Sitting up naked, pulling a sheet over her slight breasts, she talked hard sense. What on earth was the point? How was it possible? Would he abandon his career in the army and come to Paris to live? Or did he expect her to give up her children, her home, her way of life, and come to Israel, where she could not even speak the language?

"*Chéri*, you move me to tears," she said, looking not in the least tearful, "but you must forget this nonsense, now and forever. *Mon Dieu*, don't you realize how lucky we are, how beautiful this is? We can meet whenever you're free, and wherever we please. Rome, Madrid, Nice, Venice, all Europe is ours. We can ski. We can sail the Greek islands, there's no end to the pleasure we can have together —"

"But, Irene —"

"Amos, look at that window, it's growing light. Come here."

35

"We Unbelievers"

The lecture appearance by Professor Max Roweh at a bat mitzvah in a Beverly Hills temple, which Don Kishote attended with Yael, happened in this way. The father of the bat mitzvah girl, one Lew Katzman, was a film mogul of the newer sort, the lean gray chairman of GAA, as everyone called the Great Artists Agency; a solid citizen, a supporter of Israel, and a temple trustee. For the Friday night forum of Tamara Katzman's bat mitzvah weekend, her father told the rabbi he wanted the best Jewish lecturer in the world, money no object.

"The best in the world, Lew? Depends," said the young rabbi. "If you're talking fame, you want Elie Wiesel or Isaac Bashevis Singer. If you want substance, it's Isaiah Berlin or Max Roweh, but Berlin won't fly here from England. Roweh's at Columbia."

"Isn't Roweh the guy who married a Rothschild, and heads some big foundations?"

"Well, nominally he does, but he has managers for that."

"And did he write that book, *The Fork in the Road*, or whatever, that got such incredible reviews?"

"*Vico and Descartes*. Yes, that's Roweh."

"Real class. Get him."

The rabbi beamed. "Great. He's my mentor for the Ph.D. thesis I'm writing. I love Max."

"What does he cost?"

"Ten bills." The rabbi was picking up movie parlance. "The whole fee goes to his foundations. I warn you, he'll talk over some people's heads."

"So what? In his field he's a superstar. We'll have a little dinner party at home for him afterward. I'll put Tamara next to him. Maybe some of that brainpower will rub off on her."

Roweh accepted, and when two weeks before the lecture the rabbi telephoned him to ask for the title, the professor said, " 'We Unbelievers.' " Silence from the rabbi. "That troubles you? I can also call it 'Napoleon, Wingate, and Vico's Theory of the Barbarism of Reflection.' "

"No, no. 'We Unbelievers' sounds fine, Max. Catchy. It's a free forum. You won't deny the existence of God, will you, Max? In my pulpit? There are limits."

"I'll leave the question open. How's that?"

"I'm relieved."

A professorial chuckle. "So is He, I daresay, if He exists and is listening."

So Don Kishote stood at a full-length mirror in Yael's apartment that Friday night, contemplating himself in a tuxedo, the first time in his entire life that he had put one on. The rented suit fitted well, but to him it seemed a getup like a Robin Hood or Hamlet costume. "I look grotesque," he said.

"You look fine," said Yael, coming in from her bedroom in a new long Givenchy dress, putting on diamond earrings.

He pointed to the invitation on a table. "Yael, what kind of a title is that for a temple lecture, 'We Unbelievers'?"

"It's pure Max."

"Is he an atheist? And if so, why have they got him to lecture at a big bat mitzvah?"

"Listen and you'll learn something. Will you tuck Eva into bed?"

"With pleasure."

Yossi dressed his daughter in pajamas while she prattled in

Hebrew and English. For a while he sat with her over a picture book, loving the touch of her hand on his. When this elf put both hands to his face and said "Abba," or when she danced and sang for him, Los Angeles did not seem such a bad place after all. If only he still felt anything for Yael, he thought, he would certainly stay here for a while, then press her to come home with Eva. But he could not fake it.

Yael looked in. "Ready, Yossi? I am."

"Let's go."

Every seat in the temple, accommodating two thousand, was taken when they got there, except for the first three center rows roped off for the Katzmans' black-tie dinner guests. The temple was popular, Lew Katzman had a wide acquaintance, and besides, there was the sure prospect of a lavish bat mitzvah buffet. Max Roweh was also a draw. Most of the audience had read reviews of his books, and reviewers lavished praise on Max Roweh; none ventured to cry the emperor had no clothes, for fear that he might in fact be royally robed. How could they tell? When his fellow philosophers argued with him in small journals, they used jargon as remote from plain English as Swahili. So far as this audience knew, Max Roweh was a big-name intellectual, a classy ornament for Tamara Katzman's bat mitzvah.

Katzman's celebrity clients like Faye Dunaway and Dustin Hoffman caused ripples of talk as they took seats in the reserved section, but the others did not: family members, the Israeli consul-general, the Nitzans, and close business associates like Sheva Leavis and Lee Bloom. To Don Kishote this first glimpse of a big American temple was mind-boggling. What could it have cost to build? Millions and millions! Sitting next to him was the famous film comedian Cookie Freeman, in his trademark horn-rimmed eyeglasses, and beside Freeman was nobody less than Meryl Streep! Quite a change, altogether, from the bunkers of Tasa.

Max Roweh was a convincing professorial presence at the podium: badly needing a haircut, his dinner jacket baggy and wrinkled, his black tie crooked. "We unbelievers," Roweh began, after a cordial greeting to the Katzman family and a mild joke about the rabbi's half-finished thesis, "we unbelievers, I say, are confronted with a large perplexity in recent history." He paused, beaming around at the audience through thick glasses. Those were the last words he spoke at normal speed. Thereafter the speech came in machine-gun bursts of words, with quick jerky hand gestures.

"Since next Sunday is Israel's Independence Day, that perplexity will be my theme. I shall argue that the Return of the Jews to the Promised Land, though possibly the most remarkable event of modern times, is no support whatever for the notion of divine intervention in human history" — he glanced over at the purple-robed rabbi in his ornate chair — "a notion no doubt regularly promulgated from this pulpit."

In the audience, slight titters, nods, and nudges among the regular worshippers.

"We unbelievers hold, you see, that our majestic old Hebrew faith is a naive if long-lived and splendid dream, extinct as believable truth since, let us say, the year 1687, when Newton published his *Principia*, or even earlier, when Descartes wrote *On Method*. Since these two giants and the other luminaries in the galaxy of the Enlightenment — Hobbes, Galileo, Copernicus, Spinoza, Hume — battered down the immense gloomy walls of dogma which imprisoned man's intelligence, and let the sunlight of naturalism into the human condition, most well-educated men can no longer take the Bible literally and believe, as our fathers did, in the old Jewish God. Instead our knowledge of the measurable realities in deep time and deep space, however incomplete, has become our poor ersatz Book of Genesis; sadly inferior as poetry and profound vision to the scriptural Genesis, but displacing it as fact. We do not have to assert with Nietzsche's Zarathustra that God is dead. We unbelievers rather hold with Comte's view of God; and I much appreciate your forbearance, and that of your rabbi, in giving ear to an unbeliever, in this magnificent shrine to what Comte called 'an unnecessary hypothesis.' "

Audible rustlings and murmurs in the audience. Roweh flipped over several small sheets and rattled on.

"Now for our perplexity. We unbelievers have to face up to the striking chain of events and accidents of recent history, leading —

almost as though by the will of Providence, I readily grant — to the fantastic Return of the Jews, a historical anomaly nearly as unlikely, to the mind of a naturalist, as the resurrection of the dead. I shall very briefly trace this chain, before going further.

"One must, of course, start with Napoleon."

Another rustle, and something like a collective sigh, went through the enormous auditorium, as the audience perceived that it was in for a long wait before the buffet. But Yossi Nitzan found himself captivated by Roweh's amiable effrontery, as step by step he traced the extraordinary origins of Zionism, at each step denying that God had had anything to do with it. Roweh's general theme was that the major powers of the world, without any intent whatever to promote the interests of the Jews — in fact, sometimes with the opposite purpose — had each forwarded the most unlikely historical process that had created Israel.

Treating each power at some length but with express speed, he started with France because, as he said, Napoleon's campaigns in Egypt and Syria had opened the Middle East to modern times, and his spreading by armed force of the French Revolution's ideas of liberalism and equality had freed the Jews of Europe. When Roweh spoke of Russia, his rapid-fire delivery became tinged with passion. He stemmed from Russian Jewry, he said, and the pogroms of 1881 were a family memory. They had convinced millions of Russian Jews that they had no future under the Czar, so they had gone into the socialist underground, or to America like his own parents, or to Palestine. Zionism in its true beginnings was sparked by anti-Semitic Russian hooligans. Herzl and ideology came later.

The passage about England was fervent too. The British part in creating Israel, he had to admit, was the nearest thing to a show of God's hand. The King James Bible had stamped in British culture so vivid a vision of an eventual Jewish return to Palestine, that an army general like Orde Wingate could risk his career training Jewish settlers in night fighting against Arab raiders, foreshadowing the Palmakh. The Balfour Declaration of 1917, the entire legal basis of Zionism and of Israel, seemed an outright miracle; but in fact the British were simply making such a declaration ahead of Germany, so as to win American Jews to their side in World War I. There was much more, about Lord Palmerston, George Eliot, and Winston Churchill, which was quite new to Kishote.

Roweh turned brusque and arid about America and Germany, rapidly flipping his handwritten notes. The American immigration law of 1924 slammed shut the Statue of Liberty's "golden door," he pointed out, compelling emigrating European Jews to consider Palestine instead; and the German Holocaust created a short-lived mood of world favor for the Jews, resulting in the UN partition vote and the establishment of the Jewish State.

Picking the microphone from the bracket, trailing the wire to walk directly before the splendiferous Holy Ark, his notes left behind, Roweh exclaimed, "Ah, but the Arabs, dear friends, how can we unbelievers possibly account for the Arab contribution to Zionism? More than all other nations combined, more one is tempted to say than the Jews themselves, the Arabs have created Israel."

In one of his infrequent pauses for breath, a murmur rose in the audience, which he seemed to welcome. "Absurd? Perverse? Self-contradictory? But just consider and bear well in mind, my friends, the words of George Bernard Shaw: '*My best friend is my worst enemy, the one who keeps me up to the mark.*'

"Who but the Arabs forced Jews to learn the art of war again, forgotten since the Romans crushed Bar Kokhba? Who woke in them the dormant genes of Joshua's warriors, by making the very first settlers fight to survive in the ruined and barren Holy Land?

"Dear friends, how could the Arabs rationally have rejected early British proposals which would have given them control of Palestine, ended Jewish immigration, and made present-day Israel an impossible dream? How could they have rejected the UN partition which awarded them a Palestinian State?

"What did they do instead? They invaded newborn Israel on five fronts, giving the Jews a brief chance to capture enough territory, in defending themselves, to make their borders viable. And in 1967, by threatening a second Holocaust, they triggered the Six-Day War, a triumph that won Israel the whole world's reluctant admiration, and made Zionists of nearly all the world's Jews.

"Moreover, to this day their terrorism sustains sympathy for

Israel. Arab thinkers have themselves told me, in confidence and in despair, that this persisting blindness of their own people to what they are doing can only be the will of Allah. Though we unbelievers do not accept that explanation, we can certainly understand it."

Concentrate as he might on Roweh's iridescent flow of words, Yossi was befuddled by what followed, a rapid run through Vico's theory of 'the barbarism of reflection,' as it related to the civilization of Islam, which Roweh clearly admired, and in which he saw the bedrock of future peace between Arabs and Jews. "Like Egypt in Moses' time," Roweh concluded on this theme, "Islam is a crucible of rejection for the Jews, in which the nation is being forged and tempered for another twenty centuries of survival against all odds."

He went back to the podium, fitted the microphone into its bracket, and looked around at the vast expanse of faces with a benign smile. "Have I gone on too long? I have simply done my best, in the forty minutes your rabbi allotted to me —" A ripple of audible amusement spread through the temple. "Sorry, I'm accustomed to a classroom bell to cut me off — I've done my best, I say, to suggest that for us unbelievers purely natural causes have propelled the Jews back into history. The accumulation of favoring events and coincidences, and I could cite many more, is exceedingly unusual, I concede. But in the end, the most unusual element of all is the will of the dispersed tiny Jewish people to survive forbidding odds through more than twenty centuries, and on the brink of annihilation, to come back to life and create the third Jewish commonwealth. Today, facing nuclear or environmental annihilation, all mankind needs such a will to survive. In that sense, if not in any Godly sense, the Jews may perhaps be called 'a light to the nations.'

"Yet to the believers among you in the supernatural explanation of Israel's rise, I can only say — and with this I conclude and take my leave — I can only say that you *almost* have a case. Tamara Katzman, my blessings on your bat mitzvah."

"Well, for a temple lecture it was all right," Cookie Freeman commented at the Katzman dinner party afterward, answering a query by the society columnist of the *Los Angeles Times*, Holly

Jonas, who sat beside him. Four tables for ten were set in the spectacular cathedral-ceilinged dining room, looking out through an arched picture window at the Los Angeles lights far below. At each table there was a celebrity, and Freeman had just taken his seat opposite Kishote with an irked glance through his black-framed glasses toward the number-one table, where Max Roweh sat with Yael Nitzan, the Katzmans, their bat mitzvah daughter, and Meryl Streep. "On the whole, a little too high-flown. And his windup about the Jews as a light to the nations was just ridiculous, in view of Israel's crappy image nowadays."

Holly Jonas gestured with embarrassment at Kishote. "Cookie, this is General Nitzan of the Israeli army."

"Sorry, General," said Freeman coolly. "You're well disguised. No offense meant."

"No problem," said Yossi. "I'm a fan of yours, sir, I've liked all your movies. But tell me more about our crappy image. I'm interested."

"It's not a topic to pursue, is it?"

"Why not? You made a frank remark, and I'd like to understand you. A lot of Israelis might agree with you."

"Are you here for fund-raising, General?"

Sheva Leavis said in a weak voice, "General Nitzan and I are looking into matters of mutual interest, Cookie." He looked frail and very old. "Go ahead and tell him just what you think. He can handle it."

"I'm sure of that." Freeman turned to Yossi. "You know the nursery rhyme Humpty-Dumpty?"

"Sure," said Yossi. "Humpty-Dumpty had a great fall, and couldn't be put together again. It's a riddle, and the answer is an egg."

"Just so, and Israel is Humpty-Dumpty, General," said Freeman. "You've had a great fall, and you can't be put back together again. Your image is gone, smashed for good and all. Israel now comes across as a sort of Jewish Albania that almost got wiped out, was saved by an American airlift, yet still blocks all American efforts to make peace in the Middle East."

"Do you believe that," Yossi inquired, "or are you talking about image?"

"Mainly I'm talking image."

"And what do you believe?"

"If you really want to know what I believe, General Nitzan, I believe it's a pain in the ass to be blamed on talk shows for what you Israelis do, and to be asked whether I'm for Israel or America."

"Yossi, he's right about the image," Sheva Leavis quietly put in. "A movie about Israel now couldn't possibly be a success."

"Okay," Yossi said to Freeman, "but we weren't saved by the airlift. Mostly it arrived after we crossed the Canal. It was a magnificent help, but we saved ourselves."

"That's not what people think here."

"Are you sure? I think most of them know that the one thing we've learned is to save ourselves. What's Israel all about, if not saving Jewish lives? If terrorists snatched you, for instance, Mr. Freeman, while you were doing a promotion tour in Europe — and it's a risk you'd better bear in mind these days, sir — we'd try to save you."

"Why?" Freeman looked amused. "I'm a pretty poor Jew, I'm just an artist."

"You could be a pretty poor artist," said Yossi, "but to us you'd still be a Jew."

Holly Jonas laughed and scrawled in a notebook. Cookie Freeman grimaced and changed the subject.

When the dinner party was breaking up Yael came to Kishote, flushed and bright of eye, followed by Professor Roweh. "Look, dear, can you make your way back to my apartment if you take my car? Very easy to find, drive back down to Sunset and west half a mile."

"No problem at all."

"You're sure you don't mind?" She handed him the car keys. "The professor and I have been talking, and he's asked me to join him for a nightcap."

"That is, if you'll allow me, General," said Max Roweh diffidently.

"Of course. I admired your lecture, sir, but I should tell you I'm a believer."

"From what I've heard of you, Don Quixote," the professor returned, "you have better reason than most."

Hours later Kishote was sitting up in bed, reading a travel book on Alaska and making notes, when Yael breezed in, saying cheerily, "Hi. What did you really think of the lecture?"

"He's got a brain like a focussing lens. Excellent, only the Vico stuff lost me."

"Oh, that's Max. I could feel the audience slipping away and so could he, he cut it short. Max believes he invented Vico." She stood smiling at him. "I hear you gave Cookie Freeman a hard time at Holly's table."

"Not at all. Just chatter."

"Yossi, we have to talk."

"Anytime," he said. "Now?"

"Not now. I'm falling into bed. First thing tomorrow."

In the morning he sat on the terrace conning an Alaska tourist map. At his feet the little blond girl played with a large cat. The sky was deep blue, the green-brown hills startlingly clear and close, and a high snowcapped peak rose stark in the distance, for a spell of high winds had blown off the smog. Yael came out in a flowing peach robe, carrying a newspaper. "Well, well, Mount Baldy," she said. "First time I've seen it in months." She showed him the society page, with a picture of the table where Max Roweh sat between Meryl Streep and Tamara Katzman. "Big story, and guess what, you're the headline, not Max or Streep or the bat mitzvah girl."

Holly Jonas's column began "COOKIE FREEMAN HAS A GREAT FALL." In the account Holly Jonas had changed "crappy" to "negative," noting that Freeman had used a ruder word. The item ended, *"It was Cookie's night to be Humpty-Dumpty."*

"So, I'm famous. What's on the front page? Anything on Israel?"

"No, it's all about the smoking gun and impeaching Nixon. Don't tell me!" She pointed in mock horror to the Alaska map. Since arriving in California, Yossi had been driving a rented car all over: the redwoods, Yosemite, Yellowstone, the Olympic rain forest. "Kishote, enough sightseeing already! When will you get to work with Sheva Leavis? He asked me again about it only last night."

"Yael, I'm enjoying myself. Anyway, the week I spent with Lee in Las Vegas discouraged me about Leavis's business altogether. It's the sewer of the world, Las Vegas. Hell must look like Las Vegas, electric signs and all."

"That's Lee's taste. You needn't have anything to do with Las Vegas. Mainly you'd be travelling in the Far East with Sheva. You should spend more time in our offices here." She sat down in a lounge chair, and put up shapely sunburned legs. "Now listen, Kishote, Max Roweh would like to marry me."

"Oo-ah!" He put aside the map and pushed up his glasses to look at her. "Max Roweh? Has he asked you?"

"How can he, when I'm married? A shy man like Max? Still, I can tell. Just take my word for it."

"You and Professor Roweh. Amazing."

"I know, I know, I'm illiterate and I'm nobody, but he's lonesome, and he likes me."

"Hm! I've sometimes thought about you and Sheva Leavis, but —"

"Such suspicions!" she said with a wily grin. "Well, Sheva is religious, and he has a wife who's been paralyzed for years, and that's that. I respect Sheva and I owe him a lot, but Max, he fascinates me. Him and his Vico! He's scary, but he can be sweet as a child."

"So you want a divorce?"

"Are you willing to discuss it?"

"Why not?"

The humiliation of Yossi's indifference had smoldered in Yael for years, and his easy acquiescence was not flattering. The maid came and took Eva off to play in a park while they probed the subject, agreeing on most matters. Money was no issue, for she had plenty and he had none. The sticking point was Eva. Yossi said she must grow up in Israel. "Let her run away to America, if that's how she turns out," he said, "after she's done her army service. She's my daughter. If you marry and come to live in Israel, fine, you take her."

"I have to think about that, Kishote."

"Okay."

"I know that Max does have a house in Jerusalem, in Yemin Moshe," she mused aloud, "which he hardly ever uses."

"Really? Mighty fancy, Yemin Moshe."

"Yes, his wife bought it long ago." Yael hesitated, and shrugged. "Oh, listen, this is all so premature. Right now I guess I'll ask my lawyers whether we should file here or in Israel. I'll do whatever you say about Eva." She held out a hand. "Gemacht?"

He got up and shook hands. "Gemacht."

She wryly laughed. "Now he won't ask me, and I'll be out in the cold."

"Out in the cold, you? Ha. I'll call Leavis, but anyway, I'm going to Alaska."

"I've never been to Alaska," said Yael, heavy at heart, and half hoping he would invite her along, even in jest. The break she had asked for was painful now that it was happening. But he said nothing, so she forced a gay tone. "The Eskimos had better look to their wives and daughters."

Don Kishote learned a lot in his Alaska tour. Confined as he had been in the nutshell of Israel, preoccupied with geographical flyspecks like the Golan Heights and the Sinai, he had never quite perceived the minuteness of his field of action. In the American West he had glimpsed the vastness and beauty of the earth, and in Alaska his vision further cleared. The boundless majesty of the mountain ranges, glaciers, forests, and snowfields stopped his breath. He saw salmon schooling at a river mouth in the millions. He rode two days with a dog team over the snow, encountering no human being besides the driver, who talked only about oil and gas deposits and bear hunting. He figured out that into the area of Alaska alone, seventy Israels could be fitted with ease. *Seventy!* Sobering. If ever he did leave Israel, he thought, he would come to this giant nearly empty American paradise to start life over.

Los Angeles by comparison, when he returned, struck him as

just a bigger and grimier Tel Aviv. Two letters awaited him in Yael's apartment. The one with Australian stamps he ripped open the instant he saw it.

July 2, 1974

Dear Yossi:

I arrived yesterday and am still very, very jet-lagged. A long trip! It looks as though I'll be too busy in the next couple of weeks to write a real letter, so this is just to let you know, as I promised, that I'm here. Melbourne is nice, a little like Toronto, and it's strange to be having winter weather in July, but of course that's how it is "down under." I'll be staying with Lena and Mendel (her husband, very good-natured man) until I find a flat, the sooner the better. Write me here meantime, if you feel like it. Reuven is terribly thin, but he was so happy to see me! Last night at dinner he ate like a tiger, Lena said he hadn't eaten that much the whole week before.

My department head at the Technion was nice about everything. I had earned a sabbatical anyway, and it starts in September, so I'll be here at least a year, and I'll be looking for things to do. Meantime I'm happy. Since Michael died and Lena took Reuven away I've been drawing my breath in misery, but no more. I'll always miss Michael, he was a wonderful man, but as long as I can be with Reuven I'm all right. I'm not looking any farther into the future.

I hope California doesn't seem too glamorous to you. Enjoy it, but then go home. You belong in Israel, and you're needed.

Love,
Shayna

The other letter was from Zev Barak. He had been against Kishote's departure, and now he was writing every week or two, urging him to cut short his leave and return to active duty.

Dear Yossi:

Things are very bad here. Kissinger squeezed a terrible price out of Golda for that disengagement in the north, and now that we have done our part and pulled back on the Golan Heights, the

Syrians are fudging on releasing prisoners and returning the dead. The army was demoralized enough by the firing of Dado. This retreat from our positions outside Damascus, to a line that actually gives back some territory to the beaten Syrians, has got all Zahal seething. But Golda needed the deal to stop the casualties and release the reserves, and she was too weakened politically to fight anymore. She's a sick old lady. Rabin has started off well, except that he's kept me on as military secretary. I pleaded for *any* other duty, or for retirement, in vain.

Motta Gur has repeatedly asked me about you. With so many officers vying for the few star staff posts, he can hardly offer one to a general who's left the country in a huff. Most of us feel badly about what was done to Dado, but with leadership goes responsibility, and Dado was Ramatkhal when Israel had its near-catastrophe. It's all in the past, the army is undergoing a convulsive reorganization, and you've got much to contribute. Anger and withdrawal are no contributions, Yossi, so by your life, don't get bogged in Los Angeles and dollar-chasing, leave all that to Yael. Come back where you belong.

Zev

Kishote sat on Yael's terrace for a long while in a sunny afternoon, rereading both letters and pondering.

"Let me understand you," said Sheva Leavis. "You've definitely decided to go with me on my next Far East trip?"

"If you still want me, sir."

"And what decided you?"

"I've had a chance to think things over. My army service will soon end. The world's bigger than Israel, and you're offering me a chance at something interesting and worthwhile to explore for my future."

"You and Yael are getting divorced."

"I'm afraid so."

"A pity." The window behind Leavis's desk faced downtown Los Angeles and City Hall. He swiveled and looked out on tall buildings, half-obscured by smog. A silence. "Los Angeles is not what it used to be. Neither am I." He turned back to Kishote. "If you're serious, fine. Your brother has proven himself very able, and you have an outstanding army record. Finances we can discuss. Have you any questions for me?"

"Do you go to Australia?"

"Why do you ask? Not usually."

When Yossi started to tell him about Shayna, the old man raised a hand. "So, Mrs. Berkowitz has gone there, has she? I know about Mrs. Berkowitz, and I have a question for you. Are you accepting my offer to learn a business, or so that you can see Mrs. Berkowitz?"

"Frankly, both."

"Not good enough. I don't plan to go to Australia this time. Maybe not for the next year or two. And you can't detour to Australia when you're with me, the distances are tremendous and my schedule is tight. Think it over some more."

36

Shayna and Kishote

Don Kishote thought it over and accepted Leavis's terms, including the proviso against side trips to Australia. Travelling with the old Iraqi Jew was an eye-opener like Alaska, a discovery of experiences as remote as the moon from Israeli army life. During the long flights passed in the luxury of first class, and the many nights in posh hotels, the withered little man talked and talked about his business, educating Kishote as they went. Each of Leavis's circuits in the Far East took many weeks. An ultimate middleman, Kishote gradually learned, was what Leavis really was, and his stock-in-trade was his word, backed by large quantities of ready money.

The old trader brought Kishote with him to meetings in Manila, Taipei, Hong Kong, and Singapore, and in remote small towns, too. Sometimes they dealt with Jews, more often with Orientals. Kishote saw for himself how hard-bitten Filipinos who looked like murderers, and old Hong Kong Chinese in western clothes, with gracious manners and blank eyes, talked business with Sheva Leavis. Whether the deal concerned a shipload of Indian cloth, a year's output of a Korean toy factory, a collection of rare works of antique Chinese art, or the entire sugar crop of a small Philippine island, Leavis could close for a million dollars with a handshake, and the deals went through as though sealed by a twenty-page contract. There was sometimes the matter of "taking care," as Leavis put it, of the people who closed the sales. Whether they were businessmen or government functionaries, "taking care" included limousines, apartments, hard cash, and — though here Leavis drew the line — women. His competitors routinely supplied women, he did not. He made up for that, he told Kishote, with the best prices and quick payment.

The heart of the matter was buying cheap in the East and selling dear in the West. Leavis knew East and West as Yossi knew the Centurion tank and the Sinai terrain. When Yossi on an early trip protested that he could never learn to conduct such trade himself, Leavis tiredly told him that the whole world was now one place, and wherever Yossi went when he was on his own they could still talk as though they were together. At first Yossi would be his eyes and ears, and he, Leavis, would make the decisions. But after a while Yossi would be able to handle it. "What it comes down to, once you know the business," Leavis said, "is contacts with people who have the power to make deals, people you've known for years, and who know you and trust you. By now you've met many of them, and they've met you. The rest is numbers, certain key numbers. They differ with each kind of deal, each type of merchandise. You'll learn. I'm not wasting my time or yours."

The itineraries eventually took them not only to India, Burma, Malaya, and Indonesia, but even into mainland China, where Yossi's Israeli passport was useless; Leavis did not disclose how he got him in, but he did say this was one place Yossi by himself probably would have to skip. The sights of these exotic lands were not novel to Kishote after so much exposure in movies and magazines, but the long long grinds in airplanes were. He once asked Leavis how he could have endured it all these years. The trader uttered a dry laugh. "Long? The jets are magic carpets. I travelled for thirty years in piston planes, and before that in trains and boats. My father did that, too. His father before him sometimes went on donkeys and camels. In this business what you do is travel."

Yossi gave up the notion of flying to Australia on his own when Leavis could spare him. The long haul to that continent, even in jets, was a discouraging prospect, and from Shayna's letters he gathered that he could accomplish little anyway by showing up in Melbourne. Her reaction to his news of the divorce was reserved and cool, and she evaded or ignored his words about marriage. She had let her Technion position lapse and was working at Melbourne University as an assistant mathematics instructor, low-paying but something to do. Being near Reuven was enough for her, she wrote, the future could take care of itself. Between the melancholy lines Yossi hoped he discerned the old love, obscured by great doubt that his divorce would come off. The match of Yael and Max Roweh, whose books Shayna had read, she regarded as preposterous and unreal.

Winding up a very long journey, Leavis at last put two deals in Yossi's hands to manage, one in Tokyo, one in Seoul. Yossi had met these businessmen on previous trips, and had in fact once gotten hilariously drunk with the Japanese trader. He negotiated while Sheva sat by silent, and each time he shook hands on terms Sheva had instructed him to get. As they dined in the Seoul hotel the evening after that deal was closed — or rather as Kishote dined, while Leavis ate his usual travel dinner of bread and raw fruit — the old man abruptly said, "Yossi, I'm sending you on to Melbourne. That's why we were visiting those aluminum refineries yesterday. Two or three years down the road the Korean government plans a big expansion in aluminum, and they'll need much more bauxite, huge quantities. I'll put you in touch with some bauxite people in Melbourne. One of the main executives is Jewish, from Lithuania."

"Elohim, that's marvellous. Thank you, Sheva."

"For what? You mean Mrs. Berkowitz? That's your business. Keep it out of ours, which is bauxite."

The card on the door read DR. BERKOWITZ. The gray-haired lady secretary of the department knocked and called in Aussie accents, "Dr. Berkowitz, you have a visitor."

Shayna came to the door, looked out, and staggered against the doorpost. "Good God, Kishote, why do you do this to me? Do you want me to drop dead?"

He stood there in brown tweed and a red wool tie, holding

out both hands. "Hamoodah, I tried to call from Seoul, but your flat didn't answer and I had to catch the plane in a hurry, so I just came."

Tears were starting to her eyes. The secretary discreetly withdrew. "Oh, Yossi, crazy Yossi." The startled look melted to a smile. She grasped his hands. "It's so good to see a face from home! How long has it been, dear? More than a year, a lot more, no?"

"A lot more, Shayna."

"Well, God bless you for coming. I've loved your letters, but it's not the same, is it? And listen, it's about time for me to pick up Reuven, come along, my God, will he be pleased to see you!" She led him out through the grassy campus to a parking lot, her walk as light-footed as in the old days. She wore a bright blue cardigan sweater over a white blouse, and a heavy brown skirt. The rattletrap old Vauxhall she drove made so much noise that they had to shout at each other, catching up on news since the last letters.

Reuven was sitting on a bench in the play yard of the Hebrew school, watching his classmates roughhousing with skullcaps flapping. "Dode Yossi!" He hobbled with his crutch to meet him, pouring out questions. Where had he come from? How long would he be here? Would he be staying in Australia? How was Dode Zev? How was Aryeh? Kishote picked him up and exclaimed, "Oo-ah, Reuven! This is more like it. You've gained weight." He was smaller than the other nine-year olds gambolling around, but felt solid now.

"He eats when I'm with him," said Shayna. "I have to call your mother, Reuven, and tell her about General Nitzan."

"Oh, come home with me, Yossi," the boy laughed. "I live in a nice big house."

Bulkily pregnant, thick arms folded, Lena was waiting on the porch of a brick row house, with a small front garden turned autumn brown in April. "What a surprise! Welcome, General. You'll stay to dinner, of course. Mendel can't wait to meet you. He's on his way home. Come, Reuven, eat something and do your lessons."

Shayna and Yossi sat down on the porch, and he told her about his latest trip with Sheva Leavis, and the success that had earned him the trip to Melbourne. "Come on, Yossi," she said. "I'm really puzzled. Surely you aren't going in seriously for such business, just buying and selling. That's not you."

"Well, after the army I have to do something. I'm becoming interested."

"Oh, nonsense. Yael has put you up to it, that's all." With a wise look she added, "I daresay you're having fun, though, you no-good. All the ladies in far-off places —"

"Shayna, it's given me a chance to see you, and here I am."

Shayna reddened, and tossed her head much as she had as a small girl. "Now look, about Lena's husband, don't mind anything he says. He's not a bad person, Mendel. But a fool? Heaven watch and preserve us."

He showed up shortly, a paunchy man with heavy jowls and thick rippling black hair. "Good-o, General, what an honor!" He pumped Yossi's hand there on the porch. "I say, those Ay-rabs gave you Israeli chaps a proper walloping this last round, didn't they? Luckily Uncle Sam was there to save your arses, what, what? Come in, come in."

The table reminded Yossi of the Berkowitz flat in Haifa before Lena's divorce, for while he sat with Mendel and Lena, Shayna and Reuven were at the other end with different cutlery and plates, eating different food. Mendel explained to Yossi that the kosher laws were just for hot countries in ancient days before refrigeration, and made no sense now, but he respected Reuven's upbringing and his late father's wishes. "You can't beat pork sausages and eggs for breakfast," he said. "Snorkers, we call them here. You can't beat snorkers and eggs, General, but since Reuven came, all pork is out of this house."

Rattling along in an accent half Aussie and half Yiddish, he said this country was a good place for Jews, and many South Africans who could get their money out were coming here, also some Russians, and a surprising lot of Israelis. His late father had made a big mistake, going into kangaroo leather. That business was all dog-eat-dog. He now owned a fine piece of riverfront land in a Melbourne suburb, and he meant to develop it when he could find a partner with capital, probably a South African. He ran on at some length about how well off Jews were in Australia, no Ku Klux Klan as in America, no wars as in Israel, and the weather was much better than Canada's, and the Canadian dollar was too wobbly.

Under Shayna's coaxing Reuven ate a plateful of chicken and dumplings, and when dinner was over the boy implored Kishote to stay. "I wish I could go home with you," he said, stumping outside with him and Shayna. "I don't like it in Australia, except I like my mother."

"I'll be here a few days, Reuven, but then I'm just going to California."

"Will you ever come again?"

Yossi hesitated, and looked at Shayna. "If I have to, I will."

"Back into the house, Reuven," said Shayna, and he obeyed. "There's a nice park near here, Yossi. A lake, swans. Are you tired?"

"Not a bit."

As they walked in the cool moonlit night he got her to talk about herself and her plans. The university was starting a nuclear institute, and an appointment was open for her. Also, at Reuven's Hebrew day school, where she had taught for a while, they wanted her as assistant principal, for better money. The trouble was that the principal, a widower, had proposed to her and she had turned him down. "Makes it awkward," she said with a small laugh. "Actually, I've had one other proposal here. Orthodox ladies are in short supply, down under."

His arm went around her waist. "Yes, I'm sure that's the attraction, the orthodoxy," he said.

"Easy now, Kishote." But she did not pull away. "It's no trouble to chill them. I just say my husband must plan to go back to Israel with me one day. That does it. These Australian Jews think Israel's as dangerous as Chicago in the gangster days."

"You'd go back without Reuven?"

No immediate answer. "Here's the park. Nice in the moonlight, isn't it? The lake's down this path. Yes, Reuven's the problem. Lena has every right to him, but he's not happy. He misses his friends, but mainly it's the religion. A lot of the Australian Jews are religious, but not Mendel, and Lena never has been, of course. She tries to feed him kosher food, she truly does in her fashion, but he sits there apart with his different dishes — and Passover's coming, and all they do about that is put a box of matzoh on the table. They don't prepare, and he can't eat there all week, he'll have to live with me. It's all so unsatisfactory . . ." She took his arm and hugged it. "Oh, let's talk about something else. You know, I've been sitting in my flat, Kishote, playing tapes of Israeli songs — 'Shoshana,' 'Finjan,' 'Sycamore Garden,' the old ones — it's my one pleasure besides being with Reuven, reliving my childhood. Remember when you dumped my pail of water over your head during the siege? All the water for my whole family for the day? It's a wonder I ever talked to you again."

Kishote had spent the night before that carrying sacks of flour on his back to besieged Jerusalem, marching with other volunteers on the secret bypass road through the wilds, used mainly by supply mules and piled with their dung.

"You complained I smelled of mule shit, and I did."

"Yossi, you didn't mind what Mendel said about the war, did you? He has kangaroo leather for brains."

"I've heard worse things said about Israel at home, by smarter people."

"Look, look, Yossi, the swans, little white gliding ghosts on the black water."

He took her in his arms.

"No, no, none of this, by your life, no." She permitted a reluctant few kisses, then spoke in muffled tones. "Be honest, I beseech you. The divorce isn't for real, is it?"

"Shayna, it's been filed in the rabbinic court in Israel, uncontested. It's taken forever, but it'll soon be final."

"Amazing. I swear I never believed she'd give you up."

"She didn't have me to give up. Moreover Professor Roweh is quite somebody. That's for real too."

"I don't want to go home without Reuven, no. The truth is, I've talked to Mendel about adopting him, and he was noncommittal, but I suspect he wouldn't mind too much, now that a child of his own is coming along. Reuven's a burden to Mendel. No snorkers, and so on. But I can't approach Lena, I just can't."

"Let me think about it."

He pulled her down on a bench. She held him off at first, then they were kissing with the passionate abandon of twenty years ago, in the week before their breakup, when she had been sure she was about to become a bride.

A call from Mendel woke Kishote next morning in his hotel room. Distances weren't great in Melbourne, Mendel said, and the office of the bauxite firm was on the way to his land property. He would be glad to show Yossi the acreage, then take him to his appointment. Too sleepy to argue, Yossi agreed. In that case, Mendel went on, he would join him for breakfast at the hotel, so he could have snorkers and eggs. "Can't beat snorkers and eggs," he said. "I do like a decent breakfast when I can get it."

The land was pleasantly situated on high ground overlooking a river. Mendel broadly hinted that it was a marvellous investment for a forward-looking party like Mr. Leavis, and Yossi let it go at that. His meeting at the bauxite firm was short because the Jewish executive was on holiday, expected back in a day or two. Mendel waited for him and drove him to the university campus, where he was meeting Shayna for lunch. "Shayna's a fine woman, but difficult," Mendel said. "She could make herself a nice life here, and I'll tell you something, adopting Reuven might not be so impossible then, sooner or later." With a wink he added, "Think about Australia yourself, General, one day. Lots of opportunities for a Jew with some get-up-and-go."

On the long, long flight back to Los Angeles, since he was not flying with Sheva Leavis, Kishote returned to the narrow seats and cramped legroom of tourist class, more his own style. When he was not thinking joyfully of his time with Shayna, or puzzling over the problem of recovering Reuven for her — which seemed to be the key to marrying her, anytime soon — he slept away the hours. After the clear air and antipodal peace of Melbourne, the Los Angeles airport was a vast foggy tumultuous letdown. Mendel might have something at that, Kishote thought, if a Jew wanted to settle outside Israel.

When he carried his luggage into Yael's apartment, he came on her sitting in a blue suede travelling suit with two bags packed.

"Yossi, do you know that Dado is dead?" He stared at her, dumbfounded. "That's right. Died while you were flying here. Sudden heart attack."

He murmured the blessing on evil tidings, "*Blessed be the True Judge*. When's the funeral, Yael?"

"Sunday."

"Sunday. Then I can still make it."

"Barely. I've been checking passenger lists on the flights from Australia, so I knew you were due. I've made TWA reservations for both of us. You have time to clean up and repack, but not much —"

"You're coming?"

"I may as well. We can wrap up the divorce papers, also I want to check on Max's house in Yemin Moshe. And there's some hotel business I can do for Sheva —"

"I should call Sheva."

"Not necessary, he assumes you're going straight on to Israel. How did you make out with the bauxite people?"

"All right. If the Korean government bid comes through, Sheva will make a lot of money."

In an altered tone, elaborately casual, she asked, "And how did you find Shayna?"

"That's a very long story."

"No doubt."

Golda Meir's car was stalled in the dense traffic and the pedestrian mob outside the cemetery. Zev Barak, sent by Prime Minister Rabin to escort her, jumped out to clear a way through the honking pileup, and at the wheel of a Hertz car he spotted Don Kishote. "Yossi!" he shouted. "Back at last? I thought you were in California!"

"I got here an hour ago," Yossi yelled back.

"Kol ha'kavod. Pull in behind us."

Prime Minister Rabin brought the tottery Golda to the section of seats near the grave site reserved for cabinet ministers, Supreme Court justices, and former Ramatkhals. In full uniform, six generals of the Yom Kippur War were carrying the big coffin on their shoulders through a tearful throng, a chaplain in the lead reciting psalms, more generals trudging before and behind the coffin. Don Kishote knew every one of these generals well. Whatever their jealousies, jostlings for power, and unseemly finger-pointing after the war, he was one of them, a brotherhood of death and fire. It was right that he had come so far and so fast to be here.

Rabin spoke over the open grave in his clear slow Hebrew. The eulogy was in part a comment on the Agranat Report, with all the commission members sitting there listening. *"Dado did not deny his responsibility, but he found himself singled out to shoulder the burden. . . . He resigned, and bore his great pain in silence, and with rare nobility of spirit . . . but his heart was not up to it, and it faltered and gave out . . ."*

Watching Golda, Kishote could see her put a handkerchief now and again to a rigid face. As he started to walk away in the crush of departing mourners, he felt a tug at his elbow. "Yossi, the Ramatkhal is astonished to see you here," said Barak. "He wants to talk to you."

"What about? He's extended my leave through September."

"Never mind. Call him. Are you really getting rich in Los Angeles?"

"Absolutely. Streets paved with gold."

"So I've heard. Don Kishote stooping to pick up California gold! Sad, sad." Barak gave him a rough embrace. "I've got to take care of Golda, she's a wreck. Don't fail to call Motta."

Back in the Tel Aviv flat, Kishote found Yael sorting the apparel in her closet. "Hi. I didn't remember I had so much stuff here. The moths have been at it, but I'll be all right. It's not for long. How did the funeral go?"

"A great tribute."

"You missed Aryeh. He waited here until noon for you, then he had to return to his base."

"I'll drive up to see him."

"He left you this note." She handed him a folded slip. "You won't recognize him. He has a fierce black mustache, like an Arab. He's terribly lean. I hugged him and he's all bones."

"That happens the first year, and the Sayeret Matkhal course is tougher than most. I have to shower and go see the Ramatkhal."

"Aren't you jet-lagged? I'm staggering around in a daze."

"I'm okay."

"Don't let him cut short your leave, no matter what, understand? Sheva's counting on you for the July trip. It's his main swing."

"I know that very well."

Seeing Motta Gur behind Dado's desk jarred Don Kishote. Once Chiefs of Staff had seemed superbeings to him, but as the years passed and Ramatkhals came and went they had been shrinking to human dimensions. Dado had retained a trace of heroic stature, but Motta Gur was just Motta, with that same round open face, thick hair, and clever eyes, a high flyer one career step above Yossi's own stratum. "Poor Dado," were the Ramatkhal's first words as they shook hands. "A fitting funeral. Honored him as he deserved. Sit down. So, Yossi. You're doing well in Los Angeles, are you?"

"No complaints, Motta."

"Dado meant to make you deputy chief of operations, you know."

"Yes, then the Agranat axe fell on him."

The Ramatkhal gave him a long calculating look. "You're not due back until September, are you? It happens — in confidence — that the slot's opening up right now."

Yossi was taken aback. The present deputy chief was an old friend, and he had no idea what the problem might be. But asking questions was inadmissible. "Sir, several brigade generals are ahead of me for such a post."

"Not if I decide otherwise." The Ramatkhal laughed. "I still remember you coming up through the trapdoor of the Rockefeller Museum roof, all bandaged and bloody, in '67. And I know how you performed in Sinai."

"I'm so out of touch, sir —"

"You'd be back in touch in a week. Your fresh outlook might be a plus. It's a different army now, Yossi, a huge machine. We're still digesting the war, still reorganizing. But for this job you must come back now. I can't wait until October. It's what Dado wanted for you, remember. Talk to Yael, and let me know this week. She's in Los Angeles?"

"No, she came with me."

"Give her my warm regards."

Driving to Aryeh's camp in the north, Yossi mulled over the proposal, much less dazzled than he had been by Dado's original offer. It meant a sudden return to the small space of Israel, and the smaller space of Zahal. He was planning to come back, he coveted the vine leaf of an *aluf,* a major general, and Dado's death had put period to the sordid aftermath of the war. But with the commission Leavis was paying him, a small percentage of each deal they made on the trips, he was accumulating a surprising amount of money, and he had gotten used to the pleasures of what Israelis wistfully called "the big world"; not excluding, as Shayna had surmised, the ladies in far-off places. An abrupt cutoff of all that?

The paratroopers' camp where Yossi had once been based had a new concrete command building, a new mess hall; and the area of barracks, formerly a small clearing in the woods, now stretched out of sight. But all army camps, small or big, looked much the same: boyish and girlish soldiers hurrying about the paths, signs hopelessly urging smartness of uniform, unit banners and Israeli flags flapping in the dusty wind. The base commander greeted him with a glad hail. "Yossi, you'll have dinner with me."

"Depends, Yigal. Where's Aryeh's outfit?"

"Up on the Golan. Big combined armor and air exercise starts before dawn."

"Lend me a jeep, then. My time's short, and my Hertz car is too dainty for the Golan."

"No problem."

It was a rough long climb from the Daughters of Jacob bridge up the escarpment, and night was falling when he saw a line of Centurions silhouetted on a ridge. Taking a jolting shortcut over stony fields, he passed a crowd of soldiers sitting on a hillside in the cold starry night. Inside the operations tent, the battalion commander and his staff were conning a map under one glaring lamp. The commander jumped up and saluted. "This is very fortunate,

General Nitzan. We're having a bonfire ceremony in memory of Dado, with army singers. I was going to speak, but you served with him. Will you talk, sir? Just a few words, whatever comes to mind? Will you honor us?"

Yossi was tempted, his heart and mind were full of Dado thoughts, but he recalled old times when big brass had visited sons in the field; so he declined, knowing Aryeh would much prefer a low-profile visit. He returned to the soldiers, hundreds of them, ranged on the hill that sloped down to an unlit pile of wood. A soldier heaping on more wood called to him, "Abba! Abba, don't you recognize me?"

A torch was thrown just then, and the pile flared up in a cloud of red fire and black smoke. The bespectacled mustached soldier, taller than himself, came loping to him and hugged him. "How are you, Abba?"

"I'm fine. Why are you croaking like a frog?"

"Caught a cold, running fifteen kilometers in the rain."

As the bonfire blazed high the troops started to sing, and Don Kishote felt a tug back to his soldiering days. The rough male voices, the firelit young faces, the fragrance of Golan herbage, the myriad stars one never saw over Los Angeles, or for that matter over Tel Aviv, the heat of the bonfire on his face, his son beside him in uniform, a hard-bodied recruit of Sayeret Matkhal: all this rekindled in Don Kishote's spirit a spark dimmed by time and circumstance — love for Zahal, love for the Jewish people, love for the freckle on the globe called Israel.

The troupe of singers, two girls and two boys, mounted a low platform near the roaring bonfire, and performed old army songs to the wail of an accordion — "The Unknown Platoon," "The Paratrooper Song," "To the North with Love" — all with the recurring sad undertone about the fallen. The soldiers joined in the refrains, Aryeh too in a hoarse baritone. They had not yet had the experiences, thought Kishote, but at least they knew the songs. The performers began an air force song that tore at him, with words too poignant to give pleasure; "We Must Play On," likening the air force to a harp of many strings which kept breaking.

And we play on with one string less
And again one string less
And some strings that break will not be mended
And some are mended and again they sound
And this song can never stop
And we're forced to play on, play on —

Aryeh looked at his father, who had a hand over his eyes. "Abba? You okay?"

"Dov Luria," muttered Don Kishote. "Dado."

"I know," said his son, and Kishote felt a muscular arm tighten around his shoulders.

Yael was awakened by Kishote, talking on the telephone in the hallway. Where was she? What day was it? Memory returned of the impulsive air trip and her jet-lag collapse into bed. Pulling aside heavy drapes, she winced at the blinding morning sun, and looked at her watch.

"Sheva Leavis sends you his love," said Kishote as she came into the kitchen.

"I swear, Yossi, I must have slept twelve hours. Is that who you were on the phone with?"

"Yes. I told him I wasn't coming back to Los Angeles."

"You *didn't*!"

"He was decent about it. Said he half expected it, and we'd stay in touch."

Yael rubbed her eyes. "I need coffee and a bath. Have you been up long, or what? You look bleary."

"I went to see Aryeh on the Golan. We talked into the small hours. I just got back."

"Yossi, you must sleep, or you'll be sick."

"You're right."

When she came out of the bath in the best silk robe she could find, he was on the bed in pajamas. "I'll sleep two hours," he said, setting the alarm, "then I have to see Motta again."

She sat down at the foot of the bed. "Are you being fair to Sheva Leavis?"

"He assured me he understood."

"He did? How did you explain yourself?"

Kishote said he told Leavis of his feelings at seeing the generals carry Dado's casket, his sense of being back home again, the challenge of the post he was offered. She fixed him with a knowing eye. "All right, that's what you told Sheva. Now, what happened on the Golan? What went on with you and Aryeh?"

That his mind had been made up by some old army songs, the warmth of a bonfire in the cold Golan night, and an embrace by his son in uniform, was incommunicable, though it was more or less the truth. He recounted Aryeh's tales of hardships and triumphs in the Sayeret training. "I want to be here with him while he goes through all that. A lone soldier has a hard time of it."

"Yossi, he's gotten very close to Dzecki Barkowe. Every weekend that he's off, he stays with the Barkowes in Haifa. He even has his own room. Galia Barak comes and visits Dzecki, and they have a nice young group. He's quite happy there."

"So he told me, but I'm staying."

Her skeptical look softened. "You'll stay because you'll stay, right?"

"More or less. I have one real regret, Yael, I'll say that."

"Which is what?" Her tone became dulcet. An affectionate word for her at last? Regret that she had to travel back alone, or even that this might be the real parting?

"The money. Leavis has been generous, but —"

"Stop right there," she broke in briskly. "Half a percent wasn't generous. Either you were worthless, or you were worth much more. He was trying you out. If you come into the business after the army, he'll give you two percent, I know that." Kishote only shrugged. "Anyway, since when is money so very important to you?"

"I'm interested in a land deal."

"Land deal? You? Where?"

"Suburbs of Melbourne."

"Australia?" He mutely nodded. A thought struck her. "Oo-ah, has Shayna Berkowitz gone into real estate?"

"Don't be silly. Shayna? She's a brilliant mathematician, but in business hopeless. She's already lost what little her husband left her."

He described the man in the kangaroo leather business, who required a partner with capital for land development. He had given Mendel to understand, before he left Melbourne, that if the Australian could induce his wife to let Shayna adopt the unhappy Reuven and bring him back to Israel, he, Kishote, would be inclined to invest with a man of such good heart.

"Why, Yossi," Yael said, amused despite her sore spirit, "that's a real business maneuver. Something I might do myself. Did he bite?"

"I'm not sure, but he wasn't outraged."

"Look, get a bank loan for the rest, that's all. Sheva will go on the note, and you can carry the interest."

Kishote shook his head. "Sheva doesn't go on notes."

"Right, right, it's an absolute rule of his. Well, then I'll lend you the money."

"What's this, Yael? I'm not taking money from you, of all people! Why should you lend me money?"

"Because I have it."

"That's no reason."

"All right, because I love you."

That silenced him. After a while he spoke low. "Hamoodah, look here —"

She overrode him. "You don't believe me? How many years were we together? Didn't I have Aryeh? And Eva? Listen, no use talking, it's all past and dead, and you're just being proud and stupid about a loan from me. That I do understand." She stood up. "Get some sleep, Kishote."

He caught her swinging hand. "That kangaroo guy would just piss away all your money, Yael."

"So what? You'd be buying Reuven for Shayna, wouldn't you? Isn't that what you want? Besides, who can tell about land deals? Even in Australia, land is good."

"So are you."

He pulled her down for a kiss. They were both in nightclothes; and Yael, returning the kiss, rather wondered what might happen next. Another kiss, and another. He let her go, wryly smiling. "Well, if that's what you call love, I love you, too. But when you and Max Roweh are kissing, don't go thinking so hard. He can think for both of you."

She punched him. "Never you mind about Max Roweh."

"Yael, thanks."

"Thank me by never telling Shayna about my money. I'll pull the drapes. Sleep."

Two months later Yossi and Shayna were married by the Ezrakh in the courtyard of his little Jerusalem yeshiva, under a drooping velvet canopy lifted on rods by four skullcapped yeshiva boys. Her face heavily veiled in white, her dress a plain dark blue frock, Shayna held Reuven by a hand. Yossi wore only a sport shirt and slacks, for the June night was very warm, the moonless sky ablaze with stars. There were no guests but the few yeshiva students who made up the minyan and — very strangely — air force major general Benny Luria, dressed like Kishote, with a scraggly new blond beard.

This very quiet wedding was not Kishote's idea, he had planned an exuberant celebration with all their friends at a modest hotel. But Shayna was self-conscious about marrying a man fresh out of divorce court, and she felt that a quick remarriage upon setting foot in Israel somehow affronted the memory of Michael, to whose grave she had brought Reuven the day they arrived. Yossi had talked her into the immediate wedding, but the compromise was this very private ceremony.

The Ezrakh was addressing the couple in Yiddish when into the courtyard bounded a tall dusty black-mustached soldier, causing a buzz among the yeshiva boys. He strode to the canopy and grasped Kishote's hand. "*Slikha,* Rebi Mori [Pardon, Master and Teacher]," he said to the Ezrakh, who with a gentle smile switched smoothly in his weak but clear voice to Aryeh's colloquial Hebrew, for few in the younger generation understood Yiddish. Yossi could not imagine how Aryeh had managed this. Last he knew the Sayeret Matkhal was out on a supersecret mission, which probably meant in enemy territory, and release from such an exercise was unthinkable.

By way of thanking his son he squeezed the callused hand, and got a powerful squeeze in return.

With his hand in his son's heartwarming grip, Yossi's mind wandered from the Ezrakh's words. He was getting into something, with this strong-willed little woman beside him! She had already given away all the dishes in his flat, made the silver kosher by boiling it, and brought from Haifa her bedroom furniture to replace Yael's. She had informed him, moreover, of some surprising marriage-bed rules they would be living by. All in all, when the moment came to slip the ring on her finger, it felt a bit like a parachute jump. *Kfotze, Kishote!* But the look she gave him, lifting the veil to take a sip of wine from the Ezrakh's old goblet, shook him with its deep sweetness and answered all qualms.

He stamped the glass to bits, the yeshiva boys broke into dance and song in a ring around them, and Aryeh snatched Reuven up in his arms and also cavorted, a big incongruous figure in green uniform amid the yarmulkes and the flying small prayer shawls. Benny Luria too held hands with the students and danced. Yossi had heard rumors that he was on medical leave with psychological problems, and he gathered that the aviator was studying the Talmud here, but why? A puzzle.

When the dance died down Aryeh told his father that the Sayeret commander, Lieutenant Colonel Netanyahu, had released him when one phase of the exercise ended, but only for twenty-four hours. "I have to start back right away, and don't ask me where, but I wasn't going to miss Abba marrying Aunt Shayna."

"I'm told you're doing well in the Sayeret."

"I'm in the junior group, Abba. Still learning. Since I came in there's been no big challenge."

37

The Challenge

The rumors Yossi had heard about Benny Luria were not wrong. Some weeks before the wedding the aviator had been diagnosed by an air force psychiatrist as close to a breakdown, what with insomnia, inability to concentrate, fitful disorientation, and an unshakable sense of worthlessness and of oncoming doom. Before accepting the recommendation that he take medical leave, Luria had gone to see the Ezrakh.

"General, what is troubling you?" the ancient asked, stroking his thin beard and fixing him with sunken but bright blue eyes, as they sat together in his book-crammed study.

"My son's death."

"But there are so many fathers like you in Israel. When the time to mourn has passed, they take heart and return to their work."

"I've tried."

"It's a sin, General, to mourn beyond the appointed time. The Holy One says, as it were, *'You don't accept my decree? Cease the prolonged mourning, lest I give you something really to mourn about.'* "

"Rabbi, I don't know why Dov died."

"You say that? *You*? An air force general? To guard the rebuilt Holy Land, and to sanctify the Name."

"I know those words, Rabbi. I've spoken them, all too often, to pilots' parents myself. They don't stick to my son Dov. I can't put it any other way. They aren't an answer, not for me. What shall I do? I'm not well."

"Can you make time to study? Three months?"

"I can get three months' medical leave, yes."

"Study the Talmud for three months, then we'll talk again."

"Talmud? I'm not capable, and what has that got to do with Dov?"

"The Hebrew you know. The head you've got. For the Aramaic I'll assign you a *haver*. Do as I say, General."

"All right, rabbi."

The psychiatrist, strongly doubting that Talmud study was what Major General Luria needed, recommended a tour of the Orient with Irit, and then a month in Switzerland. Luria followed the Ezrakh's advice instead, immersing himself in the Talmud day and night at the yeshiva. His haver (study companion) was a youngster of fourteen from a pious Lithuanian family, who read difficult Aramaic passages twenty centuries old as though they were front-page news stories. Although it was all absolutely novel to him, Benny Luria quickly picked up a taste for the Talmud's recondite logic and hard sense, and by whatever obscure workings of his psyche, he began to feel better. For one thing, he was treated by the other students as just one of them. The Ezrakh's little yeshiva was a noisy untidy place where, past ninety but unchanged in frailty of body and vigor of mind, he presided over a student body decidedly heterogeneous; for he delighted to take in at any age Jews who wanted to learn, and to get them started. Though most were young, some were married and bearded, some bald as well as bearded, and even an air force general did not stand out as peculiar.

One evening shortly after Yossi's wedding the monitor of the study hall, a rabbi in his forties with a bristly red beard, came to Luria as he and his haver were arguing an abstruse detail of divorce law. "General, an urgent call."

At a wall telephone in the corridor he put a finger in one ear to shut out the loud *beit medrash* drone. "Luria here."

A familiar gruff voice. "Luria, do you know about this Air France plane that was hijacked on leaving Athens? Or is your nose never out of the Talmud?"

"I resent that, sir." He adopted the air force chief's waggish tone. "I always listen to the news while I flog myself before break-fast. That plane's in Uganda now, isn't it? Or has the French gov-ernment got it freed?"

"It's still in Uganda. Now listen, Luria, I want you to come to the Kirya." Air Chief Peled turned brisk. "We have a crisis here, and it's life or death, or I wouldn't disturb you."

Luria took his Talmud volume and drove to Tel Aviv, where to his astonishment the Kirya buildings were all dark and the park-ing lot almost empty. If a real military crisis were on, cars should jam every space and all windows in the compound should be ablaze. He hurried to the air force building, where typewriters clattered, officers bent over maps and photographs or argued at charts, and female soldiers hurried in the corridors. Standing at a desk spread with blurry blown-up photos, Peled waved a magnifying glass. "Elohim, Luria, you look a lot better, beard and all."

"I am, sir."

"What's doing it? The Talmud?" Benny Peled gestured at the tome Luria carried. "Maybe I should try it. Today I was called a mental case or a charlatan to my face, by nobody other than the Ramatkhal."

"Oh? Why?"

"This Entebbe business. What else? These are old intelligence pictures of the terminal." He threw the glass down in disgust. "Luria, the government's decided to negotiate with the hijackers! Its public stand is just noise. And to cover its collective ass, it has asked Motta Gur officially whether a military option exists. And to cover *his* ass, Motta called a staff conference for opinions. I crossed Motta up, I said it was feasible to rescue those hostages."

"You said *what*?"

"I said we could transport twelve hundred troops to Entebbe, if we had to, and keep them supplied for two weeks. In fact" — Peled grinned, spreading the RAF pencil mustache — "I said if the government wanted to take all of Uganda, the air force could handle its part. That may have irked Motta."

"No wonder he called you a mental case."

"All right, Luria, but if I had just said we couldn't do it, that would have been that. The army would have been off the hook, and the government could have proceeded to cave in publicly to the hijackers. No military option!" The short slender air force chief paced, shaking a fist in the air. "But I tell you, Luria, if they do that I'm going to take off this uniform. I swear it. There's no point in being an Israeli airman, because it'll mean we haven't got an Israel, or won't have in a few years." He paused and barked, "You have nothing to say?"

"Isn't the French government responsible for all the lives on that aircraft?"

"The French have been ding-donging with that subnormal dictator, Idi Amin, since the plane landed. No progress. He may well be in cahoots with the hijackers."

"But why twelve hundred troops, sir? This isn't a war. Uganda's not our enemy. It's a question of getting to Entebbe, killing the terrorists, and taking out our people. If you're serious, and if it's possible to get there, it's a task for Sayeret Matkhal, a replay of the Sabena airplane rescue."

"I'm serious, don't fool yourself, but that was here in Lod airport. Entebbe is two thousand miles away, and it'll take troops to secure a foreign airfield. Look, first things first, Luria. Our Hercules transports don't even have the range to make it there and back. Give me your thoughts on that."

The two generals sat down, facing each other across the desk. Peled ripped open a pack of Players and smoked. Drumming his fingers on the Talmud volume, Luria said, after a pause, "If Idi Amin isn't in with the hijackers he can refuel our planes himself, right there in Entebbe, and become a world hero for frustrating terrorism."

"Don't depend on that."

"No. Otherwise, three possibilities. *One*, after the rescue we can land the hostages in some African country friendly to France, and let the French come and get them; then later, sort out the return of our aircraft. *Two*, assume Idi Amin is hostile, and plan to help ourselves to fuel in Entebbe at gunpoint. *Three*, money talks in all languages. Refuel secretly wherever we can, and pay."

The air force chief nodded, squinting through smoke. "A Talmudic analysis. I'm assembling sheaves of intelligence on Entebbe. Stay here until this balagan is over. It can't go on long, and this building is a madhouse. I need one detached good mind to talk to."

"Sir, I'm at your orders, but the rest of the Kirya's asleep, the army's not moving. How can you expect to make this happen?"

"Convince Motta Gur. There's no other way. He doesn't believe it's possible, so the army's clanking along in its old nine-to-five grooves. Convince the Ramatkhal, and this place will blaze up like Dizengoff Street on Friday night."

"B'seder, sir, I can study the Talmud anywhere. I'll miss my haver, though."

Shayna Nitzan stood at the french doors to a flower-lined balcony in a peach negligee Yossi had bought her; more diaphanous than anything she had ever worn or would have chosen, but if it pleased him, why argue? Looking out over the lake at snowy Alps lit by the morning sun, she felt at once radiant joy and dark fear. Until the moment she was in his arms under the Ezrakh's canopy with the ring on her finger, Shayna had never fully believed that Yossi Nitzan would at last be hers. All her imaginings of lovemaking with him, those rosy fantasies haunting her from girlhood onward, were vaporous nonsense from books, compared to the rough sweet burning reality of their nights in this bedroom in Lucerne. The fear stemmed from her lifelong experience that any joy coming her way was balanced too soon by something unexpected, evil, and shocking. An ominous telephone call at dawn had gotten him out of bed, interrupting a sleepy moment of morning rapture.

From behind, strong arms around her, a kiss on her neck. "Blighted honeymoon, motek. Sorry."

"No, no. Beautiful, glorious, no matter what. Tell me."

"Okay." He was dressed except for sandals on bare feet. "I've been down talking to the concierge. He's arranging a taxi and our air tickets. No problem, we have several hours to pack."

"Is it the hijacking?"

"Yes. That was Motta Gur himself who called." He came beside her and hugged her close. "Shayna, Shayna, will you ever forget this balcony, these flowers, those mountains, this room?"

"I'll remember everything. Even the wallpaper, Yossi, I'll remember these blue and yellow parrots with the spreading wings —"

"Well, here it is. The French are getting nowhere with Idi Amin, and the hijackers' deadline is day after tomorrow. Unless Israel delivers some forty convicted terrorists to Entebbe, they'll start killing Jewish passengers, and they'll keep killing them until our government gives in. They've got more than a hundred of them, mostly Israelis."

"But what can the army do? Uganda's thousands of miles away, and —"

"The air force proposes to fly there and rescue the hostages."

She pulled away from him, staring with big round eyes.

"Yes, Motta thinks the scheme is crackbrained, too. The air force and the army are like different planets, you know. I'm to be liaison with the aviators. Do nothing else, just check and check air force plans with a microscope for flaws as things develop. Motta's under terrific pressure from the government to give a yes or a no in a day or two."

"But who would do the rescuing? Paratroopers?"

"It would have to be Sayeret Matkhal."

She was holding his hand to her breast, and her grip tightened as by a spasm. "Aryeh, then."

"Possibly. He's in the junior group, so he might not go. If he does go, it'll be what he's trained for and yearned for. Let's eat something from room service, then pack. Look, is there nothing but dry cereal you'll order for breakfast? What's wrong with soft-boiled eggs, for instance?"

"Let me alone. Next you'll be urging me to have snorkers."

He laughed out loud, seized her, and they embraced and kissed with passion.

Don Kishote returned on Wednesday to an awakening Kirya, where ongoing meetings in all the armed services were debating rescue scenarios. An elaborate plan for a mass parachute jump near Entebbe airport was being analyzed away as too chancy. The navy was about to try out, in the waters off Haifa, a scheme to drop sea commandos into Lake Victoria, so as to take the terminal by surprise from the water side. On the Ramatkhal's orders, Yossi went along in the helicopter to observe the exercise. It was a discouraging fiasco. The commandos never got down into the sea, for their rubber boats, on hitting the water, exploded like melons dropped on a stone floor. In this way one impractical scheme after another was being eliminated, and a landing by Sayeret Matkhal in Hercules transports was emerging as the only conceivable option. But it too required the latest intelligence on Entebbe airport, apparently impossible to ascertain in the time left. Above all, the refueling problem remained unsolved.

Amos Pasternak was in Africa, Kishote found out, on a hush-hush quest for a fuel stop; and he recalled with irony how Amos, now high in military intelligence, had once said that Air France was no target for hijackers, the French being so cozy with the Arabs. By now it was clear that Idi Amin was playing the terrorists' game. The French could do nothing with him or them, and the burden of the crisis was falling on Israel, where public clamor for action was rising. The families of the passengers were staging anguished demonstrations, even bursting in on the Prime Minister to demand that he negotiate with the hijackers.

And then, with the deadline for the killing on Thursday only hours away, the terrorists took dramatic action. In an eerie process recalling Auschwitz, they separated the nearly three hundred passengers into Jews and non-Jews, and sent off the non-Jews to Paris on Air France rescue planes. This made their death threats against those who remained, immured in the old unused terminal building, frighteningly more credible. Prime Minister Rabin asked his cabinet for a unanimous vote to deal with the kidnappers, obtained it, and went public with the decision.

The news was blazoned and broadcast around the world: *"ISRAEL SURRENDERS!"* Arab countries were jubilant. The Israeli public was in shock. The French went on futilely pleading with Idi Amin and the hijackers to moderate their demands, and the other Europeans and the Americans expressed sympathy with Israel, mingled with regret at such yielding to terrorism. In order to arrange the trade of the criminals in Israeli prisons for the hostages, the hijackers agreed to postpone their deadline to Sunday, while issuing dire warnings against any rescue attempt. Field Marshal Doctor Idi Amin Dada, in a genial telephone talk with an Israeli colonel he knew, confided that the hijackers had packed the old terminal inside and out with dynamite; and that if they so much as heard an airplane pass overhead that was not cleared by the control tower, they would instantly blow the building and everybody in it sky-high.

That night the Kirya parking lot was chock-a-block. Every window in the compound was alight. The intelligence picture was beginning to improve, for in Paris the freed non-Jewish hostages were talking. A squad of Ugandan soldiers, they disclosed, were posted in the old terminal building to foil any rescue; and an officer on Kishote's staff who had trained Ugandan troops swore that, rather than stay in a building wired up with dynamite, those soldiers would desert or mutiny. So that threat was evidently a bluff. Israeli contractors who had helped build the Entebbe airport years ago were also filling in much information. At a midnight conference with the key military men, Defense Minister Shimon Peres at last authorized the start of preparations for the attempt with the words *"Roll it"*; preparations only, since the Ramatkhal alone could give the green light, and Motta Gur remained unconvinced. The landing in an unfamiliar airport in total darkness was too wild a gamble, he maintained, especially since no reliable refueling expedient was yet forthcoming.

Still, by Friday morning Don Kishote discerned that all aspects of the operation were starting to cohere. A sense was spreading in the Kirya that something real was happening; something arising out of the embattled soul of Israel, and the peculiar improvisatory nature of its armed forces. Gaps were filling in. Ideas were surfacing and getting put into action. The thousand elements that had to go into the rescue — arms, ammunition, aircraft maintenance, medical preparations, vehicles, signal equipment, almost endless lists of urgent requirements — were streaming in from all over the little country. There was not much talk about what all this was for. The knowing knew. The rest did as they were told, and by tribal instinct shut up about it to a surprising extent, especially for Jews.

By nightfall Friday the electricity in the air of the Kirya had the acrid feel of an oncoming thunderstorm. Focussed down to an attack with four Hercules transports on Saturday night, the operation had even acquired a code name, THUNDERBALL, borrowed from a James Bond thriller. In the first plane would ride the Sayeret Matkhal fighters *(therefore maybe Aryeh!)* who would kill the terrorists and bring the hostages to the rescue aircraft. In the next two aircraft would go a covering force of paratroopers and elite infantry with vehicles, trucks, jeeps, and armored personnel carriers for sealing off the airport, and neutralizing Ugandan forces while the rescue was accomplished. The fourth aircraft would bring massive fuel pumps with fueling personnel. A great last-minute to-do was going on about commandeering these huge pumps, so as to refuel if necessary at Entebbe. So far Amos Pasternak was reporting from Africa only that "fuel might not be an insoluble problem," implying that he had found a government not unsympathetic to Israel, or at least not uninterested in hard currency. But he could not as yet confirm it, so the pumps were going to Entebbe.

Toward evening Air Force Chief Peled came back to his office and found Benny Luria in the outer conference room where he had ensconced him, sitting with a shabby teenager at the big open Talmud volume. "Who's this, Benny?"

"My teacher."

The youngster regarded the handsome uniformed air chief with very bright dark brown eyes, awed but unafraid.

"Surely you're joking."

"Well, supposedly we're studying together, but whenever I hit an Aramaic stretch I can't move hand or foot without him. So I sent for him. His name's Eli."

Peled pointed to his private office. "Eli, go in there."

Eli scampered out, taking the Talmud with him. The air chief dropped in a chair and lit a cigarette. "The situation's rotten."

"I thought the plan was snowballing."

"The snowball has hit a stone wall and smashed."

"The refueling?"

"No. Motta reluctantly buys the fuel pumps. It's the landing. Black-dark airport, no control tower, no runway lights, the pilots have never landed there, and they're coming down from a two-thousand-mile run. He accepts that they'll find Entebbe. He can't accept that they'll land without risking some mishap that'll cause the immediate murder of a hundred and three Jews."

"Show him."

"Show him what?"

"Show that it can be done without a mishap."

"Brilliant." Peled peered at him. "How?"

"Stage a black-dark landing at Sharm. No lights, no guidance beam, nothing. Those transport pilots can do it."

"I know they can, but okay, I stage it and I tell Motta it's been done, and he'll only give one of his skeptical shrugs. Nobody can shrug like Motta."

"Invite him to ride in the plane." The air chief sat up, his eyes gleaming. Luria went on. "Why not? You go with him, of course. If you'll risk your ass, and he won't, then once it works, that's that. No more shrugs."

"What are you studying with Eli?"

"Divorce law."

"Must sharpen the mind." The air chief called through the door, "Okay, Eli, come back in. Is the general a good Talmud student?"

Eli sat down with the volume beside Luria. "The general has great potentiality, sir."

"Happy to hear it. What's the topic, Eli?"

"Whether a divorce written on the horn of a cow is valid, sir."

"Well, is it?"

"Yes, sir, if the husband gives the wife the cow."

The air chief ironically grinned at Luria. "So, that's Talmud?"

Luria nodded. "Law requires husband physically give wife an instrument of divorce. Act, not instrument, decisive. Talmud takes the case to its most unlikely extreme. Pushes the envelope, so to say. Sound familiar? You were a test pilot."

"Crazy Jews," said Peled. "Well, let's see whether Motta's got the balls I think he has. Sorry I interrupted your learning, Eli."

"No problem, sir," said Eli.

The day before the hijacking, Madame Irene Fleg had been scuba diving in Eilat while her husband was attending to business in Tel Aviv. Amos Pasternak had managed to get away from his desk in army intelligence to join her overnight, so she had telephoned her husband at the Tel Aviv Hilton around midnight, to say that it would be a rush for her to get to Lod airport for a departure to Athens and Paris at 9 A.M. Could they take a later flight?

"Of course," said Monsieur Fleg. He was in Israel with other French financiers, for a meeting with lawyers and bankers on the debt restructuring of a Dead Sea potash plant. "The fact is, our executive board will be lunching with the Prime Minister, and in that case I'll be able to join them. No problem, we'll take the evening plane."

So the Flegs missed Air France Air Bus 139, and once the hijacking occurred they stayed on in Israel to follow the drama. Knowing people in high places, Armand Fleg thought he was well informed, and the decision to deal with the hijackers astounded him, and struck him, as it did nearly everyone in Israel except the families of the passengers, as catastrophic. But after a telephone call he received while at dinner in the grill, his wife thought she noted a change in the imperturbable Monsieur Fleg. "What is it, dear?"

"Let's go to the suite. I expect a visitor."

Amos Pasternak arrived shortly in a sweater and slacks, unshaven, pale and puffy-eyed. Armand Fleg told his wife to leave them alone, and she slipped off into the bedroom.

"Monsieur Fleg," Amos began without ado, "on instructions of the Defense Minister I confide in you the gravest of national secrets." In brief flat terms he revealed the rescue plan in its entirety, including the refueling problem. "If it were not Friday night, sir, I wouldn't be approaching you. You're aware how totally this country shuts down on Shabbat. To insure the return of the hostages, once they're freed, the flight leader will need seventy-five thousand American dollars in hand. It may prove unnecessary, but he must have it. Can you raise that sum in cash, sir, without disclosing the purpose to anyone?"

Fleg did not answer for almost a minute, sitting and thinking, half-closed eyes on Amos's face, fingers rotating a diamond ring on his left hand. "By when?"

"Ten tomorrow morning, the absolute latest."

"All cash, you say?"

"All cash."

"Can you wait here?"

"For how long?"

"In one hour I can let you know, one way or another. If the answer is yes, maybe sooner."

"I'll wait."

Fleg opened the bedroom door and looked in. "Irene, my dear, I have to leave this minute."

She returned to the sitting room as he went out, and she had to clear her throat to talk. "Quite a surprise, this."

"Strictly business, Irene."

"Amos, I feel haunted. Right now Armand and I should be trapped in Entebbe."

"Not so. Your passports don't say you're Jewish. You're both totally French in dress, speech, manners. By now you'd be in Paris with the others."

"No. I'd never have gone without Armand, and he says he wouldn't have left. One French passenger acting with guts, he says, insisting on staying with the hostages, could have snarled the hijackers' plans. And he says he'd have done it."

"Maybe. Sitting here in the Hilton, he may well believe he would have, but —"

"You've never really gotten to know Armand, have you? He's tough, that quiet little man. You could have used him in Beirut. Now listen, Amos, I have to tell you something. We were having too glorious a time in Eilat, and I kept putting it off, but the fact is,

Armand and I met your father at a ski lodge in Klosters back in April. He came there with his young wife." Irene Fleg hesitated, biting her lips. "A dazzler, isn't she?"

"A former Miss Israel, or maybe a runner-up. Rather simple-minded."

"To some tastes, the perfect woman, then," said Irene Fleg nervously. "Now here you are and I'm very shaken up, so I'll tell you about it. Your father invited me for a drink, and said I'm compromising your army career and any chance you have to become a brigadier general."

"Pure nonsense."

"Is it? We've been observed wherever we've been, he said. Rome, Florence, Vienna, even on the coastal boat we took in Norway, it's all in a dossier, and —"

With a vexed sweep of a fist, Amos said, "Irene, if romances made that much difference, the whole army structure would collapse. That father of mine! Now that he's cooled down and been put out to pasture, he marries an old Miss Israel. Good for him, but it's got nothing to do with you and me."

"Put out to pasture? He's in the Knesset. He'll probably be a cabinet minister."

"That's what I said."

She seized his hand and pulled him out on the breezy balcony overlooking the darkling sea and the golden lights of the shorefront. Here she put her arms around his neck, and kissed him in a motherly way. "Listen to me, my very dear. Because of our overdone craziness in Eilat, Armand and I missed that plane. I'm ready to believe that it was destiny, that it was why we met in Beirut in the first place. Now the circle's closed. The story's told. It's ending in a deliverance, and let's just thank God for that —"

"My father's an interfering old worrier, Irene. Forget it —"

"Amos, your government hasn't really capitulated, has it? Isn't it stalling, while you prepare to rescue those people?" He turned cold and said nothing. She persisted, "If you're coming to Armand, it can only involve money, a lot of money —"

The telephone rang inside. She answered it, then held it out to Amos.

"Hello? Yes, sir. . . . Well, that's a start, anyhow. . . . Of course, Shabbat is the bottleneck, as I told you. . . . Right. At once."

He hung up, and swept her into a sudden hot embrace. "Ai!" she cried struggling. *"Méchant! Non! NON!"* She struck at his straying hands with small fists. *"Non!"*

With a laugh he let her go. "Discarding me, are you?"

"Where are you going?"

"None of your business, and by your life don't ask your husband questions when he comes back."

She straightened her disarrayed dress. *"Alors, va-t-en!"*

"Je t'aime."

"Cochon, va!"

The Ramatkhal returned to the Kirya from the landing exercise at Ophir airport near Sharm el Sheikh a changed man. "We have a long way to go in the next twelve hours," he said to Don Kishote, in a new excited tone, "but those Hercules pilots can do it. They're real professionals. If the Sayeret Matkhal rehearsal comes off nearly as smoothly — well, I'll have something interesting to say to the Prime Minister."

"They're rehearsing now at Sirkin, sir," said Kishote. This was an unused old British airfield. "The air force is bringing the planes there, and the entire attack will be staged for you, start to finish."

"When? Time's getting very short."

"Whenever you get there, sir."

"Let's go."

Air Chief Peled too had a different look, coming into the room where Benny Luria sat, murmuring over the open Talmud. "So, where's your haver?"

"Went home for dinner."

"What are you doing about the Aramaic?"

"Faking it, what else?"

"Ha!" Peled dropped into a chair and lit a cigarette. "Exactly what we did. Lucky Motta Gur's no aviator."

"What happened?"

"Hairiest landing you ever saw, that's what happened. I swear to you, Luria, my heart was in my mouth all the way down. We descended in black dark, but at two hundred feet the tower turned on the lights. No sense killing the Ramatkhal in the remote case of a mishap, Motta had agreed to that, very big of him. Well, by my life, when the lights came on those dumb bastards were way off course, the runway was far to the left, if they'd landed in the dark they'd have killed us all, not just the Ramatkhal. Naturally they sideslipped in slick as water, and Motta never knew the difference."

Luria closed the Talmud volume, holding his place with a thumb. "Isn't that serious, sir? Suppose they do that in Entebbe?"

"No, no, no problem, that's an international airport, the landing strip is enormously wide. They'll be okay. Luria, the thing is on."

"Then God bless everyone who's going."

With no trace of irony, the air chief said, "Amen. I've got to get to Sirkin in a hurry."

When Peled walked into the crowded command tent at Sirkin airfield, Motta Gur was already there, pelting General Dan Shomron, the paratrooper commander of the operation, and the other leaders with sharp queries. Through the open tent flap, soldiers could be seen under floodlights frantically finishing a mock-up of the old Entebbe terminal, a high wall of sandbags with three wooden-framed doorways. Gur pointed out, on a huge blown-up map of Entebbe airport, the big *V* formed by the meeting of the new and the old landing strips, and the short diagonal connecting them. B'seder, he said, the transports could land on the new runway. He was convinced of that. But the old terminal was at the far end of the other strip. Suppose a new sewer line, or power line, or something like that, was being dug across that old strip? How reliable was this map? How recent was it?

"It's very recent, Motta. Jeppesen's, the best there is," Peled interjected. "I've checked all that. Updated with all supplements and corrections, to last week. Besides, we've gotten high-altitude aerial photos of Entebbe, and they show no such obstacles."

"Pictures taken when?"

"Day before yesterday. More being taken today."

The Ramatkhal finished his questioning and nodded. The

floodlights were extinguished, all was dark night, and the full rehearsal for his benefit began. A Hercules rolled up in the gloom, the ramp squealed and dropped open, and out leaped a black Mercedes simulating Idi Amin's limousine, followed by two Land Rovers. The vehicles sped within yards of the sandbag mock-up. The commandos jumped to the ground and ran for the three doorways, raising clouds of dust, with much shooting of fiery blanks, confused yelling among themselves, and yells over bullhorns.

"What's going on here, exactly?" Zev Barak asked Kishote. Sent to the rehearsal as eyes and ears for the Prime Minister, he could make little of all this shooting, yelling, and rushing around in the darkness. Nor did he believe the Ramatkhal could. For those who were not in the know, it had to come down to faith in the planners and leaders, and in the people all the way down the line, to the ground crews now going through the long Hercules maintenance checkoff list, to the very tighteners of screws on the cowlings. Only a divine miracle of errorless efficiency could make this thing come off, Barak thought. Of all the operations he had ever observed, this was one in which the battle could be lost for want of a horseshoe nail.

No reply from Yossi. Barak pressed him, raising his voice over the tumult. "Come on, Kishote, by your life, the truth! Plan of genius, or frightening fashla in the making?"

Don Kishote had seen THUNDERBALL grow with confounding speed from a grotesque notion, and a lot of arguing in stuffy conference rooms, to this mock attack involving hundreds of men and many vehicles of war dashing about an abandoned airfield. Now twelve or so hours remained before THUNDERBALL would go or abort; the slow-flying Hercules transports had to depart Saturday afternoon for a late-night landing. Barak was observing all this, Yossi well realized, for Yitzhak Rabin, who in the end would have to take the responsibility and the consequences.

"Plan of genius," he said.

Visible only as vague running shadows in the night, paratroopers were fanning far out over the airfield to blocking positions when Kishote heard Aryeh's voice. "Well, Abba, give me a blessing, I'm going." There he was, Uzi in hand, breathing hard.

"So you are, are you? I didn't think you would. You're pretty junior."

"I was in on all the briefings and rehearsals. A couple of the juniors are going, and Yoni picked me." Yoni was Lieutenant Colonel Netanyahu, commanding the Sayeret. Aryeh threw an arm around his father's shoulders. "Don't worry. *Yih'yeh b'seder* [It'll be okay]. I wouldn't miss this."

"I know. Go with my blessing. God guard your way."

Aryeh vanished from the side of a very anxious father. Behind that fierce mustache, Kishote knew, inside that frame now bigger than his own, was a kid not long turned nineteen, hungry for derring-do. Kishote felt that he had done his own rash exploits in Israel's precarious early years, so that his son would not have to take such risks while he was so young and so raw. But there was as yet no peace, and Aryeh was his father's son, and the rest was with God.

About one in the morning, the operation leaders reassembled in the command tent. Motta Gur stood in front of the map, his round face somber and tired. "Well, gentlemen, the military option exists. I see that." *(A few handclaps.)* "The risk remains very high. But the curse of terrorism must be lifted from mankind, or civilization will break down. If you go, the prayers of the Jewish people will go with you, and the whole civilized world will bless your success."

Zev Barak left the airfield as a final rehearsal was about to start. In these dark hours of a Sabbath morning, he had observed the top leadership of Zahal reacting like a platoon of good soldiers under attack. The question no longer was whether THUNDERBALL could go, but rather, whether it could be stopped. It had taken on a life of its own. As he was leaving he overheard an exchange between Netanyahu and his deputy, Muki Betzer. "Yoni, by the book we'd plan and game this thing for six months, and then the big brass would probably drop it as too risky."

"Right, so it's good we have twelve hours instead of six months," Netanyahu returned. "Those hostages are our people."

"I have several nightmares about this," Yitzhak Rabin said to Barak that morning. The two were alone in his inner office. Barak had just passed through a big conference room where some twenty academic and political experts were gathered, noisily exchanging ideas for advising the Prime Minister. The cabinet was shortly to meet, to vote the operation up or down.

"A couple of thousand people are now involved, Zev," Rabin went on, crushing a cigarette in an overflowing brass tray. "From the cabinet on down. Just one loose-mouth has to talk to his wife. Just one. She talks to her neighbor. A Soviet spy in this country — and there are all too many, as you know — picks it up. The Russians alert the PLO, they alert Idi Amin, and a Uganda army brigade with tanks meets our planes at Entebbe." Hunched over almost in a crouch, he peered sidewise at Barak. "Impossible?"

"I hope unlikely, Prime Minister."

"All right. Next. The airport's shut down for the night, so a fuel truck is left standing on the new runway. Why not? The first Hercules smashes into it in the dark and alerts the terrorists. They at once shoot all the hostages or kill them with grenades, as they did the schoolkids at Maalot and the Olympic athletes in Munich, and as for the Sayeret —"

"Pardon me, there I have good news, Prime Minister."

"Oh? Tell me."

"African international airports take turns as emergency landing fields. It's Entebbe's turn tonight, that's fresh intelligence. The runway will be lit and clear."

"Really? Excellent. That's one good omen." The Prime Minister sat up, with a wan grin. "Zev, have you pictured a failure? One thing going wrong, just one little thing? The hostages all murdered, and Israel blamed for their deaths, for negotiating in bad faith? One more fashla on the world stage, by the Jewish shleppers who produced the fashla of Yom Kippur? It will be more disgraceful than losing a war. My government will fall. My name will be a curse in Jewish history. All this can be avoided, simply by handing over forty or so dirty thugs in our prisons to the dirty thugs in Entebbe." He gave Barak a long stare. "Nu?"

"Prime Minister, the choice isn't that clear. That the hijackers negotiate in total bad faith is a given. They're insisting on delivery of the terrorists only to Entebbe, where they're in complete control.

For all we know, they'll give you ten hostages in return for the forty terrorists and tell you you'll get the rest when you withdraw from the Golan Heights, the West Bank, and Jerusalem. Then what?"

"Is it confirmed that they also want five million dollars from the French?"

"That's new, sir. We're still checking."

Rabin looked at the wall clock and stood up with a sigh like a groan. "Let's go to the cabinet meeting. Golda told me you were her Mr. Alarmist. Are you alarmed, Zev?"

"By the choice before you, yes, Prime Minister, I'm very alarmed."

"So am I."

While the cabinet still debated, the THUNDERBALL mission took off for Entebbe. The timetable required it, and the pilots understood that they might be recalled in mid-flight. When they were almost an hour out, the signal came. *Unanimous government decision: Go.*

38

Why Dov Died

Aryeh lies gasping, stripped to the waist, on the canvas seat that stretches all along the Hercules' fuselage. The four transports are flying almost due south down the Red Sea, staying at wave-top height to evade detection by Saudi and Egyptian radar; and the torrid sea-level July air blowing into the plane is hardly breathable. The heat, the *heat*! How can anyone sleep in this sweat bath? Yet he can hear snores from the Land Rover, where boys from his squad are curled up. Aryeh thought the low canvas might be cooler than the car, but if anything the coarse sagging hot cloth, slippery with his sweat, is worse. He is too beat to move again. Lie and endure.

Lieutenant Colonel Netanyahu goes by, sidling between the Land Rover and soldiers lying on the deck. *Ha'm'faked,* the commander, is in full uniform, of course, above the discomforts of ordinary soldiers like Aryeh Nitzan.

"Aryeh, get some sleep."

"I'm trying, Ha'm'faked."

"This heat won't last. Take salt tablets."

Aryeh has no recollection of falling asleep. Next thing he knows he is shivering, and his skin is sticky with dried sweat. The plane is freezing cold and bouncing around. His watch shows that he has slept three hours or more. His bewhiskered pal Yudi Korff, a year older and also the son of a general, is on his feet, struggling to put on a sweater.

"What the devil, Yudi, where are we?"

"Over Ethiopia, crossing the high mountains. Two hours to go."

As Aryeh hustles on his clothes, he sees on the other side of the plane Yoni Netanyahu slipping toward the rear. Has Yoni slept at all? Probably not.

Aryeh has never known anybody like Yoni Netanyahu. As Amos Pasternak once displaced Aryeh's father as his idol to emulate, Yoni has now displaced Amos. In nerve, skill, and brains Amos and Yoni are nearly matched, he thinks, but beyond that they could not be more different. Amos Pasternak is easy to figure out, strictly army, all drive and ambition, his eye on General Staff rank; and, Aryeh suspects, already on the number-one spot, Ramatkhal. But Yoni is an enigma. Every bit as tough as Amos, just as demanding a leader, he is an austere original, in and out of the army, spending years in America, studying philosophy at Harvard. What is Yoni's goal? Where is he headed? One night, finding himself beside Yoni by a fire in the wilds, eating field rations, Aryeh ventured to ask him his opinion of Max Roweh, for he himself has found the books of his future stepfather impenetrable.

"Roweh? Important thinker, brilliant author, serious Zionist. Altogether an outstanding mind. Why do you ask?"

"He and my mother are getting married." Awkward pause. "My father is already remarried."

Long silence. Then Yoni, level and low. "Your father is a great soldier, Aryeh. His march on El Arish in the Six-Day War is a classic. I've studied it hour by hour, and lectured on it. You have a name to live up to, and you're not doing badly." With that Yoni got up and left the fire. It was the first time he had referred to Don Kishote, and those few words healed raw scars of some severe chewings-out he had given Aryeh.

As the Hercules wallows and pitches in icy air, Aryeh reflects that there is Yoni Netanyahu for you, able to grasp both his father's warmaking and Max Roweh's thoughts. Yoni has his detractors in the battalion — what commander doesn't, in any unit large or small? — but to Aryeh Nitzan he is a nonpareil, a leader he would follow into the cannon's mouth. About this coming action, Yoni said to the strike force, just before they boarded the plane, "Remember, soldiers, we'll be the best fighting men on that field." Simple fortifying words. Surprised befuddled terrorists and sleepy Ugandan guards will be the opposition, and even if the surprise fails — well, it won't!

Aryeh crawls into the Land Rover, careful not to wake the sleepers, and snuggles down. Two hours to go, then *action*. His squad is assigned to clear out the second floor, not the toughest job. Those Ugandans will be less alert than the hijackers guarding the hostages, but they're posted to stop a rescue, and the orders are stark. *"Shoot to kill."* Problem, the rehearsal mock-up showed only the main hall on the first floor, where the hostages are. His squad drilled with crayon diagrams showing the separate entrance to the staircase. Still, it's simple enough to find a staircase and scramble up . . .

Yudi Korff shakes him by the shoulder. "One hour out, Aryeh. Time to get ready."

Fell asleep again! Pretty relaxed, at that, for a guy going into his first gunfight! So Aryeh thinks, as he puts on his battle gear. Throughout the plane the other commandos are doing the same. Murmur of talk, clanking of weapons. Yudi says casually, "Well, this is it, Aryeh, hah? Kill or be killed."

With that, to his own astonishment, Aryeh's knees weaken, and he breaks out in a sweat. So far he has followed Yoni into enemy territory twice; sabotage incursions into Egypt and Jordan, peculiarly peaceful though scary enough, in and out without meeting a foe, without firing a gun. He wants to say something lighthearted to Yudi, but the words die in his throat. Aryeh knows all about the sweat of fear before battle. He has read about it, heard much talk about it. Okay, it has hit him. Clench the chattering teeth, quake and endure.

Now the Hercules runs into a storm. The turbulence over Ethiopia was nothing compared to this rolling and plunging, the changing roars of the engine, the creaks of the fuselage, the fitful lightning flashes on the wings, the *cracks* of thunder all around, the heavy rattle of rain on the fuselage, or is it hail? Fastened down to the deck, the Land Rover rocks and totters. Aryeh hangs on, wondering how the transports can stay in formation through this. If they get separated the whole operation collapses, doesn't it?

Okay, this was what I wanted, Sayeret Matkhal, and here I am. *Yih'yeh b'seder, yih'yeh b'seder . . .*

All at once they are in smooth air again under a clear starlit sky. Behind, lightning still flashes. Peering out the windows, Aryeh sees the other three transports. A relief, one worry the less.

"Start vehicle engines."

Yoni's command passes down the aircraft. First the Mercedes, then the Land Rovers snort and belch fumes. The rear ramp of the aircraft opens, letting in a rush of cool air. Aryeh can see past the Mercedes to the black waters of Lake Victoria. Almost there! Like a bad dream, Aryeh's anxious fit is gone. Wild swing of mood to confidence, even elation. About to land in Africa and rescue Jews, two thousand miles from home! Plane dropping rapidly, landing wheels groaning into place. Well, here we go. Jolt, jolt, *down*. The Hercules has landed, rolling along a brightly lit runway. Roar of engine braking, plane slowing, turning. Even before it stops, there goes the Mercedes down the ramp. Aryeh's vehicle after it, crammed with his squad. Teeth-jarring BUMP as it drops to the tarmac. Not so different from Lod, this Entebbe, and strangely quiet. An airport is an airport. Nice cool fresh air.

Now everything has to go very fast. Seconds count. The air controllers in the tower saw this huge plane land, they must be wondering, what the devil? The three vehicles race down the old runway past ragged uncut grass in the fields. Sloppy maintenance. Strange big gray things rise up from the grass here and there, six or seven feet high. Anthills! Africa. The grass smells pungent and strange. Not a word spoken in the Rover, every man tensed to jump out on command.

Firing ahead.

Two Ugandan soldiers up there on the runway. One falls, the other starts to run. Blaze of an Uzi, down he goes. Who fired? Surprise blown? But here they are already at the old terminal. The Mercedes halts at the dark control tower as planned, and Aryeh sees Yoni hit the ground first, his squad tumbling out after him, running toward the three doorways to the big main room. Well, this is it, racing pulse, hammering heart, pile out of the Rover, there's the door to the staircase. Yudi Korff running side by side with Aryeh, Uzis at the ready. Powerful voice of Yoni ahead, *"Kadimah! Kadimah! Kadimah!"* ("Forward! Forward! Forward!")

Aryeh plunges after the squad leader into the staircase entrance. My God, no staircase. Where is it? Dim-lit corridor here, corridor there, room to the left, door closed. Squad leader: "Yudi, Aryeh, clean out that customs room. Rest of you, here's the staircase around this corner, follow me."

Yudi pushes open the door. Three soldiers inside, one asleep on a mattress, one squatting against the wall smoking a cigar, one in a chair eating a sandwich, his mouth open for a bite. His eyes widen in horror as Yudi pulls his trigger, Aryeh a split second later. Bullets spray the three men, they writhe on the floor and scream, they are done for. Did I kill one? Did Yudi get them all?

"Aryeh, they're finished, come on, up the staircase."

Firing above. Firing echoing from the big room. Words roared on a bullhorn, audible through the wall in Hebrew and English. *"We are Zahal, lie flat, lie flat, we are Israeli soldiers. We're rescuing you, lie flat, don't move."* Up the staircase, confusion in the broad dim corridor. Running figures, blazing *rat-tat-tat,* Ugandan soldiers sprawled on the floor, bleeding and groaning. Squad leader's hoarse shout: "They're trying to hide, don't let one get away, find them all."

Then soon, quiet. Gun smoke drifting in the corridor, bodies scattered on the floor. Squad leader: "Okay, they jumped down into the fields and ran for their lives. This floor is secure. Yudi, what about that room downstairs?"

Yudi: "We killed three guys, sir. It's secure."

Aryeh, voice shaky: "Nobody got away."

"Well done."

Next, down to the main waiting room, according to plan. If the fight with the terrorists is still on, reenforce Yoni's squad, if it's over, start moving out the hostages, because it'll be a big job. The squad clatters down the staircase and outside. Now the moment

Aryeh will never forget. Shadowy Israeli running by in the semi-darkness: "YONI'S BEEN SHOT, I THINK HE'S DEAD." And there lies the commander on the pavement outside the terminal, on his back, eyes closed. Yoni Netanyahu down, two medics bending over him, crackling of gunfire close by and flashes in the distance.

Squad leader: "Terrible, terrible. Maybe he'll be all right. Into the terminal!"

What a sight in here, huge room, filthy, awful toilet stink, wretched-looking people lying all over the floor, young, old, stunned and scared, mattresses, blankets, clothes, papers, garbage. Three terrorists lying in blood, one a woman. Yoni's deputy, Muki Betzer, holding the bullhorn, lean smart major, terrific reputation as a fighter. Betzer, his voice booming: "I say again, you are saved. Lie where you are, till we're sure the criminals are all disposed of. Then we'll take you to an airplane and fly you all to Israel. It's over. You're free. Be strong and of good courage. Just do as we tell you." He hands the bullhorn to another officer, who paraphrases in English.

To Aryeh's squad leader Muki Betzer says, "I think we've got them all, all the ones who were on watch here. What about upstairs?"

"The ones who didn't jump down and run away are all dead. Second floor secured."

"Excellent."

Aryeh is dazed and numb. Yoni shot, maybe dead. After that endless plane trip the swiftness of it all, over in minutes, the swiftness! He has killed men, Ugandans, either he or Yudi, or both together, three black soldiers left wallowing in blood in the customs room, a frightful thing but they were posted there to shoot rescuers, to shoot him and Yudi Korff. There outside lies Yoni Netanyahu, not moving. Several medics by him now, plasma bottles, nervous movements, anxious mutters . . .

Getting the hostages to the plane not so simple. They are weak, shocked, and still very frightened, for the gunfire never ceases, now close by, now distant. A double line of paratroopers has formed outside the terminal to keep them from straying, and to protect them from Ugandan soldiers. Aryeh is now an escort of old ladies and decrepit men, in the long walk to the plane which was the last to land and will be the first to take off. Those too weak to walk, and the few injured, are being brought there in the Rovers. It's a real race against time now. The Uganda army must surely be alerted, all that gunfire! It'll be up to the paratroopers at key locations to block any attempt to halt the rescue. The primary objective is to get the hostages out. Once their plane departs with every freed Jew aboard or accounted for, the mission will be a success. The Israelis still in the airport will have to stand their ground, and put up a rearguard fight until the last plane leaves . . .

Half an hour later, as Aryeh and Yudi are helping stragglers up the ramp into the jammed Hercules which will carry the hostages to freedom, huge explosions rock the ground and fires blaze high into the sky.

"Now what?" Aryeh shouts to Yudi, who knows a lot more about all this than he does.

"That's what used to be the Uganda air force," Yudi exultantly yells back. "Our farewell compliment to Idi Amin."

The ramp closes. The Hercules crawls over the diagonal strip to the main runway, gathers speed and heaves up into the star-strewn sky, toward Lake Victoria. *Mission accomplished.* Is Yoni dead or alive? Aryeh saw the stretcher go by as the commander was carried aboard the second aircraft, which is now taxiing to take off. Whether he himself will get out of Africa alive, Aryeh Nitzan still does not know. If not, he will be no worse off than Yoni, who by what he has been hearing, will not live. If Aryeh does get away to live and tell the tale, and his gut says he will, it will be a tale of the long arm of Israel rescuing Jews in peril of their lives, and of his brave commander who fell to save them.

Max Roweh's lecture at the Library of Congress on the Bicentennial, "Proclaim Freedom," has earned him and Yael invitations to the ceremonies aboard the aircraft carrier *Forrestal* in New York Harbor, where a column of tall sailing ships from all over the world is passing in review before President Ford, to honor America's two centuries of independence. They sit with Ambassador Dinitz in the diplomatic section of the reviewing stand, all three bleary from staying up through the night to follow the fragmentary reports of the rescue at Entebbe. Rumors and news flashes of a rescue have kept coming, but the Israel government has blacked out all information, and whatever Dinitz knows, he is being close-mouthed about it.

President Ford is speaking before a battery of TV cameras when a bristle-headed marine sergeant comes to Dinitz and murmurs in his ear. He slips away, and returns to his seat in a glow. "Okay, it's officially confirmed," he whispers. "Now I can talk. They've landed at Lod airport. All safe."

"Incredible, miraculous!" Yael chokes out the words and kisses him.

Commentators have been guessing that the rescue planes may still be in the air, or down somewhere in Africa refueling. Now the hard news of the success is beginning to spread aboard the *Forrestal*. Amid whispers in the diplomatic section, eyes are turning to the Israeli ambassador. Sitting directly in front of him, a black diplomat in colorful African garb faces around smiling and shakes his hand. With the brilliantly uniformed marine band playing "The Star-Spangled Banner," and the tolling of a big bell — thirteen times for the thirteen original colonies of 1776 — the ceremony on the flight deck ends.

In the cavernous hangar deck, where a buffet lunch is set out to lessen the crush of departing VIPs at the ladder to the launches, Ambassador Dinitz is so beset with attention that Yael and Roweh become separated from him. But soon a marine colonel with golden shoulder loops is leading the diplomat to them through the mob. "Something has come up, my friends," says Dinitz with a delighted grin. "It seems the President has invited me to return to Washington in his helicopter."

The marine officer says to Roweh, "Yes, and if you wish, sir, I can see that you and your guest go ashore in the next launch without waiting."

"That will be most appreciated."

Dinitz says as the colonel goes off, "How about this? I've hardly spoken to President Ford since he took office, and now suddenly I ride in his helicopter."

"Enjoy your moment, Simcha," says Roweh.

In the launch he and Yael hear much excited talk among the packed-in VIPs about the rescue. The general tenor is that the Israelis have gone and done it again, and that America should be more like Israel in dealing with its enemies and with terrorism. One beefy man well over six feet tall, in an elegant cowboy hat, polished cowboy boots, a pin-striped suit and a western string tie, capsulizes the matter so: "I'm an unholy son of a bitch if those amazing fucking Jews haven't gone and fucking upstaged the Bicentennial!"

As they settle into the back seat of Roweh's waiting limousine, he remarks, seeing her twist a handkerchief in her hands, "It won't be long now, Yael. You'll phone from the apartment. Philippe, turn on WQXR."

"I'm *sure* Aryeh's special unit did it," she says, "that's their kind of mission. I'll call Kishote first chance."

"I wonder when the Arabs will at last suspect," Roweh says, speaking through a Mozart piano concerto as the car crawls in Battery Park traffic, "that in some strange fashion they may be doing the will of Allah. Nothing could have restored Israel's world position overnight in such a total stunning way — absolutely nothing, Yael — except this hijacking."

"Oh, come on, Max! It's not the hijacking, it's the rescue."

"My dear, exactly. Over and over the Arabs create these occasions, and the Israelis rise to them, thrill mankind, and compel very reluctant admiration."

The Mozart piano concerto ends. The first news bulletin is, *"A report just in, not yet confirmed by the Israeli government. In the daring Entebbe rescue three hostages and one Israeli soldier were killed."*

Yael turns scared eyes to Roweh. He takes her hand. "Yael, my dear, you don't know that that's true, you don't know that your son took part. And if he did, that he was that one soldier is very, very long odds."

She mutely nods, but her eyes remain scared. Back in his River

House apartment, she tries and tries to call Kishote, and keeps getting the maddening high ding-a-ling that signals overloaded circuits. But she persists, figuring he will stay late, though by now it is ten at night there. At last comes the welcome *bleep* of a call going through. "Oh, Yael, hi!" Miriam, his longtime secretary sounds exhilarated. "He's speaking to the Ramatkhal. Can he call you back?"

"No, no, I'll hold. God knows when he'll get another overseas line. Miriam, how about Aryeh, is he all right?"

"Why not? He's fine. He was here in the office an hour ago." Yael gasps with relief. "Wait, here's the general."

Earlier that afternoon, on the outer fringe of the dancing, singing, cheering mob at Ben Gurion airport, Don Kishote was watching and waiting for Aryeh. When he espied his son wearily descending from the Hercules, he darted over the tarmac and caught him in a fierce long bear hug. Haggard, hoarse, Aryeh gestured at the hundred raggle-taggle hostages coming down the ramp of the leading Hercules. "The question is, Abba," he said bitterly, "whether all of them are worth one Yoni."

"They're Jews, Aryeh," Kishote said. "Yoni thought so."

Benny Luria and his son Danny, now a Phantom pilot, were also watching the jubilation. Towering over his father, his flaming red hair clipped air force style, Danny had searched for and found Luria on the thronged airfield, the Talmud volume under his arm. As they watched the hostages stream out on the tarmac to be rushed, embraced, and tearfully kissed by their families, Benny Luria said to his son, "Now I know why Dov died."

* * *

In the early days of cinema, a much-used comic device was to reverse the film. A diver would fly up out of the water and land dry on the board, or a collapsed building would rise out of its rubble and stand upright. With the Entebbe rescue, something like that happened to Israel's smashed Humpty-Dumpty image, as Cookie Freeman had put it to Don Kishote. The shattered egg pulled itself together, the shell fragments coalesced around the albumen and yolk, the cracks disappeared, the egg leaped up on the wall, and behold, there was Humpty-Dumpty again, smooth, whole, smiling. And the world now knew that whenever and wherever Jews were threatened because they were Jews, Humpty-Dumpty would have to be reckoned with.

39

The Peacemaker

November 16, 1977

Dearest Queenie —

As always, hearing your voice for a few minutes has brightened my day. I've just this minute hung up, and as promised I'm writing in more detail about the incredible Sadat development. By every indication the man is really coming. Not an hour ago, for instance, the Foreign Ministry notified me that poor sick Golda wants me to escort her to the airport to meet him. So I have to try on the uniform I've put on only once or twice since Rabin relented after Entebbe and let me retire. I hope it still fits.

You ask, what is the mood in Israel? I would say, "dumbfounded." The public can't believe that it's happening. Rumors and guesses are flying. At one extreme people say it's Messiah's time, at the other that it's only one more Arab trick before another surprise attack. I myself cautiously hope it's a real peace move, based not on Egyptian good will but on the bizarre shift in our politics that's put Menachem Begin into power after nineteen years. He's been our ultrahawk and perpetual opposition leader, and Sadat may figure that if anyone can sell our people a tough peace deal, Begin can.

You also ask what my work at Rafael is all about. Well, Rafael is the Armament Development Authority, and it produces advanced weaponry for one of two reasons: either to give us an edge in battle, or because our enemies have acquired stuff which no big power will sell us. I'm a political appointee, my lump of sugar for my long service as Rabin's military secretary. My dream of going back to biochemistry is forgotten, I can't make up those thirty years as a soldier. This is as near to science as I can come, but the genius and self-sacrifice of the scientists and engineers under me make me feel humble. I'm not in their class, and never could have been. Half of them could go abroad for two or three times the salary we pay them, but they love Israel. My brother Michael, may he rest in peace, was the scientist in the family. If he'd lived he might have been up for a Nobel Prize, and I'm an idiot by comparison. I did well to serve in the army, after all.

I must be doing this job well because Begin is keeping me on, though I've become a crusading dove, making speeches, signing petitions, organizing rallies. Was it Napoleon who said no king could sit long on bayonets? A democracy certainly can't. There must be a political solution to the historic bind we're in. I'm as suspicious about Sadat as any hawk, like my son Noah, but at least I'm willing to hear the man. Noah and I can't talk about the territories anymore. He would hang on to every square inch and make the Arabs learn to like it or leave, if it takes a hundred years. I would withdraw even unilaterally. I know we can't keep a million helots in perpetual subjection. So my rising sea commander and I don't talk politics, Nakhama and I delight in our two granddaughters, and all's well.

The big family news is that Galia's engaged at last to "Jackie," a rich American such as Israeli girls dream of, making good money in Haifa real estate. He's a distant relative of ours, and they've been going together for years. He lost an arm during the war, but that was more of an obstacle for him than for her. It's taken her a long time to convince Jack that she didn't just pity him. The cousin business also gave them pause, but it's on, and Nakhama and I are happy about that. He's a good man. We're happy about Ruti, too. She's been in Galia's shadow for years, but now that she's turning seventeen she's come to life, and the boys swarm. She's beautiful enough to be a model, and almost as tall as I am.

Yes, Queenie, I assure you Nakhama did love Paris. She still talks about it. She told me she'd never forget her lunch with you in the restaurant boat, but she's never said anything more about it. I know she came back to the hotel that day stone drunk. I presume that you were in a comparable state, and that you two ladies dissected me between you like an anatomy class cadaver. Anyway she's had some kind words for you since, which is all to the good.

(Pause while I try on that uniform. I'll give a truthful report.)

. . .

Guess what, it fits! Barely. No matter, I need it only on such ceremonial occasions. Unless, God forbid, another war comes along, then I'll be invited to stand around the War Room and give advice. Through four wars, I've smiled at those poor has-beens in their tight old uniforms. Now I'm one of them. So I pray to our old Jewish God that Sadat is serious, and that I'll never have to put it on in earnest.

Love always,
Wolf

"She talked me into it," said Sam Pasternak, holding out his glass to Amos. His son had brought a full bottle of cognac to the maternity ward lounge, and it was now half-empty. The wall clock showed past 3 A.M. "She changed my mind."

"Eva talked you into it? Eva, your slave? Abba, Eva couldn't talk you into changing your shirt."

"Oh, no? Wait till you're married, my boy," mumbled Pasternak, downing cognac. He had been there alone on the shabby couch of the lounge since almost midnight, and Amos had come at half-past two. "Just you wait. You'll find out about these women who are your slaves. We had agreed on no kids. Then she wanted one. The doctor warned her about a first baby at her age, with her pelvic problem. I said forget it, aren't we happy enough? No, no, she didn't feel fulfilled, so — Well?" A dark skinny young nurse was looking in. "What now, Sister?"

"She's doing better, but the doctor urges you to go and get some sleep, it'll be a long time yet. He has your telephone number, and —"

"What about the baby's heartbeat?"

"It's all right. False alarm."

"Look, Amos, just leave that bottle and run along," Pasternak said. "You've got your hands full with the Sadat business. I'm all right."

"You do believe he's coming, Abba?"

"Who, Sadat? Oh, he's coming all right."

"To address the Knesset in Jerusalem? You really believe that?"

"Why do you ask? Does military intelligence have contrary information?"

By habit Amos glanced around and spoke low. "Even if he's serious, and that's doubtful, he may be prevented. Of course his parliament applauded the speech, why, even Arafat did, but nobody there could conceive that his offer was serious, let alone that Begin would take him up on it. His Foreign Minister and Chief of Staff are threatening to resign. That's hard intelligence, Abba, and they've got the bureaucracy and the army with them."

"He's coming, all the same," said Pasternak, "I *know*."

"L'Azazel, Abba, what do you know about Sadat that army intelligence doesn't?"

Pasternak drank, and said with a mulish headshake, "Never mind. You'll find out about these women who are your slaves, Amos. Now, how are you getting on with Ruti Barak?"

"Why do you keep harping on Ruti Barak? She's cute, yes, but young, young. I happened to take Ruti to a movie once, you saw us there, and now you've got us engaged."

"Lovely girl, Amos. Great family. Sure, she's very young. But compared to that Parisienne yenta of yours —"

Amos held up a flat palm, and bit out three words, "No more, Abba."

"I'll put it to you short and clear, my son, you'll have to choose very soon between the lady and your future. I told the lady herself that once, and —"

"Yes, I know you did, and you had your nerve."

"I'm your father. You've got an outstanding record, and an intrigue like this —"

"Abba, how about Dayan's intrigues, did they ruin his career?"

"Dayan's been a rotten model for a whole generation of army officers, and I was no model myself, but standards were looser in our time, and —"

The nurse came scurrying in. "Well, what do you know, things are starting to happen. Surprising, but good."

"Aha!" Pasternak jumped up. "And the doc wanted me to go home! How much longer?"

"You may as well stay. She's very brave, your wife, and very sweet. Gorgeous, too."

"You're telling me?"

As the nurse left, Amos baldly cut off the Irene Fleg topic by saying, "Abba, do you know that Motta Gur intends to speak out tomorrow to denounce Sadat's visit, call it a trick to disarm us?"

"So? Well, I love Motta, and it's his job to be suspicious and on guard. All the same, Sadat's coming to make peace."

"Is he? The Japanese were in Washington talking peace, remember, when they bombed Pearl Harbor. Egyptian deployments these days are damned disquieting, I can tell you that as a fact."

Pasternak fell silent, emptied his glass, and held it out for more. "Very well. I can tell you something, too. Right now three people in Israel know what I know. The other two are Begin and Dayan. I'll make you the fourth, since I know you can control your tongue, if not your *yetzer horah* [sinful urge]."

In low tones, Pasternak described two trips to Morocco that he had arranged for Moshe Dayan, now Begin's Foreign Minister. The King of Morocco had invited Dayan, he had gone disguised in a beatnik wig, mustache, and dark glasses, and there he had met with emissaries from Sadat. What had emerged was that, if Begin was interested in exchanging the Sinai for a peace treaty, so was Sadat. But President Carter had unexpectedly called the Soviet Union, the Arabs, and Israel to a conference in Geneva next month, and his State Department had drafted a "comprehensive peace plan" for the Russians and Americans to cosponsor. This had thrown a huge monkey wrench into Sadat's secret separate deal.

"Whatever possessed Carter to drag the Soviet Union back into the Middle East," said Pasternak, "when for years Anwar Sadat and the Nixon and Ford administrations had been pushing them out, remains a mystery, Amos. But that's why Sadat's coming to Jerusalem."

Comprehension was dawning on Amos's intent face. "Elohim! So that's it. Sadat saw his secret negotiations through Dayan going down the drain."

"You've got it. Sadat's torpedoing that Geneva conference, whatever it costs him in the Arab world, by coming out into the open as a peacemaker. Carter's driven him to it. But this way of doing it — flying to Jerusalem to address the Knesset — is a stroke of absolute political genius. He's a great man, damn him. We're going to have a peace. At high cost, but a peace."

"By my life," Amos pounded fist into palm, "then I win the argument we were having at Intelligence, when you phoned me that Eva was in labor. *You're* the one who made me study American history so hard, Abba, and I was comparing this visit to Robert E. Lee's surrender at Appomattox. Half of them didn't know what I was talking about, and the others said I was crazy."

"Appomattox? You *are* crazy. Sadat will get the Sinai back for a piece of paper. Some surrender!"

"Abba, he's coming here *to surrender the entire Arab war aim.* Can't even you see that? He's breaking the perimeter. He's recognizing that we're back in the Land to stay. Just watch the Arab response! No matter what he says to the Knesset, no matter how tough he talks, they'll call it a catastrophe, a complete abandonment of the cause. They'll ostracize him for twenty years, wait and see, and from their viewpoint they'll be right. But it's a bad cause, just as slavery was a bad cause, and that's why I compare the visit to Appomattox. Sadat's abandoning a bad lost cause, and Robert E. Lee had to do the same —"

"It's a girl." The nurse darted in, looking as happy as if she were one of the family. "Big and pretty, and your wife is fine."

"Thank God!" Pasternak embraced his son. "Can we see her?"

"Your wife? No, not yet. The baby, sure. Come with me."

In a glassed-off room full of bassinets, a basket freshly labelled PASTERNAK was at the window, with a yawning wrapped pink baby in it, blinking brilliant blue eyes.

"By God," murmured Amos, "how beautiful."

Barely getting the words out of his throat, Pasternak said, "I'm too old for this."

"Glad you changed your mind, Abba?"

"Might as well be glad. There she is."

Barak sat in a worn red armchair, in the parlor of Golda's little house outside Tel Aviv, remembering the old crisis days when she had slept here instead of in the Prime Minister's Jerusalem residence. Many an hour he had spent in this chair, and some entire nights, too. Now, though Golda was out of public life and under a cloud in Israel, she remained a favorite of American Jews, and she had cut short a fund-raising tour to fly home for Sadat's arrival. The same cigarette smell came wafting down the stairs, and hearing her tread, much lighter than in former days, he stood up. "How do I look?" she said as she descended.

A hard question to handle. The leukemia had been thinning her terribly, yet in a strange way it was now restoring an ethereal semblance of the beauty which had long ago made her romances the talk of the Yishuv. Her best blue wool suit hung very loose on her, her hair was carefully styled, and he thought her cheeks were touched with rouge.

"Very elegant, Madame Prime Minister."

"Yes, I'm sure. Belle of the ball," she said in her sarcastic cigarette rasp. "At least that man is not going to see me looking down and out. Will I need a coat? This suit is warm."

"It'll be windy at the airport, Golda."

She grumbled, pulling a dark cloth coat from the hall closet. "*Now* he comes. Did he need a war, with nearly three thousand of our boys killed and maybe twenty thousand of theirs, to convince him? Why did he keep making those tricky peace proposals that I couldn't possibly accept? Why didn't he just do this long ago?"

"I guess he'd answer that his people first had to redeem their honor," said Barak, helping her on with the coat.

"What honor? We crushed them, didn't we? They were pleading for mercy at the end. They had the whole world forcing us to let them off." Barak did not comment, and she turned on him. "Well, am I right or wrong?"

"Golda, what they remember is October sixth. It's their new national holiday, October Sixth. They name bridges and boulevards after it. That's when they shattered our Six-Day War image and almost beat us."

"Almost." Sharp snap.

"Yes, but it took us three weeks to recover, and in their version only America saved us. So they got back their honor."

"Yes, I know that version. *Ha!* And now they'll get back the Sinai, too." She was tucking in her collar at a mirror. "And *that* they could have had, all of it, without bloodshed. Poor Levi Eshkol offered it for a peace treaty, right after we won the Six-Day War. And what was their answer? All those no's of Khartoum. *'No negotiation, no recognition, no peace, no nothing!'* "

"That was Nasser's doing, Golda."

"Nasser, Sadat, is there a real difference? I hope I'll live to find out. Well, let's go."

Guli Gulinkoff possessed not only the one silver Lincoln in Israel, but also the one Hollywood-style villa with a private screening room, and the only supernew Japanese TV system projecting images the size of theater films. Invitations to watch basketball, soccer, or American miniseries at Guli's villa were much sought after among Haifa's smart set; but for the greatest TV spectacle in Israel's short turbulent history — the arrival of the President of Egypt at Ben Gurion airport to offer peace — no invitations could be had. Daphna Luria and Guli had invited, for that same night, a small party of families and friends to announce their engagement. They considered calling off the party, but decided not to. "After all, how long will it take the mamzer to land," said Guli, "and go through all the ceremonial shit? Half an hour? No reason to cancel. That's bad luck, anyway."

"You're absolutely right, motek," said Daphna. "We'll just serve the drinks and hors d'oeuvres down in the screening room."

"Terrific idea," said Guli.

On all evidence Daphna had actually given her heart to the gorilla. At the Jericho Café she had endured a protracted ragging from her friends about her notorious romance with the rich Haifa kablan, twenty years older than she was, until one night she turned on them, on her feet and shaking her fists, shouting over the rock-and-roll din, "*Kvetchers!* Envious impotent kvetchers! Good for nothing but to sit around and criticize, and complain, and jeer, and find fault, and mock, and sneer, and eat olives, and drink beer, and belch, and talk about Brecht and Kafka, and feel each other under the table, and pretend you're in Paris or in New York! Why don't you go there? Who needs you here? You don't build like Guli, you don't work the land, you don't do *anything*. If somebody in this crowd turns out to be talented like Shimon he leaves, or to be brave like Yoram he dies. None of you is worth one of Guli Gulinkoff's farts. Kvetch away for the rest of your lives, I've heard your last kvetch!" And out she stalked into the rainy night, never to return. As between Guli and bohemia, she was going with Guli.

The Barkowes arrived early at the villa with the engaged couple, Dzecki and Galia. It was big-hearted of them to show up, for Dzecki and his father were suing Guli over a shopping mall project into which they had sunk some three hundred thousand dollars, with nothing to show for it but a vast brown hole on the outskirts of Haifa. For three years Guli had been assuring them that "it will all hang itself out." Since the court clerks of Israel were on strike again, it looked as though the thing would not hang itself out for years and years. Meanwhile Guli had their three hundred thousand or had spent it, and he remained unfailingly affable to them. "By all means sue," he had said with great good cheer. "Maybe the courts will help me pin down those *ben-zonahs* [sons of whores], the subcontractors. It's all their fault."

Nevertheless Dzecki had insisted on coming to Guli's party. "The greatest favor anyone ever did me," he said, "was when Guli started up with Daphna. I'm the world's happiest man, and we're going there to wish them well. While we're there we can snoop around, and maybe find our money stashed in the woodwork." Dzecki's parents were utterly disgusted with the Holy Land, which, aside from Guli's prestidigitation with their money, had cost their son an arm. On the other hand they loved their future daughter-in-law, and were much taken with their Barak relatives; they thought Noah dashing, Zev noble, and the women exceptionally warm and nice.

Noah and Julie came with their two babies, both yelling their heads off, and the party split up by sexes, the men going downstairs to get away from the screams and watch the doings at Ben Gurion airport, while the women huddled around in the master bedroom, calming the infants. "So where are Yossi Nitzan and Shayna?" Daphna's mother asked her. "You said you invited them."

"Shayna's at the airport because General Nitzan's there, commanding the military security for the whole visit," said Daphna, rocking Julie's older baby in her arms. "It's like a mobilization for war, Shayna told me, three thousand troops at the airport alone."

Julie said, "Look, my Sarah's quieting down. You have a way with babies, Daphna." Her Hebrew was much improved, if the French accent was ineradicable.

"Thanks, dear." Daphna ruefully laughed, the jealousy between them long since forgotten. Daphna was beautiful as ever and Julie was getting fat, but Julie had Noah and Daphna no longer wanted him. "Just don't say that around Guli. He says he wants five kids. He's got it all figured out, but who has to have them? Me, and one is frightening enough."

"The man does think big, doesn't he, darling?" Daphna's mother said a shade tartly. The Lurias were not enchanted by the match of their sabra daughter with a gross kablan of vague immigrant background, no matter whether Guli was really rich, or a fast-moving fraud. In banking circles where they had made inquiry, this was a highly moot point.

Galia said, "Me, I'll settle for one, and quit. Dzecki agrees."

When the babies were at last quieted and asleep, the women went down broad marble stairs to the screening room. "Just in time," said Guli, as they settled in the overstuffed leather armchairs. "Golda's arriving." On the big projector screen a car with a motorcycle escort was driving up to the airfield gate, and the police were holding back a turbulent crowd.

Julie tapped Noah on the shoulder. "Look, look, *chéri*, there's your father."

It was a long camera shot, but the white hair was unmistakable. As Barak helped Golda from the car, the crowd broke into cheers and applause. *"Golda! Golda! Golda!"* The camera zoomed in on her looking around amid the general roar and waving in pleased bewilderment.

Benny Luria said, "Now they cheer her. In the war she was a rock, and afterward they spat at her. Sadat's coming only because she defeated him."

Over the noise, the excited announcer was trying to describe the scene. "I see tears on Golda's face," he enthused, "tears of joy! Surely she never expected this acclaim."

"Who did?" said Guli. "All you heard after the war was that Golda was a disaster, and that it took her too long to resign."

The Barkowes, who had never learned Hebrew, were sitting mum through all this, but now his mother exclaimed, "Jack, translate. What is the man saying?"

"Just that the people love Golda, Mom."

"Now they love her again? I lose track."

When Ruti Barak and Danny Luria, who had started going out together, arrived in the screening room, the lights of Sadat's plane were just appearing in the sky. "So you made it," Benny Luria said to his son. "Come sit by me. You too, Ruti." The Lurias were hoping that at least this second match with a Barak girl might come to pass. They made an attractive pair, Danny in uniform with his heavy red hair well groomed, Ruti in a swirling pink skirt and white sweater, both tall, both laughing as they came in.

On the screen, as the plane descended in a blaze of searchlights, Arabic markings and ARAB REPUBLIC OF EGYPT became plain to the eye. The airfield was a sea of color with a hundred huge flapping flags, Israeli and Egyptian. Deep lines of soldiers guarded the landing area. A red carpet stretched from the plane ramp to the microphones, where a large military honor guard was drawn up, and the army band waited with brass instruments flashing in the TV floodlights.

The plane swooped in, the wheels touched the tarmac, and scattered applause broke out in the crowd as it slowed down with a roar, turned, and taxied back. A hush fell on the crowd, and in the screening room too. As the plane halted, Guli spoke out in his gravelly baritone. "I tell you what, people. That door will open and a monkey will come out."

On the black-and-white set in Max Roweh's Yemin Moshe house the picture was too streaky and blurry even to show the plane. Aryeh was trying in vain, with all his Sayeret Matkhal know-how in electronics, to make it work. His new girlfriend meantime had gone out to look for a TV shop, and she now returned, saying, "Hard to find a store open on Saturday night, but I did." She reached into the back of the set, fussed with its glowing entrails, and the picture sprang into sharp focus. There was the airplane under floodlights, the exit door still closed.

Yael exclaimed, "You're a genius, Bruria." The girl was sixteen or seventeen and not much to look at, short, sallow, unpainted, with heavy brown eyebrows. "Come, Max, it's working," she called. "You can see the plane."

Roweh hurried in from the balcony facing the illuminated Old City walls, the shawl around his neck flying. "Has he appeared?"

"Not yet. Bruria fixed the set."

"Kibbutzniks are handy," Aryeh said. "They have to be."

"We have that Grundig set in the kindergarten," said Bruria. "The same tube usually goes bad."

The thronged airfield was singularly quiet. A long time seemed to go by, and the door failed to open. Even the announcer's frenetic gibbering trailed off. Silence on the field. Silence on the tube. "Pharaoh comes to the children of Israel offering peace," Max Roweh mused aloud.

"An unusual circumstance," Yael said.

"Possibly the most unusual circumstance, my dear, in the thirty-odd centuries since we left Egypt. But not in the least supernatural."

When the door opened there was a disorderly outrush of Egyptian journalists and photographers down the ramp and out on the field. A long pause, the empty door dark; then out stepped Sadat. He stood very erect in a well-tailored gray suit, his face grave, blinking at the strong light that engulfed him. Trumpeters blew a long spine-tingling flourish, and distant guns began to thunder a salute.

"Look how dark he is," said Aryeh, as other officials were emerging behind him.

"A son of Ham," said Roweh.

THUMP . . . THUMP . . . went the guns.

"I hope he trips coming down those stairs and breaks his neck," said Bruria.

"The man's on a peace mission, Bruria," growled Yael.

"My oldest brother was killed in Suez City," said Bruria.

"By God, there's Abba," exclaimed Aryeh, pointing.

"Where?" Yael peered through glasses she had just started wearing.

He put a finger on two figures in front of the honor guard ranks. "That's the Ramatkhal, and that's Abba."

So it was. Kishote was stiffening at attention as Sadat came down the ramp. Here was the man responsible for the graves of thousands of Jewish soldiers, including hundreds of his own men, yet he felt no hatred for Sadat. Rather, he felt something of Max Roweh's historical awe, and also a strong sense of unreality, seeing Prime Minister Begin shake hands with the Egyptian and, while flashlight bulbs popped like fireworks, exchange smiles and pleasantries.

Zev Barak, standing beside Golda Meir, did not hear the two leaders' words, nor Sadat's greeting to Motta Gur as he returned the Ramatkhal's salute. With measured step and majestic mien, Sadat came to Moshe Dayan, and these words of his Barak heard. His English was clear and mellifluous. "Ah, General Dayan! You must let me know in advance when you're coming to Cairo." Dayan smiled, and Sadat went on, "I will have to lock up all the museums." The dig at Dayan's penchant for helping himself to ancient artifacts brought nervous chuckles among the dignitaries. Dayan made no response, and Barak thought his face fell. Sadat then shook hands with Abba Eban, and went on to Arik Sharon. "Ah, the famous Sharon. If you attempt to cross my Canal again I'll put you in jail."

Sharon was unfazed and ready with the counterpunch. "Oh, no, I'm Minister of Agriculture now, sir, a man of peace."

Sadat laughed, moved on, and came face to face with Golda Meir. His countenance hardened, and he shook hands with a bend just short of a bow. "Madame Prime Minister, I've wanted to talk to you."

Looking him full in the face, she said, "Why did you wait so long?"

A shadow, almost a wince, flitted across Sadat's face. "I'm here now." He walked ahead and shook hands with cabinet ministers. Side by side with Begin and the President of Israel he stood at attention, while the band played the unfamiliar Egyptian national anthem, followed by "Hatikvah." He reviewed the honor guard, then drove off with the President and Begin in a long black limousine to cheers. Israel owned no such limousine. It had been borrowed from the American ambassador.

Max Roweh's Rothschild wife had long ago bought the old Yemin Moshe house and renovated and furnished it with elegant pieces, now somewhat worn. Max had inherited it with her Bentley and her loyal old driver, minus two fingers from a mortar misfire in the Six-Day War. After taking Eva to school next morning, the driver reported that all Jerusalem was going mad with Egyptian flags and welcoming placards, and throngs were lining up to glimpse their erstwhile foe on his way to the Knesset. So the Rowehs set out early in dense traffic, and crawled toward the Knesset in a bluish miasma of fumes.

"Let me say, my dear," Roweh remarked, "that the way you're taking on Edith's funds and boards is a joy. The managers tell me that they're delighted to be rid of me."

"Ha! They're appalled. They were cats in cream, Max. Now the party's over."

His pouchy eyes twinkled through thick glasses. "Do you suppose I wed you for your charms?"

"No, you old serpent. You married an executive director for Edith's charities."

"*Mea culpa.* It did occur to me that you might wield a sharp pencil."

Outside the Knesset, an enormous unruly crowd, hemmed in by iron barriers and doubled police lines, was pressing toward the entrance gate. Yael had never seen Knesset security so tight. As cars trickled through, the passengers' identities and passes were minutely scrutinized by frozen-faced special police. Suspicious guards were checking and rechecking all visitors on foot, however harmless-looking, as they passed inside. In the great chamber only half the Knesset members were at their desks but the galleries were already packed. Yael saw her nephew Danny Luria in a reserved front row with the Barak girls, and the American with the empty pinned-up sleeve. She told Max Roweh the story of Dzecki Barkowe while the Knesset floor filled up and the cabinet members took their seats at tables in front.

"A poignant story," said Roweh. "Most American Zionists are prudent enough to keep their distance. A gallant young man, but he should have known better."

"I'm puzzled how those kids managed to get front seats," she said. But in fact, it was no puzzle. On coming in they had encountered Colonel Amos Pasternak, pacing the main corridor holding a walkie-talkie. With a quick word to Ruti he had slipped them in there.

In a glare of TV lighting, after a few brief formalities, the President of Egypt mounted to the podium under the portrait of Herzl, to deliver an unsmiling uncompromising address, taking the most extreme Arab positions on all issues, with a threatening undertone. The warm excited atmosphere in the chamber chilled by the minute. "Who wrote this for him, the Politburo?" whispered Yael, her heart misgiving her, her vision fading of Aryeh living free of military service.

Roweh whispered back, "Churchill: *'In defeat, defiance . . .'* "

Dzecki Barkowe was staring glassily at Sadat. He had long since blanked out of memory the night that now came flooding back in all its horror — the moment of glory when the traffic first went roaring over the bridge, then the shattering explosions, and his awakening in the hospital bus with a bloody bandaged agonizing stump where his right arm had been.

Danny Luria's reaction to Sadat was utterly different. He never talked about it afterward. He came to the Knesset fearing that Sadat would be a convincing peacemaker, that the wars would all be over, his skill as a Phantom pilot irrelevant, his years of training wasted, the chance gone to avenge his brother in combat with Arab pilots; fearing, moreover, that his fighter-pilot prowess would no longer matter to girls like Ruti Barak. Danny was not yet twenty-one. An infatuation with Ruti was sweeping him, with a vision of having a son and calling him Dov, so as to give the mingled Luria and Barak strain the life that Dov's death had cut off. The more uncompromising and belligerent Sadat now sounded, the more Danny cheered up, while most of the hearers sank into gloom. He paid little mind to Menachem Begin's ad-lib response, full of Holocaust and Bible references as usual. The historic moment had passed when Sadat sat down.

In the crush of visitors headed out of the chamber afterward through lines of soldiers and police, Danny and Ruti went by Amos Pasternak, stationed at a staircase and surveying the scene with a cold commanding eye. Amos gave the willowy Ruti a brief wave and a fetching grin.

"How well do you know him?" Danny inquired.

"Amos Pasternak? Oh, not well."

"He seems to like you."

"Him? I think he likes them older." The bitter twist of Ruti's mouth would have suited a woman of forty.

Not far behind them in the slow-moving crowd, Yael said to Max Roweh, "Why are you so quiet?"

"Am I?"

"You haven't said a word for a quarter of an hour."

Roweh drily laughed. "I'm trying to come to terms with a very strange thought, Yael, which may be nonsense, but then again, may be the truth."

"Tell me."

"It's just that of all the unusual turns in Zionist history, this is the most unusual — that Islam may have produced a new Saladin, a Saladin of world peace."

40

Moshe

After six years, Zev Barak was once more en route to Washington, because Moshe Dayan had decided he wanted somebody along who wasn't burned out, angry, and stale at this next-to-last stage of the tortuous Camp David negotiations. The first meeting at Camp David in September 1978, inconclusive and at times stormy, had produced tentative "Accords"; but peace between enemies who have warred for decades is no simple business when a conqueror is not dictating the terms, and since Sadat's flight to Jerusalem more than a year of the harshest wrangling had by now intervened. Foreign Minister Dayan, the former world hero, in disfavor at home and discredited even in his own party for serving in Begin's cabinet, had been at the center of the risky abrasive dealings throughout; and he was returning with some reluctance to Camp David for yet another go-around with Sadat's Foreign Minister.

His old confidant Sam Pasternak could not very well come, being a Knesset member. Sam had suggested Zev Barak, and Dayan had at once telephoned him at Rafael. Before his abrupt departure, Barak had tried to call Emily Halliday at the old McLean house, for he knew her father had died and she had gone there from Paris to settle his affairs. But she had never been in.

It was a rough flight through the February weather over the North Atlantic. Even Dayan, who could sleep through anything, was tossing and muttering in his recliner. They were alone in the upper cabin, and as the El Al captain tried to climb above the towering thunderheads, and the jumbo jet wallowed and plunged like a rowboat in surf, Barak's eyes began to hurt after too much reading of the voluminous Camp David documents. He buzzed for the stewardess. "Is a scotch and soda possible?"

"Possible, why not?" She staggered down the spiral staircase.

He was sipping the scotch and hanging on to an armrest, his seat belt as tight as he could pull it, when he heard Dayan say, "So, can you make anything of all that bumf?" The Foreign Minister was sitting up and rubbing his face with both hands.

"Well, Minister, I can see the problem with Article Six. It's deadly. How can the Americans possibly support the Egyptian position?"

"What are you drinking?"

"Scotch and soda."

"Not the best thing for my ulcer." He rang for the stewardess, who almost fell into his lap as he ordered sherry. "Zev, I dozed off thinking of the first time you and I flew to America together. Remember that?"

"I do indeed. Dutch charter plane for transporting racehorses, us sleeping on mattresses, and Mickey Marcus's coffin chained to the deck in a reek of horse shit."

"Thirty-one years," said Dayan, lying back with an arm over his eyes.

Mickey Marcus!

I'm living through a light-year of history, Barak thought. When he had been Colonel Marcus's aide back in 1948, peace with Egypt had seemed fully as unlikely as men walking on the moon. A bullet in his elbow during the fight for the Jerusalem road had put Zev out of combat, so Ben Gurion had assigned him to Marcus, the Jewish West Point graduate who knew no Hebrew, and for that matter not much war, either. Marcus was a civilian lawyer, his army experience limited to some reserve staff work in World War II, but B.G., enthralled by Marcus's West Point credentials, had entrusted him with command of the Jerusalem front; and in the end, because he couldn't speak a Hebrew password, he had got himself shot by a sentry. So it was that Dayan and Barak had accompanied his body to the United States for a hero's interment at West Point, and Barak had glimpsed for the first time the New York skyscrapers, the mighty Hudson River, and a twelve-year-old brat named Emily Cunningham, now in her forties. Lately she had stopped sending pictures of herself in her letters. Why? Was she becoming fat or wrinkled or gray, or all three? Didn't she realize how little that would matter to him?

Cut the wandering thoughts, here comes the stewardess with Dayan's sherry. Back to the Camp David papers, and that impossible Article Six . . .

The stewardess wobbled to Dayan with a little wine in a highball glass. "I hope you don't mind, Minister," she said with a worshipful look. "Just to make sure it doesn't spill."

"Very sensible, thank you." Dayan sipped. "B'seder, Zev. Let's say I'm Cyrus Vance, the American Secretary of State. Go ahead, convince me not to support the Egyptians on Article Six."

Barak glanced toward the stewardess. Without a word she slipped away down the staircase. "I'll try. What's the key phrase in these minutes, Minister?" He tapped the pile of papers in his lap. " '*Priority of obligation*'?"

"Yes, priority of obligation."

"All right." Barak assumed a pseudo-Dayan crisp manner. "Secretary Vance, unless Article Six gives us priority of obligation, the deal breaks down, and Israel can't sign."

Amused, Dayan played along with Vance-like dignity. "Sorry, I truly don't see that. Why not?"

"Very simple, sir. Egypt has treaties with the other Arab countries to enter any defensive war against Israel —"

"Well, what of that? That's her legitimate right, isn't it?"

"Mr. Vance, *any* war Arabs start can be called a defensive war. Why, even on Yom Kippur they claimed our navy attacked Egypt first and —"

"Good, Zev." Dayan nodded and smiled. "My very words to Vance. I also reminded him that after their October sixth success they laughed that off as a *'strategic deception.'* But go ahead, 'Secretary Vance' is listening with both ears."

"And therefore, Mr. Secretary, it's imperative that this treaty be a binding obligation on Egypt, *taking precedence over all other treaties*. Otherwise it's an empty piece of paper."

"I can't say I agree." Formal Vance voice. "In effect, you're questioning the good faith of Egypt. You're requiring her to sign a guarantee that she *won't* act in bad faith. That's insulting."

"Secretary Vance, I admire your great political and diplomatic achievements, but you're new to the Middle East."

Dayan crookedly laughed. "Well done. I can hint that, but I can't say it."

Almost as though taking off, the plane passed from groaning and bouncing to a smooth climb. Glancing out the window, Barak said, "Well, well, stars and a moon. The storm's still swirling below down there."

Dayan lay back on the recliner, hands clasped behind his head. "All right, you've got that picture. That's the worst of it, but there are a hundred other disputed items, some of them dangerous snags. This trip had better settle everything, because Sadat's advisers would really rather sabotage the treaty, and they'll succeed if we don't get it signed soon."

Driving from Camp David to Washington in a sunny afternoon, Emily detoured toward Middleburg and turned off into a winding side road to the Foxdale School. The car began to slip and slide on frozen puddles. "This may not be such a great idea," said Barak, clutching the door handle.

"Relax, puss, I've driven over ice on these roads a thousand times." She twisted the wheel violently. The car took a curve broadside, scraping a snowcapped mailbox with a screech of metal. "I swear, these damn mailboxes," exclaimed Emily, fighting the wheel. "Always right in the middle of the damn road."

She had not changed all that much recently, he was thinking. Same nervy lovely Queenie. More gray in her hair, face rounder, figure a bit more curvaceous. No reason to stop sending pictures, but he understood, she was Queenie.

"Em, did you telephone ahead to Foxdale?"

"No."

"Why not?"

"Look, love, when I picked you up at Camp David it just occurred to me that the school's on our way back. The headmistress used to run the English department. She's a fluttery type, and if I called her she'd fly apart at the seams." They were driving through sunlit rolling woods and farmland blanketed with fresh snow. "Isn't this lovely? I do miss Virginia in the winter. Paris is so glum. Rain, rain, rain."

"Camp David's like this." He was wearing the blue windbreaker with the presidential seal. "Sort of snowed in, hard to get around, but beautiful."

"Is that meeting going well?"

"No. Very badly. Bargaining with Arabs through Americans is a weird business."

"Can you tell me about it?"

"Too complicated and technical."

"I see. As Bud used to say, *'Don't bother your pretty little head.'* Well, we're almost there. Two more turns and over the bridge. We'll have a look-in at the Growlery for auld lang syne, and then on to McLean. Bud's bringing the real estate agent at five. There's plenty of time."

As they went across the narrow bridge spanning the creek, Emily exclaimed, "My God, it's gone."

"What, the Growlery? You're crazy, it's up there beyond those pine trees."

"Don't I know where it was? You could *see* it through the trees. I tell you it's gone, Zev, gone." She stopped near the gate at the top of the hill. Where the Growlery had been there was a white expanse of fenced-in tennis courts, smooth with untrodden snow. "Oh God, what a letdown! Why did you let me come here? Why didn't you argue? It's *always* a lousy idea to chase the past."

"Not when Queenie's in the past," said Barak.

That made her laugh tearfully and kiss his cheek. "Well, they can't level the Growlery in our memories," she murmured, "and put in tennis courts, can they?"

"It'll always be there, Queenie, fireplace, wagon wheel, and all. Just as it was, till we die."

"Lamartine's *'Le Lac.'* " Her voice was husky. *"Ils ont aimés."*

"Just so, darling. *Ils ont aimés.*"

She slammed the gearshift into reverse. "Let's get the hell out of here." They were back on the highway before she spoke again. "I have something for you at the house. It was in an old file in Chris's desk."

"What is it?"

"A memo to Admiral Redman at the CIA. The cover page says *Subject: The Sacred Region.* The date's 1956, and the paper's gone all yellow. On his deathbed he remembered that you once asked for it, and told me to send it to you. So help me, he was clearheaded to the end."

In the plowed-out driveway of the McLean house two tracks of deep footprints led from a small car to the house. "Rats, they're early," said Emily. "Good thing Bud's got a key. I'm showing the house to a hot prospect. Agent for an Iranian businessman, who got out just before Khomeini came in."

Halliday was in the living room with a rotund little bespectacled man wearing big galoshes. It was freezing in the house, and they still had on their coats.

"Hello, there, Mr. Thompson, the place is mighty dusty and dreary," Emily said to the agent, gesturing around at the covered furniture, the sheeted piano, the drawn curtains. "I've just been camping out in one room upstairs. My father didn't really live in the house in the last years, he haunted it."

"Oh, it's spacious and elegant," said the real estate agent, with a polite cringe. "One sees that right away. Gracious living. They don't build them like this anymore."

"Well, guys, while I give him the tour," said Emily, "you'll find some Jack Daniel's in that sideboard." She led the agent upstairs.

"Good to see you, Barak," said Halliday. "You know that we're releasing the first F-16s to Israel?"

"What? We're not due to get them for three years yet."

"You weren't, but this Khomeini fellow cancelled the Shah's

order for more than a hundred of them, so you move up on the delivery schedule. Decision made today."

"My God, that's wonderful news."

"Yep. Your boys will be coming over soon to train in them, and they'll love the F-16. The Phantom's a big Mack truck, a great machine, but you have to fly it hands-on a hundred percent of the time. The F-16's a light racing car, great range, a honey." He was at the sideboard, pouring. "Bourbon, Barak?"

"I'd better not."

"Well, cheers. Say, let me ask you something about the Yom Kippur War. It's been on my mind for years. Weren't you caught by surprise because you figured the Arabs would never attack, since you had atom bombs?"

Barak's response was swift and chill. "There's been no confirmation whatever at any time that my country has unconventional weapons."

"Look, even the Egyptians talked to us about it. Your 'basement bomb,' they called it."

"General Halliday, any Israeli leader who'd rely on such weapons — if we had them — to keep us out of war would be an imbecile. A first use of a nuclear weapon since Hiroshima would be the end of Israel."

"Mm." Halliday nodded and drank. "I've been hooted down at the Pentagon, but I say Sadat started the war counting on your *not* using them, for the exact reason you just gave. He felt his time was running out, he figured the whole region would go nuclear sooner or later, and mutual deterrence would freeze the status quo. He attacked to get back the Sinai at any cost, even defeat. And this treaty, whatever it costs him with the other Arabs, will do it. He broke their front, and he got beat, and still his attack is paying off."

Not unimpressed, Barak said, "Maybe. Much as I've thought about the war, that angle hadn't occurred to me. It's interesting."

"I'm pleased that you think so."

On the staircase they heard the flopping of galoshes. Flappity-flap, the agent strode in followed by Emily. "Splendidly proportioned rooms, excellent possibilities. May we have a look at the grounds now?"

"Sure thing, and I'll just have a snort of this Jack," said Emily, pouring, "if I'm to go traipsing up to my hips in snow. Down the hatch, men!" Emily tossed off the whiskey, winked, and went out.

Halliday took more bourbon. His attitude was strange today, Barak thought. He looked much older, dried-up and grizzled, and he seemed to be reaching out for contact. "You know, you Israelis have a better promotion system than ours. You retire young," he said. "You can start a new life from scratch, almost. By the time we get out, with what inflation does to retirement pay, we generals can find ourselves selling pencils. Generals like me, anyway, who have sold good real estate and bought bad stocks. I've been offered a base command at Yokota, a great chance to make business contacts, but I may have to turn it down on account of my son Chris. I don't want him spending years in Japan at his age. Not in Paris, either. His friends and his school are here. It's a dilemma."

"Why don't you ask Emily to come back here while you're over in Japan, General, and make a home for Chris?"

Halliday blinked and pondered. "She wouldn't consider it. She likes Paris. So do the girls."

"Are you sure? My wife and I have seen her in Paris. She misses Chris terribly, that I can tell you."

"By God," said Halliday, drinking, "if only she would."

"But could you give up your son for years? Wouldn't you miss him?"

"Like all hell. But I have to see him through college, don't I? And the girls, too. I have to think about money."

A cold gust blew in through the front door, and they heard stamping. "It's a superior property," said Mr. Thompson, as he flapped in, cringing and trailing snow. "River views nowadays are diamonds. I will recommend it to my client, Mrs. Halliday, and I'll telephone you. General Halliday, did you promise me a ride back to town?"

"Right. Barak, so long," said Halliday. "I've never forgotten that helo tour and those battlefields."

"Come again," said Barak, as the airman was leaving. "See us at peace."

Emily said as the door closed, "Looks like a sale, but one never knows. Come out on the terrace. No fireflies, but it's beautiful."

As they trudged down the snow-piled stairs, the setting sun through bare trees was painting the snow pink. Barak recounted his talk with Halliday, and his suggestion about Chris. Emily halted in her tracks and glared at him. "Just like that, I'm to move to Washington, hey? Always quick with bright ideas that keep us farther apart, aren't you?"

"Come on! You cried on my shoulder for hours in Paris about how you missed your boy. This way you can have him again for years."

"Oh, yes? And then give him back to Bud and that blue-eyed stick insect, Elsa? Break my heart all over again? Fat chance."

"Queenie, in four years he'll be a roaring teenager, and you'll be relieved to hand him over to his father."

She did not answer, staring out at the reddening river. Taking his cold hand, she brushed it with warm lips. "Well, it's a nutty notion. Would our once-a-year deal still be on if I came back here?"

"Yes."

"Though it's four times as far as Paris?"

"I'd do it."

"How about Nakhama?"

"I said I'd do it, Queenie."

Heaving a big sigh, she looked at her watch. "Chilly out here, at that. When does the car leave town for Camp David?"

"Half-past six."

"Let me give you that document."

In the library, which was all draped with dust covers, he flipped the yellowed pages. "Strange that he kept this so long."

"Chris never threw anything away. I'll be digging out for another month. Look, Wolf, you said you're here only three more days. Will we see each other again?"

"I'm at Dayan's disposal. Keep in touch, I'll try."

"Great. Anyplace but this house."

A note from Dayan lay under the door of Barak's cabin: *See me when you get back.* He went straight to the large cottage, treading carefully the icy narrow moonlit path through the snow. Dayan sat on a couch in his Camp David windbreaker, a tray of sandwiches on the table before him. He was not wearing his eye patch.

Never before had Zev Barak seen Dayan in this startling aspect. That small black patch, he perceived with shock, was nothing less than Moshe Dayan's persona. The dead socket was frightening, the countenance strange, the man himself transformed from the famous flamboyant hero, whatever his failures and blemishes, to a pale worn pitiable old handicapped person. And yet Barak also sensed that Dayan was, perhaps without intent, paying him a rare compliment. He knew that Sam Pasternak had often seen him so. Dayan was at last accepting Barak as someone with whom he could be himself.

Dayan caught Barak's glance at the patch lying on a side table. "For what there is to see in this lousy world, Zev, one eye is enough. Have a sandwich. The team's in the dining hall, but I'm not up to table talk."

"Thank you, sir."

"L'Azazel, Vance was playing dumb today. Perhaps he was ordered to. On Article Six, for hours and hours he backed Khalil to the hilt." This was the Egyptian Foreign Minister. "Nothing went right. They were even fudging on the oil arrangement. We've slipped back six months, Zev. I see only one thing to do. Call Begin and tell him to summon me home." He looked to Barak. This stare of one live bloodshot eye and one dead socket was terribly distracting and dismaying.

Barak forced a level tone. "How is the rest of the team doing?"

"Oh, drafting settled points, hundred percent. We have geniuses for fine-tuning legal concepts and language. But the impasses go to the top. Khalil says that's him, he has plenary authority. Vance speaks for Carter. I'm just a negotiator. It isn't working. Especially since I think Khalil really wants to torpedo the treaty."

"Moshe, there are three more days. You're being leaned on because your position's weak. Stick it out. Get all the progress you can on the drafting, and let Carter send for Begin."

Abruptly Dayan picked up the eye patch and put it on. "I need some air."

The moon was bright on the snow. They could barely walk

abreast on the path. "Good air," said Dayan. "Like on the Hermon." They passed through the cottages and were climbing a hill before he spoke again. "Golda's death has hit me hard." Crunch of feet on snow, long silence. "I respected her, but we never saw eye to eye. Unlike Golda I was born among the Arabs. I've lived with them. I've fought them, but I understand them. They were there in the land for centuries upon centuries, minding their own business. And then, along come these Jews pouring in from Europe, waving something called the Balfour Declaration and the Bible, and they say, '*Gentlemen, this land is ours, God gave it to us, be good enough to pack up and leave quietly.*' Unbelievable chutzpah."

"Not so, Moshe, it was they who swore to drive us out, and tried, and keep trying, or we'd have been living together in peace long ago."

"Look, I said just that today to Vance. He asked, 'Why can't you Jews accept coexistence with the Arabs?'. I replied, 'Cy, that's exactly what we've always wanted and still want.' *But*, I told him, for them to blow up the busses, and for us to collect and bury the bodies, that's not what we call coexistence."

"Well said."

"Oh, that was plain Golda-style arguing. For Golda it was always so simple and clear! She came to Palestine from Russia and America, already twenty-three and married. All she knew was doctrinaire Zionism. For us or against us? Capitalist or socialist? Labor or Rafi? Jews or Arabs? Black or white?"

Dayan was puffing hard, though the hill was not steep. The path had ended, and they were plunging their legs deep in snow. He stopped, looked around, and gasped, "Very pretty landscape." Behind them, the lights in the cabins and cottages gleamed through the trees, and a plume of smoke rose from the main lodge. "Well, forward, then. The top isn't far." His breath smoked in regular puffs and he did not speak until they came to the crest. "So, here we are. Nice little climb. Clears the lungs and the mind, no? Let's go back." But he stood where he was and went on. "I expected too much of the Jews. That was the mistake of my life. I thought they could hold the lines we won in the Six-Day War. I was wrong, and I bear that burden. Labor calls me a traitor for joining Begin, and for him I'm just a discardable outsider. I did it because, once he won the election, my nose told me peace with Egypt was possible. I was right about that, and it will happen. We must, and we will, have this treaty, but this second Camp David is a misbegotten sterile business. You're right, Zev. It'll soon be over. I won't tell Begin to call me home." He started down the tracks they had made in the snow, and did not speak again until they were passing the cottages. "Zev, isn't this where you stay?"

"Yes, it is."

"Good night." Dayan strode off into the dark.

At the sitting room table, a plump young man with an intensely earnest look, wearing the unlikely combination of a Camp David windbreaker and a yarmulke, was murmuring over a small Talmud volume. He looked up smiling. "Hi. Did I hear Dayan out there?"

"Yes. We took a walk. He's low."

"Tough job," said the young man, a lawyer named Eliakim. "Responsibility without authority."

"Right. Especially since the Egyptian comes as a plenipotentiary."

"Khalil, a plenipotentiary?" Eliakim grimaced, closing the book on his forefinger. "Yes, to make demands that he knows the Americans will support, and to accept our concessions. Not to concede anything, Dayan's been summoned here for that. He's not well, but he's holding the line. What willpower! He was tremendous back in September, too, with Begin and Sadat."

"You were here?"

"Oh, yes, straight through the thirteen days. They got the Nobel Peace Prize for it, but believe me, the architect of the Accords was Dayan."

Barak got into bed with Christian Cunningham's document, but the faded typing blurred and slid before his drooping eyes. Turning to the last pages, he came on a heading: "Conclusion: How It Will All End." Now he recalled the CIA man telling him, as they drove through Rock Creek Park long ago, about this memorandum to Admiral Redman. He put it aside, too tired to concentrate; and as he was dozing off, he half remembered that the lawyer Eliakim had some special tie to Dayan that made his praise of the Minister highly suspect.

It was barely light outside when he woke. Shuffling to the coffee machine in the other room, he found Eliakim pacing in phylacteries and a prayer shawl.

"Good morning. Am I interrupting?"

"I've prayed."

Barak drank coffee and asked, "Say, didn't you help prepare Dayan's defense for the Agranat Commission? Do you believe the outcome was just?"

Eliakim began removing the phylacteries and winding up the leather straps on them. "The outcome? The outcome was that Dado died a beloved national hero, while Dayan lives under a cloud of blame that never lifts." Folding his prayer shawl, Eliakim gave him a keen look. "You disagree with that outcome?"

Neat, thought Barak, and his opinion of Eliakim went up. "Tell me about Dayan's role in the Accords."

"He was the bad Israeli. Sadat had a warm feeling for Begin, sincere, or brilliantly acted. He called him *'My great friend Menachem.'* But he and Dayan rarely met, and when they did the encounter was frosty. Sadat knew who his true opponent was."

"Surely, Eliakim, it was Begin."

"It was Dayan. On the day we packed to go home, it felt like a funeral, a total fiasco, over the issue of East Jerusalem. Carter called in Dayan — Dayan, not Begin — for a battle royal. When Dayan held firm, Carter finessed the East Jerusalem issue and got Sadat to go along. Moshe knows when to hold and when to give. All those thirteen days, on every sticking point, he kept finding substance and language that Sadat could live with, and that Begin could hope to have the Knesset pass. He fashioned the main breakthroughs."

"Then maybe he deserved the Nobel Prize."

"Not so. The burden was on Begin. He had to get the Accords through the Knesset, and that was as difficult a feat as Sadat's coming to Jerusalem. He did it. Ever since, Sadat's been doing his damnedest to back away from the terms that have got him in trouble with the Arabs. This second Camp David is his last attempt to fuzz the aspect of a separate peace. Pharaoh kept changing the deal with Moses, you remember. Backed away and backed away to the last."

"But there'll be no smiting of the firstborn," said Barak, "to make Sadat stick to his deal."

"No. This time there is only Moshe."

When Barak returned to his cottage that evening, the telephone was ringing. "Wolf! At last! I've called and called and *called* —"

"It's been a heavy day, Queenie. Maybe tomorrow we —"

"Listen. Let me talk. There's been a massive earthquake in the Halliday region today, Zev. It's on, it's *on*, and I'm in heaven. I haven't been this happy in years, and as for Bud —"

"Hold it. What's on, Emily?"

"The switch is on, that's what. I've agreed to come home, Bud will go to Japan, and I'm getting Chris back. I've spent the afternoon with the boy, and he *talked*, Zev, my God how he talked. He's been pining away for me, and as for that Elsa, he can't *stand* her. The ultimate stepmother. Zev, I'd never have done it, if not for you!"

"Nonsense, you two would have worked it out, sooner or later."

"Never, I say, never. What, me? Accommodate that sonofabitching Bud after he threw me over for that animated Scandinavian coatrack? You brokered the deal, and I adore you for it. Now *listen*, can we meet tonight?"

"Em, things are boiling over here. However, tomorrow night —"

"No go. I'm leaving on Air France at two. I called Foxdale, and if I can shoot the girls in there before March first, they'll be okay, they won't lose a semester. So I'm popping over to Paris to wrap things up, help them pack, turn the key to my flat, and make a lightning return. You're *sure* we can't meet tonight, my dearest? I long to hug you, you've turned my mourning to dancing."

"I can't do it, Emily. I just can't."

"Damn, then is this one more telephone goodbye? Welladay!

That you came at all is marvellous, it's a miracle, my life is ablaze. I kiss your eyes. Darling, about the Growlery, I gave the headmistress holy hell, but she explained that nobody was using it, termites had got into it, and the school needed tennis courts. So there you are. What does it matter, if love lasts?"

"We'll go up there together, Emily, next time I'm here," said Barak, "and I'm coming, I promise you. And in a far corner of a far court we'll dig a hole and bury a little bronze plaque. And on the plaque will be engraved, '*Ils ont aimés.*' "

"Oh, God, White Wolf, you wretch, you've made the tears start. Goodbye."

Click.

The darkened El Al plane was halfway back to Israel and Dayan was fast asleep when Barak took Christian Cunningham's memorandum from his despatch case. The first paragraph hooked him and he read on to the end.

> Christmas Day, 1956
>
> THE SACRED REGION
>
> Christians and Jews alike hate to face one stark truth: that the Mosque of Omar has stood on Mount Zion for thirteen hundred years. That is longer than the First and Second Jewish Temples combined stood there — about a thousand years — plus the Crusader occupancy, a mere ninety years. To a believing Christian like myself, the long Moslem reign in Zion must be serving some occult purpose of Our Lord. Now the saved remnant of the Jews, a brand snatched from the burning, has returned to Jerusalem, halted by the Moslems just a few hundred yards short of the Temple Mount. If the Jews succeed in retaking that Mount, mankind will surely have come to a turning point of sacred history. That is of no concern to the Central Intelligence Agency, but it will be a turning point of global political trends as well, and that is our whole business.

The memo wandered off into Cunningham's archaeology hobby, his religious notions, and the Communist threat. There was much about "the three Abrahamic faiths" — Judaism, Christianity, and Islam — and their common root in the land between the sea and the Euphrates. All modern boundaries in the region, Cunningham wrote, were tissue-paper fictions; either sanded-over former Ottoman border markers, or arbitrary lines drawn by the departed Europeans. In nature, in archaeology, and in religion it was all one land, God's dwelling place, the primal Eden. The brotherhood of man had first been prophesied in this land. The three Abrahamic faiths had spread the vision to half the earth. The Return of the Jews to the Temple Mount would signal that the Second Coming was at hand, when the vision of Abraham would go out to the rest of humankind, and usher in world peace.

Then came the summing-up he had long ago mentioned to Barak.

Conclusion: How It Will All End

You asked me to write down, Admiral, what I said over brandy as we were talking the other night about the Suez War. I've tried to do so. The coming of the Messiah is not, as I say, the business of the Central Intelligence Agency. However, political trends in this volatile region, which contains the major reserves of the world's energy, are indeed a prime concern.

The pacifying of the region can only come, I believe, on the religious basis of the oneness of the region, and the underlying Abrahamic bedrock. Christianity and Islam fought each other to a bloody standstill in the Middle Ages, while despising their teachers, Our Lord's people, the Jews, as a dry dead fossil of history. When those dry bones revive and stand again on Mount Zion, that will signal a new political time, an epochal if slow reconciliation, a digging down to the common bedrock, so as to defeat Marxist atheism and forestall the nuclear devastation of the planet. The Second Coming may be a matter of my personal belief. But I predict that when the clouds of polemic and ancient prejudice clear, the New Politics of the Sacred Region will emerge, with a burst of peace and prosperity beyond all present imagining.

Christian Cunningham

This was followed by a red-inked scribble: *"Chris — You should only live so long. Redman."*

Cunningham had written in pencil underneath, in a wavering hand,

> *January 12, 1979*
>
> *Zev Barak — You once said you'd like to read this. Here it is. After 23 years, I still think this is how it will all end. But then, I'm departing a believing Christian.*
>
> *Farewell from the far shore,*
> *Christian Cunningham*

The date was four days before his death. Barak's eyes smarted from reading the faded typescript in the cone of dim light from the overhead hole. He let the papers fall on his lap, musing for a long time on this strange farrago. A man of paradox, poor Cunningham: a devout believer in Jesus Christ, and as good a friend as the Jews had had in the labyrinth of American bureaucracy. Barak had never talked religion with him, but what could Chris have thought of a Pope who averted his eyes and kept silent while the Germans were massacring European Jewry? What had he made of the inquisitors who burned Jews in public squares, all in the name of his Savior, well into the eighteenth century? Secretive, brilliant, obsessively suspicious, naively believing; Christian Cunningham was gone, taking his contradictions with him to the far shore. He had fathered Emily. Rest in peace, Chris.

Under Cunningham's farewell Barak wrote one word in Hebrew, HALEVAI, and settled back to sleep.

When President Carter came to Cairo and Jerusalem to iron out the last stubborn wrinkles in the treaty himself, Dayan did not consult Barak again. Nor did he invite him to Washington for the signing ceremony. Barak watched on TV the historic three-way handshake on the White House lawn, noting how different their demeanors were: Carter all smiles at a foreign policy triumph he badly needed, Sadat formidable and stiff, as though sensing the life-threatening danger of his move, and Begin genially stealing the show with a coup de théâtre straight from the Yiddish stage, putting on a large black yarmulke to declaim Psalm 126 in Hebrew. Carter, Sadat, the VIPs and the media people listened uncomprehending; Barak of course understood the words, and why Begin had chosen this psalm.

When the Lord returned us to Zion,
We were like dreamers.
Then our mouths were filled with laughter,
And our tongues with song . . .

And so on, every word to the last.

He who went forth weeping,
Bearing sacks of seed,
Will surely come rejoicing,
Bringing in his sheaves.

Was this the Prime Minister of Israel? This was an old skull-capped Polish Jewish tailor saying *t'hilim*, psalms; a Holocaust survivor, praising God for the confirmed miracle of the Return. It was a gesture at once awesome and faintly embarrassing, a final steamrollering of the old galut whisper, "What will the goyim say?"

At a party in Jerusalem not long afterward, Eliakim met Barak and told him about the gala dinner that had followed, in a tent outside the White House. "The Night of the Big Givers," Eliakim jocosely called it. Fifteen hundred people sat at small tables in a deafening din of chatter and music, he said, mostly American Jewish leaders with a sprinkling of Washington notables, freezing in the March night air or roasting if too close to the electric heaters. Not knowing how kosher the kosher food was, Eliakim ate nothing and yearned to leave early, but he feared offending a Vermont senator and three UJA chairmen he sat with. When he saw Dayan get up from the table of Cyrus Vance and the President of Israel, he seized the excuse to follow his Foreign Minister, and walked with him through a bitter cold wind to their hotel. Dayan spoke not a word until in the elevator he invited Eliakim into his room. "What a balagan that was, eh?" he said as they came in. "Would you like to order something to eat? Sardines, cheese?"

"I'm okay, Minister, thanks."

Dayan rattled a box of Oreo cookies at him. "These are good. Have some."

Though he avoided American packaged foods, not sure of what was in them, Eliakim took an Oreo, but did not eat it. Dayan ate several, staring out the window at Lafayette Square and the floodlit White House. From a pile of hardcover books on a table he picked up a copy with his smiling much younger face on the cover. "Eli, have you ever glanced at this?"

"I've read it twice, Minister. It's a classic."

"Don't exaggerate, it's just a plain story of my life. I had no time to be elegant. I have to sign these for ten big givers back there in that tent." He sat down and penned brief Hebrew on the flyleaf: *To the good Jew Eliakim, from Moshe*. "They'll get nine, and let them fight it out."

"Thank you, Minister. I'll treasure this."

"Well, good night." Dayan opened another copy of his life story, and as Eliakim left he was reading it and eating Oreos.

Eliakim recounted all this to Barak on the narrow flower-lined terrace of a flat belonging to a Hebrew University professor, while behind them a stereo played Beethoven over the party talk, and from the apartment below rock-and-roll music blasted the Jerusalem night. "I still don't know just why," Eliakim added, "but I've never felt sorrier for anybody."

"On television you hardly saw Dayan," Barak said. "It was all Begin."

"Yes, I thought of that at the signing. Not the New Jew, the famed sabra warrior, the effacer of the Wandering Jew image," said Eliakim. "Just an old shtetl Jew."

Eliakim left Barak sitting alone on the terrace, thinking long melancholy thoughts about Moshe Dayan, and about the river of time swiftly flowing away. Amos Pasternak came out in a short-sleeved shirt, carrying a Pepsi-Cola. He dropped in a lounge chair, "Hi. Noisy in there."

"Amos, tell me about Toulon."

A nuclear reactor assembly that France was committed to ship to Iraq had been blown up in a warehouse outside the seaport. The incident was causing an international stir.

"Well, Zev, you've heard the latest, haven't you? The French say every key item was destroyed by precise planting of plastic explosives. An inside job of some sort."

"Did we have anything to do with it?"

Amos's round face wrinkled in an innocent smile. "Why, an outfit nobody's heard of is claiming responsibility. 'The Group of French Ecologists.' "

"And how much of a respite does this give us? A couple of years?"

"Dubious. The French can replace the stuff out of their own reactor reserves. Saddam Hussein will grunt, *'Deliver, or no cut-rate oil.'* They'll deliver."

"A year, anyway?"

"Well, a year, yes."

"I tell you, Amos, Camp David or no Camp David, we are in great peril. This Iraqi reactor frightens me as I haven't been frightened since June '48."

"What happened then?" inquired Amos. "I was three years old."

"We were at the end of our rope. If the Arabs had kept going for one more week, they'd have overrun us and ended the whole thing then and there, for good and all. We caught our breath during the cease-fire, made it through the war, and here we are. But two atomic bombs exploding over Tel Aviv and Haifa would spell doomsday. Poor Golda used to call me Mr. Alarmist. By my life, I only try to see things as they are."

Amos said soberly, "Well, this Toulon business puts off the day."

"It's not a solution."

"Not in the long run, no."

Barak gestured toward the party. "Have you seen my Ruti? She came with Danny Luria."

"No, I just got here."

"Amos, just between the two of us, aren't you giving Ruti a hard time?"

"I don't mean to."

"If you didn't see her at all, that would be one thing. But you do."

"I like her."

"She more than likes you. Did she tell you that she intends to apply to the California Institute of Technology?"

"Cal Tech? Oo-ah! No."

"Well, she's out to live my dream that failed, and become a scientist. She's a math and physics whiz like my brother Michael, and amazingly ambitious. If she does go to California, will that end it?"

A silence, then, "Zev, can you picture what it's like to be in love with a woman in another country, a woman you can only see rarely, a woman with kids, a love which won't die, which has nothing to do with casual romance, which is *it*? Can you picture something like that?"

"Well, I'm getting on, but I can try," said the White Wolf. "So what?"

"I'm up for operations officer, Northern Command, and —"

"Why, that's tremendous, Amos."

" — and I know I'm coming to a crossroads. It's tough."

"Is this woman a widow?" Amos shook his head. "A divorcée?"

"No. Married. A lot older than I am. Three children."

"*Alleh myless* [All the attractions]," said Barak.

It drew a sad laugh from Amos Pasternak. He stood up. "Ruti couldn't be sweeter or prettier or smarter. Cal Tech! I bet she gets in, too. Danny Luria is lucky."

"Not while you're seeing Ruti, he isn't."

"Are you telling me to stop seeing Ruti?"

"Absolutely not."

"Or to give up the lady?"

"That only you can decide."

"You're a big help," said Amos. "I appreciate your frankness. By your leave, I'll now go and look for Ruti."

"With my blessing," said her father. "It was just a quiet word."

"Yes, I've got the idea."

41

Doomsday

THE PRIME MINISTER

invites

Major General & Mrs. Barak

to the Weekly Tanakh Circle

Topic

Isaiah and Deutero-Isaiah: Contrasts in Style

At The Residence *November 27, 1979*
8 P.M. after Sabbath *Please bring this card*

Nakhama showed the card to her husband. "*Oy vavoi,*" she exclaimed. "It sounds stupefying. Do I have to go?"

"No, but I'd better show up."

"Why does he ask us to a thing like that, Zev?"

"I have no idea." A fib for security reasons. This was about the reactor. The Tanakh Circle was an unobtrusive cover for the meeting to come afterward.

The small scholarly audience listened raptly to three experts on the Book of Isaiah, while the few military men in mufti struggled against falling asleep. When the other guests left they gathered in Begin's office, where he laid aside the yarmulke he had worn for the

Bible talk. "*Rabotai* [Gentlemen]," he said, "this is a secret informal consultation. No minutes will be taken."

He nodded at the chief of the Mossad, a small man in a brown knitted sweater, who might have been another Isaiah savant by the look of him. He talked about the rapid progress of the reactor outside Baghdad since the Toulon setback. France and Italy were again supplying technicians and main components. The West Germans, perhaps ashamed of doing it openly, were selling elements to Brazil for resale to Iraq. The uranium was coming from France, Brazil, and Portugal, and Iraq had demanded and was receiving the uranium in certain chemical forms that most readily yielded plutonium, the bomb stuff. Building a reactor for electric power made no sense, Iraq was awash in oil. Barak's background in chemistry enabled him to follow all this in detail. The implied short time frame appalled him.

Sunk in his chair, the Prime Minister listened with closed eyes. When he opened them, they were glazed and bloodshot. In a weak weary voice he said he saw only a few alternatives. Israel could try harder with diplomacy to stop the Europeans from rushing Iraq into a nuclear capability. Or it could hope with its superior air force to deter Iraq when it went nuclear. On the other hand, was an attack from the air feasible, to take out the whole complex? Or was a commando raid on the pattern of Entebbe the answer? He concluded, "I've asked the chief of planning branch to address the commando option."

The graying Don Kishote stood up to give his somber report, and Barak had a memory flash of the lanky immigrant boy on a mule at Latrun. A far cry! To begin with, Yossi asserted, Entebbe and Baghdad were not comparable. At Entebbe the objective had been a civilian airport, defended only by a PLO terrorist gang and some local soldiery. The Iraqi complex was a hardened military target, heavily fortified, strongly guarded, ringed with antiaircraft and ground defense forces. A commando raid in brigade strength, with heavy vehicles and main battle tanks, might have a fifty-fifty chance of wiping out the complex, with a large cost in dead, wounded, and prisoners. The chance of a surprise success with such a raid was zero.

Benny Luria spoke next about the air attack option, for he was in charge of the Etzion air base in Sinai near Eilat, whence an air strike would depart. In his full blond beard Benny looked much aged, and sad with good reason. He had been called out of retirement and given the mournful task of liquidating the base, perhaps the most advanced in the world, as part of the Camp David treaty; having been in on its construction, his job now was to demolish it so utterly that the Egyptians could never use Etzion against Israel. None of the aircraft on hand, Luria said — Skyhawks, Kfirs, Phantoms, and F-15s — were right for the job. The Phantoms could be refueled in the air, but over enemy territory that was a high-risk gamble. As for the new small superplane, the F-16, it might not be delivered in time, and anyway the Americans gave its range as much too short.

Begin nodded. "You're eliminating the air attack option, then."

"Well, let me say, Prime Minister, that the Americans are cautious in stating range. Equipped with special fuel tanks, the F-16s might just make it, but without testing them we can't know."

"Zev Barak." Begin turned abruptly to him. "What will the Americans do if we destroy the reactor?"

"Prime Minister, the Americans admire venturesome boldness, the cowboy myth, but if it's a fiasco, with civilian deaths in Baghdad, we can expect bad trouble."

"How bad?" Begin sounded a shade plaintive.

"No support in the inevitable UN condemnation. Halting of F-16 deliveries. Cutoff of all aid for years, if not for good."

The bald head dipped slowly and tiredly, and Begin asked the rotund Sam Pasternak, markedly fattened by a happy marriage, what France would do if many French technicians were killed. "They'll break diplomatic relations, Prime Minister, and push hard in the UN for sanctions against Israel, maybe for our expulsion." Pasternak paused. "I don't believe they'll send their air force to punish us." This arid comment elicited wry grins all around.

Various ideas were floated short of a raid, like interdicting the uranium shipments en route to Iraq. The Prime Minister appeared to be dozing, he looked more and more glassy-eyed, and, Barak thought, the rumors might be true that he was physically failing. When a clock struck eleven behind Begin's desk, he sat up and rubbed his eyes hard. "Rabotai, we have been talking about the life or death of the Jewish State. One way or another, we will stop this thing. Please forget that we have met. Goodnight."

The little Jewish tailor all at once sounded to Barak like David Ben Gurion, ordering the sinking of the *Altalena*; and this was the man who had sailed on the *Altalena* into Tel Aviv harbor to overthrow Ben Gurion.

On the highway from Haifa to Afula, where he was building high-rise apartments on a government subsidy, Guli Gulinkoff's luck ran out. Careering down the wrong lane to pass a convoy of army tank transporters, Guli had to swerve so as not to pile head-on into a horse pulling a hay wagon, and this time he hit a stone wall. End of a kablan, and of the only silver Lincoln in Israel.

Numbed by grief, because she had grown genuinely fond of the brutish Guli in two wedded years, Daphna went through the mourning rites in a daze, but in a month or so her mind cleared. She might be a rich young widow, she realized; or she might owe millions of shekels she could not possibly repay. Guli had never said a word to her about his business affairs. Suspicious of the lawyers and accountants who swarmed in on her, and of Guli's office staff too, she turned for help to Dzecki Barkowe, though his lawsuit against Guli was still pending. Dzecki had once loved her, and he knew the law and the real estate trade. Moreover he was an American, not a local shark.

Dzecki found, to his surprise and Daphna's pleasure, that once he settled several lawsuits, including his own, Daphna was still very well off. As to whether the mysterious Guli had been a fraud or a genius, the answer was, a bit of both. Guli on principle had never paid anybody anything unless forced to. Going to law had been his delight, for it meant long years during which he collected interest on large disputed sums; not to mention that plaintiffs often wearied, or died, or like Dzecki's parents left Israel in disgust, or that his Chinese-puzzle contracts sometimes even befogged the courts to find in his favor. In short, there were two beneficiaries of

Guli's sudden end; the hay wagon horse had its life, and Daphna had the departed kablan's money.

Within the year Daphna, widowed at thirty, was coping with her new status in a costly private house with a garden in north Tel Aviv, a favored neighborhood of Israel's beautiful people, and the Haifa villa was for sale. "Haifa has the Technion, the navy, and oil refineries," Daphna said to Dzecki about her decision to move. "Without Guli to liven things up I'll go mad here. As for the view of the harbor, I've had it."

Just about all the beautiful people came to her housewarming. Her brother Danny showed up at the afternoon garden reception in uniform, and Daphna, svelte, smartly coiffed, and merry in a black cocktail frock from Paris, introduced him around proudly as an F-16 pilot until he couldn't stand it. He broke away to a corner of the garden, where he stood glowering at the authors, artists, journalists, actors, film producers, models, and politicians drinking, talking, and looking at each other. Pretty waitresses passed shrimps and cocktail sausages, steering clear of the scowling aviator. When Don Kishote arrived in an open-necked white shirt, conspicuous among the suits and ties of the smart crowd, his was the first face familiar to Danny. He had recently seen the chief of planning branch on Etzion air base, at the briefing for an abruptly aborted strike. After a while Don Kishote approached him, drink in hand, and said quietly, "Hello, getting over the letdown?"

"Not yet, sir. We were a long time building up to it, you know."

"And am I wrong, or are you not having much fun here?"

"You're not wrong."

"Why didn't you bring Ruti Barak?"

"She couldn't come. I asked her."

"Would you like to go for a drive with me?"

"Anywhere."

Kishote took Danny off through the crowded house to his army Volvo, a perquisite of his rank. "Where are we going?" asked Danny, as they started off.

"An old border kibbutz near Nablus. My son Aryeh lives there, he married a kibbutz girl." He glanced at Danny. "That abort was a bad business, but why can't you take it in stride? Your chance will come, and you'll do a great thing."

"The abort was just as well. I don't think Israel is worth dying for."

The car stopped at a red light, and Kishote looked hard at the aviator. "You volunteered to fly the F-16, didn't you? You broke your neck to be selected."

"That I don't regret. The F-16 is a marvel, a rocket to Mars, it's America with wings, the F-16. That Ogden air base where we trained was heaven. But after that we came home."

"And then what?"

"And then what? Okay, here's what. Maybe as chief of planning you should hear this."

A tirade burst from Danny Luria. Fresh from America he had looked at Israel with new eyes, he said, seeing it on a crazy consumer binge, with a hundred percent inflation, people living on bank overdrafts and yet buying color TVs, new cars, luxury furniture, modish clothes, in a pitiful futile mass attempt to live like Americans. Every week a new bank scandal or government bribery case made big black headlines, as did the incessant strikes by doctors, teachers, and bus drivers. Everybody who had any money was gambling on the stock market, where the prices had gone insane, while poverty was getting worse among the poor in the cities and the small towns. The popular music was all ersatz American rock-and-roll. The magazines were all about American movie stars and multimillionaires, or about squalid Israeli crimes and squabbling politicians. Was this what his brother had died for?

Danny Luria poured all this out for about an hour, as Kishote drove in silence across the country and headed down the highway twisting through the arid brown Judean ridges. "Understand me, General Nitzan, we'll fly the mission. The air chief knows we will. But we'll fly into a hornet's nest of SAM-6s and AA, and some of us won't come back. I feel no reason to give up my life, except group loyalty. You know, at the base they call our unit 'the Chosen.' A graveyard joke! Chosen to die, and for what? For Zionism?" He sourly laughed and broke off, stared out at the vacant stony hills, and after a while went on, "And as for my father's buying the

Ezrakh's idea that Israel may be stage one of the messianic era, he just loses me. That Ezrakh lived and died in an Old City yeshiva dream. Kol ha'kavod, but dreaming in an F-16 cockpit can lead to trouble."

"Granted," said Don Kishote, the first word he had spoken in quite a while.

This break in Danny's impassioned soliloquy made him stop and laugh more naturally. "Well, okay, that's about it. I haven't talked this much since I saw Ruti Barak in Pasadena. I was as high then as I'm low now."

Kishote said, "In 1974 I left Israel for two years, feeling much as you do. I wasn't sure I'd ever return."

"So why did you?"

"I sometimes wonder. How was Ruti?"

"Too thin. Working like a horse. She'll come back, all right."

"You know, Danny, the whole world imitates the Americans. You can't get away from that."

"Not like Israel. Last Friday night a few of us did the Tel Aviv nightclubs. What a scene! *Shabbat shalom!* La dolce vita, Zionist style, Jews imitating Europeans imitating Americans. In one fancy club, at three in the morning, we saw half the big Labor politicians with their ladies, busy building the just socialist society."

Brown, muscular, in a grease-stained shirt and rolled-up shorts, Bruria was changing a bandage on Aryeh's leg when they came into the bleak little cottage. Not my type, thought Danny; sunburned pleasant face, bright brown eyes, thin determined mouth, a future kibbutz chairwoman, or possibly a far left Knesset member. Aryeh exclaimed, sitting up in the double bed which filled the room, "Danny! Ma nishma? What a surprise! Bruria, this is my fighter-pilot cousin who missed our wedding."

"Hi." She gave Danny a hard handshake. "You were training then in Utah, I think."

"How are you doing?" Kishote asked his son.

"Flesh wound. Doctor says I'll be up and around in a week."

"Wound?" said Danny. "What kind of wound?"

"Gunshot."

"L'Azazel!"

"Yes, I surprised some infiltrators on my night rounds. They left a bloody trail and I may have killed one. I hope so."

"You have that trouble here still?"

"Still," said Bruria, "and too often."

Kishote and Danny visited with Aryeh while Bruria bustled out and after a while bustled back in, inviting them to supper. "Our chairman wants to talk to you," she told the pilot. "Come, Aryeh, I'll get you ready."

Kishote led Danny on a tortuous path through cottages and blooming fragrant trees to the brightly lit dining hall. "A stagnant little kibbutz," he said. "Nice people, though."

At the community tables, where the kibbutzniks were already eating, the uniformed pilot caused stares and whispers. Bruria brought Aryeh in a wheelchair. The chairman, a thickset heavily wrinkled graybeard, told Yossi over the chopped vegetables and baked carp that the army was getting slack. The highest fences, the most tangled barbed wire barriers, weren't enough to stop infiltrators. Security meant men and guns! The Arabs were always close by with wire cutters, full of hate and looking for trouble.

As the meal ended, the old kibbutznik turned to Danny. "Will you talk to my people? They'll be thrilled."

"That I doubt, but okay."

With noisy shuffling of chairs and benches when the chairman introduced him, all turned to hear the aviator, weary-looking men and women in farm clothes or shorts, many elderly and middle-aged. The chairman murmured to Danny as he stood up, "Urge the youngsters to stay on the kibbutz. That's our biggest problem, not infiltrators."

Danny talked in a monotone about the F-16, as though giving a briefing, but the kibbutzniks listened with intent faces and shining eyes. About to sit down, he laughed and said, "Ai, I almost forgot. I'm supposed to tell the young folks not to leave the kibbutz for the big city. That I can't do. Who am I to advise you? But one thing I can say, because it's the truth. I've just driven down here from the big city. There I was feeling terrible about Israel, and here I feel good." He was astonished, and so was Kishote, at the loud applause in which the young kibbutzniks heartily joined.

As the Volvo rolled out through the gate to a dark dirt road lined with tall trees, the aviator said, "Nice people is right. I loved them. But isn't the kibbutz movement finished, sir, an anachronism from the pioneer days?"

"Well, I used to think so myself, but since Aryeh married that Marilyn Monroe back there, I've been wondering." Danny chuckled. "I mean it. An iron girl! And a sweetheart. These border kibbutzim are important for security, no argument."

They drove on the moonlit main road to Jericho without talking. Kishote was turning into the highway that climbed to Jerusalem when Danny spoke up. "I really do feel better, sir. Talking my heart out to you helped. You're a good listener."

"Everything you said was true, and well put. Too well."

"Look, why was the strike aborted?" No response. "We should have been told why. We're used to scrubs in the air force, but this last-second abort was alarming. It gave us a feeling, I tell you frankly, that the government doesn't know what it's doing. All aircraft were on the ramp, loaded up with bombs, extra fuel tanks full, engines roaring —"

"All right, Danny. This goes in one ear and out the other."

"Trust me."

"The French were having an election then. We've got an election coming up too. At the last minute, Begin came under pressure to wait and see whether a new French government would cut off the Iraqi nuclear connection. He gave in. They got the new government, but went right on supplying that reactor."

"Okay." The aviator nodded. "Now, confidence for confidence, I'll tell you something. When we unloaded the bombs and checked the time fuses, *they had all been set wrong*. It's still being investigated. If the mission had flown not only would it have failed, but the mistimed explosions might have killed some of us diving in."

"My God, you're telling me," Kishote almost groaned, "that the abort was a good thing, for the wrong reasons?"

"For the wrong reasons, it was a miracle from heaven."

"At least," Yossi said after a shocked silence, "a very unusual circumstance."

"You said it. Our level of maintenance is marvellous, but a million things can go wrong in such an operation and it only takes one . . ." He broke off, as Yossi swung swiftly past a bus grinding uphill. "Sir, will the mission ever go?"

"It will go."

"Well, and even if it succeeds, what will it accomplish, in the long run?"

"What do you call the long run? The days of the Ezrakh's Messiah? It will give us ten years."

When Ruti Barak came home for the summer, it was like having a teenager in the Barak flat. The telephone rang and rang. To her father she appeared to have faded; scrawny, peaked, and for the first time wearing glasses. All the same the young men obviously disagreed. They kept pestering her for a date on Shavuot, until Danny Luria snared her. The one-day festival celebrating the Revelation on Sinai fell on a Monday, so the beach hotels were all booked for a holiday weekend. The day after Ruti said yes to Danny, Amos Pasternak also called, to her visible vexation. But on Friday she showed up all smiles at breakfast, chirruping that Danny had backed out, and she and Amos were going to Eilat together.

Nakhama said, "*Danny* backed out of a date with you? Impossible."

"Well, he did! If you think I did it, you're wrong."

"Did he say why?" Barak asked.

"Not a word. Just called it off." Ruti gave her parents a deep dark-eyed look which ended further inquiry into her love life.

To Zev Barak this was a red light. He had been watching the calendar anxiously as Sunday after Sunday slipped by. A strike on the reactor would go on a Sunday, if at all, when the French and Italian technicians would not be in the structure. The absolute deadline was the first of July. The reactor was scheduled to go critical that month, according to intelligence gleaned from friendly Frenchmen on the project. Once the uranium rods were in and "hot," bombing was out, for it would spew a lethal cloud all over Baghdad. Was the decision then, after all, really to do nothing and let a dictator acquire atomic bombs, a man who openly boasted that he would *"burn half of Israel"*? The French government had pooh-poohed that statement as overheated Arab rhetoric, but Barak took it very seriously. Danny Luria's cancelled date with Ruti was a hint that this Sunday the air force was at last going to strike. It all fitted together.

But by now Israel's election was only three weeks away. If the strike was a failure, Menachem Begin would fall in execration. The thing would have to be a flawless success, and even so, the voters might simply take it for granted. Wasn't the IAF the most accomplished air force in the world? What else was new? And when the opposition raised the howl — as it surely would — that he had played petty politics with pilots' lives and Israel's world repute in desperate grandstanding for votes, how could he prove in rebuttal that the reactor would have gone critical in July? Zev Barak had never liked Begin as Prime Minister in Golda's shoes, but he had guts. One had to give him that.

On Saturday night Danny could not sleep, thinking about the morrow, and regretting his missed weekend with Ruti. He put on a quilted jacket and took a walk under glittering Sinai stars. At Ramat David the June nights were becoming warm and hazy, but here in Etzion it was a night of crystal air and desert cold. Ah, this gloomy doomed Etzion base! Ah, his father's melancholy duty to destroy this marvel of underground hangars and advanced avionics which he had helped to build!

Wandering into the recreation room, he found Mussa, number three in his attack foursome, drinking beer. Mussa was the silent one of the Chosen, short and swarthy, with thick curly black hair. His home was in upper Nazareth, a mixed Arab and Jewish town. Even among the pilots, who tended to reticence except about flying, he was considered taciturn. Danny did not so much as know whether Mussa was married or single. As an aviator, he was professional as the best. Taking a beer from the refrigerator, Danny said, "Tell me something, Mussa. What's our motivation for tomorrow?"

Mussa looked up at him with veiled brown eyes. "Our motivation? Why?"

"Okay, forget it. Dumb question."

"No, I'll answer you. My mother's a survivor. Both her parents died in Maidanek, and if I can help it, nobody will ever incinerate Jews again. That's my motivation. What's yours?"

"To gain ten more years for Israel."

"Not all that different," said Mussa. "One decade at a time."

* * *

June 7, 1981, 3 P.M.

"Okay, Dov, here I come."

The words break unbidden from Danny as the screaming shaking heavily overloaded F-16 struggles into the air. At once it strikes him that this blurt is a bad omen. Is he really on his way to join his brother in death?

The eight fighter-bombers flash over the deep blue Gulf of Aqaba and the barren Saudi coastal range, then drop to ground-hopping level to evade radar. Brown desert sands race backward under his wings, and the words return to haunt him. His first combat mission is in fact as hazardous as anything his brother ever did. Within two hours he is going to draw even with Dov or die. He drove himself to qualify for the F-16 so as to measure up to his dead brother. Hence the blurt, no omen but the truth, one way or the other.

Excellent weather, a bumpy ride through the thick hot air above the sunbaked sand, the escorting F-15s in sight, flying along in line with the eight F-16s. So far everything on the mark, but the departure started badly. In the leader's plane all electronic systems failed just before takeoff, no explanation, and he had to leap into a backup F-16 he had never flown. There was an omen, a bad one! Malfunction in one of these single-engine mechanical wonders, on a three-hour attack mission over enemy territory, is almost as grave a hazard as enemy opposition. The most fanatical maintenance and checking by ground crews cannot forestall a crump fated to happen.

And the probable enemy opposition is hazard enough. The force is running the gamut of Jordanian, Saudi, and Iraqi radar. The Iraqis, at war with Iran, have to be on highest radar alert, for

Iranian planes have already ineffectually attacked the reactor. A single radar report, or a secrecy leak in Israel, and the attack on arrival will touch off a volcanic eruption of SAM-6 missiles and AA fire, and a scrambling cloud of MiGs from three nearby air bases. That is why the F-15s are along, to patrol over those fields, two for each field, to hold off the Iraqi air force . . .

The first operational hazard: time to discard the two detachable wing tanks, each snugged up against a two-thousand-pound bomb. American doctrine for the F-16 prohibits such loading, but the IAF is chancing it, as the only way for the planes to get to Baghdad and back. The risky arrangement has not been tested, no detachable tanks to spare. Danny's eye is on the leading plane of his foursome, off to the left in echelon with Mussa. *There!* The tanks are tumbling away. Now there go Mussa's. He trips his release, feels the jolt, feels the new lightness of the plane. B'seder, one big hurdle passed. Now for the job ahead. Review, review, review the approach plan. In radio silence there can be no orders, no calls of correction, the whole attack has to run off as rehearsed, come what may . . .

Okay. When the objective is sighted, turn on the radar jammer of the SAM-6s and pray it works. Accelerate to throw off the mobile ack-ack, which sprays heavy shells like an Uzi but loses accuracy as targets speed up. Remember, every minute of afterburn adds risk of flameout on the way home, so watch it. Up to five thousand feet. Pair up with Mussa for the bombing dive. Fix the bomb-fall line in your sights on the white dome over the reactor. It's just a concrete vacuum chamber for radiation leaks, the target itself is buried thirty feet underground, but there's where your bombs go in, that's all in the computer. When the "death dot" on the line merges with that dome, hit the bomb button. Be ready with flares and chaff if the radar warns of incoming SAM-6s. Go to afterburner again, pull four G's on a fast climbing turn and activate IFF identifier. We'll be coming out of the setting sun. We don't want our own F-15s shooting us down for MiGs . . .

And still the sand flies past a few yards below and the plane jolts on in the heated air, needing hands-on flying all the way with the right-side control handle instead of the old joystick between the legs, a bit strange yet, even after so many months in the F-16. Plenty of time left to think. Too much. *Roar, roar, roar of the engine . . . Longest hour and a half of my life . . . Random thoughts . . .*

. . . The hollow jocularity of the flight leader after the briefing, passing around a plate of dates, "to get you used to the Iraqi cuisine." The rumor that he refused to distribute Iraqi money to the pilots: *"Money won't help a Jew falling into Iraqi hands."* The rumor of a high-brass decision against using "smart bombs." The F-16s could have stood off beyond SAM-6 and ZSU range and released those superaccurate guided bombs at the reactor. Why not, then? *"Because you need smart bombs with a dumb plane, not smart bombs with a smart plane."* The supersmart F-16 can drop its dumb bombs with greater accuracy than any smart bomb could achieve. Greater risk for the pilots? *Zeh mah she'yaish.*

Ah, is that the lake at last or a mirage, that shimmer of blue ahead beyond the brown desert? By my life, the lake, bigger than described. The crucial landmark. Great navigation by the flight leader. Baghdad buildings, as in the photos. So this is it, and sure enough there's that big cursed white dome, slightly pink in the low sun. In minutes they'll cross into the zone of AA fire. So far, not a sign of enemy action; the winding Tigris glittering off to the right, the Baghdad high-rises far ahead, not a MiG in the clear sky, and there go the F-15s, climbing to circle high over the airfields. One of the great things about the F-16 is the visibility; you sit in a bubble atop the hurtling machine and see everything, everything, in all directions . . .

Slow down and drop back four miles, so as not to dive into the first unit's bomb explosions. All this was calculated long ago and cranked into computers for visual display on the transparent screens. And there goes the first unit, popping up two by two for their dives . . .

Worked out long ago to a hair, the strike plan is a balance between least time over the target for the whole force, and enough time between dives to avoid blowing each other up with bomb fragments. Solution: diving in pairs at intervals of thirty seconds.

Four pairs, a half-minute for each pair; total time of the bombing attack, two minutes. For those two minutes, these pilots — and their backups who are not flying — have drilled and drilled for months, not informed of the target until just before the aborted strike. Yet they have guessed it long since, from practicing six-hundred-mile bombing runs. A circle of that radius on the map, drawn around Israel, shows only one target . . .

Ahead and below, concussions, flame, smoke.

Danny and Mussa are the last attacking pair, most likely to catch the heat from a surprised defense. Yet their plunge at the dome, which already looks like a broken eggshell, is all but unopposed; a few white AA puffs, nothing more, no SAMs in sight, no SAM warnings on the buzzer. Death dot crawling down the pipper toward the smashed dome. Einsteinian ballistic calculations, reduced to a simple picture for a pilot to follow and obey. Dot on dome. Okay, bomb button. Heavy jolt, plane instantly lighter, turn and climb on afterburner, pull as many G's as possible and — *Ow! OWW!*

Terrific pain shoots through Danny's head and neck. The G suit is working, but he bent his head when he turned instead of bracing it against the headrest, and he has taken the murderous G's in his neck muscles. Never mind the pain, it will pass, he is conscious. Zoom up into the sky, form up with those F-16s in plain sight overhead, trapping the last red rays of the setting sun on their white Stars of David. God, what an exciting sight! Behind and far below, smoke billowing up from the smashed egg. Next question, have they all made it?

"This is Knife Edge! Report!" The flight leader somewhere up there, breaking silence.

"Knife Edge Two, b'seder."

"Knife Edge Three, b'seder."

"Knife Edge Four, b'seder."

Voices of friends, all recognizable, young, excited, charged up.

"Cluster One, b'seder."

"Cluster Two, b'seder."

"Cluster Three, b'seder."

Silence.

The leader: *"Cluster Four, are you there? Cluster Four, Cluster Four, report!"*

A moment of worry for Danny, through all his neck agony, about the fate of poor Cluster Four. Oo-ah! *He* is Cluster Four. The code names were given just before takeoff, the pain made him forget it. He shouts, "Cluster Four, b'seder," but makes no sound, his vocal cords still strangled.

"Cluster Four, answer up, Cluster Four!" Pause. *"Danny, are you there, are you all right? Answer, Danny!"*

With all his might, Danny strains and croaks, "Cluster Four, b'seder!"

"Carbon, Carbon, from Knife Edge One. CHARLIE. I say again, CHARLIE." Thus the leader exultantly reports all planes safe, to the command plane circling many miles in the rear.

"What are the results?"

"Target appears totally destroyed according to plan."

The eight F-16s are already formed up as they climb steeply at thirty thousand feet in the lilac evening sky, four by four as in a parade flyby.

"Return to base, good luck."

The voice of the flight leader, brisk and cheery: *"Knife Edge and Cluster, go to forty-two thousand feet, head for home, make six hundred knots."*

The pain in Danny's throat, head, and shoulders is subsiding. He turns off the microphone to shout in his bubble as the aircraft soars, "Dov, Dov, we did it. Now let's see what those mamzerim, the politicians, can do with ten years!"

The strike force races home through the thin upper air, scoring contrails against the stars, breathing through oxygen masks, consuming mile by mile a fraction of the fuel they burned going in, lighter by two tons of bombs, the detached tanks, and most of their fuel. Even so, they land one by one on the illuminated Etzion runway almost dry. The ground crews greet them with joy, having no idea of where they have been, but sensing that they have done something momentous. Danny runs and embraces Mussa as he steps off the ladder from his bubble. "Well, we did it."

"That's what we're paid for," says Mussa, and he walks off into the darkness.

Benny Luria comes out of the gloom at a trot, wearing a knitted skullcap, most unusual for him while on duty. He fiercely hugs his son, puts his hand on his thick red hair, and says in a choked voice, "Repeat this: '*Blessed are you, O Lord, Ruler of the Universe, who grants favors to the unworthy, and has granted me supreme favor.*' " It is the blessing on deliverance from danger. Danny knows the words. Without sharing his father's growing religiosity, he repeats them from the heart. "Abba, Dov flew with me all the way."

His father squeezes an arm around his shoulders. "I know. Mission fulfilled, and all pilots Charlie! A great feat, Danny, a feat for the generations. Highest professionalism, plus the hand of God."

Epilogue

"And He Shall Reign"

April 1982. Deadline for all Israeli forces to withdraw from the Sinai and seal the Camp David peace.

In the media, and in many governments including the American, much skepticism has prevailed as to whether the Israelis would not in the end, find some pretext to stay put. What, leave behind their networks of modern roads, their airfields, their many military camps and underground command bases, constructed at such enormous expense? Give up the oil fields they have developed, which have made them energy-independent and balanced their national budget? Abandon the vital Sharm el Sheikh naval base, the great Etzion air base, the beautiful coastal town of Yamit? Meekly hand all these priceless installations over to the Egyptians, who tried and failed to recover them by force of arms? Just wait and see.

The Israelis are indeed full of surprises. As they surprised the world in the Six-Day War, and at Entebbe, and in the Reactor Raid, so they now surprise the world by hauling down their flags and quietly departing from the last of these irreplaceable assets. That is not to say the departure is a gladsome business. Moving day even in private life tends to be lugubrious; how much more so, in the life of a nation.

The dismantling is over at Sharm el Sheikh. Everything of military use has been removed or blown up, and only the ransacked buildings remain standing. The base commandant, Noah Barak, is having a last look around his rubble-strewn office when his father walks in. "Hi, I came down with the admiral. In case you're not feeling bad enough, I brought you this. Remember it?"

He hands the commandant a framed snapshot of a skinny boyish lieutenant in shorts and a helmet, raising the Israeli flag over a building by the sea.

The commandant nods. His beard is flecked with gray, and he is far from skinny. "I remember more than this, Abba. I remember you bringing me here in '57 when we gave the base back to the Egyptians." Bitterly he adds, "For the first time, that is."

"Remember by chance what you said way back then?"

"Do I?" Noah shifts to a childish treble. " 'Abba, why do we have to give it back? We won the war!' And you said" — Noah puts on a deep voice — " 'We're doing it for peace.' "

"Good memory. You also said, 'We'll get it back. *I'll* take it back!' " Barak gestures at the picture. "And you kept your word."

Noah puts on his white dress-uniform blouse and his cap. "Yes, and here we go again, doing it for peace. Maybe this time it will work."

As the blue-and-white flag slowly comes down, green-clad soldiers on the parade ground, and navy girl soldiers lined up on the wharf in their pretty white uniforms, stand at attention singing "Hatikvah," tears pouring down the girls' cheeks. Zev Barak tries to sing, but cannot bring out a sound. Six Dabur patrol boats are leaving the wharf in a column. As the anthem ends, they sail in a tight circle round and round, their sirens wailing.

At Etzion air base Egyptian officers and soldiers wait to take over, keeping a discreet distance from the parade ground. Danny Luria has come from Ramat David for the ceremony, and now wishes he had not. The spectacle of the wrecked hangars and blasted facilities is bad enough, but not since Dov's death has he seen his father so brought down. Yet Benny Luria goes stiffly through the flag-lowering, singing "Hatikvah" with the ranks of aviators and ground crew. The ceremony over, he exchanges salutes with the much taller, heavily mustached Egyptian general in resplendent dress uniform who approaches for a low-toned colloquy. Then Benny Luria comes to his son, takes his arm, and murmurs, *"Blessed are you, O Lord our God, Ruler of the Universe, the True Judge,"* the blessing on evil news, usually spoken at a death.

"Amen," says his son. "Let's go home, Abba."

"Amen!" Benny's voice turns loud and hard. "Back to the Promised Land."

At Yamit (Seaside) on the Mediterranean, the ghost of Moshe Dayan hovers over the dismantling. Yamit is not a military base at all, but a beach and farming town constructed just across the Sinai border after the Six-Day War; as Dayan then put it, "to create *uvdot* [facts] on the land." Several such "facts" were strung inside Sinai in a strip along the borders. In the end they almost wrecked the Camp David talks, for Sadat demanded, in return for peace, every last inch of the Sinai. So Dayan sadly reversed himself and agreed to the uprooting of the *uvdot,* including prosperous Yamit, his crowning fact. Before concurring, Begin telephoned Arik Sharon, the toughest of the tough, for his approval to give up Yamit. Now Dayan is gone, and the uprooting is for other hands. Whose but Arik Sharon's?

"Kishote, I have to evacuate and bulldoze Yamit." Early in April, Sharon, a civilian minister, is talking to the chief of planning branch in the Kirya. "We can't leave a town on the Sinai border for the Egyptians to move into. That's asking for trouble. We can't leave ruins for terrorists to hide out in, either. Every stick and brick we can't remove, we'll have to plough under. It's heartbreaking, but not one stone must remain on another."

"I can see that."

In a grating tone Sharon goes on. "Then there are the townspeople. They're getting a dirty deal. We induced them to come and make their lives in Yamit, and now they have to give up their homes, their schools, everything. The diehards won't go quietly.

There'll be protests, women lying down in front of the bulldozers, and so on. As usual with the charming jobs, I've got it. I need a deputy. Will you take it on?"

"All right."

"So quick? It doesn't bother your conscience one bit, Yossi, evacuating settlers and razing a settlement?"

"Yamit isn't a settlement, Arik. Planting those people inside the Sinai was a strategic brainstorm of Dayan's, and a misguided one. It doesn't bother my conscience, no."

"It does mine, and mark my word, it'll haunt us as a precedent."

"For the Holy Land? Show me in the Bible, Arik, where God promised Abraham the Sinai desert," says the chief of planning branch.

"Okay, Don Kishote. Draw up a plan for the evil day."

There is no flag-lowering at Yamit, only the crash of the bulldozers into crumpling walls, the yells of protesters, the sirens of police vans coming to take away the violent ones, the swelling murmur of crowds of onlookers. Some shoving, shouting, wrestling, a lot of camera work, and the people are out. It becomes a protracted long day of monotonous eradication of wreckage.

The crowds fade away. April 25 is the last day for Israel's compliance with the Camp David Accords, and the chief of planning remains there to the last, to assure that all happens in full compliance with the treaty. As the sun sets on the place that was once Yamit, its dying rays slant down on level sands, departing bulldozers, and the lone figure of Don Kishote, surveying the patch of desert that was once Yamit.

The Lebanese War starts as a triumph and becomes a controversial bog, but it is the making of Danny Luria. After scoring six victories in the air battles, to his father's bursting pride, Danny becomes a leading instructor in F-16 combat. He speaks no more of disenchantment. He speaks very little altogether for a long while after the elegant Hilton wedding of Amos Pasternak and Ruti Barak, a sort of feudal festivity for the top management of Rafael and Kivshan. At the wedding Danny is as jocund as anyone, kisses the abashed bride on the cheek, and leaves early.

He then blossoms out as an old-style devil-may-care tayass, toothbrush mustache and all, drinking and wenching in the obsolescent RAF pattern of the Weizman era. Girls either fall hard for him, or they steer clear of him so as not to be smirked at. "What, you're going out with *Danny Luria*? Hmmm! Really? Well, kol ha'kavod!" The girls who fall take the teasing with superior smiles, for they have in tow a noted tayass, while it lasts.

Professionally, Danny remains dead serious, and his advancement in the air force year after year is steady and rapid. When he requests a long travel leave before assuming a squadron command, he gets it as his due. He plans it meticulously, as he does all things that matter — his love life is not one of them — and trots around the globe touching all five continents. His return date is locked into one week before Israel's Independence Day 1988, completing the biblical cycle of the first forty years. Back in 1948 the date was May 14, but this year, by the vagaries of the Jewish lunar calendar, the anniversary falls on April 22. The celebration promises to jam all air traffic into Israel for weeks, so he reserves the El Al flight from Zurich to Tel Aviv half a year ahead, and repeatedly reconfirms it. He is all the more astonished, when he boards that plane, to find it taking off only two-thirds full. As soon as the seat belt sign is off he goes to the flight deck to find out why.

"Where have you been, Danny, anyway?" The bald captain, once a wingmate of his father's, sounds peevish. "This is a good planeload. Tourism is dead. Independence Day will be a total disaster. Don't you know about the intifada?"

"Don't blame the intifada," objects the copilot, who wears a *Shalom Akshav* (Peace Now) button. "Blame our crazy government, setting free *five thousand terrorists* in exchange for eight guys captured in Lebanon. What did we expect all those terrorists to do? Go to New York and become bloody taxi drivers?"

"The intifada is kids throwing stones and burning tires," says the captain, "not terrorists."

"That's just for American TV. The ringleaders are getting smart, sending the kids out front," says the copilot. "It's a terrorist uprising, and the tourists are right to stay away."

Danny feels himself back in an unchanged Israel, though when he left the intifada was only starting. Emerging from the quiet airport into the steamy Tel Aviv afternoon, he sees Yossi Nitzan, in shorts and a sport shirt, talking to a paunchy grayhead, sharply dressed in Hollywood style. Yossi gives him a friendly wave as he goes by.

"But Lee, where are Spencer and his wife?" Yossi is saying to his brother. Lee's son Spencer and Tamara Katzman were married some time ago, in a Beverly Hills wedding of Babylonian magnificence.

"Cancelled their trip at the last minute," Lee Bloom says. "Intifada."

"What nonsense! Why, they planned this first visit to Israel for months, I've got a car and driver for them, a great itinerary —"

"Look, she's a nice Jewish girl, Tamara." Lee Bloom shrugs. "It's the TV, Yossi. She thinks Israel is like wartime Stalingrad. I know better, but —" He looks around, taking a deep breath. "Twelve years since I've been here! The air smells nice, the ground feels good."

"You're too fat, Lee."

"I eat when I worry. Since Sheva died and Yael settled here, it's all on me. I'm rich, I worry, I eat."

Four people stand on a grassy hillside north of Yemin Moshe, around a low stone veiled with cheesecloth. The engraving on the stone is visible through the thin threads:

To
a Friend
CHRISTIAN CUNNINGHAM

with the dates of his birth and death. Teddy Kollek, the corpulent old mayor of Jerusalem, says to Emily, "Well, this is it, Mrs. Halliday. Not something to publicize, but the inscription says it all. To honor your father as befits what he meant to us, we dedicate this stone on Israel's fortieth Independence Day. Will you do the unveiling?"

She nods, stoops, and pulls aside the cloth.

Sam Pasternak says, "He made a difference. Bless his memory."

The mayor gets into his waiting car. Pasternak, even more portly than the mayor, walks off with his slow rolling gait toward Yemin Moshe.

"Where is this party we're going to, Wolf?"

"Where Sam's heading, that big house down at the foot of the staircase, with all the flowers on the balconies. It's not a party, exactly. We'll be watching the Independence Day celebration."

"What does Sam do now?"

"Sam heads a big conglomerate. Among other things, he's building thousands of homes for the Russian Jews. He's also been very involved in the rescue of the Ethiopians, on the secret end. Covert action is in that fat old warhorse's blood." He takes her arm. "Come, we won't be early, and it'll be crowded."

"Wolf, I won't know anyone there."

"Nonsense, you know Sam, and you know Nakhama. In fact, she told me she's looking forward to showing you our grandchildren."

"She did? Well, that sounds good. Four now, isn't it, dear?"

"Five. Galia had her second in March. And Ruti's expecting."

"Prolific tribe, the Baraks. Bless them all."

She gets down on a knee and touches her lips to the stone. He helps her up, for Queenie has grown quite stout and is all gray. She stands silent for several moments. "All right," she says, "let's go." They start to descend a long stone staircase. She gestures at the Old City wall across the ravine, golden in the late sunlight, where many figures are bustling about. "There it is, Wolf, the light one sees nowhere else on earth. And what's all that activity over there?"

"Readying the fireworks, no doubt."

"My God, Jerusalem is so lovely, so lovely, Zev. Even Bud, that cold customer, always said so."

"Beautiful in elevation, the joy of all the earth," Barak says. "So sang the psalmist. He and Bud Halliday agree, so who am I to argue?"

Emily stops walking, and tugs at his arm. "Explain yourself."

"Explain what?"

"That sarcastic tone. Those bitter words."

"Oh, Emily!" He whips an arm toward the Old City panorama. "This is the tourist fantasy of Israel, so your father's stone is well placed. Chris held that fantasy in his heart. He never lived here."

"And the reality, dear?"

"The reality?" A tart laugh. "Not for the Independence Day mood, but okay, where do I begin? A government paralyzed by peanut politicians, that barely functions with sleazy horse trades? Chronic blowups between the religious and the secular? People working at two and three jobs to make ends meet, lives broken by reserve callups, tax evasion as a way of life, sons and daughters leaving the country and not coming back? The dark mutter of Islam all around us and right here, at our very heart, behind those beautiful walls? Will that do as a taste of our reality?" Enfolding her arm in his, he walks on down the flower-lined stone staircase. "Come along, let's forget the reality for today."

"Then is what my eyes are seeing, Zev, just a pretty lie?"

"Oh, Queenie, Queenie, call it a dream trying to come true. Listen, is the reality of America the Lincoln Memorial and the Manhattan skyscrapers, or the terrible mess you're in yourselves? The old countries, Japan, England, Russia, worse off or better off, they just *are*. We're both still *trying to be,* you the giant of the world and we the crazy little nobody in the Middle East. Who knows whether we'll make it in the end, either of us?" His laugh is warmer. "And what set me off this way, anyhow? Thinking of Chris, I guess, and his vision of how it will all end. God make it so, and God rest his soul. Such friends are rare."

She touches a handkerchief to her eyes, and he puts an arm around her. "This may sound morbid, dear White Wolf," she says, "but I hope to God I die before you do. As long as I know you're somewhere in this world, I'm okay."

Yom Ha'atzma'ut! Independence Day! And if the tourists are not showing up, who cares? The Israelis are turning out in huge crowds. Intifada, shmintifada! Forty years! Parades, speeches, concerts, dancing in the streets, have been going on all day, all over the land. The crowning daytime event has been a flyby of Phantoms, Kfirs, and F-16s over Haifa, Tel Aviv, and Jerusalem. Now toward evening, everyone in Israel who can drive, walk, or ride an animal to Jerusalem is doing so, for the laser-beam show to be projected on the Old City wall, and Handel's *Messiah* to be performed in the amphitheater below by the Philharmonic and massed choral societies, concluding in an all-time extravaganza of fireworks.

Yemin Moshe is a perfect site for viewing this spectacle, and its residents are under much pressure to invite their friends. The front-row mansion of Max and Yael Roweh, with balconies on two floors plus a rooftop, is the hottest ticket in town, in a manner of speaking. Yael has arranged chairs and refreshments for viewers on all three levels; places on the roof for the romantically inclined, for viewing in starlit darkness; more places downstairs for young anxious parents, where their offspring can fall but a foot or so to soft flower beds, and grandparents can baby-sit and dote; the big party in the main living room and on its spacious balcony.

Zev brings Emily Halliday downstairs, and Nakhama happily sorts out her small fry from the boil of children, displaying them for Emily's admiration. Emily notes with a trace of chagrin, and faint amusement at herself for feeling so, that Nakhama — always the fleshy one — has stayed reasonably shapely, and almost unreasonably beautiful, into her sixties; her hair still dark, her arms smooth and rounded. Genes, or something. Lucky Zev, having it both ways to the last, the monster. She is grateful when he takes her up to the roof, where the first stars are appearing. "Dearest, just leave me here," she says, with a light kiss on his cheek. "It's beautiful here, it's where I'm comfortable. I'll come down when I feel like it."

"As you wish, Queenie."

Arriving about sundown, Amos and Ruti Pasternak find the house abuzz, and straight off encounter Irene Fleg in the main room. Amos knows (the wise Yael has warned him) that the French couple will be at the party, but the cane and the limp surprise him. Ruti gives the Frenchwoman a brief sharp head-to-toe scrutiny, and goes off looking unworried, leaving Amos to chat with his old friend.

"So that's Ruti. She's very pretty," Irene Fleg says.

"Come on, Irene. What she is *very*, is smart. Ruti's all right. She's expecting again."

"Glorious. Congratulations, *chéri*."

"Why the cane, dear?"

"Oh, Amos, my skiing days are over. Third time I've broken my leg."

They talk back and forth about her children and his one boy. In an abrupt change of tone Irene Fleg says, "You're happy, aren't you? I was right, wasn't I? Look at me, an old wreck."

"Ridiculous! You're lovely, Irene. Your leg will heal."

For a fact the stringy face is not what it was, but it brightens in the subtle thin-lipped smile which he has not seen for several years. "Never mind! Was I right?"

"You were right, Irene, yes."

She takes and squeezes his hand. "And just quick enough, *mon vieux*, to beat you to it. Now it can be said, *n'est-ce pas*?" She laughs. He hesitates, then reluctantly laughs too.

In a corner of the room on two sofas, a vigorous argument is going on among four powerful Israelis about the cancelled Lavie (Lion) aircraft. Very senior gentlemen they are now, with wrinkled faces and padded midsections, and each has his decided viewpoint. Benny Luria is furious, for Israel Aircraft Industries, of which he is vice chairman, has taken the main blow. Designed and built in Israel, the Lavie was touted after its test flights as the best fighter-bomber in the world, but the Americans have decided to sell Israel the F-18 rather than fund the Lavie. Sam Pasternak is arguing that the decision was forced, prudent, and in Israel's national interest. Kishote and Barak are mostly listening.

"Sam, you can be very detached and budget-conscious," says Luria. "You're in fine shape with the Merkava tank, chewing up a fat chunk of the military budget. But the air force —"

"Nobody in the world will sell us a frontline tank," Pasternak interrupts, "so we're building one. The F-18's a frontline plane."

Barak says, "What's more, Benny, the air force approved the cancellation."

Luria turns on Don Kishote, who heads an influential advisory board to the Prime Minister, called Future Assessment. "Approved, with a budgetary knife at its throat. Right or wrong, Kishote?"

"Yes, it was a little like cancelling a seventh-month pregnancy, but —" says Kishote.

"There!" exclaims Benny.

"Wait, I'm not finished, listen to me," Kishote exclaims. The youngest of the four in his mid-fifties, he still sometimes raps out words like a field commander. "There are three reasons for us to produce our own weapons systems, Benny. One, we can do it cheaper. Or two, we can make a Jewish leap in technology that puts us ahead of the enemy, if not of the world. Or three, we can't buy the system anywhere. The Lavie's a great aircraft, but when we can get the F-18 —"

"There go the lasers," somebody calls, and there is a rush to the balconies. Ruti hears that Danny Luria has just showed up and is on the roof, so she trots upstairs. She has seen very little of Danny, but has heard plenty. Ruti is very happily married, and her Amos is even talked of as an eventual contender for Ramatkhal, but she does wonder a bit whether any of her old power over Danny remains. Let's see! She isn't pregnant enough to show.

Under brightening stars in the twilit sky, to the orchestral thunder of a Bach toccata and fugue, the pencil-thin rays of the lasers — crimson, green, blue, white — are crisscrossing the valley to paint fantastic patterns on the Old City walls. Ruti sees the back of Danny's head in the crowd at the rooftop rail. Push in there to him? No, no. Just wait, and watch the pretty lasers . . .

"Here we are, Abba!" On the big balcony below, Aryeh and Bruria in uniform come to Don Kishote and hug him, both excited and aglow from having marched in a parade. The laser colors are weaving and coruscating on the wall across the valley, forming melting pictures — a roaring lion, a bounding deer, an F-16 — then dissolving into abstract designs. The massed singers in the amphitheatre are bursting into a major chorus of the *Messiah:*

Who is this King of Glory?
The Lord of Hosts
He is the King of Glory!

"Here's your Uncle Lee, Aryeh," says Kishote. "Lee, this is Bruria."

"So this is Uncle Lee. But where are Spencer and Tamara?" Bruria blurts.

"At the last minute, Bruria, they couldn't make it," says Lee. "They were very sorry. So am I."

"What! They've never been here, and now they miss this?"

Aryeh says in a tone to cut off Bruria, "I'm sure they had good cause."

Lee is staring at them and smiling. "Aryeh, you were a scrawny kid when I saw you last. You're a man, and you've got yourself a magnificent wife."

And He shall reign . . .
King of Glory, King of Glory . . .

"Ha!" says Bruria, and goes on in her broken kibbutznik English, raising her voice over the music. "Uncle Lee, we had made such plans for them! Tomorrow Jericho and the Dead Sea, and after that —"

"Is it safe there?"

"It's safe everywhere here," snaps Bruria, then amends it somewhat nearer the mark. "As safe as Los Angeles, anyway."

"Come." Aryeh takes her arm. "Let's watch from the roof."

Looking after them, Lee murmurs, "What fools Spencer and Tamara were. And I too, Yossi, if the truth be known. When all is said and done, I missed it all. Didn't I?"

"Never too late," says Don Kishote.

"Forty years too late." Lee shakes his head. "No regrets, regrets are pointless, but I missed it all."

On the roof, Ruti and Danny are drinking at the bar. He is cordial, as to any old friend he seldom sees. They talk casually about his travels, and her job in high-tech industrial intelligence. Then she ventures, "I hope you're happy, Danny."

"No complaints, Ruti."

"That's nice. I hope to hear one of these days that you've settled down."

"Me? Maybe when I'm forty and want a family, who knows? I'm having a great time, Ruti, happy as a wild bird. A free wild bird, motek!"

And He shall reign . . .
Hallelujah,
Hallelujah!

The first fireworks spring into the sky. Ruti leaves. Danny can see the fireworks here at the bar, away from the crowd, better than among them. Moreover the whiskey is here. He is quite content to stand here and watch the rockets and flares soar into the darkness with the triumphant blasts of the choral voices.

Hallelujah!
(Boom!)
Hallelujah!
(Boom!)

The pyrotechnics have been timed to explode to the beat of the music. What a tricky effect! Mighty spectacular, colored fire punctuating Handel's high notes.

And He shall reign
For ever, and ever —

Danny is pouring himself another whiskey, and feeling as though he himself may reign for ever and ever. Tomorrow he'll be back at the controls of an F-16, a squadron commander in Heyl Ha'avir. He looks up at the stars, and raises his glass with the silent thought, *To you, Dov.*

King of Kings,
(Boom!)
And Lord of Lords
(Boom!)
For ever, and ever!
Hallelujah!

And now yet more gorgeous and astonishing effects! All along the base of the wall, fireworks pour forth a red cascade, as the lasers vividly paint a white dove of peace, winging along the wall with a green olive branch in its mouth. And on top of the wall there blaze forth on flaming frames the Star of David, the Cross, and the Crescent. The four old comrades in arms are standing with Max Roweh when this gaudy climax lights up the sky above and the valley below.

And He shall reign,
King of Kings!
And Lord of Lords!
Hallelujah, Hallelujah,
HAL–LE–LU–JAH!

"There's Teddy for you, and his togetherness," Luria growls, referring to the mayor of Jerusalem. "Questionable taste, that."

"That's what Teddy believes," Barak says.

"Even with the intifada?" says Pasternak sadly.

"*Davka,*" says Kishote, "with the intifada."

"So is that it?" Lee Bloom inquires. "It's over?"

"Not till they play 'Hatikvah,' " says Pasternak.

"Oh, of course," says Lee, " 'Hatikvah.' "

"Forty years," says his brother. "But the main thing is, we were gone for nearly two thousand years. Now we're back, and there's Mount Zion before our eyes, in our possession. I call that an unusual circumstance, Max, don't you?"

"Decidedly unusual, yes."

"And think of this," says Pasternak. "About a hundred years ago a few crazy Russian Jews dreamed of a Jewish State. Now that

State is taking in Russian Jews in the hundreds of thousands. Wouldn't you call that unusual?"

"Unusualler and unusualler," says Max Roweh, who likes to drink freely on such occasions.

Now the orchestra strikes up "Hatikvah," "The Hope." The guests on the Roweh balconies join the powerful choral voices below, and voices are sounding from everywhere, singing the minor-key melody borrowed from Eastern European folk music, the mournful-triumphant anthem of the Jewish State. Lee Bloom sings along with the others in his rusty Hebrew,

We have not lost our Hope
Of two thousand years
To be a free people
In our land
Land of Zion
And Jerusalem . . .

There follows a prolonged trumpet flourish, and a giant shower of fireworks. "Independence Day ends," says Barak, and he goes off to the roof.

Aging and frail, Max Roweh still stands erect, as he did while singing the anthem. If he had a beard and a broad-brimmed rusty black hat, Kishote thinks, he could be taken for the Ezrakh. "Well, the Great Trumpet has sounded," Roweh says to the others, and with a twinkle in his eye he quotes Maimonides. *"Yet the Messiah tarries . . ."*

". . . And all the same," Don Kishote completes the quote as a last dazzling burst of blue-and-white fire rises to the stars, *"I will wait every day for him to come."*

Historical Notes

And so our story ends, though the saga of Israel continues to the present day, when pink streaks of a dawning peace seem to be appearing in a sky darkened for half a century by war.

Some readers turning the last page of *The Glory* may well wonder, "How much of all this has been accurate, how much imaginary? Did that fireworks display, for instance, really happen in Jerusalem on Independence Day 1988, with lasers painting changing pictures on the walls of the Old City, and Handel's *Messiah* thundering from the ravine below?"

It happened, all right. I was there, consulting with knowledgeable Israelis about the historical novel I had just begun, which in time became two books, *The Hope* and *The Glory*. Even then those Israelis were asking me, "How can you possibly end the story, when it's still going on?" Standing there on a Yemin Moshe balcony, as voices from everywhere sang "Hatikvah" and colored fire poured from Mount Zion, I said to myself, "This is where it will end."

As in *The Hope*, the history in *The Glory* is offered as reliable, but accuracy about the recent past has a built-in limit, especially in a country still in a state of war with several neighbors. As one approaches the present day, stubborn controversy accumulates. The facts dramatized in this novel are drawn from the available serious sources in English and Hebrew, and from consultations in depth with experts, Israeli and American. Where head-on disagreements persist, I have told the truth as nearly as I could discern it. One caveat: my characters do sometimes occupy posts held in those days by real very different people, many of whom are still alive; and for this dramatic license I must beg the indulgence of some distinguished Israelis.

All political figures, and all military personnel of general staff rank — except, of course, for my four fictional leading men — appear by their right names.

A few comments follow on sources, reliability, and ongoing controversy in specific scenes of *The Glory*.

PART ONE: THE DREAMERS

The *Eilat* sinking and the reprisal against the oil refineries happened as described, causing the frantic acceleration in the Security Council debates which led to Resolution 242, with the famous dispute over the "two little words."

The "Wild West show" of Israeli derring-do during Nasser's War of Attrition, such as the Green Island raid, the armored incursion across the Gulf of Suez, and the capture of the Soviet radar, are documented in Israeli military literature. *The Boats of Cherbourg*, by A. Rabinovich, gives a full account of that sensational escapade, and much other history of the Israeli navy as well.

The victory of Israeli fighter pilots over the Soviet air force in 1970 was not publicized at the time by either side. Former chief of the air force Avihu Bin Nun, who fought in this engagement, helped me with facts and color.

The move of the missile sites to the Canal, a clear violation of the War of Attrition cease-fire, gave Egypt a decided advantage three years later in the Yom Kippur War. After it was a fait accompli, our State Department laggardly acknowledged that it had occurred, but that nothing could be done about it.

The raid on terrorist headquarters in Beirut in April 1973 made world headlines. No declassified records are available at this writing of the secret elite strike force called "The Unit," or Sayeret Matkhal. It is known that Ehud Barak, the present (1994) Army Chief of Staff, took part, as did Muki Betzer, later important in the Entebbe rescue, and Yoni Netanyahu, the unit commander killed at Entebbe. This chapter is based on journalism and personal interviews. Invention has perforce filled out the account, and though the general facts of the exploit are correct, details are improvised. Amos Pasternak is of course an imaginary character. Unofficial accounts mention a blond woman who aided the raiders, but Madame Fleg is a figure of fiction.

The *Concepzia* which lulled "The Dreamers" before the Yom Kippur War remains a matter of much rueful analysis by Israeli strategic savants.

The roller bridge scenes are dramatized from a detailed unpublished report by Lieutenant Colonel Fredo Raz, the officer in charge of the bridge. Scattered references to this extraordinary structure occur in the literature on the war. It is presented here as a picturesque instance of Israeli improvisation, late in arriving but still important in the crossing.

PART TWO: THE AWAKENING

The controversies about the sanguinary Yom Kippur War are to this hour many and bitter. The last word about some matters in dispute may not be spoken in our lifetimes, and the account in *The Glory* is not to be taken in any way as such a last word. I tell the tale as I have come to understand it, after an arduous effort to master the almost infinite, often terrible facts of Israel's fateful test of fire.

Avigdor Kahalani, the "Black Panther" of the Syrian front, is today a Knesset member and an author. He was awarded the Medal of Heroism, Israel's highest military honor, and his books are valuable sources on the Golan Heights campaign. Yanosh Ben Gal and Yossi Ben Hanan today are retired major generals.

Chaim Bar-Lev, former Ramatkhal and cabinet minister, has been one of Israel's eminent leaders. As pictured in the book, he was in deep disagreement during the war with General Sharon, a figure of enduring controversy.

General Avraham ("Bren") Adan's memoir, *On the Banks of the Suez,* is a key military treatise on the Sinai battles; a formidable field commander, he was also an early peace advocate. Henry Kissinger's *Years of Upheaval* is an indispensable source for the diplomacy of the war. In these memoirs both authors give themselves the best of it, of course, as did Churchill, De Gaulle, and for that matter Julius Caesar. *Dado*, a meticulous biography of General David Elazar by H. Bartov, offers a unique day-by-day, hour-by-hour account of the command aspect of the war. An expert combat overview is *The War of Atonement* by Chaim Herzog, former President of Israel.

The nuclear alert on Thursday, October 25, now virtually forgotten, caused a great international tumult. I was in London at the time. I met my wife at a theater where we had tickets for a comedy, and rushed her back to the hotel so that we could pack up, and board the next plane to our home in Washington. Since Washington was Ground Zero for a nuclear attack, my conduct in retrospect cannot be called cool. I get growls about it from her to this day.

The project of an American airlift to the trapped Egyptian Third Army was dropped when, just before Kissinger's visit to Cairo, Golda Meir agreed to a second "humanitarian convoy."

The Agranat Commission's verdict remains a sore subject in Israel. Its subtle distinctions between the responsibilities of "the political echelon" and "the military echelon" did not convince a large sector of the public; and for them the forced resignation of Dado made him a heroic figure unjustly treated, while the exoneration of Dayan damaged him.

PART THREE: THE PEACE

The main facts of the Entebbe rescue are beyond challenge; the terrorists in the terminal were wiped out, the Jewish hostages were saved, and Lieutenant Colonel Yoni Netanyahu was the only Israeli fighting man killed. Disagreement has sprung up about details of his death, about the attack on the terminal, and most of all, about the credit due to the many participants in the exploit. The peripheral adventure of the fictitious Aryeh Nitzan is based on facts not in serious dispute.

Yoni Netanyahu has become a mythical hero not only of Israel, but of the diaspora, and to some extent of the world. Revision of myths is part of every nation's historiography. Yoni fell at Entebbe no flawless superman, but a thirty-year-old commander with human faults and blazing courage. In my view his myth is imperishable, and in essence true.

The exchanges of Sadat with Golda Meir, Dayan, and Sharon on his arrival at Ben Gurion airport are culled from the memoirs of all four.

My portrait of Dayan in *The Hope* and *The Glory* is based on the available literature including his memoirs, on unpublished academic material, and on consultation with eminent Israelis who knew him best. The paradox of this great man of war is that he rose to his full stature only near the end of his life, in the Camp David negotiations, as a main architect of Israel's first peace treaty. The character Eliakim at Camp David is a real person, Eliakim Rubinstein, appearing on television screens as I write, as Rabin's chief aide in negotiating peace with Jordan.

The 1981 air strike which destroyed Iraq's nuclear reactor evoked worldwide criticism. The American government even held up deliveries of aircraft to Israel, to signal its disapproval. Ilan Ram-On, the youngest of the eight pilots who made the strike, was my source for many details. At one point I asked Ilan, who had risen to command an F-16 squadron, what he would have my book say about the attack, if he were to write it himself. He replied after a pause, very seriously, *"That it took the Gulf War to prove the need and worth of the operation."*

Right on target. Only when Saddam Hussein's Scud missiles were falling on Israel, and on American troops in Saudi Arabia, were all questions answered about an exploit that deprived Iraq of nuclear warheads.

DESTRUCTION AND RESURGENCE

A final word to the readers of *The Glory*.

Menachem Begin once told me that when his term as Prime Minister was over, he would retire from politics to write a book about the Jewish epic of the twentieth century, which he would call *Dor Hashoah V'hat'kumah,* literally *The Generation of the Destruction and the Resurgence*, embodying both the Holocaust and the rise of Israel. The mischances and tragedies of the protracted Lebanon War overwhelmed him, and he retired into a depressed solitude and died. The book might have been a great one, but he never wrote it.

Though I have had no such conscious plan or ambition in mind, the historical novels I have written over the past thirty years — *The Winds of War, War and Remembrance, The Hope, The Glory,* and *Inside, Outside* — come near at least in scope to the scheme Menachem Begin envisioned. *The Winds of War* began, in fact, as a book about the Battle of Leyte Gulf; yet the art of fiction has its own strange workings. As they finally evolved, my two World War II novels tell of the Holocaust in the only way I believe that the unparalleled crime can be grasped, if never completely understood; that is, as the covert deed of an outlaw major power governed by mass murderers, and screened off too long from the rest of mankind by the fog of a global war. In *The Glory* and its prologue, *The Hope*, I have tried to limn Israel's early heroic half century; and in *Inside, Outside*, a novel of the American Jewish experience during those years, I have as it were scrawled my small signature in a corner of the panorama.

These five books have occupied the central years of my working life. Their merit is for others to judge, today and in years to come, if they last. Looking back, I perceive them as a single task of bearing witness, my *Generation of Destruction and Resurgence*. That task is done, and I turn with a lightened spirit to fresh beckoning tasks; concluding my work on *The Glory* with old words often found at the close of our rabbinic commentaries, which express what is in my heart.

תם ונשלם
שבח לאל עולם

Finished and complete,
Praise to the Lord Eternal.

Herman Wouk

1964–1994
5724–5754